THE GRAMPIAN QUARTET

Anna (Nan) Shepherd was born in 1893 and died in 1981. Closely attached to Aberdeen and her native Deeside, she graduated from her home University in 1915, and went to work for the next forty-one years as a lecturer in English at what is now Aberdeen College of Education. An enthusiastic gardener and hill walker, she made many visits to the Cairngorms with students and friends and was a keen member of the Deeside Field Club. Her last book, a non-fiction study called *The Living Mountain*, testifies to her love of the hills and her knowledge of them in all their moods. Her many further travels included visits to Norway, France, Italy, Greece and South Africa, but she always returned to the house where she was raised and lived almost all her adult life, in the village of West Cults, three miles from Aberdeen on North Deeside.

Nan Shepherd wrote three novels, all well received by the critics: *The Quarry Wood* (1928), followed by *The Weatherhouse* (1930) and *A Pass in the Grampians* (1933). A collection of poems, *In the Cairngorms*, appeared in 1934, and *The Living Mountain* was published in 1977. She edited *Aberdeen University Review* from 1957 to 1964, contributed to *The Deeside Field*, and worked on editions of poetry by two fellow North-east writers, J.C. Milne and Charles Murray. She was awarded an honorary degree by Aberdeen University in 1964, and her many friends included Agnes Mure Mackenzie, Helen Cruickshank, Willa Muir, Hugh MacDiarmid, William Soutar and Jessie Kesson.

NAN SHEPHERD

The Grampian Quartet

THE QUARRY WOOD

THE WEATHERHOUSE

A PASS IN THE
GRAMPIANS

THE LIVING MOUNTAIN

Edited
with Introductions by
Roderick Watson

CANONGATE
CLASSICS
70

This edition first published as a Canongate Classic in 1996
by Canongate Books Limited
14 High Street
Edinburgh EH1 1TE

The Quarry Wood first published in 1928 by Constable and Co. Ltd.
The Weatherhouse first published in 1930 by Constable and Co. Ltd.
A Pass in the Grampians first published in 1933 by Constable and Co. Ltd.
The Living Mountain first published in 1977 by Aberdeen University Press.

British Library Cataloguing in Publication Data
A Catalogue record is available on request

ISBN 0-86241-589-6

The publishers gratefully acknowledge
general subsidy from the Scottish Arts Council
towards the Canongate Classics series
and a specific grant towards the
publication of this title.

Set in 10 pt Plantin
by Alan Sutton Publishing Ltd,
and Hewer Text Composition Services, Edinburgh
Printed and bound in Denmark by Norhaven Rotation

The Quarry Wood

INTRODUCED BY
RODERICK WATSON

for my Mother

Contents

Introduction

Nan Shepherd once said that she didn't really like writing prose fiction and that she only wrote 'when I feel that there's something that simply must be written'. What *had* to be written amounted to three remarkable novels which appeared in the years between 1928 and 1933. These books, *The Quarry Wood*, *The Weatherhouse*, and *A Pass in the Grampians*, were published on both sides of the Atlantic to immediate critical acclaim. The *Times Literary Supplement* found 'a richness of expression astonishing in a first novel', while the *New York Times* Book Review commented on the 'vivid imagery' in her last book, '. . . sometimes as compact and condensed as poetry'. Miss Shepherd continued to write articles and poems for the rest of her long life, but these novels, produced in the five years before her fortieth birthday, mark a creative mastery which seems to have been attained, fulfilled, and then just as suddenly concluded. They have been most unfairly forgotten.

In her later years, Nan Shepherd edited the *Aberdeen University Review*, and I first came across her work with an essay she had written for it in 1938, on MacDiarmid's later poetry. This piece showed a fine insight into the poet's linguistic experiments at a time when many readers were merely puzzled or exasperated by them. It was too many years before I discovered that Nan Shepherd had also produced fiction of the first quality, or that her novels deserve a key place in that line which runs from *The House with the Green Shutters* to *A Scots Quair* and beyond.

Indeed, reading *The Quarry Wood* is to read what might have happened to Chris Guthrie, had she decided to go to university after all, for Martha Ironside makes the same difficult journey towards intellectual and emotional matur-

ity at a time when such space was seldom freely given to
women. An even greater gain, perhaps, is the unforced way
in which Matty manages to bridge what Chris Guthrie felt to
be the division between her 'English' and her 'Scottish'
selves. Nan Shepherd's achievement is to make us feel this
integrity, and to attain it herself in her narrative style. Her
protagonist's home life is difficult, squalid and narrow,
indeed her parents and neighbours would seem to be at
home in any village between Barbie and Kinraddie. Yet
Shepherd's wry and humane vision utterly eschews sentimental naturalism, and she never once slips into Kailyard or
polemical anti-Kailyard postures. This alone is a considerable feat, and, for a first novel published only two years
after *A Drunk Man* and four years before *Sunset Song*, it is a
creative triumph.

Nan Shepherd's modest middle class upbringing was
quite different from Martha's home circumstances; nevertheless, like so many first books, *The Quarry Wood* is a
'development novel' clearly derived from the author's own
life experience. The village of West Cults, King's College
Library, the students' torchlight procession, the lectures of
J. Arthur Thompson on Natural History and those of
Herbert Grierson on Literature ('Professor Gregory'), all
these are recognizably part of the Aberdeen scene that
Shepherd knew. Indeed, 'the Quarry Wood' itself (now no
longer there) rose towards the Black Top hill behind the
houses where she lived almost all her life. In later years she
was to recall its beauty on misty dawns when she used to
walk through the trees to fetch milk from a nearby farm,
before travelling to town and university classes each day. Yet
The Quarry Wood is not a naive nor a 'student life' produc-
tion, for it displays a striking maturity of style and insight.

Shepherd has an acute and unsentimental grasp of character and motivation—witness her account of Stoddart
Semple, for example, in chapter four, or her very sharp eye
for the intolerable social and sexual complacencies of young
men—yet she never loses compassion. When such insight is
matched to the reserve and dry humour of her prose, Nan
Shepherd's writing has all the grace of Chekhov, not least in
its delight at how revealing the casual juxtapositions of

everyday speech and action can be made to be. The most ordinary domestic events come alive under this subtle touch, made even more dynamic by a splendid ear for the vigour of common North East speech. In this respect the novelist honours the community she depicts—notwithstanding the often hilarious direness which she finds there—as for example in the plight of the Leggatt sisters, led by the dreadful Jeannie who learned from an early age to use religion and respectability like a two-handed engine for subduing her timorous mother and the rest of her dust-free household.

The limitations of Martha's point of view are dealt with equally fairly. Matty is an intellectual being who has yet to find that one 'does not learn from books alone', and indeed for a time in the novel she remains unaware of her own emotions and her own passionate and jealous nature. She resists and resents the coarseness of home life around her— and it's coarse enough—yet Shepherd's skill lets us see that there's more there than her protagonist has yet realized despite the scandals that are told against her. Then, too, Martha has to learn that the claims of the ideal can turn into a burden or a kind of exploitation, if they are divorced from physical expression and common life. Her own infatuation with Luke and the unfairness of his spiritualization of her, teaches Matty this.

Such wisdom is not to be found in lectures, and its spokesperson is Great Aunt Josephine, whose formidable and friendly influence opens and closes the tale. Josephine possesses 'the same sure capable grasp of life' that Matty finds in one of her most gifted professors, and that she herself will eventually inherit. Thus it is Josephine who will restore to Matty what is best in her roots, without denying the possibilities of a wider intellectual life beyond them. Paradoxically, perhaps, she does this by the manner of her death, which is where the novel ends.

In re-reading *The Quarry Wood* it becomes clear that an apparently episodic unfolding has been rather carefully controlled from the start, for its delightful opening paragraph has given us what amounts to a summary of the book's central theme and evolution. When Josephine Leggatt dies, 'aged seventy-nine and reluctant', it is after an agonizing and extended struggle against cancer, a grim vigil which Matty (and the reader with her) has assumed responsibility for and has had to undergo. It is a harrowing sequence, and yet Josephine's end comes as a triumph of affirmation, linked as it is to the turning of the seasons, and to the evocation of the dour and delicate moods of the weather at which Nan Shepherd particularly excels. There is no melodramatic heightening here, such as the Gothic crescendo which makes a 'clean sweep o the Gourlays' at the end of George Douglas Brown's novel; nor does the narrative conclude with the sweet fatalism of Chris's ebbing away at the end of *Grey Granite*. Nan Shepherd's vision is not without its own wry ironies, but she speaks positively and wholly on behalf of life. Like Josephine Legatt, she has an eye that sees everything, 'a serene unclouded eye', but 'an eye, moreover, that never saw too much'.

In the last chapter, Matty's father helps her to wring a hen's neck for the family meal:

> Geordie stood with an admirer's eye upon the fat breast of the fowl, holding her out from him until her spasms of involuntary twitching were over. Martha watched, breathing the clean sweet air of a July morning. When she raised her head she saw the wet fields and the soft gleam of the river. 'How fresh it is,' she said.
>
> 'Ay, ay,' answered her father, still holding the hen. 'It's a grand thing to get leave to live.'

Roderick Watson

ONE

Aunt Josephine Leggatt

Martha Ironside was nine years old when she kicked her grand-aunt Josephine. At nineteen she loved the old lady, idly perhaps, in her natural humour, as she loved the sky and space. At twenty-four, when Miss Josephine Leggatt died, aged seventy-nine and reluctant, Martha knew that it was she who had taught her wisdom; thereby proving – she reflected – that man does not learn from books alone; because Martha had kicked Aunt Josephine (at the age of nine) for taking her from her books.

Mrs. Ironside would have grumbled on for long enough and Aunt Josephine knew it.

'Ye'll just tak the craitur awa fae the school Emmeline,' the old lady said. 'Ye'll never haud book-larnin' in a wizened cask. Stap it in, it'll aye rin oot the faister. The bairn's fair wizened.'

'Oh, I ken she's nae bonny, Aunt Josephine—'

'O ay, ye were aye the beauty yersel, Emmeline, I'se nae deny it. But ye've nane to blame but yersel that the bairn's as she is. "There's Emmeline, noo," I says to Leebie, "throwin' hersel awa on yon Geordie Ironside, and the bairn's as ugly a little sinner as you'd clap e'en on in a month o' Sabbaths." "Dinna mention the wean," says Leebie, "nor Emmeline neither. If she hadna the wit to pit a plooman by the door, nor the grace to mind on fat was due to her fowk and their position, she can just bide the consequences. Dinna speak o' Emmeline to me," says Leebie. "She's never lookit richt upon her man if she's gotten a surprise that the bairn's nae a beauty."'

'Geordie's nae that ill-looking, Aunt Josephine.'

'Na, mebbe no. But look at his sister Sally – as grim's an auld horse wi' a pain in its belly. Matty's an Ironside, ma dear, and ye've gotten fat ye hae gotten by mairryin' aneath ye.'

Aunt Josephine said it calmly, without passion or malice, as one delivers an impersonal truth. She alone of the Leggatt family had recognised Emmeline since her marriage; but she would never have dreamed of denying that the marriage was a folly. She had even, in the early years, attempted on her sisters the thankless task of persuasion in Emmeline's behalf. After all, she was the only bairn of their own brother – 'blood's thicker nor water,' Aunt Josephine had the audacity to remind Aunt Jean, even after that lady had delivered her ultimatum with regard to Emmeline.

'But it's nae sae easy to get aff yer hands,' said Jean.

That made the matter conclusive. To have Emmeline on their hands would have been an impossible disaster for the respectable Leggatts.

Emmeline tossed her head at their opinion. With base effrontery she married the man she loved, and after twelve pinched and muddled years, with her trim beauty slack, two dead bairns and a living one mostly nerves and temper, she stood in her disordered kitchen and fretted that she could not offer her aunt a decent cup of tea.

'Beautiful, my dear, just beautiful,' said Aunt Josephine, sipping the tea; and she returned to the question of Martha's schooling. Emmeline, to be sure, had a dozen reasons against taking the child away. Reasoning to Miss Leggatt was so much moonshine. Fretful little girls are solid realities (if not so solid as their grand-aunts might wish): reasons, merely breath. It was not to be expected that a vapour would impede Aunt Josephine. She announced calmly and conclusively that she was taking the child back with her to Crannochie.

'We'll just cry on the craitur,' she said, 'and lat her know.'

The *craitur* all this while, serenely unaware of the conspiracy against her peace, was dwelling on a planet of her own. A field's breadth from the cottage, where two dykes intersected, there was piled a great cairn of stones. They had lain there so long that no one troubled to remember their purpose or their origin. Gathered from the surrounding soil, they had resumed a sort of unity with it. The cairn had

settled back into the landscape, like a dark outcrop of rock.
There Martha played. The stones summed up existence.

Aunt Josephine walked at her easy pace across the field.
Mrs. Ironside followed for a couple of steps; then stood
where she was and bawled across Aunt Josephine's head.

Aunt Josephine paid no attention: nor did Martha. The
one plodded steadily on through the grass, the other made a
planet with her dozen stones; both thirled to a purpose:
while Mrs. Ironside behind them shrilled and gesticulated to
no purpose whatsoever.

As her mother acknowledged, the child was no beauty:
though impartial opinion, at sight of her, might well have
decided that the mother was; intensifying the description by
aid of the sturdiest little helot of the local speech – 'a gey
beauty': inasmuch as the bairn's frock was glazed with dirt
and drawn up in a pucker where it had been torn; and of her
two clumsy boots, one gaped and the other was fastened with
half a bootlace and a knotted bit of string, and both were
grey. Her hair was a good sensible drab, not too conspicuous
when badly groomed; and she had a wicked habit of sucking
one or another of its stribbly ends.

'She's just a skin,' said Miss Leggatt, pausing at the foot of
the cairn, while Mrs. Ironside's voice came spattering past
her in little bursts:

'Tak yer hair ooten yer mou', Matty . . . and say how-do-
you-do . . . to yer aunt. Mumblin' yer hair . . . like that . . .
I never saw the like.'

'She's hungry, that's fat she is, the littlin,' said Aunt
Josephine.'Ye're fair hungerin' her, Emmeline.' And she
put out her hands and drew Martha towards her by the
shoulders.'Now, my dear,' she said. It was a finished action
and a finished phrase. Miss Leggatt's simplest word had a
way of suggesting completion, as though it conveyed her
own abounding certainty in the rightness of everything.

Emmeline told her daughter what was in store for her.

'Wunna that be fine?' said Aunt Josephine.

Martha firmly held by the shoulders in Aunt Josephine's
grasp, answered by the action and not by word. Words came
slowly to her need; and her present need was the most
unmanageable she had ever experienced; for school to

Martha was escape into a magic world where people knew things. Already she dreamed passionately of knowing all there was to know in the universe: not that she expressed it so, even to herself. She had no idea of the spaciousness of her own desires; but she knew very fervently that she was in love with school. Her reaction to the news she had just heard, therefore, was in the nature of protest – swift and thorough. She simply kicked out with all her strength of limb.

'I wunna be ta'en awa fae the school,' she screamed. 'I wunna. I wunna.'

'Did ever ye see the likes o' that?' panted her mother. 'Be quaet, will ye, Matty? I'm black affronted at ye. Kickin' yer aunt like that. Gin I cud get ye still a meenute, my lady, I'd gar yer lugs hotter for ye.'

Martha kicked and screamed the more.

Aunt Josephine let them bicker. Troubling not even to bend and brush the dust of Martha's footmarks from her skirt, she walked back calmly to the cottage.

Aunt Josephine Leggatt was a fine figure of a woman. She carried her four-and-sixty years with a straight back and a steady foot. She would tramp you her ten miles still, at her own pace and on her own occasions. Miss Leggatt made haste for no man, no, nor woman neither: though she had been known to lift her skirts and run to pick a sprawling child from the road or shoo the chickens off her seedlings.

'We'll need to put a fencie up,' she said.

It was just a saying of Aunt Josephine's, that – a remark current for any season. She said it as one says, 'It's a bonny day,' or, 'I dinna ken fat's ta'en the weather the year.'

'Josephine'll mebbe hae her fencie ready for her funeral,' said Sandy Corbett, Aunt Jean's gristly husband.

The fence was not neglected from carelessness, or procrastination, or a distaste for work. Still less, of course, from indifference. Miss Leggatt had a tender concern for her seedlings, and would interrupt even a game of cards at the advent of a scraping hen. But deep within herself she felt obscurely the contrast between the lifeless propriety of a fence and the lively interest of shooing a hen; and Aunt Josephine at every turn chose instinctively the way of life. The flame of life burned visibly in her with an even glow. A miracle to turn aside and see – the bush burning and not consumed. One could read it in her eye, a serene unclouded eye, that never blazed and was never dimmed. An eye, moreover, that never saw too much.

But pleasant as one found her eye, it was the nose that was the feature of Aunt Josephine Leggatt's countenance. It was as straight as her back. A fine sharp sculptured nose that together with her lofty brow gave her profile a magnificence she had height enough to carry. A good chin too: though Jean, as Josephine herself was the first to acknowledge, had the chin of the family. Jean's chin spoke.

To look in Aunt Josephine's face, one felt that life was a simple matter, irrationally happy. Temper could not dwell with her. On this June day, hot and airless, with the spattered dents of early morning thunder-drops still uneffaced in the dust, not even Emmeline could withstand her serenity.

'She's ta'en a grip o' ill-natur,' Emmeline grumbled, shaking the child. 'She's aye girnin', an' whan she's nae she's up in a flist that wad fleg ye. An ill-conditioned monkey.'

'Leave the bairn's temper alane,' said Miss Leggatt. 'The inside'll clear o' itsel, but the ootside wunna. A sup water and some soap wad set ye better'n a grumble.'

Martha was accordingly washed, and another frock put on her. She possessed no second pair of boots, and therefore the existing pair remained as they were. A bundle that went under Aunt Josephine's arm, and a hat pulled over Martha's tangled wisps of hair, completed these preparations for the child's first sojourn from home: a sojourn upon which she started in wrath.

TWO

Crannochie

Aunt Josephine made no overtures. She trudged leisurely on through the soft dust, her skirt trailing a little and worrying the powder of dust into fantastic patterns. If she spoke it was to herself as much as to Martha – a trickle of commentary on the drought and the heat, sublime useless ends of talk that required no answer. Martha heard them all. They settled slowly over her, and she neither acknowledged them nor shook them off. She ploughed her way stubbornly along a cart-rut, where the dust was thickest and softest and rose in fascinating puffs and clouds at the shuffle of her heavy boots. She bent her head forward and watched it smoke and seethe; and ignored everything else in the world but that and her own indignation.

But in the wood there were powers in wait for her: the troubled hush of a thousand fir-trees; a light so changed, so subdued from its own lively ardour to the dark solemnity of that which it had entered, that the child's spirit, brooding and responsive, went out from her and was liberated. In that hour was born her perception of the world's beauty. The quiet generosity of the visible and tangible world sank into her mind, and with every step through the wood she felt it more closely concentrated and expressed in the gracious figure of old Miss Leggatt. She therefore drew closer to her aunt, looking sidelong now and then into her face.

Beyond the wood they were again on dusty road, and curious little tufts of wind came *fichering* with the dust; and suddenly a steady blast was up and about, roaring out of the south-east, and the long blue west closed in on them, nearer and denser and darker, inky, then ashen, discoloured with yellow like a bruise.

'It's comin' on rainin',' said Martha; and as the first deliberate drops thumped down, she came close up to Aunt Josephine and clutched her skirt.

'We're nearly hame, ma dear, we're nearly hame,' said Aunt Josephine; and she took the child's hand firmly in hers and held back her eager pace. Thunder growled far up by the Hill o' Fare, then rumbled fiercely down-country like a loosened rock; and in a moment a frantic rain belaboured the earth. Martha tugged and ran, but Aunt Josephine had her fast and held her to the same sober step.

'It's a sair brae this,' she said. 'We'll be weet whatever, an' we needna lose breath an' bravery baith. We're in nae hurry – tak yer time, tak yer time.'

They took their time. The rain was pouring from Martha's shapeless hat, her sodden frock clung to her limbs, her boots were in pulp. But Aunt Josephine had her stripped and rolled in a shawl, the fire blazing and the kettle on, before she troubled to remove her own dripping garments or noticed the puddles that spread and gathered on the kitchen floor.

Martha was already munching cake and Aunt Josephine was on her knees drying up the waters, when the sound of a voice made the child glance up to see a face thrust in and peering. A singular distorted monkey face, incredibly lined.

'It's Mary Annie,' said Miss Josephine. 'Come awa ben.'

A shrivelled little old woman came in.

She came apologetic. She had brought Miss Josephine a birthday cake and discovered too late that she had mistaken the day; and on the very birthday she had made her own uses of the cake. She had set it on the table when she had visitors to tea, for ornament merely. Now, in face of the wrong date, her conscience troubled her; and what if Jeannie should know? Jeannie was her daughter and terrible in rectitude; and Jeannie had been from home when Mrs. Mortimer had held her tea-party.

'Ye wunna tell Jeannie, Miss Josephine. Ye ken Jeannie, she's that gweed – ower gweed for the likes o' me.'

'Hoots,' said Aunt Josephine, 'fat wad I dae tellin' Jeannie? Jeannie kens ower muckle as it is. There's nae harm dane to the cake, I'm sure, by bein' lookit at.'

Her heartiness restored Mary Annie's sense of pleasure; but she went away with no lightening of the anxiety that sat on her countenance.

Aunt Josephine had a curious belief that it was good for people to be happy in their own way: and a curious disbelief in the goodness of Jeannie.

'She's a – ay is she – ' she said, and said no more.

'An' noo,' she added, looking at Martha, 'we'll just cut the new cake, for that ye're eatin's ower hard to be gweed. It's as hard's Hen'erson, an' he was that hard he reeshled whan he ran.'

She plunged a knife through the gleaming top of the cake, and served Martha with a goodly slice and some of the broken sugar.

'Yes, ma dear, he reeshled whan he ran. Did ye ken that? An' the birdies'll be nane the waur o' a nimsch of cake.'

She moved about the room all the while she spoke, crumbling the old cake out at the window, sweeping the crumbs of the new together with her hand and tasting them, and breaking an end of the sugar to put in her mouth – with such a quiet serenity, so settled and debonair a mien, that the last puffs of Martha's perturbation melted away on the air.

But even in the excitement of eating iced cake, following as it did on her struggle and the long hot walk through the dust, was not prickly enough to keep her waking. Half the cake still clutched in her messy fingers, she fell asleep against Aunt Josephine's table; and Aunt Josephine, muttering, 'She's clean forfoch'en, the littlin – clean forfoch'en, that's fat she is,' put her to bed, sticky fingers and all, without more ado.

Martha awoke next morning with a sense of security. Like Mary Annie, she proceeded to be happy in her own way. That consisted at first in following Aunt Josephine everywhere about, dumbly, with grave and enquiring eyes. By and by she followed her to the open space before the door, and plucked her sleeve.

'Will I dance to you now?'

'Surely, ma dear, surely.'

She had never been taught to dance. Frock, boots, big-boned hands and limbs were clumsy, and her dancing was little more than a solemn series of ungainly hops. An intelligent observer might have been hard put to it to discover the rhythm to which she moved. A loving observer would have understood that even the worlds in their treading of the sky may sometimes move ungracefully. A young undisciplined star or so, with too much spirit for all its mastery of form . . . Aunt Josephine was a loving observer. She had never heard of cosmic measures, but she knew quite well that the force that urged the child to dance was the same that moved the sun in heaven and all the stars.

So she let her work alone and stood watching, as grave as Martha herself, and as happy.

'Lovely, ma dear, just lovely,' she said: and forgot about the tatties to pare and the dishtowels to wash before another thunder-plump came down. For be it understood that nothing so adaptable as work was allowed to put Aunt Josephine about. She was never harassed with it. She performed the meanest household task with a quiet gusto that made it seem the most desirable occupation in the world. But as soon as anything more interesting offered, she dropped the work where it was, and returned to it, if there was reason in returning to it when she was again at leisure, with the same quiet gusto. If there was no longer any reason in completing the work, why, it was so much labour saved.

'Josephine sweeps the day an' dusts the morn,' Leebie once said with her chilliest snort.

But Leebie's attitude to labour had been subtly deranged by her many years' sojourn in Jean's immaculate household. Early left a widow, and childless, Leebie had lived for nearly thirty years with Mr. and Mrs. Corbett. To the discipline of Jean's establishment she owed her superb belief in labour as an end in itself. To rise on Tuesdays for any other reason than to turn out the bedrooms, or on Fridays for a purpose beyond baking, would have seemed to both sisters an idle attempt to tamper with an immutable law of life. Indeed it is to be doubted, had Mrs. Corbett not been too much engrossed with the immediate concerns of this world to have any attention for a world beyond, whether she could possibly have envisaged a Tuesday spent in singing hymns. Bedroom day in heaven . . . the days in their courses, splendid and unshakable as the stars. . . .

Aunt Josephine, on the other hand, had time to spare for the clumsy young stars, not at all splendid and still rather shaky as to their courses. She stood in great contentment and watched the one that was dancing on her path. Peter Mennie the postie, coming up the path, was drawn also into the vortex of the clumsy star.

'See to the littlin,' said Aunt Josephine.

'She'll need a ride for that,' answered Peter.

He was an ugly man – six foot of honest ugliness. He could never be ugly to Martha. She stopped dancing at sight of him, too shy even to run and hide. He hoisted her on to his shoulder and she went riding off in terror that soon became a fearful joy.

Next day she watched for Peter and went with him again; and the next day too. At Drochety – the farm west from Aunt Josephine's where they delivered the newspaper – Clemmie had always heard them coming and was there at the door, waiting. A raw country lass, high-cheeked, with crude red features and sucked and swollen hands, she managed Drochety and his household to the manner born. Mrs. Glennie, Drochety's feeble wife, lay upstairs in her bed and *worritted* – Aunt Josephine told Martha all about it as though she were a grown-up and Martha listened with grave attention. But she need not have *worritted*, for Clemmie, though she came only at last November term, had the whole establishment, master and mistress, kitchen and byre and *chau'mer*, securely under her *chappit* thumb.

Clemmie had a soft side to Peter, and for his sake was kind to Matty: though she would not of her own accord have made much of a lassie. 'It's aye the men-fowk I tak a fancy to,' she said with perfect frankness. Martha could hear her *skellochin'* with the cattleman in the evenings, 'an' him,' said Aunt Josephine, 'a merriet man.'

The rest of the day Martha trotted after Aunt Josephine or played among the broom brushes above the house. And each day was as sweet smelling and wholesome to the taste as its neighbour.

On the tenth of these days Miss Leggatt straightened herself from the rhubarb bed, where she had been pulling the red stalks for Martha's dinner, and saw young Willie Patterson come cycling down the road. And when young Willie Patterson visited Miss Leggatt, three things always happened: they played a game of cards; they talked of old Willie and the crony of his young days, Rory Foubister; and Miss Josephine forgot the passage of time.

She forgot Martha also. The child stood gravely by, watching; and heard for the first time the name of Rory Foubister. Willie and Miss Josephine took him through hand – a likely lad he had been, 'the warld fair made for him,' said Miss Leggatt. 'But he wasna a gweed guide o' himsel. Never will I forget the day he cam to say fareweel. "I've been a sorrowfu' loon to my parents, Josephine, an' mebbé I'll never come back."'

'Well, well, now,' said Willie, 'it's just as well you spoke of Rory' (as though Miss Josephine ever neglected so to do), 'for didna I just look in on his cousin, old Miss Foubister at Birleybeg. "Tell Miss Josephine," said she, "that Mrs. Williamson and Bella will be here in an hour's time, and we'll be looking for her to make the fourth, and stay as lang's she can," she says.'

'Weel, weel, noo,' said Miss Josephine.

The good humour shone in her. She was burnished with it. When Mrs. Williamson and Bella came to Birelybeg, the summoning of Aunt Josephine followed as a matter of course. So did whist: and it was no idle game.

Aunt Josephine was in a delightful bustle. There was her best black silk *boady* to fetch and air, her boots to polish, her clean handkerchief to lay in readiness beside the bonnet with the velvet pansies. One thing Aunt Josephine forgot was the dinner. The beheaded stalks of rhubarb lay in a heap in the garden where she had left them when Willie Patterson appeared. Their skin had tightened and toughened in the sun and shreds of it were curling up like tendrils. The mince was still upon the shelf.

'We canna wait noo or it's cookit,' said Aunt Josephine when she remembered. She was standing in her petticoat and slip-body in the middle of the kitchen floor. 'We'll just hae a cup of tea an' an egg, an' you'll carry hame the mince to yer mither in yer bundle.'

On the strength of the cup of tea and the egg Aunt Josephine locked her house door and pocketed the ponderous key. On the strength of the cup of tea and the egg Martha watched her go and turned to face her first revisitation of her home.

THREE

Family Affairs

When Aunt Josephine had walked off westward in her best silk *boady*, Martha turned back alone to Wester Cairns. Life was a queer disappointment. Its Aunt Josephines had incomprehensible transactions with the world. Its very woods were dumb. She crawled in among the bracken to rest. Its great tops swayed above her, smelling good. The earth smelt good too; and she fell asleep.

When she awoke the shadows had altered. Thin blades of sunshine had stolen into the wood, shadow had stolen over great patches of the sunny land. She had slept till evening. But Martha was as yet unskilled to read the light and did not know that she had slept so long. She rose and left the wood.

The iron gate to the field was open and two small boys lay on their stomachs beside the puddle. Beyond, a black-eyed girl was strutting, an old cloak tied round her middle.

'Ye micht lat me by, Andy,' said Martha.

Neither of the boys budged.

The lady in the cloak here intervened. Martha had never seen her before; and suddenly she noted that it was her own mother's cloak that dangled from the stranger's waist.

'You can't get this way,' said Blackeyes. 'It's to my house.'

'It's nae to your hoose,' cried Martha. 'It's to my hoose and it's my mither's cloak ye've got on.'

'It's her hoose richt eneugh,' said Andy. 'She bides there.'

'She disna bide there,' said Martha. 'It's nae her hoose and it's nae her cloak. Ye've stealed that cloak. It's my mither's cloak.'

And with that Martha sprang at the puddle, leaped short, and fell in the mire on the farther side.

13

'Sic a mucky mess ye're in, Matty,' said Andy with deep satisfaction. '*You*'ll get yer hi-ma-nanny when ye win hame. Yer mither's in an awfu' ill teen the day. Isna she, Peter?'

'Ay,' said Peter, without looking up from his mud-grubbing. 'She's terrible short i' the cut.'

'Ye'll fair get it, Matty. I wadna hae a mither like yon. She's a tongue, yon woman, an' nae name feart to use it,' went on Andy, repeating lusciously the judgements current in his home on Mrs. Ironside. 'Hisna she, Peter?'

'Ay,' said Peter, intoning his portion of the antiphon from the mud. 'She's a tongue that wad clip cloots.'

'An' a gey heavy han' as weel,' chanted Andy. 'She fair gied it to Peter the day as she gaed by. She fair laid till him. Didna she, Peter?'

'I dinna care a doit,' said Peter, altering the antiphon abruptly under stress of recollection.

Martha attended to neither. She was now on the black-browed stranger's side of the puddle and promptly laid violent hands on the cloak. Blackeyes wrenched herself free, pirouetted out of reach, and over one shoulder, with the most mischievous little sparkle in the world, thrust out her tongue at Martha.

Martha flew upon her, her limbs dancing of themselves with indignation. The black-burnished lady raised a pair of active sun-browned arms in readiness for the onslaught, and as soon as Martha was near enough, flung them tempestuously round her neck and smacked down a slobbery kiss upon her mouth. Martha had no time to adjust herself to the astonishment of a kiss. Her lifted hand came against the stranger's cheek with a sounding slap, and turning she ran until she reached the cottage.

On the flag by the door she paused and stared for a minute or two at the untidy thatch, the jagged break at the bottom of the door, the litter of cans and leaky pots and potato parings beside the pump. When she went in, her father was alone by the fire, in shirt sleeves, his sweaty socks thrust up against the mantel.

'Ye're there, are ye?' he said to his daughter.

Martha said, 'Imphm,' and climbed into the chair opposite her father.

Not a word from either for a while.

Then: 'Faither.'

'Weel?'

'Fa's the lassie wi' the black pow?'

'It's a lassie come to bide,' said Geordie slowly, 'Yer mither brocht her.'

Silence again, through which Martha's thoughts were busy with the queerness of family relationships. Other people's families were more or less stationary. Martha's fluctuated. It was past her comprehension.

'Faur's mither?' she asked.

'She's awa oot.'

Geordie did not think it necessary to add that she was out in search of more family. His wife's preoccupation with other people's babies was a matter for much slow rumination on the part of Geordie. He knew well enough that she did not make it pay. But Emmeline would undertake any expedition to mother a child for gain. She liked the fuss and the pack in her two-roomed stone-floored cottage. The stress of numbers excused her huddery ways. Some of the babies died, some were reclaimed, some taken to other homes. Martha accepted them as dumbly as her father, brooding a little – but only a little – on the peculiarities of a changing population.

Geordie himself interrupted her thoughts this evening. It had occurred to him to wonder why she had come home.

Martha explained. Roused from her brooding, she realized that she was hungry.

'Is't nae near tea-time, faither?' she asked.

Geordie took his pipe from his mouth and surveyed his daughter with trouble in his eyes.

'The tea's by lang syne,' he said. 'Did ye nae get ony fae yer aunt?'

'Nuh . . . Ay . . . I some think I had ma tea, but it was at dinner-time. I hadna ony dinner. She was ower busy wi' the cairds to mak' ony, an' syne whan she heard she bude to ging to Birleybeg there wasna time.'

This preposterous situation slowly made itself clear to Geordie's intelligence. Aunt Josephine had neglected for a new-fangled triviality like cards the great primordial busi-

ness of a meal. It was a ludicrous disproportion. Geordie
flung back his head against the chair and roared with
laughter.

There was something elemental about Geordie's laughter.
It flooded up out of the depths of him – not gurgling, or
spouting, or splashing up, but rising full-tide with a steady
roaring boom. It had subterranean reserves of force, that no
common joke was able to exhaust. Long after other people
had fatigued their petty powers of laughter at some easy joke,
the vast concourses of Geordie's merriment were gathering
within him and crashing out in mightily renewed eruptions
of unwearied vigour. He found a joke wholesome until
seventy times seven.

So he laughed, not once, but half a dozen times, over Miss
Leggatt's departure from the common sanities. But after his
seventh wind or so, he put his pipe back in his mouth and
drew at it awhile in silence. Then he hitched himself out of
his chair, with the resolution of a man who has viewed the
situation impartially and made up his mind.

'Yer mither disna like me touchin' her thingies,' he said,
'but we'll need to get a bit piece till ye.'

Martha did not budge. She lay back in her chair with her
legs dangling, and awaited the pleasure of her Ganymede.

'Here's a sup milk an' a saft biscuit,' said Ganymede,
returning (silent-footed as became a banquet). 'That'll suit
ye better'n the cakes.'

Martha nodded and bit deep into the floury cushion of the
biscuit. She loved soft biscuits.

She lay still in the chair and nibbled luxuriously, her
thoughts drifting.

Ganymede resumed his leisure. He sprawled, his stock-
inged feet upon the arm of Martha's chair. They gave her a
happy, companionable feeling. She moved the least thing in
her corner so as to nudge them gently. Ganymede gave her in
response the tenderest, most tranquil, subjovial little kick.
Father and daughter shared a silence of the gods, in which all
is said that need be said.

The clatter of a distracted earth broke by and by upon
Olympus. Noisy voices, with anger in the flying rumours
they sent ahead.

'Here's yer mither comin' in aboot,' said Geordie, disposing of his legs, 'an' I some doot she's in ane o' her ill teens.'

Geordie's diagnosis of his wife's spiritual condition was correct. Mrs. Ironside appeared, herding in Blackeyes. Her very skirts were irate. The three-year old bairn who hung in the wind of them was in some danger of blowing off. A baby kept her arms steadier than they might otherwise have been. Mrs. Ironside had multiplied her family by two.

Her wrath against Blackeyes was checked by the sight of Martha, motionless in the depths of her chair.

The situation was explained.

'Ye maun jist ging back to the school, than,' said Mrs. Ironside, eyeing her daughter.

Passionate tears broke over Martha's cheeks.

To make herself conspicuous by marching back to school when Aunt Josephine herself had made arrangement for her absence, publicly to give report of the drab conclusion to her travels, was more than Martha's equanimity could face. She went hot with shame at the very thought.

She battered the arm of the chair with her fists.

'I canna ging back,' she sobbed. 'I canna ging back.'

'You're a queer ane,' said her mother. 'Ye hinna a please. Temper whan we tak ye fae the school an' temper whan we pit ye back.'

'She can bide aboot the doors, surely,' said Geordie.

'I canna hae her trallopin' at my tails a' day lang. An' look at the mess she wad be in. She's a gey lookin' objeck as it is,' said Emmeline, whose appreciation of cleanliness varied inversely with the godliness of her calm. The more serene she was, the more she tolerated dirt.

'I gaed dunt intil the puddle,' said Martha miserably.

'Fit way cud she help it, whan she hadna had ony dinner?' said her father: a notable man for logic of a strictly informal variety.

Blackeyes was crying, 'It was me that made her do it,' and Martha, suddenly remembering her parcel, jumped up and said,

'But I got the mince.'

A pound of mince may not go far to counterbalance an

increase in family, but it helps. It abated Emmeline's aggressiveness. Mollified with mince, she put her family to rights. Martha was *beddit* side by side with Blackeyes, who fell asleep with one swarthy arm curved round her middle.

The newcomers were Dussie, Madge, and Jim. In August the elder children went to school again. Soon it was dark by supper-time, then by the closing of afternoon school. Winds were up. Mornings of naked frost changed to afternoons of black and sullen rain. There were nights when the darkness blared and eddied round the thatch and sang in the chimney; white nights, all sky, with the moon riding overhead and round her half the heaven swirling in an enormous *broch*; moonless nights when Orion strode up-valley and the furred and fallen leaves glistered on the silken roads.

The children saw nothing of these night festivities. They were jammed together in the huddled kitchen, under the smoky and flaring lamp. But one evening Geordie, from the open house-door, whence a guff of caller air flapped through the stifling kitchen, called the girls out to the night.

At Geordie's call, Dussie was up on the instant. Martha came reluctantly, stooping back over the table to add another stroke to her map.

Outside, after the flare of the lamp and the burnish of firelight, they stepped into a bewildering January dark. Bewildering, because not really dark. Their eyes accustomed to it, they found it was a dark that glowed. No moon; infrequent stars; but when Geordie led them round the end of the house they saw the north on fire. Tongues of flame ran up the sky, flickered, fell back in the unstable pools of flame that gathered on the horizon, rose to crests again and broke into flying jets. The vast north was sheeted in light; low down and black, twisted firs, gnarled, shrunken, edged the enormous heaven. The Merry Dancers were out.

A shudder ran over Martha. Something inside her grew and grew till she felt as enormous as the sky. She gulped the night air; and at the same time made a convulsive little movement against her father. She was not afraid ; but she felt so out of size and knowledge of herself that she wanted to touch something ordinary.

'Some feart kind, are ye?' said the ploughman, taking her hand tight in his own. Dussie clung to his other hand, rapping his knuckles, waggling his fingers, stroking his leg, sneaking a supple hand in his trouser pocket, all the while that she made lively comment on the sky. Geordie and Dussie had half a dozen private finger games before Martha had had enough of gazing upon the light.

It was Dussie who put the eager questions Geordie could not answer.

'Weel, I dinna richtly ken fat they micht be. They ca' them the Northern Lichts. Fireflaughts.' Then an ancient memory stirring (a rare occurrence with Geordie), 'I min' fan I was a laddie there was a bit screed I used to ken. It was some like the geography, Matty, gin I could get a haud o't. Arory . . . arory . . . bory . . . syne there was a lassie's name on till't. Fat div ye ca' yon reid-heided craiturie o' Sandy Burnett's?'

'Alice,' said Matty.

'Ay, ay, that's the very dunt. Arory-bory-Alice. Weel. Noo, Matty, fat is there a' roun' Scotland, lassie?'

'The sea,' said Matty, 'a' the way roun', except faur there's England.'

Geordie stood so long considering it that Martha grew impatient. She was jumping up and down against his hand in her excitement.

'An' fat aboot the Arory-bory-Alices, faither?'

'Weel, I canna get a richt haud o't,' said Geordie deliberately, 'but it gaed some gait like this: On the sooth o' Scotland there's England, on the north the Arory-bory – Burnett's lassie, the reid-heided ane – Alice; on the east – fat's east o't?'

'The sea,' said Martha, turning eastward, where a span of sea, too dull a glint under the Dancer's light to catch an ignorant eye, notched their eastern view.

'Weel, aye, but it wisna the sea. It was something there was a hantle mair o' than that.' Geordie's thoughts, like Martha's, glanced upon their private notch of sea. 'I some think it was the sun – the risin' sun. Ay, fairly. That's fat it was. Noo, the wast. Fat's wast o' Scotland, Matty?'

'The sea,' said Martha again.

'It's nae that, though, i' the bit rhyme. It was a bigger word nor that.'

'Ye cud ca't the ocean – that's a bigger word,' suggested Dussie.

'It's the Atlantic Ocean,' Martha said.

Geordie could get no further with the boundaries of Scotland: but his assertion of the northward edge was too obvious at the moment to be doubted. They stood on Scotland and there was nothing north of them but light. It was Dussie who wondered what bounded Scotland when the Aurora was not there. Neither Martha nor Geordie had an answer.

Some weeks later Geordie had a shaking and shuffle of excitement in the middle of the kirk. He nudged Martha with signs and whispers she could not understand. She held her eyes straight forward and a prim little mouth, pretending not to see or hear. It was dreadful of her father to behave like that in church. Once out on the road again,

'Yon's the wordie, Matty – fat's the meenister was readin' aboot. Eternity. That's fat wast o' Scotland. I mind it noo.'

Martha said it over and over to herself: *Scotland is bounded on the south by England, on the east by the rising sun, on the north by the Arory-bory-Alice, and on the west by Eternity.*

Eternity did not seem to be in any of her maps: but neither was the Aurora. She accepted that negligence of the map-makers as she accepted so much else in life. She had enough to occupy her meanwhile in discovering what life held, without concerning herself as to what it lacked.

She repeated the boundaries of Scotland with the same satisfaction as she repeated the rivers in Spain. Up to her University days she carried the conviction that there was something about Scotland in the Bible.

The Merry Dancers danced in storm.

Huge galleons of cloud bore down upon the earth, their white sails billowing on the north horizon. Swiftly their glitter and their pride foundered in a swirl of falling snow. The air was darkened. The sun crept doubtfully back to silence. Shifty winds blew the road bare and piled great wreaths at corners and against the dykes. An unvarying wind chiselled knife-edged cornices along the wreaths.

Thaw blunted them, and filled the roads with slush. Rain pitted the slush and bogged the pathways.

The children went to school through mire. There was no scolding now for mucky garments; boots were clorted and coats sodden and splashed. Their ungloved hands were blue and swollen with chilblains.

There was east in the spring. Summer winds tumbled the sky. Dykesides smelt of myrrh and wild rose petals were transparent in the July rain.

Dussie and Martha were each a year older. So was Madge. She was not communicative. Her conversation was yea and nay – except to Geordie, and her own small brother Jim, to both of whom she would occasionally impart much astonishing information. Geordie received it with composure, Jim with fists or chuckles according to the edge of his appetite.

In August Mrs. Ironside brought home another baby boy.

One result of this was that Madge, who because she took frequent colds had hitherto slept in the unfreshened kitchen, was sent to share the west room with the other girls. Dussie and Martha found her inconvenient. She interrupted their disclosures to each other regarding the general queerness of life. Not that she seemed to be paying any attention; but one day Martha overheard her solemn and detailed recital to baby Jim of one of their dearest secrets. Martha had shaken her till her yells resounded from the Quarry Wood; and Emmeline had shaken Martha till she was sick and had to have castor oil.

It was some consolation for the castor oil that Dussie heartily approved her action. Dussie also commandeered two sweeties from Andy Macpherson and raced home with them triumphantly to Martha as an aid to the castor oil in its kindly office.

Dussie and Martha had things to tell each other that were not for the ear of infants.

FOUR

In Which a Latin Version Is Spoilt

On a February evening, when sleet lashed the window in tides of deepening violence, and spat upon the flames, and sluiced under the ill-fitting outer door, was debated with pomp and circumstance the question of whether or not Martha should go to the University. For days the wind had streamed up-valley; a dull, grey wind, rude and stubborn, that subdued the whole landscape to its own east temper. The howl of it was in the ear at night, long after dark had hid its bleakness from the eye. Gulls screamed and circled over-head – a wild skirl against the drone of the firwood. Spring was late. Hardly a peewit, not a lark, to hear. A drab disconsolate world.

Martha had pushed against the sodden wind four miles and a half that morning, her heavy bundle of books tied on behind her cycle. She was eighteen now and in the highest class at school; but the bursaries on which she had carried herself so far ran to no unnecessary railway fares – not in the Ironside family, where a penny saved had a trick of turning to a penny squandered – and in most weathers she cycled back and fore to town night and morning.

That morning Emmeline had said:

'Ye'll nae get in dry. It'll be a doonpour. Yon win's nae for naething. Hae. There's yer coppers.'

She gave her daughter the pence for her return fare to town. Martha had never had money of her own. She handed over all her bursary money to her mother and had to ask back what she needed. She very seldom asked back. It was too unpleasant being made to feel an undue drag upon the house. Not an exercise-book was purchased but it was audibly grudged. Martha felt a felon when her teachers ordered her to buy a pencil. Her journey home at night was sometimes

22

spent devising ways and words to approach the theme of another new text-book; she would sit all through supper-time with a sickening twinge pulling and twisting inside her body; her back would not hold up; when she washed the supper dishes her knees were sagging. Emmeline had no understanding of her own tyranny. She objected for the sake of objecting.

Martha put the train fare in her pocket and looked at the sombre sky. It had been just as heavy for days and she had escaped a wetting. She pulled her cycle from the shed and raced along the beaten path that crossed the field. The field was lately ploughed. At every dozen steps she stumbled off the narrow path (moist enough itself in the sodden weather) into the heavy upturned earth. Clods hung upon her boots. She raced on, to gain the road before her mother saw her go. The pennies in her pocket jigged to a dance tune. They meant a candle (if the candles could be bought before her mother knew the pence were saved), and a candle meant peace to work at night in her own chill room.

She dared not buy the candles in town lest at the last minute the storm broke and she had to return after all by train. At half-past four the wind still screamed up-country; no change since morning, and Martha set off to cycle home. She intended to dismount and buy her candles in the last shop on the outskirts of the city; but the wind, and her own fear of being caught in rain and her mother's anger, drove her at such a frantic speed that she was already past the shop before her mind snatched at the necessity for dismounting. It would have been foolish to turn back and fight the wind – the candles could be bought at Cairns. The shop was far behind her by the time her mind had worked itself to that resolve, so irresistible a vigour was in the wind that pushed her on. She let herself go to its power, pedalling furiously on her old machine that had no free-wheel and one inefficient brake.

A long stretch of unsheltered road lay ahead, running beneath a low sky that sank farther and farther as she advanced. Suddenly the grey wind turned dirty-white, drove upon her in a blast of sleet. It chilled her neck, soaked her hair, dribbled along her spine, smothered her ears; the backs of her legs and arms were battered numb; her boots filled slowly with the down-drip from her skirt and stockings; once or twice she looked at the handle-bars to make sure that her hands were there. She had dismounted when the sleet began, to unfasten her books from behind the bicycle; her person might be soaked, but not her precious books. She rammed them in the bosom of her coat, that gaped and would not fasten over the unwieldly bundle. When she mounted again she had to pedal furiously in spite of her hampered and clammy limbs, because to pedal furiously was easier than to hold back against the sweep of the wind; but as the sleet continued to fall and filled the road with slush and semi-liquid mud, her pace slackened, till at last she was pushing with effort over the pasty ground, her front wheel bumping, splashing, squirming by reason of her inability to guide it. Darkness had come down too soon. She had a lamp but no means of lighting it, nor could it easily have been lit in the violence of the weather. A passing cart filled her with nameless dread; a chance pedestrian loomed horribly distorted through the sleet; there were no recognizable sounds. The beat of the storm upon her back had plastered her shoddy clothing to her skin. By the time she rode through Cairns, its early lights diffused and smudgy in the thickened air, she was too numb to think, even to picture the possession of a candle, much less procure it. She rode like an automaton.

At the foot of the long brae to the cottage she stumbled from her machine. Light had gone from the earth. The sleet drove now upon her side as she battled uphill pushing her bicycle. Thought began to stir again when she reached the puddle at the gateway of the field. She went straight ahead through the puddle because it mattered little now how much wetter she became; and with that she began to wonder what reproach her mother would have ready. She had not even candles for consolation; and Emmeline would say next morning, 'Ye've got yer money for the train.' She tumbled her cycle into the shed and pushed open the house-door, standing dazed a moment on the threshold.

Emmeline's back was towards the door, as she bent over the fire and stirred the sowens for supper. Without turning, when one of the children said, 'Here's Matty come,' she complained to her daughter.

'Ye've ta'en a terrible like time to come up fae the station.'

Martha's heart fluttered and thumped, and pulses beat hot and hurried in the chill of her temples. So her mother had not been in the shed and did not even know that the cycle had been taken out!

'It's a terrible night. I'm wet through,' she said. But the wetting had suddenly become of no importance. Her mind did not even run forward to the pennies she had gained; the mere relief from an immediate onslaught by her mother's tongue was joy enough. She went in a sort of stupid excitement to remove her dangling clothes; but she had to call Madge through from her Pansy Novelette to help her strip.

Geordie came in, soaked too. The fireplace was hung with dripping garments and the iron kettles perched with sopping boots. The steam of them eddied about the room, mingling with the wood-smoke blown back from the chimney. Emmeline worked herself into a lather of vituperation at the weather and the folk, but gave the latter none the less their sowens in ample measure, smeared with syrup and piping hot. She set the boys to feed the fire with branches and logs of pine. Every now and then a resinous knot spluttered and sang, flared out in blobs and fans of flame. Emmeline made no economies with fire. She loved heat. The little kitchen was shortly stuffed with a hot reek – the reek of wood and folk and sowens, wet clothes, steaming dishwater and Bogie Roll.

For once Martha did not regret her lack of candles. She was shivering violently from her exposure and glad of the heavy heat of the kitchen. She sat at the deal table, catching her share of light from the lamp upon her open school-books. Geordie was playing Snakes-and-Ladders with the bairns – Madge and the eight- and nine-year-old boys. There was no Dussie now. Something less than three years after her arrival, Mrs. Ironside had polished her one day according to her lights and taken her away. Her folk reclaimed her. Dussie was in a whirl of excitement. She had tangled the processes of washing and dressing with fifty plans for interminable futures, and Martha was to share her fortune and her favour. They had not seen her since.

A three-year-old girl was asleep in the kitchen bed, to be carried *ben the hoose* in Madge's ruddy arms when she herself retired. Madge was twelve, a strong-built girl, not tall, no great talker, knowing and not sharing her own mind.

In spite of the driving sleet, which had sting enough to keep most folk by their own firesides, Stoddart Semple lounged in the ingle nook and smoked his filthy cutty. He was a grey cadaverous man in the middle fifties, who did for himself and doggedly invaded his neighbours' homes. 'Stoddart's takin' a bide,' folk said. They growled at him but seldom put him out. He was good to laugh at.

Emmeline, still standing, a dish-towel lumped beneath one arm, and her elbows dug into the back of her husband's chair, was having her turn of the Pansy Novelette.

Geordie could rattle the dice with the best when it was a matter of Snakes-and-Ladders or so, and was unaffectedly happy in his slow deliberate play with the bairns; but jerking back his chair he chanced to dislodge Emmeline's elbows, and drove her fists against her chin, her teeth closing upon her tongue.

'Tak care, will ye?' said she. 'Garrin' a body bite their tongue. . . .'

'Haud oot ower a bit, than,' said Geordie, and he slapped his knee and roared with laughter. The game was upset, and the boys began a monkey-chase about the room. Madge climbed on a creepie to see over Emmeline's shoulder on to the jewelled-and-ermined pages of the Pansy Novelette, which Emmeline was still reading voraciously, bending as often as the boys scuttled within her reach to flick them with the dish-towel.

Martha all this while sat at another board, playing a different game: a game of shifting and shuffling and giving in exchange. Its most fascinating move consisted in fitting four flighty little English sentences into one rolling Latin period. Martha bent her energies upon it, too absorbed to heed the racket around her. Even when a bear beneath the table worried her knees, she only moved aside a little impatiently, saying nothing.

Martha had grown up quiet. After all the flaring disquietudes of her childhood, she had settled into a uniform calmness of demeanour that was rarely broken. Her silences, however, were deceptive. She was not placid, but controlled. She had the control that comes of purpose; and her purpose was the getting of knowledge. There was no end to the things that one could know.

Goerdie was still in his cups, metaphorically speaking, an honest joke suiting him as well as a dram; and Mrs. Ironside was grumbling still: 'Garrin' a body bite their tongue . . . I never heard . . .'; when Willie sprang on the top of the table and upset the bottle of ink upon Martha's Latin version. She had written half of it in fair copy, in a burst of exasperation at the refusal of the second half to take coherent form. Now she sprang to her feet and watched the black ruin, staring at the meandering of the ink.

'Ye micht dicht it up,' said Emmeline.

Emmeline had stuffed the novelette under her chin, pressing it there, head forward, to keep it in position, and had lunged out after Willie, flicking at his ear with the dish-towel. The lurch she gave as he dodged jerked the book on to the floor and Emmeline herself against the table; and the dish-towel flicked the ink.

'Blaudin' ma towel an' a',' she grumbled; and then,

'Ye micht dicht it up,' she said to Martha.

Martha gulped. She suddenly wanted to scream, to cry out at the pitch of her voice, 'I haven't time, I haven't time, I haven't time! What's a kitchen table in comparison with my Latin, with knowing things, with catching up on the interminable past! There isn't *time*!'

She set to work cleaning up the mess.

Then tears scalded her. Through them, blurred, ridiculous, all out of shape, fantastically reduplicated, she was watching her mother pick up the Pansy Novelette, bunch the towel beneath her arm again, and read.

Martha felt her mouth twist. The reeking air of the kitchen choked her. Its noises hammered and sang through her brain. The room was insufferably tight. She pushed viciously with both hands at the wet cloth she was using, smearing the table still further with pale blue stains. She licked a tear from her upper lip. Quite salt. Another – she licked that too. Her eyes and cheeks were fired where they

had run. . . . And the intolerable waste of mood! She had
been saturated with the spirit of Latin prose – it had soaked
in. Words, phrases, turns of speech, alert and eager in her
brain, drumming at her ears, clamouring in an exultant
chaos. And that last triumphant mastery, forcing on the
chaos order and a purpose – the god's security. Gone now.
Spilt like the ink, as irretrievably. A worse waste even than
the time.

'Ye're skirpin' a' ower the place,' said Emmeline.

Martha flung the cloth into the basin of water.

'Oh why can't you do it yourself!' she cried. '*Mother*!
You've more time than I have. You're just reading. Just
rubbish. – Oh, it doesn't matter – I didn't mean – you
needn't be angry anyway. It *is* just rubbish. And I've all my
Latin to do for tomorrow.'

'Latin?' said her mother.

'I'll never get it done tonight now.'

'Latin,' said Emmeline again. 'Fat sorra div ye need wi'
Latin for a teacher? Ye're nae to larn the geets Latin, I'm
hopefu', an' them disna ken ae year's en' fae the t'ither.'

Martha moistened her lips. The hot salt tears had shrivelled them.

'I need it to get a bursary,' she said.

'Oh, that's something new,' said her mother. 'It's the first
I've heard o't.'

Stoddart Semple glowered at Martha. He was a long loose
man, *ill-shakken thegither*. Useless laps of skin sagged round
his mouth. '*Nos et mut . . .* ,' he mumbled, forgetting the
conclusion. Then he broke into a tirade against learning.
Abject the people who value what we valued once and today
despise. Stoddart had hankered once after knowledge; once
he too had stormed the fastnesses of understanding. The
fastnesses unfortunately had stood fast. His father, who had
jogged for a lifetime behind his *shaltie* selling smokies and
finnan haddies to the country wives, and had jogged more
pence into his pocket than wisdom into his head, satisfied the
boy's ambition and sent him to college. Strangely, not a
professor among them could be found to endorse young
Stoddart's opinion of his brains. Old Semple would have
bribed them cheerfully, the whole Senatus, Sacrist and all, to

let the laddie through: but he died before it became plain that the laddie had stuck; and the old man's transactions began and ended with fish. Stoddart sold the fish-cart and the decrepit horse, counted (in an evil day) his father's savings, and from that day onward never did a stroke of honest labour. He lived alone in his father's cottage, meditating projects to astonish the earth: soon he would have been glad to astonish even the parish. The parish had little use for a fine phrase, and did not know what to do with learning authenticated by no official stamp. Had he passed his examinations they might have listened to him, even without understanding; once he had been ploughed, they were at liberty to laugh. He let them laugh, but in a fury of contempt. He grew increasingly morose, striding by in a sort of bickering speechlessness. He shunned society: then mooned; then slouched, body and mind settling to a habit of slackness; his features coarsened; he seeded and grew stringy. His grudge against ungrateful man blackened and rotted his powers. The devotee's indignation at the disdaining of his god had turned to a black and brooding madness on this one subject of himself.

With the passage of years he ceased himself to believe in his discredited dignity.

The neighbours saw the deterioration of face and figure, the hanging jaw, the rag-nailed thumbs, the sloven countenance; they saw refuse encumber his doors; the smell of his body *scunnered* them; they cackled at his clothing, sodden from exposure to every weather, matted and split. He trailed through any *dubs*, under any sky. A night prowler too, haunting the deep of the wood by midnight. His neighbours' premises, perhaps, as well: who could know? Labouring folk sleep early and sleep sound. But there were suspicions anent him – queer ends of talk. A dark bulk – an indeterminate shadow – a malignant *reeshle* of the leaves without wind – sorry matters, but from them grew half-broken tales. A troubler of men's imaginations, generating legend . . . a queer rôle for the *stickit* graduate. A looking-glass progression towards the object of his old ambitious desires . . . troubling men's imaginations . . . .

The neighbours saw the change in him – his rotting look:

it was not for them to know that under the external squalor
seethed horribly a spiritual regeneration.

Stoddart had need of his kind.

He blundered his way back into society by virtue of an
inlaid dambrod. Old Semple had been a craftsman of sorts
and had begun to fashion a dambrod of two varieties of
wood, each square inset with patient skill. Death made a
move on his board before the man's board was completed. It
lay where chance had tossed it, till Stoddart unearthed it one
morning and set to work to finish it. No craftsman, he made
a sorry enough job: but the board was ready for the game and
Jamie Lowden liked a game fine of a blank and blustery
winter evening. Stoddart carried the dambrod to Jamie
Lowden's.

By what processes of pity, curiosity, persuasion, the
dambrod gave him entry to other houses, would be hard to
say: but in course of time, shambling, apologetic, he slunk
his way wherever he desired: accompanied always by the
board. He loved the bit of wood. He would shuffle round
with it under his arm, 'oxterin' at it as though it were a
body.' Humbly at first, he ventured the piece of workmanship into view, claiming praise for his father's handiwork; but careful to add that it was he who had finished it.
By and by the squares that he had fashioned subtly shifted
their position on the board. He was not oversure himself
which he had made; and at the thought that he might really
be the framer of this dark beauty or of that, he regained
something of the belief in himself that he had lost. In
consequence he tidied his homestead a little and cleaned his
person; and became a more decent member of human
society. With the passage of another year or two he was very
comfortably convinced once more of his own dignity and
importance: with this difference, that he had ceased to
trouble very much whether others believed in them or not.

One house to which he did not carry the dambrod was the
Ironsides'. Emmeline could not abide him, in his days of
grandiloquence. 'He's fair clorted wi' conceit,' she said
impatiently to Geordie. 'Ye cud tak a rake an' rake it aff'n
him.' Emmeline's own conceit, in those early days of marriage, was at too low an ebb to allow her to enjoy the quality

in others: hence perhaps her ineradicable grudge against Stoddart. When he rose out of the nadir of his degradation and Geordie brought him *in aboot* of an evening, she suffered his presence but gave short shrift to the dambrod. Geordie indeed, in the natural complaisance of his soul, sat to study the play: but it exacted too much of a man wearied out and sodden still with the heavy sense of wet fields and claggy soil. Geordie carried back with him to his own fireside, stored up in his own body – his stiff and aching muscles, his numbed brain, his slow and inattentive nerves – the memory of a thousand generations wearing down the long resistances of the earth. A desperate task, to shake oneself quickly free from memory that had worked itself in. Geordie was not altogether sorry when Emmeline's tongue banished the dambrod from her kitchen.

'Sic a cairry-on he hauds wi' himsel an' yon boardie,' she said contemptuously. – 'Wheesht, wheesht, he's hearin' ye,' from Geordie. – 'I named nae names,' said Emmeline. 'Them that has lang noses can tak tae them.' Stoddart was touchy. The dambrod was effectively dismissed.

The man, however, kept coming, in spite of abuse. He was stingy with his own fuel and liked Emmeline's lavishness with hers: especially on a night of driving bitter sleet, like the one in question.

So he slouched in the heat and, diving among recollections that had gone sour, miscalled knowledge.

Martha listening did not divine the man.

Our acquaintances have no past for us until we have a past ourselves.

She was merely irritated at his opposition. Rashly, she had precipitated her fight, and the fortune of war was against her. This henchman of darkness, sunken-eyed, slack-mouthed, betrayed her to the enemy. The wastrel forces of ignorance were in power.

For Martha was set upon a purpose not yet divulged. It was understood that she was to be a teacher, after a two years' course at a Training Centre; but Martha herself was working secretly for more. She had learned as yet to be passionate on behalf of one thing only – knowledge: but for that she could intrigue like any lover. She had made her own plans for going, not to the Training Centre but to the University. So, quite unnecessarily, she was learning Latin. When her bursary was gained, it was time enough to tell.

And now, fool that she was, she had given her position away.

And to let Stoddart Semple, whom she hated, see her cry! She swallowed hot tears and listened, craning for every word, to her mother and Stoddart, disputatious, grumblers both, using Martha's preposterous ambition to justify their own particular grievance.

'Fat ails ye at bein' a teacher?' demanded Emmeline.

'Nothing ails me. – I'm going to be a teacher. But I want to go to the University.'

'An' how muckle langer'll that tak ye?'

'Two years,' Martha said.

Emmeline's exasperation had a deeper basis than Martha understood; than Martha indeed was capable of understanding, for she had never breathed a Leggatt atmosphere nor been nurtured in the *pietas* of Leggatt respectability: except, and that dubiously, at Crannochie; for Aunt Josephine was not a thoroughbred. Her social status did not exist for Martha. She had never thought about it. But Emmeline had dreamed with undiminished ardour for twenty years of being respectable again. She had consented to let Martha be a teacher for no other end than this. And after twenty years you ask an Emmeline to wait another four instead of two to see her dream fulfilled! How could a Martha, hungry for the tartness and savour of knowledge, be expected to understand? Martha saw only a slovenly and inefficient woman, given to uncertainties of temper and meaningless indulgences, and with a cankering aptitude for objection. She had never even known that her mother was beautiful; nor that men have decreed rights to beauty that reason need not approve. Dumbly, fitfully, Emmeline was aware of a trouble within her consciousness. She had been somehow foiled – blame it on any wind you will, not on Emmeline – of the right of loveliness to queen it over the imaginations of men. Ill-trickit rascal, that godling with the bow, at whose caprice she had given her love, and been thrust away in consequence to the middle of this dull ploughed field!

Emmeline hankered still after the respect men pay to beauty, though what she dreamed she wanted was the respect they pay to the respectable. She had built herself a formidable conviction of the automatic increase in reputation that would come to the family when Matty was a finished teacher. Add two years to that! – Two and two in this case made an eternity.

Mother and daughter fronted each other, antagonistic, weighing the years in a balance, but with what differing weights!

Stoddart Semple grumbled on. 'She wants to mak hersel oot somebody,' he said. All the rasping irritation of his own discomfiture was in the sneer.

'Some folks are grand at that,' said Emmeline sharply. But he took her up, not heeding the home-thrust.

'Deed they are. You cud dae fine to be somebody yersel, Mrs. Ironside, an' Matty's nae far ahin ye.'

'She wunna be't, then,' said Emmeline with tart decisiveness, furious that Stoddart should read her secret desires. 'My lassie wunna ging like Maggie Findlater, terrible goodwillie to yer face an' despisin' the hale rick-matick o' her fowk ahin their backs.'

'Maggie!' said Stoddart. 'Maggie's nae that ill.'

'A muckle easy-osy lump,' snorted Mrs. Ironside.

'If she'd keep her mou' shut an' her feet in she'd be a' richt. She taks a gweed grip o' the grun' yet an' a grand mou'fu' o' her words for a' her finery.'

'Yon's a terrible pit-on.' Mrs. Ironside's voice expressed the loftiest contempt that a woman who has married ill can possibly bestow on one who has married gorgeously. 'An' a' the men maun be like her man to be men ava'. "Do you play golf, Mr. Ironside?" she says, most gracious-like. Imagine asking Geordie wi' his sharny sheen if he played golf!'

Geordie came to the suface again. He had been out of depth, uneasy at every quirk in the conversation that his slow mind could not follow.

'I dinna haud wi' that cleverness masel,' he had said.

Nobody was listening to him. He tried in vain himself to listen to his own thoughts pounding within him. They said nothing intelligible. Now at the relief of a tried and accepted joke he let himself go, laughing immoderately. His eye on his miry boots flung sidelong in the corner – to focus the idea – he pictured their befouled and clumsy strength companioning the natty smartness of the golfers.

Sane man, seeing always in relation such things as he did see.

Martha meanwhile burned in an agony of impatience. What did they mean, chattering of these indifferent occasions while she waited for her doom? If they would only let her back to work. . . . Wasted time! She stood and fretted, not daring to interrupt, able hardly to endure. And why should her father laugh like that and she in mortal stress?

Geordie came out of the absorption of his joke and heard his wife and his neighbour dispose of Martha's pretensions to a University education. He ruminated soberly. In the cramped kitchen prodigious horizons lengthened out. There were vast unenclosed tracts within him where his thoughts lost themselves and disappeared. He pursued them deep within himself, past his land marks.

The noise of tongues went on.

'Ye're gey forcey, though,' said Geordie.

He said it very loud, with a sharp resonance that startled Emmeline and Stoddart into silence. He jerked forward on his chair, sitting unusually upright, and spoke unusually loud all through his disquisition. The voice of a man who knew the disabilities of Providence – 'deaf in the ae lug an' disna hear wi' the ither.' . . . Providence against Emmeline – it needed that.

'We'll nae be nane waur aff wi' Matty at the college than we are e'noo whan she's at the school, will we?' He boomed the question at them as though they too were a little deaf.

'But we'll be a hantle better off, it's to be hopit, whan she's a finished teacher.'

'Weel, but that's nae the pint. We are as we are an' we're nae that ill – we micht be a hantle waur. But we wunna be a hantle waur wi' Matty at the college. It wunna mak nae differ.'

Emmeline felt a little giddy. Geordie argumentative! A new departure.

Being set on concealment of the true reason for her

obstructionist policy, she could not immediately find another plausible enough to check him with.

'We've gotten a' we need,' he was saying. 'We've aye a tattie till wer dinner.'

'O ay, it's aye the meat you look till. Ye're a grand hand at yer meat, I will say that for ye. But there's mair things nor meat in *this* world.'

Emmeline laid a violent emphasis upon *this*, as though she were quite willing for her husband to circumscribe his activities at eating in a world to come.

'Ye wunna beat a tattie,' said Geordie, 'an' ye wunna ging far wantin' ane. – Nae in this warld,' he added, as though he were willing in his turn for his wife in her next existence to be freed from the encumbrance of food.

Martha crushed the ruined sheet of paper suddenly in her fists and began plucking it to pieces with a series of savage staccato rents.

'Jist you write it ower again, lassie,' said her father. 'There'll aye be a tattie for ye or ye're dane.'

Emmeline broke into abuse. She was defeated by one of the few loyalties she retained. Queer, she never taunted Geordie with her loss of status, nor *deaved* him with her dreams of respectability to come. Queerer still, she had no motive but her love for him. Her fury against Stoddart Semple increased. He had her inner argument pat. She tongued him therefore with virulence, cutting across his rumbling sentences.

'It's a mou'bag that you wad need. A body canna hear themsel's speak in their ain hoose.'

At that moment the wind flared in the chimney, driving the smoke down gustily into the room. Emmeline snatched noisily at the interruption.

'See to yon flan,' she cried, seizing the poker and beating at the fuel as though she would batter the smoke back up the chimney. 'We'll be smokit ooten existence. Haud back yer chairs a bit.' And she swung the poker with a virago brandish that made both Geordie and Stoddart scrape back their chairs. The feathery ash from the charred wood blew in their faces.

Balked of serenity, Emmeline took refuge in cleanliness.

The kitchen was certainly not out of the need of it. Slush and smoke together – smuts and soot and dribbled snow – clods of earth tumbled from drying boots – *dubs* and dung and crumbs and ink and dishwater not yet emptied out, tea-leaves swimming in it, and the rind of bacon flung on the hearth and dissolving in greasy dirtiness among the ashes – a very slattern among kitchens. Emmeline flung herself upon the dirt like a tornado.

'As black's the Earl o' Hell's waistcoat,' she grumbled, sousing the floor.

She splashed and soaped and scrubbed. The steam from her soap suds thickened the air. She lunged with her scrubbing-brush towards Geordie's seat and he moved farther and farther back before the soapy flood; she dived towards Stoddart and he retired with an edgy and raucous creak from the legs of his retreating chair.

By the time the chair was marooned against the wall Stoddart bethought himself and took his leave. Geordie tip-toed across the dripping floor and reached for his boots. Hospitality hardly requires of a man that he conduct his neighbour home (if the neighbour be so ill-advised as to visit him in such conditions) through pitch-black ploughland, an edged south-easter and a barricade of sleet. But Geordie pulled to the outer door with a terrific bang, settling the business of that impudent baggage the wind that threatened to wrench his own door-handle out of his hand with its blufferts, and steered Stoddart across the field by the elbow, roaring at him in gusts between the palavers of the gale.

'They tell me she's byordinar clever. . . . Faith, it beats me a' thegither fat way a bairn o' mine can 'a gotten brains. . . . Man, it's a sort o' judgement on a body. There ye ging, a' yer life long, rale pleased an' comfortable. Naething to gie ye a shog ooten yer ain road. An' then yer ain lassie, that's the fruit o' yer ain loins. . . . Man, it beats a'.'

In the kitchen Martha fumed miserably. She was troubled with a raging conscience. She was wrong. Of course she was wrong to burden the family for two extra years. – But might her father's authority be considered final? Was her fight really won? – She had not fought at all, then! – stood mute and foolish. She underwent a rush of self-contempt. And in spite of conscience and contempt together she was throbbing with exultation. Back to work, quick – master the throb before it mastered her; though how could she work with her mother *nyattering* like that?

'That's jist yer faither a' ower,' Emmeline was grumbling. She had already raised Geordie's aberration into a universal law governing his being. 'That thrawn there's nae livin' wi' him. Aince he taks a notion intil his heid, naething'll move him. He wad argy-bargy ye intil the middle o' next week. Ye micht as weel ging doon on yer knees an' speak to a mole that was crawlin' on the grun'. He taks a bit o' understandin'.'

Martha bent grimly to her Latin. But inspiration had fled. The four shabby sentences declined to be made less than four. The prose was completed, with much searching of the heart and the vocabulary.

Geordie came in again. Wind, water, earth, came with him, spluttered in his tracks. Emmeline dabbed at the filthy runlets – 'as muckle dirt's wad fill a kirk. I never saw. . . .'

The boys were *beddit*. They slept in the middle place, a sort of box between the rooms. Madge was sent packing. Martha pulled her books together and went too.

Emmeline's resentments were messy, but brief.

Next day Martha went to town – in a bitter downpour – by train. Her mother gave her the fare without demur: but she missed the early train home and it was already past the family meal-hour when she returned. There was sign of neither family nor meal. Emmeline on her knees, in splendid isolation, scoured the floor as though it had not felt water for a twelvemonth.

'Where's father?'

'Awa' to the wall for peats.'

Finality in that reply. Martha's heart sagged. She went through to the bedroom.

There she found Madge, curled on the bed, her shoulders hunched, devouring her penny trash. Her grunt was inarticulate; she did not lift her eyes from the page. She had an end of candle stuck in Martha's candlestick.

'Where did you get the candle?' cried Martha sharply. Was it hers? Had Madge stolen it? secreted it?

Madge smirked: not audible enough for one to say, giggled.

'It's nae yours, onyway. – Ye needna stand there and glower,' she added, raising her head. 'I've tell't you, it's nae yours. I suppose I can hide things as well's you.'

But where did she get it? Martha continued to ponder, still glowering at the child. One fragment of her brain said reasonably: Of course she can; and another cried in fever: She mustn't criticize me – she's much too young. The voices in her head circled and intersected; shortly she became aware that they were laced by actual voices, coming through the shoddy wall. She listened – noises too: the stir of industry. Her father and the boys must be in the lean-to against the house-end. She dashed out through the rain and pushed the door. Inside was a reeking, buzzing warmth – an oily lantern, unwashed and sweaty skins, stale air, animation, laughter. Geordie was cleaning Martha's neglected bicycle. The boys were also engaged on the bicycle; wreathing a towsled bit of rope through the spokes of the front wheel and ripping it smartly out again. A terrific display of industry. The flaring and smoky light from the open lantern, shifting, smearing, exaggerating what a moment ago it had suppressed, suppressing what it had exaggerated, gave their actions a fantastic air of unreality. Baby Flossie, hoisted aloft on a barrel and some boxes, a little insecure but in great content, presided over the scene like some genius of the place – an immature deity whose effort at creation had resulted in grotesquerie. She was like a grotesque herself – a very tiny baby, 'an image' Emmeline contemptuously called her: and there she squatted on her barrel, preternaturally solemn, a little above the level of the lantern, that juggled her features all askew so that she seemed to wink and leer upon the workers. But then of course the workers (Geordie excepted) were labouring a little askew.

'She'll kick up a waup for a whilie,' Geordie said when he saw his daughter, 'but it'll wear by. She'll keep's ooten languor an' inen anger.'

He wiped his oily hands on his buttocks, picked up Flossie and happed her in his coat, and extinguishing the lantern made for supper.

'Ay, ay, it'll wear by,' he said.

In spite of a sore throat and aching limbs, Martha did her lessons that night in the cold. She held an illumination, lighting two candles to elucidate *the sine of A + B*. Madge's candle-end was gone: she must have secreted the stump for future use. Martha pushed one of her candles into the candlestick and fixed the other by its own melted end to a broken saucer.

Madge poked her head in.

'You've got to come ben. You'll be perished.'

'I'm not coming. I'm quite warm.'

'A' richt, then, dinna.'

She remained staring for a minute at the twin candles, but said nothing and went away. She could keep her own counsel and was quite willing to keep Martha's also.

Martha was glad of the feeble heat the candles gave. There was warmth also in the recollection of her father's words, 'Ay, ay, it'll wear by.'

It wore by. In very short time Emmeline had comfortably persuaded herself that a daughter with a University degree was a grandiloquence worth the waiting for. She took care, however, to hide her persuasion: in case of need still protestant.

When some months later Martha's examination was over and she had gained her bursary, Geordie sat a long while in his shirt sleeves, unbraced after supper, gripping the newspaper that had published the results, 'aye takin' the t'ither keek at her name.' Emmeline too was moved by the sight of her daughter's name in print. They would see it at Muckle Arlo! She pictured Uncle Sandy Corbett spreading out the paper and reading it aloud. Aunt Leebie would sniff, no doubt, and Aunt Jean receive it in silence: but they would know!

'Ye can jist snifter awa' there' – she addressed an imaginary Aunt Leebie – 'but ye canna say ye hinna seen't.'

'She's got ma sister Sally's gump.' Geordie's voice broke across her pleasant reverie. 'She's rale like Sally whiles.'

'Sally!' screamed Mrs. Ironside, her fancies scattering like a pack of cards. 'Her that disna richt ken gin she's merriet or no.'

'Merriet or nae merriet,' said Geordie, 'she had a sicht

mair gumption nor ony ither o' my fowk.'

Sally Ironside's life, indeed, had demanded, or perhaps developed, gumption. For nine brief days she had been the speak of the place. She had left home at the age of thirty, with neither wealth nor looks to commend her, and gone through a marriage with the man whose taste in womankind had roused the astonishment of all Peterkirk and Corbieshaw and Crannochie.

'If Sally Ironside's gotten a man, an' her thirty an' nae a stitch o' providin', there's hope for me yet,' said one old crone to another.

'There's queerer things happened,' answered she. 'But fat's the notion in nae settin' aboot it the proper gait, tell me that, will ye? A gey heelster-gowdie business, this rinnin' awa' to get yer man.'

Eighteen months later, the sole addition to her worldly gear the bairn in her arms, Sally found herself on the street, her husband having given her to understand that their marriage was a form only, and invalid. Sally disputed nothing; nor did she offer any interference – legal or moral – with his subsequent marriage to a lassie with siller. Ten years later she paid a brief visit to her old home at Peterkirk, in the garb of the Salvation Army. She was well-doing and self-respecting, but what sieges and stratagems she had carried on in the interval against a callous world only Sally herself could tell. She did not choose to tell too much. The bairn had died. 'Good thing,' said Sally briefly.

Questioned as to her marriage, she acknowledged her private suspicion that the ceremony had been valid enough but that the man had taken advantage of her ignorance to get rid of her. She had no marriage lines and did not even know the name of the place where the marriage took place.

'He had a perfect right to tire of me,' she said.

Urged to set enquiries afoot, to seize what chance there was of being proved an honest woman,

'Honest fiddleyorum!' said Sally. 'I'm honest enough in myself, I hope, and a name won't make me any honester that I can see. I'm best quit of him – to start speirin' might only raise the stew. Besides if it turned out I was his true wife, it would be a gey-like pliskey on the lassie wi' the siller.'

'Like Sally!' screamed Mrs. Ironside. . . .

She added, by and by,

'It's fae the Leggatts, onyway, she gets the brains. Your fowk's a' feel.'

Which was a proposition Geordie did not take upon himself to contradict.

FIVE

Luke Comes In

Luke came in upon a day in August.

Martha was wandering in the wood.

'It's a queer like thing that ye canna bide at hame,' Emmeline would say querulously, 'an' nae a stockin' fit to ging on to the bairns the morn's mornin'. Faur hae ye been?'

'In the wood,' Martha would answer, with the same miserable sense of disaster wherewith she had confessed to tumbling in the mire on her return from Crannochie.

'That's richt, ma dear,' said Aunt Josephine, if she happened to be by: and her voice had the quiet decisiveness that suggested something absolute and took the wind from the best-sailing of squabbles. 'They say trees is awfu' gweed for ye.'

She was wandering then in the firwood on the August afternoon when Dussie reappeared: Dussie come back, true to her old fore-visioning, with fortune at heel! – If this were indeed the guise wherewith she ushered fortune in, lanky and sober-suited, a plain unsmiling youth.

Fortunate, by tale of her own appearance. Dussie had a costly look. A silken shimmer on her gown, like the play of flame when she moved and every detail exquisite, from the burnished mass of her hair to the burnished buckles of her pretty shoes: for Luke Cromar had cobbled shoes and knew a good thing in footwear when he saw it; and liked it too, upon his wife.

For nineteen-year-old Dussie, tiny, radiant, absurdly finished and mature, was a bride of five weeks' standing. She had run away from the aunts who had taken her, and married Luke.

'And of course he had no right to marry me,' she said.

'Not so soon. He's only a student – students aren't supposed to get married. But he'll be a doctor next year.'

With that Martha looked at the lanky youth. Hitherto she had paid no attention to him. How could she, with Dussie running on like that? But she gave him now her grave consideration, and he returned her a scrutiny as grave.

'It's a holy pilgrimage,' he said. 'All the haunts of her childhood. A devotee's processional.'

Was it some sort of joke, Martha pondered, walking by them out of the wood. Dussie certainly had laughed extravagantly, though on her life she could not tell whether Mr. Cromar had meant it for a joke or not; and he was very earnest when he asked if they might see the cottage.

Martha asked them in. Dussie, quick to catch her hesitation, cried 'No!' But Luke was quicker and said, 'Of course we're coming in.' So in they came.

Martha's trepidation had cause. Emmeline was complacent that afternoon and therefore tolerant. The tolerance was manifest. Dirty dishes, a bit of pudding, old cast clouts and old rotten rags, broken bark, twigs and jags of firewood, a sotter . . . . Emmeline herself had just completed the current instalment of the serial story in the *People's Treasure*. An insatiable reader, like her daughter: but seeking apocalypse in fiction, not in fact. Peeragesque, her novels. Or if there were not titles enough (bold, bad and foreign in default of English) to go round, let them at least portray the Fortunate, their reversals be from misery to style: and never, dear fate! depict a ploughman, or a ploughman's wife and family.

She had just remarked to Madge, 'I bet you she'll mairry yon chap an' come oot a great swell yet,' when the door opened and the visitors arrived.

Married she was, though not the she of the novelette. Remember her? Well, to be sure! One didn't keep a black besom under one's roof three years and forget her in such a suddenty as that. And, looking her up and down,

'Ye're nae muckle bookit, onyway,' she said. Martha was a good four inches taller. A scoring point for Martha, and scoring points had been hard to find: would be hard still, she realized, studying Dussie more closely. Martha, clothe her how you would, would never look like that. Martha's figure went straight up and down, her blouses were always in bags or escaping at the waist, her skirts drooped, her hair was stribbly and in moments of preoccupation even yet she sucked its ends. Emmeline had a sudden movement of furious hatred against this shapely apparition that rose in her own house to mock her for her daughter's lack of presence. It was imperative to disparage Dussie for the sake of her own self-respect.

'A terrible-like chase ye were in to get merriet,' she said. 'But you aye did a'thing by stots an' bangs,' – and added, her eye on the husband,

'But what a tang'l! Ye micht a' chosen ane wi' mair beef on him fan ye were at it. Like a forty-fittit Janet up on end.'

Dussie's lip stiffened. Their call was brief.

'Yes, we must go on, mustn't we?' said the bridegroom. 'There's that wonderful Aunt Josephine. We have to see her.'

Aunt Josephine! Martha felt relief. Of course, they would go there, all three of them. Aunt Josephine's hospitality was equal to any strain. Martha had been wretched; the sloven kitchen, her mother's rudeness, Dussie's pretty hauteur, sank her in embarrassed shame. The young man's voice revived her. But there he was taking leave of Emmeline with a grave courtesy that was embarrassing too. Beef or no beef, the forty-fittit Janet up on end had manners. Martha was not accustomed to men who were polite to her mother. She felt incredibly shy.

Not much grave courtesy out of doors, however.

He had Dussie by the hand.

'Gorgeous heap of stones. Come on!'

'O Luko!' she breathed, ecstatic; and away they went, stumbling and shrieking, helter-skelter between the barley and the dyke.

They stood all three on top of the cairn, breathless.

Martha said: 'It's very old. It's supposed to commemorate something.'

Luke said: 'I like this place. There's such a lot of sky round about here.'

Dussie said: 'But aren't we going to see your father?'

From her point of vantage she swept the surrounding fields. How Geordie had kittled her, let her climb upon him, sheltered her from storm – Emmeline and the elements, both.

Martha was secretly glad that he was out of sight and call. It would have meant a shame the more. Her father, with his great crunkled boots, straws caught between the soles and uppers, sharn in spatters over them, his trousers tied with string, his empty speech, his roaring gales of laughter. . . .

They set out for Aunt Josephine's.

Mary Annie was visiting Miss Leggatt.

The years had made little difference to Aunt Josephine. She had no capacity for growing old. Mary Annie, too, was hardly altered: she had grown so old already, so many ages were graven in her anxious face, that nine years or so could only trifle with the indentations that furrowed her.

Apologetic, she tried to creep away.

'Noo, noo, Mary Annie,' said Aunt Josephine. 'Ye were bidden to tea an' ye'll bide to tea. We'll hae wer tea a' thegither. It'll be a party, ma dear' – she enveloped Dussie, excitement and buckles and all, with her slow shining gaze – 'just a party. Ye canna ging awa', Mary Annie, an' Jeannie oot. Ye canna bide yer lane.'

Fetching a profound sigh at the mention of her loneliness, Mrs. Mortimer sat down again.

Mary Annie's man was dead. He had died three months after getting a complete set of false teeth. Unlucky all the ways of it, those teeth. He hadn't had them three weeks when he had a drop too much. Some late in coming home, he was, and not so able to hold his liquor as he used to be . . . 'an' him spewin' a' the road hame, in ahin dykes an' sic-like.' . . . It was next morning till he noticed that he had shed the teeth . . . 'An' a terrible palaver there was or they got them.' The police poking about in all odd corners. And he hadn't had them three months when he died.

Mary Annie's plaint against the horrible uncertainty of life started always from the teeth and returned back upon them. They symbolised for her the tragedy of life's waste. She had wrapped them in a handkerchief and put them between the folds of the nightgown laid aside in her kist for her own last dressing. She would have given them a more prominent place among her gear had it not been for awe of her daughter Jeannie. Jeannie, and no cataclysm of nature or the soul, had tortured Mary Annie's features into their ghastly fixedness of dark anxiety. She was preyed upon by the perennial sense that she was unworthy of her daughter.

Jeannie indeed had certain powers beyond her mother's comprehension. In her early teens she had developed ways of her own and displeasures for which her mother could see no kind of reason. Her withering young disapproval ran across the household. Mary Annie set herself against innovation and Jeannie had no more than looked at her father.

'I dinna see fat ye need conter the lassie for,' said he to his wife. 'Dinna quarrel her. Jeannie's nae to be contered.'

Mary Annie, painfully conscious of the honour he had done her in lifting her from her estate of servant lassie at the Leggatts' to be mistress of a four-roomed house, had sorrowfully acquiesced. Her daughter bewildered her. She was of her father's mould, superior to the breed of servants. Her own shortcomings loomed heinous in view of Jeannie's assured and incomprehensible managements. But one day when the girl was sixteen she had appropriated a crimson sateen bodice trimmed with black bugles, that had been her mother's pride some eighteen years before. Never worn now, it yet retained its valour in her memory. It was like a bit of materialized experience. Mrs. Mortimer entered by chance her daughter's bedroom (without knocking: a practice that Jeannie in vain had indicated to her as objectionable) just as the second slash was making in the crimson stuff. The girl (who did not even pay her mother the idle compliment of deceit with regard to unapproved proceedings) told her coolly that she was doing up the bodice to wear when Tammie Gleg took her next week to the Timmer Market.

'Ye needn't be in sic a takin' aboot it,' she said, the scissor poised for another cut, 'it's gey cheap-john lookin' stuff.'

Mary Annie had long ceased expostulating with her daughter by word of mouth. She simply grabbed the crimson bodice and wrested it by main force from its captor. Jeannie let go, to avoid rending it, secure of her own ultimate victory. But Mr. Mortimer, to whom the sentimental value of the garment was fudge, nevertheless on this occasion sided with his wife. He had no mind to see a lass of his gallivanting in the Castlegate with a merry-andra like Tammie Gleg, 'skraighin' an' chawin' nuts, an' nae mair sense in their heids nor the timmer spurtles.' He forbade the occasion for the bodice, whispering behind his hand to Jeannie.

'Never heed the boady. Ye'll get a better ane to yersel whan ye're a bittie aulder.'

Jeannie never forgave her mother the interference. She took a terrible, if unintentional, revenge. She took to religion. In one of her turbulent adolescent moods she underwent conversion. The process was passionate and thorough, nor was there any reason to doubt its sincerity; but she early learned to master a force that might otherwise have mastered her, and use its currents for her own purposes. Henceforward the thwarting of her will became impossible. She had leadings from above and resorts to prayer in every complicated situation. She cultivated the habit of praying – aloud – for the soul of anyone who crossed her will. Mary Annie was gifted with a humble and ignorant adoration for all that had to do with religion. She had no genius for it herself. For many years it had been the secret craving of her heart to make up a prayer out of her own head, till the attempts had shrivelled of their own useless accord and been forgotten. When therefore her daughter graduated in piety, Mary Annie abased herself and worshipped. Thenceforward she was haunted by her own unworthiness of such a daughter. There was no conscious hypocrisy in Jeannie's conduct: her life indeed was one of extreme rectitude, just as many of the innovations she brought to the home were in themselves excellent: she merely allowed herself to be deluded in accordance with her desires.

She was now a woman in the middle forties, of powerful build and marked features, that gave her the impression of a strength of character she did not really possess. She was thrawn, not strong.

Aunt Josephine was making tea.

'Ye cutty 'at ye are!' she would interrupt herself to say to Dussie.

'And shouldn't Marty get married too?' said Dussie, preening herself.

'There's Andy Macpherson has a gey ill e'e aifter her, I'm thinkin',' said Aunt Josephine complacently.

'Rubbish!' cried Martha in a savage scarlet. Andy Macpherson, who sold bacon and sweeties in a grocer's shop at Peterkirk, had considerably less to do with her present scheme of the universe than had Hannibal or Robert Peel. Her annoyance, however, rapidly subsided. A day earlier she would not even have blushed. But something in Dussie's presence, her dancing and observant eye, troubled the waters in Martha's soul. Only momentarily: anything so alien from her common world of ideas had little power to hold her mind.

'You must come and see my house,' Dussie was saying.

'House!' scoffed Luke. 'Two rooms and a half, four stairs up.'

'In Union Street,' Dussie explained.

'Union Street!' echoed Martha. Funny place to live – all shops and offices. She had not thought that folk *lived* there.

'Oh, right on the top,' said Dussie. 'Above the shops and offices. Right up at the roof.'

'And you get out on the leads,' – Luke added his touch to the picture – 'grand view. All up and down Union Street. Some sky and a few gulls besides. You must be our guest next coronation procession. Splendid facilities.'

'You must be our guest a jolly lot sooner. Waiting for any old King, indeed!'

'Well, the Torchlight, then. That's better than a coronation. You shall view that from our top shrubbery – no, it hasn't any greens, just a way of speaking. Oh, but I forgot. You'll be a student yourself by the next Torchlight. You'll be waiting in the Quad, of course, not a spectator from the gods.'

And Martha listening had a sense of widening horizons, of vistas opening insecurely on a foreign country.

There was less foreign in the country when, a week or so later, she went to tea in Union Street, four stairs up, above the shops and offices, and Luke showed her his row of books. She was at home there, glowing visibly as she touched them, turned their leaves, read in snatches. She even found a tongue, and questioned. A listener, too. Her very listening was speech, he thought. She was eloquent by what she did not say.

'Young Pantagruel!' he laughed at her: and to her look of enquiry read aloud:

'"These letters being received and read, Pantagruel pluck't up his heart, took a fresh courage to him, and was inflamed with a desire to profit in his studies more than ever, so that if you had seen him, how he took paines, and how he advanced in learning, you would have said that the vivacity of his spirit amidst the books, was like a great fire amongst dry wood, so active it was, vigorous and indefatigable."'

She went home with as many books as she could carry.

'Saw ye ever the like o' that in a' yer born days?' cried Emmeline. 'Faur are ye ga'in to pit them a'? Fat were ye needin' wi' sae mony a' at aince? There's a mids i' the sea.'

And Luke, four stairs up in Union Street, was saying to Dussie,

'Your Marty's worth the knowing, you know. She's so absolutely herself. There's such a white flame of sincerity in her. So still and self-contained too. She's like – well, if one could imagine it – a crystal of flame. Perfectly rigid in its own shape, but with all the play and life of flame.'

He liked his simile and reverted more than once to it in thought.

For Martha, she was happy in the possession of his books and gave no thought to the owner.

In October she went to King's.

SIX

Expansion of the World

Martha snatched. There was no time to build a cosmos. Her world was in confusion, a sublime disordered plenty. Some other day, far off, she would order it, give it structure and coherence. . . . Meanwhile there was the snatching.

She snatched because she lived in fever. Greedy, convulsive, in a jealous agony, she raced for knowledge, panting. Supposing, in the three years of her course at King's, she should not be able to gather all the knowledge that there was. . . . When, in March, she sat her first degree examination, and passed, she had a movement of profound disillusion. 'Is this all I know? I thought I should know everything.'

She understood that a graduate may be ignorant.

By that time her panic was over. The grey Crown, that had soared through so many generations above the surge and excitement of youth, had told her that wisdom is patient and waits for its people. The greed went out of her as she looked up morning after morning at its serenity. It was like a great rock amid the changing tides of men's opinions. *Knowledge alters – wisdom is stable.* It told her time and again that there was no need for haste. In the long Library, too, with the coloured light filtering through its great end window, and its dim recesses among the laden shelves – where thought, the enquiring experiencing spirit, the essence of man's long tussle with his destiny, was captured and preserved: a desiccated powder, dusted across innumerable leaves, and set free, volatile, live spirit again at the touch of a living mind – she learned to be quiet. One morning she thought, standing idly among the books: 'But they might come alive, without my mind.' And she had a moment of panic. The immensity of life let loose there would be terrifying. They might clutch at her, these dead men, storming and battering at the citadel of her identity, subtly pervading her till they had stolen her very self. She so poor, and they with their magnitude of thought, of numbers. . . . The panic passed, and elation possessed her in its stead. She stood a long time in a dark corner, watching the people come and go, touch books, open them, read them, replace them, carry them away: and at every contact she thrilled. 'Spirit is released.' The great room tingled with it. Even when no one was there, it might turn back to spirit, that dried powdering of words that held the vital element. But the thought no longer gave her fear. It liberated. She walked in a company.

From the company she kept in the flesh she took less consciously material for her building. She had not yet discovered that men and women are of importance in the scheme of things: though she allowed an exception of course in favour of Professor Gregory. She owed to him one of the earliest of those moments of apocalypse by which life is dated.

'Gweedsake!' said Emmeline. 'Sic a lay-aff. You and yer Professor Gregory! You wad think naebody had had a tongue in their heid afore to hear you speak.'

Martha spoke no more of Professor Gregory, but thought much. The moment of apocalypse had come in his opening lecture. She had climbed the stair, jostled a throng that pushed and laughed and shouted. Everyone was going to hear Professor Gregory's opening lecture. Martha felt herself carried violently on by the pressure from behind. At the top of the stair, separated from the girls she knew, she was flung suddenly forward. She lost her balance and her breath. . . . Then she found herself held securely. She had been pitched against a stalwart in navy uniform, who quelled the impetuous rioting throng with a gesture, a glance. They surged round him, chattering and shouting, 'I say, Daxy –' 'Hello, it's old Dak –' 'Daxy, you're a sight for sair e'en, man –'

Daxter, Sacrist of King's, an old campaigner, like Odysseus full of wiles from warfare in the East, greeted them all with one eye and marshalled them with the other; and all the while held Martha firm in a little island amid the stream.

'Now, miss, you go in.' And the way was clear for her. The old Logic class-room was filled. Greetings were shouted. Voices ran like the assorted noises of a burn. And then two hundred pairs of feet were pounding the floor, and Martha, looking round, saw a long lean man come in, spectacled, with a smile running up his face that drove the flesh into furrows.

'Funny smile,' Martha was thinking. 'Not a smooth space left anywhere.' But she forgot the corrugations when he began to speak. He spoke like a torrent. He digressed, recovered himself, shot straight ahead, digressed again. He forgot his audience, turning farther and farther round till he stood side on to them, gazing through a window and washing his hands with a continually reiterated motion while he spun his monologue. Then suddenly he would turn back upon the class with a wrinkling smile and swift amused aside; and a roar of laughter would rise to the roof, while the feet thundered on the floor. His theme was English literature, but to Martha it seemed that he was speaking the language of some immortal and happy isle, some fabulous tongue that she was enabled by miracle for once to comprehend; and that he spoke of mysteries . . . .

The confines of her world raced out beyond her grasp. When he had ended she felt bruised and dizzy, as though from travelling too rapidly through air. The strong airs had smote her. But she had seen new countries, seen – and it was this that elated her, gave her the sense of newness in life itself that makes our past by moments apocryphal – the magnitude of undiscovered country that awaited her conquest. She was carried downstairs in the crowd and at the bottom met the Sacrist, who gave her a look of recognition. At the moment Martha was thinking: 'And I shall go on travelling like that. There will be more new countries.' And she was radiant. For sheer joy she broke into a smile; but perceiving that she was smiling straight into the face of Daxter, went hot with confusion and hurried away.

Daxter, however, accosted her as she was crossing the quadrangle some days later. Shortly she counted his greeting a normal part of her day. He claimed friendship with her as from the beginning.

'You see, miss, you smiled to me the very first day you came.'

'Oh,' cried Martha, 'but I didn't mean to –' and stopped abruptly, confused again. A tactless thing to say. But Daxter did not seem to be offended. He took her into his den, a narrow room at one corner of the quadrangle, the walls and table of which were covered with photographs. From the photographs 'Daxy' could reconstruct the inner history of the University since he had become Sacrist. Here were the giants who had been on the earth in those days. He told Martha tales, such as appear in no official record, of the immediate past of the University, and tales of his campaigns in India, making her world alive for her in new directions. One day he showed her some strips of silk. They had been part of the colours of a regiment – a tattered standard that had hung in the Chapel of King's till its very shreds were rotting away. He had been ordered to remove it: but round its pole the silk was still fresh, and he had kept the remnant. He cut two snippets of the silk, a snippet of cream and a snippet of cerise, and gave them to Martha.

'That's history, that is, miss.' And he put them in an envelope for her.

Martha carried the envelope in her pocket for nearly a week, deliberating where she might keep her treasure safe from predatory fingers. She had so few possessions and no stronghold for storing them. Madge, on the verge of the teens, had developed an inordinate interest in her appearance. She brewed herself strange scents from perfumed flowers and water, and decanted the product into an ink-bottle, sprinkling her garments lavishly with the concoction; and rubbed her lips and cheeks with purloined geranium petals. Martha caught her once sneaking out of a garden where geraniums were bedded out, and preached her a very pretty sermon on the heinousness of her deed. Madge's only reply was to march without the slightest attempt at secrecy into the next geraniumed garden and abstract a goodly handful of scarlet petals. She was quite capable, if she caught sight of them in the bedroom, of using Martha's scraps of silk for personal adornment. In the end Martha flattened the envelope, that was crushed and smeared from its sojourn in her pocket, and laid it between the pages of a heavy algebra text-book that stood on the high triangular shelf in the corner of the room: with hooks on its under surface to serve the girls for wardrobe. Sometimes she slipped the envelope from its hiding-place and touched the bits of silk that a regiment had followed. At such times it seemed to her that she was touching the past.

While her universe was thus widening both in time and in space, Scotland grew wider too. Hitherto her own blue valley, the city with its spires and dirty trawlers, had been her measure of Scotland. Now it grew. The North came alive. Out of it, from cottar-houses and farms, from parlours behind country shops, from fishing-villages on the Moray Firth, from station-houses and shepherds' houses and school-houses, manses and mansions, crofts on the edge of heather, snow-blocked glens, clachans on green howes beneath the corries, where tumbling waterfalls lit the rocks; islands in the Atlantic, gale-swept, treeless; thatched cottages where the peat reek clung in stuff and fabric and carried east in clothes and books – there flocked in their hundreds her fellow-students, grave, gay, eager, anxious, earnest, flippant, stupid and humble and wise in their own conceits, dreamers and doers and idlers, bunglers and jesters, seekers of pleasure and seekers of wisdom, troubled, serene, impetuous, and all inquisitive; subjecting life to inquisition.

Out of the Islands Martha found her friends. Chief was Harrie Nevin. Harrie came from Shetland. She had the Vikings in her bearing and Martha worshipped her from a distance: until she discovered that Harrie was doing the same by her. Then they wrote each other wonderful letters. . . .

Martha suffered bitterly because she could not ask Harrie to her home. Harrie, with her regal port, in Emmeline's haphazard kitchen! In compensation she was able to introduce her to Luke Cromar.

It had not occurred to Martha that knowing Luke was a matter for public congratulation; but the girls who saw him leave a group of talkers in the quadrangle at Marischal and dash across to Martha when he saw her pass, put her right as to that. She perceived that knowing Luke gave her a social status in University affairs; but rated that at less worth than simply knowing him.

University affairs, indeed, made much of Luke. He was in everything. He was President of the Student's Representative Council and on half a dozen other committees as well. And in the flat, four stairs up, Dussie waited for him and entertained his guests. They lived on little. Luke had been an apprentice shoemaker, an orphan boy who had dreamed while he cobbled shoes of mending all the philosophies of the world. A legacy had enabled him to go through college. But Dussie played eagerly at economy. Gracious, petulant, fresh as rain, she was the delight of all his friends. She made a hundred mistakes, but proclaimed them aloud with such a bubbling candour that they were only so many assets the more to her popularity. The men loved to hear her own rapturous recital of her indiscretions, her social *faux pas*.

In the summer they held tea-parties on the leads – 'Luke's sky-highs,' Kennedy called them; and the name caught.

Martha came to few of their parties, though Dussie, whose childhood's adoration had lost none of its vehemence, would have had her come to all. She was too shy, too awkward, and her Sunday blouse and skirt were out of place. Besides, time was short. Piles of stockings to darn, of dishes to wash, ate too far into it. Emmeline, it was clear, regarded the time she spent on books as leisure, her recreation. To have pen and paper about, and open note-books, protected her: but when her pulses raced to the choruses in *Atlanta*, or, rapt away by thought, poring over *The Marriage of Heaven and Hell*, she stared out motionless upon the strangeness of its landscapes, Emmeline's voice would break in:

'Is that yer lessons ye're at?'

It took many skirmishes with her conscience to convince her that she was justified in saying yes: and by that time Emmeline was convinced to the contrary. A 'poetry book' was for fun, and its reader might legitimately be interrupted. *The English Parnassus* she recognized as a lesson book. It had been bought, not borrowed from the Library at King's; and on winter nights that were too chill for her bedroom, Martha carried *The English Parnassus* to the kitchen; she read it from cover to cover, fairly secure from onslaught.

Her leisure therefore she would not devote to parties: where, to say the truth, she was not over-happy. She went however to the Friday evening Societies – to the 'Lit.'; and to the 'Sociolog,' because Luke was its President and had made her a gift of a membership card.

'Raw ripe red wisdom every Friday at seven,' he proclaimed.

She sat astounded at the discussions she heard. Wages, industrial unrest, sweated labour, unemployment, mental deficiency, syndicalism, federation – words to her! She had given so little of her thought as yet to the present; and it amazed her increasingly to hear her fellow-students, some glib, some stuttering, some passionate, some sardonic, talk of these matters. *We are the people*, they might have cried.

In particular she stared cold-hearted at the 'Vice'. The Vice-President was a girl: Lucy Warrender by name. No matter what the theme, Miss Warrender talked with authority. She had already an Honours degree in Philosophy and was studying now for History and Economics. She seemed to know existence to its ends. Martha gulped in sheer terror sometimes when she heard her talk: so competent, flawless, master of her purposes.

'Oh, a mine of information,' Luke called her, when Martha stammered her dismay. Was it praise or disparagement? She could not tell: and when, puzzling it out, she looked at him, his long face told her nothing.

But astonishing as were some of the things she heard, Martha took them all in. One must not throw away a fact. Knowledge grew sweeter the more one ate of it. Sharp-flavoured too, though, acrid at times upon the palate.

This widening world of ideas grew more and more the true abode of her consciousness. The cottage did not reabsorb her afternoon by afternoon: it received her back. She was in its life but not of it. Its concerns did not concern her nearly. Still less did she feel herself concerned with her neighbours, the Andy Macphersons and the Stoddart Semples. She had no point of contact with these: or thought so. In this she was mistaken. The contact was there, though she did not feel it.

Its existence, however, might have been detected, less than a month after her session began, on a day when Aunt Josephine Leggatt walked down from Crannochie to Wester Cairns.

SEVEN

Sundry Weathers

Aunt Josephine, hodging steadily along the soft road in the direction of Wester Cairns, met Stoddart Semple lounging by the dyke.

Stoddart had never forgiven his February dismissal into the sleet. Having backed, in that dispute, the side that lost, he went away convinced of Martha's uppishness; and as Martha did not like the man, tasted moreover no salt in the jokes he relished with her father, and never stopped to give him a crack by the roadside, he supposed himself in her contempt when it was merely she who sat in his.

Meeting Miss Leggatt, he began to grumble sourly.

'Ye've gotten a lady in the family noo.'

He put a bitter emphasis on the *lady* and stopped to look at Miss Leggatt.

'I see the muckle feet o' her takin' awa' doon the road,' he added.

'If it's Matty ye're meanin',' said Miss Josephine – and she said it without the shadow of an alteration in mien or accent – 'she's been a lady sin' ever she was the littlin.'

'A bonny penny she'll be for books,' he grumbled.

'I wadna say. Ye get naething for naething in this warld.' Miss Leggat was quite unmoved at his grievance. She told him with an amiable serenity, 'An' naebody's biddin' *you* pay. Ye needna talk as though they hadna a penny to rub on t'ither.'

Once launched, he could not leave the theme. There was east in his weather. The old sore itched. He scratched. Moreover he was curious. He wanted to know many things – matters of price, for instance, and such gossip as he could glean regarding the *terrible lang chiel* that came about the doors sometimes, and his wife, that was here when she was a bairn. He had questioned Geordie, to be sure, but Geordie's knowledge did not go very far.

'He's a terrible ane to speir,' Aunt Josephine said to Emmeline. She had given him little satisfaction by her answers.

'Speir!' cried Mrs. Ironside. 'He wad speir the claes aff'n yer back an' than speir faur ye tint them.'

She resented his prying into Martha's affairs, and – remembering February – stiffened her resolution to see the girl through her Odyssey.

'I'll show him,' she muttered to herself. 'Speirin' indeed.'

She 'showed him' a few days later. Martha fell sick. She recovered, but dragged her limbs.

'The cyclin's ower muckle for ye,' said Emmeline. 'Ye'll get a season ticket in the train.'

Thenceforward Martha went by train, tramping down the rough brae morning by morning.

The cross-country road, through the bright winds of October, had been pleasant: but she was glad enough to put away the cycle in these faint November days. December came with rain, black pitiless unceasing rain, that hurled itself upon the fields for days together, paused sullenly, and spewed again upon a filthy earth. It was on such a day of rain that Martha went with Luke and Dussie to her first opera. Luke insisted on coming home with her, although she warned him that he could hardly hope to catch the last train back to town.

'No matter,' he said. 'I like a soaking now and then. Good elemental feel it gives you.' And he steadied her by the elbow at the turn of the road.

The road was swimming. A flat of slimy mud lay across the bottom of the brae. Cataracts poured ceaselessly into it, carrying soil from the brae. The wind drove from the east.

'Just an April shower,' he said, crossing to the weather side of her as they turned.

She looked at him, swiftly. She could not see him. It was too dark. But she had an uncanny impression of having seen his smile. Oh, it was in his voice! – that smile that she had not been able to locate. He had a laughing voice.

They were both laughing as they stumbled among the

mud and the loose stones. Weather was a joke, it seemed! And the stormy chords from *Tannhäuser* beat upon her sleep, mingled in a colossal harmony with the beat of the elemental storm, through which his laughing voice recurred like a song.

January changed the wind. The stir of spring was in the world almost as soon as the year came in. Soft airs, faint skies plumed with shining wisps of cloud, blossom on the whins, bursting willow catkins, blackbirds fluting, a gauze of gnats against the sun, and everywhere the strong clean smell of new-turned earth – a wholesome kindly world: too mellow perhaps; without the young astringency of spring.

But at the end of February, out of a cold black north a dozen meandering snowflakes fell. They drifted about the air like thrums – blown from the raw edges of the coming storm. Next morning colour had gone from the world. Shapes, sounds, the energies and acutenesses of life, were muffled in the dull white that covered both earth and sky. No sun came through. The weeks dragged on with no lifting of the pallor. The snow melted a little and froze again with smears of dirt marbling its surfaces. To the northward of the dykes it was lumped in obstinate seams, at the cottage doors trodden and caked, matted with refuse, straws and stones and clots of dung carried in about on clorted boots. The ploughs lay idle, gaunt, like half-sunk reefs among the furrows.

'We'll hae wer sax weeks' snaw in March the year richt eneuch,' said Geordie, beating his arms across his chest to quicken the circulation.

Baby Flossie wailed miserably and sucked her frozen fingers. They were hottest in her mouth. When Emmeline caught them there she pulled them out and smacked them till they tingled. That heated them too.

Martha, buffeted in the bitter winds, struggling to keep her footing on the rutted ice of the brae, arrived listless at the lecture-room. Often her fingers were dead. She could not write notes. She sat, in the chill room that gathered a clammy warmth from a hundred breaths, heavy-headed, her interest subdued: but by noon, when Professor Gregory lectured, she was alert again, fleet-footed after knowledge. No ice, no battering winds, could hold her from that pursuit.

The spring term had ended before the frost gave.

One afternoon the wind veered. It rushed out of the south-west, hot and sweet, like the breathing of a cow against one's face.

'The snaw's gotten a fleg,' said Geordie jubilantly. He leaned against the door-post, a thumb in his arm-hole, watching the wind lick the surface of the world clean. Martha, plodding home with a bagful of groceries, looked at him listlessly and made no answer. She was heavy-eyed and round-shouldered. Knowledge is inexorable to its devotees and sets its own price high. The mild air softened her resistance to her own weariness. Her month's vacation dragged.

And meanwhile the sun was gathering strength. The earth was steaming like a wet clout held to the fire, with a steam so thick and close that it floated over the fields like heavy morning mists on an autumn valley. The fog-horn boomed; and the slopes beyond the river were out of recognition, flat and pale.

The sun gathered strength. The roads blew dry. In three days' time the dust was flying. The plough land changed its colour – sharp sandy brown at last, ready for the seed. Larks sprang and shrilled, operatic, mechanical, in a series, as though a multitude of catches were successively released in the grass and stubble. The sowers were out and the harrow was on the fields.

Geordie cried to Stoddart Semple down the gale that lifted the earliest clouds of dust – a roaring, rollicking, tattering, clothes-line-walloping gale – 'Ay, ay, man, the land's dryin' fine.'

It had been Geordie's daily remark since the thaw set in. He said it to everyone he met outside, and three or four times a day at home as well. A matter of such importance could not stale.

Stoddart, slouching by the dyke, made answer,

'It would dry some quicker if your missus stood oot o' the way a bit.'

And he looked at Emmeline where she stood full in the sun, stretching out after the tail of a shirt that reared and curveted on the clothes-line.

'I see she's gettin' a terrible-like size,' he said.

Emmeline in the last few months had been putting on flesh rapidly, achieving a shapelessness that was far from her old rounded grace. The shadow she cast, standing there in the sun, was considerable. It was a sore point, and luckily she was too far away to catch either Stoddart's sneer or the reply made by Geordie, quick-witted for once as he watched the surface of the earth scatter upon the wind.

'O ay,' he said, 'gran' for keepin' the grun' doon in a gale.'

Martha, however, had been near enough to catch both. She pondered, standing by a bush of whin, plucking at the golden scented blossoms and rubbing them on her palm until her skin was yellow; she pondered whether her father's answer was really as crass as it had sounded. She remembered Luke Cromar, who was polite even to Emmeline. And behind her Geordie went off in sudden uproarious laughter, as though his witticism, so natural in face of the blowing dust, had only now occurred to him as being witty.

Martha went back to the house and read *The Land of Heart's Desire* – a silver and azure world where she did not recognize that there walked the peasant folk of her own acquaintance. Like Emmeline, she hardly desired the stories that she read to deal with ploughmen: not at any rate with sharny boots and hacked hands seamed with dirt.

In the summer term she spent her afternoons studying Natural History. The Professor, in a quiet voice that he never raised nor quickened, peopled for her the airs, glancing waters and grassblades, and the cold dark grave profundities of the sea. He had the tongue of a poet and of a humorist: a tongue like that of the fabled story-teller of Arabia, whom no one could hear without believing every word he uttered. When he spoke, incredible shapes moved through an unimaginable past; and an unimaginable present surged in on one, humming with a life one had not seen before, nor even suspected. So full the world was, and so clamorous! And placidly, without haste or emphasis, he conjured up its press and clangour, its multitudinous anxieties.

'Like Aunt Josephine,' Martha found herself thinking: and her own temerity frightened her. But she was right. He had the same luminous unhurrying serenity as Aunt Josephine, the same sure capable grasp of life.

She lunched, between her two diets of worship, between King's in the morning and Marischal in the afternoon, on a hunk of bread and a bit of cold bacon.

'Not good for you,' said Luke. 'You must lunch with us.'

Dussie seconded eagerly. She served up every dish in her repertory, and invented a few new combinations of material. Martha had never eaten so many unfamiliar things in her life.

Dussie objected: 'You are not a rapturous eater, Marty. Now Luke is. He really pays attention to what I make for him.'

And to Luke she pouted: 'She might just as well be chewing at her hunk of bread. She doesn't care what it is she's eating.'

To which Luke made answer: 'Well, of course, you know, flame is fairly indiscriminate as to what it takes for fuel.'

'Oh,' she cried, exasperated, 'you are crazed with your flame. Marty has a stomach like the rest of us, I suppose, and she should be made to know about it.'

'Lord forbid!' he said. 'The people who know about their stomachs are the devil.'

Her exasperation effervesced into laughter.

'But you know what I mean, Luke. It's only because I love her so much that I want her to be like other people.'

'I should have thought that was a reason for wanting to keep her as she is.'

Dussie's brows went up in pity. Really, to be so clever, Luke had sometimes astonishingly little common-sense.

If Martha was indifferent to the provender, she was not indifferent to the joy of sharing it. As May ran on, indeed, she was glad of the heat and the shelter. The weather changed to a black cold, hard skies, hard edges to the earth, bitter winds. Then the skies loosened at the edge, puckered into cloud.

'Ower mony upcastin's,' said Geordie, eyeing the solid lumps of cloud *birsed* up into the sky.

Next day a plaster of snow deformed the opening leaves and hung in wet semi-transparent blobs on the clusters of lilac.

'The cauld Kalends o' May,' Geordie called it.

'Fourth winter for the season,' said Luke, helping Martha out of her dripping coat and chafing her white dead hands. And such a lunch as Dussie had for them – 'hot as sin,' Luke proclaimed.

Luke graduated early in July, coming through his finals with a star. One of his professors – who had warned him against his own enthusiasms – told him drily that he had no right even to have passed. Luke seemed to spend his days doing things he had no right to do, and doing them triumphantly: marrying Dussie, for example. They were radiant both. Their weather was golden, crisp, vibrant with energy. The dark gods had little portion in their love. It was of the sunlight and flashing winds, clear and merry.

Standing in the quadrangle after his graduation, Luke held a petty court. Half the University surged up to congratulate him; and when it became known that old Dunster had asked him to stay on the following session as assistant, they surged back and congratulated him again.

'It's not official yet,' he kept saying. 'Has to be ratified by the Senatus. Doubtless they'll rise in a body and refuse.'

Professor Forbes, who had told him he had no right to pass, shook hands and said cordially,

'So you're to be one of us next session, I hear.'

Next day they left for the Continent, where Luke was to study for six weeks in a hospital. Martha saw them off. Harrie had gone too. The islands and the glens and the fishing villages and farms had taken their bairns back. Martha's life was bounded again, in its externals, by the slovenly kitchen with its heat and clatter, the low-roofed bedroom where all the family clothes were stocked and where Madge smeared her lips with her geranium petals and studied the effect in a spotty mirror that had a crack across its upper corner; by meals for which her father cast his coat and kicked his boots aside, where the bairns wrangled and slobbered, Emmeline raged, Flossie whimpered. Her privacy was in the open; and in her thoughts. There like a wrestler she tried all comers – the companies of new ideas that had crowded in upon her mind. She had received them all impartially, stored them away. Now she called them out again. Martha was beginning to think.

Emmeline had said, eyeing the newspaper on the day when the University lists were published and Martha's name appeared,

'They'll see't at Muckle Arlo' – a consolation that it required some strength of mind to accept for consolation; since she could not know that her surmise was correct. It was therefore by way of a flutter in the dovecot when Aunt Jean herself wrote to Martha inviting her to Muckle Arlo.

EIGHT

Leggatt Respectability

Emmeline was fluttered and took some pains to make Martha presentable. The girl herself had not much interest in her outfit. She was so much accustomed to her own dowdy appearance that she accepted it as in the nature of things and made no effort to alter it: but the visit itself was an excitement. Here was she a traveller, at last; though the travel carried her only twenty miles. And it thrilled her immoderately to climb a stair to her bedroom. She had never slept upstairs before and never had a bedroom to herself. She sat on the edge of a chair, when she had said goodnight and shut the door, and clenched her hands together to keep within measure the waves of excitement that washed over her. So new the world was! When the door opened gently and she looked up with a start, she was prepared for any unaccountable vision to meet her eyes.

The vision that met her eyes gave account of itself at once.

'It's just the Syrup of Figs,' Aunt Leebie was saying, creeping across the carpet with her shapeless figure hunched together. 'Yer Aunt Jean aye gars the bairns tak' a dosie the first nicht they come.'

She was standing above Martha, struggling with the cork, the spoon thrust by the handle in her mouth while she fichered. Her dim and anxious eyes searched the girl, noting the bones that protruded at her throat, the shadows round her eyes. Leebie was a kindly body. Taking her cue from Jean, she was ready to translate her relenting even more liberally than she had formerly translated her disapproval.

'A sup cream wad dae ye mair gweed,' she was moved to say. 'But yer Aunt Jean . . . . Whan the bairnies comes – ye wunna ken aboot the bairnies?' She shot off at a tangent, glad of the excuse. Mrs. Corbett's elder son was married; the two children came frequently to stay with their grand-parents. Castor-oil, Aunt Jean believed in. That was the thing when she was young and her bairns after her.

'But their mither, she has notions o' her ain. Nae castor-oil for *her* littlins. She's a prood piece,' said Leebie confident-ially to Martha, edging up until the Syrup of Figs was almost at her nose.

'Terrible ful, an' aye wears a tailor-made.'

In spite of her kindliness, Aunt Leebie was inexorable over the Syrup of Figs. The tilt of Aunt Jean's chin had commanded.

Leebie, it was plain, was spokesman. The weather being wet and the ground soft, Martha could never return from a walk, or from picking, between showers, the black currants in the garden, but Aunt Leebie, mounted dragon over the immaculate fleece of the carpets, would be meeting her at the door:

'Noo clean yer feet, aifter a' that muck. We'll hae a hoose nae common.'

Martha grew to have a fondness for Aunt Leebie; though her reprimands pursued her. She liked the funny soft giggle in which her sentences ended. Round-shouldered, wrapped always in a grey Shetland shawl that was matted by frequent washings, she watched the girl's every action, and found fault with many. On washing day it was Martha who carried out the rugs and beat them on the green. She paused for breath, too soon.

'That's nae the way,' cried Leebie from the window. 'Startin' aff like that at a bicker an' then haein' to stop.'

The aunts had undertaken Martha's domestic education with more thoroughness than consorted with holiday. She made beds under supervision and learned how silver should be laid away and the due and proper method of buying and storing yellow soap. They talked as though she knew nothing.

'But I've stayed with Aunt Josephine,' she said, 'I've seen . . .'

Leebie sniffed. 'Josephine does a'thing by instalments.'

And Aunt Jean added, in one of her rare bursts of elo-quence,

'Josephine will dee by instalments.'

On the last evening of her stay they called her into Leebie's room. The half-drawn blinds, the starched Nottingham curtains, the dressing-table with its swivel mirror set straight across the window, made the room dark: Aunt Jean, sitting very upright on a cane-bottomed chair, made it portentous. Leebie sorted her parson-grey Shetland shawl. 'It's aye slippin',' she complained, ending on her soft giggle. And pulling it closer to her throat, she moved up to the bed. 'Come richt in,' she ordered Martha over her shoulder.

On the bed was laid a lustre frock – ivory, that had deepened with age. Its voluminous skirts billowed over the quilt.

'Ye'll try it on,' Leebie said.

Fingering the folds while Martha took off her blouse and skirt, 'It was richt gweed stuff,' she muttered; and pouncing, at sight of Martha's underclothes,

'The Lord preserve's, look at yer slip-body – that's yer safety-pins. Pinnin' yer skirt up!' ('It won't keep without,' Martha pleaded.) 'Canna ye wear stays, like a Christian body?'

She dropped the gown and with her hands explored the leaness of Martha's haunches.

'There's naething there to support a skirt. Ye *maun* get a pair o' stays.' She continued to fumble with her hands at the girl's hips, muttering, as though she had a personal grievance in the make of her lanky figure. Then she lifted the lustre gown and fitted it upon her grand-niece. The full skirts sprang from the waist, covering her thinness, and at the back trailed slightly on the floor. Aunt Leebie struggled with the fastenings of the bodice, dragging Martha round, pulling her from point to point in the room to catch a clearer light. The bodice was fitted to a shaped lining, that fastened down the front with close-set alternating rows of hooks and eyes.

'It's some grippit in at the middle,' she complained in the aggrieved tone she had used with which to talk of stays. 'But ye cud sort that.' And again she giggled softly.

Martha perceived that the frock was given to her.

She wondered vaguely what she could do with it. No room at Wester Cairns for frocks like that – hardly room to store it!

And as for wearing it – ! Of course it could be remade – there were yards of stuff: but plainly that was not Aunt Leebie's purpose. *Sort* the waist, shorten the skirt a little, and there you were! Martha gave a gulp of sheer panic at the thought of wearing the gown; and she was no facile needlewoman, to transform it for herself. Shirts, underclothing, yes: but when it came to the tricksey wiles of fashion . . . she remembered Dussie's frocks and felt that she would rather die than snip and alter at this ancient dress till it was wearable.

But what was it that Aunt Leebie was saying? – She must make some sign of gratitude; and plunging she said,

'I could wear it when I'm capped.'

Her graduation was so infinitely remote – two whole years away. One could make rash promises for two years hence.

'I'll keep it for then,' she said. And fearful that her gratitude had not been warm enough, she put her arms round Aunt Leebie's neck, rubbing upon the parson-grey Shetland shawl, and kissed her. 'But where am I to keep it?' she was thinking.

Aunt Leebie was pleased. She helped Martha to take off the gown and lay it carefully across the back of a chair.

'Ye maunna fold it yet,' she warned. 'Let it air a whilie.' And anxiously, with her head pushed forward and her bent shoulders pressing in the direction of the girl, she added,

'See ye guide it noo ye've got it.'

It was plain that the maxim emanated from Aunt Jean (seated there so upright and so silent on her cane-bottomed seat), and issued by way of her square-set chin through Leebie's mouth, although the frock was Leebie's and the impulse to give it Leebie's too.

Martha suddenly wanted to kiss Aunt Leebie again. 'But must I kiss Aunt Jean as well?' she queried. And a wave of shyness flooded her.

Next morning she had to unpack the Japanese basket hamper (frayed to a hole at one of its corners) in which she had brought her clothes. She had to unpack it because Aunt Leebie came into her room too late to see her fold the gown.

'I canna hae it whammlin' aboot in there,' she said. And she giggled her soft giggle.

That Martha was affected by this solidity and order, the Leggatt respectability towards which her mother yearned in vain, the girl herself did not perceive: though she gave certain signals of it after her return. Indifference to the household laxity, the unconcern with which, sunk in a dream or hot on the tracks of knowledge, she had viewed domestic turmoil as no affair of hers, altered – spasmodically only, it is true – to irritation and that to hesitant rebuke. Emmeline took the hints with unexpected meekness. She had the makings of respect for her daughter now that she was reconquering the citadel whence Emmeline had been exiled. Martha had visited at Muckle Arlo: henceforward she was allowed to be an individual. Emmeline accepted an occasional innovation, not because it was cleanly and made for order, not even because Aunt Jean arranged her matters so, but because Martha had been at Muckle Arlo. That Martha had been at Muckle Arlo was a step on towards the shining goal round which her fancies fluttered, the respectability she had foregone: though how indeed was she to reach it? Respectability was a habit of mind beyond her powers.

It was a habit of mind beyond Martha's intentions. When the winter session opened in October, and her mind was steeped again in book-learning, she forgot household management. Respectability according to the Leggatt canons had little reality in a world of passionate pursuing, where the quarry, phantoms from a dead past flitting in shadow, grew more and more alive the hotter one's pursuit. Her contact with it had nonetheless strengthened, unknown to herself, an inborn timidity that shrank from unlikeness to its fellows. It made her more sensitive to the deficiencies of her personal appearance. It was it that operated in her, on a day in the winter session, when Luke had said,

'Oh, but you mustn't go away, Marty. You must stay to tea. Old Dunster's coming.'

His professor! Tongue-tied though she knew that she would be, Martha longed to meet him. But she said.

'Oh, I can't, Luke! Not with these old boots on.'

The *old* was a concession to public opinion. They were not really old; nor had she any better; but they were rough, clumsily cut, of thick unpliable leather that had crunkled into lurks about her ankles; country boots, and all the more unsuitable for the reception of Professor Dunster that Dussie was wearing the daintiest of black court shoes, with buckles whose silver gleam was lit with blue that answered the blue shimmer of her frock.

And Luke said,

'Oh, your boots! – My dear Marty, do you suppose any one would ever look at your boots who could see your eyes?'

'My eyes!' she echoed, in such genuine astonishment that Luke and Dussie laughed aloud.

'They're nice eyes, you know,' said Dussie. And she plumped herself on a cushion at Martha's feet and craned up into her face.

'If you had said Dussie's eyes – ' Martha began.

'Dussie? – Oh, she uses eye-shine. Pots of it. You have stars in yours.'

He loved to disparage Dussie's beauty. She loved him to disparage it, paying him back with hot-head glee.

Seriously, he said,

'You are a very lovely woman, Marty.'

'Oh well,' objected Dussie, 'not very lovely, you know . . .' and Martha, flinging up her head, was crying, 'I don't know what you mean, Luke! I'm ugly.'

'True,' he answered promptly. 'Out of the running, you and I. We have both big noses.'

It was the same sensitiveness to any external oddity that operated on an afternoon in early spring when Luke, she felt resentfully, put her to public shame.

NINE

Beatrice among the Pots

She was wearing shoes that afternoon, trim, black, new –
big, of course, because her feet were big; but respectable by
any Leggatt standard, though, to be sure, they showed up
the clumsiness of her ankles in their four-ply fingering
home-knitted stockings. She was wearing also her Sunday
costume. Emmeline had grumbled at both shoes and
costume: wearing them to her school – a pretty-like palaver.
Emmeline continued to talk of Martha's University classes as
'school' and of the hours she spent in study as her 'lessons'.
So did Geordie, for the matter of that. 'But they will never
understand,' Martha sighed to herself.

Emmeline's displeasure notwithstanding, Martha wore
the Sunday shoes and costume. Dussie had a tea-party and
there was no time to come home and change. The tea-party
in the parlance of the hour was a 'hen-shine': until Luke
came in at five o'clock, bringing Macallister, there were no
men present. Martha felt herself a dullard in more than
clothing. The chatter was edged, and Miss Warrender, now
President of the Sociological, with her raking wit and air of
authority, turned the world inside out to the discomfort of
one at least of its inhabitants. It was after Luke came in that
someone, discussing another theme, took for granted
Martha's Honours course.

Martha said, 'But I am not taking Honours.'

'Not taking Honours? Everyone thinks you are.'

They overhauled the position. Miss Warrender in her
adequate way ('rather foolish, isn't it?' she asked) persuaded
the assembly that in these modern days the passman was a
nonentity.

'An ordinary degree is cheap,' she said. 'Everyone spe-
cialises.'

She disposed of Martha's pretensions to a share in the sunlight of the teaching profession without specialisation and an Honours degree, with the same thoroughness and decision wherewith Stoddart Semple and Mrs. Ironside had disposed of her pretensions to a degree at all.

'Even financially, the extra year is worth it.'

The thought of Emmeline obtruded itself on Martha's mind and she realized, hating the knowledge, that she did not wholly belong to the world in which she sat.

She became aware that Luke was speaking. He was speaking magisterially, with an air of authority that equalled Miss Warrender's own.

'That's nonsense,' she heard him say. 'It's quite wrong, most of this specialising. For teachers, anyhow. Teachers shouldn't specialise – except in life. That's their subject, really. A man doesn't set out to teach mathematics, but life illuminated by mathematics; or by literature, or dancing, or Double Dutch, or whatever it is he chooses with which to elucidate the mysteries. Miss Ironside is specialising in life. She does it rather well too.'

'Illuminated by what, if one may ask?'

The speaker was Macallister, the only other man in the room. A huge full-blooded bovine fellow, with inflated hands and lurks of fat ruffling above his collar, he was reading for Honours in Philosophy.

'I wish to goodness you'd stop asking that Macallister here,' said Dussie. 'He never looks precisely at any particular spot of you, but you feel all the same as if he'd been staring the whole time just under *here*. Such a sight too – all those collops of fat.'

Here indicated the waist-line. She referred to Macallister's way of looking as 'the Greek statue glare'.

'That's what comes of philosophy, you see,' said Luke. 'Aren't you thankful I gave it up? – Jolly acute mind, though, for all the encumbrance.'

He continued to bring Macallister to the house. He liked to know the latest developments in philosophic thought, having never quite forgotten that as an apprentice shoemaker he had constructed a system of philosophy which he dreamed would revolutionise the world. Macallister was a useful asset.

'Illuminated by what, if one may ask?' Macallister was saying, waving his cigarette towards Martha and giving her the Greek statue glare with his continually roving eyes.

'Illuminated,' said Luke, 'by the sun, the moon and the eleven stars. Also by a little history and poetry and the cool clear truths of the wash-tub.'

And again before Martha's quickening eye came the figure of Emmeline, towsled and sluttish, and of herself on the sloppy kitchen floor thrusting her arms in the water. Emmeline's voice rasped. 'Ye've scleitered a'ower the place,' she was saying. Martha felt sure that every other girl in the room was seeing the same vision as she saw, and her heart burned hot against Luke.

'Luke, you gumpus!' cried Dussie's ringing voice. 'Cool and clear indeed! Much you know about the wash-tub.'

And a girl in an immaculate white silk shirt said pettishly,

'My blouses are being ruined, just ruined! In digs, you know – but what can one do? Last week – '

The conversation drifted to more important matters than specialisation.

'Spanking night,' said Luke when the guests had gone. 'Say, Duss, let's walk Marty home.'

'You can walk her home if you like, but I've an ironing to do. – No indeed, Marty, you shan't stay and help.'

She despatched them into the dusk.

'Quarries car,' cried Luke, 'and out by Hazelwood.'

The twilight was luminous, from a golden west and a rising moon. The whole sky glowed like some enormous jewel that held fire diffused within itself. Slowly the fire gathered to points, focussed in leaping stars. They struck through Hazelwood. Stark boughs vaulted the sky, and they walked below in silence, along paths that the moon made unfamiliar. There was no purpose in breaking a silence that was part of the magic of the place and hour. Luke walked on in a gay content. Troubled, in a low voice, Martha at last remonstrated with him on the disclosure to which he had subjected her. 'They will despise me.'

He heard the low words with some astonishment, not having supposed her susceptible to a worldy valuation. For a moment he realized that her nature might be other than he had perceived, but speedily forgot it and saw her only in his own conception of her.

'Let them then. It's not worth minding, Marty. Merely the price you have to pay for my determination that they shall know there are people like you in the world. They don't think, these women – they don't think anywhere farther up than coffee in Kennington's and partners for the next dance.'

'Oh Luke, that isn't true. They know such a lot – things I don't know. All those books they've read and plays they've been to, and concerts. I've never heard of half the names they used.'

'Ornamentation, Marty. They wear them because they're in the fashion. When they really *think*, it's of how to remove an incipient moustache. Oh, they're not all like that, thank God, but that little lot mostly are. I want them to know you – what you're like. To understand that there are qualities of mind that make common labour grace and not disgrace the purest intellectual ardour.'

'But I'm not intellectual.'

She did not know what she was, never having analysed herself; and the disclaimer was not coquetry but disbelief.

'No,' he answered, 'you're an Intelligence – a Phantom Intelligence.'

She let the accusation pass, not knowing how to refute it; and followed her own thought.

'But Miss Warrender, she's not – she's – '

'Oh, she's different, of course. Talks well, doesn't she? Tremendously well-read. Get Miss Warrender talking and you're sure to learn something you didn't know. A perfect pit of knowledge.'

'Then you shouldn't have classed her with these others – should you, Luke? The ones that just wear what they know.'

Martha spoke slowly, pondering the question, which evidently exercised her.

'I am rebuked, gentle guardian.' Martha shrank. Luke in obeisance before her was troubling. If she were sure that he was only bantering – ! She guessed too that he was aware of her trouble. 'Of course I shouldn't. Not so very different either, though. Her knowledge is merely hers, not her. It makes no sort of alteration in the essential man. She knows a few hundred times more now than when I met her first, and she hasn't grown an atom with it all. It gets no farther in than her brain. When her brain suffers dissolution, so will the knowledge. Food for worms. She'll waken up to her next incarnation with horribly little to put on. Now you, on the other hand, Marty – you know things with the whole of you. Your knowledge pervades your whole personality. It's pure spirit. A rare and subtle essence.'

He took an arrogant delight in troubling her, having decided that she was insufficiently aware of her own worth and ought to be made to see herself through other eyes. He had a fine intellectual apprehension of her quality and tried to show her herself as he perceived her.

'You are big enough to stand the knowledge. Nothing will spoil you, Marty – there's flame enough in you to burn the danger up.'

She began to comprehend that she was for him an earnest of the spiritual world; its ministrant; his Beatrice.

'I don't worship you. You worship a goddess through flame, don't you? – But I have learned through you to worship flame. The flame of life. Like Beatrice. Making me aware of hierarchies of being beyond our own. – I'm not making love to you, you know, Marty.'

She said, 'Luke!' with a tongue so astounded that he laughed audibly; and in a moment so did she. The absurdity of the idea was palpable.

'I suppose to some fools it would sound pernicious,' he reflected. 'To tell a woman that you love her and at the same time that you haven't the least intention of wooing her – well! – It can be done, though.' He was a little magisterial again, liking his theories. 'There are two sorts of woman to whom one can say these things with impunity. There's the quite worthless woman, frivolous, nothing in her. The ichor of her life's too thin and weak to receive anything in solution – all her experience is precipitated immediately – it doesn't even cloud the liquor – simply doesn't touch her. You can say any mortal thing you like to her and be safe. And then there's the woman in whom the life is so strong and powerful that it receives all experience into solution – makes a strange rich-flavoured compound of the liquor; and crystal clear.

You can trust a woman like that with any knowledge. You can tell her the truth. We lie to most of the women we know. I'm telling you the truth.'

She remained silent so long that he turned to look at her. They had left the woodland and the moon was strong. He saw her face, held straight ahead and as though she walked without seeing where she went. Rossetti's picture of the Annunciation came irresistibly to his mind. She had Mary's rapt tranquillity.

It did not occur to him that that was her very mood; that she carried it home with her; that, lying still on her bed, among threadbare sheets that were patched with stuff of different tone and texture from themselves, under matted and dun-coloured blankets, she was undergoing the awe and rapture of annunciation. Humbly she cried, 'I am not worthy,' and the wonder deepened within her till it brimmed and flooded her consciousness. She lay without moving, nor were there articulate words even in her thought; but her whole being was caught up in passionate prayer that she might be able for her destiny. The place was holy; neither Madge's noisy and rancid breathing, nor Flossie's muttering and the constant twitch of her limbs, could disturb its solemn air. Let the whole world despise her now, in Luke's dower was her peace. He made her great by believing her so. Because unwittingly she loved him she became the more fully what he had imagined her. She fell asleep in ecstasy, and woke in ecstasy, carrying to the tasks of early morning a sense of indwelling grandeur that redeemed them all. So strong and bright was this interior life that the things she touched and saw no longer wore their own significance. Their nature was subjugated to her nature; and she handled without disgust, in the confined and reeking closet where the boys had slept, the warm and smelly bed-clothes and the flock mattress that had sagged in holes and hardened into lumps, because her mind had no room for the realization that they were disgusting. As she cleaned the bairns' boots, there fell on her so strong a persuasion of the very immediacy of unseen presences that she stood still, a clumsy boot thrust upon her fist, staring at the stubbly brush.

'You're a dreamy Daniel as ever I saw,' cried Emmeline as she poked fresh sticks beneath the kettle. 'A real hinder o' time, you and yer glowerin'. Fa's the time to wait on you? – Haud, Willie! – ye thievin' randy.' And she clutched Willie's *nieve*, *birsing* the cakes he had been stealing into mealy crumbles that spilt over the floor.

Martha returned to the brushing of the boots without comment, tied the strings of her petticoats for Flossie, who was wandering about half-clad among everyone's feet, and went back to the bedroom to make ready for town.

'Am I the daughter of this house, or are you?' she found herself asking Madge, having rubbed her sleeve against some of her untidy pastes that Madge had larded on a chair-back.

Madge, fourteen years old and done with her education, required, like Martha herself, a wider life than the cottage allowed, and was finding it in the glare of publicity afforded by the baker's shop, whither she took her jewelled side-combs and fiery bows attached to the very point of her lustreless pigtail, to enliven the selling of bath-buns and half panned loaves and extra strongs, and the delivery of morning baps and 'butteries' at the villas round Cairns. She ate in these pleasant precincts more chocolates and pastries than were at all good for her complexion, which had considerably more need now of her geranium petals than it had had two years before; instead of scarlet, however, on the assumption that the more of pallor the less of plebeian was accused by one's appearance, she spent her meagre cash on the cheapest variety of face powder, which she smeared with an unskilful hand across her features. Martha shrank from her tawdry ostentation, but was worsted in every attempt at remonstrance by Madge's complete indifference to what she had to say. It was useless to lose one's temper with Madge; and quite ridiculous to waste one's irony. She stared and answered, 'You are, of course,' and completed the tying of her pigtail bow. Madge would go her own way though the heavens fell upon her: or though Emmeline fell upon her, a much more probable, and to the girl's imagination more terrifying, catastrophe. She asked no one's advice and sought no one's approval. Martha was grateful for at least her silences, dearly as she resented the visible signs of her presence. She had long since ceased to share a bed with her, allowing Madge and Flossie the one respectable bed the room contained, and sleeping herself on a rackety trestle-bed underneath the window. There she could watch Orion, or hear, in the drowsy dawn, a blackbird fluting and the first small stir of wings.

On this particular morning she stood by the window watching clouds like green glass curving upward from the east horizon, and dressing her hair – a little perfunctorily, it must be admitted – while she gazed. She had wiped the chair-back clean herself, being in no mood to break her own interior peace by altercation with Madge. She studied now to dwell in peace. That she had suffered what was obnoxious in her surroundings – whether Madge's conceits, or Emmeline's sloven hastes and languors, or Geordie's grossness – had until now been by instinct; not from the tolerance that comes of understanding, but because, not having begun to understand them, she lived her real life apart from them, within herself. But she was now more consciously resolved to shrink from nothing in her laborious and distasteful life, subjecting herself in a glow of exaltation to the rough sand-papering of her daily courses. She would in no wise dishonour her fate. If the spirit had chosen her for shining through, she would be crystal clear. Crystal clear! Luke had used the very words. And again there rushed on her a sense of abasement that was in itself the sharpest joy. Incredible and sure – it was she who had been chosen for this rare privilege. Luke, whom she honoured, had desired her too. But what did they all see in her eyes, she queried, staring in the dull and spotty mirror. She could not even tell their colour exactly: they had something in them of Nature's greens that have gone brown, of grass-fields before the freshening of spring. What did they all see in them? She looked in the mirror longer than she had ever looked before, searching for her own beauty. It was not to be found there.

'Fat are ye scutterin' aboot at?' cried Emmeline from the kitchen. 'Ye'll be late for yer school.'

She jammed a hairpin into place and pulled her blouse awry as she poked it under the band of her skirt. The end of a shiny safety-pin looked out from below her waist-belt. The mirror had more cause than ever not to reflect her beauty.

Spring wore to summer and Martha lived in an abiding peace. She was disciplined to exaltation. Doubtless her critical faculty suffered. A course of Muckle Arlo would have done her no harm; and Emmeline fell ill, to the advantage of Martha's domestic, if dubiously (in her own eyes) of her spiritual economy.

On a day in early June she sat and read upon the cairn.

The country was indigo, its austere line running out against a burnished sky to the clear enamelled blue of the mountains. Rain at sea, a soft trail of it like grey gauze blowing in the wind. And an enormous sky, where clouds of shadowed ivory and lustrous hyacinth filed by in vast processional; yet were no more than swayed in the wash of shallows when the eye plunged past them to the unfathomable gulfs of blue beyond. Martha lifted her head from the pages and looked out on those infinitudes of light. She was reading history that year. The slow accumulation of facts and dates was marshalled in her brain, waiting for the fire from heaven to fall; and as she turned from reading and gazed on that wide country gathering blue airs about itself; saw the farms and cottar-houses, roads, dykes, fields, river, she was teased from her own inner stillness by an excitement to which all she had been reading anent the press and stir of centuries contributed. Looking up, she thought suddenly, 'I am a portion of history,' and between her glancing from the pages and the formulation of the words, that she had spoken half aloud, there passed the fraction of a second, which nevertheless was crammed with furious thought. She had seen the riotous pageant of history peopled with folk who were like herself. Wheresoever they had gone, whatsoever had been their acts and achievement, they had all begun in a single spot, knowing nothing, with all to find and dare.

'This place as well as another,' she thought; and then she said, 'But I am part of it too.'

She perceived that the folk who had made history were not necessarily aware of the making, might indeed be quite ignorant of it: folk to whom a little valley and a broken

hilltop spelt infinity and who from that width and reason-
ableness of life had somehow been involved in the monstrous and sublime unreason of purposes beyond their own
intention. The walls that shut people from people and
generation from generation collapsed about her ears; and all
that had ever been done on the earth – all she had read and
heard and seen – swung together to a knot of life so blinding
that involuntarily she closed her eyes and covered them with
her hands. She could not keep still for the excitement and
almost ran in her haste to the wood, forgot the supper-hour,
and walked hither and thither at random; but noting that
north of west the skies were flecked with saffron, and that a
June sunset is late, she turned home to resume her part in
the making of history.

Geordie was leaning against the door and seemed glad to
see his daughter.

'Yer mither's feelin' drumlie kind,' he told her. 'She's
had a dwam.'

Martha recalled her thoughts from the All and considered
this ingredient in it. Emmeline was not wont to be ill.

They went indoors together.

Emmeline, flushed and querulous, manifested a valiant
disinclination for bed. They got her there at last, and at
intervals throughout the night she proclaimed stoutly that
she was a better Leggatt than the best and 'that sair made
wi' thirst that she could drink the sea and sook the banks'.

'She's raivelled kind,' said Geordie.

In the morning it was plain that Martha must turn
sick-nurse. It was hardly the contribution to history that she
desired to make. Her examinations were coming on and
Emmeline ill was a handful. She broke every regulation the
doctor laid down. Fevered, she hoisted her bulk from the
bed and ran with her naked feet upon the floor to alter the
angle of the window screens.

'Sic a sicht ye hae them,' she grumbled to Martha when
the girl expostulated with tears. 'If ye wunna pit things as I
tell ye, fat can I dae bit rise masel'?'

'Temperature up again,' said the doctor to Martha. 'I
hoped you would have managed to keep it down.'

'Fat'n a way could *she* keep it doon?' cried Emmeline.

'Wad ye expect her to haud ma big tae to keep doon ma temperature?'

She was indignant now on Martha's behalf as she had been against her earlier. Indignation was a fine ploy when one lay idle and condemned. Emmeline was in high good-humour with herself. It was long since she had felt so important as she did lying mountainous beneath the bed-clothes, deriding her medical adviser's opinions and diagnosing her every symptom for herself with the aid of nothing more artificial than mother-wit; while round her in the heated kitchen the fervours of life went on – the steam of pots, the smell of food, the clatter of dishes, the hubbub of tongues, the intimacies of a sick-room toilet. Martha made a clearance of such articles as she could do without and Emmeline enjoyed a fresh attack of indignation. Demanding news of the whereabouts of something she had missed,

'There's a'thing ahin that door but dulse,' she cried, being told. 'Easy to tidy up when ye jist bang a'thing in ahin a door. But wow to the day o' revelations.'

'But where am I to put things?' Martha asked. 'There's just nowhere. There's nowhere in this house to put things. You shouldn't have so many of us – it's not as if they were ourselves.' And forgetting under the pressure of life the way of life she had purposed – her jubilant acceptance of every roughness – she allowed a secret desire to break cover.

'You should put these boys away now, mother. Why should we keep them when we haven't room for ourselves?'

Emmeline lay astounded. To be sure they had not room. And to be sure the boys were not her own, and stripped her stores like locusts, and brought no counter benefit in cash. The meagre sum she received for Jim and Madge was still forthcoming, but for Willie there had been more promises than pence. But put them away!

Alter an arrangement that had hardened to the solidity of a law! It was, and therefore it was right. – A belief that Emmeline was not singular in holding.

Martha did not push her argument. She dropped it, indeed, hastily, as though she had touched live coal. But the presence of the boys, their claims upon space and time, burned acidly in her consciousness. Jim she could endure, big hulking loon though he was, with Madge's own stolidity and a genius for unnecessary noise; but Willie, the younger boy, she was coming to dislike very fervently. He was dirty in habit and in attitude of mind. He sniggered. He used accomplishments hard-won at school for nefarious purposes, writing up obscene words on gates and outhouse doors: a procedure quite unredeemed in Martha's eyes by a certain merry insolence of bearing, not unattractive in itself. Her father's crassness, Martha could recognise from contact with Willie, was wholesome.

It looked like a month before Emmeline had recovered sufficiently to allow her to resume her classes. Actually the time had been so short that Luke and Dussie had not discovered her absence. But they had so many preoccupations! Luke was writing detective stories. He wrote for dear life, as though he had never had a hobby before and could not conceivably have another.

Dussie collaborated, criticising with a contemptuous common-sense the more outrageous effronteries of his plots.

They had had one accepted.

'Stout old yarn,' – Luke was telling Martha all about it, about its cruise among the editors, its ultimate haven – 'We'll go down to posterity yet: Sherlock and Missus.'

They were dreadfully – and quite sincerely – sorry to hear that Emmeline had been ill, and eagerly gave Martha the magazine to read that contained their detective story.

TEN

Dussie Enters on an Affair of Moment

Dussie had all this while been engaged on an affair of moment: to find someone for Martha to fall in love with. Happy herself, she longed to make her friend as happy, and knew only one way for doing it. But the men to whom she was introduced made little of Martha. She did not repulse them; but she seemed not to know that they were there.

'I can't get her to see,' Dussie said.

'Why should she see?' Luke asked. – 'No, she's not too innocent. She's not innocent at all. She's integral. Herself. And a singularly rare self. It would be criminal to alter it.'

Philosopher though he fancied himself, he had fallen into the plain man's error over Martha. He had made up his mind about her and was satisfied with that. She was the spirit made visible in flesh; tangible thought. He forgot that she was alive.

'No man in his senses would want Marty changed,' he said.

'A woman in her senses would,' retorted Dussie.

But Dussie did not get far that summer in the management of Martha's affairs. In August she bore a son, who lived an hour. Dussie was very ill too, for all her splendid vitality.

Luke took it hard. He had wanted his son. But in her weakness Dussie became dearer. She made no lamentation over the dead child; but sometimes in the darkness, slipping from her bright defiant capriciousness, with low words that were maternal in their solicitude, she consoled him for his loss. He divined that in comforting him she comforted herself and loved her as he had never loved her before, this new tender Dussie, comforting him in the night.

When the winter session was in swing again she was ready for company. There were merry meetings in Union Street;

but she refused passionately to have Macallister in the house again. The Greek statue glare. . . .

Luke laughed, and talked philosophy with Miss Warrender instead.

'A most informative lady,' he called her.

Martha had never lost her early fear of Miss Warrender. Less diffident now, she talked in company; but if Miss Warrender were present she sat mute, anxious and self-distrustful.

'But why?' persisted Dussie. She rather liked Miss Warrender herself. She talked so well – kept a conversation going. Martha, Dussie reflected, must be cured of this over-sensitiveness: now that she herself was growing well again it was time to resume that important undertaking to which she had vowed herself – the finding of someone with whom Martha could fall in love: but meanwhile it was pleasant to dissect Miss Warrender.

'O shut up, will you!' cried Luke from the other side of the fireplace. 'Can't you see that I'm engaged on a deathless work?' He waved his sheet of paper, and read aloud:

'Strange that the spirit's infelicity
    Should rob the world of beauty –
'That's deathless, but I can't get any further.'

'Didn't know you were a poet,' said Dussie.

'Neither did I, until today.'

He mouthed the lines again.

'That's a magnificent opening for a man's first sonnet, you know.'

He continued to write poetry. Magnificent openings that reached no conclusions. He had none of your young poet's diffidence in showing them off. No hole-and-corner self-consciousness. He displayed his accomplishment gratuitously. Why not? Had he possessed a Cloisonné vase, a fine quartz crystal, a son, he would have showed them off with the same eager gesture. Like his faculty for verse, they were among the myriad enticements that life offers to the curious.

In spring he announced the advent of his first long narrative poem.

'It's about the Archangel Gabriel. He gets tired of

hopping about heaven, so down he comes, moons about on earth for a bit and does a star turn.'

'I don't wonder – much more fun out of heaven,' said Dussie.

'Nonsense! More fun out of heaven? Fat lot you know about it. Much more fun in heaven than anywhere else. Isn't it, Marty? Don't you expect fun in heaven?'

Martha looked at him, a slow considering look. She was not an eager talker. *I can wait*, her willing silences implied; but her pauses were not hesitant, giving rather a sense of hoarded powers. Now she said, slowly:

'Of course. There will be so much to discover.'

'Of course! Hell's the sort of place where everyone sits around with a teacup and wonders what on earth to say next. O, they're a dull lot down in hell. Sensible. Everyone as like everyone else as ginger-beer bottles. Nobody with a mind of his own. Whereas in heaven you'll have all the really interesting people, the cranks and eccentrics, the fanatics and fools, all the folk who aren't afraid to be really themselves. No, my dears, there will be neither originality nor style nor humour in hell.'

'I hope we'll get some humour in heaven, then,' said Dussie. 'It would be awful to be serious all the time.'

'Never you fear. Heaven isn't serious. How do you imagine we could stand being as wise as we shall be if we weren't able to laugh at ourselves? You take my word for it, a sense of humour's a paradisal possession. It's the liberating agency. You go crawling about under a heavy tombstone, suitably inscribed, Wife of the Above and all the rest of it, until suddenly one day you see how confoundedly funny it all is, and then you come out with a great shout of laughter at yourself, and hey presto! up you walk to the next ring of the circus.'

With his arm round Dussie, he began to declaim his lines.

'What's that?' she asked. 'The new pome?'

'My latest and greatest. Wait till I tell you about it.'

Eager, impetuous, he spoke: as though the doings of the Archangel Gabriel were all that mattered in the world.

'You see, he grew tired of heaven, because he wanted to know what God was really like to the people on earth. So he visited a man, and took him up to heaven. Tremendous experience for the man, of course, but that's not what really matters. What really matters is what Gabriel discovered by taking the man up. But I've got them hung up between earth and heaven just now, and I can't get any forrader.'

He swung into the lines again, chanting them, hypnotised with his own creation:

'But the full certainty of understanding
Was his not ever. He had oft to go
Among the worlds, and knew their fierce demanding,
Sharing their troubled littleness, their woe

'Not little. For only thus could he endure
Divinity upon him, and unfold
Its thousand-fold intensity. The lure
Of the worlds had called him and their tale untold.

'So grew he, oft surrendering complete
And rounded silences and brimmed desire,
And chose bewildering war: but deemed it meet.
For though he had learnt the All, and might not tire

'Of knowing it, he knew not yet the whole
Of those inconstancies and alterations
That dwell resolved in God. God of his soul
He knew the fulfilment, but –'

'Luke dear, now listen,' said Dussie firmly, climbing on his knee and covering his mouth with her hand. 'Do you remember that we have a supper party tonight?'

'Yes, of course,' he answered, coming promptly out of his absorption. 'Fraser and young Kennedy and the beautiful Mrs. K., mostly frocks and fal-la-la-la – what Marty's mother would call with equal truth and eloquence a flee-up.'

'Well. – Don't be soulful in front of Mrs. Kennedy, Luke.'

'I shall be myself, my love. If the self chances to be soulful, all the worse for the beautiful Mrs. K.'

Soulful the self chanced to be, the beautiful Mrs. K. notwithstanding. He discussed at length the scheme and purpose of his narrative poem and declaimed the complete contents of the manuscript.

'If you'd cut out two-thirds of it and sharpen the rest, Luke,' said young Kennedy, 'you could make something of that.'

'Cut out two-thirds! My dear fellow, there's two-thirds yet to write.'

Kennedy grinned. With his Buchan accent he developed his criticism.

'It's like a half-hewn statue just now. Imperfectly disengaged from the block. You want to hew much deeper – '

'My good youth, am I a hewer of wood and a drawer of water?'

He wrote his poetry easily. Like going to heaven, it was fun; and without the travail of his soul he was satisfied.

Martha spoke little during the supper party. She sat very quiet, smiling to herself with a still, shining smile. She was intensely happy. How Luke could take her secret thoughts and transfigure them! – as though she had not always known that when the angel visits the man the deeper spiritual experience is the angel's. Since he had begun to write poetry (would he be as great as – oh, not Milton! one could not expect that – as Tennyson perhaps? or Mr. Yeats?) he had written nothing but had responded, like the vibration of a stringed instrument, to some tune within her own being. She did not look at him, but once or twice amid the nonsense he was talking he caught her eye. There passed between them a spark, swift, momentary, the flitting of a gleam, a recognition from their external and perfect selves.

Fraser called across the quadrangle next morning, 'Hello, Luke, how's the Archangel Gabriel?' It became a three-weeks' fashion to greet him with, 'Hello, Luke, what's the Archangel doing?'

The Archangel Gabriel remained in a parlous state between earth and heaven, and Luke was unable to extricate him from his plight.

'After all,' he explained, 'light takes a few hundred years to make the passage. You can't expect an Archangel to do it in a month.'

Doubtless the Archangel accepted the situation with grace

and humour, that paradisal attribute. The only person to suffer seriously from the delay was Martha, who was passionately exercised over the climax of Gabriel's experience. What did he discover about God? She wished Luke would reveal it; and brooding, devised conclusions for herself, even setting one of them, impatiently, to rhyme; though to tell the truth her verses were by no means as beautiful as her eyes had been when she tramped the Quarry Wood beating out the metre. Preoccupied thus, less than ever did she yield her inclinations to Dussie's Cupid-mongering.

ELEVEN

The Lustre Frock

'She's to hae a goon like the lave o' them,' said Geordie. 'She's nae to be an ootlin.'

Emmeline fingered the stuff of Aunt Leebie's lustre frock, holding it taut and running her thumb along its weave.

'It's richt gweed stuff,' she said. 'Yer Aunt Leebie'll be terrible offended if ye dinna wear it.'

Martha had said, when she brought the frock from Muckle Arlo:

'I promised to wear it when I'm capped.'

Graduation had looked immeasurably distant then, but how rapidly the years had sped! She had still her year of professional training to go through before she would be a 'finished teacher'; but her University course was almost over. Another month, and she would be dismissed into the world with a little tap on the head to signify that there was learning there . . . *Initium sapientiae* . . . .

Meanwhile there was the question of the frock. Martha considered it with a bad grace. The sacrificial mood was in abeyance. She had conceived a horror of the out-moded garment and would have repudiated her own hasty promise with great good-will. It was Dussie whose quick eye saw the possibilities of the lustre, her hands that transformed it. Martha was astonished by the result.

The Graduation morning arrived.

Geordie, Emmeline and Aunt Josephine came through the archway slowly. Of the three, Aunt Josephine was most at ease. She was superbly at her ease. She had travelled. She knew the ways of the world. She moved at her steady sober pace down the quadrangle, doubting nothing of the homeliness of those towers and pinnacles of granite towards which she floated with sails full-set. She would have made port as cheerfully in a barn.

Neither was Geordie perturbed, though stiff and awkward to appearance in his Sunday suit; and though he stood within the very haunt, the breeding-ground of that jeopardy that menaces a comfortable world, the virus of brains. For, holding still to his opinion that brains were a vexing agitation, he had yet of late kept silence on the matter and ruminated over what he saw; since he saw Martha reaching the very crown and proper end, the acme – as he supposed, being uninformed to the contrary and knowing nothing of the cunning whereby the university makes mention to her sons of only the beginning of wisdom* – the acme of instruction, without any alteration so far as he could see in her power or willingness to wash his sweaty socks and clear away the remnants of a meal. Moreover he had the reassuring persuasion that he had the right to be where he was. He set foot in the precincts with the confidence of a man for whom a place is prepared. Had not his daughter won it for him? And no gliding motors, no proud and peacocked women, could take away his security. It was Emmeline with her pretensions to gentility who was embarassed. Waddling under her load of fat, smelling of perspiration, with a button missing from one of her grey cotton gloves, she stared around uneasily, convinced that the majority of that animated throng had eyes for her; and with a good conceit of herself in spite of her uneasiness, keeked about in the presumptuous hope of being seen by someone who might admire and report her state. Being recognised by no one but Luke (who existed merely as husband to that Dussie) she yielded herself with but a hoity grace to his guidance, and followed behind his lean length up the stairway of the Mitchell Hall, indignant at his easy thinness and turning a critical eye upon the company with which she moved. 'Some gey ordinary jiffs,' she thought. She had been very uncertain what she was to see in a concourse gathered under the roof of the great hall of the University, and was secretly reassured by seeing numbers of men and women not too unlike herself.

* Motto of Aberdeen University: 'Initium sapientiae
  timor Domini.'

From the glens and farms, the fishing villages and country towns, the fathers and the mothers had come.

Here, and not in the granite walls, not in lecture-room nor laboratory nor library, nor even in the mind and character of those who taught, was the true breeding-ground of Geordie's jeopardy. Here, for this one day, was the creative power behind the University's glory and achievement. Twice a year she gathered for an hour the sources of her life, that he who would might look and understand. Geordie was part of this great spectacle, no spectator merely. By his ploughman's gait, his misshapen shoulders, his broken nails and fingers ingrained with earth, his slow rough speech, his unabashed acceptance of himself, he brought into that magnificent hall the sense of a laborious past, of animal endurances, of the obstinate wholesome conservative earth. With him came the mind's humbleness. He symbolised its ultimate dependences, its elemental strength.

Part also of this spectacle for the imagination was Aunt Josephine, who had been piloted by Dussie to the gallery and sat pleased with all she saw and pleasing all who saw her. In her was manifest that substantial Leggatt imperturbability, sure of its own worth and ways, positive, that gives direction and stability to the questioning mind.

Part too was the woman who sat on Geordie's farther side, and shared with him her printed list of graduands, Emmeline having fixed very securely on to the sheet served to them. With her exquisitely gloved finger she pointed out to him the name of her son ('my youngest') and he sought for Martha's and showed it her, pressing his thick discoloured thumb on the paper ('ma auldest an' ma youngest tae. I've bit the ane – ma ain, like,' he said) .

'Yon was a gey grand duchess I had to sit aside me,' he told them later, at lunch in Dussie's flat. 'A terrible fine woman.' A woman of race, mother of sons who were to make an illustrious name yet more illustrious in government and law and literature.

Part also was the washerwoman with ragnails and sucked hands where the flesh had swollen in ridges round her wedding-ring, whose daughter went in crêpe-de-chine; and the minister, hollow of cheek and with the eyes of a fanatic, and his shabby sunny wife, clapping her hands at the antics of the laddies, at heart a *halarackit* boy herself.

Martha, as part of the obvious spectacle, discovered that graduation was after all not very exciting. It was ordinary and inevitable, like stepping out of a train when you reach your destination. She was excited none the less; and her secret excitement had a double cause. Half was in Luke's parting words to her that evening – 'We're off tomorrow. Mind, you are coming to stay with us.' The other half, surprisingly in a Martha who seemed to care so little for the outer integuments of living, was the lustre frock. It was so different from every other frock she had possessed. Dussie called it her inspiration. Everything had gone right in its making. Wearing it, Martha had an uncanny sense of being someone other than herself; as though she had stepped carelessly to a mirror to dress her hair and had seen features not her own looking out from the glass. The mere wearing of the frock could not have changed her: but like the mirror it served to make her aware of alteration; and she seemed to herself farther from her folk and her home. Wearing the lustre frock, she had no Ironside instincts. She did not belong to the Leggatts. Across the mirror of lustre there flitted an unfamiliar Martha with alien desires; and when some days after her capping she received one of Aunt Jean's brusque notes of invitation, that specified the dates on which she was expected to arrive at and depart from Muckle Arlo, Martha set it aside and did not answer. The following day brought another note, as brief and as peremptory as Aunt Jean's:

DEAR MARTY,

The Beyond at whose Back we are meanwhile situated is a Gloomy Mountain Pass much infested by midges. Come at once.

LUKE

'But ye canna nae ging to yer aunt's,' said Emmeline aghast.

'I could go later.'

'Deed ye'll dae nae sic thing. Ye maun ging whan she's bidden you.'

'Not if I'm going elsewhere,' said Martha. 'I shall write and ask if I may come to her afterwards.'

Emmeline bickered for the next two days. This was a strange riding to the ramparts of the citadel that she was counting on Martha to reconquer. When the portcullis had been lifted, that the girl should turn in the saddle and canter away to other ploys! 'She wunna lat you come,' she said to Martha.

'I suppose I shan't miss a very great deal,' Martha answered. Queer contagion from a frock!

Aunt Jean having signified that the later date was approved, Martha went to Luke and Dussie.

Her fortnight in the hills had no reality. The hours floated past. Night glided after night. Muckle Arlo was on another earth. After two years Martha was amazed to find how similar everything was and how differently she regarded it. The black currants were over but there were red currants and rasps to pick. Martha again gathered currants and Aunt Leebie cried to her to wipe her feet; and Aunt and Uncle Webster came to Sunday dinner.

Yet nothing was the same. She was not excited but bored by her bedroom, and Leebie with the physic bottle was ludicrous; and when she changed on Sunday morning, after breakfast and the making of the beds, to her best apparel (which was of course the lustre frock), she chafed a little at kinship. Relations . . . but what relation had they to her soul? She set out for church living again in ecstasy her days among the hills.

'Ye've connached it,' Aunt Leebie was saying. 'Clean connached.'

She was pulling her lustre frock about, scraping with her nail at its embroidery. But what right had she to be displeased? She had given the frock. And Martha remembered how Luke had approved it and Dussie had waltzed her round the room when she saw it on.

'That's gey guideship it's gotten,' the old woman was muttering.

Martha had no leisure to be touched.

'I'm nae nane cornered wi' Matty this time,' Leebie said to Jean.

A relation . . . but what relation had she to their soul?

TWELVE

Torchlight

Martha's year of professional training began badly. After a dozen tentatives, rehearsals as it were for the grand affair, Emmeline took that autumn to her bed in sober earnest.

'There's naething ails her but creish,' grumbled Stoddart Semple.

He still came in about and smoked a pipe by the fireside while Emmeline lay, lumped and shapeless, in the kitchen bed. He would slouch about the doors: sometimes Martha, glancing up, saw him glowering through the window.

'Foo are ye the day, missus?' he would cry through the window to Emmeline; and abroad, report, 'There's naething ails her but creish' – a diagnosis that speedily came round to the lady's ears.

'So he says,' quoth she a little grimly. 'He says a'thing, that man, but his prayers.'

If *creish* were the ailment, certainly it did not serve to swacken the patient's temper. Martha was *trauchled*.

'Ye can keep Madge at hame to notice ye,' said Geordie. But Madge was earning money (if but a pittance), Martha merely expending it by her daily labour. It was obvious to plain common-sense which of the two might best be interrupted.

Martha, however, was resolved not to have her work interrupted. She knew that Emmeline would fare well enough alone by day. There was a modicum of truth in Stoddart's dictum. Emmeline was ill, though not so ill but that she might have been better had she wished. She had perhaps a pardonable temptation to indulgence in the importance that hedges an invalid about. Emmeline had been unimportant for so long! – Now her neighbours talked of her, and talked with her, comparing her ailment with their own, their sisters', their mothers', their aunts'. . . . How could Emmeline resist such dalliance? Fortified by the doctor's authority, Martha determined to do her college work by day and her cottage work at morning and evening; but stated early in family conclave the condition upon which alone it would be possible: that the bairns should be put away. Her reasoning was too cogent to be dismissed. Even Emmeline yielded; and other homes were found for the boys and Flossie. Madge remained, parting from her brother with no emotion on either side. Flossie screamed and kicked. She had had scoldings and buffetings enough in all conscience; and yet immoderate huggings too, and jammy *pieces* at illegitimate hours; and always Geordie's slow affectionate devotion.

Martha was not much concerned as to where they might be ultimately tossed. She had other absorptions. Even apart from her enraptured inner drama, her life was full enough to keep her thoughts engaged. She came home from long crowded days in schools and lecture-rooms to make the supper, set the house to rights, prepare as far as she could the next day's dinner; and rose in raw black mornings to get breakfast ready and attend to Emmeline's wants. Never, through all the weeks of Emmeline's illness, had she to clean the stove, light the fire, or carry water. Slowly and clumsily, but without fail, Geordie did these things; and he and Madge between them dished up some sort of dinner, while Aunt Josephine came frequently about, and the neighbours ran in and lent a hand. By and by Emmeline rose again, and sat heavily by the fire, putting her hand to an occasional job; and the winter wore through.

Meanwhile Martha's private drama had spun more fiercely. She had discovered, on the opening of the Training Centre session, with something like dismay, that Miss Warrender, now with Double Firsts, had been appointed to the lecturing staff; and that she would spend an hour a week under her tuition. Her reason repudiated the dismay. To feel a fool in the presence of a brilliant woman when one meets her socially, is no excuse for dread of her as a teacher: but reason was not particularly successful in her arguments. Martha continued to feel constraint in Miss Warrender's presence.

Others of the girls, who though her juniors had been the
year before the young lecturer's fellow-students, were less
abashed. The student's inalienable right to criticize his
teachers became doubly a right when the teacher had been a
fellow student the previous year. Martha therefore heard, in
the Common Room and corridors, much discussion of Miss
Warrender's affairs. It was thus that one afternoon, waiting
in the lecture room for the lady herself to appear – for with
all her brilliance Miss Warrender had no very accurate ideas
on punctuality – Martha heard her name coupled with that
of Luke Cromar, and coupled lightly. Luke, it appeared,
talked philosophy with Miss Warrender elsewhere than in
Union Street. She was reported to have said that he counted
her his greatest friend. The tone implied that species of
friendship that has laws outwith the common moral law. It
was the tone, even more than the disclosure, that played
havoc in Martha's brain. She tried to shout, 'It's a lie, a lie,'
but her lips were parched, her tongue was too clumsy for
her mouth. Miss Warrender came in. Martha could distinguish words but no ideas in the lecture. Her pulses were
pelting and in a little she rose and went out. 'Are you sick?'
her neighbour whispered. She paid no attention, walking
straight past the lecturer's desk to the door.

Outside she stood still in a fury of anger. This breaking of
the third commandment! But was it true? The blood
thundered in her ears and wave after wave rushed hotly to
her brow. She hurried at random among the mean streets
that surrounded the Training Centre, but recollecting that
her fellow-students might come out from lecture and meet
her, directed her steps towards Union Street. A filthy lie. –
But if he had given it circumstance? His walking with Miss
Warrender was so hateful to herself that she saw it as a
dishonour to his nature. That Luke should stain his
honour! – could even act so that foul breath might play
upon his honour.

In Union Street she met Dussie. Dussie cried, 'Do come
and see this frock!' and dragged her to a window. 'That
golden-brown one. Marty, you'd look lovely in it.'

'Duss,' blurted Martha, staring through the plate-glass
window, 'I heard something abominable just now. Some

girls talking. They suggested that Luke goes too much with
Lucy Warrender.'

'Pigs,' said Dussie.

Martha had spoken from an urgent impulse to thrust the
knowledge outside herself, but regretted at once that she
had thrust in on Dussie.

'I oughtn't to have told you. I –'

'Why ever not? You'll better tell me next who the
damsels were, so that I can claw their eyes out when I meet
them.'

She had broken across Martha's slower speech, so that
simultaneously Martha was saying:

' – didn't mean to make you unhappy.'

'Oh, *that* doesn't make me unhappy! It's rather fun than
not to be properly angry. I could slaughter the lot of them
and then dance upon their reeking corpses.'

She made a mouth at the shop-window and laughed at it
herself so heartily that Martha was compelled also to laugh.

'I suppose,' she said thoughtfully, 'a thing like that
couldn't make you unhappy unless you weren't sure of
Luke.'

'Marty! – You're the pig now.'

'Oh, I don't mean *you*. I mean anyone. I was only – ' after
a perceptible pause she concluded – 'theorising.'

'Don't, then. Theorising's stupid. Sure – ! I'm as sure as
death. No, as life. That's a lot surer.'

'I know you are. No one could be not sure of Luke.'

Her anguish nevertheless was because she was not sure.
Not that she doubted his faithfulness to Dussie! But she
feared lest by a careless gesture he had marred his own
shining image, made himself a little less than ideally perfect.

It was at that moment it dawned on Dussie that Martha
was in love with Luke, and the irony of her own procedure
struck her. But immediately after she was moved with a
grave pity for her friend. 'How unhappy she must be.'

But Martha was not unhappy. So long as she was unaware
of it, to be in love with Luke was bliss; and she was not yet
quite aware. She was however at the moment in an agony of
fear for him. Her love was ruthless on his behalf and would
have nothing less for him than her imagined perfection. For

two days she supped and slept with her agony, rose with it in the morning and carried it to every task she undertook. She began to understand the Incarnation. It was the uttermost shame for her to offer rebuke to the man who had dazzled her eyes until she could not see his human littleness; but if one cared enough for a person one would be thankful to suffer any shame, humiliation, misunderstanding, if so be the beloved could be saved from becoming a lesser man than was in him to become. God, put gladly to shame and reviled, because that was a lesser anguish than to see men and women fail of their own potentialities. . . . By the third day she had tortured herself into the persuasion that she must do violence to her nature and tell Luke that he had laid himself somehow open to public reproach.

She told him what she had heard.

'Do you happen to know one George Keith, fifth Earl Marischal?' he said, in the curious voice that she used to think had a smile in it.

She turned enquiring eyes, as though to ask what the Earl did there.

'As you may have heard,' Luke proceeded, 'he founded Marischal College, of which I am an unworthy member, in the year of grace 1593. Rather a magnificent Earl he must have been, since he did of his own prowess what it required kings and such-like bodies to do elsewhere – founded a University. The only one in Britain, you know, founded by an Earl. It was a separate University then, a sort of rival grocer's shop across the street from King's – whence it results that Marischal had a motto which I daresay you have heard.'

She wished he would be serious.

'What's good enough for an Earl is good enough for me.' And he quoted the old motto: 'They haf said: Quhat say they: Lat them say.'

So! – He had not understood.

She made her point clear – the high perfection he must not violate; and lifted her eyes to him, suffering mutely, imploring his acquiescence with all her simplicity of soul.

'You precious saint!' he said. 'Beatrice from the Heavenly Towers. There's an impromptu beginning for a poem. Shall

I continue? Or has any other blighter used it before me?'

But though he jested she touched him with a kind of awe.
Impossible ideas she had, of course; not of this world: but
her speech was like a lit and potent draught. What fools
men were, to think the spirit could not be manifest in
human flesh!

She kept herself in hand until the last of the evening's
tasks was over, undressed herself in darkness and went to
bed. Then she let her strung nerve snap and sobbed with
abandon. He had smiled at her and she all earnestness. . . .
Thinking after a time that she heard a movement in the
room, she quieted herself and lay, tense and listening. So
lying, she became aware of moonlight, and turned her head;
Madge in the other bed had raised herself upon her elbow
and was watching her with curiosity.

'What' up with you?' she asked.

'Nothing's up with me.'

'What're you crying for then?'

'I'm not crying.'

'Oh, all right, then.'

Madge dropped to her pillow again.

Shortly she said, 'If you'd fash yourself to do your hair a
bit decenter, you'd easy get a lad.'

'What do you mean?'

'Oh, well,' said Madge, 'you're near twenty-two and
hinna a lad yet.' And after a moment's pause she added, 'I'll
lend you my side-combs if you like.'

Her side-combs were set with a glitter of sham blue
brilliants.

Martha said sharply:

'I don't want either your side-combs, or a lad, thank you.'

'Oh, all right, then,' said Madge again. She turned her
shoulder, rubbing her greasy hair about on the pillow till
she found a comfortable nook. Soon she was sleeping
heavily.

Martha was indignant at the supposition that she
occupied her thoughts with anything as vulgar as a *lad*:
though if a *lad* be considered as a young male who cares for
one and for whom one cares in return, that was exactly of

what she had been thinking with persistence for some little time. But what relation was there between Luke and a *lad*, any . more than between Martha and an Ironside or a Leggatt? He had set their intercourse on too high a plane for the one, and kept her in her exalted mood too long for the other. Thinking of him (and no longer of his honour) she fell asleep.

The following week Miss Warrender spoke to Martha after lecture.

'Are you quite better now?' she asked. 'I was sorry you weren't feeling well.'

Martha stared, having forgotten the manner of her exit the previous week. Talking at the classroom door with the young lecturer, she was swept by a hurricane of hate. She wanted to hit her. Her fingers clenched of themselves . . . she could feel them closing on Miss Warrender's throat . . . and all the time she was saying calmly, with a smile, that she had not been very sick and was quite well now; that the sky was threatening; there had been too much wet weather lately and it would be most unfortunate if the coming Rectorial Election were marred by rain.

'For the peasemeal fight and the torchlight procession – it would be too bad,' Miss Warrender said.

Martha walked away. The corridor was endless. It seemed to roll away, like a barrel on which one tried to walk. She supposed she was tired; and, Good Lord! how she ached, now that she let herself relax. Into that imagined strangulation had gone the energy of a week's work.

She went home, climbing the long brae very slowly. There was dirty weather in the offing. A grey south; and a diffused yellow crept through the grey, giving it a still dirtier look. As Martha plodded on, absorbed, her blue-paper-covered child-observation note-book, in which she had to write her observations on every lesson she saw taught in the schools, slipped from among the books on her arm and fell in the soft road. She was annoyed at its griminess and wiped it hastily with her coat-sleeve. The smear looked uglier.

'Stupid!' she thought. 'I should have let it dry.'

And she stood staring at the stain, but it was not the stain that she was seeing. She felt as though with every step in her slow ascent she had been turning very carefully the revolving lens of a fieldglass, and had come to rest with her picture focussed to a perfect clarity.

She understood now that she was in love with Luke.

Reason told her that there should be black depths of horror in the knowledge, but all she could feel was wild glad exultancy, the sureness of a dweller in the hills who has come home. One loves – the books had taught her, though she had given the theme but little attention – as one must, perhaps against one's will and inclination: but she, sucked under without awareness, had loved the greatest man she knew. Judgment approved. She counted herself among the blest. Besides, this secret and impossible love had a wild sweetness, flavoured and heady, luscious upon the palate, a draught for gods. It was eternal, set beyond the shadow of alteration in an ideal sphere, one of the concentric spheres of Paradise. It would satisfy her eternally. There was nothing possessive in her love; or rather she possessed already all that she desired in him – those far shining, terribly intimate moments of spiritual communion.

She thought that she would love Luke forever with hidden and delectable love. It was a consummation, the final fusion of their spirits in a crystal that would keep forever its own exquisite shape, timelessly itself.

But some crystals founder in some fires.

The rain began, hesitant at first, then powerful as from an opened sluice. Martha pulled off her gloves, and throwing her face and palms upwards, let the water rush upon her naked flesh. She felt light, as though her body were sea-wrack floating in the deluge of waters; or as though an energy too exorbitant for her frame, coursing through her, had whipped her into foam.

'Ye maun be soaked,' Emmeline was saying. 'Yon was hale water.'

Martha only laughed, standing in the doorway with the water streaming from her clothes. She was remembering what Luke had said, one stormy night when he had brought her home from town: 'I like a soaking now and then. Good elemental feel it gives you.' Elemental! – That was it. Washed by the rain she felt strong and large, like a wind that tosses the Atlantic or a tide at flood –

'Ye micht shut tae the door,' Emmeline complained. 'We'll be perished wi' cauld.'

Martha smiled to herself and shut the door. She had done the biggest thing she had ever done: she had fallen in love with Luke. It was the crown of her achievement. And without changing her wet garments she began briskly to prepare the supper.

'Ye're raised the nicht,' her mother said. 'Fatever's ta'en ye?'

Martha laughed again, catching the tails of her dripping skirt for joy of the feel of water through her fingers. Raised! – of course she was – upraised to the highest heaven because she had had the wit to fall in love with Luke and with no other man on earth. And still laughing, and squeezing the hems of her skirt, she began to waltz round and round very rapidly on the kitchen floor.

Martha's procedure was by way of pantomime to her mother. Emmeline found the days very long. 'We're better wantin' yon canalye o' kids,' she acknowledged; but she missed the stir. When Aunt Josephine did not walk down from Crannochie, and none of the neighbours stepped in about for a crack, and not even Stoddart Semple flattened his nose against the window and called 'Foo are ye daein'?' her days were very empty; nor did her evenings provide much-entertainment. Geordie might have a curran remarks to make anent the doings at the farm, and Madge, when directly asked, would detail the customers who had visited the baker's shop and what their purchases had been; but Martha, with her head in the clouds, or absorbed by the mysteries of School Hygiene and Child Psychology, had no news to give her mother. Emmeline therefore enjoyed the departure of Martha's impromptu by the fireside, though her mind, untrained to the true analysis of its own enjoyments, insisted that she was distressed.

'Are ye gane clean gyte?' she asked; and anxiously: 'Haud oot ower fae the dishes. – There ye are noo! – a' tae crockaneeshion.'

Martha was still laughing. The clash of the broken crockery was like cymbals to her. Stooping she swept the

pieces together with her wet hands, flung them with a
clatter in the coal-scuttle and ran to her own room.

She was still laughing. She wished that she could stop. It
was folly to laugh like this because one had got wet. Her
clothes were clammy now and she was shivering from her
exposure. Her teeth chattered and suddenly her weariness
came back upon her. She sank to the floor, one arm upon
the bed. The walls and roof seemed to recede to an
interminable distance. The whole house was flying away;
and through an unobstructed clearness, but very far off, she
could see Luke. There was nothing between him and her
and she knew that she could reach him. She knew that she
had reached him. Her spirit flowed out upon him, encompassing and permeating his. She could give herself to him
forever by the mere outpouring of herself. She put herself at
his disposal, and rising from the floor very quietly, changed
her clothes and returned to the kitchen.

The weather cleared. The night of the Torchlight
Procession was dry and cold, and very dark; but cold only
heightened the ardour of the students and the dark threw up
the torches' glare. They poured out of the quadrangle on to
the crowded October streets – devils and pirates, wivies
with mutches and wivies with creels, knights and grinning
deaths'-heads, Japs and Maoris, *tattie-boodies* and emperors
– lit fantastically by the gleam of the torches they carried.
Spectators lined the streets, and the bairns of the poorer
quarters, yelling and capering, pressed in upon the rev-
ellers; some marvelled, some in a fine scorn criticized, some
tumbled to the tail of the procession and followed on with
shouts and mimicry. In the remoter streets, away from the
glare of the shop-lights, the procession trailed its length like
a splendid smouldering caterpillar, with fire and smoke
erect like living hairs along its back.

Dussie had pranked Luke out in a sailor suit, from which
his inordinate length of neck and limb protruded gro-
tesquely. Though no longer a student, he was too much a
boy to hold back from the fun of a Torcher.

'Wish I could go too,' Dussie had pouted as she stitched
at the sailor collar. 'Luke – couldn't I? Dressed up – no one
would know.'

'Rubbish!' said Luke. 'The size of you – it would give you away at once.'

Miss Warrender was in the flat that evening. She laughed and said, 'The men's monopoly, you see, Mrs. Cromar.' Miss Warrender was noted for an ardent feminist. Luke laughed also, and said, 'Oh, you want to share Torchers as well as Westminster, do you, Miss Warrender?'

'Why not?' she said.

'I'd do it,' cried Dussie. 'I'd do it in a twink, if I were tall enough.'

'Oh, no need to wait for your growth, Mrs. Cromar. One should do such things openly, or not at all.'

'Would you?' challenged Dussie.

Miss Warrender shrugged her fine supple shoulders and flung her arms above her head in a careless gesture.

'Why not?' she said again.

'You'd make rather a jolly gipsy,' said Luke watching the play of her arms.

Miss Warrender laughed again.

'For a freak,' she said, 'I believe I'll do it. You'd better come too, Mrs. Cromar – show yourself off. We'll let them see we are not afraid of them.'

She spoke mockingly. Luke took her in jest but Dussie in earnest; seeing which 'Rubbish!' cried Luke again, sharply decisive. 'You can hang around in the Quad, Duss, and welcome the warriors home.'

By the evening of the procession he had forgotten the jest; nor did it recur to him at all, when, marching through the streets, he found himself puzzled by a Spanish gypsy lad who walked in front of him. Something in the figure was familiar. It teased him for a little, then was forgotten.

When the roysterers had made their round of the city and gathered in the quadrangle again to fling their torches on the blazing bonfire, Dussie slipped from the crowd of waiting girls. Flushed and excited she sidled among the torch-bearers seeking Luke. Some of the men, recognizing her, shouted a welcome. 'Come on, Mrs. Cromar – into the ring!' Luke, excited himself, grabbed at her arm. At the same moment he felt his other arm seized. Turning, he saw the Spanish gypsy whose identity had puzzled him in the

street; and with something of astonishment recognized him
for Lucy Warrender. In the hilarious confusion that arose as
the torch-bearers thronged to dance around the bonfire, she
had manoeuvred herself close to Luke and thrust her arm
firmly into his. He glanced aside at her. She was wearing
heavy gold ear-rings that glittered with a barbaric
inconstancy as she swayed; and he was startled by
something lascivious in her eyes and posture, as though the
Spanish costume, like Martha's lustre frock, was a mirror
that reflected sharply an unfamiliar aspect of the woman.
He did not like the sharp reflection. Revolted, he flung her
off brusquely and drew forward Dussie, who had been
pushed back in the scrimmage, putting his arm around her
possessively. For the first time Miss Warrender perceived
that Dussie too was in the ring of dancers, and with a savage
energy she threw her torch on the bonfire and slipped back
into the shadows. A tongue of light pursued her for a
moment but shifted rapidly, and her gorgeous finery was
flattened out against the blackness and melted in it. Her
torch, flying high and falling short of the central fury of the
bonfire, spat back a shower of sparks and smuts that lit on
Dussie.

The incident made Luke thoughtful. He was still
thinking of it next morning, as he walked briskly down
Union Street through a frosty haze. In his preoccupation he
whistled as he went. Luke had a passion for making the
world comfortable. He liked setting people at their ease,
humouring them into a satisfaction with themselves that
made them the best of company; and if he had humoured
his   living-mine-of-information-and-perfect-pit-of-knowledge
into a belief that she meant more to him than she did,
well, he must disabuse her, that was all! But he hated the
necessity. He had taken all she offered him so long as it was
to his mind, and now that she was offering that for which he
had no manner of desire . . . Luke turned into Broad
Street, making for the University, and continued to whistle.

As it happened, Miss Warrender was already sufficiently
disabused. Her pride was fiercely hurt by the manner of her
throwing off, and she made public the opinion she had
always held of Dussie – a poor thing to be mated with a man

like Luke, illiterate. She could give him so much that Dussie could not give.

'A poor thing but mine own,' Luke said to his wife with the voice that had the smile in it. He had told Dussie plainly of Miss Warrender's outburst. There were always birds of the air to carry the matter.

'I prefer to be the dicky-bird myself,' he told her.

Dussie meditated, saying nothing. Then, flinging her head back and laughing merrily:

'Do you know, Luko,' she said, 'I once tried to make myself literate. I read and read at your books – oh, for hours – when you weren't in. I thought you'd hate me for being ignorant, but I gave it up 'cos you didn't seem to like me any better when I knew things out of books, and just as well when I didn't. But I was dreadfully unhappy about it for awhile.'

'I didn't think you were ever unhappy.'

'Oh! – lots of times.'

'Over what, for example?'

She looked at him with her mouth askew.

'Not over that Warrrender creature, anyhow!' she said at last.

They agreed that the Warrender creature was not worth unhappiness.

'You know, Luke,' said Dussie by and by, 'Marty never liked that Lucy Warrender. I used to try to argue her out of it, and you see she was right.'

'Marty has a way of being right on points of judgment. Spiritual instinct. She's clear-eyed. Like day.'

It were hard to say whether it was by reason of spiritual instinct that Martha disliked Miss Warrender, but very easy to say that she liked her lecturing no better as the term went on. No doubt but that Miss Warrender knew her subject and lectured, as she talked, brilliantly and with authority; but she had no power to fuse the errant enthusiasms of the young minds before her, to startle them from their preoccupations and smite them to a common ardour to which all contributed and by which all were set alight. She had not discovered that lecturing is a communal activity. For once Martha found that the getting of understanding had no charm, and confounding theme with lecturer, she hated both; though as far as Luke was concerned she gathered from both Dussie and Common Room conversation that she need fear nothing more to Luke's honour from Miss Warrender. She was therefore shining again with gladness, rejoicing that he no longer laid himself open to the mis-representations of the scandal-mongers and quite unaware that Luke was raging inwardly at that disgusting feminine folly that will not allow a man plain Monday's fare, a little rational conversation on topics of current interest, without the woman's obtruding her womanhood on him and forcing upon him the meanness of repulsing her. He had no more desire to offer love to a woman other than Dussie than to offer her a used teacup; but with his avidity for exploring other people's minds, he wanted as much intellectual comradeship as he could obtain, from men and women alike. He wanted to go on talking philosophy to Miss Warrender as he had always done, and being unaccustomed to repressing any of his energetic and multitudinous impulses, resented the make of human nature.

Seeing no alteration in Martha's shining calm, and clearly persuaded that she was in love with Luke, Dussie thought: 'She is heroic.' But Martha was not heroic. She had her paradise within herself and it sufficed her. What she possessed was more to her than what she lacked.

Luke continued to believe her a spirit: but her spirit haunted him. He was arrogant but not conceited; and that she might love him had not crossed his mind. Indeed he felt a subtle fear of her; and fear is not the way to truth. But during that spring Luke began to grow up. Though he hardly admitted it, Miss Warrender had sobered him; and Martha's rebuke had gone deeper than he knew. He was thoughtful, brooding sometimes until Dussie marvelled. He would turn from her finest dishes, light a cigarette and fling it untasted on the fire.

'A burnt offering,' he said, answering her remonstrance.

'A burnt . . . what on earth?'

'Well, a sacrifice to the gods. You set fire to valuable things, you know.'

'And what god do you sacrifice cigarettes to?'

He said: 'An unknown god.'

'But what *is* it, Luke?' she cried one evening. 'You don't eat or anything. You seem hardly to know that I'm here.'

'I don't quite know, Duss,' he said, rumpling his hair. He was rueful and puzzled; a boy who had remained a boy too long and found maturity difficult.

'It's . . . some sort of spiritual adventure, I suppose,' he said.

And he began to talk of Martha.

'Remember the time she told me I shouldn't be so friendly with Lucy Warrender? All nonsense, of course. Oh, in this particular case she happened to have some justification, but in principle she was quite wrong. But somehow afterwards I couldn't get her out of my mind. Herself. Not what she said. But her nature. Her nature is like an exquisitely chastened work of art. She does without. Rejects. Takes from life only its finest. And she doesn't *want* the other things. She's amazing, you know – to want so little and to lack so much. She doesn't really want the things we want – chocs and shocks and frocks and things – all our social excitements. But it's not because she's satisfied with a thin and empty life. I expect it's because she has something much more wildly exciting of her own. I thought and thought about it till I wanted to have it too – to get at the positive side of asceticism. What it gives you, not what it denies. It was really an intellectual curiosity – wanted to know what it was like. Inquisitiveness, you know.'

He could not humble himself far enough as yet to acknowledge that it was more than an intellectual curiosity.

'You're awfully funny, Luke,' said Dussie. 'Imagine punishing yourself out of inquisitiveness.'

'It's what scientists and explorers and people do. But it isn't punishing myself. That's the great discovery. It's the most thrilling excitement – refusing yourself things. Things you normally enjoy. The thrill of doing without them is far more exciting than having them. Comes to be a sort of self-indulgence. A Lenten orgy. A feast of fasting. A lap of luxury. I shall take to lashing myself next as an inordinate appetite. Like smoking, you know. Strokes instead of whiffs. Shan't you love ironing my hair shirt?'

Dussie's heart had gone cold. Was he in love with Martha? She turned to the piano and played a ranting reel.

'You'll have to look after your costume yourself,' she cried over her shoulder. 'I don't know how to dress for spiritual adventures. I never have any, you see. Shouldn't recognize one if I met it in my porridge.'

They were both growing up and afraid at first to share their knowledge.

THIRTEEN

Crux of a Spiritual Adventure

Throughout that spring Martha had walked enchanted. A spell was on her that altered the very contours of her body. Unlike the maleficent spells of the witches, that shrivel the flesh and destroy the human semblance, the spell that was on Martha rounded her figure, filled out the hollows of her cheeks, straightened her shoulders. In spite in her harassed and laborious winter, she had never been so strong and well. Her limbs were tireless. She carried her head high. The philtre she had drunk was of very ancient efficacy. Under the influence of her conscious love for Luke, she was rapidly becoming what Luke loved her for not being – a woman.

'That's grand hurdies ye're gettin' on you, lassie,' said Geordie, slapping her as she passed him. 'The wark suits you better'n the books.'

Martha was indignant. She felt obscurely that a change was coming on her, and though hardly aware of its cause knew well enough that it was not housework. Scornful, she tossed herself from her father's reach and strode up the brae towards Crannochie.

'Spangin' awa' up the hill in some style,' her father reported.

'Weel, lat her,' said Emmeline. Now that she had recovered sufficiently to resume most of her household duties, she was willing enough that Martha should take her liberty again. Besides, it was Sunday evening – an April Sunday – the very time of the week for young people to go walking. Madge was out too.

'Awa' oot aboot wi' her lad,' said Geordie.

'Lad!' quoth Emmeline contemptuously. 'Fat'n a way wad she hae a lad?'

'Weel she tells me whiles aboot him.'

'O ay, a' a speak. It's easy to see fa her lad wad be – a palin' post.'

On this occasion Emmeline was wrong. Madge had a lad. He came from Glasgow, clerked throughout the week in a wholesale paper store – a very genteel business – wore his tie through a ring with a flashy diamond and had alberts to his watch chain. Altogether a satisfactory person, and given to the week-end pursuit of rural delights: among which was numbered Madge's sturdy little figure. At sixteen her breasts were already swollen and her hips pronounced. Madge, when she caught gawkishly at the alberts as they walked along the road, was already in possession of her share of the spiritual mysteries. Her perceptions had attained their apotheosis. She had other uses now for her side-combs than offering them to Martha.

Martha, swinging uphill on the April Sunday evening, had no more use for the side-combs than she had had on the October night when they were offered. She was feeling splendidly alive. Life coursed through her veins, and she was glad, in a way she had hardly known before, of the possession of her body. It was a virginal possession. On the solitary uplands, throwing her arms to the winds, breasting the hurricane, laughing with glee at the onslaught of the rains, she felt as Diana might have felt, possessing herself upon the mountains. She rejoiced, as a strong man rejoices to run a race, in her own virginity, the more, as she came to fuller understanding of life's purposes, in that she felt herself surrendered eternally to a love without consummation. Her virginity was Luke's, proudly and passionately kept for him.

So strong was the life in her as she walked onwards in the tossing April weather, that she could afford to be prodigal of herself even to the extent of throwing a greeting to Andy Macpherson, who was walking, also alone, on the uplands. So might Artemis, of her condescension, have graced a mortal with a word. But Andy knew only one way of talking to a girl, and be sure, given the opportunity so long denied, made use of it: whereupon Artemis, who had amassed a very considerable vocabulary during her researches in history and literature, and in her new-found arrogance of spirit discovered she could use it, chid him with such hot scorn and vehement indignation (after making the first advances too!) that Andy's blandness frothed to bluster and his bluster collapsed like a paper bag at a Sunday school picnic; while Martha marched ahead with her chin a little higher and her shoulders more squarely set. O, cruel! – But these goddesses are notoriously unfeeling, up yonder on their Olympian crags. When Artemis takes to the heather, ware to the soap-selling, bacon-slicing helot who would follow.

Artemis was very happy on the heather. She swung up through Crannochie, hailing Aunt Josephine as she went; and on to the Rotten Moss, where she clambered upon the boulders and plunged among the heather-tufts; and like a votary of the fleet-foot goddess (for to goddess her were hardly fair and she so near the discovery of her humanity), ran races with her own swift thought; and wind-blown, mazed with distance, drunken with height and space, danced fiercely under a bare sky. Diana would have trembled, could she have seen her votary. Such wild abandon was hardly virginal.

May was a frail blue radiance. Was there ever such a summer? Day after day the sun rose softly and night after night sank in a shimmering haze. The hills trembled, so liquid a blue that they seemed at point of dissolution; and clouds like silver thistle-down floated and hovered above them. Stifling one night in the low-roofed bedroom, where Madge's cheap scents befouled the air, Martha rose exasperated and carried her shoddy bed outside. There she watched till morning the changes of the sky and saw the familiar line of hills grow strange in the dusky pallor of a summer midnight. Thereafter she made the field her cubicle and in its privacy she spent her nights. She did not sleep profoundly, but her vitality was too radiant to suffer from the privation. Sometimes the rain surprised her and she was compelled to shelter; sometimes she let it fall on her, soft unhurrying rain that refreshed like sleep itself; sometimes she awoke, dry and warm, to a cool wet world where every grass, each hair on the uncovered portions of her blanket, each hair about her own forehead, hung with its own wet drops. But oftener the nights were clear, marvellously lit. Darkness was a pale lustrous gloom. Sometimes the north was silver-clear, so luminous that through the filigree of leaf and sapling its glow pierced burning, as though the light were a patterned loveliness standing out against the background of the trees. Later the glow dulled and the trees became the pattern against the background of the light. The hushed world took her in. Tranquil, surrendered, she became one with the vast quiet night. A puddock sprawled noiselessly towards her, a bat swooped, tracing gigantic patterns upon the sky, a corncrake *skraighed*, on and on through the night, monotonous and forgotten as one forgets the monotony of the sea's roar; and when the soft wind was in the south-west, the sound of the river, running among its stony rapids below the ferry, floated up and over her like a tide. She fell asleep to its running and wakened to listen for it; and heard it as one hears the breathing of another.

In the third week of June Luke said: 'We deserve a change – we're positively grey with dust.'

The hot air quivered above the bogs. There was no wind to blow the cotton-grass. An insubstantial world, hazed upon its edges, unstable where the hot air shook. Midsummer: at their feet the sweet pink orchises, the waxen pale cat-heather, butterwort: the drone and shimmer of dragon-flies around them: and everywhere the call of water.

They were drowsed with happiness. Sometimes they walked, sometimes they stood and gazed, sometimes they lay in the long brown heather, smelling the bog-myrtle, listening to the many voices of the burns. A butterfly – a tiny blue – glided over and over them. It floated on the current of their happiness.

At twilight long shadows came out upon the hills. Their darknesses were tender purple, and stars, too soft to shine, hung few and single above. The skies were dust-of-gold.

There were no stars too soft, no purple too tender, no dust-of-gold too paradisal, for their mood.

Tomorrow – the trance will break.

Martha tossed the bedclothes off and sat up in bed. She was in the house, in the low hot room with Madge and her reek of face powder. She had been too weary, coming home from the afternoon among the hills, to carry her bed outside.

They had gone, the three of them, in an excursion train, up-country among the Saturday trippers, and back at night in a crowded compartment where sleepy children squabbled and smeared the windows with their sticky hands.

It was long past midnight when she abandoned the effort to sleep and sat up. She was not weary now, but through her body there ran a tantalizing irritation. She thought: 'It isn't pain – but what is it? It's in me. It hurts my body.' And she writhed, twisting herself upon the bed. 'I want the eleven stars,' she thought. 'But are they enough?' Her wants felt inordinate and she too small and weak. She battled against a sense of impotence.

She moved again, tossing an arm, and her hands met and clenched. She was so sunk in her absorption that for a moment she did not realize it was her own hand she had closed upon. She felt the firm impact of the grip . . . oh, it was her own! Queer, her own hand there. And then, with the suddenness of light when a match is struck, she knew what it was she wanted. Luke's hand, just to touch his hand: that would allay the agony that tore her, the pain that gnawed and could not be located, that was in all her body and yet nowhere.

She knew now. She wanted Luke. All of him, and to be her own. And the torrent of her passion, sweeping headlong, bore her on in imagination past every obstacle between her and her desire. The thought of Dussie was like a straw tumbled in a cataract. Let the whole world be swamped and broken in this cataract, so it carry her to her goal. The Ironside in her blood was up. Like her father who had swept the proud Leggatt beauty on to marriage, masterful until he had his will; like her Aunt Sally who had defied opinion and eloped with the man who roused her passion; Martha was ready to spurn the whole world and herself as well, in the savage imperious urge of her desire. Leggatt respectability! – She wanted Luke with an animal Ironside ardour. And was he not already half in love with her? – or more than half. 'I could make him love me,' she thought; and the sense of her own power rushed over her with a wild black sweetness she could not resist.

A curious part to be cast for a Beatrice. Martha was going

out of her rôle. But in truth she was neither Beatrice, nor Artemis, but Martha Ironside, a woman: of like dimensions, senses, affections, passions, with other women. If you prick her, will she not bleed? And if you wrong her –

But it was a little later till Martha began to consider whether she had not been wronged.

Morning came at last, and she could rise without exciting comment.

The day was Sunday. Impossible to see Luke that day. She passed the time in restless walking, and had one thought only: 'I can make him love me.' She had never had a strong sense of the complex social inter-relationships of life: now it was gone completely.

At night she slept in the field. Slept! – Sleep was past imagining. There was no darkness; and the diffusion of light was strange and troubling. In the very early hours of morning she slipped from bed, put on her clothes, and went to the wood.

There the light was stranger still. The wood was bathed in it; a wood from another world; as though someone had enclosed it long ago in a volatile spirit, through which as through a subtly altering medium one saw its boughs and boles. She was almost afraid to enter in; and when, ahead through the glimmering gloom, she had a swift glimpse of fire, as though a match had been struck and extinguished, she shook with an undefined terror and plunged hastily in another direction.

Roaming thus through the wood, she came in sight of Luke himself, standing among the trees. She knew of his night-wandering habits, but nonetheless at finding him there just then, an intoxication seized her. Her blood raced; her heart thumped; she could hardly stand: but recovering herself she went straight towards him. 'I will have what I want. I can make him give –' But as she glided on among the boles of the pine-trees, and he saw her coming and stood watching where he was, there was no alteration in her that he could have seen. The boiling fermentation of her passion was all within; and her habit of self-control and silence was too strong to be broken soon or lightly. The Martha who advanced through the strange shimmering night came tranquilly, stole in an exquisite quietude to shatter and plunder and riot. In her heart was havoc, in face and movement a profundity of peace. Luke, watching her coming, did not stir. She stood beside him, and neither he nor she spoke a syllable. They did not look at each other but at the night. Moon and afterglow and the promise of dawning were dissolved together in one soft lustre. They stood side by side and looked at it. After a long time Martha swayed a little, made a blundering half-step backwards, as though numbed with standing and seeking the support of a tree. He put out an arm and she swayed against it; and stood so for some minutes longer; and imperceptibly her head drew closer until she laid it at last upon his shoulder and looked up full, for the first time that night, in his face. Her whole being cried, 'Take me, take me.' But she stood so still, so poised, that it did not occur to him that she was offering herself. After a while he stooped and kissed her on the lips. There was no passion in the kiss. It was grave, a reluctance, diffident and abashed, as of a worshipper who trembles lest his offering pollute the shrine. But the flame that burned within herself was fierce enough to transfigure the kiss. It seemed to blaze upon her lips and run like fire through all her body. She closed her eyes under its ecstasy; and opening them again, slipped from his arm and went swiftly away through the wood. He did not follow her, nor did she look back, nor had either of them spoken.

Martha did not perceive that she had not had her desire. She was drunk with the sense of her own power over Luke and gulped more and more of the perilous draught until she was incapable of distinguishing any other taste. She lived only for seeing him again, but would not place herself in his path. It was three days later that, walking along the street, she heard his voice behind her and turned. The look she gave him was a direct continuance of the look with which she had left him, as though all that had passed between had not existed and they were still at their moment of exquisite communion in beauty. But he was not aware of the look. He had been much occupied in the interval and plunged at once into the theme that engrossed him.

'Tremendous news, Marty. If you have tears, prepare, etcetera.'

And suddenly very grave:

'Marty, how long have you known me? – four years, is it? And have you seen me in all that time accomplish anything? Lord, I've strewn the street with corpses! – things I've begun and cast away unfinished. And you've seen it and never said a word. Why didn't you tell me about it earlier?'

'Tell you,' stammered Martha. How could she have told what she had not perceived?

'You should have stabbed me awake to it sooner. There I've been, junketing at a thousand occupations, while you walk steadily on at one. So that's why I'm going away.'

'Away.'

'Imphm. A spell of hard labour. Hard labour and prison fare. It's you that's sending me away, you know. Aren't you upset by the responsibility?'

'Sending you away,' she said again. She had not fully grasped his meaning. He always went away in summer; but, was there more in this? And her responsibility? Wildly self-conscious, remembering the night in the wood, she queried: Was he fleeing her? Afraid of her power? And black exultation shook her. But he was speaking – she forced herself to listen.

'We're bound for Liverpool, Marty. I've just completed the purchase of a practice – a fine slummy practice, plenty of work and little pay. I'm leaving the University – old Dunster has his hanky out.'

She stared at him without speaking. Her mind seemed to have stopped working.

'Got a shock?' he said, looking down on her. 'We're giving shocks all round, it seems.'

'It's so – sudden.'

'Yes. Well, no. Not exactly. It's been under consideration for awhile, but we didn't want to say anything till it was all settled.'

She asked,

'Does Dussie know?'

'Dussie? – Rather!'

'I mean, did she know? – before.'

'Before? – When? – But of course she knew. A man doesn't do that sort of thing without consulting his wife.'

He was still unaware that Martha loved him. Rapidly though his education had progressed in the last few months, he was still able to believe that a woman could be all spirit. He had told Dussie, with a certain defiant diffidence, of his meeting Martha in the wood.

'You know when I walked the other night – sounds like a ghost, doesn't it? And it was ghosty – you wanted to say a bit out of the Litany, that bit we used to say when we went the long way round home at nights, after theatres and things, in the out-of-way streets, you know – "Fae ghaisties, ghoulies an' lang-leggity beasties, fae things that go dunt in the dark, Good Lord, deliver us." Only it wasn't things that go dunt in the dark that you wanted protection from, but things that go lithe in the light. Ghosts of light, not of darkness. You never saw such a night! Moon up and the whole sky like silk – gleamed. So did the earth. You felt like – or at least I felt like – a stitch or two of Chinese embroidery. You know – as though you were on a panel of silk. Unreal. I went as far as Marty's wood – the Quarry Wood. You've no idea, Duss – you couldn't imagine what it was like. At least I couldn't have. You know that thing – Rossetti's – about going down to the deep wells of light and bathing. It was like that. Only it was like an ocean, not a well. Submarine. Seas of light washing over you, far up above your head, and all the boughs and things were like the sea-blooms and the oozy woods that wear – you know. It was like being dissolved in a Shelley ode. Your body hadn't substance – it was all dissolved away except its shape. You walked about among shapes that hadn't substance, unreal shapes like things under the sea. Even some of the horrid rapscallion fishes out of the sea-bottom were there – one was, anyhow. That great sumph of a man that lives near Marty – what's his name? – Stoddart something. I met him just inside the wood – like a monstrous unnatural fish, one of those repulsive deep-sea creatures. Meeting him's like finding a slug in your salad. It was that night, anyhow. He had his eternal pipe in his mouth, and when he cracked a spunk the lowe of the flame was like an evil eye winking. Horrid feel it gave you. But further into the wood you forgot ugly fishes. You forgot ugly everything, and when Marty came walking through the wood you knew she wasn't real – just a ghost of light. I've no idea why she came – perhaps it really wasn't herself but just her phantom. I don't know. I didn't ask. She didn't speak a single word all the time. Just glided in and stood beside me – stood at gaze, so to speak. We looked and looked for a long time. Then she got tired, standing so long in one position, and made a stumbling sort of movement. And I put out my arm to give her support – and kept it there. And then somehow or other – God knows why I did it – I kissed her.'

He had paused there, diffident. Dussie had made no answer.

'And she just melted away – if I were a mediaeval chiel I'd honestly be tempted to believe she was an apparition. A false Florimel. An accident of light. She never spoke, you see. A voice is rather a comforting thing, don't you think?'

He paused again: and suddenly his wife was in his arms, her bright capriciousness gone out, sobbing as though she could not stop.

When he understood her fear, Luke went through one of those moments that are like eternity, so full it was of revelation. In that moment his boyhood was over. When he had held Martha in his arms in the wood, he had felt no lust for her possession but only a solemn wonder at his nearness to a thing so pure and rare: but now as he held his wife in his arms, and understood her fear that he might love Martha more than herself, he was ravaged by desire for Martha. At that moment he felt like universal Man assailed by the whole temptation of the universe; and because hitherto he had taken exactly what he wanted from life, the shock was extreme.

But there was rock in the welter: he did not know that Martha loved him. Had he been aware of her passion, there could have been no straight issue. Blindingly it flashed on him that she might be assailed. He put the thought from him. The contest was unimaginable but so brief that when he came to himself Dussie was still sobbing:

'I know she's better than me, but I love you so, oh Luke, I love you so.'

Afterwards he could hardly remember that he had thought of Martha thus. The lightning had been too keen. He was not quite sure that he saw it. But he took his wife in his arms very soberly. They had done playing at love. Henceforward they were man and woman, knowing that life is edged.

Dussie kept her own counsel concerning Martha.

'She has just to get over it,' she thought.

So when, in the street, Martha asked, 'Did Dussie know?' he looked at her with some surprise.

Martha perceived that she had not been in his innermost counsels. Hardly aware of the action she began to chafe her hands, which were clammy cold. In common daylight the insanity of her supposition – that she might be more to him than Dussie – was glaringly apparent. Hot black shame consumed her. She was too conscious of it to grasp very thoroughly the significance of his departure, but with a resolute mastery of her thoughts she forced herself to attend to what he was saying. She heard much detail about the new practice, the house they were moving into, the date of their going.

'I wish you were coming too, Marty,' he said. 'We shall miss you horribly.'

She heard her own voice saying:

'I'd have been away from you this year anyhow. I don't know where I may get a school. Not at home, likely.'

He continued: 'You've meant an awful lot to us. You've no idea how much. And do you know, it's really you that's sending me off on this new enterprise. They've been glorious, these last three years, but too easy. My work – oh well, I've done it all right, of course. Old Dunster wouldn't be so sorry to let me go if I hadn't. But somehow – well, it hasn't used enough of me. There was too much over to caper with. Another year or two of this divine fritteration and I'd be spoiled for good solid unrelieved hard labour. I owe it to you to have realized that one must have singleness of purpose. Oh, I'm not condemning the fritteration. Capering's an excellent habit. But not for me. Not just now. I feel in need of a cold plunge – you know, something strenuous that you have to brace yourself for. A disciplined march. A general practitioner hasn't much leisure for capering. G.P.'s to be my disciplined march. Instead of a hundred things I'm going to do one.'

And something cracked within her. Suddenly, it seemed,

the new self inside, that in the wood had not yet worked out
to the surface, had issue. It surged out over her. It took
form in a jest. Gaily she cried, throwing her head back and
meeting his look:

'And what about the other ninety-nine?'

'Dussie will attend to them,' he said, gay like herself.

Her mind began to work again. G.P.! – But his
greatness? He was to have been – what was he not to have
been? She saw the destinies she had dreamed for him float
past, majestic, proud, inflated. . . . She found herself
saying – and how queer it was, incongruous, unforeseen,
that she was laughing over this also, twisting it to jest –

'So it's a P. after all. Remember all the P.'s we planned
you were to be? Philosopher, Poet, Professor –'

'Piper, Pieman, Priest. Sounds like prune-stones, doesn't
it? Or there's Policeman – I'm tall enough. Or Postman.
That would be a fate worth considering. A country postie –
I'd love that. There I am again, you see! Can't stick to one
thing. A real Philanderer.'

They had reached the door in Union Street.

'Dussie's begun to pack already,' he said. 'Oh, that's
what I must be – a Packman! Come on up.'

The next five days were like a dream to Martha. Dazedly
she helped with the preparations for departure, and stood
on the draughty station platform among the crowd that was
seeing the travellers off. There was chattering and jesting,
and a ringing cheer as the train steamed slowly out. Martha
chattered and jested with the others; but the jests she
bandied, and the thoughts she had been thinking, had no
reality. 'You have been a fool,' she told herself: but the
accusation had no meaning. Even shame was burned out;
nothing had reality but his going. He saw her from the
carriage window among the waving group; so gay, so
shabby. Almost, he thought – but it was not a thought, so
quickly it flitted, so unformulated it remained in the scurry
of his mind – almost, he thought, he had rather she had not
been gay; but still, a shining symbol, herself the counterpart of the image he had made of her.

She was gay because she was no longer a counterpart. She
did not know what she was.

Climbing the long brae home she was overtaken by the lassitude of reaction. She did not seem to have strength enough left in her for passion, but she did not understand that it was only a temporary ebb. 'I don't seem to care any more,' she thought; and later, walking wearily on, with her eyes to the ground, she said to herself, 'So that's over,' and she thought she had only to exercise her will to be again what she was before, passionless, possessed only of herself.

But Martha after all was very ignorant. She could not know that a cataclysm four years in preparing does not spend its forces so easily. The waters were loosened and not to be gathered back.

FOURTEEN

Trouble for Aunt Josephine

Martha went to the Graduation. She had intended to go, and though the sap and savour were gone from every avocation and she was indifferent as to how she spent the days, it was easier to drift on the stream of former intentions than to force herself to new. Besides, Harrie Nevin was graduating, with Honours in English Language and Literature. She realized with a shock how little she had seen of Harrie recently and how seldom she had visited her thoughts. Of course she must see Harrie capped! But it was a stimulated interest.

For a time she continued to sleep out of doors, though there was no joy in the changing lights or the many voices of the country. She could no longer surrender herself and be lost in the world's loveliness. She would as willingly have slept in the bedroom beside Madge; she was quite indifferent to where she slept, and it was easier to stay in the bedroom; but that would have provoked comment and question. Anything rather than that! But she was not sorry when the weather broke and she was compelled to stay within.

At the turn of July there was already a hint of autumn. The skies were heavy grey; everything closed in unexpectedly; the wind blustered and squalls of rain broke upon the country, laying the corn in patches. The hips and rowan berries were dull brown that sharpened every day. Soon, the barley was russet. An *antrin* elm-leaf yellowed. Birds gathered; suddenly on a still day a tree would heave and *reeshle* with their movement, a flock dart out and swoop, to settle black and serried on the telegraph wires; and after a little rise again in a flock and disappear within the tree. In the wood and among the grasses gossamers floated, tantalizing the face, invisible, but flaring as they caught the sun like burnished ropes of light. Moors and hillsides, railway cuttings and banks beside the roads, glowed with the purple of heather. In a blaze of sun its scent rose on the air and bees droned and hummed above the blossom. Strong showers dashed the sun and the scent. *Hairst* began. They were cutting the barley. Scythes were out and the laid patches cut patiently by hand. Sometimes a whole field had been devastated, and through the yellow of the heads there gleamed the pink of exposed stalks. Winds rose and dried the grain. Stooks covered the fields. Nights grew longer and sharper. One morning the nasturtiums and potato tops were black. Leaves floated down. At every gust a light rain of *preens* blew through the firwood. The bracken and the birches turned golden and golden trails swayed from the laburnum trees, a foolish senile mimicry of their summer decoration. Gales brandished the half-denuded boughs and whirled the leaves in madcap companies about the roads. The whole world sounded. A roaring and a rustle and a creak was everywhere; and dust and dead leaves eddied in the gateways.

But long ere these things Martha's path had turned. Late in August she was appointed to a school at Slack of Mar, some ten miles across country towards the Hill o' Fare. There being no direct conveyance, it was not so near that she could stay at home, though not so far but that at weekends she could cycle back and fore. From Monday morning till Friday night, and later when the nights grew longer and darker from Sunday night till Saturday morning, she lodged in a cottage near the school.

'A gey quaet missy – terrible keep-yersel'-tae-yersel- kin',' the folk around said of the new teacher. The other teachers in the school tried to draw her out, but she refused their advances. She was thankful to be left alone. Her inner life was too turbulent, too riotous, and absorbed her energies too fully to leave much possibility of interest in the external world.

Martha had discovered that she was by no means done with passion. The numbness of exhaustion worn off, she found herself delivered again to its power. She let herself go to it. Only in its flame did she feel herself alive. She luxuriated even in the black depths of pain to which her craving surrendered her. They were the earnest of an intensity of life beside which all else in the world was mean and flat. She lived for the incidence of those cyclones of desire that lifted her and drove her far beyond herself, to dash her back bruised, her very flesh aching as though she had been trampled. There were times when she felt the presence of Luke so close and vivid that the things she touched with her hands and saw with her eyes were as shadows. These were the times when she had been accustomed to pour herself out for him. Since the day when, dripping wet from the pelt of rain that had overtaken her, she had crouched on her bedroom floor and felt for the first time in absence of her spirit in immediate communion with his, she had satisfied by this means love's imperative demand to give. Her life had seemed to pass out from her and be received in his.

But love's imperative demand was now to take. She wanted Luke, his presence, his life, his laughing vitality; and it seemed to her, crouching mute upon the floor with the mood upon her, that reaching him she could draw his very life away and take it for her own. 'I mustn't. I mustn't,' she thought. It was like rape. And her exultant clutching was followed by an agony of shame. But next time the mood possessed her she clutched again. 'He is mine. I can hold him. I can have his life in me.' And she felt like a dabbler in black magic, the illicit arts. There had been nothing illicit in her loving Luke, nor in the outpouring of her spirit upon him; but this reckless grabbing was like a shameful and beloved vice. She fought frantically against it, only to succumb to a blacker and more gluttonous debauchery. Reason, that had been the adversary in her effort to give, mocking her with the ultimate inability of the mind to know that what she felt as true was actually so, was now her triumphant ally. 'You cannot know,' reason whispered, 'that you really touch him. It is only idea.' And as long as she could not be sure, she could not exert her will to check her thieving. Afterwards she was hagridden, with strained miserable eyes. The hollows had come again in her cheeks. Her face was hungry.

At home she was merrier and more vivacious than she had ever been. Mirth was her hiding-place. Anything rather than have them guess she had been hurt, and how! But she hated

the effort it demanded and was thankful that the larger part
of that winter was spent away from home.

The road from Slack of Mar to Wester Cairns ran through
Crannochie, and every weekend as she passed on her bicycle,
Martha paid Aunt Josephine a visit; but preoccupied with
herself she failed to notice, what the neighbours round about
Crannochie were noticing that spring, that Miss Leggatt was
less alert than she had been. Her straight shoulder and steady
foot were failing her. She sat too often and too long by the
ingle, forgetting time; sometimes, she forgot to rise; her
blind was not drawn up, her door was not opened, till far on
in the day; but always she had a ready word for a visitor, and
Martha, for whom Aunt Josephine had been just the same
since ever she could remember her, went on perceiving the
familiar image and missed its alteration.

'Yer Aunt Josephine hasna come in aboot this lang while,'
said Emmeline one Sunday in February. 'Is she weel
eneuch?' If it was long since Aunt Josephine had been to
Wester Cairns, it was longer since Emmeline had been to
Crannochie. Emmeline, in the parlance of the neighbourhood, was like a house-side. Walking was not for her. The
mountain could not go to Mahomet, and Emmeline was
dependent on her daughter for news of Miss Leggatt.

'She was all right on Friday,' said Martha, staring out at
the weather. A storm had broken the day before and she did
not relish her ten miles' cycle run to the Slack.

'It's nae near han' by,' said Emmeline, peering out over
her shoulder. 'See to that roarie-bummlers.'

Glittering bergs of cloud knocked against the south-east
horizon, and turned and floated on again, and gave place to
others; or stayed and piled themselves in toppling transient
magnificence.

'The sooner I'm off the better,' said Martha. The ground
was coated with a powdery snow; not enough seriously to
impede progress, had it not been for the wind. Through the
lifted snowclouds a ferocious wind seethed and twisted. One
could watch its form in the writhing powder as one watches
the reflection of branches broken in a pool. A dragon-shaped
wind. With the sifted snow stinging her cheek and clogging
on her spokes, Martha was glad enough to see Crannochie;

and too grateful for Aunt Josephine's fire and cup of tea to pay overmuch attention to Aunt Josephine's appearance. On the Friday of that same week, however, she could not be blind to the alteration of the old lady.

The cold snap had gone, giving place to a muggy Monday, Tuesday, Wednesday, Thursday, days without spirit or *smeddum*. But here was a day for you, blue as a kingfisher, pungent as tang'l! – tonic. Martha sprang on her cycle and came to Crannochie flushed and towsled with the spring.

Aunt Josephine sat in her chair, dull-eyed, *dowie*, indifferent. She was without enthusiasm and without food. Even from the cup of tea that Martha prepared she turned away her head. Aunt Josephine refuse a cup of tea! But when one has been sick for days –

Martha persuaded her to go to bed.

'I'll tell you what, I'll come back and stay with you. I'll run home first and tell them.'

By light of Saturday she saw everywhere the evidences of Aunt Josephine's unfitness. The house was grey with dust, clothes smelly with dirt were flung in a corner, on the pantry shelf she found a dish with scraps of stinking meat, hairy-moulded. *Scunnered*, she turned the contents into the fire and carried the dish hastily to the door. Peter Mennie the postie was coming up the path.

'But the dish smells still,' she said, 'even though I've washed it. Throw it away for me, Peter.'

'Bury it, lassie, bury it in the earth,' answered Peter, 'the earth's grand at cleanin'.'

And thrusting on her the bundle of letters he was holding, he took the cause of offence in his hand and strode with it round the end of the house.

'It's in ahin the white breem buss,' he said when he returned. 'You dig it up in twa-three weeks an' it'll be as sweet's the earth itsel'. There's mair buried in the earth nor fowk kens o'.'

With a spasm of dismay, an hour or two later, Martha was wondering whether Aunt Josephine might not soon be laid there too. Plainly she was very ill. There was hurrying back and fore . . . by night Miss Leggatt had been carried to the infirmary. They operated thrice in all before they sent her home, haggard, shrunken, a ghost of herself; and with the knowledge that shortly she must die.

'They should 'a' lat me dee in peace,' she said, weary of hospital routine, of chloroform and the knife and all the elaborate paraphernalia by which science prolongs a life that is doomed like hers. 'They canna cure an' I micht 'a' been deid ere now an' laid in the bonny grun', an' nae trouble to naebody. Weel, weel, but here I am.' And contemplating herself in her own bed among her own belongings, she *cantled* up and looked around her with a shining pleasure. 'It's rale fine nae to be deid,' she pronounced. She *cantled* up a little farther when Aunt Jean, who had accompanied her from the hospital, began to tell her the arrangements made for looking after her. 'A nice body that had been a nurse, nae ane o' the hospital kind, ye ken – ' 'Nurse!' quoth Miss Josephine; and with that she perked up and there was no more word of dying. Never a nurse would Aunt Josephine have, no, nor any hired woman. A pretty pass things were come to, if she had to take a hired woman under her roof, she who had relished her jaunty independence through so many years. Oh, she knew there were unpleasant necessities, her wound to dress and so forth, but the district nurse was coming in about every morning to do that; and for the rest –

'There's Matty there,' she said, ''ll bide wi' me. That would be mair wiselike nor a stranger body, surely. She can easy get ower to the Slack on her bicycle. An' it's little that a craitur like me'll want an' brief time that I'll want it.'

Aunt Jean approved the suggestion. Quite right for Matty to make herself useful.

Martha was undergoing at the moment one of her fierce revulsions from a bout of passion. She wanted to dash up out of the waters that had engulfed her, to stand high and dry on common ground; and it seemed to her that the more hard work she had to perform, plain and ordinary tasks that would use her up, the freer she would become. 'Even more than I've strength for,' she thought, 'so that I'll be tired out always and never have time to think.' There would be an astringent quality in days that included an eight miles' cycle run night and morning through all weathers, the tending of an old woman stricken with cancer and the keeping of her house, in addition to the day's teaching in school: something antiseptic to draw out from her what at the moment she felt as poison. *An ounce of civet, good apothecary.*

'Of course I will stay with you,' she said; and to her father, who demurred a little at the arrangement, though conceding, 'Ye'll hae to pleesure her. It canna be for lang,' she repeated, 'Of course I'll stay with her. I can easily manage.'

Later, when the sharpest of her revulsion had worn off and she no longer thirsted to scourge herself, she had a sagging of the heart over what she had undertaken. 'Shall I be able?' she queried: and with the insidious creeping in again of desire she thought, 'I shan't have time enough for Luke.' To gather her forces and pour them out on him seemed just then the only worthy use in life: though in her heart she knew that the outpouring would turn, as it always did, to grasping. She wanted time for that too. . . . But it had never been in her nature to step aside from necessary labour and she held steadily to her task, stifling the impulses that sometimes she counted madness and sometimes the noblest sanity she knew.

Aunt Josephine made an astonishing patient. As Peter the postie said, 'I never saw her in twa minds. She's aye grand pleased wi' hersel'.' Pain, sickness, comfort, the kindliest of attentions, the most wearisome of waiting, a clean house or a dirty, won from her the same divine acquiescence. On her worst days of pain she said, 'Weel, weel, ye canna mak a better o't. There's fowk waur nor me.' 'If you knew where to find them,' Martha said once. She was humbled by Aunt Josephine's shining gratitude for attentions that were often, tired as she was by the time she arrived back at evening, scanted and hasty. 'That's richt, ma dear,' Aunt Josephine would say, when Martha had not time to shake the mats or lift the ornaments and dust behind them. 'They'll wait fine till the morn. A lick an' a promise, that'll dae grand.'

'A dicht an' a promise – it'll serve my day,' she often said. Yet as the weeks slipped by and summer came in, she seemed far indeed from dying. Every day she took a firmer grip again of life. She left her bed, sat most of the day in her chair; then moved about the room doing odd jobs for herself; by and by could take a turn in the garden.

'I'm a bittie better ilka day,' she proclaimed delightedly. 'I'll seen be tae the road again at this rate.' And jubilation shining from her countenance, 'I'll nae keep sorrow langer nor sorrow keeps me,' she said.

Did she really think she was recovering, Martha queried of herself. If she still talked of what would serve her day, in the tone of resignation that suggested a brief day and a bounded, it was only, Martha noted, in phrases where to speak so had become a habit. When she was not simply making use of a phrase, Miss Leggatt's talk was all of life. No worms, nor graves, nor epitaphs had entry there. She had turned her back on the incredible folly of dying and was setting again about the excellent business of living with all the astuteness she could muster. 'Does she understand?' Martha thought. A few months at the most, the doctors had said. And she pondered whether she ought not to recall the old lady's galloping ideas. Was it kind to let her deceive herself, build false hopes that could have no foundation?

Miss Leggat understood well enough. She knew that she was dying: but she was not going to smirch what was left of her life by any graveyard considerations. And she said to Martha, 'It's high time the kail was planted out.'

'Kail!' Martha thought, with a queer contraction of the heart. 'Where will *she* be by winter? – But if it makes her any happier, where's the harm?' And she planted out the kail.

The old woman's gallant endurance of pain astounded her. 'But it's less awful than spiritual pain,' she said to herself hastily, ashamed a little of her own cowardice in face of her black nights of craving; and ashamed a little farther at the self-excusing, she would turn to Aunt Josephine with some tender ministration. She was not always tender. Passion, that seeks self very abundantly, left her at times a poor leisure for the concerns of other folk. When the crave was on her, it was dull companionship she gave Miss Leggatt. Luckily, however, Miss Leggatt had other companions. Peter Mennie, whether he had a letter for her or not (and Miss Josephine had no great correspondence), put his head every day round the cheek of the door and cried her good morning. Clem, from Drochety Farm, the rough country lass who since the death of Mrs. Glennie had been mistress in all but name of Drochety's establishment, and held her empire with an audacious hand, ran in on any pretext, or none at all, and bandied high jests with Miss Josephine.

'Ye're a great case,' Miss Josephine would say, gleaming in spite of her nauseating pain at some of Clemmie's audacities. Clem was a thorough-paced clown. She had an adaptable body. She could squint at will and her limbs were double-jointed. She would descend rapturously upon Miss Josephine with 'eyes that werena neebors an' feet at a quarter to three,' and take off again 'bow-hoched,' her tongue lolling; while the old lady sat in her chair and beamed with pleasure.

'She's a tongue in her heid an' she can use it tae,' she would tell Martha. 'She's some terrible up-comes. She's a caution, is Clem. A cure.'

A cure she was. The bluffert of her presence did Miss Josephine good. The very sound of her voice, strident and exuberant, carrying across the fields, was companionship in the long lonely days; and when Clemmie made jam, she gave Miss Josephine a taste; when she baked she brought her a scone for her tea.

And Stoddart Semple shambled in once or twice with his dambrod and gave the old lady a game; but she was 'tired some seen' for the game to be much of a success. 'We maun jist tire an' fa' tae again,' she said, 'that's fat we maun dae. Tire an' fa' tae again.' They fell to again, Stoddart having ample leisure to await her convenience and in his glum fashion enjoying the stir.

Mary Annie, too, old widowed Mrs Mortimer, would look in, hastily and deferentially, upon her friend. Her visits were conditioned. With the years Jeannie Mortimer had become increasingly peremptory and inquisitorial. She had carried her habit of bigotry from her religion into the minutest affairs of daily life; and surer every hour of her own salvation, grew proportionately contemptuous of the remnant of mankind. For Miss Leggatt in particular, who said straight out exactly what she thought of such a misanthropic variety of religion ('I'm ane like this,' Miss Leggatt would proclaim, 'fatever I think I say.' And she thought, and said, that Jeannie Mortimer was a *besom*. 'She's blawn up nae handy in her ain conceits. Religion's nae for plaguin' ye. A bit prayer's richt bonny in its ain time an' place, but yon's fair furth the gate. She's nae near han' soun'.'), for Miss Leggatt in particular Jeannie entertained an unconcealed distaste.

'I canna bide,' Mrs. Mortimer would tell Miss Josephine. 'It's an offence if I bide awa' ower lang.'

But when Jeannie's back was turned, Mrs. Mortimer, with her head poked forward, in her curious mode of progression that was half a walk and half a run, would sneak in by to Miss Leggatt. Some mornings she would arrive a little after ten o'clock.

'Jeannie's tae the toon, Miss Josephine,' she would say. And, jubilantly, 'I've on the tatties. I dinna need muckle breakfast, but I maun hae ma dinner. I'm nae nane o' yer gentry kind o' fowk. I'm jist the common dab. I jist eat whan I'm hungry.'

'The gentry has jist three meals a day,' Miss Josephine would answer. 'It's the common dab that has five or sax an' jist eat whan they're hungry.'

'I dinna ken' – all her old anxiety was in Mary Annie's voice and countenance – 'I dinna ken. I'm jist plain Geordie Williamson.'

And she would trot away, between a walk and a run, to eat gleefully of smoking hot potatoes and salt; and then pick and fidget at the meal she shared with Jeannie.

'I dinna need muckle mate, an auld body like me,' she said.

June was a hot and heavy month. Martha found the eight miles to Slack of Mar a little longer every morning. There came a morning when, nauseated by the odour that clung about Aunt Josephine's room, she sickened and could eat no breakfast. She climbed on her bicycle nonetheless and set off up the road.

'She has her ain a-dae wi' they littlins,' Aunt Josephine was saying somewhat later to the doctor, who chanced to call that morning.

It did not occur to her that Martha might have her own ado in Crannochie as well. How could she be a trouble to anyone, sitting there so quietly in her chair, with never a word of complaint upon her lips?

Quarter of an hour later the doctor came on Martha herself, sitting by the side of the road where she had stumbled from her bicycle, her head sunk in her hands.

'If you could take me on to the Slack – ' she said.

'The Slack!' quoth he. 'It's slack into your bed that you're going.'

And to Miss Josephine he said, 'You'll have to get a woman in to notice you, or I'll be having two patients instead of one.'

'Weel, weel,' said Miss Josephine, 'what we canna help we needna hinder. We'll jist e'en hae to dae't.'

But that evening as she sat in her chair her mouth was a little grim. A woman in to notice her indeed! What noticing did she require? It was not as though she were *raivelled*, as her old mother had been, poor body, or Miss Foubister of Birleybeg, who had been a terrible handful for years before she died, getting up and dressing herself in the middle of the night and trotting away down the road to the yowie woodie in search of a sweetie shop to buy her peppermints; or clearing the dirty dishes off the table into her apron and flinging them like so much refuse on the grate, where they smashed to smithereens. No, indeed, she was not like that. And a stranger body, too, meddling among her things, preventing herself perhaps from going and doing as she pleased. Her mouth was still a little grim in the morning.

'I'm fine, auntie,' Martha insisted. 'I'm quite all right today. Really I am.'

'Wi' a face like that!' said Miss Leggatt. 'Like a deuk's fit.'

Martha laughed. 'I've been waur mony a day an' nae word o't,' she said, giving Miss Leggatt back one of her own sayings.

The old lady's mouth relaxed a little.

'I shan't go to school today,' said Martha, 'but by tomorrow, wait till you see, I'll be as right as ever. The house can do without cleaning today.'

The mouth relaxed a little farther.

'The doctor thinks ye've some muckle to dae,' said Aunt Josephine. '"Hoots, awa', doctor," I says, she's managin' grand." "O ay, grand," he says, "but ye'd better get a woman in to notice you."'

'If only she would,' thought Martha swiftly. 'O God, I'm tired.' But she read the note of entreaty in Aunt Josephine's voice.

'We don't want a woman, do we?' she said.

The grimness went quite away from Miss Josephine's mouth.

'It gings clean by my doors,' she said, 'fat'n a way fowk can like to hae strangers aboot them. They're like the craws amang the wifie's tatties. I mind fine, fan I was stayin' wi' that cousin o' yer grandpa's, her that was terrible ill, there was twa fee'd weemen in the hoose – a cook an' a hoosemaid. I crocheted a cap to the hoosemaid, but nae to the cook. I didna dae richt. I should 'a' gi'en her a cap tae. But she was sic a discontented besom. She micht 'a' been mair contented if she had gotten a cap.'

Its natural pleasant line was restored to Aunt Josephine's mouth. She talked gaily on of the fee'd woman of half a century before and forgot the project to fee a woman on her own behalf.

'Matty and me'll jist scutter awa',' she said to the doctor. 'Her play'll seen be here. We'll manage grand.'

He looked at the girl's sunken eyes. They were not sunken because of Aunt Josephine, nor yet on account of the bairns at Slack of Mar: but that was her own affair.

'Term's nearly over,' she said. 'Of course we'll manage.'

'It can't be for long,' he told her as she saw him out.

But they had said that so often. The holidays came and Miss Leggatt was still smiling and serene, and viewed her growing kail plants with satisfaction; and Martha drew in her lip and wondered what was to happen about her visit to Liverpool. That visit had been promised for a year, and for a year she had luxuriated in the thought of it. Now – ? Aunt Jean and Aunt Leebie came occasionally to Crannochie, though Aunt Leebie was fragile now and ailing nearly all the time. 'Leebie'll dee first o' us a',' Aunt Josephine had always said; and Leebie herself accepted the probability as a distinction. It was a melancholy business for her to come and look on Josephine usurping, as it were, her right. She came but seldom. Aunt Jean came, brusque and brief, and found rust on the pan lids. Aunt Margot came, once only, harassed with flesh. But none of them offered to relieve Martha, and she was too proud to ask.

'She could get a body in for a whilie, surely,' said Emmeline, who knew of the invitation to Liverpool.

'She wouldn't like it,' Martha said.

'Oh well, ye'll need to humour her. She's gey far on her way,' Emmeline responded, and thought no more about it.

'There's mair last in her nor a body wad 'a' thocht,' said Geordie, who did not know of the Liverpool project but had overheard the last few words between his wife and his daughter before the latter left again for Crannochie. He was wanting his daughter home. Matty might have her head stuffed with queer notions, but he liked her presence about the doors.

'Fat way wad she nae get a wumman?' he asked Emmeline. 'Has she nae the siller?'

'O ay, she has the siller, but she has mair, she has the sense to keep it. What ill-will hae ye at Matty's bidin' wi' her?'

'O, nane ava', but that the lassie wad need her holiday.'

'Holiday eneuch for her to be awa' fae the geets, surely to peace,' said Emmeline. Remembering a disclosure Martha had inadvertently made anent Aunt Josephine's marketing, however, she added, 'But she's funny wi' her cash.'

'We're a' funny wi' something,' Geordie answered, stretching his legs out in the sun. Matty, he reflected, was funny with her notions about book-learning, and sleeping in the field – 'like the nowt,' he thought – and now there was Madge trying on the same caper; and Emmeline was funny with her notions about other folk's bairns. There he paused, ruminating.

Emmeline had designs upon another baby boy.

Unfair, Geordie pondered, to bring another bairn there without even telling Matty. It was for Matty's sake the others had been sent away, and Matty, it was to be expected, would not be long an absentee from home.

On Martha's next visit home, meeting her in the field on her way to the house, he told her of her mother's intention.

Martha's anger blazed. She broke out upon her mother.

'Where are you getting him?' she asked, after having

intimated her displeasure. Some illegitimate outcast, she supposed.

'Hingin' on a nail i' the moss,' said Emmeline shortly.

Martha could be conclusive too.

'Well, mind,' she said, 'if you bring that child here and you fall ill again, I won't look after him. So you can please yourself. I mean it, mind.'

'Ye're terrible short i' the trot the day,' said Emmeline.

Martha's anger blazed again.

'Well,' she said, 'I want to know what my bed's doing out in the field.'

'Oh, is't oot? That's Madge, the randy. Fancy nae bringin' it in a' day. That's her sweirness – '

'Do you mean to tell me that Madge is sleeping in my bed?'

'Weel, fat's a' the temper for? Ye did it yersel! Why sudna she?'

'It's my bed,' cried Martha passionately. 'She can take her own bed outside.'

'Yon lumber o' a thing – '

'And she's had my sheets. Hasn't she? I know she has – '

'The sheets'll wash, surely to peace.'

'I'll never sleep in them again after her.'

'Weel, dinna, then. Ye wad think she was a soo.'

'She's worse,' cried Martha in a transport of rage; she had no idea that she hated Madge so much; and the girl herself coming in at the moment, she emptied out the cataracts of her wrath.

Madge gave her a contemptuous stare and began to spread a bit of oatcake with jam. She did not trouble herself to answer back. There was something horrible in her self-possession.

'Mind you about that infant, mother,' said Martha, swinging round on Emmeline. 'I won't touch it, I won't look at it. If you're ill it can starve, for all I care.' And she made off up the field. A fortnight of her six weeks' holiday was already gone and there seemed no nearer hope of reaching Liverpool; and she had realized, in a ferocity of anger against herself, that through the whole year that had elapsed since Luke's departure, she had been living for the moment of reunion. 'I need him,' she cried desperately to the night. 'I must have him. I'm only really alive when I'm with him. If I can't see him now I'll die. I'll never go through another year without him. Without seeing him. Being revitalized by him. It's by his life I live.' And in daylight, taking the ashes from the grate, 'Good God,' she thought, 'am I such a slave as that?' She wanted to kick out at the whole world to prove how free she was.

'Fatever ails her?' said Emmeline, as she swung herself away from the family conclave. 'I hinna seen sic a tantrum sin' she was a bairn.'

'She's richt eneuch aboot the loonie,' Geordie said. 'If you werena weel again it wad be a gey trauchle for her.'

'O weel,' said Emmeline, 'I wunna bring him.'

In spite of aching muscles after a long day's work among the hay, Geordie walked to Crannochie that night to tell his daughter that the child was not to come.

'O, I'm not caring,' said Martha peevishly.

What did anything matter if she was not to see Luke?

But the next time she came home Emmeline was seated by the fire with a bundle cradled in her arms.

Martha's rage had fallen. She was toneless, apathetic. Three weeks of her vacation had gone.

'So you brought him after all, mother,' was all she said.

Emmeline had been in secret a little afraid of what Martha might say. She blurted, apologetically,

'Ye sud 'a' seen the girl's face whan I said I cudna tak him, Matty. . . . Besides, I'm rale fond o' the craiturs. I've been used to them a' ma days an' it's rale lanesome-like wi' you and Madge an' yer father awa' a' day lang an' me used to a hooseful. I like a bairn aboot to get the clawin's o' the pots.'

Martha said nothing. Encouraged by the silence, Emmeline drew aside the shawl that wrapped the child.

'Did ye ever see sic an imitation?' she said, displaying the baby. 'Ye cud haud him i' the lee o' yer hand. But he hadna a chance – the lassie was that sair grippit in.'

Martha glanced incuriously at the child.

'Sax months an' mair,' said Emmeline. 'An' ye wadna think he was three.'

Six months and more, Martha was thinking. Six months and more till she would see Luke. Half her holiday was gone. Aunt Jean had visited Aunt Josephine the day before and Martha, desperate, had gulped that she was invited to Liverpool. Aunt Jean had not seemed to realize that Martha could not go to Liverpool unless someone else stayed at Crannochie. She had not made the slightest motion towards help. She had said, 'Oh. Fa's there?' 'I've friends,' Martha had said. In Aunt Jean's presence it had seemed an utterly senseless proceeding to have friends of her own outside the family cognisance. But perhaps later Aunt Jean would realize the position, and write.

At the end of another week Aunt Jean had not written. Martha wrote. She wrote to Liverpool and told them that she would never be able now to get away.

Three days later Peter Mennie, calling out cheerfully from the garden so that they might know he was coming, strode into the kitchen and struggled with something in the letter bag.

'Is't a parcel?' asked Miss Josephine, all agog with interest.

'There ye go!' he said triumphantly, dragging out from the bag first one and then another huge potato. 'A makin' o' ma new potatoes to you. Arena they thumpers?' And while Miss Josephine exclaimed upon their beauty, he held a letter out to Martha.

'O ay, they're a terrible crop the year,' he said, striding to the door again; and stepping out cried over his shoulder to Martha:

'Ye'll be awa' to Liverpool ane o' these days.'

The postmark of her letter was Liverpool: doubtless Peter had taken a shrewd glance at it before he gave it up. Clemmie had trained him well in such habits of observation: especially in regard to the letters that were delivered before he came to Drochety.

Obeying a sudden impulse, Martha blurted out her bitterness of spirit to Peter.

Twenty minutes later Drochety's Clem burst open the door. 'Foo's a' wi' ye the day?' she shouted to Miss Josephine, and, lugging Martha outside the door:

'Dinna you fret, lassie,' she said, 'awa' wi' ye an' hae yer holiday. I'll come in-by an' sleep aside Miss Josephine an' dae her bits o' things. There's nae need to hae onybody in.'

Martha looked at her coldly.

She resented Clemmie's interference in her affairs. She had almost instantly regretted her impulse of confession to Peter and was furious that he had gone straight and told Clem. She might have known! – He told Clem everything. Every day as eleven o'clock approached, she watched for his coming and had his cup of cocoa ready when he arrived; and while he sat in the big armchair in Drochety kitchen and drank it, Clemmie relieved him of the bundle of letters he was holding. . . . Hence her unique mastery of the affairs of the neighbourhood.

'But she doesn't need to know mine,' thought Martha angrily: and she was short with Clem; refusing her offer in brief politeness. It was only when Clemmie insisted – 'Ye're lucky fond, lattin' them a' ride ower ye that gait,' she said. 'Yer play'll be up or they tak ony notice o' ye. O, I ken yon Mrs. Corbett. It tak's her a' her time an' a lot mair to see that her cap's set straught. An' Mrs. – the little ane – the Leebie ane – she's aye that sair made wi' hersel, ye wadna think ony ither body had an ill ava.' She wad be a sicht waur gin onything ailed her. Jist you tak yer ways awa' an' never heed them. Miss Josephine'll dae grand wantin' ye' – it was only then that Martha had the grace to tell the truth.

'It's awfully good of you, Clem,' she said, with an effort upon herself, 'but it's too late now. My friends are going off to Spain this week.'

Dussie had written, in the very letter that Peter had handed to her that morning, 'We're frightfully sorry you can't come, but since you can't we're to take our holiday at once. It suits Luke better. We're going to Spain.'

A couple of hours later Clem came running back with a plateful of scones. Clem was the most generous of mortals, with Drochety's goods. Since Drochety's ailing wife had died, a twelve-month after Clem had taken over the rule of the place, she had slowly and very securely gathered the power into her own hands. All the countryside knew that Peter had *speired* her more than once, but Clemmie had always an off-putting answer. She had been putting him off for fourteen years now. And meanwhile with a lavish hand she distributed Drochety's belongings.

Martha ought to have been grateful for the scones. Clemmie's scones were a wonder and a treat. They melted in the mouth. But at sight of them Martha's anger flared. 'How dare she pity me?' she thought; and she pushed the plate savagely away.

She persuaded herself that she did not care. Her mind seemed to have gone dead, as her fingers went on winter mornings. Too tired to cope with her thoughts, she turned away from them and left them in confusion. School took up again. She cycled to the Slack and cycled home, absorbed herself as best she could in the bairns she taught and in Aunt Josephine, and told herself that her emotions were exhausted and nothing would stir them any more.

She had yet to reckon with Roy Rory Foubister.

FIFTEEN

Roy Rory Foubister

The coming of Roy Rory Foubister to Crannochie woke queer old memories in Martha's heart. She lay far into the night and heard, through the pelting rain, the creak of the boarding above her head as he turned himself on the improvised bed in the loft where he had insisted that he must be the one to sleep; and saw, in vivid projection, an ill-dressed awkward child of nine who stared at Aunt Josephine's hand of cards and heard her doom pronounced. Her halcyon days in Crannochie had ended because Aunt Josephine and her guest had talked of Rory Foubister: or so it had seemed to the child: and persistently as erroneous ideas will cling, she had gone on associating the name of Foubister with evil omen. The name had stuck: though to be sure that was not wonderful; seeing that Aunt Josephine had told her a hundred times since then of Rory and his stars. 'The world fair made for him, ye wad 'a' thocht . . . but he wasna a gweed guide o' himsel . . . "I've been a sorrowfu' loon to ma parents, Josephine" . . .' She had heard it all so often, and it had had the conventionality of the long familiar. It was only very recently, in the light of her own new comprehension, that Martha had divined a broken romance in Aunt Josephine's past. The serene old lady, with her boundless assurance in the rightness of life, had know heartache too. 'But it couldn't have been like this,' thought Martha, agonizing on her bed alone. 'She never went through a hell like this.'

She lay then that night and thought, in a hazy and jumbled fashion, of these old tribulations; and hearing the small unaccustomed noises above her head of the stranger within the gates, remembered feverishly the queer thump that her heart had given when he had said, shouting at her through the bluffert of wind and rain that made her hold back behind

the shelter of the door, 'Roy Foubister's my name . . . .
This is Miss Leggatt's, isn't it? She knew my father – '

'Oh yes,' she had said. 'You'd better come in, hadn't
you?'

'It would be wise,' he said. And he came in streaming.
'Gosh! but you keep some weather here. Oh, the rain's all
right. I could show you rain – ! But this cold gets into you.'

It was November, and bitter on these unprotected roads.
She knew it to her cost, cycling up to Slack of Mar in the
early mornings. That day was Saturday and she was at home:
and so Rory Foubister's son, seeking Miss Josephine, found
Martha.

Aunt Josephine was in a flicker of excitement. Rory
Foubister's laddie! Well, well! That she should have lived to
see this day! And hearing that Rory himself was dead, but
had bidden his son, on the visit home that had somehow
never happened in the old man's time, seek out Miss Leggatt
if she was still alive. 'Alive!' said Miss Leggatt quite indignantly. A funny-like thing to suppose she would not be alive.
'And Rory's deid,' she said. 'Peer laddie, he was young to
dee.'

'Young?' said the son Rory had left behind him. 'Oh no,
my father was never young. He was eighty when he died. He
was over fifty, you know, when I was born.'

And Miss Josephine, to whom Rory was an incarnation of
eternal youth, and who was seventy-eight herself, replied:

'It's been gey queer guideship he's gie'n himsel, I'm
thinkin', to be awa' sae seen. Weel, weel, we canna but feel
the way-ga'in' o' wer freens.'

She let Roy do the talking for a little then, and he talked
very pleasantly of his fruit-farm in the Transvaal. Breaking
across his evocation, for Martha's delight, of a thousand
golden oranges in their groves, Aunt Josephine came back
into the conversation with a hearty:

'Weel, weel, he's deid. Deid an' daein' fine an' ca'in' peats
to Paradise. He was gey sair keepit in aboot fan he was the
laddie, but I'se warren he's seen the ferlies sin' syne. I mind
now – ' Thereafter it was family history for what'll-you-
wager, thick and slab while Martha made the tea. And if Roy
told Miss Josephine twenty tales of what Rory had done

abroad, Miss Josephine told Roy twice twenty of what he had done before he ever went away from Mar. She even told him the famous tale of how Crookity Bella, the hotelkeeper's wife at Slack of Mar, cured Rory of the drink. 'A terrible drouthy chap he was, 'but he didna cairry it weel,' said Aunt Josephine sadly. 'Bella kent him weel an' ower weel. He cudna keep awa'.' But on a certain Saturday night she refused him his dram. 'She was as gweed at a joke as onybody, was Bella, but there was nae joke that nicht. She was in sober earnest.' Rory, it seemed, was neither sober nor earnest. 'He was in a bawlin' singin' kind o' humour, an' had mair in him already nor he kent hoo to cairry. Sae she jist said, "Na, na, Rory," though he craved her for't. An' there was him cravin' her wi' a bit sang an' a bit dird aboot the fleer, an' her gie'in Barny Tamson anither an' aye anither drappie. But nae his warst enemy cud 'a' said o' Barny that he cudna cairry his dram. He was aye drinkin' – a sodden lump – but niver drunk. Weel, fan Rory saw Bella handin' anither drap to Barny an' denyin't to himsel, he oot at the door in a flist, an' "Nae anither copper o' mine will she see," he says, "though she's in the peers-house." An' nae anither copper o' his did she see. He niver darkened her doors again, an' him was fou' ilka nicht afore. "He's ta'en the bung," Bella says. "Weel, weel, lat him tak it." He was grand company an' she thocht to tryst him back, but he cud set his mou' wi' the best o' them. She fair cured Rory o' the drink.'

'That's a great tale,' said Roy, very polite, though plainly a trifle perturbed at these evidences of a disreputable past in his immediate ancestry.

'It's nae only a tale, it's true,' answered Miss Josephine. And her eyes shone with delight. She was a girl again.

But when tea was over Roy altered the programme. He was very willing to entertain the old lady, but to entertain her by listening to her was out of his part. He liked to hear his own narration just as well as she to hear hers. There was indeed a superficial resemblance between the two. Both were pleased with themselves; both buoyant; but the old lady's imperturbable assurance in the rightness of everything was replaced in the youth by an imperturbable assurance in the rightness of himself: a distinction not immediately evident.

What was evident was that he was in spirits, hearty and pleasant. The world seemed made for Rory's son as well as for Rory; and already after a couple of hours in Crannochie he was stretching out his hand to claim a little portion of the world that he found there.

The little portion was Martha.

Martha was an uncommon listener. Tell her a tale, and you had her! And for so long she had had nothing fresh to listen to. Her life had been held in a schoolroom, a sickroom, and the room of her own dark passion. Absorbed in these, she had hardly realized how she was missing the intellectual excitements of college; and now here again came a talker who brought her light and air, space, widened horizons. Her face took fire: a subtle flattery that was not lost on the narrator. Very politely, but quite firmly, he claimed a monopoly in the conversation. Old wives' tales could rest. He seasoned his wares with a dash of cunning, watching their effect. The plain one was attractive when she listened! Such a wildfire light in her eyes. Those eyes again! But it was not for Roy to know that he was not the first to find that plain face quite redeemed by those shining eyes.

'But I've never been in London,' she had said when he expected her to understand his reference. 'I've been no-where. I've seen nothing.' And she had bent forward, dig-ging her elbows in her knees, eager as a landward child for the first visit to the sea. Such a young-girl face! Its candour at the moment quite belied her twenty-three and a half years. Delicious, he thought, to find a girl so innocent, so frankly inexperienced. Martha was not acting the *ingénue*. She felt herself very aptly the landward child and was not ashamed of her eagerness for what lay beyond her borders; and sinking her chin in her hands as she listened, she made a curious inarticulate noise of contentment.

'Whinnied,' he thought, and smiled at his metaphor. 'I'll have her nuzzling me next,' he promised himself. A riderless girl! All he need do was to mount. And he put his hand to his pocket for the knots of sugar, added the Anthropophagi to his traveller's tales.

The November night had closed in long before he was wearied of talking or she of hearing; and when at last he sprang to his feet, stretched himself splendidly and cried out on the lateness of the hour, the rain was still battering on the window.

'But in that storm,' said Martha. 'And it's pitch – you'll never find the way.'

'Na, na,' said Aunt Josephine, 'ye maun jist bide. Ye'd be like a drookit rat or ye got the length o' Beltie an' it dingin' on like that.'

'If you think you could put up with sleeping in the kitchen –' Martha ventured.

'Oh,' he laughed, 'I've slept in many a worse place than your kitchen.' He had already been there, carrying the tray for her and drying the dishes when she washed them up. But when he realized it was her own bed she was surrendering to him, nothing would serve him but that he and not she should sleep in the loft.

'But it isn't even a room,' she said. 'Just boards. We just store things there. It hasn't a stair. You have to shove a ladder up through the trap-door and climb.'

'Top berth,' he said genially. Apparently everything was to please him. They placed the ladder and helped each other up and down as they made the eyrie habitable; and Aunt Josephine sat alone in her room and beamed at the sound of their laughter.

So it came about that Martha lay and heard the boards creak above her; and saw, between sleep and waking, the world spin giddily round. 'Top berth,' she murmured; the house was a ship tossed on billows, and the rain was the lapping sea; and herself, a child, leaned over the deck-rail and saw, far below, a tiny Aunt Josephine playing a hand of cards with a boisterous black-a-visaged man whom she knew to be Rory Foubister. Roy was leaning beside her over the rail, watching too; and she knew that she had grown up again. 'It was the cake,' she thought mistily. 'No, the bottle. Alice in Wonderland. I shut up and stretched out again.' She fell asleep dreaming of flying-fishes that skim the surface of the sea like swallows; and the Karroo at evening, transfiguring the light.

She woke to a soft blue world. The rain was over. The hills were faint and clear. Roy called down to ask whether he might descend. 'Or shall I be in your way?'

'Come and look at Lochnagar,' she answered. And when he scrambled down from his eyrie and came to the garden gate, from which they could see the long panorama of the hills, she said, softly, as though her voice might smudge the frail shimmering beauty of the morning, 'Distance upon distance. Wouldn't you think it would never end?'

'Wait till you've seen the Veld,' he said. His loud cheerful voice seemed to roll echoing about in the empty morning. 'You won't talk about distances then. Or going down to Delagoa – the Low Veld. You look down and down and down and there's always more of it. You begin to think it must be the sea, and it isn't. It's always more earth.'

Martha's heart was battering in her throat. 'Wait till you've seen the Veld. Wait till you've seen – ' The words hammered themselves against her consciousness. She hardly heard the rest of his sentences. 'Wait till you've seen the Veld.'

She escaped to the house and made breakfast.

In the afternoon she walked with him to Beltie.

'You'll come back and see Aunt Josephine?' she said. 'It's been a treat for her to see you.'

'Yes,' he answered. 'I'll come back and see Aunt Josephine.'

He chose to come back and see Aunt Josephine the next Saturday. He came suitably munitioned for seeing Aunt Josephine, with a motor-cycle and a side-car; and before Martha very well understood it, she was bundled into the side-car and whirled along the road. They were through Slack of Mar before she had quite collected herself.

'That's where I teach,' she shouted up at him across the rush of air.

'Lord, is it, though!' he answered. 'It won't be long.'

'No,' she rejoined seriously. 'Was Aunt Josephine telling you? I'm being transferred at Christmas. To Peterkirk. It's much nearer.'

'You precious innocent!' he thought.

She was by no means so innocent as he imagined. Martha knew quite well that she was being wooed, and an uneasy excitement possessed her. She had never been wooed before.

Oh, there was Andy Macpherson, of course, who once in a way leered in her direction. But she knew how much that counted for! Andy's conquests were numerical. He wanted to add her to his row of scalps. But this was the authentic thing.

'Why shouldn't I know what it is like?' she thought: but she gave no sign of her awareness. Under his insinuating speeches she was as quiet, as unconcerned, as though he were asking for another cup of tea. Roy was completely in the dark. Finding her inexperienced on the levels where he could test her, he failed to realize that there were other modes of experience. It did not occur to him that she had any sort of past. He had no inkling of the still black depths through which she had gone down nor of the depths of light through which her thoughts had soared and hid.

They sped on past the Hill o' Fare, across the river at Potarch, over the Sheetin' Greens and down by the Brig o' Bogindreep. Martha let her spirit fly out on the air; the swift motion whipped her blood and paralysed her mind. Better, far better, never to think! If one could rush like this forever, too fast for contemplation, too merrily for desire, without a goal! She belonged neither to her past nor to her future. Before they rattled up the long brae to Crannochie again the hills were a uniform sombre grey, the trees and bushes a wash of shadow; inside the cottage it was already dark.

'O, I'm sorry,' she cried to Aunt Josephine, who was seated in her chair with one hand over the other. 'I didn't mean to be so long.'

As though what she had meant, or hadn't meant, had had any authority once she was caught in the machine. She had surrendered her will and knew it.

'Ay, ay, you're gey far ben, my lady,' answered Aunt Josephine, smiling at her.

Aunt Josephine smiled with the air of a woman who knows a thing or two. She smiled very frequently as the weeks and the motor-cycle ran on, and by sundry sly pokes and digs at Martha expressed her delight in what she felt to be happening. Martha suffered the digs. She offered neither repartee nor denial. Why should she? She was gliding on over a surface. She knew it was only a crust and at any moment might crack and precipitate her through its fissures; but its very insecurity exhilirated her, and plainly foreseeing a period to the excitements she was enjoying, she snatched them while she could. They galvanized her to a very fair imitation of life. She let her excitement appear, as he plied her with new experiences – rushing rides to all quarters of the country, theatres, dances – and the candour with which she showed it made her very young. Knowing women, Roy reflected, were the devil. She drew him on by her utter lack of calculation, and he made no doubt but that he rode her fancy as he intended very soon to ride herself.

Martha was under no real delusion as to his quality. She saw plainly that he was generous for his own ends.

'An' we aye get a fairin',' Aunt Josephine told Clemmie with proud assurance. 'He's that goodwillie. There's aye a pyockie or a boxie.'

Roy was astute enough to offer on most occasions the *fairin'* to Miss Leggatt. It was Martha who realized that his politeness was policy. She was coming to a surer understanding of men and women and in the abstract judged the situation fairly enough. Roy's was a cupboard love of life. Taking life, like Aunt Josephine, with zest, he could not take it, as she did, for itself; but always for what he might take from it. It was plain that he would exact of life his pound of flesh and see to it that he was not duped with carrion. Martha read it in his impatience at any interruption to his purposed enjoyments, his indifference to her concern over leaving Aunt Josephine alone: but her judgment remained in the abstract. She had not yet quite learned that the importance of things lies not in themselves but in their relations. Roy as an isolated phenomenon she had appraised, but she was still blind to the fact that Roy was not an isolated phenomenon. If it did not occur to him that she had a past, neither did it occur to her that both he and she had a future. She knew that he was wooing her and she knew that she would not be won: between these two sharp certainties the whole world lay in a confusion that her deadened intellect made no attempt to clarify. That he might count her a cheat, and be justified therein, was at present outwith her comprehension.

Meanwhile the motor-cycle ran back and fore. It enlivened the road. Motor-cycles, particularly reinforced by side-cars, were not so numerous as they have since become; and on the Crannochie road were not numerous at all. Not much doing on the Crannochie road! Folk did not congregate there; or if they did, they were the known folk, whose affairs were common property. They made no *steer* when they gathered for a *collieshangie* at a dyke corner. But add a motor-cycle and a side-car, duly inhabited by two! – Two in that case made a rabble, and the neighbourhood was agitated by the rabble.

The agitation, however, did not reach to Wester Cairns. The wood lay between, and Wester Cairns looked naturally towards Cairns and the city, while Crannochie looked towards Beltie and Peterkirk. Emmeline and Geordie heard nothing of their daughter's on-goings. She had reported Roy's first visit to Miss Leggatt – 'the son of an old friend – somebody Foubister, Rory Foubister,' she had said.

'Oh,' said Emmeline, 'I mind aboot him fine. He sud 'a' merriet yer aunt, if a' tales is true. O ay, if a' tales is true, that's nae a lee. She was terrible come-at, I mind ma faither sayin', fan he up an' laft her. But he was gey gweed at ga'in' on the ran-dan. Some ill for a dram, I doot. But a terrible fine chiel. Ma faither had a great gweed word on Rory.'

And Geordie, stumping up on a Sabbath to pay his respects to Miss Josephine – and see his lassie in the by-going – met cycle and cyclist and was introduced.

He duly related the meeting to Emmeline.

'Is he as young's a' that?' said Emmeline, with the judicial air of solicitude that must be allowed in the circumstances to the mother of a marriageable daughter. 'Wad he be aifter Matty, div ye think?'

'Na, I dinna nane think that,' Geordie answered. 'He had anither lassie i' the cairrage.'

The other lassie was a neighbour's niece, who had spent her Sunday afternoon in Crannochie. She had chanced to come in on an errand to Miss Leggatt on her way back to Beltie, and Roy with his ready affability had offered to run her in to town. Hence Geordie's misapprehension. Emmeline accepted his diagnosis of the situation and thought no more of Rory's loon. Had she known that the motor-cycle, with her own lassie in the *cairrage*, had not returned to Crannochie till the small hours of that very Sunday morning, her thoughts might have been of another colour.

Roy had taken Martha to her first dance.

He had taught her her steps in Aunt Josephine's room. The dancing lessons had delighted the old lady. She was not blither at the barn dances of her youth, the reels and *Strip-the-Willows* that Rory had shared; and when the night of the dance arrived, she watched Martha don the lustre frock with a brightening of the eye that would have done the heart good had there been a heart near enough to feel its influence. There was Martha's heart, to be sure, but it was not susceptible just then to such influences.

'Haven't you a warmer wrap than that?' Roy was asking.

'Just you wait, just you wait.' Aunt Josephine was rising from her chair and making for her high old wardrobe. 'Just you wait. You'll get my cloak.' She fumbled among garments; and Martha going to her aid they pulled out between them a long black cloak with a peaked hood falling down behind. The old lady wrapped Martha up in it, drawing the hood close round her face.

'Noo, ma dear,' she said. 'Ye're in an' lookin' oot.'

'Is it a proper sort of thing to go there with?' Martha was wondering, her eyes on Roy.

'Enchanting,' he was saying.

She was sure it was the wrong word, but would not let herself suspect a duplicity. Since he appeared to be satisfied, she said, laughing up into Aunt Josephine's face,

'My evening cloak! Imagine me possessing one.'

'And you *will* possess one,' Roy declared to himself.

Miss Josephine heard the retreating clamour of the motor. She sat smiling at the blaze of her fire, following their progress in thought; and it seemed to her that fifty years had fallen away and she was again the lassie whose heart Rory had made to *dirl*. She lived again her girl's romance, all save its dismal conclusion; and made no doubt but that Martha was dancing through a romance as sweet. There was endless wonder for her in the way things had come to pass.

Early in the year, on a stormy Saturday when Martha was busy close by her, she chanced to say aloud what she had often already said in secret:

'Weel, weel, an' to think I should have lived to see this day. I've been keepit alive for this.'

Martha caught the *Nunc dimittis* of the tone. But giving thanks for what? She glanced sharply aside at her aunt. Thanksgiving shone from her face; she was radiant with it; and her eyes rested on Martha with a joyful satisfaction. *When you have seen the Veld*. The words hammered in the girl's head. But she had not supposed that other folk had noticed whither she was drifting. She had short time, however, for speculation. At the same moment her ear caught the approaching throb of the motor-cycle and her eye the spectacle of a face flattened against the window and peering. She started violently, staring at the face.

'It's jist Stoddart Semple,' said Miss Josephine, following her agitated stare. 'The muckle sumph. He aye glowers in like that.'

'How horrible,' Martha said.

'Ye needna fash yersel,' said the old lady unperturbed. 'Ye needna be sae vexed.' She was vexed enough herself at times at the bad manners of the man. 'He's nae worth mindin'. He hasna the manners o' a soo. He's some ill-fashioned – wants to ken a'thing. But lat him in. It's kindly-like to come an' gie me a gamie.'

Martha opened the door to him and saw Roy dismounting by the gate. Stoddart had had no more time than to say, 'Foo are ye daein'?' thrusting his face forward into Miss Leggatt's as he spoke, when the young man strode in; and almost immediately afterwards the rain, which had been threatening all afternoon, fell battering.

'No ride for you in that, my lady,' grumbled Roy. And he went out to cover his machine.

On his return, 'Here's another visitor for you,' he cried, ushering in Clem. Clemmie had brought along some chicken and sauce, decorated with a wish-bone.

'I sees aul' Auntie takin' doon the road,' she said (referring to a neighbour for whom she had no great respect), 'an' turnin' in-by wi' a hen in her oxter. "Ay, ay,"

I says to masel, "if Auntie's gotten the length o'killin' a hen, it'll be a gey auld ancestor o' a hen that she's kill't." Ye had had some dividin' or ye got yon ane divided up, I'se warren ye.'

Aunt Josephine dimpled over into the most disarming of laughter.

'Weel, weel, ye're sayin' it,' she said. 'As auld's the Hills o' Birse – she wad neither rug nor rive.'

'Sae, "I'll jist tak them a bit," says I, "to lat them taste the taste o' a hen."'

She laid her offering on the table, and began explaining to Roy, behind Miss Leggatt's back, while the old lady praised both the gift and giver to Stoddart, 'She's penurious wi' her meat, but cud ye wonder?' *Penurious* Aunt Josephine was not. 'It's wersh, wersh,' was the utmost of her complaining, when food had neither sap nor savour in her mouth. But Clem continued to explain to Roy, in her hearty fashion: 'Her digester's a' tae nonsense. She gets scunnered at a'thing. Ye wadna wonder, noo, wad ye? Matty's nae great hand at the cookin' – her awa' a'day an' a' – ' and breaking off hastily, she eyed Roy and burst into laughter. 'Losh, laddie, I didna mean naething. The lassie's awa' a' day. Bit she'll come at it – she'll be a grand hand yet.' And she gave Roy a dig with her elbow and winked at him lavishly.

Roy winked back.

'She won't need to bother,' he said. 'She'll have a black boy to cook for her.'

'Losh be here!' said Clem. 'That's nae mowse.'

These savoury asides between Roy and Clemmie were meant for their own private entertainment; but they paid so little heed to the modulating of their voices that their words could be heard quite clearly by the other three persons in the room.

Martha's heart stood still. What! she thought. Were her affairs thus publicly arranged? In the innocence of her heart she had been supposing this adventure, this voyaging after the fruit of the Tree, as secret and self-contained as her adventure with Luke; inward. Seeing it thus bounced and bandied in plain daylight, focussed for her through the consciousness of others, she saw it as common and tawdry.

She had cheapened herself for her apple. Good God! she must disabuse them, and that mighty quick. But how? She was quite uncertain how to proceed.

And as it chanced she was already a little late. The four persons gathered round her were very comfortably persuaded that she and Roy were making a match of it. To Stoddart, who had not come that way for awhile, and had seen Roy only once before, the idea was new; but he seized on it with avidity. He knew a thing or two concerning Martha; and he relished a bit of gossip. Greedy once after the secrets of the universe, now he was greedy after the secrets of his neighbours; and he loved his own importance when he could divulge what others did not know. Not that he chose always to divulge such knowledge. He had a sappy mouthful, for example, concerning Martha, which he had kept to himself. In that there was malice. He had never forgiven the girl for her indifference to himself, which he termed her uppishness, and he had saved his bit of knowledge, to be used when it might harm her.

The time was now.

He growled at her across the room: 'Ye'll be ooten practice in kissin' sin' yon lang lad o' yours took to his heels.'

Martha stared.

Back over her memory rushed the night of her only kiss. Its width, its shining exaltation, caught her anew. O, to escape, leap upwards again to that sure serene communion in loveliness that had been theirs! – And crashing horribly through her moment of reconstructed paradise came the query: How did this man know? Confusion was in her brain. Conscious that there was silence round her, and that it must be broken, she blurted, 'I don't know what you mean,' and immediately cursed herself for her folly. She should have ignored his insinuation, changed the subject swiftly. She was too late now.

'I'se warren ye kent fine fat *he* meant,' Stoddart was saying. 'If it wasna a kiss ye was seekin', fat gar't ye tak a dander intil a wood in the middle o' the nicht?'

'To haud you speirin',' cried Clemmie in her loud rough voice. 'Fat sorra ither?' And she went off into a prolonged crackle of laughter. She had no idea to what Stoddart was referring, nor apart from her natural love of knowing everyone's affairs, was she greatly concerned to know: Clem was ready to defend her friends from any charge, and accuse her enemies of any enormity, that the human mind was likely to devise; truth being secondary. 'An' fat's in an antrin kiss?' she asked. 'A lassie needs to be kissed to get her mou' in.'

Clem had her mouth out. She had worked her way round to the back of Stoddart's chair and was carrying on her antics behind his back but in full view of Aunt Josephine, to the old lady's unconcealed delight. Aunt Josephine was as blithe as a bairn at a Punch and Judy show. Clem was the deftest of mummers. *Sonsy* though she was, big and ungainly of body, with huge hands and feet, she was incredibly nimble in her movements. Behind Stoddart's chair she was mocking Stoddart's clumsy gestures, shoving her mouth out till one could have tied twine round it, rolling her eyes so that the pupils seemed to meet.

'It's a fine thing a cuddle,' Stoddart was sneering, 'i' the deid o' nicht.'

'It's a fine thing an ingan,' mimicked Clemmie, 'to them 'at likes't.' And bringing her arm down with a thump on the back of the chair, 'Yauch!' she cried. 'I've yirded ma airm.'

She made a great to-do about the arm, showing off the bruise to each separate member of her audience, and talking volubly about the pain. Stoddart's drawling speech was lost in her clatter, as she had meant that it should be; and if he muttered something about lying in the arms of a man, Clemmie's arm was guarantee that no one knew distinctly what he said. And now Miss Josephine, deprived of her raree-show, was beginning to feel discomfort from the wintry air that penetrated by every chink.

'It's a wild-like nicht,' she said, drawing her shawl closer and huddling towards the fire.

The wind was rising, and the rain turning to sleet.

'O ay,' said Clemmie, 'I cud 'a' tell't ye last nicht there was a storm on the road. The moon was in the midden.'

'Yes,' Martha answered, 'she had a halo round her.'

She answered Clem's remark resolutely, holding her shoulders back and her head high. She had remembered a forgotten detail – how light had winked suddenly in the darkness of the wood and scared her: Stoddart with his pipe? Knowing the man's night-roving habits, she knew that her guess was probably correct. He had seen her hour of apocalypse. She had not time just then to realize into what foul-mouthed travesty he might turn it: all she cared for was to get his slouching evil self out of her presence; and thankful that she had noticed the *broch* around the moon the night before, she held resolute conversation with Clem anent the weather.

And luckily Aunt Josephine desired no game that afternoon. The chill was hard on her. She shivered. She was feeling sick. Her guests must go. Stoddart slouched away. He cast at Martha, 'Fan dirt begins to rise it gings an awfu' heicht,' and drew no flicker on her impassive face. She wished him good afternoon; with her chin lifted. Clem was off too, *dirdin'* on through the sleet; and Roy must follow.

Martha raised her eyes and looked at Roy. They inhabited different worlds. She had always known it, though she had chosen not to see. Now she saw; and desired nothing but to have him gone: forever if he liked. She felt she would not care. But it flashed upon her suddenly that he had not shared her experience of the afternoon; that for him there had been no re-focussing and he considered her still at his whistle. She revolted from the thought. How to disillusion him? If it could be done without overt explanation, by significant withdrawal of herself! Her mind played wildly round the problem as she followed him to the door.

'Come to the door with me,' he had said peremptorily. And she had obeyed, walking as in a dream.

'Look here,' said Roy in his loud bumptious voice, 'will you kindly tell me what that person meant?'

'Which person?' Martha asked. She was looking at him but hardly seeing him, absorbed as she was in her own thoughts.

Roy jerked his head backwards towards the road where the sloven figure of Stoddart Semple could still be seen through the sleet.

Martha came half-way out of her absorption and realized that Roy also had undergone that afternoon the necessity for re-focussing. With that half of her that was still absorbed she answered, using mechanically the same form of words as she had used to Stoddart:

'I don't know what you mean?'

'Well, you had better discover what I mean. Double quick time, too. Were you, or were you not, in a man's arms at midnight in the middle of a wood?'

Martha came three-quarters out of her absorption and realized that Roy was offended.

O, admirable! All unconsciously, Stoddart had played into her hand. She was very willing just then to offend Roy.

'It wasn't midnight,' she said. She said it without calculation. Her mind was running on that June hour that was neither dawn nor dark, and instinctively, as she might have corrected in school a child's inaccurate statement, she said, 'It was almost dawn.'

'Good Lord!' cried Roy. 'You're mighty calm about it, I will say. And you thought you would palm another man's property off on me, did you?'

Martha came all the way out, and realized that Roy was offensive.

The blood coursed hotly up her face. Brow, ears, neck, were scarlet. She was not prepared to purchase immunity from Roy's attentions at the price of insult. A double insult. He had insulted her relationship with Luke and he had insulted her relationship with himself.

She wanted to say so many things at once that she could say none of them explicitly. Words would not come to her either to justify herself, or clear Luke, or stigmatise the filthiness of Roy's misapprehension. She broke into half-a-dozen sentences and broke off from them all.

'O, damn *mistake*!' cried Roy, interrupting her roughly. 'I don't want to know what you mean by *mistake*. *You*'ve made a mistake, it seems to me. I can understand that kind of mistake –'

'Roy, on my honour –'

'Was that man telling the truth, or was he not?'

'O, go and ask him!' she cried.

'That's exactly what I mean to do.' He flung a glance back

over his shoulder to the wet road. With his motor-cycle he would quickly overtake Stoddart.

'I can't stand here and argue,' Martha cried. 'Aunt Josephine's needing me. She's sick.' She made to shut the door against him.

'Was that man telling the truth?' persisted Roy.

She gave him a queer look. He could not have read it even had he been at leisure to make the attempt.

'Of course it was the truth,' she said; and shut the door.

Aunt Josephine was miserably sick. For several hours Martha's attention was held.

'Weel, weel, ye canna mak a better o't,' Aunt Josephine would say in her moments of comparative ease. 'There's folk waur nor me.' And with a smile, 'Ye jist tak a howffie an' a kowkie an' ye're a' richt again.'

It was late in the evening, however, before she was right again; or near it; and when at last she dozed, Martha sat staring at the fire, without moving, for a long time.

The several hours respite had nerved her for the inevitable tussle with herself. She thought of her fingers, gone dead on a winter morning, and of how she had sometimes plunged them in water too hot for them, to restore the circulation. Her mind, like dead fingers, had been plunged in water too hot for it; and for a time she was conscious only of pain. Late at night a fierce clarity came in her thoughts. She saw all that had chanced in the last two years sort itself out in patterns. The patterns shifted; no two were quite alike, yet all were recognizably the same; and it seemed to her that she was looking in succession at the events of her life through the eyes of all the different actors in them.

She despised Roy very heartily now: and herself still more for her dealings with him. Under his veneer of politeness he was common: shoddy stuff. She writhed, remembering his accusation; and having forfeited her self-respect, was all the more desperate to justify herself in his eyes. To be counted wanton – ! But reason mocked. He would never understand. Though she talked with the tongues of men and of angels, he would never understand the quality of her love for Luke.

But if she could give him new perception? – If she bared her soul and forced him to look, surely he would see. 'I

could make a bigger man of him,' she thought. She thought
a good many foolish things in the course of that night; and
perhaps a few that were not foolish: but certainly her
resolution to give spiritual insight to Rory Foubister's son
had not quite so altruistic a motive as she tried to believe. 'I
have wronged him. I've wronged womanhood. I've made
light of love. I have to show him now what it's really like.'
But in her heart she knew that it was justification for herself
that she craved.

And what was love really like? Not so sheerly spiritual
after all. She recalled the frenzy of her June desire. That
was what had driven her to the wood. In intent she had been
just what Roy supposed. Shame sucked her under. So! –
There was a God after all, implacable, not to be gulled,
punishing even the fiercely smothered desires of the heart.
She had been no better than that Warrender creature she
had hated so tumultuously. Like her, she had fished for
Luke.

She sat up in bed then, remembering her agony over
Luke's part in the Warrender affair. Waste! She had
blamed him for giving to Lucy Warrender just what he had
given to herself – friendship of the mind. She laughed at the
recollection of her own torture. She should have been
tortured that he had liked her too: dishonour in that as
much as in the other – or as little. Half the agony in life
came from blinded motives, an insufficient understanding
of what one truly thought. Men's creeds are conditioned by
their desires. Martha's ideas of right and wrong were
altering under pressure of the discovery that she had
condemned Luke for giving to Miss Warrender what, given
to herself, had been the richest nurture of her spiritual life:
what, in fine, she had wanted. Of course he had laughed at
her remonstrance! She had been an intolerable fool – a prig
in the name of the Spirit.

And she began to consider how best to initiate Roy into
the spiritual mysteries. *All things are lawful.* Her mind
sagged. Roy would not believe that. Suddenly and fiercely
she saw that she did not believe it herself. Luke had had no
right to all he had had of her. He had wiled her on, taking
all she could give: as he had taken the contents of Lucy

Warrender's brain; raped her of what he wanted in her and
flung the rest aside; deflowered her, using colour and
contour and perfume for his delight, and refusing to see that
he had plucked the blossom whole to have them. Was it any
mitigation for him to say, *I did not want the flower*, since
the flower was taken? He had no right to her essence if he
did not want herself. Fiercely she resented his claim in her;
fiercely she repudiated her own proud passion of giving. She
hated Luke.

And what madness there was in the world's morality! She
had given herself utterly – all save the one thing that the
world condemns a woman for giving. Was she any whit less
guilty – if it were true that there was guilt in love – than the
woman who gave her flesh? – Or Luke less guilty in taking
her soul than though he had taken her body? – A consideration that left her only the more desperate to prove to Roy
the innocence of their kiss.

The woman who rose in the sombre and windless dawn of
Sunday felt many years older than the girl who heard Aunt
Josephine give thanks on Saturday that she had lived to see
that hour.

In the afternoon she walked to Cairns, through half-an-
inch of slush, to post the letter she had written. The writing
had taken her most of the morning.

On Tuesday evening Roy's answer was awaiting her.
When she walked in from school and saw the letter where
Aunt Josephine had propped it against the china shepherd-
boy on the mantel-piece, a deadly cold ran through her
body. Her stomach turned as at the smell of a nauseous
draught she had to swallow. She knew, even before she
touched the letter, that she had been a fool to suppose that
Roy would understand. She had profaned her Holy of
Holies; and without avail.

The letter confirmed her suspicion. Roy wrote in anger.
He had overtaken Stoddart on the Saturday, given him a lift
in the side car, and heard his story. In words Stoddart said
little beyond the truth; in insinuation much. Roy's anger
did the rest. The myth of Martha's young-girl innocence
was disposed of with finality. Well, his flesh was carrion,
but luckily he had not cut his pound. He was committed to

nothing; and if his riderless girl had been ridden before he found her, he could at least tell her so: and did it.

He had made a double discovery that Saturday regarding the girl. Another man's belongings, yes: but also with belongings of her own that he had not bargained for. She had a temper, had she! At his accusation she was like a wild thing trapped. He had not even guessed that she was wild until he saw her trapped. It came upon him with a nasty shock. He wanted neither experience nor much capacity for it in the woman of his choice.

The confession of her spiritual passion for Luke that had reached him on the Monday morning found him in no sweet mood, nor anxious in any way for the quickening of his own spiritual perceptions.

He replied at once.

Through every line of the letter Martha could hear again the distortion of his voice as he had said, 'And you thought you'd palm another man's property off on me, did you?'

Dismayed she thought, 'I've never had language like this used to me in my life before.' She burned to plead her integrity anew. This slur was not to be borne! But with a self-control that was heroic through the effort upon herself that it exacted, she put the letter in the fire and refrained from answering.

'You're some tired, my lady,' said Aunt Josephine, watching her as she leaned against the mantelpiece and saw the sheets of paper curl and glow and blacken in the flame. 'Ye're some sair ca'ed. It's a gey tyauve up yon brae in the deid o' winter.'

Martha came back with difficulty to the moment.

'Yes,' she said. 'And the roads are so soft. Slush. I'll need to get my boots off.'

'It's nae a terrible grand fire,' said Miss Josephine, glancing at the white charred remains of the letter. 'Gie't a kittlie up.'

Martha changed her shoes and made the supper; and Aunt Josephine told her about the *April eerand* that Rory had sent auld Willie Patterson (but he was young Willie then) and how Willie would tell the tale against himself. 'A terrible funny story,' she said. 'He leuch five minutes or ever he got begun to tell't. But mebbe he added a bittie on til't aince he did get begun.'

By Wednesday Roy's fury was over, and he was ready to consider (though not to confess) that he might have made a fool of himself by his hasty judgment. Oh, Martha was in the wrong, of course. Still, a peccadillo. He hated perturbation of the spirit and was very willing to be on cordial terms with all the world, provided the terms were his own. He decided to be magnanimous and forgive Martha. All would again be comfortable.

In the afternoon he went to meet her. It had not occurred to him that his letter of Monday morning had reached her only the evening before. She would have had time to forget the terms of his diatribe, which, in any case, he had not supposed to be offensive. He knew that she had been transferred to Peterkirk and on bad days took train from Beltie. He therefore went walking on the Crannochie road, and fell in with her.

Martha was still smarting under the language he had used. She had not yet had four-and-twenty hours in which to get accustomed to it. When he addressed her as though nothing had changed between them, she was astounded, then contemptuous. As he continued she began to understand that she was not believed, but was forgiven. She felt she could afford to laugh at his magnanimity; and laughed.

Here was something she had never imagined, that she should be pardoned for not having transgressed the common moral law; and should find it amusing.

'Life's funny,' she thought, and laughed still louder.

Roy's magnanimity did not stretch to being laughed at. He turned in the road and left her.

SIXTEEN

The Ironside Brand

Geordie had stopped half-way up the brae to put sharps in the horse's shoes. The wind had shifted due north, with a bite to it: a wind as hard as the ridges of slush in the road had suddenly become beneath its influence. The frost had set in keen and quick; the *neips*, when Geordie was piling them in the cart, were sodden wet; now they glistered, catching the saffron light.

The sharps in place, Geordie glanced up and saw a young man come smartly down the road. He had seen him only once before but recognized him as Miss Josephine's friend from Africa; and passed the time of day. Roy, who had just parted indignantly from Geordie's daughter, gave him back his greeting.

'Hiv ye hurtit yersel that ye're hirplin' that gait?' Geordie said, with the intimate concern of a man whom all things human must concern. Roy's walk, though rapid, was limping.

'Oh, it's nothing,' he answered in haste. 'A fall on the ice.' And as one pressed for time and thrusting trifles aside, added, 'I must be getting on.'

'Ay, ay, it'll be a terrible slipper,' Geordie answered. Roy had already gone on his way. 'Ca' awa' there then,' cried Geordie to the horse; and they climbed the hill to the crossroad.

At the corner, seated on a stone, was Andy Macpherson.

Andy took his pleasures queerly, if it was for his pleasure he was seated on an icy-coated stone, surveying an empty world. A black wind had wallopped the clouds to tatters and driven in a frost that sharpened with every breath. Footmarks, cart ruts, the imprint of tyres, all the casual traffic of days of slush, were caught and patterned in a relief of shining steel; and already, blown up from nowhere, shaken amazingly from branches and sifted from the empty sky, eddies of powder fluttered in the ruts and indentations, icy against the cheek in the sudden worrying winds. Not much comfort in Andy's choice of a seat for his half-holiday; nor much apparently to watch for but a hardening of the whole temper of the land. Yet there he sat, arms folded on his bulging chest, with the air of a man who took his ease and relished it.

'Ay, ay, Andy, ye're gey weel pleased wi' the weather, man,' said Geordie, stopping his horse and beating his arms to get up the heat.

'Grand,' said Andy.

He was in no need of getting the heat up and had a saner use for his arms than pummelling his own chest with them. Pummelling another man's chest was the better occupation; and Andy had just felled his man with all the pleasure in the world.

His man was Roy Foubister.

Andy had heard that Matty was taking Roy; and had no objection to the arrangement. He was not in love with her. Oh, once – yes: perhaps two or three times, by way of incident in a busy career. Andy knew a great deal about girls. He had made excellent use of his evenings though his earliest attempt at kissing had failed. His earliest attempt was made on Martha, years before, as they walked home up the brae after a Church *swarry*. If, as Aunt Josephine declared, he 'had a gey ill e'e aifter her' then, he quickly cast the eye elsewhere: but out of sheer *divilment*, if for no sweeter cause, he hankered still for a kiss from the only girl who had refused him.

'I'll get ye yet, ye b—!' he had sworn to himself on the April Sunday when Martha spurned him from her company. the b— was too sure a runner for him. She ran on mountains. She was unapproachable. And Andy did not put himself about to chase her. A bit of fun – that was all he wanted. A struggle and a shriek and the subsequent boasting. An American tourist of lips – that was Andy. Meeting, on his half-holiday, the lad who had had her kisses (and Andy would have found much difficulty in believing that

Roy had known Martha for nearly seven weeks and had not yet kissed her: even though three of the weeks he had spent on a Christmas visit elsewhere), meeting the lad, Andy snorted joyfully and dashed in to have his fun.

The distance between failure and achievement is infinite; but the distance between a kiss that touches flesh and a kiss that smacks the empty air may be only the fraction of an inch. One can argue away the fraction of an inch. Sheer *divilment*. Andy enjoyed himself immensely in assuring Roy that his girl had been kissed before; and bashed Roy's head less to remind him that he was not the only man in the world than just for the joy of bashing.

Roy picked himself up and thought bitterly: 'Is this the lout that she allowed to kiss her?' He was not likely to try forgiving Martha a second time.

Seated on his stone, Andy let Geordie into the joke. Geordie's wits, *i' the length o' the lang*, made this of it – that Matty was courted by the motorcyclist and that Andy had hoped to get her.

'Andy,' he said, 'ye're a gomeril.'

Andy grinned at the soft impeachment.

Fine he knew that he would never have got Martha; nor would he have known what to do with her if he had.

'She's nae for the likes o' you, Andy. She'll be upsides doon wi' her mither's fowk – her mither'll be grand suited. A richt bonny lassie her mither was,' said Geordie, his mind running baack on his own *coortin'*. 'Matty's a fine lass, ay is she, but she hisna the looks o' her mither, nor yet her speerits – singin' the best ye saw, an' aye ready for a crack, an' a pair o' cheeks,' said Geordie, 'like a weel-skilpit backside.'

Chuckling he hoisted himself on top of the glistering turnips and rode home in his triumphal car. He had got back to a comprehensible level with his daughter lost so long amid the lights and ardours of learning. Courting needed no brains. Geordie could understand that employment. But to think that he had not known! That was what came of biding at her aunt's. How he would tease her, once he got her home again!

In the course of the evening Geordie, ruminating by the

fire, let out a bellow of laughter. 'A fa' on the ice!' quoth he. 'A fa' on the ice!'

Admirable joke: but neither of his listeners seemed disposed to rejoice with him. Madge gave him a cold stare and left the room; and Emmeline continued to grumble over her own ailments.

'I've got ane o' that ill-natur'd kind o' backs,' she said. 'Girnin'.'

Madge gone, Geordie shared the joke; but Emmmeline refused to be impressed.

'Yon Andy Macpherson,' she scoffed. 'He's nae near neebor to the truth, yon ane. O ay, I'se warren ye'd gotten a legammachy fae him. "We'll believe ye the day ye're deid, Andy," I says till him.'

She paid heed nevertheless to the news; but being out-of-sorts was cantankerous; and angry that Geordie should have heard before her – and from that *sklype* of an Andy Macpherson too – treated the subject with contempt.

The following day, after supper, Geordie walked to Crannochie.

'Ye'll need to come hame, I'm thinkin', lassie,' he said to Martha. 'Yer mither's terrible bad. She's got a sair inside.' He enlarged on Emmeline's symptoms.

'You'll have to send Madge to sleep here then,' said Martha. 'I can't leave Aunt Josephine alone all night.'

'Weel,' Geordie hesitated. He had news to bring out and found it none too easy. 'She's awa',' he said at last.

'She's – But what – ?'

'Jist awa'. Tired o' us, like.'

He explained that Madge had left the house before daylight that morning, carrying her property in a bundle. They had found a note to say that she was going to lodge with the woman who kept her brother Jim.

'And did she know that mother was ill?' asked Martha bitterly. 'Was she ill last night?'

'O ay, she's been gey queer for a day or twa. She cudna bit 'a' kent.'

'And she goes away just when she might have been a little use. O, she would. *She* won't trouble herself for anyone.'

She was furious against Madge.

'Well, I can't leave Aunt Josephine alone,' she said. 'You'd better go along to Drochety and see if Clem'll sleep here for tonight.'

'Why disna she get an 'umman?' Geordie asked; and turning to Miss Leggatt he bellowed, 'Ye sud get an 'umman. Tak ye the gweed o' yer siller, Josephine. Ye wunna hae a poochie in yer last robe.'

'Oh, it's not only the money,' said Martha impatiently. 'Will you go to Clem?'

'Ay, ay, I wull that.'

Martha remembered the circumstances in which she had refused Clem's offer to sleep in the cottage. And now she was asking her!

'Well, did you see her?' she said.

'O ay, I got her,' Geordie answered. 'Dirdin' on wi' her mou' a' kail an' her heels a' sharn. She's a roch ane, yon.'

Martha assented absently and forgot to say that if Clemmie was rough she was also good.

'Don't wait for me,' she said to her father. 'I've some things to do. I'll follow.'

'Oh, I'll wait aboot,' Geordie said.

Martha wanted to be alone. She was in no mood for a conversation. But Geordie wanted the conversation. A walk in the dark with his daughter – here was an excellent chance for intimacies. He was impatient to begin that process of teasing from which he anticipated such enjoyment.

Martha, though her father failed to see it, looked little like a maid new-courted. She had gone down through another circle of her Inferno. She had lost her self-respect; and her suffering was bitten on her countenance.

When he had her out in the comfortable privacy of night, Geordie punched her very gently in the ribs with his elbow and whispered:

'It's to be hopit yer young man wunna be oot needin' ye the nicht.'

Martha drew aside from the elbow. Gentle or not, she wanted no liberties taken with her person.

'I don't know what you mean,' she said, using the same words as she had used to Stoddart and to Roy.

Geordie tried again.

'Yer lad'll be in a gey takin' fan he gets ye awa'.'

'I don't know what you mean,' Martha repeated. 'I haven't a lad, or a young man either.'

There was such cold fury in her tone that Geordie held his tongue.

Emmeline was less reticent with regard both to Madge and to Martha's courting.

In the intervals of her own pangs and groans she made diligent enquiry into the story of the courtship.

Martha took refuge in an exaggerated gaiety and cried: 'You don't mean to say you've been hearing *that*? Oh, it's just a joke. An idea of Aunt Josephine's. She hoped to marry his father, you know, and she seems to think it'll make all square now if he marries me. That's all that's in it.'

She said it laughing. Her mother was not in her counsels and she had no intention that she should be. She knew that she was less than just to Aunt Josephine, but she had to find cover somewhere.

'Weel,' said Emmeline, 'an' why sudna he? Ye're nae sae weel to be seen as lots, I'm bound to say that, but I'se warren ye cud get him if ye wanted to.'

'I've no doubt I could, but you see I don't want to. He's not my kind.'

'Oh, he's nae your kind, is he?'

'No,' said Martha, still laughing. 'He's a dandy. Fond of his pleasures. He's much more Madge's style than mine.'

It was the bitterest thing she could find to say.

'Oh, Madge,' said Emmeline. Her tone was grim.

'What's she away for?' Martha said.

'Fa wad ken? A tantrum. An' mebbe mair. She's been ettlin' aifter a shift this whilie back. "I'll be a lodger," she says. "Ye can be a lodger here," I says, "an' pey yer wey as weel here as ony road." "I'm nae treated like a lodger," she says. Feart to fyle her han's, that's fat she was. But I didna think she wad up an' awa' like that. I'm thinkin' there's mair in't nor a tantrum. She hasna been behavin' hersel. I've jaloosed it this gey while. Bit jaloosin's nae provin'. She's been ower mony for me ilka road I've tried her. She's close. She peys nae mair heed to ye nor the win' blawin' by ye. Bit she'll fin' oot or she's muckle aulder that there's some things gey ill to hide.'

'What?' Martha asked. She asked in all innocence, not having understood her mother's hints.

'A bairn wunna hide,' said Emmeline tartly, 'an' that's fat she'll see or lang, or I'll bile ma heid an' shak' the banes.'

Martha was staring at her mother in consternation.

'A bairn,' she stammered. How could Madge have a bairn? 'She's only a bairn herself.'

'A gey bit bairn. She's seventeen. If she's sense eneuch to catch a lad she's sense eneuch to haud him aff. That's you an' yer beds in a girse park.'

Martha swung away in disgust. What travesty of her tranquil nights! Her anger against Madge had turned to a furious cold contempt. If her mother were right, she was thankful at least that the girl had gone away. It would have been horrible, having the child born there. She had had enough of illegitimate bairns. She hated them. Madge herself was one, and Jim, and all that long succession of children who had trooped through her life. Dussie was one, she remembered with a queer quick stab, and so was that youngster who lay in the corner of the kitchen and sucked his finger with a loud smacking relish: the youngster at whose arrival she had been so wrathful, whom she had proclaimed so passionately she would never tend. Well, she would have to tend him now, she supposed. Did one ever order one's life as one desired?

'He's ill-trickit,' said Emmeline, following Martha's glance. 'Tak his finger ooten his mou'. He'll hae it sookit ooten comprehension.'

Martha pulled the finger from the child's mouth and thrust it, a little roughly, under the coverlet.

As soon as she turned away the baby, pulling the blanket up with one hand to screen his action, began sucking as vigorously as before.

'Ye rascal 'at ye are!' cried Emmeline, clapping her hands loudly from the bed.

A glint from two black eyes. A roguish grin upon the baby's face. The coverlet pulled higher.

'He's a droll craiturie,' cried Emmeline. 'Wad ye think they'd hae sae muckle sense?'

Martha did not want to think about them at all and made no answer.

It took short time to prove Emmeline's suspicion true. The very next day, on her way from Beltie to Aunt Josephine's, Martha fell in with a Crannochie woman going home from her marketing. The woman gave her the news with a relish. Madge, carrying her bundle in the half-light, had slipped on the ice and fallen headlong. 'She got a gey cloor,' the woman said. She had scrambled to her feet again and gone to the house of the woman who kept her brother Jim. That night her child was born, too soon. 'An ablach, they say.' The woman's avidity over detail disgusted Martha. The whole business disgusted her. Her own passion gave her no measure by which she might weigh Madge. The brae to Crannochie was undesirably long; and her companion insisted on coming in to see Miss Leggatt: she wanted a more appreciative audience for her tale.

She got it. Clem had looked in; and both she and Miss Josephine had long ears and ready tongues.

'The wratch o' a man, he deserves to be shot,' said Miss Josephine.

'Shot!' cried Clem indignantly. 'The dirty deevil, sheetin's ower gweed for him. Roas'n alive, that's mair like the thing. Shut tae the door, Matty. Ye wad think ye was born in a cairt-shed faur there wasna a door.'

Martha had left the door open on purpose, as a hint to the visitor to be gone.

She left at last, saying to Martha, 'Yer mither kens, Matty. Francie Hepburn fell in wi' Geordie on the cairt-road, an' some o' the neebors'll likely hae gi'en her a look-in as weel.'

'Oh yes,' thought Martha bitterly. 'They'll all tell us.'

Having attended to Aunt Josephine's wants, she went home.

Geordie and Emmeline were talking together, but ceased as she entered.

'That's a gey begeck we've gotten,' said Geordie, breaking the silence. He spoke heavily, a sorry and bewildered man.

'Ach!' cried Emmeline impatiently, 'you had aye a saft side to Madge. Onybody wi' their twa een in their heid cud a' seen the road she was like to tak. Wi' her palaverin' an' her pooderin' an' her this an' her that. She had a' her orders, had Madge. An' a stink o' scent 'at wad knock ye doon. Foozlin' her face an' bamboozlin' her face wi' her pastes an' her pooders. Eneuch to pit faces ooten fashion. I wadna be seen ga'in' the length o' masel wi' a face like yon. I wadna ging to the midden sic a sicht.'

'Weel, weel,' said Geordie, 'face or nae face, the bairn's here. Ye wad mebbe need to gie a lookie in, Matty, an' see 'at she's weel dane by.'

'She'll be weel eneuch dane by,' said Emmeline. 'It's nae nane o' our business, her marchin' aff like that an' a'.'

'It wad be bit kindly like.'

Martha was busying herself with the baby in a corner, so that she would not have to answer her father. Visit Madge! How could she do it? Her mind revolted from the very thought.

Geordie opened his lips twice again during the evening. The first time he said,

'Fa' wad a' thocht it? A grand sonsy lass she was – great stumperts o' legs she had on her.'

And the second time:

'The frost's loupit. Terrible coorse roads we'll hae the morn.'

He said no more of visiting Madge.

Martha knew she ought to go. She felt that they were responsible for Madge, even though she had left them; and had they had no news of her she would have gone: but they heard that she was well and well looked after; and Martha's hands were very full. On Saturday, through the filthy roads that the thaw had brought, she went back to Crannochie and found Aunt Josephine worse. Between her two invalids and her long school day, she had little time for visiting. Emmeline luckily had improved: Martha did not require to sleep at home; but invalids have privileges and Emmeline exercised hers – she did not waste her strength on housework.

On the following Saturday, early in the afternoon, Martha was walking down from Crannochie to Wester Cairns. She had taken, not the road through the wood, but an opener path that skirted the fields and ran past the Macphersons' cottage. By some rough stone steps this path crossed a low dyke into the field beyond; and Peter Macpherson, Andy's brother, with a couple of other young fellows, was idling beside the dyke. They were talking and snichering together as Martha approached, and, obstructing her path, made no offer to move. 'Are they talking about me?' she wondered; and edged her way behind on to the steps. One of the youths was whistling, and hardly had Martha passed when the other two took up the tune and gave it words. The words came clearly down the wind to Martha.

'Tak the floonces fae yer goon,
Mak a frockie tae yer loon,
For ye're like to need it soon,
Bonny lassie, O!'

The scarlet rushed to her face as she walked on. Though their snicher might have been for her, their song at least was not pursuing her; but it set her thinking of Madge. 'I'll go tonight,' she thought.

Mrs. Davie was the name of the woman to whom Madge had gone. Martha had only a vague idea of where she lived, and was obliged to ask. The passer-by to whom she applied was a stranger to her, but answered her query with, 'O ay, Miss Ironside, it's the fourth door, roon' the corner there.' Martha thought, 'You know me, and you know why I've come.' She held her head high and knocked.

'She's nae here,' said the woman.

'Not – ? Oh, I thought . . . Where is she, then?'

'Weel – ' Mrs. Davie hesitated. 'But come in-by,' she said, holding the door wide.

Martha went in.

The kitchen was light and hot. The gridle was on the fire and a good smell rose from it and filled the room.

'I was just makin' a crumpet,' said Mrs. Davie. She hurried across to the fire, seized her knife, slid it beneath the nearest crumpet and lithely slapped the smoking delicacy over.

'Sit doon,' she cried over her shoulder to Martha. 'I canna lat them burn.'

Martha sat and waited. When the batch of crumpets was turned, Mrs. Davie began her story, but interrupted herself almost immediately to lift the first of the batch and offer it to Martha.

'Het aff'n the girdle, Miss Ironside. Jist you snap it up.'

She laid it on a towel and pushed it towards the girl, who thought, 'I suppose I must,' and lifted it. It broke in her hand, a tiny portion remaining in her fingers while the larger part fell back on to the towel.

'They're that free,' said Mrs. Davie. '"Ye're a grand hand at the crumpets, Lizzie," ma man aye tells me.'

'But Madge?' Martha was thinking impatiently. She said nothing and waited.

Mrs. Davie put a second batch on to the girdle and resumed her tale.

Madge had walked away that very morning, bairn and all, just as she had walked away from the Ironsides'. She had been seen at the railway station and had told someone that she was joining her sweetheart.

'She had siller,' said Mrs. Davie, 'fatever wey she cam by it. She peyed me, an' she was buyin' a ticket as fine's ye like.'

'But with an eight-days' old baby,' Martha said. She was appalled. 'I should have come sooner,' her brain was saying, 'I should have come sooner.' The words ran like a refrain through and through her head; and aloud she added, 'Do you suppose – was she really going to him? I mean, was he expecting her?'

'Fa wad ken? She had nae letter a' the time she was within my doors, nor posted nane. I wadna say but that she's aff aifter him a' on her ain. They men's a scurvy set.' Mrs. Davie greased her girdle for another batch of crumpets and said, raising her voice above the sizzling of the hot fat, 'But ye ken that ower weel yersel, Miss Ironside.'

The thought glanced in Martha's brain that this woman also had heard of Roy; but she was too sincerely concerned over Madge to let it trouble her. She remembered her mother's saying some time before that Madge's fine lad had gone back to Glasgow whence he came. Had Madge gone seeking him in Glasgow? And with no letter sent or received. He could not even have known about the child. Martha felt herself groping in a dark oppresive place.

'Perhaps she'll come back here,' she ventured.

'O ay, she may.'

'Or – do you think she'd write to Jim? – if she – gets to Glasgow, I mean. If she does, if she writes, or comes back, do you think – could you – would you let us know?' Martha's words came out in spurts. She wanted air. She was oppressed by the ugliness of life. 'If you could send a message,' she said. 'You see, I'm so busy, I haven't much time.'

'O ay,' said Mrs. Davie genially. 'I'se warren ye've lots to dae. Yer ain loonie'll be wearin' up. Gettin' on for a year auld, is he?'

'Who?' said Martha. – 'Oh, you mean the child my mother keeps.' And she wished that outsiders would leave their family affairs alone.

'Weel, he's yours, isna he?' Mrs. Davie asked it cheerily.

'Mine?' said Martha.

She was astonished.

'Is't nae true then?' Mrs. Davie asked.

'True!' Martha began to laugh. 'I never had a child in my life,' she cried; and instantly thought, 'Of all the ridiculous things to have said!'

She stopped laughing.

Her astonishment was turning to dismay.

'An' sae it's nae your bairn ava'?' said Mrs. Davie. 'Weel, weel, fat'll fowk nae say? They've got a haud o' some story aboot a lad ye used to tryst wi' up in the woodie. "She bides oot a' nicht," Leebie Longmore says to me. "A bonny-like cairry-on." An' it's nae your bairn?' – And observing that Martha had left her crumpet lying with the little portion broken from its side, she added, pushing the towel towards her:

'But tak it up. Ye'll easy manage it. A crumpet's an idle eat. A knap-at-the-win'.'

She would have been just as hospitable had Martha owned to the child.

Martha's dismay had turned to sickness. She remembered the snicher and the ribald song of Peter Macpherson and his companions. And the woman who had called her by her name when she asked the way that evening. Filthy place the world was! She pulled herself together and said:

'You'll let me know if there's any news,' and rose to go.

'Ay, ay, I'll fairly lat ye ken,' said Mrs. Davie; and added, 'But dinna be sae upset at an idle word. I says to Leebie, "I dinna ken Miss Ironside," I says, "to speak to, like, but a nicer quaeter lassie ye wadna wish to meet. Ye've ta'en the story up wrang," I says.'

Martha walked out without reply.

She had to pass through the village, in front of the lighted shops. The women were doing their Saturday shopping. They stood in *bourrachs* about the doorways. She felt the curious eyes, guessed the purport of the whispering. She supposed herself to be in every mouth and her heart sickened within her; but she recollected the motto of Marischal College, that Luke had quoted: 'Quhat say they? Lat them say.' Pride came to her aid. She walked truculently past the women; reported at home what she had heard concerning Madge, shut her lips upon what she had heard concerning herself, and returned to Crannochie.

The weather had cleared. On the Sunday, Emmeline walked to the field end and held some lively discourse with Bell Macpherson, mother of Andy and Peter. She had just returned from her expedition when Martha came home.

She opened fire at once.

Martha perceived that her mother had heard the scandal. She hardened herself to hear what would come. Emmeline's indignation, however, was all for the scandal-mongers: she had championed her daughter with gusto and let her daughter know it.

'"It's a sair peety," says she,' – Emmeline reported at length the conversation between herself and Bell – '"that Matty didna get him aifter a'." "Fa didna Matty get?" I speirs. "Weel, weel, that's fat ye've nae need to speir, I'se warren," says she. "A'body kens that." "Dear me," I says, "ye're farrer ben nor me, than, the lot o' ye." "Nyod, noo, Mistress Ironside," she says, "ye needna be sae blate aboot it. A'body kens that Matty near got the laddie." – "Fatna laddie are ye meanin'?" – "The laddie Foubister," she says. "Fa' else? Him an' Matty was terrible chief awhile. But he up an' awa' fan he heard the wey she's misconducted hersel. An' wad ye wonder?" "Misconducted hersel?" I says, rale

gypit-like. "O ay, she didna behave hersel richt." "Behave?"
I says. An' than she up an' gied me i' the face wi' the bairn.
"Deil tak ye," I said, "an' may the Lord forgie ye the evil o'
yer blabbin' tongue! Fat'n a wey cud it be Matty's bairn?
Matty was aye at her school." "O," she says, "ye're sayin't.
But we werena to ken. Her sae muckle awa' fae hame an' a'."
"Nursin' her aunt," I says. "Ay, ay," she says, "the auld
body was beddit up at a likely time, wasna she? Matty was
grand suited to be awa' fae hame an' nae tales tell't. Nine
month fae midsummer," says she sleekit-like. "Midsummer?" I says.'

'Oh!' cried Martha, 'I've heard it all already. You needn't
tell me it again.'

She wanted to brush her mother past the one incident of
the story that was not conjecture.

Emmeline was for leaving nothing out.

'Oh, ye've heard it?' she said. "'An' fat had midsummer to
do wi't," I says. "I'll be at the reet an' the rise o't," I says.'

Martha rose abruptly and began tidying away the papers
and dusters and dirty garments that littered the room. She
kept her back to her mother. Emmeline fought her battle
o'er again, too absorbed in her indignation to pay much heed
to her daughter. She tongued Bell Macpherson a second
time.

"'It's a sair haud-doon for a girl," she says. "A haud-
doon," I says. "It's you that wad need to be hauden doon," I
says. "It's yer lugs nailed to the gallows that you wad need.
Ye wad gar a deid dog tak the kink-hoast. But I'll pit the
Deil's trot on the lot o' ye if I hear ye at yer lees again. I'll ram
yer lees doon the ugly throats o' ye." "Lees," she says.
"Weel, weel, there's some lees gey like the truth." "It's
mebbe the truth," I says, "but it's gey like a lee. Yer wits is
hairy-moulded if ye suppose I cudna see a thing like that
aboot ma ain lassie an' her back an' fore ilka week an' whiles
twa-three times a week a' the time. An' her as flat's a
bannock for a' to see. Sic a say-awa'," I says, "aboot naething. They're an ill-thochted crew, the fowk hereaboots – the
best at ransackin' ither fowk's affairs 'at ever I heard tell o'.
As happy's a blake amon' traicle fan they're cairdin' honest
fowk."'

Martha remained silent.

Emmeline, surveying the landscape that had been presented to her view, came back in course of time to Stoddart Semple's tale. Cross-examined, Martha admitted its basis of truth.

'An' fa micht you be meetin' in the deid o' nicht?' demanded Emmeline. Her indignation swirled to a new channel.

Martha remained silent.

'I'll be bound it was yon lang-leggit doctor chap, Dussie's man. It's fat I've aye said, ye canna trust a skin. A jolly fat chap, noo – a' on the surface – a body kens faur they are wi' them. But wi' a thin man ye never ken faur ye are.'

Martha did not know where she was with Luke. She did not know where she was with herself; and she longed to be again what she had been – possessed only of herself, unbroken. She saw that Luke had broken her integrity, and by not loving her had put a larger wholeness beyond her reach. 'He had no right,' she cried savagely to herself. Emmeline's accusation against Luke stirred all the smouldering resentment in her own mind: she did not trouble to refute the charge on his behalf.

'But that Dussie,' Emmeline continued, 'she was aye a besom. She was aye amon' the loons.'

Martha knew the singleness of Dussie's eye, but neither did she defend Dussie.

She heard her mother out, sullen, murky-eyed, saying nothing. Her flame had gone to smoke.

'Oh, ye're in an' the door steekit, are ye?' said Emmeline. Having failed to draw any answer she was left to her own conjecture over her daughter's affairs; which did not prevent her from continuing her indignant denunciation of the scandal-mongers.

'Fat ither wad ye expeck fae a hoose like yon?' Bell Macpherson was reported to have said. 'Steerin' wi' weans an' nae ane amon' them 'at's honest come by. That's yer Ironsides for ye!'

Even her Aunt Sally's story was revived to swell the evidence against Martha. To be an Ironside was apparently sufficient to brand her.

'Gin onybody said the likes o' that to me,' declared
Geordie, ruminating over his wife's report upon the current
gossip, 'I'd be aweirs o' takin' the graip to them.'

No one however said it to him; and there was no assault.

'Ach!' said Emmeline. 'If ye're to start believin' that lot,
ye micht as weel eat a' ye see.'

'Bit fa wad a' startit it?' said Geordie.

'Deil kens,' his wife replied. 'An' the Deil has nae
business to ken.'

Her Aunt Sally came often to Martha's mind in the weeks
that followed. Madge had not been heard of. She stayed, a
dull rankling spot of offence, in Martha's consciousnesss.
She remembered that her aunt had been working among
outcasts in Glasgow. If Madge were there, an outcast too – .
Martha did not allow herself to formulate definite thoughts
on the subject, shelving as far as she could her sense of
responsibility towards Madge; but as the weeks passed her
secret uneasiness grew.

She was not alone in harbouring a secret uneasiness. Aunt
Josephine too was troubled. Roy had given over his visits;
and Martha was unapproachable on the theme. Aunt Josephine teased, and hinted, and openly marvelled, and finally
held her tongue; and Martha held hers. If Clemmie spoke,
or Stoddart Semple, Aunt Josephine had more wit than to
believe their idle havers.

On an evening in February Martha was walking home.
She was late and the weather was heavy. Dark fell from a
brown sky and had not far to fall. As she came nearer she
saw that the light was shed from the lamps of a motorcycle
and that the cyclist was bending over his machine. She
knew him at once for Roy and stopped. He visited, she was
aware, at a house in the vicinity of Slack; doubtless it was
there he had been. Her instinct was to turn before she came
within the radius of the light, go back and through the
wood: but despising her own dread of meeting him, she
went on; and glancing up he saw her.

He was embarrassed but polite. Martha was amused to
see how polite: but there was not the semblance of intimacy
between them.

'I'm judged and found wanting,' she thought amusedly.

'I'm just a common slut, I suppose – not even worth his anger. We're like chance acquaintances. We're polite to each other.' But in spite of her amusement she was piqued by his indifference and remembered hotly the letter she had sent him. The futility of her confession mocked her; but putting restraint upon herself she said aloud, 'Will you come and see Aunt Josephine before you go away? She's wondering that you haven't come' – and could not resist adding, 'You can come on a school-day, you know, when I'm not there.'

He ignored the remark; and came the next Saturday. 'Just to spite me, I suppose,' said Martha to herself.

He came, and Aunt Josephine was jubilant; but learning that he had come to say farewell, and was about to sail again for Africa, looked from her niece to her visitor and back to her niece with a puzzled concern.

Neither niece nor visitor took heed. They continued to be polite to each other. Roy was very entertaining and kept Miss Josephine delighted by his talk. Martha sat silent and wished she had never had occasion to look beneath his pleasant veneer. They parted at the door, still politely.

'We're done with each other,' she thought. 'We're strangers. He's come to see his father's old friend and I'm just her grand-niece.'

Roy too was thinking, 'We're done with each other.' They parted with relief and supposed they would not meet again. In this they were wrong. He was back in Europe not so very long afterwards, fighting in France; and on his first leave came straight to Martha. Aunt Josephine was dead by then and Martha still teaching in Peterkirk. He wanted to marry her then and there, but she gave him a steady and smiling refusal.

She was smiling now as she shut the door upon Roy and returned to face Aunt Josephine, but the smile was not steady.

'Well, that's our visitor gone,' she said as lightly as she could.

'Ay, ay,' said the old lady, 'but I'se warren he'll be back or he gings awa'.'

'Oh no! Why should he? He has said goodbye.'

Aunt Josephine remained puzzled and in distress.

Geordie also had his secret anxiety. He was bothered about Matty's lad. He knew well enough what folk had said about his daughter; he knew well enough that it was false: but plainly it had driven away the young man who was courting her; and plainly she was not happy. Geordie sought a remedy in vain. He had no great opinion of a youth who allowed the clack of tongues to prejudice him against his sweetheart. Still, the lass was fretting. Geordie was sorely exercised. He tried more than once to open the subject with the girl, but the most delicate insinuation was enough to waken the nastiest furies that inhabited Martha's mind. She snubbed him brutally.

One evening in March he met his daughter at the corner of the field. It was gloaming, and in the dusk he gathered courage to say, as they crossed the field together:

'I'm main stupid, lassie, I ken that fine. I canna un'erstan' a lot o' things, but I can see fine that ye're frettin'. I thocht it was aboot yon lad o' yours, but it seems I was wrang. Weel, we'll nae say nae mair aboot that. But I canna bide to see ye fret, Matty ma lass, an' nae dae naething to pleasure ye. I'm nae askin' fat ails ye, I'm nae bit askin' to be lat help ye gin I can.'

To his surprise, and perhaps to her own, Martha answered him.

'Father, do you know anything about your sister Sally? Where she is, I mean? Is she still in Glasgow?'

'Sally?' said Geordie, stopping on the path. He required time to adjust himself to this sudden change of theme.

Martha began to explain why she wanted news of Sally. If she was fretting, she said, it was over Madge.

'Ay, ay.' Geordie approved. His knowledge of Sally's whereabouts, however, was vague. She had come home but the once. She never wrote. She might be still working for the Salvation Army in Glasgow; or she might not.

'I could find out,' said Martha.

'O ay, ye cud try a letterie.'

Martha was silent. She had other intentions. She wanted to go herself to Glasgow and seek her aunt. By letter she could not effectively secure her co-operation in what must seem at best a hopeless search for Madge. Common-sense suggested that it would be wise to discover first, if she could by letter, whether her aunt was still in Glasgow; but Martha thrust the suggestion under. She wanted the hardest way.

She was suffering from a festered conscience: not that she held herself responsible in any way for Madge's fault or flight; but she had dishonoured her own nature in her dealings with Roy; and obscurely she felt that there was evil in the disruption her self had undergone in her dealings with Luke. He had neither claimed her nor let her alone. She had been tampered with; defaced; and she felt it in her like the degradation of disease. She tried but could not reason it out with herself in how far the breaking of her integrity had involved the breaking of the laws that governed her being. All she could be sure of was that she felt unclean; and she hankered after purgation – some expiation, arduous, impossible, that would restore her soul. To pursue a half-apocryphal Aunt Sally on behalf of a Madge she had hated offered at least the consolation of activity. Emmeline demurred but yielded. Easter was approaching; and when her holiday began Martha set out alone one morning in pursuit of her wild geese.

As far as her aunt was concerned the chase was easy. Sally was still in the Salvation Army and still in Glasgow. A brusque woman, harsh-featured, big-boned, she had no need of her kin and did not think of writing; but there was honesty in her ugly face and Martha felt at home. She blurted out her tale, but Sally interrupting dragged her niece to the light and scrutinized her closely.

'Thank the Lord He's made you with a big mouth, Matty,' she said; and forthwith prepared the supper. Not till the meal was over did she say, 'Now let's hear your story all over again.'

'I suppose it's impossible that you'd ever come across her,' Martha said when she had told Madge's story.

'Just about it,' said Sally cheerfully. 'Still, there's no knowing. There's queerer things happen than we've the right to expect.' And she began to tell her niece the queer things that happen.

'I've had a venturesome life,' said Sally.

A footnote to her life might have run: For *venturesome* read *betrayed, persecuted, forsaken, hampered and undaunted*: but the general public finds footnotes uncomfortable reading and leaves them alone.

'She's come through the hards, yer Aunt Sally,' Geordie had said to Martha. Sally had thriven on the hards. She had her brother's hearty capacity for life – a big eater and a big endurer, with power to exist spiritually for a long season on one joke or one idea.

Martha returned home the following evening. She felt happier than for long. 'Because,' she told herself, 'I've done something about Madge.' She did not realize how much the lightening of her heart was due simply to the hurry and excitement of her journey, and to her contact with the vigorous personality of her aunt. The very rushing of the train had brought her exhilaration.

SEVENTEEN

Martha Flies in a Rage

Aunt Josephine grew steadily weaker.

'She's gey far awa' wi't, I'm thinkin',' said Geordie; and though Geordie had said that already more than once, this time, in the shimmering June evening that made all the earth look new, it seemed truer than it had ever been.

Even Emmeline dragged her unwieldy bulk up the hill and sat *pechin'* beside her aunt.

'I wunna see her again,' she said to Martha across Aunt Josephine's bed and body.

Talked over thus, Aunt Josephine waxed indignant. There was a subacid flavour in the tone in which she answered Emmeline's 'Ye're gey sair made, I'm thinkin', aunt' with a ready 'O ay, auld age disna come its lane'; and when Mary Annie, frail now herself and useless, crept in about and said in a small and pitiful voice, 'I'm richt sorry to hear that ye're sae far yer road,' – 'Weel, than, I wasna ga'in ony road the day, Mary Annie,' responded Miss Josephine tartly.

She brooked no public mention of her disease, talked (out of a mouth twisted and drawn with pain) as though every tomorrow would see her on her feet and active, and met every reminder of death with an obstinate flare of the little life that was left in her.

'If I jist had a guff o' the earth I'd be gran' – that wad seen hae me weel again,' she said to Emmeline; disconcerting Mrs. Ironside, who had arrived in pious frame for a death-bed meditation. 'She'll be the death o' me yet, yer aunt,' she grumbled afterwards to Martha. 'Garrin' a body aye believe she's deein' an' nae deein' after an' a'.'

'I wad jist like to howk a holie i' the earth an' get a waucht o' it – the smell o't aye gaed aboot ma hairt an' me the lassie at the fairm,' Aunt Josephine continued; and Emmeline, collecting herself, answered, 'O ay, ye were aye fond o' yer bit gairden.'

The old lady dragged herself laboriously up on her pillow, whence she could just see her patch of ground.

'There's a gey bicker o' weeds,' she answered Emmeline, letting herself fall again in the bed. 'I tell Matty whiles to rug them oot, but she's some hard ca'ed – she hasna time. They'll be a' the langer an' she'll get the better haud o' them fan she has time.'

And as though there were tonic properties in the weeds, she turned to Emmeline with a brisker air and demanded her news.

Nothing loath, Emmeline fell to gossip.

Martha slipped away from the gossiping and into the weedy garden. The air was limpid, the hills a frail smoke-blue. She looked at them dully and told herself that they were beautiful; but their beauty did not move her. Her old vivid sense of the life of earth and sky had gone. She was no more of their company; and as she stood there, listless and sorry, she caught the words upon her lips and repeated them aloud:

'Strange that the spirit's infelicity
Should rob the world of beauty –'

the opening of Luke's first sonnet, that had shaken her so fiercely years before; the sonnet he had begun and left unfinished, as he had begun and left unfinished so much besides; as he had begun, and left unfinished, the evocation of a new woman from the aloof and alien dreamer that had been Martha Ironside. No dreamer now! But what instead? And she smiled, a bitter mirth. 'I'm an uncompleted work of art. My creator has flung me aside.' But stung suddenly by the admission the thought implied, 'Good Lord!' she exclaimed. 'Am I such a slave as that? Dependent on a man to complete me! I thought I couldn't be anything without him – I can be my own creator.'

And for a moment she slipped outside herself and regarded the thing she was with a smiling inquisitive detachment; but the point of vision was too novel and uncomfortable and she quickly returned to the safer ground of self-scorn. In a fever of fury she turned back from the hills and began to tug at Aunt Josephine's weeds – tangles of dead-nettle, fistfuls of groundsel, mats of chickweed; but when her fury had spent itself she rose in a sort of disgust and left the garden.

She paced the road outside and wished she had not thought of Luke. It disturbed her peace. She had shunned the thought of him, living in holes and corners of her being where he was not. The past was too painful to be courted. It shamed her and she did not know where. It puzzled her and she could not resolve its contradictions. So she had run away from it, and hidden herself in the present. She did not want to see Luke. She was glad that this year she could not go to Liverpool: Aunt Josephine's tenure of life was from day to day. And Luke and Dussie could not come north for their holiday, as once they had talked of doing. In April Dussie had given birth to another son, who lived and throve. They named him Ironside and called him Ronnie; and Dussie was aching to show him off: but the journey was too long for a three months' baby. Martha wrote that she was sorry and in secret was glad. She did not want to see Luke's son.

The summer wore on. August was harsh, hard on the frail. One day the sisters were summoned. They came, Aunt Margot older and larger, Aunt Leebie older and smaller, Aunt Jean older and more majestic; but before they arrived Aunt Josephine had got the turn again and talked of bonnets instead of grave-clothes.

'She's a thrawn auld buckie, ye wunna rug her aff,' said Uncle Sandy Corbett when he heard the report on Aunt Josephine.

Aunt Leebie remained for some weeks at Crannochie, dottling in and out, getting into Martha's way, and providing Aunt Josephine with a mirror of frailty in which she never thought of looking for her own reflection.

'Ye're gettin' terrible crined, Leebie,' she said. 'Ye're rale auld like. Yer face is pickit.'

When school began again Martha was glad enough to have Leebie there. She had never imagined another session beginning with Aunt Josephine still alive. Yet there she was!

September came in sweet and mellow, and Aunt Josephine sat up in bed.

'The sunshine gars a body cantle up,' said she.

A few days later, stumbling painfully and exultantly between the district nurse and Martha, she reached her armchair. Soon she was sitting up most of the day. One afternoon Martha, coming home from school, found her dragging a timid and unstable Leebie across the floor. Leebie, ostensibly the supporter, looked by far the feebler of the two.

'I'm hippit wi' sittin' sae lang,' said Aunt Josephine, collapsing on a chair. 'But I'll be as fleet's a five-year auld aince I get ma legs to wark.'

She got her legs to work, and Leebie departed.

'I'm nae needed ony mair,' she told Jean. 'Forbye she's that restless – a body canna get sitten doon.'

And Aunt Josephine, smiling triumphantly to Martha, was saying:

'We're best by wersels. She had her fingers inen a'thing.'

So another winter began.

To Martha it seemed that she stood outside life. The world went by her, colourless shapes on a flat pale background. Nothing had solidity or warmth. She felt numb, as though she could never be passionately alive again.

'I suppose one gets like this as one grows older,' she said to herself, remembering that she was twenty-four and a half. 'One stops feeling acutely.'

It did not seem to be true, however, of Aunt Josephine, who had just celebrated her seventy-ninth birthday with every token of exquisite enjoyment: nor yet, Martha was forced to admit, of her father, whom she discovered time after time on her hasty visits home taking with a relish the hobgoblin liveliness of little Robin, Emmeline's latest addition to the household. Not much evidence of numbness there! Geordie kittled the loonie with appetite.

He was now some twenty months old, being three months older than the gossips would have had him, though his size might have justified their belief that Emmeline had lied anent his age. 'An ablach,' Emmeline had called him when she brought him home, 'a sharger.' 'A deil's limb,' she called him now; but with pride; delighting, as Geordie did, in his quick and tricksey nature. 'There's mair nor the speen pit in in that ane,' she would declare. Martha's early resentment against the child's presence had worn down to indifference. She seldom gave him a thought: but one day coming home before supper-time and finding Emmeline out, she had set to work tidying the slovenly kitchen.

Emmeline had increased in flabbiness of temper as of body. She indulged seldom now in the clean sharp rages that drove her to scour and scrub. 'It's a thocht to me to begin,' she would say: or, waiting for the kettle to boil, 'I wad need to be scrapin' the brook affen ma kettle – it's barkit. It'll never bile': or, impatiently to Geordie, 'Fat needs ye tak the loonie oot in a' that muck? In ye come the pair o' ye an' scatter it a' aboot, an' than I get a' the jollification o' the dirt.' But the dirt remained.

Habituated to the dirt, Martha as a rule ignored it: but on this particular evening she was having supper at home and had no mind to eat among filth. She had been busy for several minutes before she became aware that she was watched: Robin was in the room; though she had not seen him where he stood, motionless as a caryatid, under the shelf that projected from the window ledge. His head and elbows were pressed against the shelf and his two big eyes stared out unwinking.

Martha was embarrassed by his scrutiny into a closer attention. Queer grave little imp! – bowed forward as though some massive weight were resting on his uplifted arms. And though she stared back at him he neither moved nor spoke. She resumed her work; but the caryatid had fascinated her and she looked again and again. An engaging little face, she decided. And this was the child they had mothered upon her! – Hers! Suddenly she thought, 'I wish he were!' The swiftness and power of the desire astonished her. She wanted to crush the child against her body, cover him with passionate kisses. Her fastidiousness revolted: a dirty waif . . . Then she clutched him fiercely, pressing him in a savage grip. It was the child's turn to be astonished. He fought and screamed, battling with his fists against her face; and wrenching himself free just as Emmeline and Geordie entered together, he ran to Geordie and sobbed out his terror in his arms.

'Fat's a' the tae-dae aboot?' said Emmeline. 'He disna aften greet. He's a biddable bairn. Fat wad a' angered him, wad ye think?'

'Oh, nothing, said Martha, arranging spoons on the supper table.

The meal began.

Martha made only a pretence at eating. Robin sat on Geordie's knee. Sometimes he looked rapidly round at Martha, but if she were looking at him hid his head instantly against Geordie's waistcoat; and once when Martha spoke to him he screamed. Martha sat and fiddled with her bread and was absurdly angry and quite incomprehensibly upset.

After supper a couple of neighbours dropped in. There was tobacco smoke and a clatter of tongues. Emmeline, luxurious in an armchair and the sweet savour of gossip, called out to Martha to put the bairn to his bed; but when Martha approached him the child beat her off with his hands, crying.

Martha was furious. She made a wild grab and caught his arm. Robin screamed the louder.

'Michty me, sic a skirlin',' cried Emmeline looking round. 'He's ta'en an ill-will at ye, Matty. Ye've surely bad-used him.'

'I'm sure I never did, said Martha, flaring. She was indignant that outsiders should see her defeated by the child.

Emmeline began to argue the point with alacrity.

Geordie's voice interposed, cool and equable.

'Fat needs ye pit the lassie's birse up? Canna ye lat her be? She's gotten the teethache.' Martha flashed a curious glance at her father. 'It's a sair bide, the teethache,' went on Geordie, settling stolidly down to the first imaginative falsehood of his life. 'I've had it masel.'

The company discussed teeth. Emmeline hoisted herself out of her chair and began undressing Robin. Martha under cover of her apocryphal ailment slipped out and returned to Crannochie.

'Hap ye yer mou' weel up,' Geordie cried after her; and added to the company, 'It's the cauld that does't,' but immediately after was overcome by the glorious absurdity of discussing solemnly a thing that had no existence. Laughter rumbled within him. Within him also was a blurred perception of those loyalties that force a man to do violence to his appetites; and heroically he repressed the surging tide. But not to have his laugh out was a continence as foreign to Geordie's habit of body as any other continence. It was a physical distress.

The placid talk went on.

Geordie could restrain himself no longer. He broke into a prolonged stentorian bellow, that considerably startled the auditors, who seeing no cause for mirth demanded leave to share the joke. Now was the deceitful man caught: for Geordie was in evil case unless forthwith he could invent a glorious lie, a lie with heat and *smeddum* enough to justify that uproar of laughter.

Shuffle as he might he could invent nothing. His wits went out on him.

'She hadna the teethache ava,' said Emmeline contemptuously. 'That's fat he's lauchin' at. I dinna see onything extra funny aboot that.'

Geordie rubbed his neck and admitted defeat. Still, the lass had got away.

The lass came back the following week and found Geordie and Robin taking their game with gusto. Geordie was prodding the bairn to the accompaniment of an old rhyme:

'The craw's ta'en, the craw's ta'en,
    The craw's ta'en wee pussie, O!
The auld cat, she sat an' grat
    On Robbie's thackit hoosie, O!'

and the bairn shouted with glee as Geordie's clumsy fingers ruffled his hair. Martha watching was shaken by a passion of jealousy. She sat smouldering at the supper-table, crumbling her bread and leaving it uneaten on the plate.

'So he won't look at me, will he?' she thought angrily.

She began to intrigue for his affections as she had intrigued for candles years before. She took to coming home more frequently than she had hitherto considered necessary. Perhaps Aunt Josephine was a little lonelier in consequence, but no one asked her and she said nothing. On her first two visits Martha ignored the boy. She kept herself well in his presence, but neither looked at him, mentioned him nor spoke to him. On the third occasion, Emmeline being in a snooze, she sat down on a stool by the fireside and began telling the fire a story. It was a jolly story, with hens clucking, dogs barking and pussy-cats scampering one after the other. When she had come to the end of it she began again at the beginning and told it all over again to the fire. There was no sound in the room behind her and she did not dare to turn and look for Robin. At the end of the second recital Emmeline awoke and Martha began immediately to talk to her.

Her next visit was on a Sunday afternoon. Emmeline was sleeping on the bed. Martha again took her stool and sat by the fire and again told the story of the hens and dogs and cats. Towards the end of the story she heard a very quiet movement behind but did not turn her head. Then Robin came into view, dragging his own little stool, which he set in line with hers, sitting on it in the same attitude as Martha. When the story was done, ''Gain,' he said; and when Martha made capering motions with her hands to indicate the scampering, Robin made capering motions too.

Martha's heart bounded. She had the same impulse as before to snatch the child and press him to her; but she contained herself and did not even look aside. At that moment Geordie put his head round the door.

'Come oot-by a meenutie, Matty,' said he.

Martha was exasperated. Just when the bairn was coming to! And what could her father want that was of any importance? She rose impatiently and went outside. A light rain was beginning to fall.

Geordie was holding a baker's bag.

'Ye're nae eatin' naething, Matty ma lass,' he said. 'Ye used to be terrible fond o' a saft biscuit.' And he thrust the baker's bag into her hand, saying, 'Fu' sorra's better'n teem,' and made away round the corner of the house.

Martha stood staring at the paper bag. Waves of resentment surged over her. What right had he to interfere? And what did it matter to him, or to anyone, what she ate, or what she did? With a churlish movement she flung the bag from her and watched it fall against a broken pail that had lain there time out of mind. She watched until the rain soaked through the thin paper, that clung transparent against the bumpy rounds of the soft biscuits. Then she went back to the kitchen.

'And my story's spoilt and all,' she thought.

Robin was bouncing up and down on her stool. He keeked round at her with a roguish grin and instantly turned back his head again, hunching his shoulders as though for cover. She made a feint of catching him, but he slipped from the stool and hid. When she made to seek him, he beat her off.

Martha gulped, and went through to the bedroom. She was both angry and sorry. 'If I hadn't thrown it where he'd see it,' she said to herself: but she was too proud, and too resentful still, to go outside and pick the baker's bag from the ground. By and by she heard Geordie come in; and in a while, knowing that it was tea-time and that her father did not like waiting for his tea, she pushed open the kitchen door.

Inside the door she paused. She wanted to laugh, but her lip quivered as though she was going to cry. Geordie had the child between his knees. His hand was fumbling in his jacket pocket, and Martha saw him pull some tousled paper out and fling it on the fire. It was the sodden baker's bag. Then he broke the fragments from the rejected biscuits and began putting them in his mouth. The child clamoured for a share, and got it. Martha shut the door as softly as she could and hastened back to the bedroom. Shame and vexation blinded her. She squeezed her eyes hard to keep back the tears; but they came scorching. When at last she heard Emmeline rise, she put on her outdoor things and called in at the kitchen door, 'I'm off. I'm not waiting for tea,' and went.

On her next visit she sat again on her stool and told the fire a story. Robin came almost at once and ranged his stool alongside. At the end of the tale, "Gain,' he commanded; and "Gain' at the second conclusion; but in the middle of the third recital he grew tired. 'Ga'in to Mama,' he said, setting off to find Emmeline in the shed. 'Tell 'tory to 'at,' and he pointed Martha imperiously to the fire. Martha continued her tale for a sentence or two and then sat gazing into the flames; but the child, turning at the door, ran back and shook her arm, 'Nae tellin' 'tory,' he remonstrated. 'Tell 'tory to 'at.' Martha took up the tale again, thinking he might linger within hearing: but he joined Emmeline in the shed and did not return.

The following day she met Emmeline trailing through the field for a bout of gossip at Bell Macpherson's. The child was trailing after her, some distance behind, and making no very expert job of his progress. Martha walked past him without speaking. She gave no overt invitation; but hardly a minute after she had entered the house she saw Robin had followed her. Without comment she sat down on her stool. Robin sat on his; and the routine began.

In the story there was an old woman who prodded her pig to see if he was fat. Martha prodded the chair beside her: Robin prodded the chair beside her. Then somehow, Martha hardly knew how, she was prodding Robin and Robin her. They prodded each other ecstatically, shouting with laughter. In another minute they were rolling tumbled together on Emmeline's grubby floor.

Martha was ridiculously happy. Geordie came in, *dubbit* and weary, and stretched himself by the fire. She was so happy that her resentment evaporated. She was no longer put to shame by the recollection of her father nibbling at the soft biscuits she had flung away. Suddenly she loved him for it. A passion of ruth laid hold of her – tender, amused, affectionate, profoundly moving. She wanted to tell him she was sorry, but the words would not come. So she poked him instead, a little, hesitant poke on the knee, as though inviting him to share the game. It suited Geordie better than an apology. He poked back, at Robin and at Martha alternately. They were all breathless and merry. It was a gracious interlude.

Emmeline burst upon them, hasty and flustered from too long a diet of chatter.

'Sittin' there wi' yer mou's open,' she grumbled, 'like a lot o' gorbals waitin' to be fed. Ye micht a' had the supper set, Matty. I didna fash masel fan I kent ye were in.'

Martha jumped from the floor and caught Robin under

one arm. She had been too happy to remember supper. She
balanced the bairn by his middle across an arm and with the
other hand began placing cups and plates upon the table.

'Oh, nae sae forcey there,' cried Emmeline. 'Ye'll be
brakin' something.' And as she spoke a cup crashed to the
ground. 'There ye are, ye see.'

'Hard words break no bones,
    Happy words break the cups,'
chanted Martha to a nondescript tune. She caught Emmeline
suddenly with her disengaged arm and whirled her round on
the floor.

'Gweed sake, lassie, ye're fey whiles,' panted her mother.

'I know,' said Martha. But it was so long since she had
been fey! She gathered up the fragments and flung them on
the ashes; then catching Robin, made to fling him after
them.

'Throw him away! Throw him away!' she cried.

'Dae't again, dae't again!' breathed Robin at every feint.
He was bounding so with laughter that she could hardly hold
him securely.

'That wad be a geylies sicht,' said Geordie behind their
backs to his wife, 'for them as thocht he was her ain.'

'Thocht!' snorted Emmeline. 'Naebody ever thocht it – it
was jist a speak.' She added, 'Fa wad believe fat yon Stoddart
Semple says – a face like a diseased pancake.'

'That's the bit about Luke,' thought Martha, who had
heard the dialogue through Robin's laughter. And she wondered what her mother really believed about Luke. Though
apparently it did not matter much: the nine days' talk was
over. Folk had forgotten her affair already; though she
supposed they would be quite ready to revive it if they had
opportunity. 'But I'll never give them the opportunity,' she
thought savagely. She might have remembered that they had
revived her Aunt Sally's story when the opportunity had
certainly not been given by Sally. But remembering Sally all
she thought was, 'I'm sure they may say what they like if I
can be as independent of their tongues as she was.'

'I don't believe mother thinks about Luke at all,' she
thought; and with a sigh she wished she were less sure of
what Aunt Josephine thought about Roy.

Aunt Josephine was openly distressed about Roy.

For awhile she had watched the post, sure that he would write to Martha. Martha evaded her hints and ignored her teasing. One day exasperated she cried,

'Why do you suppose Roy should write to me? He doesn't want to write to me and I don't want to hear from him. – Oh, I know you thought we were to marry each other, or some such thing, but you're quite wrong. I wouldn't marry him if he came back tomorrow. And what's more he won't come back.'

Aunt Josephine listened and was unconvinced; but as the posts went by and no letter came, a new conviction took hold on her: Roy had deserted the niece as Rory had deserted the aunt.

Martha repudiated the suggestion with disdain. She laughed in Aunt Josephine's face at the idea. Aunt Josephine was the more settled in her conviction. Martha was annoyed and warded off the theme.

Being friended now by Robin, she filled her visits home, never very lengthy, exclusively with him; and hardly lifted a hand to redeem the house from its bondage to Emmeline. One Saturday, however, Emmeline being from home, Robin climbed upon her in such a welter of filth that she cried out in disgust: and looking round the room seemed to see it in a flash of revelation. Her stomach rose. Her blood was up. She felt a raging anger against her mother, a passion of divine intolerance against dirt and disorder. She was possessed of a devil. A tearing energy possessed her and would not let her be. It drove her down a steep place violently. She cried to the boy, 'Come on, Bobbin, we're going to have a grand game!' and had off her frock and was wrapped in a wincey apron in the twinkling of an eye.

She chased the boy, about with a broom. 'Here's a muckle big c'umb,' he cried, running in front of her brush. She swept grimly but with a violence of vitality that allowed her energy for play. The 'muckle big crumb' had his fill of delight. She sent the window roaring wide to the chill air, and pitched a wilderness of rubbish out. The chairs went reeling. She dived savagely beneath the bed. Choked with the dust she shook herself like a terrier. Robin gurgled and shook himself too. Then she got on her knees with a pail of water and scrubbed. 'Flood's coming, Bobbin. On you go!' And the loonie, driven back, made forays on the wet and was driven back again. It was a game for the gods. How they must glory, now and then, in clearing up the mess that mortals leave behind them!

Martha scrubbed and sang. Like her mother she had to be angry to be intolerant of dirt. She was angry now to singing-point. Martha seldom sang, was not in her normal moods a song-bird, and her indulgence over the scrubbing was proof enough that her blood was up. The song she chose was not, strictly speaking, appropriate. It was *Ye Banks and Braes*. But her repertory of songs was limited and it served as well as another.

Martha scrubbed and droned her tune; but her heart went to a larger music than her lips. How clean this scrubbing made one feel! She could scrub to all eternity. A jolly kind of heaven, an eternity of this vehement physical action, that cleared the head and set the body glowing! Wholesome and strong – a cosmic harmony. . . .

'Sae ye're makin' a ceremony o't,' said Emmeline's voice behind her.

'Not on that patch, Bobbin,' Martha cried; and sprang up to face her mother. Bright defiance was in her countenance.

'No, we're making a game of it,' she said.

'A bonny-like thing, a body's goods an' chattels meetin' them at the mou' o' the place, an' the yaird packit an' a'.'

'Oh, *that*,' said Martha. 'What's outside's useless, the lot of it. It's not coming back here. We're making a bonfire of that.'

'Ye can mak a kirk or a mill o't for a' I care,' said Emmeline; and she picked her way across the floor and plumped upon a seat. 'I canna get lived for a sair heid,' she grumbled, plaintively, as though in exoneration of the state of her dwelling. 'Yon Bell Macpherson – she's a tongue that wad deave a dog.'

Martha got on her knees again and wiped the floor. She saw that Emmeline was secretly relieved and would make no commotion.

'Your turn to be scrubbed next, Bobbin,' she said.

They made a game of that too.

'Weel, weel,' said Emmeline, watching. 'Ye're daein' dirdums. Ye've fair been eident.' She kicked her dirty boots off her feet and let them tumble on the floor, where the mud in contact with the damp ran in little spreading streaks. 'An' there's me fylin' the fleer,' she cried; and tossed the boots on to the coal-scuttle. The dirty streaks spread through the damp.

Martha having washed Robin was looking with distaste at his filthy clothing. She rose from her knees and rummaged in all the drawers and boxes.

'Ye'll jist hae to shak' his shirt an' pit it on again,' said Emmeline. 'There's nae anither ane clean.'

Martha turned back from her fruitless search.

'He's going to have some new clothes as soon as ever I've time to make them,' she proclaimed.

'Ye're michty concerned wi' him a' at aince,' said her mother.

'Am I? Well, yes, I am. And I'm going to be concerned with him. He's going to be mine.'

'Weel,' said Emmeline, 'ye micht dae a lot waur nor gie the bairn a shog alang.'

'Once I get home again,' Martha answered, 'he'll maybe get two or three shogs along.' She had had her eye on Robin's table manners and was determined they should improve.

'O ay, we'll a' be gettin' that, I'se warren,' said Emmeline. 'Ye've been that ta'en up wi' yer aunt. But it canna be for muckle langer noo.'

'No,' said Martha. And she wondered what she would find it like to be at home again.

EIGHTEEN

Death of Aunt Josephine

Aunt Josephine grew steadily weaker.

The flaring of her life in September that had sent Aunt Leebie home, died out with the month. By mid-October she was bedded up again, and for good. She was helpless now and could do nothing for herself. It was impossible to leave her alone, and Martha engaged a woman from Beltie to stay with her while she was at school. Aunt Josephine appealed against the sentence, but Martha was obdurate. She marched straight out of the house and found her woman, made her terms and engaged her before she showed face again in Crannochie. She had had no idea she could be so masterful. Something of the security of her handling of Robin seemed to have passed into her relations with other folk. Her old diffidence was gone. The current of her life was running strong and sure; but underground; deeper as yet than her own knowledge.

In the early autumn she was too excited over Robin to give Aunt Josephine much but the *ootlins* of her mind; but one Saturday she bethought herself and took Robin to visit the old lady. He had new clothes now and was very important and in high glee over his excursion. Aunt Josephine was as pleased as the bairn.

'Eh, the littlin,' she said.

And her very tones rejoiced. A kind of song, Martha thought. After that she fetched Robin every Saturday; and every Saturday Aunt Josephine was just as pleased. Her life was shot through with pain now and riddled with sickness.

'Whan we canna dae naething else, we can aye thole,' she would say; and as soon as the pain released her she *cantled* up and told Martha interminable stories from the past; but always when the tales were of Rory Foubister she sighed, looking at Martha with a rueful countenance. Martha read her thought; and at first it annoyed her; till she began to perceive that the old woman suffered. Her grief was deep and tender; the more that it was not for herself. A second time she had seen the promise unfulfilled. Her *Nunc dimittis* was a betrayal.

'Foubister flesh an' blood's nae to lippen till,' she said one evening, sorrowfully, by firelight.

'If only she would understand,' thought Martha. 'She hurts herself.' And she slipped to the floor beside Miss Leggatt's bed and laid one arm gently across the old lady's body.

'But auntie,' she said, 'you mustn't make yourself unhappy over what isn't true. I didn't love Roy. I wouldn't have married him though he had stayed till Doomsday. I don't want to marry him.'

'O ay. O ay,' was all Miss Josephine's rejoinder. She herself had made the same protestations when Rory went away.

Martha sighed a little, and remained where she was on the floor, touching with her strong firm fingers the cold and wrinkled skin of Miss Leggatt's hand. Impossible to disabuse Aunt Josephine. But did she want to disabuse Aunt Josephine? She sat a long time quietly on the floor, leaning against Miss Leggatt, and it seemed to her that the heavens were opened and the spirit of God descended and brooded on the frail and wasted frame of the old woman. She had taken upon herself what she conceived to be the young girl's sorrow and was carrying it. Martha understood that her mistake altered nothing of the grandeur of her action. The strong serenity of life that dwelt in the old woman seemed to possess and inhabit the girl, purchased for her – was it idle to suppose? – by the love and suffering she had divined.

That night she wept into her pillow noiseless and flooding tears, tears without salt in them, that washed the last bitterness from her heart; and in the morning rose and went about her work marvelling at the redemptive vitality of an old woman's misapprehension.

She knew now that her heart-break was of no one's causing, but in the nature of things; that the shame that had torn her was as wrong as her resentment against Luke; and the shattering of her selfhood not evil, but the condition of growth. She had given love and had received only adoration: and love is so much bigger a thing than adoration – more complex and terrible. At its absolute moments it holds resolved within itself all impulses and inconsistencies, the lust of the flesh, the lust of the eyes, the pride of life, the spirit's agonizing. Martha seemed to herself that morning to touch one of its absolute moments. She had no more fear of what love might do to her.

In the watches of that winter she was closer in spirit to Aunt Josephine than at any time since she was a little child. Together they enjoyed Robin and laughed at Clemmie's *upcomes* and antics; and upbraided Jeannie Mortimer (though not to her face) for her treatment of her aged mother.

'Lattin' her ging aboot a ticket like yon,' said Aunt Josephine indignantly. 'Jist an objeck. A rickle o' banes. An' her claes! – patched an' yea-patched. Ye cudna tell the maisterpiece. Forbye some bits as thin's ye cud pick bird's meat through them. A tink's mair weel-to-be-seen than yon.'

'She's not much better to look at herself,' said Martha. Jeannie's pride of person had been slowly going down before the advancing tides of her religion.

'Na,' Aunt Josephine agreed. 'It's a gey whilie sin' she was in-by, bit the hin'most time she cam' I jist sat an' beheld her. "That's gey-like coats ye've gotten, Jeannie. If ye dinna sell them ye'll come aff by the loss." "They're gweed eneuch to pray in, Miss Leggatt." Weel, weel! She's an awfu' wife wi' her tongue fan she speaks to common fowk like you an' me, fatever like she be fan she's speakin' to the Lord.'

In November Mary Annie took to her bed. It was not easy to visit her: Jeannie brooked no interference. For the intrepid few who entered she prayed in loud and offensive terms: but on a Sunday she left her mother alone locked in the cottage, and tramped to town to meet her brethren and sisters in righteousness.

'See if ye cudna get in,' suggested Aunt Josephine to Martha.

'Oh, if there's a way in I'll find it,' said she. They giggled together like two conspirators. 'There's an upstairs window open,' said Martha after reconnoitring. 'I'll have a shot at it.'

Aunt Josephine was like a lassie again at the idea. Many was the time she had clambered in at windows. 'I was a wild limmer,' she said, 'aye at some prank or ither. – But dinna fleg the auld body,' she added.

Martha got on the roof from the branches of a tree and squeezed her thin body through the window. In the kitchen Mary Annie looked at her with bleared and uncomprehending eyes. After what seemed a long time she began to understand who Martha was and what she wanted. 'Miss Josephine's terrible kind,' she said. Then clutching Martha's arm, in an importunate whisper and pointing with a claw-like finger at the dresser, 'Tak it doon,' she said. 'Tak it doon. I wad richt like a haud o'it for a meenutie. Tak it doon.'

Martha tried the japanned tea-caddy, but it was not that. She tried the blue kiln-cracked sauce-boat, and the greedy glitter in Mary Annie's eyes told her she was right.

In the sauce-boat was a wedding-ring.

Mary Annie grabbed it from her and began rubbing it gently with her hand. Martha noticed that her wedding finger was bare.

'I tint it,' she said. 'I tint it mair nor aince, an' it cudna be gotten. She thinks I dinna ken that she's gotten't, bit I ken fine. She disna want me to ken case be I tine't again. I'm an auld dane craitur, ma finger's awa' to naething – it aye slippit aff.'

She had put the ring in its place and was twisting it round and round, touching it with light caressing fingers. There was love in the movement.

'Dinna bide,' she said after a minute to Martha. 'Dinna bide. She micht come hame. Hae.' And she pulled the ring off and held it out. 'Pit it back again. Pit it jist faur it wis afore.'

Pity and indignation rushed upon Martha.

'Why should you put it back?' she asked. 'She's no right to keep it from you. It's yours. You keep it. She needn't know.'

'I micht tine't again,' said Mrs. Mortimer. 'I'm a peer dane body, I canna anger Jeannie. She's that gweed – she's ower gweed for the likes o' me.'

Martha put the ring in the sauce-boat and the sauce-boat on the dresser, exactly as she found it; and went away by the upstairs window.

A few days later, having risen early in the morning to give Aunt Josephine a hot-water bottle, she heard a harsh powerful chanting through the still air. She knew at once that it was Jeannie Mortimer. Jeannie was an inconvenient riser. She rose at five in winter, at any hour in summer – 'makin' wark to hersel,' Miss Josephine declared. 'Hain yer licht, Jeannie,' she had said to her once. 'Ye'll be gettin' up the nicht afore or lang.'

Miss Josephine too had heard the singing. Jeannie's psalms and spiritual songs rent the morning air frequently. 'She's coorse,' said Miss Leggatt, 'raryin' aboot the hoose at this time i' the mornin' an' keepin' her mither fae her sleep. Peer auld stock, I'm hairt-sorry for her. Ging ower, Matty, an' speir if there's onything she wad like.'

Martha demurred. At that hour in the morning, to penetrate the arcana of the Babylon inhabited by Jeannie! But perceiving that Aunt Josephine was set on it ('Though she does pray for yer soul,' said Miss Leggatt, 'it wunna dae ye nae ill.') she humoured her and went.

The raucous singing dropped suddenly as she approached, and she knew that she had been seen. Through the deathly silence that followed she stood uncertain in the raw grey air. At last she tried the door. It gave and she pushed it open. A gabble reached her ear, and looking in she saw Jeannie on her knees in the middle of the floor, unsupported by any furniture, gesticulating to the Almighty. At the eddy of chill air she raised her voice, spluttering and screaming her frenzied ejaculations. Martha closed the door and waited. The thin knob of greyish hair, the great boots sticking out behind, the clumsy evolutions of her powerful frame, the clutching skinny hands, the strident voice – all seemed the crude material for some grinning modern caricature of death.

As the prayer continued, Martha walked past Jeannie and spoke to Mrs Mortimer.

'She's terrible kind, is Miss Josephine, terrible kind,' said the old done voice – 'extinct,' Martha thought – ' Naething, naething. Jeannie there – she's ower gweed for the likes o' me. She's prayed for me. There was a while she wadna dae't – I wisna gweed eneuch for her.'

Her habitual expression was unchanged, but the horrible graven stare of anxiety had become a mask. She was secure in Jeannie's prayers.

Late that night Mary Annie died. Aunt Josephine was great-hearted, and talked of her own end. She bade Martha take the feather-stitched nightgown from its drawer and hold it up for her to see. It was flecked with mould. 'Ye'll need to air it,' she said. 'I cudna lie quaet in ony but that.'

'But it's so narrow,' Martha was thinking; and she was heart-sick, looking down upon the old woman's body swollen and monstrous with disease.

'Ye canna pit that on her,' said Clemmie, coming in aboot as she shook it in the sun and wind.

'I have to say I will, or she'll be miserable.'

'Ach,' said Clemmie, 'slit it up the back an' stap it in ahin. She'll never be a penny the wiser an' her deid.'

Alive still, Miss Leggatt regarded the nightgown with a jealous eye; though once she had seen it comfortably airing by the fire, her talk was but little on the grave. There was too much else to be interested in.

The back-end of the year was open, kindly to unwell folk. A dead November, heavy-skied; but the year went out in sunshine, after weeks of warm uncertain winds. Aunt Josephine had seen another new year, and she liked it. She sat a little higher up in bed. 'I've diddled you all yet,' said the wrinkles round her mouth. She had the same complacent serenity over her doing as when she set out so long ago for Birleybeg and left Martha dinnerless and forlorn. There was no question at all as to the absolute rightness of her continuing to live. The world was hers and the fulness thereof, and she had no intention of giving it up.

And such mornings January brought! A sky of silver-point, the east like mellowed ivory. Floating in saffron, the morning star was there and gone. No breath of wind: but gusty, blowing from one tree to another, the song of the blackbirds.

Later a powdery sunlight filled the room, irradiating the feathery *caddis* from the blankets that had drifted into corners. The *steer* of life floated in from the road. Hens cackled, dogs barked, women scolded, crying on their bairns in sharp resonant voices that carried far through the empty winter air. Peter Mennie stamped along the road with the post-bag, his greeting still in the air when already the echoes of his voice clanged up from Drochety. The *littlins* bickered past from school, chasing cats and hens, flinging stones, calling names after an occasional stranger or carrying on for his benefit a loud and important conversation mainly fictitious. And the bigger the loons, with stolen *spunks* that had all but burned holes in their *pooches* through the day, fired the whins along the roadside. Prometheus with a vulture indeed! – They tortured the wrong side of his body, those undiscriminating gods. A good old-fashioned *skilping* would have served the nickum better. What had he to do with anything as sophisticated as a liver?

The crackle of the flame reached Aunt Josephine's ear, the pungent odour of the burning delighted her nostril. Sometimes the flame would roar up, towering into view beyond the dyke; but for the most part the laddies were cautious and struck no matches till they were round the bend and out of sight of the clachan. But there were other fires to see as the year wore on – all the cleansing and renewing fires of an out-of-door winter, fires of refuse, whin fires, heather fires. All up and down the valley they were visible, long trails of smoke blowing the one way, smudged brown thinning to blue, lit with the sun; or soft and inconspicuous like morning mists. At night an eye of fire would wink – elemental, evil, uncanny, on the homely land.

And in the dusk Drochety's two pair of horse clumped home, young Drochety himself on the offhand beast of the first pair, whistling like a mavis and always first to *louse*; the hired man with the second pair, dour and silent.

There were crows too, vivid black eddies of them, and sometimes a ploughshare of wild ducks flew overhead. And when the wind rose and blew from the south, the smell of the new-turned earth went about Aunt Josephine's heart.

As though anyone, thirled to pain and days and nights of sickness notwithstanding, could possibly want to leave a world like that!

That January Martha loved the earth as she had never loved it before. Her pilgrimages in the growing and waning light, to and from school, were exquisite initiations. On the homeward way she loitered, steeping herself in the life of earth and air. Once, at the head of the brae, she saw the brown ploughed field stretch out, empty and dark against a golden afterglow; but turning to look back on it she saw a plough left in the furrow, catching the glow and gleaming. It seemed to focus for her the life of the soil. And once she had a far-off glimpse of Geordie, in a steep field some distance from the road. She watched the horses straining up the furrow, back and neck one rigid line. She watched them turn. Then horses and plough and man were swallowed up in the darkness at the far end of the field, against the upturned earth and the blur of wood. Only when the team swung round and their white foreheads and noses glimmered through the brown could she distinguish where they were. It was surely impossible that Geordie could see longer to cut the furrow; but his eyes had been bent so long upon the darkness of the earth that he seemed to share its life, know his way with it by touch. Martha brooded, her eyes on the slow sombre darkening; then lifted them and saw the arch of sky. When she looked again her father and his team were blotted out, one with the earth.

She thought, 'I've come from him.' She too was at one with the earth. 'I'd like to follow a plough,' she thought: and she laughed, 'What boots I'd have! – and what legs I'd have! and what a back!' and shook herself and hastened home.

In middle February snow began to fall – few and irresolute flakes.

'The snaw's comin' doon as if it didna care gin it cam' doon or no,' said Geordie. 'There'll be a terrible storm.'

Next day each bough and telegraph wire and paling post was piled with snow, light, fluffed, that seemed to float in air rather than lie upon substantial surfaces. Then the wind rose; for two days there was *blin' drift*; and the wind went as it came, leaving the roads choked and the sky blown bare. Frost followed. Martha's hands were chapped and *tangles* hung from the cottage eaves. Aunt Josephine shivered and shrank within herself. Her face grew smaller, disproportionate above the bloated horror of her body; her hands shrivelled and were deadly cold to the touch.

'She's geal cauld,' said the woman who noticed her when Martha came in glowing and breathless from her long tussle through the storm.

'She may go at any minute now,' the doctor said.

The sisters were again summoned.

They came: Aunt Margot and Uncle Webster in the Ford over roads that were *byous coorse*. Uncle Webster sat in the kitchen and talked in a loud assertive voice of the hazards of the journey – the block, the digging out, the skidding upon icy braes. *Ben the hoose* Aunt Margot stood with Jean and Leebie, and gazed melancholy on Josephine's grim and yellow face.

'She's nae takin' nae notice,' said Leebie. 'She's oot amon't a' thegither.' Josephine, as though to repudiate the libel, looked up and became aware of her sisters.

'Ye're come to see me dee,' she said. 'Sit ye doon. – Na, na. Sit faur I can see ye. An' Matty – faur's Matty? Bid Matty come an' see me dee.'

Leebie called Matty through.

Martha found her aunts in a row upon the sofa; and at Aunt Josephine's peremptory command sat herself down beside them.

'I'm jist hingin' on by the brears o' the e'e,' Aunt Josephine said.

A silence fell upon the room. The aunts breathed hard. Once Leebie sniftered; and once snow slurred upon the roof and thudded *reeshling* to the ground. 'Fresh,' Martha thought, 'what roads there'll be.' Aunt Josephine seemed to doze. No one spoke or stirred; but Leebie sniftered for the second time.

Aunt Josephine looked sharply up. She had always hated a snifter. Her eye fell upon the row of sisters – an ironic antagonistic eye.

'Fat are ye sittin' there glowerin' at me for like a puckle

craws a' in a raw?' she demanded; and fixing her eye upon
her youngest sister, 'Leebie,' she said in a reproachful
voice, 'are ye nae ga'in to dee afore me yet?'

'She fair sorted me, glowerin' like yon,' said Leebie
afterwards.

Aunt Margot too thought it well to shelter from the
glower. She had done her duty by Josephine (though she
had not seen her die) and departed with Uncle Webster in
the Ford.

Aunt Jean and Aunt Leebie slept in the kitchen bed. 'It's
a sort of eternal recurrence,' thought Martha as she lay
down on the sofa in Aunt Josephine's room. 'We do the
same things again and again.' She was to waken Aunt Jean
at two in the morning and take her place in bed for the
remainder of the night: but a little after twelve she came to
the kitchen, hurriedly, and shook Leebie, who was nearest
the door. 'She's going, I think. You'd better come.'

Leebie got out of bed and began to pull on some clothes,
but pausing for a moment to meditate on mortality, from
very weariness fell asleep at the bedside. Waking again with
a start, she envisaged in horror her unfaithfulness; but
deciding, with the optimism of the sleeper, that her nap
could have lasted only a matter of seconds, she resolved to
say nothing of the delay to Jean; and rousing her with a
stern serenity she made her way across the passage to fulfil
her sober task.

Thus it came about that when Leebie thrust her head
fearfully round the door-cheek, she was met by the extraordinary apparition of Aunt Josephine sitting up in bed and
clutching an egg-cup to her bosom with one claw-like hand,
while she supped the contents of the egg with vigour:
having cantled up during Martha's absence from the room,
and decided on her return that she would enjoy a little
nourishment. Thus also it came about that Leebie,
withdrawing her head hastily from the doorway, met the
further apparition of Mrs. Corbett ghastly in candle-gleam
and white nightgown and fallen puckered mouth without its
garnishing of teeth, and clutching her by the arm whispered
vehemently, 'Faith, Jean, she wunna dee.'

After two days Mrs. Corbett departed. She was uneasy.

The routine of Muckle Arlo required her, and Josephine apparently did not.

Leebie remained and dottled in and out as before.

On the fourth day the doctor thought her gone: but she *warstled* through and spoke in weak uncertain syllables.

'She can't last the night,' he said.

'If onything happens, than, doctor,' said Leebie, whose habit of mind was dependent, 'we'll jist send for you.'

He shook his head. 'There's nothing I can do,' he said, 'nor yet anyone else. I'll come back first thing in the morning,' he said, 'and bring the death certificate with me. Her fight's done.'

It had been a magnificent fight, he reflected. She had the quality of life in her that the antagonists in ballad and in saga must have had – dour, obstinate, invulnerable; withstanding the repeated hack and shock of battle.

In the morning Aunt Josephine was drinking tea.

'Weel, doctor,' she said genially, 'I'm aye livin', an' livin' like.'

'Ay, ay, and so you are,' he answered her, marvelling when the epic would end. He carried the death certificate away again in his pocket. He carried it for five days, because Josephine Leggatt, seventy-nine years of age, and grievously afflicted with cancer, would not die.

In the end she died swiftly and unexpectedly, having rallied a little just before and spoken in a loud and firm voice.

The following week, on the second day of March, Martha went home to Wester Cairns. Aunt Josephine had left her her house and what money she possessed: which was more than she had allowed folk to suppose. Martha might have made her abode at Crannochie and ordered her life and surroundings at her pleasure. She was tempted sometimes so to do. A few months before she would hardly have hesitated; but now there was Robin. He wiled her back. Afterwards, perhaps, when he was older . . . and her mind rioted across the future. She meant to educate Robin. He was now two years and two months old, and already his mind was alert and his speech engaging. Another game for the gods was ahead of her.

So she went home.

NINETEEN

The Pillars of Hercules

'You must thraw her neck for me,' said Martha, crossing from the hen-house with a plump Rhode Island Red under her arm.

'Fairly that,' Geordie answered; and having despatched the business added, 'Ye'll need to larn to dae't yersel.'

'I can manage the cockerels,' said Martha, laughing, 'but I haven't strength of grip for that big fat duchess.'

'Ay, ay, she's a fair size. A bit o' the packin' o' that and a new tattie wad wark awa' fine.'

'Just you wait till Sunday then, and you shall have it.'

Geordie stood with an admirer's eye upon the fat breast of the fowl, holding her out from him until her spasms of involuntary twitching were over. Martha watched, breathing the clean sweet air of a July morning. When she raised her head she saw the wet fields and the soft gleam of the river. 'How fresh it is,' she said.

'Ay, ay,' answered her father, still holding the hen. 'It's a grand thing to get leave to live.'

Martha took the hen, which had stopped twitching, plucked it and hung it in the shed. On Sunday Luke and Dussie 'were coming to dinner, with their fifteen-month-old son, her name-child Ronnie. It was three years since they had parted. Now they were coming to spend their holiday in the cottage at Crannochie that had been Aunt Josephine's. Later Martha was to let it and use the money for Robin's education.

'Them that disna like hen can just tak want,' Emmeline declared triumphantly, setting the ashet on the table with an air that proclaimed her utter incredulity in anyone's not liking hen. 'We'll gar Matty divide. She's grand at dividin'.' And she pushed the ashet towards her daughter, deranging Martha's carefully appointed table.

'She's some sair birstled, mither,' said Geordie with an eye on the dish.

'I thocht ye likit it like that.'

'O ay, ay. I div that. But there's mair nor me to be considered.'

'We like it bristled too,' cried Dussie smiling.

'Birstled, lassie,' said Geordie, coming out with a great roar of laughter at the mispronunciation. 'Ay, ay, I mind fine. You were aye the ane for the birstled bits oot o' the pots.'

'An' mony's the skilpin' ye didna get for't,' said Emmeline.

'I know. Marty got half my skilpings and scoldings, I think.'

'Weel, weel,' said Geordie benignly, 'she's been skilpit the richt gait ony road – she can mak grand packin' till a hen. We'll hae a bittie mair o't, lassie, jist to help awa' wi't, like.' And he held out his plate for a second helping of oatmeal stuffing.

He helped away with it to such good purpose that at the end of the meal he pushed his chair back, *pechin'*. 'I'm fair stappit fu'.'

'Ye'll need to sit an' swage a while, than,' said Emmeline.

'We'll ging oot to the doors, than.' They sat in the July afternoon, idly, till Dussie said, drowsily, her baby asleep in her arms, 'This is perfect. I couldn't move for toffee. But Luke's aching for a walk. Do go with him, Marty.'

Watching Martha, and feeling (though she did not reason it out) her gay strong assurance, the poise of her whole nature, Dussie had been thinking, cheerfully, 'She's got over it. Of course she would.'

Luke too had been watching Martha. He knew life better now and was less sure of his theories; but until he saw her again he had continued to think of her as of spirit. Now he understood that he was wrong. She too had understood that this was no demi-god but a man; and there fell between them a constraint that neither knew how to break.

Watching her, Luke thought, *A sword of Spain, the ice-brook's temper*; and suddenly the lightning that had blinded him for a moment when he held Dussie weeping in his arms, lit up his universe from end to end. He knew now that passion had gone to the making of this new Martha and for the first time he realized that it might be for him. The blood thudded in his temples. His thoughts were in confusion. A thousand meanings were in the air and he dared grasp at none. The brightness of the blade turned him back.

He began to tell her of his work in Liverpool. For both of them the afternoon was inconclusive. Life was stranger than they had supposed. Of the two Martha was the happier: she had acquiesced in her destiny and so delivered herself from the insecurity of the adventurer. *Sail not beyond the Pillars of Hercules.*

As they neared the house a gentle rain was falling. It sent the idlers in. The kitchen was filled with their clatter, till Emmeline cried, 'Haud the lang tongues o' ye or I see if ma kettle's bilin',' and made the tea.

And they all drew in about their chairs and ate.

The Weatherhouse

INTRODUCED BY
RODERICK WATSON

Contents

Introduction

Scottish literature is rich in novels which have taken the life of small communities for their setting: Dalmailing, Thrums, Barbie, Brieston, Kinraddie, Segget and many others, are memorably located on the maps of our imagination In modern times, however, these locations have been less than happy places, and in *Gillespie* and *The House with the Green Shutters*, they have been revealed as appalling microcosms of all that is mean, petty and cruel in the human spirit.

The spirit of Fetter-Rothnie in *The Weatherhouse* is more balanced from the start. As an account of Scottish rural life and character in the first decades of this century, it is a humourous delight. (Fetter-Rothnie is imagined to be near the coast, a few miles from Nan Shepherd's native Aberdeen.) As a social document, *The Weatherhouse* tells of a community of women—girls, widows, wives and spinster ladies—and of the many links which bind them together to make our world into a whole and humane place. Finally, as an exploration of human nature itself, and of the mysteriously personal and fluid well-springs which underlie what we think of as truth or reality, it is a small masterpiece, and a very fine modern novel in its own right.

This was Nan Shepherd's second book, published in 1930, and it is by far her most complex and subtle achievement. As with Chekhov, whose dryly compassionate wit she shares, there are no truly central characters to her story, for its themes are advanced through almost every person in the novel. There are no villains and heroes either, and what we are left with is a vision of mortal existence and human reconciliation which is transcendent, liberating, and even frightening at times. And yet all is achieved with the lightest of touches in what seems to be the most domestic and parochial of tales about poor Louise Morgan's fantasy engagement to David Grey (who has died T.B.), and Garry Forbes's determination to make her confront her self-delusion.

Shepherd keeps a wry distance from her world, as the section headings show: Garry Forbes's unseemly fervour and Louie Morgan's feeble untruths scarcely qualify as 'The Drama', after all, and the author's use of 'Prologue' and 'Epilogue' serves to place the affair even more ironically against the longer perspectives of time and local legend. Within the book itself the presiding genius of this detachment is Mrs 'Lang Leeb' Craigmyle, matriarch of the Weatherhouse and, at over ninety years old, 'an ironic commentator' with 'an intelligent indifference to life'. Her impudence is delightful, for there is 'no spectacle like what's at your own doors,' and as her creator observes, 'Life is an entertainment hard to beat when one's affections are not engaged.' Yet Lang Leeb's disinterestedness can strike a more sinister note, and this delicate and non-judgemental balance between the comic and the disturbing is characteristic of Shepherd's humour:

> Mrs Craigmyle had few gestures; she held herself still; only her eyes glittered and her lips moved, and often her fingers went to and fro as she knitted — a spider stillness. The film of delicate lace upon hair as fine as itself was not the only thing about her that betokened the spider. One had the sense of being caught upon a look, lured in and held.

The life that Leeb delights to observe is all around us in the book, for Shepherd has created a complex web of relationships in a community largely bound together by women in a tangle of connections through birth, friendship, work, debt, widowhood and marriage. The list of characters at the end of this introduction provides ample evidence of this web and will also serve, I hope, as an aid to understanding Nan Shepherd's most ambitious portrayal of how the social fabric is held together in small communities.

In this respect *The Weatherhouse* is a feminist text of considerable sensitivity, not least in its author's understanding of the position of women in a society where female status is still chained to bridal veils and apron strings. Thus the sweetness of Lindsay Lorimer's romance with Garry Forbes is countered by the sharper pains of Ellen Falconer's fantasies as she seeks to be the girl's mentor. At the age of sixty, Mrs Falconer is looking for vicarious fulfilment in Lindsay's youthful enthusiasms, and then again in the excitement of uncovering the 'truth' in the Louie Morgan affair. Finally, and most pathetically of all, she hopes to impress Garry Forbes, ostensibly on her daughter's behalf, but actually in her own right as a fellow idealist (as she sees herself) in a community of clods. What Lindsay sees, on the other hand, is 'a poor old thing', and later, 'a horrid old woman'. Nan Shepherd has the most piercing eye for the differences between how we like to think about ourselves and how others perceive us. Like Lang Leeb 'her cruelties [come] from comprehension, not from lack of it.'

Long widowed and isolated by her own dreamy, imaginative and uneducated nature, Ellen Falconer has to discover that she is just as sadly removed from the real springs of life (which she always thought to value so much), as the pitiable Louie Morgan. In fact their two fates are bound up in the most poignant fashion as Ellen, that 'shy, baffled soul', decides to visit Louie in a harrowing scene at the end of the book, only to recognise a mad version of herself. Yet reconciliation is possible, and she makes a kind of peace with Louie and Lindsay and herself. We, too, are kept from a more tragic sense of closure, for although the book ends with Ellen's death, the moment is lightened by a tribute paid to her by the bold Stella, who leaves a flower in her hands in memory of an unconsidered and unpretentious moment's kindness shown to her by Ellen long ago.

Garry Forbes has to learn, too, that things are not quite as they seem, nor as he would have them be. Shaken by grim experience and the trauma of the trenches, he returns to the parochial world of Fetter-Rothnie only to have his faith in the stability of the world undermined yet again, and at an even more profound level. Nan Shepherd uses a

destabilising imagery of light and dark and space to mark
the point at which Garry moves on from the simplicities
of his engineering trade ('making boilers and bridges as
stable as one could', with 'right and wrong as separate as
the bridges he helped to build'), to a perplexing vision of
ordinary life as something far more fluid, dynamic, dangerous and uplifting:

> Garry's thought went back upon the evening
> when he had seen the land emerge and take form
> slowly from primordial dark. Now its form was on the
> point of dissolution into light. And the people whom
> the land had made—they, too, had been shaped from
> a stuff as hard and intractable as their rock, through
> weathers as rude as stormed upon their heights; they
> too (he thought) at moments were dissolved into light,
> had their hours of transfiguration. In his aunt dancing
> her wilful reel on the kitchen floor, in Lindsay as
> she had grieved for Louie's hurt, he had seen life
> essentialised.

In such images Nan Shepherd manages to invest the
dourness of the Scottish land—a very familiar theme in our
fiction—with aspects of imagination and grace. For her the
natural world is full of such insights, and they are repeated-
ly evoked in brilliant descriptions of weather, light and
the North East landscape. In the realm of human affairs,
equivalent moments of generosity and delight are provided
by Shepherd's unsentimental affection for her characters.

Chief among these delights is Garry Forbes's maiden
aunt Barbara Paterson. Loud, boisterous and unconven-
tional, she is something of a natural force, 'elemental, a mass
of the very earth, earthy smelling, with her goat's beard, her
rough hairy tweed like the pelt of an animal.' Both Garry
and Lindsay (who is frightened of her at first), have much
to learn from 'Bawbie' Paterson's vivid enjoyment of the
moment, not least the grand carelessness with which she
sets fire to the roof of her farm at Knapperley, and then the
hilarious confidence with which she sets out to repair it. The
job is attacked with her usual gusto as she enlists the aid of
her untrained nephew and the hapless journeyman Francie
Ferguson. 'Up on the heid o' the house, like Garry Forbes

and his twa fools', becomes a local proverb on the strength of the event, and yet Garry comes to a crucial recognition (all the more timely since the bloodiest of wars is still being fought in Europe), that 'his folly on the housetop was a generosity, a gesture of faith in mankind.'

Such faith, like the imagery of light, fluidity and reconciliation, illuminates this extraordinary novel throughout, as Bawbie, at first an earthy 'boulder' in Garry's inner eye, finally becomes perceived by him as a 'dancing star'. Even Louie's pale and pathetic delusions are not without some saving grace in the end, for in the Epilogue, as Lindsay thinks of her childhood and happier days with the older girl, she seems to remember Louie's faithful whippet hound, Demon, who used to follow her wherever she went. ' "Nonsense!" rapped Miss Theresa. "Louie had never a dog . . . She wanted one . . . And after a while she used to pretend she had it—made on to be stroking it, spoke to it and all." '

Lindsay looked doubtfully.

'Did she? I know she pretended about a lot of things. But Demon –? He seems so real when I look back. Did she only make me think I saw him? He used to go our walks with us. We called to him—*Demon, Demon*—loud out, I know that.'

She pondered. The dog, bounding among the pines, had in her memory the compelling insistence of imaginative art. He was a symbol of swiftness, the divine joy of motion. But Lindsay preferred reality to symbol.

The last line returns us to common sense, but Nan Shepherd has already made her point. Once again she has managed a bitter-sweet and creative disturbance of our equilibrium, as she has done, so subtly and so memorably on almost every page of *The Weatherhouse*.

Roderick Watson

The Main Characters

THE YOUNG PROTAGONISTS

Captain Garry Forbes (30), ('the Gargoyle'), son of the timid Benjamin Forbes who was half-brother to Barbara Paterson. Wounded in the trenches of the First World War.

Miss Lindsay Lorimer (19), daughter of Andrew Lorimer; sister of Frank, who served in the war with Garry Forbes.

Miss Louisa (Louie) Morgan (35), at Uplands, daughter of the previous minister at Fetter-Rothnie. Louie claims to be engaged to David Grey, Garry Forbes's engineer friend, who died of T.B.

THE LADIES AT THE WEATHERHOUSE

Aunt Craigmyle (Lang Leeb) (90+), cousin to Andrew Lorimer, the solicitor father of Lindsay and Frank. Widowed at 54, Leeb retired to the Weatherhouse and left things to her three daughters, namely:

Miss Annie Dyce (Paradise) Craigmyle, raised by her father to look after the farm, she took charge of it when he died until crippled by rheumatism.

Mrs Ellen (Nell) Falconer (60), married at 27 to Charlie Falconer who died in poverty, leaving Ellen to return to her old home along with her daughter, *Kate Falconer* (30), cook at a nearby convalescent hospital.

Miss Theresa (Tris) Craigmyle, Leeb's youngest daughter, housekeeper to her mother and sisters at the Weatherhouse.

FROM THE NEIGHBOURHOOD

Miss Barbara (Bawbie) Paterson (55), of Knapperley, maiden aunt to Garry Forbes.

Francie Ferguson, son to Jeames Ferguson who helped adapt the Weatherhouse; brother to 'Feel Weelum', finally husband (after 22 years engagement) to 'Peter Sandy's Bell', already father to her children, Stella Dagmar and Sidney Archibald Eric.

Mrs Barbara Hunter, of Craggie, ex servant girl and friend to Bawbie Paterson at Knapperley; wife of crofter Jake Hunter; mother of Dave, who returns wounded from the war to re-educate himself as a graduate and a school teacher.

Jonathan Bannochie, cobbler to trade, originator of the phrase 'Garry Forbes and his twa fools', referring to Garry, Bawbie and Francie.

The Prologue

The name of Garry Forbes has passed into proverb in Fetter-Rothnie.

One sees him gaunt, competent, a trifle anxious, the big fleshy ears standing out from his head, the two furrows cutting deeply round from nostril to chin, his hands powerful but squat, gift of a plebeian grandfather, and often grimed with oil and grease—hardly a figure of romance. Of those who know him, to some he is a keen, long-headed manager, with a stiff record behind him in the training of ex-service men and the juvenile unemployed, tenacious, taciturn, reliable, with uncanny reserves of knowledge; to others, a rampageous Socialist blustering out disaster, a frequenter of meetings: they add a hint of property (some say expectations) in Scotland; to some he is merely another of those confounded Scotch engineers; but to none is he a legend. They are not to know that in Fetter-Rothnie, where the tall, narrow, ugly house of Knapperley is situate, his name has already become a symbol.

You would need Garry Forbes to you. It is the local way of telling your man he is a liar. And when they deride you, scoffing at your lack of common sense, *Hine up on the head of the house like Garry Forbes and his twa fools*, is the accepted phrase. As the ladies at the Weatherhouse said, A byword and a laughing stock to the place. And married into the family, too!

ONE

To the Lorimers of a younger generation, children of the three Lorimer brothers who had played in the walled manse garden with the three Craigmyle girls, the Weatherhouse

was a place of pleasant dalliance. It meant day-long summer visits, toilsome uphill July walks that ended in the cool
peace of the Weatherhouse parlour, with home-brewed gin-
ger beer for refreshment, girdle scones and strawberry jam
and butter biscuits, and old Aunt Leeb seated in her corner
with her spider-fine white lace cap, piercing eyes and curious staves of song; then the eager rush for the open, the
bickering around the old sundial, the race for the moor;
and a sense of endless daylight, of enormous space, of a
world lifted up beyond the concerns of common time; and
eggs for tea, in polished wooden egg-cups that were right
end up either way; and queer fascinating things such as
one saw in no other house—the kettle holder with the
black cross-stitch kettle worked upon it, framed samplers
on the walls, the goffering iron, the spinning wheel. And
sometimes Paradise would show them how the goffering
iron was worked.

Paradise, indeed, gave a flavouring to a Weatherhouse
day that none of the other ladies could offer. Round her
clung still the recollection of older, rarer visits, when they
were smaller and she not yet a cripple; of the splendid
abounding wonder that inhabits a farm. Not a Lorimer
but associated the thought of Paradise with chickens newly
broken from the shell, ducks worrying with their flat bills
in the grass; with dark, half-known, sweet-smelling corners in the barn, and the yielding, sliding, scratching feel
of hay; with the steep wooden stair to the stable-loft and
the sound of the big, patient, clumsy horses moving and
munching below, a rattle of harness, the sudden nosing
of a dog; with the swish of milk in the pail and the
sharp delightful terror as the great tufted tail swung and
lashed; with the smell of oatcakes browning, the plod of
the churn and its changing note of triumph, and the wide,
shallow basins set with gleaming milk; with the whirr of
the reaper, the half-comprehended excitement of harvest,
the binding, the shining stooks; with the wild madness
of the last uncut patch, the trapped and furtive things one
watched in a delirium of joy and revulsion; and the comfort, afterwards, of gathering eggs, safe, smooth and warm
against the palm.

Of that need for comfort Paradise herself had no comprehension. Rats, rabbits and weakly chicks were killed as
a matter of course. There was no false sentiment about Miss
Annie: nothing flimsy. She was hard-knit, like a home-
made worsted stocking, substantial, honest and durable.
'A cauff bed tied in the middle,' her sister Theresa said
rudely of her in her later years, when inactivity had turned
her flabby; but at the farm one remembered her as being
everywhere.

It was Andrew Lorimer, her cousin, who transformed
her baptismal name of Annie Dyce to Paradise, and now
his children and his brothers' children scarcely knew her by
another. Not that Miss Annie cared! 'I'm as much of Paradise as you are like to see, my lad,' she used to tell him.

The four ladies at the Weatherhouse, old Aunt Craigmyle
and her daughters, could epitomise the countryside among
them in their stories. Paradise knew how things were done;
she told of ancient customs, of fairs and cattle markets and
all the processes of a life whose principle is in the fields. The
tales of Aunt Craigmyle herself had a fiercer quality; all the
old balladry, the romance of wild and unscrupulous deeds,
fell from her thin and shapely lips. And if she did not tell
a tale, she sang. She was always singing. Ballads were the
natural food of her mind. John, the second of the three
Lorimer brothers, said of her, when the old lady attained
her ninetieth birthday, 'She'll live to be a hundred yet, and
attribute it to singing nothing but ballads all her life.'

Cousin Theresa cared more for what the folk of her
own day did—matter of little moment to the children.
But she had, too, the grisly tales: of the body-snatchers
at Drum and the rescue by the grimy blacksmith on his
skelping mare; of Malcolm Gillespie, best-hated of excise-
men, and the ill end he came by on the gallows, and of the
whisky driven glumly past him in a hearse. To Cousin Ellen
the children paid less heed; though they laughed (as she
laughed herself) at her funny headlong habit of suggesting
conclusions to every half-told tale she heard. Cousins Annie
or Theresa would say, 'Oh, yes, of course Nell must know all
about it!' and she would laugh with them and answer, 'Yes,
there I am again.' But sometimes she would bite her lip and

look annoyed. It was she too, who said, out on the moor, 'Look, you can see Ben A'an today—that faint blue line,' or talked queer talk about the Druid stones. But these were horizons too distant for childish minds. It was pleasanter to hear again the familiar story of how the Weatherhouse came to be built.

Mrs Craigmyle at fifty four, widowed but unperturbed, announced to her unmarried daughters that she was done with the farm: Annie could keep it if she liked—which Annie did. Theresa and her mother would live free. Theresa was not ill-pleased, when it became apparent that she was to be mistress of the new home. Theresa could never understand her mother's idle humour. The grace of irresponsibility was beyond her. But Mrs Craigmyle, whose straight high shoulders and legs of swinging length had earned her the family by-name of Lang Leeb, had been a wild limb, with her mind more on balladry than on butter; and her father, the Reverend Andrew, was thankful when he got her safely married into the douce Craigmyle clan. She had made James Craigmyle an excellent wife; but at fifty four was quite content to let the excellence follow the wifehood.

'We'll go to town, I suppose,' said Theresa, who liked company.

'Fient a town. We'll go to Andra Findlater's place.'

Annie and Theresa stared.

Andra Findlater was a distant cousin of their mother, dead long since. A stonemason to trade, he had lived in a two-roomed cottage on the edge of their own farmlands. When his daughters were seven and eight years old, Mrs Findlater decided that she wanted the ben-end kept clear of their muck; and Andra had knocked a hole in the back wall and built them a room for themselves: a delicious room, low-roofed and with a window set slanting.

'But if I could big a bit mair—' Andra kept thinking. Another but-and-ben stood back from theirs, its own length away and just out of line with the new room—now what could a man do with that were he to join them up? Be it understood that Andra Findlater had no prospect of being able to join them up; but the problem of how to make the

houses one absorbed him to his dying day. It helped, indeed,
to bring about his death; for Andra would lean against a
spruce tree for hours of an evening, smoking his pipe and
considering the lie of the buildings. He leaned one raw
March night till he caught cold; and died of pneumonia.

Lang Leeb, as mistress of the big square farmhouse, had
always time for a *newse* with her poor relations. She relished
Andra. Many an evening she dandered across the fields, in
her black silk apron and with her *shank* in her hands, to
listen to his brooding projects. She loved the site of the
red-tiled cottages, set high, almost on the crest of the long
ridge; she loved the slanting window of the built-out room.
A month after her husband's death she dandered down the
field one day and asked the occupant of the cottage to let her
see the little room again. 'It's a gey soster,' said she. 'The
cat's just kittled in't.' Lang Leeb went home and told her
daughters she was henceforth to live at Andra Findlater's
place; and her daughters stared.

But Leeb knew what she was doing. She took the cottages
and joined them. Andra's problem was, after all, easy
enough to solve. She had money: a useful adjunct to
brains. She knocked out the partition of Andra's original
home and made of it a long living-room with a glass door to
the garden; and between the two cottages, with the girls'
old bedroom for corridor, she built a quaint irregular hexa-
gon, with an upper storey that contained one plain bedroom
and one that was all corners and windows—an elfin incon-
sequential room, using up odd scraps of space.

The whole was roofed with mellowed tiles. None of your
crude new colourings for Leeb. She went up and down the
country till she had collected all she required, from barns
and byres and outhouses. Leeb knew how to obtain what
she wanted. She came back possessed of three or four quern
stones, a cruisie lamp and a tirl-the-pin; and from the farm
she brought the spinning wheel and the old wooden dresser
and plate racks.

The place grew quaint and rare both out of doors and
in. One morning Leeb contemplated the low vestibule that
had been a bedroom, humming the gay little verse it often
brought to her mind:

The grey cat's kittled in Charley's wig,
There's ane o' them livin' an' twa o' them deid.

'Now this should be part of the living-room,' said she.
'It's dark and awkward as a passage. We'll have it so—and
so.'

She knew exactly what she wanted done, and gave her
orders; but the workman sent to her reported back some
three hours later with instructions not to return.

'But what have you against the man?' his master asked.

'I've nothing against him, forbye that he's blind, and
he canna see.'

She refused another man; but one day she called Jeames
Ferguson in from the garden. Jeames was a wonder with his
hands. He had set up the sundial, laid the crazy paving, and
constructed stone stalks to the querns, some curved, some
tapering, some squat, that made them look like monstrous
mushrooms. 'Could you do *that*, Jeames?' 'Fine that.'
Jeames did it, and was promptly dismissed to the garden,
for his clumps of boots were ill-placed in the house. Mrs
Craigmyle did the finishing herself and rearranged her curious possessions. Some weeks later Jeames, receiving orders
beside the glass door, suddenly observed, 'I hinna seen't sin'
it was finished,' and strode on to the Persian rug with his
dubbit and tacketty boots. But no Persian rug did Jeames
see. Folding his arms, he beamed all over his honest face
and contemplated his own handiwork.

'That's a fine bit o' work, ay is it,' he said at last.

'You couldn't be angered at the body. He was that
fine pleased with himself,' said Mrs Craigmyle.

But the house once to her mind, Mrs Craigmyle did no
more work. Dismissing her husband in a phrase, 'He was a
moral man—I can say no more,' she sat down with a careless
ease in the Weatherhouse and gathered her chapbooks and
broadsheets around her:

Songs, Bibles, Psalm-books and the like,
As mony as would big a dyke—

though, to be sure, daughter of the manse as she was,
the Bible had scanty place in her heap of books. *Whistle
Binkie* was her Shorter Catechism. She gave all her household dignity for an old song: sometimes her honour and

kindliness as well; for Leeb treated the life around her as though it were already ballad. She relished it, but having ceased herself to feel, seemed to have forgotten that others felt. She grew hardly visibly older, retaining to old age her erect carriage and the colour and texture of her skin. Her face was without blemish, her hands were delicate; only the long legs, as Kate Falconer could have told, were brown with fern-tickles. Kate had watched so often, with a child's fascinated stare, her grandmother washing her feet in a tin basin on the kitchen floor. Kate grew up believing that her grandmother ran barefoot among tall bracken when she was young; and probably Kate was right.

So Lang Leeb detached herself from active living. Once a year she made an expedition to town, and visited in turn the homes of her three Lorimer nephews. She carried on these occasions a huge pot of jam, which she called 'the berries'; and having ladled out the Andrew Lorimers' portion with a wooden spoon, replaced the pot in her basket and bore it to the Roberts and the Johns. For the rest, she sat aside and chuckled. Life is an entertainment hard to beat when one's affections are not engaged. Theresa managed the house and throve on it, having found too little scope at the farm for her masterful temper. Her mother let her be, treating even her craze for acquisition with an ironic indulgence. Already with the things they had brought from the farm the house was full. But Theresa never missed a chance to add to her possessions. She had a passion for roups. 'A ga'in foot's aye gettin',' she said.

'She's like Robbie Welsh the hangman,' Lang Leeb would chuckle, 'must have a fish out of ilka creel.' And when Mrs Hunter told Jonathan Bannochie the souter, a noted hater of women, that Miss Theresa was at the Wastride roup, 'and up and awa wi' her oxter full o' stuff,' she was said to have added, 'They would need a displenish themsels in yon hoose, let alane bringin' mair in by.' 'Displenish,' snorted Jonathan. 'Displenish, said ye? It's a roup o' the fowk that's needed there.'

Miss Annie too, when she gave up the farm brought part of her plenishing. Ellen was the only one who brought nothing to the household gear. Ellen brought nothing but her child; and there was nowhere to put her but the daft room at the head of the stairs that Theresa had been using for lumber.

'It's a mad-like place,' Theresa said. 'Nothing but a trap for dust. But you won't take a Finnan haddie in a Hielan' burnie. She's no way to come but this, and she'll just need to be doing with it. She's swallowed the cow and needn't choke at the tail.'

Ellen did not choke. She loved the many-cornered room with its irregular windows. There she shut herself in as to a tower and was safe; or rather, she felt, shut herself out from the rest of the house. The room seemed not to end with itself, but through its protruding windows became part of the infinite world. There she lay and watched the stars; saw dawn touch the mountains; and fortified her soul in the darkness that had come on her.

TWO

Of the three Craigmyle sisters, Ellen was the likest to her mother. She too was long and lean, though she had not her mother's delicacy of fingers and of skin; and to Ellen alone among her daughters Mrs Craigmyle had bequeathed the wild Lorimer heart.

How wild it was not even the girl herself had discovered, when at twenty seven she married Charley Falconer. There was no opposition to the match, though Falconer was a stranger; well-doing apparently; quiet and assured: which the family took to mean reliable, and Ellen, profound. Her life had hitherto been hard and rigid; her father, James Craigmyle, kept his whole household to the plough; not from any love of tyranny, but because he had never conceived of a life other than strait and laborious. To work in sweat was man's natural heritage. His wife obeyed him and bided her time; Ellen obeyed, and escaped in thought to a fantastic world of her own imagining. The merest hint of a tale sufficed her, her fancy was off. Her choicest hours were spent in unreality—a land where others act in accordance with one's expectations. Sometimes her toppling palaces would crash at the touch of the actual, and then she suffered an agony of remorse because the real Ellen was so unlike the Ellen of her fancies. 'There I am again—I mustn't pretend these silly things,' she would say; and taking her Bible she would read the verse that she had marked for her own especial scourging: 'Casting down imaginations and every high thing that exalteth itself against the knowledge of God, and bringing into captivity every thought to the obedience of Christ.' For a day or two she would sternly dismiss each fleeting suggestion of fiction, striving to empty a mind that was naturally quick and receptive, and finding the plain sobriety of a Craigmyle regimen inadequate to fill it. Shortly she was 'telling herself stories' again. It might be wicked, but it made life radiant.

Concerning Charley Falconer she told herself an endless story. The tragedy of her brief married life lay in the clash between her story and the truth. Charley was very ordinary and a little cheap. He dragged her miserably from one lodging to another, unstable, but with a certain large indifference to his own interests that exposed his memory to Craigmyle and Lorimer contempt, when at his death Ellen could no longer deny how poor she was.

She came back to her mother's house, dependent, the more so that she had a child; at bitter variance with herself. She had been forced up against a grinding poverty, a shallow nature and a life without dignity. By the time she returned home her father was dead, the Weatherhouse built and Theresa comfortably settled as its genius. Ellen found herself tolerated. Power was too sweet to this youngest sister who had had none: the widowed and deprived was put in her place. Since that place was the odd-shaped upstairs room, Ellen did not grumble; but Theresa's management made it perhaps a trifle harder for her to come to terms with the world. Her own subordinate position in the house was subtly a temptation: it sent her back to refuge in her imaginings. After a time the rancour and indignity of her married years faded out. She thought she was experienced in life, but in truth she had assimilated nothing from her suffering, only dismissed it and returned to her dreams.

Two things above all restored her—her child and the country. It was a country that liberated. More than half

the world was sky. The coastline vanished at one of the
four corners of the earth, Ellen lost herself in its immensity.
It wiled her from thought.

Kate also took her from herself. She was not a clever
child, neither quaint nor original nor *ill-trickit*; but never out of humour. She asked nothing much from life—too
easily satisfied, her mother thought, without what she could
not have. Ellen, arguing from her own history, had schooled
herself to meet the girl's inevitable revolt, her demand for
her own way of living. But Kate at thirty had not yet revolted. She had wanted nothing that was not to her hand.
She had no ambition after a career, higher education did not
interest her, she questioned neither life nor her own right to
relish it. Had she not been brought up among Craigmyles,
their quiet domesticity was what she would have fancied.
She liked making a bed and contriving a dinner; and since
she must earn her living she took a Diploma in Domestic
Science and had held several posts as housekeeper or school
matron; but late in 1917 she entered (to the regret of
some of her relations) upon voluntary work in a Hospital, becoming cook in a convalescent Hospital not far from
her home.

Ellen had therefore carried for nearly thirty years the
conviction that she had tested life; and mastered it.

At sixty she was curiously young. Her body was strong
and supple, her face tanned, a warm glow beneath the tan.
She walked much alone upon the moors, walking heel first
to the ground with a firm and elastic tread. Her eyes
were young; by cause both of their brightness and of
their dreaming look. No experience was in their glance.
She knew remote and unspeakable things—the passage
of winds, the trembling of the morning star, the ecstasy
of February nights when all the streams are murmuring.
She did not know human pain and danger. She thought
she did, but the pain she knew was only her own quivering
hurt. Her world was all her own, she its centre and inter-
pretation; and she had even a faint sweet contempt for
those who could not enter it. The world and its modes
passed by and she ignored them. She was a little proud of
her indifference to fashion and chid her sister Theresa for

liking a modish gown. She saw—as who could have helped seeing—the external changes that marked life during the thirty years she had lived in the Weatherhouse: motor cars, the shortening skirt, the vacuum cleaner; but of the profounder revolutions, the change in temper of a generation, the altered point of balance of the world's knowledge, the press of passions other than individual and domestic, she was completely unaware.

Insensibly as these thirty years passed she allowed her old fashion to grow on her. Fancy was her tower of refuge. Like any green girl she pictured her futures by the score. After a time she took the habit of her imaginary worlds so strongly that hints of their presence dropped out in her talk, and when she was laughed at she would laugh or be offended according to the vehemence with which she had created; but among the gentle scoffers none guessed the ravishment her creations brought her, and none the mortified despair of her occasional revulsions from her fairyland.

It did not occur to her that when Lindsay Lorimer came to Fetter-Rothnie her fairyland would vanish into smoke.

Lindsay came to stay at the Weatherhouse on this wise: her mother, Mrs Andrew Lorimer, arrived one day in perturbation.

'We don't know what to do with Lindsay,' she confessed. 'If you would let her come here for a little—? We thought perhaps the change—and away from the others. These boys do tease her so. They can't see that she's ill.'

'She's ill, is she?' said Theresa. 'And what ails her, then?'

Mrs Andrew took some time to make it clear that Lindsay's sickness was of the temper.

'Not that we have anything against him,' she said. 'He's an excellent young man—most gentlemanly. When he likes. But she's so young. Nineteen. Her father won't hear of it. "All nonsense too young," he says. But I suppose she keeps thinking, well, and if he doesn't come back. It's this war that does it.'

'It's time it were put a stop to,' said Miss Annie.

'Yes,' sighed Mrs Andrew. 'And let things be as they were.'

'But they won't be, said Ellen.

'No,' she answered. 'Frank'll never go to college now. He swears he won't go to the University and won't. And it's all this Captain Dalgarno. It's Dalgarno this and Dalgarno that. Frank's under him, you know. I wonder what the Captain means by it. He's contaminating Frank. Putting ideas into his head. He was only a schoolboy when it began, you must remember—hadn't had time to have his mind formed. And now he swears he won't go to the University and won't enter a profession. All my family have been in the professions.'

She sighed again.

'He wants to *do* things, he says. Things with his hands. Make things. "Good heavens, mother," he said to me, just his last leave—the Captain was home with him on his last leave, you know; it was then that Lindsay and he wanted to get married, and her father just wouldn't have it. "Good heavens mother, we've *un*-made enough, surely, in these three and a half years. I want to make something now. *You* haven't seen the ruined villages. The world will get on very well without the law and the Church for a considerable time to come," he said, "but it's going to be jolly much in need of engineers and carpenters." Make chairs and tables, that seems to be his idea. "Even if I could make one table to stand fast on its feet, I'd be happy. I won't belong to a privileged class," he said. "There aren't privileges. There's only the privilege of working." It *sounds* all right, of course, and I'm sure we all feel for the working man. But if Lindsay marries him I don't know what we shall all come to.'

Mrs Craigmyle, attentive in the corner, began to hum. No one of course heeded her. She sang a stave through any business that was afoot. She sang now, the hum developing to words:

Wash weel the fresh fish, wash weel the fresh fish,
Wash weel the fresh fish and skim weel the bree,
For there's mony a foul-fittit thing,
There's mony a foul-fittit thing in the saut sea.

And Ellen's anger suddenly flared. A natural song enough for one whose home looked down on the coast villages of Finnan and Portlendie; but it was Ellen the dreamer, not the sagacious Annie or Theresa, who had read in her mother that the old lady's was an intelligent indifference to life. She took no sides, an ironic commentator. Two and thirty years of Craigmyle wedlock had tamed her natural wildness of action to an impudence of thought that relished its own dainty morsels by itself. Her cruelties came from comprehension, not from lack of it. And had not Mrs Andrew said the word? 'Contaminating,' she had said. Ellen did well to be angry. She was angry on behalf of this young girl the secret of whose love was bandied thus among contemptuous women.

'But I know, I know, I understand,' she thought. 'I must help her, be her friend.' Already her fancy was off. She had climbed her tower and saw herself in radiant light, creating Lindsay's destiny.

She looked from under bent brows at her mother, who continued to sing, with a remote and airy grace, her long fine fingers folded in her lap. She sat very erect and looked at no one, lost apparently in her song. Ellen relaxed her frown, but remained gazing at the singer, falling unconsciously into the same attitude as her mother, and the singular resemblance between the two faces became apparent, both intent, both strangely innocent, the old lady's by reason of its much withdrawn, Ellen's from the enthusiasm of solitary dreaming that hedged her about from reality.

THE DRAMA

ONE

Proposal for a Party

Miss Theresa Craigmyle opened the kitchen door in response to the knock, and saw Francie Ferguson holding a bag of potatoes in his arms.

'Ay, ay, Francie,' she said, 'you've brought the tatties. Who would have thought, now, there would be such a frost and us not to have a tattie out of the pit? It was a mercy you had some up.'

'O ay,' said Francie, 'and the frost's haudin'. There's the smell o' snaw in the air. It'll be dingin' on afore ye ken yersel.'

Miss Theresa took the potatoes, saying cheerily, 'And a fine big bag you've given us, Francie. But you were aye the one for a bittie by the bargain.'

Francie shuffled to the other foot and rubbed a hand upon his thigh.

'Well, ye like to be honest, but ye canna be ower honest or ye'd hae naething to yersel.' He added, spreading a dirty paw against the door-jamb, 'The missus is to her bed.'

'Oh,' said Miss Theresa. She said it tartly. The bag poised in her arms, she was judicially considering its weight. 'Not so heavy, after all,' she thought. Francie's way had formerly been, 'I just put in a puckle by guess like.' He hadn't been long at the school, he said, wasn't used with your weights and measures. But his lavishness, Miss Theresa could see, was receiving a check: beyond a doubt the work of the *missus*. Miss Theresa was not disposed to sympathy. 'She's a din-raising baggage,' she reflected, and heard Francie out with a face as set as the frost.

Francie was grumbling heartily at life. He knew fine that the potatoes were scanty measure. He did not confess it, of course, but since Miss Theresa was sure to discover,

he detailed the mitigating circumstances: a sick wife, a
cow gone dry, forty barren besoms of hens and a daughter
soft-hearted to the point of letting all the rabbits off the
snares—ay, and giving them a bit of her *piece*, no less, any
one that looked pitiful at her. Francie had remonstrated, of
course, but might as well speak to the wind blowing by. 'A
gey-like swippert o' a queyne, she is that,' he said, not without a certain conscious pride. And meat-whole, he added,
'They're a' that—the wife as weel.'

'She would be,' said Miss Theresa. 'She's about stotting
off the ground with fat. And what is't that ails her, like?'

Francie laboured to explain.

'Oh, a stoun' of love,' said Miss Theresa shortly. 'It'll
have come out at the wrong place. Wait you.' And laying
down the potatoes, she brought a good-sized pudding from
the pantry and thrust it on Francie.

'You can't take that before the court and swear to it
that you're hungered,' she said, and shut the door on him.

In the parlour she repeated the conversation.

'He does all the cooking himself, he tells me. I wouldn't
be any curious about eating it. He stewed a rabbit. "It was
gey tough," he says, "it gart your jaws wonder." '

'Fancy the little girl and the rabbits,' cried Lindsay.
'That's the child we saw yesterday, isn't it, Katie? With
the coal-black eyes. She looked a mischief! She's not
like her father, anyway. You'd never suppose she was his
daughter.'

'You never would, for the easy reason that she's not.'

'I'm glad to see he calls her his daughter, it's kindly
of the body.'

'What other could he do? You can't give a gift a clyte
in the mouth, and the bairns were her marriage gift to the
craitur, as you might say.'

'They looked so neglected, these children,' cried Lindsay.
'And with their mother ill. Couldn't we give them a party?
They can't have had much of a Christmas.'

'Oh, party away at them,' conceded Theresa. 'Would
you really like it, Lindsay?'

Lindsay was aglow with eagerness. 'And a Christmas
tree?' she said. 'Oh, I know it's January now, but I

don't believe they've ever seen a tree. One of those big
spruce branches would do.' She was given over entirely to
her excitement. A mere child, thought Theresa. Well, and
here was a change of countenance from the earlier days. The
affair could not mean much when she threw it off so easily.
The pale and moody Lindsay who had gone wanly about the
house on her arrival, displeased Miss Theresa, who disliked
a piner. Like many robust people, she resented the presence
of suffering; pain, physical or mental, was an inconven-
ience that she preferred not to see. A Lindsay absorbed
in trifling with a Christmas tree was a relief Miss Theresa
might well afford herself; and she afforded it with grace.

'Have you time, Kate,' she asked of her niece Kate
Falconer, who was spending her hour of leave at home,
'to go round on your way back to the Hospital and bid
them come?'

'Why, yes,' said Kate, 'if we start at once. You come
too, Linny.'

'Go in by to Craggie,' pursued Miss Theresa, 'and bid
Mrs Hunter too. We've been meaning to have her to tea
this while back. She'll be grand pleased at the tree. She's
like a bairn when you give her a thing.'

Kate went to make ready, and Lindsay would have followed; but as she passed, her grand-aunt detained her with
a look. Mrs Craigmyle had few gestures; she held herself
still; only her eyes glittered and her lips moved, and often
her fingers went to and fro as she knitted—a spider stillness.
The film of delicate lace upon hair as fine as itself was
not the only thing about her that betokened the spider.
One had the sense of being caught upon a look, lured in
and held.

Lindsay drew up to her, and stood.

'So, so, you are to turn my house into a market, Leezie
Lindsay?'

'Why do you call me that, Aunt Leeb?'

Lang Leeb sang from the old ballad.

'Surely you know,' she said, 'that Leezie Lindsay came
to Kingcausie with that braw lad she ran away with, and
it's not far from Kingcausie that you've come, Mistress
Lindsay.'

The scarlet rushed on Lindsay's brow and stood in splatches over neck and chin.

She pushed back her mop of curls and stared at the old woman; and her words seemed to be drawn from her without her will.

'Kingcausie? That's—isn't that the place among trees, a line of beeches and then some scraggy firs? Beyond the Tower there.'

'Hoots! Never a bit. That's Knapperley. Daft Bawbie Paterson's place. Kingcausie lies to the river.'

The scarlet had deepened on Lindsay's throat. 'Have I given myself away?' she was thinking.

She had discovered what she had wanted to know since ever she came to Fetter-Rothnie. Often as she had visited the Weatherhouse, she had not stayed there, and its surroundings were unfamiliar. It had seemed so easy, in imagination, when she walked with Kate, to ask it in a careless way, 'Isn't that Knapperley over there, Katie?' or 'What place is that among the trees?' But when the moment came her heart had thumped too wildly; she was not strong enough to ask. Now that she knew she sheered off nervously from the subject, as though to linger were deadly. And she plunged, 'But why a market, Aunt Leeb? I'm sure we shan't be very rowdy.'

'A lot you know about the fisher folk, if that's your way of thinking. It was them that cracked the Marykirk bell, jingle-janglin' for a burying.'

'But they're not fisher folk here—Francie?'

'She is.'

And Lindsay, because she was afraid to hear further of the lady who had brought the black-eyed bairns as a wedding gift to her husband, glanced rapidly around, and saw Mrs Falconer put her head in at the door and look at them. There was something pathetic about Cousin Ellen, Lindsay thought—her straying gaze, her muttering to herself. A poor old thing. And what was she wanting now, watching them both like that?

A poor young thing, Ellen was thinking. She must protect her from her mother's sly and studied jests. So she said, 'Kate must be off, Linny,' and the girl fled gladly.

Francie was shouting a lusty song as he worked:

I'll never forget till the day that I dee
The lumps o' fat my granny gied me,
The heids o' herrin' an' tails o'cats—

He broke off abruptly and cried, 'Are ye cleanin' yersels, littlins? Here's ladies to see you.'

The children hove in sight, drying their half-washed hands on opposite ends of a towel. Bold-eyed youngsters, with an address unusual in country bairns. Each hurried to complete the drying first and so be saved from putting away the towel; and both dropping it at one moment, it fell in a heap. The children began to quarrel noisily.

'Put you it by, Stellicky,' said the man, who stood watching the bickering bairns for awhile with every appearance of content. Francie had a soft foolish kindly face, and while the girl, with black looks, did as she was bidden, he swung the loonie to his shoulder and said, 'He's a gey bit birkie, isna he, to be but five year auld?'

'And how's the wife?' said Kate.

Francie confided in her that whiles she took a tig, and he thought it was maybe no more than that.

'They were only married in August,' said Kate, laughing, as the girls followed a field path away from the croft.

'Oh, look,' cried Lindsay. 'A bramble leaf still. Blood-red.'

'So it is,' Kate replied. 'And engaged for over twenty years.'

'I don't particularly want to hear about it, Katie.'

'But why,' said Kate, 'it's an entertaining tale.'

And she began to relate it.

Francie was son to old Jeames Ferguson, who had helped to make the Weatherhouse; and Francie's taking of a wife had been a seven days' speak in Fetter-Rothnie. He had been betrothed for two and twenty years. All the country-side knew of the betrothal, but that it should end in marriage was a surprise for which the gossips were not prepared. A joke, too. A better joke, as it turned out, than they had anticipated.

The two and twenty years of waiting were due to Francie's brother Weelum. Weelum in boyhood had discovered an astounding aptitude for craftsmanship. He had been apprenticed to a painter in Peterkirk, and in course became a journeyman. From that day on Francie referred invariably to his brother as 'The Journeyman.' Weelum's name was never heard to cross his lips; he remained 'The Journeyman,' though he did not remain a painter.

Weelum's career as a journeyman was mute and inglorious. He was a taciturn man: he wasted no words; and when his master's clients gave orders about the detail of the work he undertook he would listen with an intent, intelligent expression, and reply with a grave and considering nod. Afterwards he did exactly what he pleased. Folk complained. Weelum continued to do what he pleased. In the end his master dismissed him; reluctantly, for he had clever hands.

He established himself with Francie. There was not work on the croft for two men; but as there was no woman on it, Weelum took possession of the domestic affairs. He did what he pleased there too, and made much to-do about his industry. Francie could not see that there was much result from it all. 'He's eident, but he doesna win through,' he would sometimes say sorrowfully. 'Feel Weelum,' the folk called him. 'Oh, nae sae feel,' said Jonathan Bannochie the souter. 'He kens gey weel whaur his pottage bickers best.' To Francie he was still 'The Journeyman.'

When Weelum came home to bide, Francie was already contracted to a lassie in the fishing village of Bargie, some twenty miles away, down the coast. A bonny bit lass, but her folk were terrible tinks; they had the name of being the worst tinks in Bargie. Weelum had some family pride, if Francie had none, and there were bitter words between the brothers. The Journeyman set his face implacably against the marriage, and stood aggrieved and silent when Francie tried to thresh the matter out. 'He has ower good a downsit, and he kens it,' said the folk. Francie's respect for his brother was profound. On the Sunday afternoons when he cycled across to Bargie, he would slink out in silence by the back way from his own house. One Sunday the brothers came to high words. Francie mounted his cycle,

and trusted—as he always did trust—that all would be well
on his return. That Weelum did not speak on his return
gave him no anxiety: Weelum often *stunkit* at him and
kept silence for days. But this time Weelum kept silence
for ever. He never again addressed a word to his brother,
though he remained under his roof, eating of his bread,
for over twenty years. Through all that time the brothers
slept in the same bed, rising each in the morning to his
separate tasks.

One afternoon the Journeyman fell over with a stroke.
That was an end to the hope of his speaking. 'I some think
he would have liked to say something,' Francie declared.
He climbed in beside his brother to the one bed the room
contained, and wakened in the hour before dawn *geal cauld*
to find the Journeyman dead beside him.

Some months later Francie was cried in the kirk. A
burr of excitement ran through the congregation. So the
Bargie woman had waited for him! When the day of the
wedding came, Francie set out in the early morning, with
the old mare harnessed to the farm cart.

'Take her on the hin step o' yer bike, Francie, man,' cried
one of the bystanders. 'That would be mair gallivantin' like
than the cairt.'

'There's her bits o' things to fesh,' Francie answered.

'She'll hae some chairs an' thingies,' said the neighbours. 'The hoosie'll nae be oot o' the need o' them. It's
terrible bare.'

Francie had not dreamed of a reception; but when, late
in the evening, the bridal journey ended and the cart turned
soberly up the cart-road to the croft, he found a crowd about
his doors.

Francie bartered words with no man. He handed out
his bride, and after her one bairn, and then another; and
then a bundle tied up in a Turkey counterpane. The bride
and the bairns went in, and Francie shut the door on them;
and turned back to tend his mare.

'She'll hae been a weeda, Francie?' said Jonathan Bannochie. A titter ran round the company.

Francie unharnessed the mare.

'Weel, nae exactly a weeda,' he said in his slow way;

and led the mare to stable.

Next morning he harnessed her again and jogged in the old cart to town. All Fetter-Rothnie watched him come home with a brand-new iron bedstead in the cart. 'For the bairns,' they said. 'He might have made less do with them.' But the bed was not for the bairns.

'Aunt Tris was the first of us to see her,' Kate told Lindsay. 'She invented an errand over. Aunt Tris would invent an errand to the deil himself, Granny says, if she wanted something from him. She came home and sat down and took off all her outdoor things before she would say a word. And then she said, "He was fond of fish before he fried the scrubber." She told us about the bed. "She won't even sleep with him," she told us. "Him and the laddie sleeps in the kitchen, and her and the lassie's got the room. It's six and sax, I'm thinking, for Francie, between the Journeyman and the wife." And she told us the bairns' names.'

The bairns' names were a diversion to Fetter-Rothnie. In a community that had hardly a dozen names amongst its folk, Francie's betrothed had been known as Peter's Sandy's Bell; but she was determined that her children should have individual names, and called the girl Stella Dagmar and the boy Sidney Archibald Eric. Bargie treated the names after its fashion. The children became Stellicky Dagmaricky and Peter's Sandy's Bellie's Sid.

'Granny sat and listened to Aunt Tris,' Kate continued. 'Licked her lips over it. Granny loves a tale. Particularly with a wicked streak. "A spectacle," she said, "a second Katherine Bran." Katherine Bran was somebody in a tale, I believe. And then she said, "You have your theatres and your picture palaces, you folk. You make a grand mistake." And she told us there was no spectacle like what's at our own doors. "Set her in the jougs and up on the faulters' stool with her, for fourteen Sabbaths, as they did with Katherine, and where's your picture palace then?" A *merry prank*, she called it. Well!— "The faulter's stool and a penny bridal," she said, "and you've spectacle to last you, I'se warren." Granny's very amusing when she begins with old tales.'

Lindsay's attention was flagging. 'Besides,' she thought,

'I don't like old tales. Nor this new one either.' They had come out of the wood on to a crossroad and the country was open for miles ahead.

'And that's Knapperley, is it, Katie?' she asked.

'Yes,' said Kate. 'But we don't go near it to get to Mrs Hunter's.'

TWO

The January Christmas Tree

Snow fell that night, and the night following, and the frost set harder than before. The guests were stamping at the doorstep, knocking off the snow that had frozen in translucent domes upon their heels, shaking their garments free from the glittering particles of ice that hung in them. The children eyed the house with awe, mingled in Stella Dagmar with disdain. 'It's a terrible slippery floor, I canna get traivelled,' she objected in the long, polished lobby. But the glories of the Christmas tree silenced criticism for awhile. Lindsay had made a very pretty thing of it; and when by and by she slipped from the room and Miss Theresa said ostentatiously, 'She's away to take a rest—she's been ill, you see,' the girl herself was as deliciously excited as any bairn. She giggled with pleasure as she draped an old crimson curtain round her and adjusted her Father Christmas beard. 'Now what all nonsense shall I say?' And she said it very well, disguising her voice and playing silly antics.

'My very toes is laughin',' Mrs Hunter declared.

The room grew hot, and Lindsay in her wrappings choked for air. She slid her hand behind the curtain that covered the glass door to the garden. But the door blew open at her touch. The wind and a woman entered together: a woman in the fifties, weathered and sinewy, clad in a rough, patched Lovat tweed and leggings caked with mud and battered snow. On her head sat a piece of curious finery that had been once a hat and from it dangled a trallop of dingy veiling.

'Bawbie Paterson,' cried Miss Theresa. 'Who would have expected that?'

Miss Paterson marched across the room.

26

'It's you I'm seekin', Barbara Hunter,' she announced. 'Will you send for Maggie? There's my lassie up and left me. The third one running. Will you send for Maggie? Maggie's the lass for me.'

'Barbara Paterson,' said Mrs Hunter, 'that I will not. Maggie's in a good place. I'd be black affronted to bid her up and awa'. And mair than that, Miss Barbara, nae lass o' mine'll ever be at your beck and ca'. Ye dinna feed your folk, Miss Barbara. I've seen my chickens hanging in to the bare wa's o' a cabbage as though they hadna seen meat this month an' mair, and your kitchen deemie, Barbara Paterson, had the same hungry e'e. Ye'll nae get Maggie.'

'And what am I to do wanting a kitchen lass?'

'Ye can tak the road an' run bits, Miss Barbara.'

'Since you are in my house, Bawbie Paterson,' said Miss Theresa, 'you'd better take a seat.'

'I'll not do that, Tris Craigmyle. You'd have me plotted with heat, would you? But I'll wait a whilie or I go in a lowe. And who might this be?' And she wheeled round to stare at Lindsay, who had dropped the curtain and was staring hard at her.

'A likely lass,' said Miss Barbara; and she clutched at Lindsay, who did not resist, but allowed herself to be drawn closer. 'And are you seeking a place? Can you cook a tattie? A' to dross?'

'Hoots, Miss Barbara,' cried Mrs Hunter, scandalised. 'That's nae a servant lass. That's Miss Lorimer—Andrew Lorimer the solicitor's daughter. Ye're nae at yersel.'

Lindsay's heart was beating fast. She said nothing, but stared at the great rough face above her. She had a feeling as though some huge elemental mass were towering over her, rock and earth, earthen smelling. Miss Barbara's tweeds had been sodden so long with the rains and matted with the dusts of her land, that they too seemed elemental. Her face was tufted with coarse black hairs, her naked hands that clutched the fabric of Lindsay's dress were hard, ingrained with black from wet wood and earth. 'She's not like a person, she's a thing,' Lindsay thought. The girl felt puny in her grasp, yet quite without fear, possessed instead by a strange exhilaration.

Held thus against Miss Barbara's person and clothes, the outdoor smell of which came strongly to the heat of the parlour, Lindsay, her senses sharpened by excitement, was keenly aware of an antagonism in the room: as though the fine self-respecting solidity of generations of Lorimers and Craigmyles, the measured and orderly dignity of their lives, won at some cost through centuries from their rude surroundings, resented this intrusion into their midst of an undisciplined and primitive force. The girl waited to hear what Miss Theresa would say, sure that it was Miss Theresa who would act spokesman against this earthy relic of an older age.

But before Miss Theresa could speak, Stella Dagmar, angry at her interrupted play and offended that no one noticed her, began a counting rhyme, running about among the women and slapping each in turn:

I count you out
For a dirty dish-clout.

Miss Theresa's wiry hands were on the culprit. 'A clout on the lug, that's what you would need. Francie hasn't his sorrow to seek.'

Stella dodged and screamed. The whole room was in an uproar. And suddenly Miss Barbara, loosening her grasp on Lindsay, broke into a bellow of laughter; and in a moment was gone.

Miss Theresa was scarlet in the face from fury.

'Saw you ever such an affront to put on a body?' she cried, cudgelling Stella to the rhythms of her anger. 'Coming into a body's house at a New Year time a sight like yon. Coming in at all, and her not bidden. And I'm sure you needn't all be making such a commotion now. You couldn't tell what's what nor wha's Jock's father.'

They were all talking together. Lindsay stood amazed. The voices became appallingly distinct, resounding in her very head; and the hot, lit room, the excited ladies in their rich apparel, burdened her. She wanted to run after Miss Barbara, to escape; and, picking up her crimson curtain, she said, 'I'll put this past.'

'I kent it was you all the time,' Stella flung at her. But Lindsay was already gone. She closed the door from the parlour and stood in the cold, still hall. Through the windows poured the light of full moon. And Lindsay had a vision of the white light flooding the world and gleaming on the snow, and of Miss Barbara convulsed with laughter in the middle of the gleam.

She threw the curtain about her, drew on a pair of galoshes, and ran into the night.

The night astonished her, so huge it was. She had the sense of escaping from the lit room into light itself. Light was everywhere: it gleamed from the whole surface of the earth, the moon poured it to the farthest quarters of heaven, round a third of the horizon the sea shimmered. The cold was intense. Lindsay's breath came quick and gasping. She ran through the spruce plantation and toiled up the field over snow that was matted in grass; and, reaching the crest, saw without interruption to the rims of the world. The matted snow and grass were solid enough beneath her feet, but when she looked beyond she felt that she must topple over into that reverberation of light. Her identity vanished. She was lost in light and space. When she moved on it surprised her that she stumbled with the rough going. She ought to have glided like light over an earth so insubstantial.

Then she saw Miss Barbara.

Miss Barbara Paterson came swinging up the field, treading surely and singing to herself. Her heavy bulk seemed to sail along the frozen surfaces, and when she reached the dyke she vaulted across it with an impatient snort.

'O wait for me!' Lindsay cried. She too was by the dyke, and would have leaped it, but was trammelled with her curtain.

'Wait for me,' she cried. 'I want to speak to you.'

But when Miss Barbara turned back, there was nothing she could find to say.

'Were you wanting over?' asked Miss Barbara. She leaned across the dyke, lifted the girl in her arms and swung her in the air. 'You're like the deil, you'll never hang, for you're as light 's a feather.'

'Oh, put me down. But I want to go with you. Will you show me Knapperley?'

'Ca' awa' then.' Miss Barbara, without further ado, made off up the top of a furrow, pushing the girl firmly along by the elbow. Lindsay kept her footing with difficulty, sinking ever and again in the deep snow that levelled the furrows. She wondered what her mother would think. It was like an escapade into space. Her safe and habitual life was leagues away.

Miss Barbara made no attempt to speak. They passed through a woodland and came out by a gap.

'There's Knapperley for you,' its owner said.

Lindsay stared. From every window of the tall narrow house there blazed a lamp. They blazed into the splendour of the night like a spurt of defiance.

'But the Zepps,' she gasped.

'They don't come this length.'

'But they do. One did. And anyway, the law.'

'That's to learn them to leave honest folks alone.'

A spasm of terror contracted Lindsay's heart. Miss Barbara had clambered on to the next dyke. She made little use of stile or gate, preferring always to go straight in the direction she desired. She stood there poised, keeping her footing with ease upon the icy stones, and pointed with an outstretched arm at the lights, a menacing figure. Then she bent as though to help Lindsay over.

'Will she lift me again?' thought the girl. The insecurity of her adventure rushed upon her.

'Will she kidnap me and make me her servant girl? But I couldn't live in a house with lights like that. There would be policemen if there weren't Zepps.'

She twisted herself out of reach of the descending hand and fled, trailing the scarlet curtain after her across the snow.

THREE

Knapperley

Meanwhile in the Weatherhouse parlour Mrs Hunter was discussing Miss Barbara.

'If she wasna Miss Barbara Paterson of Knapperley she would mak you roar. You would be handin' her a copper and speirin' if she wanted a piece.'

'O ay, she's fairly a Tinkler Tam,' said Miss Theresa. 'Coming into a body's house with that old tweed. But she hasn't any other, that's what it is.'

'That's where you're mistaken, Miss Craigmyle. She's gowns galore: silk gowns and satin gowns and ane with a velvet lappet. Kists stappit fu'. But whan does she wear them? That's the tickler. It's aye the auld Lovat tweed. And aye the black trallop hangin' down her back.'

'It's her only hat, that I can wager.'

'It or its marra. Wha would say? She bought it for a saxpence from a wifie at the door and trimmed it hersel' with yon wallopin' trash. "If you would do that to your hat, Barbara Hunter, it would be grander." "God forbid, Barbara Paterson, that I should ever wear a hat like that." But she's aye worn it sin' syne. Some says it's the same hat, and some says it's its marra and the auld ane gaes up the lum on a Sabbath night whan there's none to see.'

Mrs Hunter talked with enjoyment. She was entirely devoted to the spanking mare on whose land she and her husband held their croft, and entirely without compunction in her ridicule of Miss Barbara's departures from the normal. She liked to talk too—gamesome cordial talk when her hard day's work was over; and the Craigmyle ladies, with their natural good-heartedness, allowed her to talk on.

'Auld Knapperley gave her an umbrella and her just the littlin, and she must bring it to the Sabbath school as prood's

pussy. "What'll I do with my umbrella?"—hidin' it in ahin
her gown—"it's rainin'." "Put up your umbrella, Barbara."
"I won't put it up, Barbara. I won't have it blaudit, and it
new." And aye she happit it in the pink gown. Me and her
was ages and both Barbara Paterson then, and she took
a terrible notion o' me. If I had a blue peenie she must
have a blue peenie as well. And syne I was servant lassie
at Knapperley for a lot of years. I couldna but bide, her
that fond of me and all.'

'But you won't let Maggie go, Mrs Hunter?'

'I will not that. She was queer enough whan the auld
man was livin', and she's a sight queerer now. I was there
whan he dee'd and whan Mrs Paterson dee'd an' a'. Ay, I
mind fine, poor body, her thinkin' she would get him to mak
her laddie laird o' the placie and nae Miss Barbara. She liked
her laddie a sight mair than ever she liked her lassie. But she
married Donnie Forbes for love and Knapperley for a downsit. And she thought, poor soul, that she had nae mair a-do
than bid him say the word and Knapperley would be her
laddie's. But she aye put off the speirin'. And syne whan
she kent she wouldna rise again, she bids Knapperie in to
her bedside. "What's that you're sayin'?" says he. "Say't
again, for I'm surely nae hearin'." So she says it again. "And
him a Forbes," she says, "a family of great antiquity." "O
ay, like the shore porters o' Aberdeen, that discharged the
cargo from Noah's Ark." "You're mockin' me," she says.
"I'll grant you this," he says, "there was never a murder in
this parish or the next but there was a Forbes in it. There
was Forbes of Portlendie and Forbes of Bannochie, and a
Forbes over at Cairns that flung his lassie's corp ahin a
dyke. But there's been nae murder done at Knapperley
and nae Forbes at Knapperley—" "But there wasna aye
a Paterson at Knapperley, and some that kens," she says,
meanin'-like, "says the first that ocht the place didna rightly
owe the name." "It's a scant kin," he says, "that has neither
thief nor bastard in it, and for my part I'd rather have the
bastard than the thief. The lassie'll mak as good a laird
as the laddie. The place is hers, and you needna set any
landless lads on thievin' here. I'll keep my ain fish-guts
for my ain sea-maws." She didna daur say mair, but aye

whan he gaed by her door there cam the t'ither great sigh.
"You can just sigh awa' there," he would say. And whiles
he said, "Jamie Fleeman *kent* he was the Laird o' Udny's
feel." Well, well, he was a Tartar, auld Knapperie. But
he's awa' whaur he'll have to tak a back seat. He dee'd
in an awfu' hurry.'

'And Mr Benjamin has never come back since.'

'O ay. O fie ay. He cam' back. But just the once.
"This is a great disappointment to me, Barbara. Bawbie's
getting near. You see the weather it is, and you could
hold all the fire in the lee of your hand. There's the
two of us, one on either side, and greatcoats on to keep
us warm. And nothing but a scrap end of candle to light
you to your bed." "You may thank your stars, Mr Benjamin, she didna stand and crack spunks or you were
in ower." So he never cam again. But he let his laddie come.'

'She'll be making him her heir,' said Miss Annie.

'I wouldna wonder. They're chief, Miss Barbara and
Mr Garry.'

'A halarackit lump,' Theresa said.

'O, a gey rough loon. Mair like auld Knapperie's son
than Mr Benjamin's. But a terrible fine laddie. Me and Mr
Garry's great billies. "Will you dance at my wedding, Mrs
Hunter? I'll give you a new pair of shoes." "I will do that,
laddie. But wha is the bonny birdie?" '

'Yes, who?' thought Mrs Falconer. She made a running
excursion into the past. Once she had fancied that Kate was
not indifferent to Garry Forbes. At one time they had been
much together, when he came on holiday to Fetter-Rothnie.
But Theresa's tongue had been so hard on the boy—the intimacy ceased. Mrs Falconer remembered her own impotent
fury against her sister. And, after all, Kate had given no
sign. 'Another dream of mine, I suppose,' thought Mrs
Falconer. And she sighed. It was not easy to include Kate
in any dream. 'And she's all I have to love,' thought her
mother wistfully.

Mrs Hunter ran on. ' "O, that's to see," he says. "I've
never found a lassie yet that I love like your ain bonny self."
"You flatterer," I says. "Unless it would be my aunt." And

we both to the laughin'. But he's fair fond of her, mind you. There's nae put-on yonder.'

'He would be,' said Theresa. 'Sic mannie sic horsie. She's a Hielan' yowe yon.'

Mrs Hunter bridled. 'She's a good woman, Miss Craigmyle. There's worse things than being queer. There's being bad. There's lots that's nae quite at themsels and nae ill in them, and some that's all there and all the worse for that. There's Louie Morgan, now—queer you must allow she is, but bad she couldna be.'

Whether because the affront put on her by Miss Barbara's rash incursion was still rankling, or whether by reason of the naturally combative quality of her mind, Miss Theresa stormed on the suggestion.

'Louie!' she said. 'Hantle o' whistlin' and little red land yonder. And you don't call it bad to bedizen herself with honours and her never got them?'

'Meaning' what, Miss Craigmyle?'

'This tale of her engagement,' said Theresa with scorn.

'Poor craitur! That was a sore heart to her. Losin' young Mr Grey that road, and them new promised. It'll be a while or she ca' ower't.'

'She never had him.'

'Havers, Miss Theresa, she has the ring.'

'Think of that, now.'

'She let me see the ring.'

'She bought it.'

'She didna that, Miss Theresa. It's his mother's ain ring, that she showed me lang syne, and said her laddie's bride would wear whan she was i' the mools.'

Miss Theresa took the check badly. To be found in the wrong was a tax she could not meet. She had grown up with a hidden angry conviction that she was in the wrong by being born. As third daughter, she had defrauded her father of a son. It was after Theresa's birth that James Craigmyle set himself to turn Annie into as good a farmer as himself. He never reproached Tris to her face, but the sharp child guessed her offence. When he was dead, and she in the Weatherhouse had power and authority for the first time in her life, she developed an astounding genius for being in the right. To prove Theresa wrong was to jeopardise the household peace.

She was therefore dead set in her own opinion by Mrs Hunter's apparent proof of her mistake. The matter, to be sure, was hardly worth an argument. Louie Morgan was a weak, palavering thing, always playing for effect. The Craigmyle ladies knew better than to be taken in with her airs and her graces, that deceived the lesser intellects; but they had, like everyone else, accepted the story of her betrothal to David Grey, a young engineer brought up in the district, although David Grey was already dead before the betrothal was announced. Even Theresa had not openly questioned the story before. Irritation made her do it now, and the crossing of her theory drove her to conviction.

'It's as plain as a hole in a laddie's breeks,' she said. 'There was no word of an engagement when the young man was alive, was there?'

The whole company, however, was against her. The supposition was monstrous, and in view of Mrs Hunter's evidence upon the ring, untenable.

'And look at the times she's with auld Mr Grey,' said Mrs Hunter, 'that bides across the dyke from us, and him setting a seat for her that kindly like and cutting his braw chrysanthemums to give her.'

'She had sought them,' said Theresa.

'Oh, I wouldna say. She's fit for it, poor craiturie. But she wouldna tell a lee.' Mrs Hunter frankly admitted the failings of all her friends, but thought none the worse of them for that. 'She's her father's daughter there. A good man, the old Doctor, and a grand discourse he gave. It was worth a long traivel to see him in the pulpit, a fine upstandin' man as ever you saw. "Easy to him," Jake says. Jake's sair bent, Miss Craigmyle. "Easy to him, he's never done a stroke of work in his life." His wife did a' thing—yoked the shalt for him whan he went on his visitations, and had aye to have his pipe filled with tobacco to his hand when he got hame.'

'Where's Lindsay gone to?' Theresa cut abruptly across the conversation. 'She's taking a monstrous while to put away her cloak. And it's time these bairns were home.'

She pulled the coloured streamers from the tree out of Stella's hands.

They called for Lindsay, but had no answer. When it became plain she was not in the house, there was a flutter of consternation.

'Out?' said Miss Annie. 'But she'll get her death. And what could she be seeking out at this time of night?'

Only Mrs Falconer held her peace. A light smile played over her features, and her thoughts were running away by the upland paths of romance. She had a whole history woven for herself in a moment—a girl in love and escaping into moonshine on such a pure and radiant night as this: did one require pedestrian excuse?

She said, 'I'll put on my coat and take these children home. I'm sure to meet her on the way.'

Like Lindsay, she had the sense of escaping into light. She went along with a skipping step, her heart rejoicing; and almost forgot that she had come to look for a runaway whose absence caused concern.

She delivered over the children to Francie, who shut the door on them and said, 'I'll show you a sight, if you come up the park a bit.' Mrs Falconer followed, caring little where she went in that universal faerie shimmer. It seemed to her that she was among the days of creation, and light had been called into being, but neither divisions of time nor substance, nor any endeavours nor disturbances of man.

'What think you o' that in a Christian country?' Francie was asking; and Mrs Falconer saw, as Lindsay had seen, the blazing lights of Knapperley.

'What a strange pale beauty they have,' she said, 'in the moonlight.'

'Beauty, said ye?' echoed Francie, with supreme scorn. 'It's a beauty I can do fine wantin' in a war-time, and all them Zepps about.'

'Hoots, Francie,' said Mrs Falconer, recovering herself, 'it's as light as day. The house lights 'll make little difference in the sky tonight.'

'I've seen that lights, Mrs Falconer, in the darkest night o' winter. It's nae canny. She'll come by some mishaunter, ay will she, ay will she that.'

'A fine, maybe. Don't you worry, Francie. If she carries on like that the police 'll soon put a stop to her cantrips.'

Francie went away muttering. Mrs Falconer returned home, having forgotten to look very hard for the runaway. Lindsay was still absent.

'You can't have looked sore all the time you've been,' said Theresa.

Ellen did not, of course, confess that she had forgotten the girl. She said, 'What harm can she come to? She's gone out to see the moon.'

'Fiddlesticks and rosit! Everybody's not so daft about a view as you.'

'I'll go again,' said Ellen, nothing loth; but as she opened the door Lindsay arrived, running.

She was plainly in terror, and throwing herself on the sofa broke into sobbing.

'Whatever made you want to go there?' they asked when she told where she had been.

'I don't know,' sobbed Lindsay. She was like a little frightened child, and very lovely in her woe. They made much of her, and miscalled Bawbie Paterson to their hearts' content.

Lindsay told her story over again to Kate, when Kate had arrived home for the night and the girls were in the windowed room that Kate shared habitually with her mother. Ellen had yielded her tower to the guest.

'They wanted to know why I went, Katie, but they mustn't. Oh, I wish she weren't like that—she's dreadful.'

'But you needn't go near her, need you?'

Lindsay began to laugh and to sob. 'Katie,' she whispered, 'she's his aunt, you know.'

Kate was silent from astonishment.

She had heard her aunt's account of Mrs Andrew Lorimer's story—'Captain Dalgarno,' Mrs Andrew had said.

'I see,' she said at last. Captain Dalgarno was therefore Garry Forbes.

'Mother told you about me, didn't she? Didn't she, Katie? She had no right—they treat me like a child. She did say, didn't she?'

'I wasn't here, Linny. Yes, she said.'

'Said what? How much, Katie? Oh, I couldn't bear them to know that was why I ran after her. I wanted to see—Do you suppose they know, Katie?'

'I am sure they don't. But is it secret, Linny?'

'No. But running after her like that—' She began to writhe on the bed. 'I'm so unhappy, Katie.'

'Yes,' said Kate.

Kate was dumb before emotion. Her own was mastered and undivulged. She remained silent while Lindsay sobbed, and in a while the girl grew quiet, and fell asleep.

But Kate, after her young cousin slept, stole out of bed and crossed the room. Bending, she pulled the cover over Lindsay's naked arm. 'In this frost—she'd starve.' And for a moment Kate stood looking down on the flushed young face. So this was the woman whom Garry Forbes had chosen. Kate returned to bed and went to sleep. She had a long day's work ahead of her and a long day's work behind; and lying awake brought scanty profit.

FOUR

Coming of Spring

Lindsay's escapade on the night of the Christmas tree provided much matter for talk and for allusion. The ladies had their ways. Paradise, genial and warm, would cry, 'Out again, Lindsay. Stay you by the fire, my lass. But you don't seem to feel the cold, stravaigin' in the snow. You'll be stiffer about the hunkers before you come to my time of life. Put some clothes on, lassie, you'll starve.'

Theresa, hearing, would retort, 'She's not like you, rowed up like a sair thoomb. She's youth to keep her warm.'

'Ay, ay, here's me that needs the fire. And me to have been so active all my days.'

'Like Vesuvius.'

'Don't you heed her,' said Paradise, laughing. 'I could dander at night with the best when I was younger. O ay, frosty nights and all. Many's the lad that's chased me up the park and in by the woodie side.'

'But she aye took care of herself. Catch a weasel sleeping. You'd better have a care, Lindsay, going out alone by night, in a place you don't know.'

'There's somebody you would have liked fine to be meeting out there, my lady,' Paradise would add.

And Lindsay's face burned, as she watched them under narrowed lids. They had no mind to disconcert her, but had lived too long and heartily to remember the reticence of youth; and old Mrs Craigmyle, with her fine regard, Lindsay felt, enjoyed her young discomfort—not in a thoughtless frankness, like the others, but pondering its quality.

'Leezie Lindsay,' her grand-aunt would say—the very name made Lindsay's cheek grow hot—'you never ask the old dame for a song. When you were a littlin, it was, "And now a song, my grand-aunt," and when she sang you danced and you trebled. You have other ploys to please you now.'

Lindsay, knowing that she avoided the old lady's presence, blushed the more. And there was nothing in the words, yet everything. Her rare low words had a choice insolence that astounded the girl; but she dared not take offence, so delicate was the insinuation, lest she had mistaken her grand-aunt's meaning and herself supplied the subtle sting she felt. She would leave Lang Leeb's presence bewildered, in a sorry heat of shame that she had a mind so tainted.

Mrs Falconer had other modes of leading to attack. She would make up on the girl as she tramped the long moor roads and walk musing by her side. An ungainly figure, Lindsay thought. And rather a nuisance. She could never get accustomed to Cousin Ellen's habit of muttering to herself as she walked, and when Mrs Falconer began to address her, in her low hesitating voice, it was hard to be sure that she was not still talking to herself. Hard, indeed; because Ellen had no plain path out from her dreams, and her queer ends of talk were part of the story she had woven around herself and Lindsay.

'There's hard knowing what to do,' she would say. 'I've had to suffer, too. I fought for my own way of seeing things.' That battle of thirty years before came fresh and horrible to her memory. 'One generation forgets another's war. But, you see, I came out the conqueror.'

She let her thought hover upon her own past. It was a glancing embroidery now, pleasant to sight. But Lindsay saw only a tarnished and tangled thread or two that had no connection with herself, and thus a scanty interest.

'So I didn't hurry you,' Cousin Ellen went on. ' "Seek her out," they said, "seek her out. There's danger." But I knew, you see. Oh yes, I knew. Not the danger *they* meant. So I didn't look sore. I let you bide your time. There's some sorts of danger you have to meet, and where better to meet them than under a moon like yon? Oh yes, I knew.'

'Knew what?' Lindsay pondered. 'Why I went out at night? But I am sure she doesn't. What danger was there?'

Only Kate, who knew, said nothing. Kate had no words. Lindsay thought her callous, and writhed angrily to remember how she had given her secret self away. But she could have given it to no better heart than Kate's. Kate took it in and loved it.

Lindsay, unaware of her devotion, had hours of embarrassment among these elderly women who barbed their chance words with a story half heard from her mother and an escapade whose reason they did not understand. The allusions were sufficiently rare, except on the part of Mrs Falconer, who continued to puzzle Lindsay with her air of secret communion; but their mere possibility was enough to alarm the girl and soil the pleasantness she had always expected of a Weatherhouse sojourn. When, therefore, the frost gave and the roads were filled with slush and the whole countryside was dirty, Lindsay went home without regret.

It was a black February, wet, with an east wind 'hostin' through atween the houses.' At the end of the month trains were blocked by snow and fallen trees, and March came in bleak and bitter. Lindsay found the time long. She had wanted to be a nurse and they would not let her—she was not strong enough, they said—and there was nothing else that she particularly desired to do. So she made swabs and waited at the Station Rest Room Canteen, and thought herself a little hardly used by fate, but would not confess it, since she saw others around her used more hardly. She was to think it shortly with more justice, for Garry ceased to write to her. She would not confess at home to the lapse, but searched casualty lists and grew pale and restless. Before March ended spring suddenly filled the world. Buds were swollen in a night. Crocuses and scilla broke from the black earth; and Mrs Andrew Lorimer, watching her daughter's thin, strained face, sent her back to the Weatherhouse. She knew well enough that no letter had come for Lindsay, but would show no sympathy in an affair of which she disapproved.

The Weatherhouse ladies had had time to forget Lindsay's escapade. It was no longer matter for stupid allusion. They seemed also to have forgotten the love affair. There were no covert allusions to that either. Perhaps the girl's bearing, a little proud, steeled to show no hurt even when hurt was taken, made a hearty farm allusiveness fall flat. Kate remembered in silence. Mrs Falconer again waylaid the girl with queer talk that she could not understand. Lindsay could have no idea of the rush of life that came to Cousin Ellen by touching even so distantly the vital experience of a young girl's love and growth. Ellen had touched no vital experience other than her own. Kate had apparently had none to show her. No one had opened a heart to her or shared with her the strange secrecy of living, and in the hours of remorse when she chid herself for the false fictions of her brain she recognised sadly that she created these because she had had so little of the real stuff of living to fill her mind. So Lindsay, coming to Fetter-Rothnie charged with the splendours of a real romance, intoxicated Mrs Falconer. The elderly woman watched her with a sort of adoration, and would have purchased her confidence at a price; but she did not know how to reach the girl's confidence. Lindsay thought her queer and avoided her.

The others she did not avoid. Suspense, she found, was easier to bear up here in the sun and wind, where no one knew that she was waiting. It surprised her to find how she slipped into the life of the countryside, learned its stories, its secret griefs and endeavours. She had not dreamed how much alive a few square miles of field and moor could become. Miss Annie taught her to understand the earth and its labourers—the long, slow toil of cultivating a land denuded of its men. She learned to despise Peter Cairnie, a shrewd shirker in a rich farm by the river, who ploughed Maggie Barnett's land to her at an exorbitant figure; and to honour Maggie, wife of a young crofter at the Front, who managed the croft and reared her three bairns alone.

'Do you hear from him often?' Lindsay said to Maggie.

'Whiles, whiles,' the wiry woman answered. 'But he's nae great sticks at the pen. I heard five weeks syne.'

Five weeks, Lindsay thought, and she takes it as of course. She watched Maggie whack the cow round in her stall and set to milking, and followed Miss Theresa a little thoughtfully to Mrs Hunter at Craggie.

Another croft; its man not gone this time, but slow and frail; Dave, the eldest boy, in the Gordons.

'And does he write?' asked Lindsay. It was something to say.

'Write!' cried Mrs Hunter in her glowing fashion. 'There was never a lad to write like our Dave. And money coming home to keep the loonies at the school. "Keep you Bill and Dod to their books, Mother," he says. "This war's bound to go over some time, and the boys'll need all the education they can get. I'll put them through college," he says. It's himsel should have been at the college, if I had my way of it. His heart was never in the joinering, but there, it couldna be. But the young ones, they're to town to the school, a gey lang way, and a gey lang day; their father could do fine with a hand from them with the beasts and about the place, but there you are, you see. "Keep them to their books, mother," says Dave. "They'll get what I couldn't get." And I can aye lend a hand with the beasts mysel.'

Lindsay went often to Mrs Hunter's. Mrs Hunter had been servant lass for so long at Knapperley, and she talked freely of Miss Barbara and Mr Garry, not suspecting the avid interest of her listener. Talk lightened the heart to Mrs Hunter. Good reminiscent unprejudiced talk was the salt of earth to her; and she had earth enough in her laborious life to require salting.

Lindsay would come in, swing herself to the table or squat upon a creepie, and manoeuvre Mrs Hunter to the subjects she desired. It was thus that she heard the story of David Grey. David had been Garry's friend. And he was dead. His father, John Grey, lived across the dyke from Mrs Hunter. This indomitable old man, approaching the seventies, spare, small and alert, lived alone except for the woman who kept his house. Son of a petty crofter in a Deeside glen, he had laboured on the croft, taken his schooling as he could, and fought his way to apprenticeship in an engineering shop. The master of the country school where he had spent his winters did well by him; in night school he rose steadily, until by the end of his apprenticeship he was teaching draughtsmanship and mechanics. He went out

early on Sunday mornings and took long walks in the coun
try, in the course of which he studied botany and learned
by heart the works of the English poets. He even wrote
verses, in Tennyson's early manner; and studied Carlyle
and Ruskin, John Locke and Adam Smith. His books were
bought from second-hand bookstalls; it was thus that he
became possessor of an eighteenth-century *Paradise Lost*,
leather-bound, with steel engravings of our First Parents in
a state of innocence. To these engravings he had added, for
Eve a skirt, for Adam short pants, of Indian ink. He married, became Works manager of the Foundry where he had
served his apprenticeship, settled within reach of town and
cultivated his garden. He rose with daylight, laboured in
the earth till the breakfast hour, made a rapid but thorough
toilet, went to town. At the end of his garden, the beauty of
which was celebrated through all the district, was a workshop: there was nothing connected with a homestead that
he could not make or mend. His fingers, clumsy, broad and
seamed, were incredibly delicate in action. His figure was
squat and plebeian, but redeemed by its alert activity and
by the large and noble head. The brow was wide and lofty,
the nose aquiline, shaggy eyebrows emphasised the depths
of the eye-sockets, in which there shone a pair of dark,
piercing and kindly eyes. Children loved him. His voice
was soft and persuasive. His men revered him and trusted
his judgment. He spoke evil of no man.

In youth his hair, brows and beard (which he never removed) were intensely black, but by the time of this story,
white; and so much of his forehead and temples was now
bare as gave a singularly lofty and serene appearance to his
head. One felt him as a man of peace. In the spring of 1914
he had retired from work and given himself with a child's
delight to his garden; but early in the war, feeling that
his specialised knowledge and training should be put at the
service of his country, he offered himself to the Munitions
Department of his city, and was engaged as a voluntary and
unpaid Inspector of Shells; he stipulated only that his travelling expenses should be paid—his salary had always been
small, and he had saved no more than would suffice for his
old age. The lifting and handling of shells was too much for

his failing strength. He toiled home at night exhausted; but was up on the following morning to work in his garden. He had even taken in another piece of ground and was growing huge crops of potatoes and green vegetables, which he distributed among the local hospitals.

His wife was dead. His only son, a brilliant boy, unlike his father in appearance and temperament, had inherited and intensifed his genius. David was tall, red-headed, fiery-tempered, wild and splendid, but with his father's capacity for engineering and his power over those who worked for him. John Grey saw his own dreams fulfilled in his son. The boy marched triumphantly through school and college, and, entering Woolwich Arsenal in the war, became night manager of a new fuse factory. His work was his passion. Brilliant, inventive, steady in work as his father, he lacked the older man's composed serenity. The artist's sensibility, the lover's exaltation, went to his work; and broke him. He developed tuberculosis, and in three months' time was dead.

John Grey took the blow in silence. He spoke to no one of his son, but went on his steady, quiet way. Only the professional books that he and the boy together had amassed ceased to interest him. He never read them again, and his tired mind had no further concern with the modern developments of which, for the boy's sake, he had kept himself informed.

When Lindsay learned, through Mrs Hunter, that David Grey had been Garry's friend, she placed both the old and the dead man in her shrine of heroes. This shy and undeveloped girl at nineteen had the Lorimer passion, exemplified in Mrs Falconer's day-dreams and the balladry of Lang Leeb her mother, for a romantic enlargement of life. Lindsay was given to hero-worship. On these spring evenings and on Saturday afternoons she would watch the old man at work in his garden. Sometimes, as he crawled weeding among the beds, in his old garments that had turned the colour of earth itself, with his hands earth-encrusted, he seemed older than human—some antique embodiment of earth. One could fancy a god creating an Eden. Steady and happy. Absorbed. Like a part of what he worked in, and yet beyond it. The immanent presence.

The stooping figure, moving back and forth like a great silent animal, would raise itself, the noble forehead come into view; and rising on stiff knees, the old man would greet the girl with a perfect courtesy, sit by her pulling at his pipe. Once, in the sun, he fell asleep as he sat beside her, nodding in an old man's light and easy slumbers.

Once or twice Louie Morgan came to the garden. Lindsay had heard her story too; how she was betrothed to young David Grey—an unannounced betrothal, to which she had confessed only after his death. One evening, walking away with her from the garden, Louie showed Lindsay a ring, which she wore about her neck.

'Why should I flaunt it for everyone to see?' she had said; and with her head on one side she gazed at the ring. Her face was all curious little puckers—a study for a Lady in Anguish. She made funny twists with her mouth. But Lindsay was excited. It was her first intimate personal contact with the bereavement of war, and she exalted Louie also to a place in her shrine.

So the spring wore on. There on the upland one saw leagues of the world and leagues of sea, all milky-blue, hazed like the bloom upon a peach. And how good it was to watch the country changing with the spring!

'Come,' Paradise would say. 'Tomorrow the chickens should be out. We'll sprinkle water on the eggs today.' Tomorrow came, and the shells broke—small, soft, delectable living things were there.

'Oh, how I love them! I have never seen them so young. Oh, it's running, it's running on my hand! But why can't I feed them?'

Paradise, taking the broken shells from the coop, told her they were too young for food; but Lindsay was not listening. She had heard somewhere a loud harsh cry.

'Look, look! Oh, there! See them! What can they be?' And she pointed far overhead, into the height of the blue sky. Birds were flying there, one bird, and others following in two lines that made an open angle upon the blue; but while one arm of the angle was short, the other stretched far out across the sky, undulating, fine and black.

'One, two three—twenty, twenty one—Oh, I have counted ninety birds! My neck is aching.' She held her hands to her neck, moving her head about to ease its pain. 'Paradise, tell me what they are.'

'Why, that is the wild geese. Have you never seen them fly before?'

'Never. Wild geese, wild geese! How wonderful the country is!'

When Cousin Ellen walked with her she assailed her with questions.

'And see, Cousin Ellen, this one. Look at him. Has he a nest there, do you think? Where do you look for nests? What kind is he? What is his name?'

Ellen shook her head.

'I hardly know their names, Linny.'

'But don't you love birds?'

'Oh, yes.' Ellen paused, gazing at the eager girl. 'They are a part of myself,' she wanted to say; but how could one explain that? Where it had to be explained it could not be understood. 'You are a part of me, too,' she thought, with her eyes fixed on Lindsay's where she waited for her answer. Her lips were parted and her eyes shone; and Mrs Falconer longed to tell her of the strange secret of life—how all things were one and there was no estrangement except for those who did not understand. But all that she could find to say was, 'I know hardly any of their names.'

The girl's clear regard confused her, and she dropped her eyes. She felt ashamed. 'Names don't matter very much, do they?' she asked hurriedly.

'Oh, yes. Names—they're like songs.' And she chanted in a singing voice, 'Wild duck, wild duck, kingfisher, curlew. Their names are a part of themselves. Can you tell me where to see a kingfisher, Cousin Ellen?'

'No . . . I'm afraid not.'

Ellen had been found wanting, Lindsay felt. To walk with her held no allurement.

Only once a spontaneous feeling of love for Cousin Ellen welled up in her heart.

Lindsay had come to the Weatherhouse bringing gifts.

'I've brought presents for you all. See, a poor woman made them. She can do nothing for the war, so she makes these lovely things and gives the money.'

Theresa and Paradise took their boxes, which were of embroidered silk exquisitely fashioned, and put them instantly to use. But Cousin Ellen's gift lay on the table.

'Don't you like your gift? I'm sorry you don't like it.'

'Oh yes, I like it. It is very beautiful. Please don't think because I don't use it that I am not grateful for it. I have never cared for many possessions. I have never had many possessions to care for,' she added, smiling brightly. 'A man's life consisteth not in the abundance of things that he hath.'

A week later Miss Theresa stamped into the parlour.

'Well, really, Nell! To give Lindsay's beautiful box away. Something commoner would have done, surely to peace, if you must be throwing things at that Stella Ferguson's head. A nice appreciation you show, I will say.'

'Yes, I gave it to Stella. Possessions mean a lot to her.'

Theresa continued to bluster; but Lindsay jumped from the stool where she had been seated with her book, and cried, 'Oh, I love you for giving it to Stella, Cousin Ellen.'

'Lindsay'—Miss Theresa changed the subject sharply— 'you'll spoil your eyes, poring over these great books. You are quite wrinkled.'

Lindsay turned a flushed and troubled face, pushing the hair from off her brow.

'But I must be ready. The world will need us all. I'm doing nothing now, but I can prepare myself for afterwards. There will be ten years of trouble to live through.'

She quoted the phrases she had heard from Garry's lips, and set herself to study the books that he had read. 'We shall all have our part to play in the reconstruction.'

Into this life Garry Forbes came in the second week of April. All spring was in that week—its tempestuous disinclinations, its cold withdrawals, its blaze of sun, its flowers, its earthy smell. On all hands was a breaking: earth broken by the ploughshare, buds broken by the leaf. The smooth security of seed and egg was gone. Season most terrible in all the cycle of the year, time of the dread spring deities, Dionysus and Osiris and the risen Christ, gods of growth and of resurrection, whose worship has flowered in tragedy, superb and dark, in Prometheus and Oedipus, massacre and the stake. Life that comes again is hard: a jubilation and an agony.

Garry was at this time some thirty years of age. Tall, dark-skinned, black stubbs on his chin and cheek that no shaving would remove, with prominent nose and cheek bones and outstanding ears, the two deep furrows that were later so marked a feature of his appearance already ploughing their way from above the nostrils to encircle the mouth, and just now lank and haggard from war and influenza; he came to spend a brief sick leave with his aunt, Miss Barbara Paterson, at Knapperley.

'What do you want with a kitchen lass?' he said to her. 'I'll be your kitchen lass.'

Miss Barbara sat back in her deep chair and flung yowies from her pockets on to the blazing fire. She, who could spread dung and hold a plough with any man, disliked the petty drubs of housework.

'You're Donnie Forbes's grandson,' she said, watching her nephew as he washed the supper dishes. 'I'm a Paterson of Knapperley. A Paterson of Knapperley doesna fyle their fingers with dishwater.'

Benjamin Forbes, Miss Barbara's half-brother, son of the despised Donnie Forbes whom Mrs Paterson had wedded merely for love, had, like his mother, been timid and incapable in his relations with other people. He lived with his boy in the mean suburb of an inland town. When charwomen cheated and neglected them, it was the boy who found fault, dismissed and interviewed. The fiction was faithfully preserved between father and son that the father habitually did these things, but delegated them upon occasion to the son. Garry put a bold front upon the business, and won the praises of the women in the block for his assured and masterful bearing. They could not know that the child sometimes cried himself to sleep, and he would have perished rather than confess to it. When service was not to be had, Garry waited on his father;

and broke the nose of the boy who taunted him with it at school.

'I'll sweel out the slop-pail if I like,' he shouted.

He was a powerful fellow, able easily to wipe out insults, and far too proud to acknowledge his own secret abasement at doing a woman's jobs.

Benjamin talked often to the boy of Knapperley. 'Yon's the place, laddie,' he would say. Garry choked as he listened; he felt he must perish of desire for the burns and the rocky coast. But when he begged his father to let him go to Knapperley, Benjamin demurred. He shrank from a second encounter with his half-sister. One day, when Garry was twelve years old, Benjamin came home to find the boy on the next-door roof, mending a broken gutter-pipe, and learned that his son mended for all the women in the row—and took his wages. Shamefaced but voluble, Garry produced his money-box; he had not spent a penny of his earnings; all was saved—to pay his fare to Knapperley. Benjamin swore softly, but wrote to Miss Barbara; and though no answer was received, the boy set off alone as soon as his holidays began. He tramped the eight miles out from Aberdeen with his belongings on his back, and was dismayed at the ease of the journey. It was unbearably tame to walk in to Knapperley and sleep in a bed; and his secret hope (that his aunt would not receive him: a contingency for which he had made elaborate preparations) vanished like smoke when he saw the actual place. He was sure she would take him in and bid him wash his hands.

'That Knapperley?' he asked a man who was lounging against a gate.

'Who was ye seekin'?'

'Oh, nobody much. I just wanted to know.'

He walked away.

'Ay is't,' the man shouted after him

Garry did not turn.

He came in a little to the moor and saw the sea. That night was full moon. The boy wandered all night like a daft thing. He had drunk magic. At dawn he fell asleep, and the sun was well up when he awoke, furiously hungry, and made

for Knapperley. He had no intention of telling where he had
spent the night.

But the first person he saw was the fellow who had
spoken to him by the gate. Miss Barbara was standing on a
cart, forking straw from the cart into a great bundle beside
the stable door.

'Ay, ay,' said the man. 'Ye've gotten your way. I tell't
her ye was in-by the streen.'

'Let's see you with the graip,' said Miss Barbara, descending from the cart and handing the fork to her
nephew.

Garry threw his knapsack from his shoulders and clambered on to the cart. He would not be outdone by anybody;
but the horse moved and set the cart in motion; he lost
his balance, plunged violently and swung his graip high
in the air.

Miss Barbara and the man roared with laughter. A dozen
dogs, as it seemed, arrived from nowhere and barked.

'I'll show you how to laugh at me!' cried Garry, recovering his footing. He was mortified to the soul, and
began to handle the straw with all the skill and vigour
he could command. Miss Barbara folded her arms and
watched. Rabbie Mutch could be heard recounting the
affair to the kitchen lass, and there followed a guffaw
of laughter from them both.

'You'll be ready for your porridge, I'se warren,' said
Miss Barbara in a little; and she led the way to the kitch-
en, where breakfast was ready for herself, her man and her
kitchen girl. 'Where spent you the night?'

'Up beside a tower kind of place.'

'You never got in?'

'Oh no, just outside.'

'Gweed sakes!' roared Rabbie. 'Like the—nowt.'

'Dinna you do that,' said the kitchen lass earnestly.
'The moon'll get you. You'll dwine an' dee.'

Far from bidding him wash his hands, Miss Barbara let
her nephew come to table with his clothes sullied from the
moor. The rough free life she led suited the spirited lad.
His manners grew ruder. Rabbie Mutch kept up on him
the joke about his sprawling from the cart. He would say

at dinner-time, 'O ay, ye can haud the forkie better'n the graip. Yon was a gey like way to haud a graip. Forkin' the lift, was ye?'

The sensitive boy was too proud to show his resentment. He retaliated in kind. Rabbie and he made rude jokes at each other's expense and became fast friends.

For his aunt, the boy admired her wholeheartedly. She knew so much that he had never heard. The country became a new possession. He was free, too, from the indignity that harassed him at home; the endless squabbling with washerwomen. Miss Barbara found fault often enough, but in a coarse and hearty manner, that was followed by guffaws of laughter from all concerned. Garry developed a poor opinion of his own and his father's assertion of authority, and determined to try Miss Barbara's methods on the next woman who offended.

He would secretly have preferred to leave these offenders unchallenged, but, being plagued with a passion for the ideal, could not let ill alone.

When, at the age of twenty nine, on leave at the Lorimer's house with the young Frank, he met and loved Lindsay, this passion had not abated. 'Well, I've done it now,' he thought. He rushed about the house, forgot his manners, played absurd practical jokes, swore himself to secrecy over his love, and blurted it out immediately to Lindsay. To his consternation she flung her arms around his neck.

'I've loved you for ever and ever so long,' she cried. 'You should hear how Frank talks of you.'

Her girl friends called him the Gargoyle.

'One could forgive the ears,' her mother declared, 'if he knew how to conduct himself.'

Garry's lapses from a Mrs Andrew Lorimer standard were not always due to ignorance. He resented those refinements that suggested privilege. This shy lover of the ideal, this poet who clowned away the suspicion of poetry from himself, burned in his heart with no less a fire than love for all mankind. A simple fool, not very fit for Mrs Andrew Lorimer's drawing-room, where such an enormous appetite was found ill-bred. The well-bred love with discrimination.

'Such waste of furrow,' said Mrs Robert Lorimer. 'Those architectural effects of feature. In a gentleman, how distinguished! A man of race and breeding could arrive where he liked with a face of that quality.'

Garry's race being that of the despised Donnie Forbes and his breeding of the back street, his ugliness was pronounced not distinguished, but common.

'You've got a rarity there, Miss Lindsay,' mocked her aunt Mrs Robert.

'I know he is rare,' the girl answered steadily. She and Frank alone appreciated the rareness. Both listened vehemently to his interminable plans for reconstructing the universe. They talked far into the night, until Mrs Andrew despatched her husband from his bed to round them up.

'Leave them alone,' he grumbled. 'There's a war on. Those boys'll be in the trenches again soon enough, God knows.' But he obeyed the mandate.

'Your mother thinks it's time you were in bed, Linny.'

He blinked in the glare of light. Standing there in his pyjamas and dressing-gown, an unimaginative man, he felt nevertheless the tense elation in the room.

'So courting's done in threes nowadays—eh?'

Lindsay flung back her head. 'O daddy, nights like this don't come again.'

She met her mother's morning eye with a clear regard.

'Europe is in the melting-pot, mother—is a slight alteration in one's bedtime of importance?'

'Ler her keep her phrase,' said Mr Lorimer. 'She'll outgrow that.'

Inflamed by Garry's letters, she continued to keep her phrase.

The letters ceased when Garry took influenza, after a day and a night's exposure in a shell hole, where, up to the thighs in filthy water, he had tried to suck the poison from another man's festering arm. The other fellow died where he stood, slithered through his fingers and doubled over into the filth, and Garry was violently sick. He stared at the horror beside him, and now he saw that blood had coagulated in the pit between the man's knees and his abdomen. Poor beggar, he must have had another wound . . . He must get out of sight of that, but his feet were stuck, they would never pull free again. He stooped, plunging his arm in the slimy water. Branches came up, dripping long strings of ooze. Now he had detached the other man's feet; the body canted over, a shapeless rigid mass, and he saw the glaring eyes, the open mouth out of which slime was oozing. He pushed with all his might, thrust the thing under; barricaded himself with branches against its presence. Rain fell, sullen single drops, that burrowed into the surface of the slime and sent oily purplish bubbles floating among the ends of branch that were not submerged. Clots of blood appeared, washed out from the body.

'A wound I didn't know of,' he thought. 'A wound you couldn't see.' Perhaps his own abdomen was like that—black with blood. Squandered blood. Perhaps he too was wounded and did not know it. 'I put him there—I thrust him in.'

Delirium came on him. A wind roared hideously. He knew it was an advancing shell, but shouted aloud as he used to do when a boy in the hurricanes that swept the woods at Knapperley. Again the rushing mighty wind. Night came at last. He knew he must escape. 'Can't leave you here, old man.' In some queer way he was identified with this other fellow, whom he had never seen before, whose body he had thrust with so little ceremony under the slime. 'Tra la la la la,' he sang, tugging at the corpse. 'Come out, you there. Myself. That's me. That's me. I thrust him in—I am rescuing myself.'

He was found towards morning in a raging fever, dragging a grotesque bundle at his heels—a corpse doubled over, with bits of branch that protruded from the clothing, plastered with slime. They had to bring him in by force.

'Don't take him from me, you chaps. It's myself. I have been wounded—here, in the abdomen. Here,' he shouted. And he put his arms round the shapeless horror he had dragged bumping from its hole.

He never knew what came of the body, nor whose it was. When he regained his senses he was in hospital, too weak to think or speak, but sure he had been wounded. 'Queer business that,' he said later, 'about my wound. I

was convinced I had a wound. I saw myself. Oh, not a
pretty sight. Obstinate old bag of guts. I had to haul myself
out. I hauled for hours. And I knew it was myself and the
other man too. I thrust him in, you see, and I had to haul
myself out. Queer, isn't it, about oneself? Losing oneself
like that, I mean, and being someone else.'

He lay pondering the hugeness of life. Sometimes he
was so weak that he cried. Nurses said to one another,
'Poor fellow—that huge one in the corner. Crying like a
baby. He has delusions.'

He fumed at their pity as he had fumed at ridicule
in his boyhood; but in a gush of charity allowed himself
even to be pitied. One could not refuse to meet other people
halfway.

'It's because it's so big,' he tried to explain to one
of the nurses.

'Yes, I know,' she answered, pressing his hand.

Of course she didn't know. It wasn't the war that was
big, it was being alive in a world where wars happened—that
was to say, in a world where there were other people, divinely different from oneself; whole Kingdoms of Heaven,
clamouring to be taken by violence and loved in spite of
themselves. No nurse could know that; but he permitted
her to put her hand on his, and even when she pressed it he
did not fling it off. But then he was so tired.

Some weeks later Garry left his valise at the station and
set out to walk the four cross-country miles to Knapperley.
Night had fallen—a night of war-time, unrelieved. Behind
him, along the line of railway where the houses were clus-
tered, dull blurs of light were visible; in front all was dark.
Slowly the vast heaven detached itself from the earth. Trees
took shape—bare, slender branches striking upward into the
sky. It seemed as though out of the primal darkness the
earth once more were taking form: an empty world, older
than man, silent. In a while Garry became acutely aware of
the silence. It burdened him. He stood to listen. A bird
was stirring, dead dry leaves rustled in the beech hedge;
far off, a dog barked. The lonely echo died, there was no
wind, the world was still as dream. Life had not yet begun
to be, man had not troubled the primordial peace. Strange

stagnant world—he hated its complacency. Standing there on the ridge, dimly aware of miles of dark and silent land, Garry felt a sort of scorn for its quietude: earth, and men made from earth, dumb, graceless, burdened as itself.

'This place is dead,' he thought. The world he had come from was alive. Its incessant din, the movement, the vibration that never ceased from end to end of the war-swept territory, were earnest of a human activity so enormous that the mind spun with thinking of it. Over there one felt oneself part of something big. One was making the earth. Here there were men, no doubt, leading their hapless, misdirected, individual lives; but they were a people unaware, out of it. He felt almost angry that Lindsay should be dwelling among them. He knew from her letters that she was in Fetter-Rothnie, and, convalescent, had written her that he would come to Knapperley; but that her young fervour should be shut in this dead world annoyed him. She was too far from life. The reconstruction of the universe would not begin in this dark hole, inhabited by old wives and ploughmen.

But as he mounted farther into the night, the night, growing upon his consciousness, was a dark hole no longer. The sky, still dark, brooded upon a darker earth, but with no sense of oppression. Rather both sky and earth rolled away, were lost in a primordial darkness whence they had but half emerged. Garry felt himself fall, ages of time gave way, and he too, was a creature only half set free from the primordial dark. He was astonished at this effect upon himself, at the vastness which this familiar country had assumed. Width and spaciousness it always had, long clear lines, a far horizon, height of sky; yet the whole valley and its surrounding hills could have been set down and forgotten in the slum of the war territory from which he had crossed. All the generations of its history would not make up the tale of the fighting men.

He paused a little, contemplating that history. Fierce and turbulent men had made it: Picts and Celtic clansmen, raiders and Jacobites. Circles and sculptured stones, cairns and hill-forts, tall grim castellated strongholds, remained as witness to its past. In its mountain glens there were recesses, ledges at the waterside under overhanging crag a hundred feet in height, where fugitives had hidden from their foes; on its coasts dangerous caves, where smugglers had operated, caught the resounding seas. Craft put out and were tossed on the waters in adventures of piracy and merchandise and statesmanship. Fishermen knew its landmarks. Wrecks were strewn about its shores. Monarchs and chieftains had ridden its passes; a king had fled that way to his destruction, a queen watched the battle on which her fortune hung; and its men had gone to every land on earth following every career. Yet, a small land; poor; ill to harvest, its fields ringed about with dykes of stone laboriously gathered from the soil. Never before had Garry felt its vastness; and he paused now, watching and hearkening. A sound broke the stillness, faint bubble of a stream, the eternal mystery of moving water; and now the darkness, to his accustomed eyes, was no longer a covering, but a quality of what he looked upon. Waste land and the fields, in common with the arch of sky, and now a grandeur unsuspected in the day. Light showed them as they were at a moment of time, but the dark revealed their timeless attributes, reducing the particular to accident and hinting at a sublimer truth than the eye could distinguish. Garry felt for a moment as though he had ceased to live at the point in time where all his experience had hitherto been amassed.

He was recalled to his accidental point in time by a woman's voice, shrill and clamorous, carrying across the night. A man's voice answered, like a reverberating boom. Garry walked on. Knapperley was just ahead.

The dogs were on him as soon as he entered, but not before he had seen Miss Barbara, alone on the kitchen floor, in her swinging Lovat tweed, dancing a Highland fling. How she lifted her supple sinewy legs, and tossed her arms, and cracked her fingers! 'That's you, is it?' her nod seemed to say as she glanced towards her nephew and went on with the step. Garry laughed, weary as he was, and swung into the dance. How much of the character of the land had not gone into this vigorous measure, which a hard-knit woman of fifty five was dancing alone on her kitchen floor in the middle of a world war, for no other reason than that she wanted to!

But in a moment he caught his breath and sat down. Miss Barbara sat also, pulled a handful of raisins from her pocket and began to munch. She asked no questions of her nephew, accepting him as she accepted rain or a litter of pups.

'That's better than jazz, aunt.'

'And what might jazz be?'

'It's a thing some people do.'

'Don't you come here, my lad, with your things some people do. This is a decent house.'

The man lay back, face seamed and drawn, eyes sunken, and looked at the house. Since the war began he had not come to Knapperley till then.

'Not a mortal thing is changed. The war just hasn't touched you, has it, aunt?'

To which she answered with an indignant flash, 'Change and change enough. There's nae near so many bodies about the roads. Tinkler bodies. There's just nane ava, and they're a terrible miss. I aye liked them coming in about for a sup and a crack. Many's the collieshangie we've had in this very ingle—Jeemsie Parten that has nae teeth but on the Sabbath, and Tammas Hirn, he had aye a basket with trappin' and aye time for a newse, and an auld orra body that hadna a name—pigware he brought, bowls and bonny jugs. I hinna had a new bowl since I kenna the time. And Johnnie Rogie, a little shauchlin' craitur, but the king o' them a'.'

Garry went to his room and fell asleep; but awoke in a little shivering violently. The bed—he might have known it—was damp. He dressed and crawled shaking down to the embers. The dogs stirred, but soon were quiet. An owl called. Miss Barbara made no sign; and for the rest of the night Garry sat by the blaze that he rekindled, staring into its heart and attempting to reconcile his aunt's vivid enjoyment of the moment with the dark truth he had been thrust upon in his walk that evening, where time and the individual had ceased to matter.

FIVE

Problem set for Garry

Lindsay was on the moor next morning to meet her lover. She was glad that she had taken his letter herself from the postman, that the old women need not know. The five last empty weeks had collapsed, the moment was enough.

'There are tassels on the larch, Garry. Look, and purple osiers. And oh, do you smell the poplar? I forgot—you are laughing, you know all these places so much better than I. I have never been in the country in spring before.'

'But now that I think of it, neither have I.'

'Not here?'

'Why, no. They were schoolboy holiday visits. Once or twice since, in midsummer.'

'You've never bird's-nested here?—I am so glad. Then I can show you things . . . These are the osiers.'

'No matter what they are. They are too lovely to require a name.'

On the willows by the pool the catkins were fluffed, insubstantial, their stamens held so lightly to the tree that they seemed like the golden essence of its life escaping to the liberty of air. Once, as the two wandered in the wood, they saw a rowan, alone in the darkness of the firs, with smooth grey branches that gleamed in the sun. The tree had no seeming substance. It was like a lofty jet of essential light.

But farther into the wood, in a sheltered clearing, the sun blazed upon a woman, picking gleams from her feathery yellow hair. She was kneeling on the ground, her hands clasped together and her head thrown back. They could see that her eyes were squeezed close and her lips were moving.

'Saying her prayers,' cried Lindsay. 'It's Louie Morgan. She's pi, you know.'

Louie continued to pray. They could hear now the words that issued from her lips. Bowing and smirking to an audience that was not there, Louie was petitioning: 'I'm on the Fetter-Rothnie Committee—may I introduce myself? I'm on the Fetter-Rothnie Committee—may I introduce myself?'

Lindsay checked her gurgle of laughter. 'But it's a shame to laugh at her. Poor soul, she's had so hard a time.'

'How?' Garry asked, carelessly; amused at the creature's antics.

'But don't you know? Your friend David Grey.'

She told him the story of Louie's betrothal.

There began for Garry at that moment the tussle that made his name a byword in Fetter-Rothnie.

'Dave,' he repeated stupidly. 'Dave.'

He had shared rooms with David Grey when they were students at Glasgow Technical College. David's death had touched him closely. Lindsay knew little of the depth and strength of that affection, of which indeed he had never spoken.

'David Grey,' he repeated. 'That creature there.'

Louie was still becking and bowing, swaying upon her knees, with clasped hands and eyes squeezed close. The exhibition, which had been ludicrous, became offensive. But the eyes opened suddenly, and the antic creature scrambled, not ungracefully, to her feet.

Louie Morgan was a slight, manoeuvring figure, in the middle thirties. Her large eyes were melting and beautiful. She studied her movements of arm and throat. When a stranger asked the way of her, she heard him think, 'What a beautiful girl! What poise! I am glad I missed my way. That is a face one must remember.' She studied to have a face one must remember. She had solid respect in Fetter-Rothnie as the daughter of her father, who had been its minister; and of her mother, who made the tea at every Sale of Work and Social Meeting. As Jonathan Bannochie had said, in proposing her a vote of thanks at the last Congregational Meeting, 'It would be a gey dry tyauve wantin' the tea, and Mistress Morgan's genius lies in tea.' She had a further genius in her admiration for her

only child. She thought Louie only a trifle less wonderful
than Louie thought herself. Mrs Morgan was small, plain
and collected. Louie, she said without a tinge of envy, took
her charm and temperament from the father's side.

As became the daughter of her father, Louie was devout.
She carried a pocket Testament and read it on ostenta-
tious occasions. She wanted to hear strangers think, 'What
beautiful piety! How fine the expression it gives the countenance!' And it was always in her prayers that the perfect
lovers of whom she dreamed made their appearance. Always
when she reached a certain point in her petitions they appeared. 'God bless father and mother . . . and all my little
cousins . . . and make me a good girl—' She had a vision
of herself as a good girl, a charitable Princess giving alms to
footsore men, and one of them saying, out of parched and
swollen lips, 'She is more radiant than the sun, and blesses
what she looks on. It is she that the King my father sent me
to seek.' As she grew older, *make me a good girl* changed its
wording, but the sentiment remained and so did the vision,
changed also. Her prayers had long footnotes, in which she
had visions of herself in all the splendid roles she pleaded
with Heaven to let her play; and always a hero came, whose
comment on herself she heard, and whom she answered. She
was a missionary in a dangerous land, and a ferocious chief-
tain knelt sobbing at her feet. 'You are more wonderful than
all the gods of my people. Your God will be my God, and
you shall be my queen.' She was a nurse in hospital, and the
sick and wounded blessed her name. A great surgeon saw
her pass, noted her touch. An emergency operation must be
performed. The man's life hangs on it, he is delirious, fights,
will not take the anaesthetic. 'You will come, hold him.' He
is calm in a moment, his life is saved. 'Yes, the first time I
saw my wife she helped me with a critical case. Saved the
man. She has a wonderful touch.' Or perhaps the hero was
diffident and would not speak. 'I'm on the Fetter-Rothnie
Committee—may I introduce myself?' 'Ah, beloved, had
you not had the courage to speak to me that fateful day,
how drab life would have been.'

The immediate words that broke upon her prayer, however, were not these; were not, indeed, intelligible. Aware

merely of voices, she opened her eyes; then rose and faced the two intruders, flushing with satisfaction. She had always wanted to be discovered at prayer in the woods. *Into the woods my Master went.* She composed the face one must remember, and heard Lindsay and Captain Forbes think, 'Her face is shining. It is by such devotion that the world is saved.'

Louie lifted her eyes from her subconscious play-acting to look at Captain Forbes.

'How ugly he is! It must be years since I've seen him.' Her satisfaction was marred. Garry's face was working. He was still thinking, 'That creature there.' She felt an antagonism. Was it not a waste of effect? 'The wrong sort of man to appreciate me. Life's like that—never the right people.' Distinctly, the wrong sort of man. Louie decided to have nothing to do with Captain Forbes; but immediately she tilted her head a little sideways and held out a hand. 'I am so glad. And what was doing at the Front? Oh, Captain Forbes, now that we have you here; you must say a few words at our concert. Next week. Comforts for the troops, you know.'

'Comforts? Oh yes, you protect yourselves against us with comforts, I believe.'

'Protect—?'

'Parcel us up your comforts, and then feel free to forget all about us.'

'But, Captain Forbes! Linny, do tell him he is absurd.'

'He always is. Garry, you'd better go to her concert and *tell* them about the comforts.'

'Tell them—Good Lord, I will! But it won't be a happy concert. You'd better not ask me, Miss Morgan. No, on the whole better not. Let's get on, Linny. Good afternoon.'

'So you won't come?' she called after them.

'No, no. Lin, where did that gossip get a start? I hope it hasn't spread far. What you told me, I mean. Who could have spread such a story? About David Grey.'

'But it isn't a story.'

'Isn't a story?'

'Not a story. It's true.'

'No.'

'Yes.'

'It'll need a jolly lot of comforts to protect me against that. Where did you get the tale?'

'But, Garry—don't you believe it?'

'Comforts. Believe it? Did you know David Grey?'

'No.'

'Well, I did.'

'But—'

'David was the cleanest thing on God's earth. And not killed, you know. Not a clean, sharp death. Rotted off. Diseased. To die like that! It's an insult. A stupid, senseless, dirty joke. I wish they hadn't added this to it. These scandalmongers. They must always be at something. This tale about an engagement. Another dirty joke. Senseless and dirty. Accusing him of moral disease, as though the physical were not enough.'

'But she told me—'

Lindsay compelled him to understand that the story was no mere rumour. Louie herself asserted it.

'Of all the brazen— Clawed him up from the dead and devoured him. I wish her joy of the meal.'

'I can't understand you, Garry. Why should you disbelieve her?'

'Did you know David Grey?'

'You know I—'

'Well, I did. David was utterly incapable of fooling around with a woman he didn't mean to marry. And utterly incapable of marrying a woman like that thing there. It's obscene. See that tree there, Linny? It's like phosphorescence on decaying fish. Evil look, hasn't it?'

'Why, it's just the sun.'

It was the naked rowan they had seen before. Garry felt a poison in the air. He strode to and fro.

'But your precious Louie shall disgorge. I'll see to that. Give him back his character. In public, too.'

In their restless turning they came face to face again with Louie.

'Captain Forbes, I am sure you will reconsider. It would be such an attraction for our concert.'

Garry stood swaying upon his parted feet. A hand rumpled his forehead. He glared down. Like an ogre, Louie said. One did not fling liar at a woman: still, the thing had to stop.

'I thought perhaps a short address. Some aspect of life at the Front. Of course we want to know the truth.'

The truth, did they? That was easy. David was not cheap. He said aloud, 'Sorry. Been ill, you know. Really don't feel fit for that sort of business. And look here, by the way, this story that's going the rounds. About Grey. Couldn't we do something—fizzle it out somehow? They've got you mixed up in it too, I understand.'

He did not look at her. Louie's eyes melted into Lindsay's. She drew a long breath, then spoke with a guarded frailness in her speech. A mere trickle of sound.

'I don't quite follow, Captain Forbes.'

Lindsay was standing watchfully. A great unhappiness surged within her. Misery, she thought, had ended yesterday, when Garry's letter came at last, when he had said, meet me on the moor. Today had been so perfect that she had thought unhappiness was done with for ever. Why should it begin again? And when Louie's eyes melted into hers, she could have cried for the strangeness of life, its pain, its mystery. She, who had thrilled to her lover's denunciation (in the abstract) of injustice and hypocrisy, stood now aghast while he exposed one hypocrite. But Louie was true, that was the trouble. There was some hideous mistake.

'I don't quite follow, Captain Forbes.'

And then that Garry should say straight out the hideous thing! Now Louie was weeping, talking swiftly. 'But why should I say these things to a stranger? Oh, I know you were my dear David's friend, but some things are too sacred even for a friend's ear. Too secret. How could you know the secret sacred things I shared with David?'

It wasn't Garry's voice she heard. 'I'm sorry, Miss Morgan, I simply don't believe the story.' And Louie still weeping. Garry was going away. What! He could insult a woman like that and then march off and leave her! Louie's sad eyes were watching her.

'Men,' said Louie, 'never begin to understand what we

women have to suffer. The loneliness. The awful emptiness.'

'Oh, I know,' Lindsay cried, remembering her own anxiety. 'Tell me, tell me, Louie. He's quite wrong, isn't he?
Oh, I don't know what he means by it. It's horrible. I'm so
sorry, so sorry.' She began to sob.

Louie put her arms round the child. 'Ah, we women. We
understand one another, don't we?' Lindsay let herself be
comforted. There was a subtle flattery in Louie's accepting
her as a grown woman, meet for a woman's suffering. She
couldn't know all this if she hadn't been through it, thought
the girl. Louie was like a priestess divulging mysteries.

'You *were* engaged, weren't you?' she whispered.

'I *am* engaged. As you call it. Betrothed, I prefer to
say. My troth plighted unto eternity.'

'Forgive me for asking. Forgive me for asking.' In some
deep fashion she felt that it was forgiveness for Garry that
she requested.

To Garry the problem thus set seemed on the first evening
simple, if a trifle disgusting. He had always disliked Louie
Morgan. When he had first come to Knapperley, she, doubly entrenched as daughter of the manse and a young lady
five or six years older than the boys, had administered
reproof to David and Garry for their behaviour on the
way to church. To Garry: 'Even though you do come
from a godless house—' To David: 'And you should be
all the more ashamed, a saintly man for your father.' The
boys lay in wait for my young miss. On the day she wore
her first long skirt they walked behind her, whispering and
laughing. They sang in chorus, then in antiphon:

O wot ye what our maid Mary's gotten?
A braw new goon an' the tail o't rotten.
O wot ye—O wot ye—A braw new goon—
The tail o't—the tail o't rot-ten—

Louie could hardly wait till they desisted before ducking
round to see that the tail of her skirt was in its place. A shout
of laughter came from the ambushed boys.

Later they bribed a small girl to be their victim. In
full view of the minister's daughter, they pulled her hair
and punched her arms. The victim expiated all the sins of

her sex in the way she wailed. Miss Louie was scarlet with indignation. She read the boys a homily they would remember. But suddenly all three had joined hands and danced round Her Indignation, whooping. The daughter of the manse spluttered with disgust. Assailing the victim: 'Are you not ashamed, you who come from a Christian home, to play deceitful tricks with these boys?' The victim (who was Kate Falconer) being sturdy and stolid, made a face. That night the boys took Kate to the harrying of a bike.

In the years of their apprenticeship the boys ceased to see each other. They served their time in different towns, and holidays were spent in camp. But with their Technical College Course they were again together. In the last of their student years David chanced to remark, 'Old Morgan's gone. Decent old soul.' 'And what's come of Miss Hullabaloo?' 'Oh, husband-hunting still, I suppose.' Garry could not remember that they had ever talked of her again.

He was therefore sure that the story, wherever it originated, was false. At first it had seemed a simple matter of gossip. That Louie herself asserted its truth made it hardly less simple, though more unpleasant. The claim was a lie, and must be exposed as such. Here was a small but definite engagement in the war against evil, and Garry's heart, on the first evening of the engagement, rose pleasurably to the fray. It was not often one could deliver so clear a blow against falsehood.

SIX

Tea at The Weatherhouse

In the course of the following morning Miss Theresa Craigmyle ran out of cornflour. Theresa made no objections to running out of necessaries. It provided an excuse for running out herself. Theresa's slogan—*A ga'in foot's aye gettin'*—embraced more than what she purchased at a roup. She would come home with all the gossip of the neighbourhood.

This morning she brought in the cornflour and said, 'Mrs Hunter tells me that Bawbie Paterson's nephew is come. Sick leave, she says. And a terrible sight. Influenza and not got over it. All nonsense too thin. "Bawbie won't fatten him sore," I says. "Oh, there's aye a bite and a sup for him here," says she. "Mr Garry kens where to come whan he's teem. He'll aye get what's goin'. The tail o' a fish and the tap o' an egg, if it's nae mair." O aye, he would. He had a crap for a' corn and a baggie for orrels, yon lad. He could fair go his meat. You would have thought he was yoking a pair of horse.'

'Well, well,' said Miss Annie, 'what would you expect? A great growing loon. He needed his meat.'

Kate, who had come home that day with a week's leave from hospital, heard and said, 'Better ask him to tea. Well, why not? You ask all the young men home on leave, don't you? Even if you do object to his aunt—well, even to himself, then—but I daresay he's sobered down by now. We haven't seen him for donkey's years.'

Miss Theresa conceded the tea. It was one of her ways of helping on the war. For every young man of the district home on leave she baked her famous scones and gingerbread, while Miss Annie and Mrs Falconer asked the same series of questions about the Front.

'I'll tell you what,' said Kate. 'Linny and I will walk round by Knapperley. She's never seen the place.'

'She's seen Bawbie. That should be enough. Well, Lindsay, don't you take her tea if she should offer you any. Spoot-ma-gruel.'

'He'll be waiting for me, Katie,' murmured Lindsay when they were outside.

'That's all right. I'll go away.'

'You'd better give the invitation— Or— As you please.'

Garry said, 'You, Kate— Remember the wasp's bike?'

'Why, yes, I do. Will you face my aunts tomorrow?'

'Will you face mine today? Yes, do come, Katie. Linny must see Knapperley. And I want to talk to you. How are we to set to work killing this lie about Davie? That Morgan creature, you know.'

'Is it a lie?'

'Oh, Katie,' cried Lindsay, 'do help me to convince him. He's taken such a dreadful idea into his head—that poor Louie has invented the whole story. He's hurt her so.'

'That sort doesn't hurt. Does it, Kate?'

'Why, yes. Very badly, I should fancy.'

'What! Hullabaloo? No. You thrust, and she closes up round. Unless she's changed a lot.'

'But why a lie?'

'You think David would have married that?'

'I don't know. Why not?'

'Lord, Kate!'

'Well, I don't see what's preposterous in the idea. She's a good woman. Feckless, a bit. Rather conceited. I'm not particularly fond of her. But David Grey may have been, for all I know. I presume he was, since he asked her to marry him.'

'But he didn't.'

'Didn't?'

'Garry, you don't *know*,' cried Lindsay.

'Look here, Kate, you wouldn't dishonour David, would you? You wouldn't think him capable of such meanness?'

'But why should it be meanness to marry a woman? Most men do.'

'But that Louie.'

'Louie's all right, Garry. I don't see why you should be so angry. I don't like her much, as I said, but lots of people do. You haven't seen her for so long. Of course, she was a bit—you know—self-important. Put on airs. But that sort of thing wears off. Or else one gets accustomed to it. She'd make as good a wife as another. I don't see why David shouldn't have chosen her.'

'David, Kate? As good a wife as another, yes. But for the other man—not for David.'

'David is merely the other man for me, Garry. Any man. I hadn't seen him for years. How could I know what he might or might not do? And a lot of men make fools of themselves when they marry, anyhow.'

'So at least you acknowledge that such a marriage would be folly.'

'No. I was talking of a general principle.'

'Katie, can't you see what is at stake? It's a lie. A blasted, damnable lie. She's false as hell. It must be killed. She must be forced to acknowledge there was no engagement.'

'But what an idea! You propose to put it to her?'

'Oh, Katie,' cried Lindsay, 'he isn't only proposing. He's done it.'

'And she acknowledged it, of course?'

'No, she denied.'

'Well, what more do you want? Why do you suppose it's a lie? I didn't know there was any doubt over it.'

'I suppose it's a lie because it can't be true.'

Kate stopped in the road and gave him a long, considering look.

'Because you refuse to believe it's true, you mean. Do you *know*? David ever say anything about it to you? You've no proof? Look here, Garry, you'd better be sure you're not doing this because you hate Miss Louie Morgan. You never used to miss a chance, you know, of tormenting her.'

'Of taking her down a peg, you mean. She needed it.'

'Yes. But it was good fun, taking her down.'

'Well . . . it staled. You never could take her down. Just what I said: you thrust and she closed up round. Oh yes, good fun enough. But you don't suppose there's any fun in this business about Grey, do you?'

'I think you are persuaded by your own dislike.'

'Katie,' Lindsay's clear, sharp voice rang out, 'you have no right to speak to Garry like that.'

'You don't want him to make a fool of himself in the countryside, do you?'

Garry winced.

'Louie Morgan is too much respected—her father—her mother. People would simply gape. It's your word against hers, isn't it? And they'll all remember the things you used to do to her. Even David Grey thought you went too far. That time you made on to be fighting, and she separated you and you carried her off and shut her in the old Tower.'

'And forgot to let her out.'

'A willing forget.'

'No, I don't think so. No, I'm sure we were doing something else. Queer how hard it is to remember. We did mean to let her out.'

'Do tell me,' said Lindsay.

'Nothing to tell. Horrid rumpus. Dr Morgan purple in the face. And David's father— That was something to remember. Davie said it happened only once before. Davie's father told him off. Six words, no more. No more needed.'

'No one could understand how you got in.'

'We pinched the key.'

'Are you quite sure you are not pinching the key this time? I'll leave you two,' Kate finished abruptly.

'But, Katie—about going home. I came out with you. They'd think it funny.' Lindsay did not wish the old women to understand Garry's identity. They would make uncomfortable remarks.

'Yes,' agreed Kate, 'they do chatter. Very well, I'll wait for you. Behind the spruce trees.'

'But,' Lindsay questioned as she watched Kate melt against the moor, 'need we go to Knapperley?'

Garry had been thinking of Kate: 'How she has altered! She's growing like her aunts. What, not go to Knapperley? But you must see my aunt. She is not fearsome,' he added, smiling.

'But I fear her.'

'Why?' he asked, smiling protectively down upon her.

'No, it's not that—I am not a child.' She could find no way to express her thoughts about Miss Barbara. They were not thoughts—that was it. They were something felt, apprehended in her dumb silent self. The image of Miss Barbara loomed above her, as she had appeared in the winter night, elemental, a mass of the very earth, earthy smelling, with her goat's beard, her rough hairy tweed like the pelt of an animal. She had thought John Grey too like a portion of earth, as he crawled on all fours weeding; but he embodied the kindly and benignant earth; Miss Barbara its coarser, crueller aspect . . . Has no mythology deified a bearded woman as its god of earth? Lindsay, unable to find words to explain her terror, which could not be explained by anything as yet within her experience, blurted, 'It was the lights. They were awful, Garry, truly. Every window blazing, in mid-winter, and it war-time.'

'What's this?' said Garry. 'Good old Barbara! She would win every war that ever was.'

'Win it? Keep it from being won. Defying orders.'

'But that's just it. The spirit of it. We shan't have won this war until we're all defiant. Haven't you understood that yet? My aunt's enormously herself. She'll never alter, except to get more herself. I don't suppose the lights mattered. The police would have seen to it otherwise.'

'But they did. She was fined, I think. Warned, at any rate.'

'Very well. Now come and see her after her warning.'

'You think I am a child, to be afraid.'

But perhaps she was. The warm glad sun danced over her. The earth shimmered away into idle space. And now she had seen a blue tit.

'What is he, what is he? I do so want to know his name. Garry, there are herons in the lower wood. I saw one yesterday with Kate. Flying. A great grey heavy one.'

'They are all like that.'

'Are they?'

'Then it had been herons we were hearing yesterday while we were talking.'

'Yes.'

'And are you satisfied now that you know?'

'Oh, to know makes me so happy . . . You think that strange?'

He took her through the high, bare rooms of Knapperley.

'But these are dreary rooms.'

'Not the kitchen. I don't know where my aunt can be.'

'No matter. Let's go out.'

'I was giving these outer doors and windows a coat of paint. Look how warped they are. The wood's shrunken. Do you mind if I go on?'

'How neatly you work, Garry! Do you hear that bird? I must follow.'

He gave himself to the consideration of Kate. She was wrong to be so sure: he was sure, moreover, that she was wrong. And to bring this ignoble motive in to a clean fight against falsehood! It was petty on Kate's part to suppose that he still harboured these boyish animosities. He fought for greater issues now. And if the victim in each case was the same, was he at fault? It was not as a person that he wanted Louie punished, but as the embodiment of a disgrace. He brought the brush down with neat furious strokes. But Mrs Hunter, when he had called the night before at Craggie, had scorned his suggestion of duplicity in Louie's tale.

'She has the ring, Mr Garry—his mother's ring that she showed me herself, and her dying, and said her laddie's love should wear. That's nae ca'ed story, Mr Garry. Louie fairly has the ring.'

'His mother's ring,' muttered Garry.

'I'm nae saying but it's a queer whirliorum, a matter like a marriage to come out in a by-your-leave fashion like that. Miss Craigmyle, now, was of your way of thinking—that she made the story up, But "Na, na," I said to her, "na, na, she has her credentials." And her credentials is more than the ring, Mr Garry. There's the name she has, and her family.'

Miss Theresa Craigmyle? Very well, then, he would go to their tea.

Lindsay came bounding back.

'Garry, your aunt knows—why didn't you tell me? Your aunt knows all kinds of things. There's a heronry in Kingcausie woods, my heron must have come from there. They have to shut the doors and windows at breeding time. Against the clamour. And there are oyster-catchers' eggs on that bit of shingle. Lying in the stones. You stumble on them. Oh, Garry, I like your paint. You have made a difference.'

'So you found my aunt.'

'I was watching a bird. I didn't know what it was, I am so ignorant. I crept in, under the trees there, following. She found me. I thought it was something wonderful. It was only a chaffinch. But even a chaffinch is very wonderful, if you know just nothing at all, like me.'

'Wonder what Aunt Barbara thinks of this Louie Morgan affair?'

'What does it matter, now? It's ended, isn't it?'

'Ended?'

'Surely Kate convinced you? Do you still think Louie made the story up?'

At the Weatherhouse, after tea that evening, Mrs Falconer followed Kate to the garden. How still the air, how shining pure the sky! Waiting—all waiting for the revelation of spring. But it was so hard to talk confidentially to Kate. Her mother stumbled, came in broken rushes against the girl's tranquillity.

'Garry is coming? I thought, I used to imagine—long ago—you were such friendly you two. I wondered sometimes—but then he went away. I used to think you cared.'

Kate knit her brows, considering the implications of her mother's insight; decided that the secret was not hers to divulge.

'Why, yes,' she said, unbending her frown. 'But there was no need for you to know.'

'And now? It hasn't altered?'

'No. No, I think not.' She thought, 'As good a way as any to cover Lindsay.'

Mother and daughter parted.

'Stop your bumming, Ellen,' sharply said Mrs Craigmyle. Leeb was accustomed to say, 'Not one of my daughters has tune in her, and there's Ellen would bum away half the time, if I would let her.'

Ellen laughed and forebore. She went out to the long brown Weatherhill, where no one would resent her bumming. It was that hour of waning light when colours take on their most magical values. The clumps and thickets of whin, that had turned golden in the few days of sun, glowed with a live intensity, as though light were within them. The colours of life had for Ellen the same bright magical intensity. She was more excited than she knew. Had Kate a hidden life her mother had not suspected? She was so placid, so contained; Ellen had schooled herself for so long to the disappointment of believing that her daughter was thus contained because there was nothing to spill over. Had she misjudged her Kate? Ellen's thoughts turned back to Kate's girlhood, and she remembered how the girl had run about the moor with this Garry Forbes—a great awkward lad, she had never seen much in him. Wild ruffian, Theresa said. Yes, they had all condemned his madcap ways, and Kate had suffered in silence. But Ellen had woven a whole romance around the two and hidden it in her heart, hardly believing it had more foundation than the hundred other romances that she wove. But it had, it had. Foundation, and a new miraculous lustre. Kate took on a new dignity in her mother's eyes—perhaps the grandeur of a tragic destiny. But no, that must not be—unless he were slaughtered. No, no, I must not fancy things like that. Kate's love would reach its consummation. They would be wedded. He would call her mother. The boy had had no mother—and now he would tell her the things that a son keeps for a mother's ear. 'Mother, it is so easy to tell this to you. You have a way of listening—' No, no. I must not fancy things like that.

But on the morrow, when Garry came to the Weatherhouse, Mrs Falconer tingled with her excitement. She pressed herself upon the guest, eager to know him. 'For Kate's sake, I must get to understand him.'

'You've no knives on your table, Nell,' scolded Theresa.

'No, no. No.' She *scuttered* at the open drawer, sat down again by Garry, smiling.

'See that your mother has those knives put down,' said Theresa to Kate. 'When my back's about I can't know what she'll do. She's been the deed of two or three queer things this day. I've got two or three angers with her.'

'She's tired today, I fancy.'

'Tired! Your granny in a band-box.'

Kate returned from the kitchen and set the knives herself. Mrs Falconer was smiling, looking up in Garry's face, asking senseless unimportant questions.

'You might have the wit to know *that*,' Lindsay was thinking, impatient at the trivial turns the conversation took.

'Mother, don't giggle,' said Kate, aside, passing her.

'Why shouldn't she giggle?' Garry thought, watching for the first time the elderly lady with interest. 'So, Miss Kate, you are growing like your aunt Theresa. You put people right.' He gave Mrs Falconer's questions a serious attention.

Theresa brought in the tea.

'There', slapping down her pancakes before the guest, 'you don't get the like of that at Knapperley. It's aye the same thing with Bawbie, a stovie or a sup kail.'

Garry drawled, 'A soo's snoot stewed on Sunday and on Monday a stewed soo's snoot.' And he did not look at Miss Theresa, whom he hated, with her air of triumph, her determination to show him that man must live by bread alone.

Miss Annie laughed delightedly. 'When did I hear that last? And whiles it'll be as tough's the woodie, I'm thinking, your soo's snoot.'

Lindsay cried, 'Garry, do you know them too, all these funny picturesque phrases? You must teach them to me.'

But Theresa muttered, 'Sarcastic deevil.'

'I would have you know'—he addressed himself mentally to Theresa—'I can't stand people who humiliate me. The pancakes are excellent, Miss Craigmyle,' he said aloud. 'And now please tell me, why do you suppose Miss Louie Morgan was not engaged to David Grey?'

'Did ever you suppose such a thing, Aunt Tris?' asked Kate.

'Garry has taken a dreadful idea into his head,' cried Lindsay, 'that Louie made the story up.'

'There!' cried Theresa triumphantly. 'Didn't I tell you that long ago, but you weren't hearing me. I was right, you see. I'm not often wrong.'

But was she right? Now, where did the tale begin? Let's trace it out. But nothing came of that, except to disturb everyone's sense of security. No, not a whisper before his death: that was plain. But shortly after, 'I haven't the right to wear mourning,' she had said to Mrs Hunter. And she had the ring. And Mr Grey received her often. But counter-balance that with her character: well, a good character, a moral character. But they all knew she was out after a man. Oh yes, a flighty thing, always ogling the men. 'Though there's lots that's taken in with her airs and her graces.' Would a man like Grey be taken in? His character against her known assertiveness, her pretty dangling. But where does all this lead? Since the man is dead, it can't be known for certain.

'Since he is dead, I must put it to the proof. His reputation must be cleared. And publicly.'

'Be wary, Garry,' said Kate. 'If you are wrong—no, accept the possibility for a moment—if you are wrong, you will have pilloried your friend.'

'Publicly,' Miss Annie cried. 'You wouldn't do the like of that. She's a harmless craiturie that nobody seeks to mind.'

'And it would hurt her. Garry, you don't understand—it will hurt her horribly,' Lindsay pleaded. 'Suppose he did love her, after all.'

'And David Grey,' said Miss Theresa, 'is hardly of the place now, as you might say. Since he went away to go to the college we've hardly seen or heard of him. Except his medals, to be sure, and prizes. But he might marry anyone you pleased to point at, and who would care? Not a soul would let their kail grow cold with thinking of it.'

'And anyway,' said Kate, 'now that he's dead, does it matter?'

'Captain Forbes matters,' said Mrs Falconer.

Ellen's hands were clasped tight together above her breast, and they shook rapidly from her excitement. They were like a tiny bald nodding head that gave assent

to her speech. Her head nodded too, slightly and rapidly.

The gaunt young man looked across the table; and
remained looking, his jaw down, as though, having opened
his mouth to speak, what he was about to say had become
suddenly unimportant.

'I mean,' she continued, 'honour matters. Whether people care or not, and whether she's to be hurt or not, you've
to get the truth clear. Because of truth itself. Because of his
honour. And it matters to you, because you feel his honour's
in your keeping now he's gone.'

'Yes,' he said, 'that's why. Because of truth itself. It's
good of you to see that.'

If one had never seen a bird before, never seen a flake
of earth, loosened and blown into the air, change shape and
rise, and poise, and speed far off, beyond the power of eye
to follow; seeing one would understand the sharp delight
that Mrs Falconer experienced at hearing the young man's
words. She kindled, her face became winsome, like that of
a young girl. She laughed—a low, sweet laughter. When he
talked to her, words bubbled on her lips.

'But must you go so soon?' she pleaded. '—Yes, yes,
a pack of women, we can't entertain you very hard.'

Indeed, as he walked away the man felt relief from
the pack of women. On the other side of the dyke Francie
Ferguson, slicing turnips, droned a song. Garry leaned his
arms on the dyke and looked over.

'Ay, ay, you're having a song to yourself.'

Francie straightened his shoulders, pushed his cap farther
back on his head, answered, 'Imphm,' scratched himself a
little, added, 'Just that,' and returned to the turnips.

'Decent fellow,' thought Garry. Yes, that Morgan creature had to be corrected. Beside the honesty of Francie she
showed unclean.

In the Weatherhouse: 'Stop your bumming, Ellen,'
commanded Mrs Craigmyle.

'Mother, don't giggle,' said Kate apart.

As on the evening before, Mrs Falconer left them and
walked alone on the Weatherhill. Again the sky was shining
pure. Again the wide land waited. Annunciation of spring

was in the brown ploughed fields, the swollen buds, the blackbird's sudden late cascade of song, the smell of earth. A wood of naked birches hung on the hillside like a cloud of heather, so deep a glow of purple was in their boughs. And a bird had gone up out of Ellen's heart, pursuing its unaccountable way into the distance. A flake from her earth had risen. Life had a second spring, and it was opening for this woman of sixty who had lived so long among her dreams. The earnest young man, his brows drawn in that anxious pucker, his eyes unsatisfied, roving from face to face, burdened with the pain and ugliness of life—yes, she was sure that that was it, that haunted look of his betrayed a soul unhappy over the torment and mystery of life, its unreason and its evil—this young man had brought her suddenly back into its throng and business. She who had been content to dream must now do.

And her fancy was off. She saw that it was she who was to help the young man (she called him mentally her son-in-law) to establish the truth, to rout Louie.

'How can I have lived among trivial matters for so long?' she thought. 'This is real, and good. I feel alive.'

She wandered back slowly to the house. Light still lingered in the sky; the hills, that had been dissolved in its splendour, like floating shapes of light themselves, grew dark again. Ellen too, emerged from the transfiguring glory of light in which she had been walking. What did her happiness mean? Why, of course, she was happy because of Katie. This mysterious and tranquil glow that had irradiated life had its source in a mother's satisfaction. Kate loved, Kate would be loved, Kate's mother would be satisfied.

But in the house there was no satisfaction. They were all talking together. Lindsay tossed back her disordered hair, angry tears were in her eyes. The leaping firelight gleamed on her face, her agitated movements, and on Theresa's fingers as she put away the knives and silver, and on Leeb's busy knitting needles and the glittering points her eyes made in the gloom.

'Cousin Ellen,' cried the girl, 'Cousin Ellen, Louie is true. Oh, she is! Garry is wrong, wrong, wrong.'

'It's not worth the to-do, Lindsay,' said Miss Theresa.

Ellen flamed magnificently from the exaltation with which she had been suffused. 'But yes. Always worth, always worth to follow truth. The young man is doing the right.'

'To hurt her? Even if it wasn't an engagement. If she just loved him—and never told?'

'She never did. She just couldn't stand being unimportant.'

Ellen said it suddenly. She had not known it herself till that moment. 'There's all the girls round about, they all had their lads, and some of them killed and some wounded, and everybody making much of them and them on everyone's lips. And Louie had nobody. She had a lot of talk one time about *missing, missing,* as though she wanted us to believe she had someone and him lost.'

'What an idea, Mother!' said Kate.

'But she had. "It's cruel, this *Missing, Presumed Dead,*" she would say. "It keeps one from starting fresh." '

'Yes, she said that to me.' Lindsay stared across at Mrs Falconer. 'She said, "It's the faithfulness that is unto death. It deadens you. Keeps you from beginning life anew." What a curious thing to say!'

'Always what we couldn't disprove, you see. And then she hit on David Grey. And so she paraded her tragedy. It made her important. They may say what they like about Louie looking miserable—she's never looked so *filled out* as she has of late. She was a starved sort of thing before.'

'But, Cousin Ellen, I can't believe that it's all a lie. If you had heard Louie talk about it. So tenderly. You can't imagine. A lie couldn't be lovely like that.'

'There's lots you can't believe in life, Linny. Angels of darkness masquerading as angels of light. I'm some afraid she's lived so much with her lie that she can't feel it a lie any longer. Her head must know, but her heart is persuaded.'

Lindsay's eyes, mournful and still, were fixed on her. 'Why, the child herself had some affair,' Ellen remembered. Surely it was over. This eager Lindsay, following bird song, catching at country ways and sights, gathering windflowers, was quite changed from the pallid girl who had come to them at Christmas. 'Yes, yes, she was too young. It must be over.' But the girl's eyes burned in the dusk; not eyes of light forgetfulness.

Theresa put the last of the knives away, and stood scratching the side of her nose.

'Such a to-do about a dead man,' she said, 'that can't come back to set the matter right. I've had an itchy nose all day—itchy nose, you'll hear of fey folk. It's to be hoped no more of you are doomed, the way you're carrying on. I always told you Louie made the story up. But to hold this parliament about it—'

'Cousin Theresa, don't you dare to mention it to anyone. Not anyone. That Louie made it up, I mean. Not till it's proved, if Garry ever does prove it. To disgrace her publicly— If *you* begin to talk, she'll have publicity enough.'

Mrs Craigmyle chuckled from her corner. 'Take you that to butter your skate.' Without lifting her eyes or altering a muscle of her face, she began to hum a little tune.

'You're turning as rude as that young man, Miss Lindsay,' retorted Theresa. 'But you will note that he enjoyed his tea. You needn't be in such a taking over Louie, bairn,' she added, more kindly. 'Grows there skate on Clochnaben? She was born with a want—you'll get no sense yonder. But *you* needn't turn your head about it. You greetin' like a leaky pot, and Nell with a great baby's face on her—I never saw the like. Worse than you's useless.'

The face that Ellen turned towards the fire was indeed strangely child-like. A soft smile played on it, pleased and innocent. She was still thinking, 'I shall help him to proclaim the truth.' But the sharpness of truth was not visible on her countenance. She had the look of the dreamer who has not yet tried to shape his dream from intractable matter.

In the firelit room Mrs Craigmyle's hum grew more audible. The words became clear:

Duncan Forb's cam here to woo,

sang Mrs Craigmyle, with a subtle emphasis upon the altered word:

Ha, ha, the wooin' o't.

Ellen looked up. Her face quivered. She began to talk loud and quickly.

'Hateful,' she thought, 'making it uncomfortable for Kate.'

Later she found her mother alone. Mrs Craigmyle raised her voice (but not her eyes) at her daughter's approach:

Duncan Forb's cam here to woo.

She sang gaily, her foot tapping the time, and her snow-white head, crowned with its mist of fine black lace, nodding to the leap of the flames. And her face was innocent of any intention. She was singing an old song.

'Mother,' said Ellen, with burning cheeks, 'you shouldn't do that. Hinting. In your song. It isn't nice.'

Mrs Craigmyle turned an amused, appraising eye upon her widowed daughter.

'You're right, bairn,' she answered blandly. 'The young man has a good Scots name that won't fit into the metre. You're right. I shouldn't spoil an old name as though I had an English tongue on me—feared to speak two syllables when one will do. I'll not offend again.'

She watched her daughter with a fine regard that had malice in it. Mrs Craigmyle, through her apparent uncon-cern, had noted Ellen, habitually so quiet and reserved, kindle and crackle, and it amused her.

'Well,' said Ellen, 'but if Kate doesn't like it.'

'That's right my lass, study you to please your family.'

Ellen went away, her cheeks still hot; and a mocking laughter followed her, faint, that seemed to echo from very far off, centuries away, in ancient story.

Lindsay was leaning from her open window. The spring night, hushed and dim, yet held a tumult. Out there, in every field, in boughs of the secret wood, life moved. Kate slept, but Lindsay could not sleep. Everything—the promise of spring in the air, an owl's call up the valley, the tranquil radiance that the young moon had left above the hills, water tumbling with a thin clear note, the shame and trouble of her nature—all conspired to keep her exquisitely awake. And Lindsay thought, 'I want everyone to be happy. It shouldn't hurt like this—all that beauty.'

She could not tell herself what the hurt was. All was vague and confused in her mind. Garry was different from what she had supposed him. But she had known him so little—only his kisses and those amazing talks, far into the night, until her father came and sent them all to bed. This Garry with the worried frown and haggard eyes was someone else. Worrying because he wanted to do a wicked thing—Lindsay was still convinced by Louie's phrases. Or—were her confusion and trouble because she was no longer quite convinced? Was Louie, whom she had set admiringly in her temple, no god at all, but brittle clay?

'I don't understand,' she cried, leaning to the night. 'Life's so strange. It isn't what you want.'

One grew and things altered, people altered, just being alive was somehow not the same. Spring was like that, changing the world, taking away the shapes and colours to which one was accustomed. Were seeds afraid, she wondered, and buds? Afraid to grow, afraid of life as she was afraid of it. Evil, and wrong—one knew there were such things in the world, but to find them in people, that was different. In people that one knew. Garry cruel, and Louie false; and all the while earth and sky brimmed with beauty. And she leaned farther into the tranquil night.

Below her on the grass someone was moving. Who should be in the garden so late? If it were Garry! How good to have him seek her presence in the dark, in the still, sweet April glamour! A very night for lovers.

But the figure on the lawn moved farther off. Now it was against the sky, and she saw that it was a woman's. Her eyeballs were stinging. 'I only want to be happy,' she cried. The sound of her own voice, breaking unexpectedly upon the silence, affrighted her. But Katie did not stir, and in a moment another voice was borne to her upon the air. She recognised it for Theresa's. 'Come in to your bed, Ellen.' The voice floated from the next window. 'Walking there like a ghost.' There was no answer, but the figure in the garden moved back towards the house; and Lindsay heard a stair creak. Cousin Ellen! Why should she walk in the night? Why should anyone walk in the night but the young and the untranquil and the lovers who cannot wait for morning?

SEVEN

Why Classroom Doors should be Kept Locked

Morning changed the temper of the spring. Plainly the lady had no more mind for honeyed promises. Her suave and gracious mood was done, and those who would win her favours must wrestle a fall with the insolent young Amazon. Sleet blattered against the ploughman's side as he followed the team; or, standing in a blink of sun, he saw the striding showers cross the corner of the field like sheeted ghosts. Never tell me, ghosts took to sheets for the first time in a Deeside ploughman's story, who, bewildered in an April dusk, saw white showers walk the land, larger than human, driven on the wind.

'Where are my birds today?' asked Lindsay. 'And oh, the poor thin petals! Look, Garry, on the whin.'

But Garry answered, 'I'm going to take you home.'

At the Weatherhouse door Mrs Falconer met them, running.

'Come in, come in. You must be wet.'

She did not pause to question why they were together.

'They never seem to guess,' Lindsay thought. 'Old people don't see.'

Doors flapped, sleet scurried along the lobby.

'Come in, come in,' Mrs Falconer cried. 'She will be angry at this mess.'

She drew them in and, stooping, plucked with her fingers at the melting flakes of sleet, and dabbed at the runnels with a corner of her skirt. 'There, she'll be none the wiser.'

'Not a whit,' Garry said. He had taken out his handkerchief and wiped a smeared wet patch from the hat stand.

But Theresa was safely in the kitchen, so they sat and talked by the living-room fire, with old Aunt Leeb spider-quiet in her corner, and Paradise in a happy doze. She opened her eyes and smiled at them. 'I'm dozened,' she said, and slid away again.

Garry began to talk of after the war. 'It will be a very different Britain before we're done with it.' He told them all that was to be accomplished to make life worthier. Lindsay glowed. This was the talk she loved to hear. Her young untried enthusiasms delighted in the noble. Above all she wanted her lover to be good. These splendid generalities were like the fulfilment of all her own vague adolescent aspirations.

Ellen also glowed. 'Why, what a barren useless life I have lived!' She felt a smoulder of shame run through her at the thought of the evanescent fancies in which her inner life had passed. 'But *this* is real. How I hate these shams and unrealities!' And, without noticing what she did, she began to form a new fancy. 'Katie loves him. If they should ever marry—when they marry I trust they will let me live with them.' How good that would be—to live in daily touch with men's enterprises, to know what was done and thought in the world. Hearing the young man speak, she would never slide again into these wicked imaginings. And she remembered how he had taken out his handkerchief and wiped away the smear of sleet. 'But when I live with them, I shan't need to go in terror of Tris.' She could open the door then, without fear of what came in, to strength and manhood and new ideas, and even to brave young folly that laughed in the sleet when it might sit warm at home.

All this she fancied at the very moment that Lindsay, lifting her eyes to smile into her lover's, was thinking, 'I thought if he came here there would be all their stupid jokes to face, but not one of them seems to notice.' Then she saw Miss Annie's eye upon her. But Miss Annie only said, 'I think I'm taking a cold. Lindsay, you've no clothes on.'

Lindsay ran behind the old woman's chair and put her arms round her neck. 'Girls don't wear clothes nowadays, Paradise, you dear.' And she wanted to tell Paradise that Garry was her lover. 'Because I'm sure you saw,' she thought. And, after all, it was pleasant that Paradise had seen. 'It's the others who would talk. Paradise, your hair's so soft behind. Paradisal hair.'

'It's got most terrible grey.'

'Silver, you mean. Silver of Paradise. Apples of gold and silver of Paradise.'

'You're a wheedling thing—what are you wanting now?'

'Only a kiss.'

She dropped a kiss in the nape of Miss Annie's neck and danced round the back of Garry's chair, running her fingers across his shoulders as she passed; but Cousin Ellen she did not touch. Even grand-aunt Leeb she had breathed upon, blowing a kiss so light upon her ancient head that the gossamer of her lace hardly trembled.

'How strange!' she thought. 'Last night I was miserable. And now today I'm glad. I don't know what to make of life.'

And Mrs Falconer, whom she had not touched, was unaware of the omission. A warm glow suffused her body. She was thinking, 'This false betrothal, that is something true. To expose the falsehood is something real that I can take my part in.'

Garry went away. The sleet eased off, but the roads were like mortar and the land looked bleak. An empty land—he remembered his vision of it as taking form from the primordial dark. Some human endeavour there must be: like Lindsay unaccustomed to a country year, he had hardly realised before today how much endeavour, skill and endurance went to the fashioning of food from earth in weathers such as these. His midsummer holidays had not told him of wet seed-times, of furious winds blowing the turnip seed across the moors, of snow blackening the stooks of corn. He saw a man lead home his beasts through mire, fields not yet sown were sodden wet again. He had never thought before of these things. There must be grit and strength in the men who sowed their turnips thrice and ploughed land that ran up into the encroaching heather. A tough race, strong in fibre. Yet since he came how little he had seen of them! Women mostly—Lindsay like whin blossom on the cankered stem of her people; his aunt like an antique pine, one side denuded, with gaunt arms flung along the tempest; Mrs Hunter like a bed of thyme . . . pleasant fancies, dehumanising the land.

Across them he felt suddenly as though a teasing tangle

had been flung—nets of spider-web, or some dark stinging
noxious weed from under ocean. He had thought of Louie
Morgan. He disliked the thought—no question as to that.
And how this mean affair had tangled across his vision!
Wherever he turned he saw it. Three days ago, when they
came on Louie at her base devotions and he had heard the
story first, it had seemed a simple thing to dispose of it. Now
it was less simple. He had recoiled instinctively from the tale
as something false, but his instinct was to be taken as no
proof by other people. These women with whom he had discussed it insisted, moreover, after the fashion of women, on
treating it as a personal matter, a matter of Louie Morgan,
not of truth. His aunt, to be sure, had raised the issue to a
matter of principle, but not one that helped him much.

'What's she wanting with a man ava?' was all he got
from Miss Barbara.

The others saw it purely on the personal plane; and
Kate's assumption that he himself was moved by a personal rancour smote him to wrath. Even Lindsay could
not see that truth and justice were beyond a personal
hurt—Lindsay, who had looked so sublimely lovely in her
pleading that he resisted her hardly. Her eyes had been fixed
on him, mournful and limpid. She was lovelier than herself.
She had identified herself with Louie. She too, was hurt and
was transfigured in her acceptance of another's suffering.

He had thought, 'But you can't ask other people to
pay the price. You can't ask Lindsay.' Was truth, after all,
more important than the pain you inflict on others for its
sake? It was only that long, lean, nice Mrs Falconer who
understood that truth and honour were at stake. A curious
champion of truth. He remembered her furtive ducking in
the lobby to dab the runlets of sleet with her petticoat. Well,
he supposed, one could tilt at error even in petticoats and
in spite of an abounding fear of one's sister in her domestic
cogencies.

He had as yet, in these three days, had no man's opinion
upon his problem. Not, for instance, John Grey's. But to
visit John Grey, as he knew he must, David's father, was
of necessity to find some expression for what he felt over
David's death; and he could find none.

At that moment, through the darkening light, he saw Miss Morgan approach.

'The deil has lang lugs to hear when he's talked about,' muttered Garry.

Miss Morgan picked her way towards him along the puddled road, and her face was as puddled as the road itself. She was weeping. She stood with downcast eyes in front of the astonished young man and said, 'Oh, Captain Forbes, what shall I do? I've been a wicked woman. Help me, Garry—I may call you Garry? We are such old friends, we used to play together.'

A man stumped past and regarded them with curiosity.

'Well, we can't talk here,' Garry said.

'No, no. The school. I was going there. I have the key.' And she led the way, looking back at him over her shoulder with eyes that languished and saying, 'The concert, you know. For those comforts. Garry, I understand what you meant about comforts. We think our responsibility is over, and it isn't. Our responsibility is never over. We are our brother's keeper all the time. You must be my keeper.'

She unlocked the school door. 'I have a key. I am in charge, you see. A little sketch they are doing—there are so few hereabouts that understand these things.'

The school was a two-roomed building, built close upon the church. The church having no hall, and a vestry like a cupboard, the adjoining school was used for many parochial purposes. Miss Morgan went in. 'I have to measure something—curtains, you know.'

Garry followed in spite of a remarkable distaste. To chatter of curtains amid tears of contrition argued, to him, a blameworthy lightness. But were the tears of contrition? He waited.

'No, I think in here,' Louie was saying. She led him to the inner room, and with some ostentation locked the door. She had an indescribable air of enjoying the situation.

Then she came swiftly at him.

'Help me, help me. What am I to do? I've done such dreadful things. I've lied and I've stolen. I am a miserable sinner, and my transgression is ever before me.'

He stopped her torrent of words with a cold: 'It is easy

to bring such general accusations, Miss Morgan. We are all sinners. If I understood what you referred to—'

She darted him a glance of hatred.

'Of course you understand. But you will make it as hard for me as you are able. Oh, what shall I do? What shall I do? People must never know what I have done. Promise me that—they mustn't know. Promise me.'

'When I know myself—'

'Yes, yes, make it as hard for me as you can. It's right, it's just. I want to confess to the uttermost. Abjectly. I will tell you—I want to tell you everything. You. But no one else. Oh, do not make it public! My name, my mother, afterwards.—Yes, yes, I will tell you all.'

Garry stood in the dark schoolroom and marvelled. He had never seen an emotional abandonment so extreme, and it seemed to him as ignoble as her perfidious clutch on his friend. He would not have helped her out in the confession, determined that she should taste its dregs by telling all; but disgust drove him to shorten the affair.

'You mean that there was no engagement.'

'No, no, it's not like that.'

'You made it up.'

'No, no, I did not make it up.'

'What then?'

'It wasn't like that. Yes, yes, I made it up. Oh, how wicked I have been! Quite, quite wrong. Evil. I see that now.'

Suddenly she raised her head, listening.

'Yes, there's someone there,' said Garry.

He had heard before she did a sound of voices outside and of feet. Now the outer door of the school was pushed open and men came in. They heard their tramp and the noise of speech.

Louie's whole expression altered. She snatched her companion by the arm and whispered, 'Caught. It's a session meeting. I had forgotten it was tonight. What shall we do?'

He shook her off. 'There's nothing to make a fuss about. You have the right to be here, I suppose, since you have the key.'

At that moment someone tried the door of the inner room. The voices rose.

'But you,' said Louie, weeping. 'And alone here. And it's dark. Oh, what shall I do?'

'Do what you please. I should imagine you could invent a sufficient story.' He flung the window up and leaped out on to the ground. 'Better shut that window again,' he called back. Then he strode off.

Louie wiped her eyes and opened the door.

An oil lamp, new-lit and smoky, hung in the outer room. Louie blinked. Her eyes, bleared and tender, smarted in the smoky atmosphere; she stood shaking, thus ruthlessly thrust back from her attempt at truth to the service of appearances. To these men she was still Miss Morgan, daughter of their late minister. She put her head to the side and apologised, and in a minute speech came freely to her and with it relief: she had escaped from the terror of her attempted encounter with her naked self.

'I really didn't remember—that concert, you know. I was measuring. I didn't remember your meeting. But I'll go— Well, if you don't mind. I could get on with those curtains.' Aided by one of the elders, she took her measurements, which were in the outer room, and went.

Outside Garry stood in the gloom. It was lighter here than in the school. It was lighter than he had expected. Forms of men passed him and entered at the school door: elders of the kirk, on their way to deliberate. An odd idea seized him—to walk in upon their deliberations and state his problem. He remembered the old kirk session records: *Compeared before the Session, John Smith and Mary Taylor*—the public accusation and punishment. If he were to go now: *Compeared before the Session, David Grey and Louisa Morgan.* She was still there. Why should she not answer for her guilt, her moral delinquency? But to drag the dead man there—

He put the idea from him and walked on; but, considering that he had better have the interrupted matter out with Miss Morgan, returned towards the school.

Jonathan Bannochie the cobbler came from the school door as he hesitated.

'The birdie's flown, ma lad,' said Jonathan. 'Ay, she's awa'.'

Garry stared, but turned and walked on.

Jonathan kept step beside him. 'I'm for the same way mysel'. I've a pair o' boots for Jake Hunter's missus. They can just cogitate awa' wantin' me or I win back. Yon was a gey grand jump you took out at the windock. The laddies wouldna need to ken yon, or the missy'll hae her ain adae to haud them in. Ye're nae takin' us on? Man, it was a grand notion to get the door locked on the pair o' you. Ye're nae takin's on, I'm sayin'. Well, well, and what was the door locked for, my lad?'

'On a point of honour.'

'Eh? What's that? O ay, it's a gey honorable business, a kiss.' And he bellowed:

Some say kissin's a sin

But I say it's nane ava.

'Is the construction your own?' said Garry, stopping short. 'Or the finding of the Session?'

In the grey half-light he eyed his man. Jonathan Bannochie was a power to reckon with in Fetter-Rothnie. That the man had character was very evident: his mouth was gripped, a sardonic and destructive light glimmered in his eye. The man was baleful, yet not in action, but in speech. To have one's reputation on the souter's tongue did not make for comfort. If the souter's thumb was broad, in accordance with the rhyme:

The hecher grows the plum-tree

The sweeter grows the plums,

And the harder that the souter works

The broader grows his thumbs—

(and Jonathan was a smart and capable workman), the souter's tongue was sharp as the thumb was broad. He could destroy in a phrase, spread ruin with a jest. It was he who, in a few days' time, with a twist of mockery, was to make the name of Garry Forbes the common possession of Fetter-Rothnie speech.

Of this Garry could have no foreknowledge; but he saw in front of him a man of parts whose life's achievement had narrowed itself to a point of tongue. Undoubted that Jonathan had made his shoemaking a success, and Garry's philosophy set high the man whose common labour was achieved with skill and honesty; but that Jonathan's gifts would have been adequate to more than the cobbling of country boots he was very sure. The man had been dissipated, though by no overt system of dissipation. He did not even drink: in Mrs Hunter's eyes a downward step. 'I dinna ken what's come over him,' she said, 'he doesna even drink now. And a kinder man you needna have wished to meet when he had a dram in him.' His domestic life had come to grief. The wife whom Mrs Hunter could never understand his having chosen ('I dinna ken what gar't him tak her. A woman with a mouth like yon. The teeth that sair gone that the very jaws was rottin'. And nae even a tongue in it to haud her ain wi'.') moved early from the scene, and left him two daughters, both spiced with their father's temper. Both decamped. A few years later the elder girl, choosing her time with a knowledge of her father's habits, descended on the homestead, 'and up and awa' wi' the dresser under one arm and the best bed under the other.' Jonathan found the house stripped. In compensation a puny child was left on the kitchen bed. But Kitty did not prove another Eppie. She grew up scared and neglected, the butt of her grandfather's scorn, with rotting teeth like those of her grandmother, and her grandmother's lack of tongue.

In addition Jonathan Bannochie was an elder of the kirk, feared but hardly respected, a shrewd and efficient critic of other men's business and bosoms.

'Is the construction your own?' Garry asked, watching his man. 'Or the finding of the Session?'

'Ach, haud your tongue, Mr Forbes. A bonny lassie in ahin a door—we're nae the lads to blame you.'

There flashed across Garry's mind: *Compeared before the Session, Louisa Morgan and John Dalgarno Forbes.* Apparently, the finding was acquittal. He laughed.

'You've the wrong soo by the lug this time. Mrs Hunter, did you say? I'll hand over the boots. But as I've a matter to lay before the Session, I'll take it kindly if you'll step back with me now and hear it.' He stowed Jonathan's parcel away in his pocket.

EIGHT

Compeared before the Session

'Gentlemen,' said Garry, facing the assembled Session, 'forgive this interruption, but I see you have not yet begun your business. And I've some business of my own—yours too—I want to make it yours.'

He looked earnestly round the men. Some he knew, others were mere faces; one lined and puckered like a chimpanzee's, one spare and shrewd; one fat, without distinction, one keen and cultured; enormous brows; black beards; an oppression of watching eyes. He felt the impact of them like a mob; but as he talked, he scanned the countenances, swiftly computing how each would answer to his challenge. At his shoulder he was aware of the sardonic semi-grin of Jonathan Bannochie, that haunted him like an echo of all that grinned within himself, his contempt of his own sensitiveness to ridicule, his fear of the humiliation of failure. In front was the long, serious face of Jake Hunter, a crofter on his aunt's estate, husband to the jolly woman who was his aunt's old servant and faithful friend. Jake, too, was a faithful soul; a stern fighter against the odds of poverty, sour soil, bad harvests and uncertain prices. His bit of land was seamed with outcrops of rock and heather. He cut laboriously with the scythe, both because the land was too steep and uneven for the reaping machine he did not possess, and also because the scythe cut closer to the ground and no inch of loss on stubble could be afforded. Jake had fought his slow, obscure way upwards, quenching errant enthusiasms. Books had been one such enthusiasm. He was already a man over forty, toughened and worn by exposure and labour from his earliest childhood, when he wedded Barbara Paterson, Miss Bawbie's servant girl, and her uncle settled them on the meagre croft. Then for the first time Jake hoped to satisfy his craving for knowledge. He bought some books, a miscellaneous lot picked up from a second-hand bookstall, and settled it with Barbara that he would read for an hour each night. Barbara put the book for him and took her shank to sit and watch. But the reading did not thrive. A day's work is a day's work, and a man must stretch himself.

'I'm nae nane swacker o' anither day's wark, 'umman,' he would say; and then he would *ficher* with the pages awhile and nod a little. By and by it would be up to have a look at the weather.

'I'll just rax mysel' to be mair soople for the book,' he would tell Barbara, and coming back, dropped to sleep again. Not as you would say a real sleep. Still less of course, a feigned one. A sample, rather—three-four grains between finger and thumb for earnest of the wide fields of slumber that would be his at night. Waking from one of these offhand naps, he would stretch himself largely, move to the door again, and restore the book to the shelf before sitting down.

'I'll just be puttin' it by for the night,' he would say, smothering a mighty yawn. 'It's as you might say a habit, the readin', it beats you at the start. It'll come mair natural-like come time.'

Vain expectation. These habits do not grow on one. They have none of your fine Biblical ease in pushing, a man going to sleep and rising night and day while they adjust themselves to the requirements of the universe. Each year that made the rent queerer to come by and the stomachs of his hungry bairns harder to find a bottom to, made Jake swacker neither in the muscles nor in the wits. He stiffened by living. But his fervour for book learning passed to his eldest son Dave, who united the serious humour of his father with the drive of his mother's vitality. Dave, serving his time as a joiner, read far into the night, and fired by his new experiences at the Front, wrote home, as Mrs Hunter had told Lindsay, that he would put the younger boys through the University. As it happened, Dave, returning from the war with a single arm, went through the University himself on his pension and an ex-service grant, and turned schoolmaster, to his parents' great content.

Garry, in the rapid glance by which we can review at times many years' knowledge of a personality, saw the long, grave anxious face of Jake Hunter as that of a good man, a man upright in all his dealings, but too limited in the reach of his experience to understand the matter on which Garry desired a judgment.

His next door neighbour, John Grey, David's father, was not in the company. Garry felt freer to speak, but regretted not to meet him for the first time since David's death among other people.

The minister, who watched the young man curiously, was a latecomer to the district, not very old, pale and shrunken. To him, Garry felt, he was not speaking, but to these elder men who knew both Louie and David and had some pretensions to knowledge of himself.

'Gentlemen,' he said, addressing the pale young minister, 'I had a friend, a man you all knew and I believe respected—as you respect his father, Mr John Grey. He's dead. I lived with him—that tells you what a man is like. Well, I believe in David's honour with all my soul. I come here and I find—we make honourable images of our dead, don't we?—I find the image left of him in your memories defaced. By a woman. The woman who came out of that room there just now. I am given to understand you knew that I was in there too. Well, I was. In the dark. Locked in and all the rest of it. And I jumped out of the window, as I gather you also know. Because, gentlemen, I wanted to prove—I have every reason to believe'—he spoke very slowly, measuring his words— 'that her claim to be engaged to David Grey was an impudent forgery. She is a woman whose word is not to be trusted—'

'Tell her that, and seek a saxpence,' said Jonathan at his ear.

'I am convinced there was no engagement. The thing–the thing's immoral.' He began to talk wildly, blurring his words. Jonathan's interpolation angered him. 'It's an insult to my friend. Tell me—that's what I want you to do, once it was the duty of the Session to regulate the morals of the community, it doesn't seem to be so any longer—tell me what I am to do now.'

The men were embarrassed. The affair at issue was curious. But the man with the keen face, whom Garry did not know, and who was a petty landowner not always resident in the parish, said, 'There would seem to be the man to answer your question.' And turning, Garry saw John Grey, who had come quietly in while he was speaking.

It was a number of years since he had seen Mr Grey, and he was aghast at the change he saw. He was now an old man. His shoulders were bent, what was left of his hair had gone white; but the receding of the hair served only to expose still further the noble and lofty forehead and give his figure a serene dignity, a majesty even, that his smallness of stature hardly led one to expect. He had come in late. Weariness was in his bearing. He had lifted shells all day. But as he stood listening to Garry, his face was alert, and a deep still glow burned in his eyes. He came forward now, a pleasant briskness in his spare figure, and taking Garry by the hand, very courteously gave him welcome, neither mentioning what he had overheard nor inquiring the young man's business among the elders; but the former speaker pressed his point, saying, 'Mr Forbes has a matter here for your attention.'

'Let the matter rest.'

There was a stern authority in John Grey's tone. Without raising his voice, which was habitually soft, he yet conveyed in its intonation a settled finality that caused Garry to tremble. He had heard that note in his voice only once before, when David and he as boys had locked Louie in the tower.

'I know no more than you do,' John Grey said, 'the truth of this engagement. My son never mentioned it to me. The boy is dead. Let there be no more said about it.'

No more could be said. Garry felt a fool. He got himself out of that room and stood fuming on the road, having distinguished nothing in what was afterwards said to him but Jonathan Bannochie's whisper, 'Try her in the Tower, Mr Forbes.'

Inside the schoolroom there was an awkward moment. Most of the men resented vaguely this intrusion into the ordinariness of living. The landowner with the keen face said, 'A curious affair. Has the young man any grounds for his suspicion?'

Another man answered, 'Now here's a funny thing. Just yesterday my lassie had a letter from a friend, a boy in Captain Forbes's Company. Went queer, they said. Left out in a shell-hole and brought back clean off—raving mad. A corpse bumping at his heels that he insisted was himself. Wouldn't leave go of it. Touched, I'm afraid.'

'Is that the way of it? Poor chap! The war has much to answer for. He certainly looked raised.'

Garry, indeed, hollow-eyed, taut with the terrible earnestness of his purpose, breaking upon the Session to propound his riddle, looked hardly sane.

The pallid young minister wiped the sweat from his brow. A bookworm, he liked life plain. The promise of confusion among his people smote him to a sort of panic. Now, wiping his brow, he breathed deep in his relief. The threatened confusion to his peace was no worse than this, the meanderings of a poor fellow not quite responsible for what he said. He had never before seen Garry, but was ready to believe in any mental aberration in a nephew of Miss Barbara Paterson. John Grey interrupted his thoughts.

In his quiet, courteous fashion Mr Grey asked leave, if nothing demanded his presence in the meeting, to follow Garry.

'Yes do, do go,' the minister said. Sweat broke again upon his brow. He had come to this country parish to escape the impact of life, but there were moments when he recognised himself a coward. The sweat breaking on his brow bore witness to such a moment.

'Do go, Mr Grey,' he said.

Garry was still standing on the puddled road. All his boyhood's discomfort in the face of ridicule was working in him. At first he could hardly speak with civil tongue to Mr Grey; but the old man's quiet refusal to note that anything was wrong, as they walked and talked, in time restored him to a sense of deeper hurt than that to his own vanity; and he felt better. He went home with Mr Grey. Garry was unfed, and his host called for food. The room was shabby but gracious. All it contained, if old and worn, was good:

engravings after the Masters, some photographs of hills and of machinery, a Harvest Home, hung in oak frames of Mr Grey's own making. The bookcases, also of his making, were filled with books, like the furniture, good and worn. While Garry ate, the old man, seated by the fire, fell asleep; and awoke in a little to say, 'I'm getting to be a done old chap.' He stooped forward and picked a child's doll from the fender. Garry had observed it there, with china face and blue eyes that stared towards the fire.

'The eyes came out,' said John Grey, as he lifted the toy and examined it with care, 'and her little mistress brought her to me. She believes I can mend everything that breaks, but this was as hard a task as I have tried. I had to work the eyes back into place and fill the head up with cement to keep them fixed. See, it has set.

Garry took the doll and examined the workmanship.

'Jolly neat. I saw a youngster, two evenings ago, as I went past, following you around while you were weeding. Slip of a girl. Her arms were round your neck as you knelt. Once I declare I saw her ride on you, bare leg across your shoulder, and you paying no attention.'

'That is the child.'

'Confident little sparrow, wasn't she just!'

'She was not in my way,' said the old man smiling.

Garry thrust plate and cup from him and buried his head in his hands.

'Perhaps I am not in your way either,' he said at last; and without waiting for an answer he began to talk, pouring out to David's father his bitter distaste at David's betrayal. 'You can't think that ever he meant to marry that woman.'

John Grey talked in his turn; but with reticence. It was plain, however, to Garry that Louie Morgan as a daughter was not a welcome thought. Yet he defended her, even, as it seemed to Garry, to the detriment of his son. He slowly gathered that the old man was unsure of what the brilliant boy, who escaped beyond his father's experience at many points, might not have done. Besides, David and Miss Morgan had certainly met, many times, not long before his death. She had been staying in the south, with friends, very near his lodgings. David's own letters had referred to her presence, even to her quality. 'There's more in her than ever I thought.' They had had long and intimate talks. No, David had never hinted at love, certainly never a betrothal.

'But this confession she was making to me,' stammered Garry. Death was in his heart. To find Mr Grey believing that the thing was possible made Garry face it for the first time, and the thought that David might indeed have kissed that vapid mouth weighed on him like death.

'Think nothing of the confession. Never mind it. She was overwrought. Leave the matter as it is. Let there be no more said.'

Of what was he afraid, pondered Garry. Surely of something. He could not leave the theme, returning to his own contempt of the woman. But the old man silenced his complaint. Garry felt uncomfortably that in his presence one could disparage no human being; not even a woman for whom he had confessed that he did not care.

'You are too good for this world,' thought Garry. 'Or too simple.'

Mr Grey put the theme aside with decision.

'We'll just leave it where it is, lad.'

Garry was profoundly dissatisfied, but drew his chair to the fire and smoked; and they talked for over an hour. Garry would have enjoyed the talk (for he had a deep respect for John Grey, and they had many tastes in common) had his secret uneasiness not kept growing. At last its torment worked through even his interest in shells and fuses, and he rose to go.

The night had cleared. Spring had danced her caper, and sat now dreaming and demure. Under the wide dim sky, where single stars hung soft, the man walked out his torment. He had to face the issue he had evaded: someone he must despise if his convictions were to go unchanged. Was it John Grey, who could believe of a splendid son that he would sully his honour? Or David himself, who had sullied it? Had David loved—no, David could not have loved this woman, but had he perhaps, incredibly, become infatuated with her? Had the ancient madness worked, the old invincible gods snuffed up their reek of sacrifice? David's face rose before him, brooding, strong, ironic as in life, and at the thought that he had lost not only the face but what it meant to him, desolation fell so strongly upon his spirit that David died a second time. His mouth was filled with ashes, loathing took his soul. So it was the Cyprian John Grey had feared, and, prudent man, stayed his eyes from looking lest the goddess smite. It is not well for man to pry into the doings of the gods. But as he paced in his bitter misery the thought returned: what was this incomplete confession that Mr Grey desired him to ignore? It must have had some meaning, and he must know its end.

He had reached the gate of Knapperley when his hand came against the bulge that Mrs Hunter's boots made in his pocket. Jonathan Bannochie had told him they were promised for tonight. He turned, then turned again and took another road that came to Craggie by way of the house inhabited by Mrs Morgan and her daughter.

The house, standing back from the road, was dark, but against the shadowy trees a pale figure moved. Garry leaped the wall and strode across the lawn.

Miss Morgan was as restless as himself. Her mother and the maid had gone to bed, but she had come seeking into the starlight—and found Garry.

'Let's finish that talk we were having,' he said.

She cried indignantly, 'What do you mean, breaking into my garden like this, so late? You are as rude and wild as when you were a boy. Haven't you done me harm enough today already, locked in with me like that?'

'Don't be a fool. Who's to know I'm here?—Listen, Miss Morgan'—he gripped himself and spoke less roughly—'you began tonight to tell me something. Will you finish it?'

He saw, however, that he was dealing with another Louie. Instead of tears he found defiance. Louie's attempted excursion into truth had been too hard. But he was determined this time to hold her fast.

'Yes or no—were you engaged to marry David Grey?'

Louie twisted her hands together.

'What is it all about? Won't you tell me what you meant this evening? Why are you a sinner? You said—'

'Yes, yes, I said! I said! Do you suppose words ever

mean the right thing? I said. And I suppose I meant it then. But you are to blame for what I said. You, by your suspicions and your accusations. I am too sensitive, that's what it is. I see other people's point of view too quickly. I said dreadful things about myself, and they all seemed true then. Because you had moved me and I was seeing with your eyes. Don't you understand? One can accuse oneself of any enormity under the stress of an emotion. You tell me how my conduct looks to you, and I see it. Yes, I see it. I acknowledge my sin and my transgression is before me. But that vision isn't me. When the emotion is over, I recover myself. I realise to what an enormity I have confessed.'

'But you haven't confessed to anything,' said Garry wearily.

'You think I made the story up—that David didn't love me. I will tell you what I meant, what I was trying to confess. But all those tears were quite wrong. I was too humble. It's nothing so very bad, after all. We were not actually engaged—no formal engagement, I mean. I could never bring myself to that—I wouldn't do as David wanted. Because, you see, I was not sure that he was saved. I couldn't say yes until his soul was safe.'

Garry was staring in the chill of horror.

'You think you knew David—you didn't know my David. You think I wasn't good enough for him. Perhaps I was too good. There was a side to him you didn't know. I developed it. I created him. My own part of him. And *you* can't take it from me. You didn't know how much we were to each other in those last months before he died.'

'I heard—something.'

'Oh, something. But no one knew. Do you suppose we blabbed? No, but we talked and talked—six weeks we talked. Oh, just in snatches, when he had the time. He slaved all those weeks. But when he had an hour—how we talked! We threshed out all the religions in the world, I think. You didn't know David cared for that. You thought his machinery and his music were all he thought about. But he did. I made him care. Only—he died so soon I never knew, never was sure that I had saved his soul. And now

I never can be. So, you see, I couldn't enter into a formal engagement, could I? But it would have come to that. Am I so very wrong to claim it before the world? To me it is like a proclamation of my faith in David—that his soul *was* right at the last. It is a mere formality I am assuming. But surely I am justified. The truth that was the truth of our hearts is expressed in it—that is all.'

Garry said slowly and with difficult utterance, 'That is a morality more involved than I am accustomed to.'

'Morality is always involved. Only truth is clear and one. But we never see it. That's why we must live by morality.'

Garry got up from the garden chair on which he had been seated.

'This is too much for me. I don't pretend to understand you. And was this what distressed you in the evening?'

'Yes, yes. You made me feel a cheat, to claim the reality without my formal right. But I do not feel a cheat now.'

'Then I suppose I had better go away?'

'Yes, go; yes, go.'

He went in misery. He could not disbelieve this tale of David. Talk they must have had. More of David—and more of Miss Morgan—than he had known became apparent: new stars slipping from the dusk. He walked bewildered.

In a little he came to Craggie. All was dark and silent. He rattled on the door, and the sound, rolling into the night, roused him to observe that all the countryside was folded. It must be late: he had not thought of time. He made out the figures on his luminous wristwatch—half past eleven. The Hunters were a-bed; he regretted having come and turned to go quietly away.

But shuffling footsteps were approaching, bolts were shot back, and the long knotted figure of Jake Hunter appeared in the doorway, trousers pulled hastily up over his nightshirt. His face was twisted in a look of apprehension.

'What's wrong, ava?'

'Nothing, nothing.' Garry apologised, explaining his errand.

'Man, it's a terrible-like time o'night to tak a body out o' their beds.'

'So it's you that's the death o' them,' cried Mrs Hunter,

coming to the door. 'And me callin' Jonathan Bannochie
for a' thing—nae boots for Bill the morn's morn. An' it's
nae like Jonathan to be ahin hand wi' his work. He doesna
seek nae to put to his hand. And it's you that was poochin'
my laddie's boots.'

'Man,' said Jake, 'you feared me, comin' in about at
this hour.'

'O ay, now, Mr Garry, sir,' Mrs Hunter interrupted,
'what's this you were up to with Miss Louie? She came
by this house with a face begrutten that you couldna tell
it was a face, and when I but said "Good evening"—quiet-
like and never lettin' on I saw the tears—ran as if she saw
reek. Bubblin' an' greetin'—tears enough to make the porridge with.'

'Hoots, wumman,' said Jake, 'let the thing be. Seein'
there's naething a-dae, let's to our beds. But man, you fair
feared me. Would it be our laddie, I thocht, killed maybe
or wounded.'

Garry apologised again.

'Miss Morgan's all right,' he told Mrs Hunter. 'I saw
her a little ago. Very cheerful.'

The couple went in and shut their door. But Garry stood
on the road, struck dumb. Mrs Hunter's voice had brought
to his memory what he had forgotten—the assurance she
had given him that Louie had her betrothal ring: the ring
that David's mother had reserved for his bride.

Not betrothed to David, yet wearing his mother's ring:
now what should that forebode?

NINE

The Andrew Lorimers go to the Country

The sleet had vanished in the night. Airs were soft as summer, and over the last golden clumps of crocus, wide open in the sun, bees droned and buzzed.

'A flinchin' Friday,' warned Miss Annie, who had a farmer's knowledge of the weather signs. 'There'll be storm on the heels of this.'

Storm! thought Ellen, bumming as she cleared the breakfast dishes. Youth was in her heart, she had risen up at the voice of a bird, and the world for her was azure. She could not understand this flood of new life that welled up within her.

The postman came, bringing the letters, and told them the story of Garry before the Session.

'He had no call to shame her like that,' said Miss Annie.

'Pity for her in her snuffy condition,' scoffed Theresa. 'The lad's as thrawn as cats' guts, he'll do as he pleases.'

'But it's not to laugh at,' said Ellen, with an unexpected heat. 'It was a noble thing to do.'

'Locking her in a schoolroom, the same as he locked her in the old Tower—where's your nobility in that? Well, well, Louie'll be having him next, wait till you see. The cow dies waiting the green grass, and if she can't get one to her mind, she's well advised to take what she can get.'

Lindsay thrust her thumb into the envelope of a letter and ripped it savagely open, and glared at Theresa above a trembling lip.

Ellen said, 'Tris, you're an old fool. As if the boy would mind her.'

'If he can't get a better, where's the odds?

Are ye hungry?

Lick the mills o' Bungrie,

103

Are ye thirsty?

Kiss Kirsty.

'What stite you talk!' said Miss Annie. 'The lad was scunnered at her.'

'There was once a lad that took a scunner at butter, and after that he could never eat it thicker than the bread.'

'Oh, they're coming here,' cried Lindsay, reading from her letter. 'The children—for a picnic.' She began to read aloud, hastily, to hide the trembling of her mouth, and even she was less indignant than Ellen at the monstrous suggestion that Theresa had made. The sisters were still bickering, and Theresa had just said, 'Oh, no, to be sure I know nothing. What should a silly tailor do but sit and sew a clout? It was me that had the right of it in the other affair, I would have you remember. I told you she wasn't engaged to him'—and was making for the kitchen, but paused to hear Lindsay read her mother's letter.

Mrs Andrew Lorimer wrote that as the holidays had begun the children were eager for a picnic. They were taking lunch out, and would the Weatherhouse ladies give them tea?

'And there's them turning in at the foot of the brae,' said Theresa. 'What a congregation! We'll need our time to tea all that.' She went to the kitchen and began to bake. Theresa liked nothing better than to provide a tea. Lindsay ran flying down the brae to meet the children, and as she ran the words spurted from her lips, 'Brute, brute, brute. I hate her. Brute.'

'She's never away in these thin shoes,' said Miss Annie, following Theresa to the kitchen. 'She'll be ill.'

'Fient an ill. She's that excited you would think she was a bairn herself. That's her that was so dead set on marrying. There's no more word of that affair, it seems. And she doesn't get letters from any at the Front but Frank.'

About the same hour Garry Forbes was walking up to Mrs Morgan's door. He was stern and ill at ease, but determined to go through with the task that he had set himself. Louie, too, was ill at ease. When she saw him her face crumpled up, puckering as though she were to cry, and she lowered her eyes and would not meet his. He was sure she had already been weeping.

'Forgive me,' he said, 'I haven't slept. I must know this: that ring you wear—it's David's mother's. How do you come to have it if you were not betrothed?'

'Why do you pursue me like this?' She sat down with a gesture of despair and motioned him to a seat. He saw the tears trickle between the hands with which she covered her face.

'I did try to tell the truth yesterday,' she said at last, looking up. 'Perhaps if they hadn't come in—and yet I don't know. Oh, must I tell you? Can't you understand how it is? I am so covered with shame—will you let me try to show you how it was? Will you let me try?'

He assented gravely.

'I think sometimes I can't tell the truth—can you understand that?'

He was embarrassed, not knowing what to answer.

'Yes,' she continued, 'truth to me is terribly hard. I am made like that. I live all the time—oh, I am going to scourge myself—in what I want other people to be thinking about me, until often I don't know—indeed, indeed I don't—what I really am and what I have thought they are thinking I am. I understand myself, you see. But I can't give it up, I can't. I've nothing to put in its place.'

Garry was looking in amazement.

'I should have thought the difference between truth and a lie was clear enough,' he said as she paused.

'Oh, no, it's not—not clear at all. Things are true and right in one relationship, and quite false in another. It's false, as a mere statement of fact, that I was betrothed to David, but true as an expression of—an expression of—' She faltered and burst into tears.

'I was going to say, an expression of feeling—our feeling. But it's my feeling. David—I am to tell you the truth now—David never mentioned love to me, or marriage. We had those talks—yes, yes, you must not think those were invented. We talked—all sorts of things, deep, intimate things. And I was always thinking: I am making an impression, I am altering his ideas. I wanted to save his soul. I think—I think I wanted it to be *me* that would save his soul, not just that his soul would be saved. I am trying to be honest, you see. And then I thought: he will recognise how much I have done for him, I shall become needful to him, and in time—in time—yes, I hoped that in time he might marry me. Don't you understand? I think that about every man. There have been so few—just none, just none. No one ever before with whom I even had an intimate conversation, like this with David. It was luscious, it was so good! I wanted to be at the heart of life instead of on its margins.'

'Yes, yes, I can see that. But I don't see that it justifies you in grabbing David.'

'Grabbing! But I didn't grab. Oh, you haven't understood at all! That part of him is mine. I created it. No one can touch it but me.'

'But you said he never—'

'No, no, he never did. I suppose it was all a tiny thing to him—just some occasional talk. He liked it at the time. But between times he was absorbed, he forgot. And I thought and thought until that was all that was alive for me. And yet he liked the talks. He would say, "Now there, what you said last week—I've been thinking about that." He made me feel, somehow, as though what I said was tremendously important, as though I were tremendously important to him. And then I came to believe I *was* important. You see how well I understand myself.'

Garry was at a loss. He felt as though a roof had blown away and he was looking in amazement at a hive of populous rooms where things were done that he had never imagined.

'So when he died it was myself I felt for, that my hope would never come to be.' Garry made a motion of disgust. 'Yes, yes, it was hideous. But don't you see my desperation? "What are the men thinking about?" they said. "Not about me"—I couldn't answer that. Don't you understand? I had to save my self-respect. Confess no man had ever wanted me? "What are the men thinking about, that *you* are still unmarried?" "Ah, I could tell you that an I would." You needn't tell a lie, you see. A hint is all. But it saves you from humiliation—from yourself. Yes, I know it is in your own eyes that you are saved. The others forget, but you keep on remembering that they know.'

'So David had to suffer that people might think—the right thing about you.'

'To suffer! But I forgot. You think it is a degradation for David to be thought in love with me. That is why you have wormed all this out of me.'

He could not deny, and so was silent.

'But why should it be a degradation? I'm not wicked. I'm not ugly. I have charm. I'm thirty five—you wouldn't dream. I've kept astonishingly youthful.'

Juvenile, was the word that flashed across his brain.

'I have such girlish ways. Oh, God, what am I doing? Why did you let me go on? You can't expect me to acknowledge that it would have been a degradation. And yet I know it was only—what was the word you used?—*grabbing*. That I grabbed David. But it didn't feel like that to me. It felt like— Oh, I tried to explain it to you. Like the seal and signal of the great belief I had in him. A high and holy thing. I see now that it wasn't—that it was only—was bad and wicked. The human heart is deceitful above all things and desperately wicked. That doesn't mean that you tell lies. Self-deceitful. You think you are doing a brave thing, and it turns out mean. And you don't deliberately persuade yourself about it. You really are deceived. Only some people—like me, I'm one of them, you should pity us, we are of all men most miserable—, some people see the deceptive appearance and the deceit both together, as it were, only they can't quite distinguish. Or won't let themselves. Just now, for instance, I am hoping that I am saving your soul. As I hoped with David. I am saying, years after, he will look back on this hour and say, "My life was changed—that was a crucial hour for me. I had a new revelation of life given to me." That's what I meant by saving your soul. But you won't, will you?'

'No. No.'

'No, of course not. I know that. Only you see I go on thinking and acting as though I knew you would. There, I have revealed my innermost being to you. No one has seen it before. But you—you have forced me to see how vile it is. Will you not have mercy? Are you to make of me an outcast in the eyes of men?'

Garry found his thoughts in confusion; but remembered suddenly that she had not yet explained her possession of the ring.

She went very white, threw her head back and breathed deeply. 'I took it. Why don't you say something?' she added after a pause. 'I took it. *You* would say stole, I suppose. But it wasn't really that.'

'No?'

'Oh, you are cruel! You are saying, double meanings again. But I shall tell you how it came about. His mother wore that ring. I used to watch it when I was a girl—the strange old set and chasing of the gold. And I was with my mother when we saw her dying. She said, "It's not of value, it's only a square cairngorm, but the setting is old and rare. My son's bride shall have it." I thought nothing then, but you know how unimportant words like that may stay with you. You forget that you heard them, and then one day back they all come. It was Mr Grey himself that showed me it. I asked him, "Have you nothing for our jumble sale?" And he said there might be some useless odds and ends. He pulled out a drawer, and there was the ring. I knew it at once. He put it aside and some other things, and then he said, "If you find anything there of any use, just you take it." So I rummaged in the drawer. But afterwards I couldn't keep my thoughts off the ring. Nor off his mother's words, "David's bride." I said them over and over, and then I felt: if only I could have the ring a moment on my finger I should feel better. David's bride. It would feel real then. I thought about it till I couldn't keep away, and I went back to the house and opened the drawer and slipped the ring on. I felt so happy then, I can't explain to you. It seemed as though something had come true. I could have danced and sung. I couldn't bear to take it off again, and I went and stood by the window—it opens like a door, I had come in that way—and watched the light shine on it. And then I heard a sound, and there was his old housekeeper coming in at the door. So I slipped it in my pocket, meaning to put it back in the drawer, and I said, "Mr Grey gave me leave to take some things from that drawer for the Jumble Sale. I knocked, but you couldn't have heard. I'm glad you've come in, for I was just wondering if I could take the things away when nobody was here." Then I went into the room again and played about among the things in the drawer, always hoping I'd be able to slip the ring back. But she watched me all the time. So I had to carry it away. And I slept with it on that night. Oh, I can't make you understand—in a few days it felt like a part of me. All I had wanted of David seemed to be concentrated in that little piece of gold. I loved it. I couldn't bear to have it off my finger—though I was prudent, and wore it only when I was alone. He wasn't dead a month by then. Well, one day I had it on, and my glove was off, when I happened to meet Mrs Hunter. It was on my wedding finger, you understand, and she pounced at once, and said, "What, what!" and then she stood staring at the ring and cried, "But I've seen that ring before," and I felt like death and said, "Dear Mrs Hunter, it hasn't to be known. We hadn't made it public, and now—" "You poor bit bairn!" she said, and I began to weep. It was such a relief to weep, I felt so frightened. But then I recollected myself and told her on no account to speak of it. Especially not to Mr Grey. "You know that he never mentions David's name," I said. "And at any rate, since the betrothal had not been announced, it's better to keep it secret still. I prefer to suffer in silence." But I couldn't, you know. That was just it. I wanted everyone to know that I was suffering. Mrs Hunter promised faithfully to say nothing—'

Garry gave an involuntary exclamation and clapped his mouth shut on it at once.

'I know, I know. You are to say: she spoke to me, she told me. It *was* Mrs Hunter who told you the ring was his mother's, wasn't it? But you see she did not break her promise, it had got known without her, and she was free to speak. Got known, I say. I made it known, was what I mean. I couldn't keep it, you see. I gave other people hints—it was so sweet, oh, if you knew how sweet their pity was! No, not their pity—their admiration. For the way I bore my suffering, I mean.'

Garry sighed profoundly. The whole interview oppressed him. Her speech was an unseemly mockery of human pain. Yet she was terribly in earnest. He could not refuse to listen to the end. In some tortured and labyrinthine way she was revealing a soul. All was not sham. He sighed and listened.

But the door was opened, and Mrs Morgan came in, cordial but inquisitive. Louie's demeanour changed. She jumped to her feet, laughing, and said, 'Mother, I'm defeated. I've tried to persuade Captain Forbes to give a brief talk at our concert, and he refuses.'

Mrs Morgan sat down. She took possession of the room.

'Mother dear,' said Louie softly at last, 'Captain Forbes was so good—he called to—to tell me some things about David. Do you mind?'

Mrs Morgan did mind, plainly, but she rose and went. Garry sighed again. She was so enmeshed in falsehood, he supposed, that she hardly noticed when she told a lie.

'Now, where was I?' she was asking. Was it possible that she enjoyed this too, that her tale was one huge ostentation? She would have another invention for her mother's ears, of that he was sure. Mrs Morgan's knowing smile would invite till she received—received what? What had he to 'tell her about David'?

She continued. 'But I didn't dare to wear the ring, so I hung it round my neck and bought another not unlike it. I wore that, and trusted that Mrs Hunter, who was the only person who knew, would never notice the difference. It does sound deceitful, doesn't it?'

He did not reply.

'What are you to do now?' he asked after a pause.

'Do? Does anything need to be done?'

He rose and paced the room impatiently.

'At least I hope you will restore Mr Grey the ring.'

'The trouble is, how am I to get in without attracting notice?'

'Without— Good God, you don't mean that you would put it back and say nothing?'

'What can I say?'

'The truth, of course.'

He saw the sheer pain in her eyes.

'What I've told you?'

'If that is the truth, yes.'

'*If* it is the truth! Oh, do you not believe me yet?'

'Very well, of course you must tell it to him.'

'And then—then you'll proclaim it abroad. You'll tell everyone I am a common thief. That's what you wanted, wasn't it, to tell them all?'

He shook his head. To clear David's honour was one thing, but a very different matter to set the tongues wagging over such a sordid story. He would have felt it an indecency to expose her, and smiled a little soberly as he thought that those who could not see his point when he talked of his friend's dishonour would see quickly enough the point of a stolen ring. A profound sadness invaded him as he saw by what strange ties honour and reputation may be bound.

'No, no,' he said, 'this is not a matter for the public. But you must go by what Mr Grey decides.'

She was weeping now and said, pleading, 'Captain Forbes—Garry. I shall tell him, but need it be now? Listen. Our concert—it's just two days ahead. And I have so much to do in it. I'm playing. And there's that sketch. I've the curtains to finish, and final rehearsals. And if I tell—I'm so, so—I feel so keenly, it will kill me. I know I shall be ill. I feel I might collapse. Perhaps at the concert. I know that I'll be prostrate after I tell. Mayn't I wait? It's—it's a sort of public duty, to keep fit for the concert.'

Garry rose to his feet. Blind blundering emotions had hold on him. To his surprise he felt surges of pity where he had thought to feel only disgust; but it was a pity that it hurt him to give, as though some portion of himself had been rent to make the pity possible; and he was profoundly uncomfortable.

'Yes, yes, tell him when you please.'

'But you will say—'

'Nothing, nothing. Till your concert is over, then.'

She accompanied him to the door, talking loud and laughing. Mrs Morgan reappeared. He supposed she had come to hear what had passed. Louie, of course, would dissemble. He went rapidly out.

He was astonished at the pure sweet morning into which he walked—as though he had come from a murky den where the air oppressed. It was incredible that there could be a world as fresh and unashamed as that he saw around him. For a time he stood, breathing the sweet air, then rapidly climbed to the summit of the ridge. There space encompassed him. Space sang again its primal song, before man was, before the tangle of his shames began. Infinite sky was over him, blue land ran on and on until it seemed itself a ruffled fold of sky, a quivering of light upon the air; the blue sea trembled on the boundaries of space; and the man standing there alone was rapt up into the infinitudes around, lost for awhile the limitations of himself. He came back slowly. Strange how the land could be transfigured! A blue April morning, the shimmer of light, a breath, a passing air, and it was no longer a harsh and stubborn country, its hard-won fields beleaguered by moor and whin, its stones heaped together in dyke and cairn, marking the land like lines upon a weathered countenance, whose past must stay upon it to the end; but a dream, wiling men's hearts. In the sun the leafless boughs were gleaming. Birches were like tangles of shining hair; or rather, he thought, insubstantial, floating like shredded light above the soil. Below the hills blue floated in the hollows, all but tangible, like a distillation that light had set free from the earth; and on a rowan tree in early leaf, its boughs blotted against the background, the tender leaves, like flakes of green fire, floated too, the wild burning life of spring loosened from earth's control. On every side earth was transmuted. Scents floated, the subtle life released from earth and assailing the pulses. Song floated. This dour and thankless country, this land that *grat a' winter and girned a' summer* could change before one's eyes to an elfin and enchanted radiance, could look, by some rare miracle of light or moisture, essentialised. A measure of her life this morning had gone up in sacrifice. Her substance had become spirit.

Garry's thought went back upon the evening when he had seen the land emerge and take form slowly from primordial dark. Now its form was on the point of dissolution into light. And the people whom the land had made—they too, had been shaped from a stuff as hard and intractable as their rock, through weathers as rude as stormed upon their heights; they too (he thought) at moments were dissolved in light, had their hours of transfiguration. In his aunt dancing her wilful reel on the kitchen floor, in Lindsay as she had grieved for Louie's hurt, he had seen life essentialised.

A shouting caught his ear. The swarm of young Lorimers, skimming the moor, hummed about him. He gave in gladly to their merriment, lunched with them beside the old tower, and led their games. Lindsay's gaiety, however, was assumed. She was still furious against Miss Theresa for her cynical suggestion of the morning; but though she tried to convince herself that her misery came from that, as the day wore on she was compelled to acknowledge that there was a deeper hurt in what Garry had done the previous evening in the school. After all, he had exposed Louie to public scorn. Her eyes sought his many times, reproachful and sad, but it was only on the homeward way that, lingering by common consent, the two could talk.

'I thought you would have done what I wanted you to do,' she said.

She did herself injustice by her complaint. She had no sense of personal grievance; but she had been quite sure that Garry would be good—that he would do nothing out of accord with her creed and standards. Her rebuke was the grieving of a bewildered child.

Garry kept silence. He could not tell her the collapse of Louie's story. The purloined ring had altered his attitude to the affair, and he almost hoped that Lindsay need never know of it. In any case he could not assert his knowledge of Louie's perfidy without revealing its proof. Constraint fell between them. They made up on the others, and reached the Weatherhouse in a bunch.

'What's *he* seeking here again?' said Miss Theresa, looking from the window.

Mrs Falconer looked from the window too, and saw Garry, as it happened, toss an empty basket laughingly to Kate. The bird sang in Mrs Falconer's heart—that fugitive bird, that flake from Ellen's earth that had escaped, far out into the blue air, across distant seas and islands of romance. She ran to set another cup and plate, thinking, 'How happy they look together!'

'You needn't bother yourself,' said Theresa. 'He's away.'

Ellen turned to the glass door, and saw him passing through the gate. She flung the glass door open and ran across the garden with hasty, unsure steps, her long angular body bent forward from the hips, and she reached the low wall before Garry had passed beyond it.

'Just a cup,' she panted. And when he would not come she continued to talk, leaning upon the stone-crop that covered the wall.

'A pack of old women—I don't wonder. We must seem unreal to you. A picture-book house.'

'Well.' He stood considering. Unreal—he could not know all that she had put into the word, her lifelong battle against those figments of her fancy that had often held her richest life, yet it expressed what he had vaguely felt when he took tea with these women. 'After out there,' he said.

Mrs Falconer had the curious sense of having run, in her stumbling progress through the garden, a very long distance from her home.

'You're a dimension short,' he continued. 'Or no. You have three dimensions right enough, but we've a fourth dimension over there. We've depth. It's not the same thing as height,' he added, looking up. 'It's down in—hollowness and mud and foul water and bad smells and holes and more mud. Not common mud. It's dissolution—a dimension that won't remain stable—and you've to multiply everything by it to get any result at all. You people who live in a three-dimensional world don't know. You can't know. You go on thinking this is the real thing, but we've discovered that we can get off every imaginable plane that the old realities yielded.'

'We can perhaps imagine it a little.' She kept her adoring eyes upon him, and smiled at undergoing this initiation into a soldier's world.

'Imagination's no good. Imagination has to save the world, but the people who haven't it will never believe what the others say. Your sister's beckoning.'

Mrs Falconer turned and saw Theresa signal from the window. Cups clattered, talk and laughter eddied into the garden. Everyone had gone in: except old Mrs Craigmyle, who walked serenely to and fro on the garden path, knitting and carolling. Mrs Falconer looked, and turned back to Garry. She had a certain elation in disregarding Theresa's summons. There were plenty of them there to serve; but she was choosing a better part. She said, 'That's what I've always wanted—to have imagination.'

'You shouldn't. It's too cruel, too austere. You should pray your God of Comforts to keep you from imagination. Lead us not into imagination, but deliver us from understanding.'

Mrs Falconer shook her head, slowly, as though to shake away an idea that bemused her.

'They laugh at you,' Garry continued (he had not talked like this to anyone since his return, not tried to share, even with Lindsay, the thoughts that had haunted his delirium and convalescence), 'they laugh at you as foolish or pity you as not quite sane if you try to get past the appearances of things to their real nature. That's what they said about me: beside himself, cracked. I was in a fever, you see. But I'm convinced I saw clearer then than in my right mind.' He began to tell her of his adventure with the dead man in the hole. 'I wasn't rightly sure which was myself, you understand. And it's like that all the time. You do things, and you're not sure after they're done if it is yourself or someone else you've done them to.'

She was listening absorbed.

'Yes, yes, that Louie Morgan now. She did it just to please herself, but look what she has done to you. You were right to expose her, I think.'

But Garry was thinking (also of Louie) that in un-masking her he had done something to himself regarding

which he was not yet quite sure. Nor did he want Louie
on the public stage. He stepped back from the wall, said,
'But she's not exposed. Now I am keeping you from your
tea,' and walked away.

Not exposed! thought Mrs Falconer, turning back across
the garden. But she would be! A fire ran through her veins.
Too austere! How could imagination be austere? Your
God of Comforts. Another dimension. His words bubbled
in her ears. She had run farther than ever from this idle
garden, and the air beyond it was sharp and pungent to
her nostrils.

The garden was not empty, after all. Lang Leeb still
walked the path, serenely singing; and as her second
daughter came near with wide unseeing eyes, Leeb raised
her voice and sang on a gay and insolent note. She did not
look at Mrs Falconer, but kept her fingers on her shank and
her eyes straight ahead:

Auld wife, auld wife, will you go a-shearin'?
Speak up, speak up, for I'm hard o' hearin'.
Auld wife, auld wife, will you hae a man?—

The glass door slipped from Mrs Falconer's hand and
clashed, and Mrs Falconer did not even apologise. She let
Miss Theresa talk.

The children had finished tea. It was time they were
off. There was noise and bustle.

'For the love of Pharaoh,' cried Miss Theresa, 'wash
your faces. They'll charge you extra in the train for all
that dirt.'

Mrs Falconer sat to her solitary tea. The children's voices
came ringing up from the road, fading as the distance grew.
Lindsay and Kate had gone with them.

'Your God of Comforts,' Mrs Falconer continued to think.
The phrase brought Louie to her mind. 'Why, we must go
to that concert. But how can she appear in front of them all?
Not exposed, he said. Not. But she must be. And playing,
they say. Well, if it's like the last concert, I'm sure I shan't
care if I don't go. Terrible grand music, she said it was—just
a bumming and a going on. But how can she face them? Your
God of Comforts.' Her mind came back always to the phrase
A comfortable God—what had the young man meant?

Lindsay and Kate returned. Night came. Lindsay leaned again from her window. She was trying to control her thoughts. They were like horses new let out to grass; brutal and beautiful; unbridled energies. She had never before had so many thoughts at once. Life was too intricate. New complications rose upon her. Getting to know Garry was not what she had supposed it would be like. And now the children would go home and tell that Garry was here, and there would be her mother's disapproval to be faced. She should have been more stern that afternoon, but he had kissed her, her throat was burning still where he had pressed it. Oh, where was she venturing? The sea grows more immense as the distance widens between us and the shore.

Kate was asleep. The whole house had withdrawn. Only she, awake and aware, tussled with life. She felt creep over her the desolation of youth, that believes no suffering has ever been like its suffering, no heart has been perplexed like it. 'They're all happy,' she thought, 'and I don't know what I am. They're all asleep, and I can't sleep.'

She did not know that through the wall, kneeling upon the floor, Mrs Falconer endured an agony of prayer. She too, wrestled, and as she wrestled a strange sense of triumph overwhelmed her, exultation filled her soul.

'Help me, O God,' she prayed, 'help me to overcome the evil and expose the wrong, that Thy great cause may be triumphant. Through our Lord Jesus Christ, Amen.'

The words sang to her spirit. No more for her the pallid shadows of her dreams. She would labour now for truth.

'Grant, O Lord, in Thy mercy, that I may be equal to that which Thou wouldst have me do.'

A shudder ran through her frame. The seraph with the live coal from off the altar touched her lips, and as she rose, chill and quiet, from her prayers, the dreamy innocence habitual to her face had changed to a high and rapt enthusiasm.

TEN

Andrew Lorimer does the Same

The following days deepened the furrows that became so characteristic a feature of Garry's countenance. Life had always been to him a serious affair, but, till the delirium of his recent illness, simple. One worked hard, making boilers and bridges as stable as one could, and played equally hard and sure; and men were good fellows. Evil there was, of course, but always in the next street—the condition that gave fighting its vehemence. The complexity of human motive and desire had not come home to him, and he supposed, without thinking much about it, that right and wrong were as separate as the bridges he helped to build and the waters over which he built them. But in what he had been irresistibly impelled to say to Mrs Falconer that afternoon, his discovery in the dissolution of the solid land of a new dimension by which experience must be multiplied, he was only giving articulate expression to thoughts that had for some time been worrying in his brain. Limits had shifted, boundaries been dissolved. Nothing ended in itself, but flowed over into something else; and the obsession of his delirium, that he was himself the dead man whose body he had lugged out of the slime, came back now and haunted him like the key note of a tune. But what a tune! How hard to play—rude and perplexing, with discords unresolved and a tantalising melody that fluted and escaped. His mind sounded the note again and again throughout that night, but always the tune itself eluded him.

The night was like the morning, soft and still. Earth floated in the radiance the young moon had left above the hills; stars, remote and pure, floated in the wide serene of heaven; nothing moved, yet all was moving, eternally sustained by flight; and Garry walked for hours in troubled impotence, angry at a world that would not let him keep his straight and clean-cut standards. To refute what he had thought a false conception of his friend's honour had seemed a simple and straightforward matter, but it had led him into a queer morass; and now, as he tramped in the night, he was filled with panic lest the story of the ring should become public through his agency. It would be a degradation to expose that. He was glad he had resisted the impulse to tell Lindsay, though her disapproval had been difficult to bear. He had longed to justify himself, and the frustrate longing had made him rough. He had caught her to him with violence, clutching at her throat until the mark burned upon her flesh. Her young primrose love had not yet learned to endure such heats.

In time he went to bed, but sleep did not come. Instead came fever and a new throng of disordered visions. He saw the solid granite earth, on which these established houses, the Weatherhouse and Knapperley, were built (less real, as he had said to Mrs Falconer, than the dissolution and mud of the war-swept country), melt and float and change its nature; and the people fashioned out of it, hard-featured, hard-headed, with granite frames and life-bitten faces, rude tongues and gestures, changed too, melted into forms he could not recognise. Then he perceived a boulder, earthy and enormous, a giant block of the unbridled crag, and behold! as he looked the boulder was his aunt. 'You won't touch me,' she seemed to say. 'I won't be cut and shaped and civilised.' But in an instant she began to move, treading ever more quickly and lightly, until he saw that she was dancing as he had caught her dancing on the night of his return. Faster and faster she spun, lighter of foot and more ethereal, and the rhythm of her dance was a phrase in the tune that had eluded him. And now she seemed to spurn the earth and float, and in the swiftness of her motion he could see no form nor substance, only a shining light, and he knew that what he watched was a dancing star.

It was already morning when he fell asleep, and he woke late, heavy-eyed and languid. Miss Barbara brought him a cup of tea—a visiting star, perhaps, but of peculiar magnitude. Thereafter she left him alone, and he lay swamped in lassitude and dozed again.

In the afternoon she went out. The house grew intolerably still. Not even a dog broke the uneasy quiet. He dozed, and struggled awake in a joyous clamour, a merry and tumultuous barking that did him good. Later he heard the stir around the ingle—sticks broken, fire-irons clattering, even, in the stillness of dusk, a sudden explosive crackle from the burning logs. He wanted food and a shave, the warmth and life of fire; speech, and the comfortable feel of paws and noses; and rising, he went downstairs.

To his surprise his aunt was just coming in. He had supposed her in the kitchen, where she, having seen the lamp lit, was supposing him. They pushed open the kitchen door together, and entered.

The fire was roaring on the hearth, the room was light and gay; dogs snuggled to the heat, tobacco smoke eddied on the air, the lid of the kettle danced and chattered and steam rose invitingly and bellied and wavered towards the chimney; and deep in Miss Barbara's favourite chair there sat a little man, as abundantly at home as if the place were his. As Miss Barbara and Garry came in he was in act of rocking back his chair, stretching his arms with a luxurious content, and singing to a merry tune:

> He took his pipes and played a spring
> And bade the coo consider—

'If it isna Johnnie Rogie!' cried Miss Barbara. 'Man, but you're a sight for sair e'en.'

The little man turned in the chair, nodded gaily to Miss Barbara in time to his music, beat vigorously with his arms and continued to sing:

> The coo considered wi' hersel
> That music wadna fill her—

Ay, ay, Bawbie, but I've the reek risin' and the kettle on, an' you shall hae your supper, lass:

> And you shall hae your supper.

'You'll have a dram first, laddie,' cried Miss Barbara. 'I've aye a drappie o' the real Mackay—none of your wersh war rubbish, dirten orra stuff.'

'We'll have it out, Bawbie.'

Miss Barbara fetched it running. She polished the tumblers and set them before her guest, who poured the whisky with the air of a god. Not more benignly did Zeus confer his benefits upon humanity than Johnnie Rogie the tramp handed Miss Barbara Paterson of Knapperley a share of her own whisky; and Miss Barbara took it with a gratitude that was divine in its acceptance, and called Garry to come forward and have his glass.

Unshaved, with hollow cheeks and sunken eyes from which the sleep was not yet washed, Garry came to the fire.

'Come awa', my lad,' cried Johnnie. 'Sojers need a dram like the lave o's.' He poured the whisky and conferred it upon Garry. 'Take you a' you get an' you'll never want.' And, raising his own glass, he let the golden liquor tremble to his mouth. 'And sojers need to live and sojers need to pray. Live, laddie, live? Ay, sojers need to live mair than the lave o's. Clean caup oot, like the communicants o' Birse'—his head went back as he drained his glass—'that's the way a sojer needs to live. Tak' you a' that life can give you, laddie. Drink you it up, clean caup oot. It's a grand dram as lang's ye're drinkin' it, and ye'll be a lang time deid.' And seeing that Garry had not yet emptied his tumbler, he added, 'But drink clean in, tak it a' at ae gulp. Life's a dram that's better in the mou' than in the belly.'

He poured himself another draught, and drank.

Apparently he found it good; for when he had swallowed it the sun-god himself was not more radiant, and when he spoke the words flowed out like song.

On Garry, too, unfed and over-strung, the golden liquor was having its effect. The shabby, under-sized man with the matted dingy hair and a little finger wanting, pouring the whisky and swaying his whole body to the rhythm of his chant, was hypnotising him, and with his will. He seemed a ministrant of life, bringing for a moment its golden energies within one's grasp, making the visionary gleam look true. Garry thrust his elbows on his knees and leaned forward, talking eagerly. Miss Barbara was moving from room to room upstairs. When she came in again her face was aglow and she slapped Johnnie heartily on the shoulder.

'And where have you been this long weary while?'

'Where you could never follow, Bawbie.'

'Nae to the wars,' she mocked.

'Just that.'

'Eh? And you near sixty, and a cripple muckle tae and but the ae cranny.'

'For a' that, an' a' that, I've been wi' the sojer laddies, Bawbie.' He reeled off into a popular soldier song. 'Ay, ay, the sojers need to live an' the sojers need to sing. An' wha wad sing to them if it wasna Johnnie? There's nae a camp an' nae a barrack but Johnnie's been there. An' whan the sojers are wearied an' whan the sojers are wae, wha but Johnnie wad gar them cantle up, wi' his auld fiddle an' his auld true tongue?'

He quaffed the golden fire again: Medea's fire, it made him young and reckless. He chanted more uproariously.

'An' mebbe whiles when pay day cam, a sojer here, a sojer there, wad mind on singing Johnnie. Ay, ay, the sojer lads, they're free wi' their siller, the sojer lads, whan they ken the next march is the march to death. They've a lang road ahead o' them, a lang road an' few toons, the road to death; an' lads that wadna pairt wi' the dirt aneth their nails, in the ordiner ways of living, 'll gang laughin' doon to death an' toss the siller fae them like a lousy sark. What's the siller, what's the siller, give's a sang, they say.'

'You'll have a bonny penny in your pooch, Johnnie,' commented Miss Barbara. 'You'll have made your fortune.'

'Fient a fortune.' The little man ascended again to prose. He drew himself together, sat up straight and squared his shoulders. The reckless fire died down, the cadence of his voice altered. He talked of supper, and Miss Barbara made haste to prepare it.

Supper over, the dogs set up a barking.

'Did you hear a step?' said Miss Barbara.

She rose and let in Francie Ferguson.

Francie stood sheepishly in the glow of light. 'I didna ken ye had company, Miss Barbara. It was the lights. Yon's a terrible blaze, 'umman. I was feart you would dae us some hurt.'

'Ach!' said Barbara sturdily. 'What's in a puckle candles?'

The soldier and the tramp had tilted back their chairs and with sprawling legs and arms flung easefully abroad, trolled out old tales, recitative and chorus. Johnnie had slid away again from prose. The boom of their laughter ceased when Francie entered. Now Garry rose from his seat, crying, 'But hang it all, you know, aunt—' and thereupon went off again in a round of laughter. Recovering himself he said, 'I give you my compliments. He's worth an illumination. Still, you know, *noblesse oblige*. There are weaker brothers—prime ministers and such-like fry.'

'I'm a Paterson of Knapperley, my lad, a Paterson of Knapperley can please himself. It's only your common bodies that need your laws and regulations, to be hauden in about. The folk of race have your law within themselves. Ay, ay, I'm a Paterson of Knapperley, but you're Donnie Forbes's grandson and seek to make yourself a politician. But go your ways.'

He went through the house, and found candle or oil-lamp burning in every window; and put them out: with a queer contraction of the heart as room after room was left dark and dead behind him. The war was putting this out too—this impetuous leap of exhilaration, this symbol of joy. When he returned to the kitchen Francie had been drawn into the charmed circle. He and Miss Barbara together were making lusty chorus to Johnnie's song:

I saw an eel chase the Deil,
   Wha's fou, wha's fou?
I saw an eel chase the Deil
   Wha's fou noo, ma jo?
I saw an eel chase the Deil
Roon aboot the spinnin' wheel,
   An' we're a' blin' drunk, bousin' jolly fou, ma jo!'

Francie too, had drunk of fire, and was like one that prophesied. Warmed by the whisky, heartened by honest song, he began to talk of what sat closest to his own bosom: what but Bell his wife and her incomprehensible trick of not sitting close, of holding off. 'He doesna seek to kiss me. I canna do with that kind o' sotter,' she had proclaimed abroad. A libel on a man. 'A blazin' lee,' shouted Francie. 'Doesna seek to kiss her. Doesna indeed.' For what but that had he waited twenty years, to be thwarted in the end by a woman's caprice: a woman who had the impudence to say, 'Fingers off the beef, you canna buy,' to her own lawful spouse. 'But she'll be kissed this very night,' he shouted. He banged the table and swaggered home at last in glee. His habitual sheepish good-humour had turned to a more flaming quality. A man greatly resolved.

'He needs all his legs,' said Miss Barbara.

Garry went drunk to bed, but not with whisky. Again he had seen life essentialised. Its pure essence had been in Johnnie as he usurped the rites of hospitality and in Miss Barbara's extravaganza of candles; in Francie too, revolting against a niggard life.

He was interrupted in his soliloquy by the opening of the door. Johnnie shambled in, without apology, and asked for money: which Garry gave, amusedly, too much exalted still to resent this degradation in the golden godling; finding it indeed no degradation, but a glory the more. So few people had the grace to take what they wanted with such unabashed assurance. Oh, if all the world would turn audacious—! He fell asleep at last to the sound of Johnnie's voice on the other side of the wall:

> There's twa moons the night
> Quo' the auld wife to hersel.

Meanwhile for Lindsay the day had crawled. At every moment she had expected to see her mother arrive, and there would be an awkward moment when the ladies learned that the lover she had been sent here to forget was Garry Forbes. She detested the clandestine, yet merely to have sheltered from distasteful pleasantry was not a sign of guilt. She felt guilty nevertheless, and devised a score of speeches to convince her mother that the secrecy was not deceit. Her mother, however, did not come to be convinced.

Lindsay's feverish anxiety increased. She was ready to defend Garry against anything her mother might say, but as the day wore on she found it increasingly hard to defend Garry against herself. Always her accusation was the same—he had wantonly exposed Louie to the clack of tongues, without any proof that what he alleged was true. If he thought evil so readily of one woman, what might he not think soon of another, of herself? The child tossed upon dark and lashing waters, and was afraid. It had been safe and very beautiful on shore.

As dusk drew down she stole from the house, not unobserved by Kate, and shortly afterwards a car panted up the hill, and Andrew Lorimer himself came in.

Mrs Lorimer, as Lindsay expected, put it down to deliberate deceit on her daughter's part that they had not been told of Garry's arrival. Andrew refused to be annoyed.

'I'll talk to her myself,' he said. 'To the young man, too, if I clap eyes on him.'

Andrew Lorimer was a burly, big-nosed man, more like a farmer to the eye than a lawyer, thrawn and conservative, devoted to his children, but determined that they should have their good things in the shape that he saw fit to give them. He was quite willing that his little linnet should ultimately go to Miss Barbara's rough and rather ugly nephew, for he knew that the fellow had sound worth in spite of his execrable opinions; but the child was far too young. He wanted her for himself a long time yet.

'A nice condition you've cast my wife into,' he grumbled to the Weatherhouse ladies, 'letting that daughter of hers run round the country with her sweetheart at her tails.'

There was consternation and surprise. Andrew liked to hector.

'What,' he cried, 'you didn't know? So she takes you in, does she—cheats her mother on the sly?'

Kate looked up calmly from her sewing.

'There was nothing sly about it,' she said. 'Lindsay was perfectly frank. When she came at Christmas she told all there was to tell. And as we understood your objection was merely her age, what harm should we suppose in their meeting?'

And to Miss Theresa, who was still indignantly exclaiming, she said, with the same unmoved demeanour, 'Perhaps *you* may not have heard, Aunt Tris, but it wasn't because Lindsay didn't tell.'

'To be sure we knew,' put in Miss Annie with a chuckle. She remembered the day Lindsay had dropped kisses in the nape of her neck. 'And blithe we were to see the bairn so glad and bonny.'

Andrew Lorimer was in high feather. Theresa, disconcerted, took the check badly. He remembered how, from their childhood up, Tris had liked to be in the know, and he enjoyed her discomfiture. It was not unlikely that Kate also, calmly as she continued her needlework, with frank and placid eyes lifted to look at her aunt, relished the moment.

Theresa began to give Mr Dalgarno Forbes his character.

'You can just hold by his doors, then,' thundered Andrew.

Mrs Falconer sat stupefied. Her mind registered the incredible fact, but she could not feel it. And Kate, who on her own confession loved the man, sat there collectedly and sewed. She had known, even when she confessed, that Garry was Lindsay's lover. Mrs Falconer's dreams were dust.

Lang Leeb warbled from her corner. The fragile sounds were blown like gossamers about the room and no one heeded them, but Ellen moved her head impatiently as though they teased her face. Leeb sang:

My mother bade me gie him a piece,
    Imphm, ay, but I wunna hae him,
I gied him a piece and he sat like a geese,
    For his auld white beard was newly shaven.

Ellen turned and looked at her mother. The old eyes, bright and sharp, glittered like the reflection from a metal that has no inner illumination of its own. She was subtle and malicious, this old woman for whom life had ended save as a spectacle. Ellen, as she looked, read her mother's mocking thought. Theresa too, had said to her, when she ran across the garden to bid Garry stay for tea, 'Nell, you old fool.' What did they think—that she was running after the boy for her own sake? Dastardly supposition, so vile that she blushed, went hot and cold by turns. But wasn't it true? In a flash she realised it, that this sense of tragedy in which she had foundered came not from any grief for Kate, but for herself, because she loved the youth and wanted him

near her. But it was life she wanted, strong current and
fresh wind, no ignoble desire.

Theresa continued to sneer at the boy's expense. Leeb
changed her song. The mocking voice teased like a gnat
round Ellen's consciousness:

She wouldna slack her silken stays,
sang Leeb.

What! Not be generous to this young man who had
wakened her out of her unreal dreams? They could call
her what kind of fool they liked, she would not be guilty
of that cowardice. She would give. She cut across Theresa's
denunciation with an incisive thrust.

'He is a very fine young man.'

Andrew turned and looked at his cousin, whose long
lean cheek was from him.

'Very fine fiddlesticks. He's a very ordinary decent fellow, with some high-falutin ideas that ought to have worn
themselves out by now. Better, I grant you, than the low-
falutin that seems to be the fashion nowadays. I've no
objection to an idealist, always provided he can keep his
own wife when he takes one. And what ails you at Bawbie?'
he added, swinging round again to disconcert Theresa.
'Bawbie's folk's as good's your own. A Paterson was settled
in Knapperley as long since as the seventeen-thirties, and a
Paterson was married on the son of an Earl, if you didn't
know it, in 1725. A collateral branch, that would be. Let
me see, let me see, it was the same branch—'

The door was opened, and Lindsay thrust unceremoni-
ously in by a little wiry wrinkled man who bounced rapidly
after her.

'It's yourself, Mr Lorimer,' said he, too excited even
to greet the ladies into whose house he had thus bounded.
'Then pass you judgment, Mr Lorimer.' He rattled a tin pail
under their noses. 'Pass you judgment. Here's me sortin' up
the shop with the door steekit, and what do I hear but the
jingle-jangle of my pail, that was sittin' waitin' me on the
step. So out I goes and sees my lady here makin' away pretty
sharp. "Ye're nae away wi' my pailie, surely," I says. Bang
goes the pail and away goes she. So I puts on a spurt and up
wi' her. "Ye needna awa' so fleet, Miss Craigmyle," I says.

"I see you fine. You werena needin' to send my pailie in ower the plantin'." But losh ye! It's nae Miss Craigmyle I've got a haud o', but this bit craiturie. A gey snod bit deemie, I wouldna mind her for a lass.' He turned the crunkled leather of his countenance towards Lindsay, in a wrinkled effort at a smile. 'But she would have been up and off with my pailie, Mr Lorimer, and nyod man, see here, the cloor it's gotten whan she flung it frae her into the plantin'.'

Andrew watched his daughter with amusement. Flushed, panting, near to tears, she stood in the middle of the room and threw defiant glances around.

'Clap it on her head, Mr Gillespie,' he answered to the indignant grocer, 'and up on the faulters' stool with her.'

'She has a gey canty hat there of her own,' said the grocer, whose wrath had fallen now that his grievance was recounted. 'But,' he added, glancing round the assemblage of ladies, 'it was Miss Theresa there I thought I had a haud o'. We a' ken she canna keep her hands off what she sees. She maun be inen the guts o' a'thing.'

Andrew bellowed with delight. Didn't he know the ancient habit of his cousin Tris, to appropriate all she fancied: failing roup, barter or purchase, then by simple annexation! The shades of sundry pocket-knives, pencils and caramels grinned humorously there above her ears. So the habit had not died, but was matter of common talk. To have seen his excellent cousin twice confounded in one evening was luck. He rose in fine fettle.

'Well, well, Gillespie man, but we can't let the lassie connach your goods like that.'

'Na, na, Mr Lorimer, sir,' answered the honest grocer, refusing the proffered money, 'I dinna want your siller. The pailie's nane the waur. It'll serve as well wi' a cloor in the ribs as wantin' it.' Mr Lorimer saw him out and came back to challenge Lindsay.

'Well, my lady, what have you been up to?'

'Daddy, I wasn't going to steal his pail—you know that.'

'What were you going to do, then?'

Lindsay looked round. They all awaited her answer. She wondered if they had been talking of Garry and her. Throwing her head proudly back, she answered, 'It's very silly. I don't know what made me do it. But Knapperley was all blazing with light. I thought—I really thought for a minute it was on fire, and I had a sort of panic. I saw the pail and seized it and began to run. I know it sounds absurd—as though my little pail could have helped any if there really was a fire. There wasn't, you know. The lights were blazing, right enough, but we saw them go out just after.'

'There's your Bawbie for you,' Theresa flung at Andrew Lorimer. Theresa was in a black anger. Her slogan, *A ga'in' foot's aye gettin'*, had covered numerous petty assaults on property, never (as of course one would understand) of magnitude to be called theft; but the grocer's calm recital of her obsession took her by surprise. She glared furiously at Andrew, and pounced triumphantly on Miss Paterson's aberration as a shelter from her own.

'Andrew's wanting a word with Lindsay,' Miss Annie interrupted in her pleasant way. 'We all know Bawbie's gotten a dunt on the riggin', Tris. Leave her alone. Andrew, I'm getting stiffened up like a clothes rope after rain. I'm terrible slow. But we'll all go through and let you talk to your lassie.'

'Indeed no, Paradise. Daddy and I will go through.'

Andrew trolled a song in his deep strong voice as he went to the other room. He had quite enjoyed the little episode. Theresa's exposure was part of the ruthless comicality of life. 'O ay, he's a comical deevil, your cousin Andrew,' Lang Leeb had been wont to say. 'He might laugh less if it was some of his own.'

One of his own was now involved. He had yet to deal with Lindsay's affair.

'Your mother,' he said, 'hasn't made the acquaintance of your proposed aunt-in-law. On the whole, we'd better keep this dark. She doesn't relish eccentricity in the family. What's this about the lights? And fined, was she? Well, you keep that to yourself. Your mother needn't know you were chasing round the countryside with the grocer's pail.'

'You're a dear,' said Lindsay.

'And you'd better tell me what to say about this man of yours. All fair and square, I suppose?'

'You bet.'

'What'll I say, then? Hurry up, I can't stay here all night. What am I to say to your mother? Lord love you, bairn, don't weep. Make up the triggest little tale you can.'

A burning tear splashed down upon his hand. Lindsay's face was against his coat, and he felt the shaking of her sobs.

'Daddy, daddy, I'm so miserable.'

'Here, here, cheer up. It's war-time, after all. Do you want to marry him?'

Lindsay raised her head and stared with blank eyes at her father.

'We'll bring your mother round,' continued Andrew.

Lindsay wept the harder.

'Well, well, that's settled,' said her father, drying her tears with his handkerchief, and he plunged exuberantly into talk of Theresa and the pail.

'But daddy, what could Mr Gillespie have meant?'

'Just what he said—your Cousin Theresa can't go past a thing she wants.'

'But taking things—? She's perhaps beginning to get old. Old people do things like that.'

'Don't you suggest it. Tris won't be thought old. No, no, it's not a sign of her decrepitude. Tris wasn't to be trusted with property at any time. If it was movable property that was concerned, she lee'd like a fishwife and thieved like Auld Nick.' He began to entertain his daughter with tales from his youth. 'But this won't do. What am I to say to your mother?'

'Why, daddy,' said Lindsay, with very bright eyes, 'it's your business to make up explanations for people.'

'What am I to say to your mother?'

'Don't eat me up! Are you to be everyone's advocate but mine?'

'What—'

'Well, say then—oh, say that he's a gruff old bear and you can't get a word in edgeways and it wouldn't have been safe to let her know that he was here. Say that he's a terror to the neighbourhood, that he has enormous ears, the better to hear you with, my dear, and perfectly enormous teeth, the better to eat you up. Oh, say what you like, daddy, I leave it to you.'

She clung about her father's neck, convulsively kissing the roughness of his coat.

Andrew fondled her.

'Well, if we let you marry him—you're not very old yet. Sure that you know your own mind? Quite sure you love the bear enough to spend your life with him? Eh?'

'Quite.'

Andrew enjoyed the arrogant lift of her head.

But later, hunched on her pillow, she queried in the dark of Kate, 'And you told daddy I was out with him, Katie?'

'And weren't you?'

'I said no, didn't I?'

'But I supposed—'

'You shouldn't suppose.'

'Oh, I'm sorry if I was wrong. But your father wasn't very angry, was he?'

'Oh, not particularly. It's mother that thinks he is not good enough for us. We're so grand, aren't we? Daddy only says I mustn't be turned into a woman too soon.'

'Well, neither you must, Linny.'

'Oh, you're all the same. As if age—Louie's the only one—'

'What about Louie?'

'Oh, nothing.'

'But it will be all right, Linny, when you're older? Your father won't make objections?'

'Oh, quite all right. It's perfectly all right, isn't it, not to make objections to an engagement that doesn't exist?'

'That doesn't— But it will exist when they give their permission.'

'I've broken it off.'

'But whatever—'

'Tonight. I wrote it. I was posting it when I was out, if you want to know.'

'But Lindsay, this is terrible. Whatever for?'

'Oh, for everything.' She slipped under the bedclothes and lay rigid, her face hidden. 'Don't speak to me, please, Kate.'

Kate held her peace.

'Katie.'

'Yes.'

'Life's so terribly strange, isn't it?'

'Is it? I don't know.'

'Don't *you* think it strange, Katie?'

'No, not particularly.'

Lindsay sat up again.

'But truly, Katie? Have you never thought life was tremendously queer? One day one thing, and the next day all
changed. Don't you find yourself wanting one thing at one
moment, and then in a trice you know that wasn't what you
wanted at all, but something different? Don't you?'

'No, I can't say that I do.'

'Then is it only me that's unlike everyone else? How
could I be anyone's wife, Kate, if I'm like that?'

'But—'

'Oh, it wasn't for that I broke it off. At least, partly
that. He's—he's not what I thought quite, Katie, and I'm
not what I thought, and I don't know what to do. I wish I
had been like other people, but I don't know what to make
of life. I don't know what I want. It's all so queer.'

'Lindsay, you're hysterical. Lie down and sleep. It'll
all be right in the morning.'

'No, it won't. You don't understand. I don't seem to
be like other people, Katie. I'm queer. It must run in the
blood.' Kate smiled to herself at the thought of queerness
running in the respectable Craigmyle-Lorimer veins. 'Look
at Cousin Theresa,' continued the girl's impatient voice.
'That's her that cavils at Miss Barbara for being queer. I
was never so ashamed in my life as when that grocer man
shouted, "You hold your hand, Miss Craigmyle, we know
you like to nab a thing fine." '

'In the house—I know she claims all she wants as hers.
But outside— And so Miss Barbara's lights were up again,
Lindsay? The police will be on her. She's been fined
already, you know. Crazy old thing. A public nuisance.'
Kate chatted on, in hope of distracting Lindsay's mind and
persuading her to sleep. But the girl flared out, 'I don't see
why you're all so bitter about it. I think she's splendid. She

knows what she wants, and wants it enough to have it, too. She's magnificent. She's herself. She can burn her house up if she likes.'

'And it doesn't matter if other people suffer?'

'Not in the slightest. Oh, don't let's talk any more, Katie.'

Kate was silent as she was bid.

The night air grew colder. Lindsay tossed restlessly. The wind rose. A sough ran through the pines. Blinds shook, and somewhere in the house a door rattled. Lindsay shivered. How cold the night was now!

'Don't tell them I've broken it off, Katie. You see—we don't know yet what he may say.'

'Very well. Now sleep. It will be all right tomorrow.'

In the next room, preparing for bed, Theresa rapped out, 'Sleekit bessy she's been. And such a bairn to look at. Butter wouldn't melt in her mouth. And Kate's no better, Ellen, let me tell you that. To think of the two of them, and them up to such a cantrip.'

'They've done no wrong.'

'Ask Mrs Andrew as to that.'

'I can decide for myself without any Mrs Andrew.'

'Well, if you don't think it wrong, I'm sure—! Sleekit, I call it. And raking about with him like yon after dark—you never know what harm she might take.'

'Oh, pails are easy to come by,' said Ellen.

Theresa held her tongue and got into bed.

'Hist ye and get that light out,' she commanded in a while. Ellen raised her eyes from her Bible and said nothing. 'Your chapter's lasting you long tonight.'

Ellen dropped her eyes, but did not speak. She had read no chapter. One uncompleted sentence only: the sentence with which she had been wont, in her hours of abasement, to scourge her fleeing fancy. 'Casting down imaginations and every high thing that exalteth itself against the knowledge of the Lord.'

Imaginations! It mattered nothing to her what the commentators said, the word for her summed up those sweet excursions into the unreal that had punctuated all her life. She thought she had forsworn them, fired as she was by the glimpses that Garry had provided of man's real travail and endeavour. But all she had achieved was a still more presumptuous imagination; and as she saw the ruins of her palace lie around her, she realised how presumptuous, and at the same time how desirable it had been. Now she would never open the door of her dwelling to youth and arrogant active life. Desolation came upon her. The cold wind searched her and made her shudder. Her prayer was a long and moaning cry, 'Me miseram. I have sinned. I have sinned.'

ELEVEN

Garry and his Two Fools on the Housetop

Mrs Falconer awoke suddenly and could not remember what had occurred.

She knew that she had been hurt. Her mind was aware of its own suffering, but could not find the cause. She lay very still, grappling with memory. This impotence was horrible. It gave one a sense of calamity too huge for the mind to master. Her eyes went straying, and across the window she saw the passage of a falling star; then another, and another. 'That's someone dead,' she thought; but instantly came recollection. Her mind cleared and the weight of disaster lifted. Stars did not fall from heaven in the course of ordinary living; one's pain had other sources. Kate loved a man she would not marry: that was all. Kate— But Kate remained unmoved. The blackness of desolation was not for that, but was born of shame and of despair. There was no escape for her from unrealities to the busy world of men, and when she sought to break away she did shameful and presumptuous things. The gnat-bites of her mother's song had swollen now, poisonous and hateful seats of pain.

Outside, the shooting stars were still falling across the window. They could not be stars—so many, so continual. They eddied and fluttered. Mrs Falconer raised herself and stared. Sparks! Something must be on fire. She was fully awake now and her mind was alert and vigorous; as she got out of bed and crossed to the window she reviewed in a flash the whole story of the preceding days. 'There's no good not confessing it,' she thought. 'I do love that boy. I want to live the kind of life he would approve, to fight with real opponents for a real cause. I want to find the dimension that he said was lacking in our lives.' And then she thought, 'I can at least help him to expose the falsehood about that betrothal. That is something real I can help to do.'

Even if her fond dreams of his saying to her, 'Mother, no one understands what I mean like you,' could meet with no fulfilment, she must still do all she could to fight the evils he detested.

All this passed through her mind as she hastened to the window, at the same time as she was thinking, 'Can the fire be in this house?'

When she reached the window she saw that the air was full of large, floating flakes of snow. A shaft of light lay across them and made them glow like tongues of fire. And now a voice rose from the garden. Mrs Falconer leaned out, and saw Francie Ferguson standing in the whirl of snowflakes, moving a lantern.

'Ay, ye're there, are you? Ye're grand sleepers, the lot of you, nae to hear a body bawlin' at your lug.'

'But what's the matter, Francie?'

'A dispensation of Providence, Mistress Falconer. Ay, I tell't you whan a' that lights was bleezin' to the heaven, I tell't you the Lord would visit it upon her heid. Knapperley's up in a lowe, Mistress Falconer—'

'What! But are you sure?'

'As sure's a cat's a hairy beast. Ay, ay, I've twa e'en to glower wi' an' I'm gey good at glowerin'. And thinks I, Miss Craigmyle'll never ca' ower it if there's a spectacle and she's nae there to see. So I e'en in about to let you know.'

'But surely, in that snow—surely it won't burn.'

'The snaw's new on.'

Mrs Falconer roused Miss Theresa.

'What's that? Knapperley? It's just the price of her.'

Theresa was out of bed on the instant. As Francie knew, she would have counted it a personal affront to be left out from a nocturnal fire. Mrs Falconer too, put on her garments, with trembling and uneasy fingers.

'What can we do, Tris? We'll only be in the way.'

But though she offered a remonstrance, she was drawn by some force beyond herself to complete her hasty dressing and follow Theresa to the garden.

As they went out the snow ceased falling and they could see that dawn had come. The sky cleared. Francie put out his lantern, and in a while the sun rose in splendour, touching the leafless tangles of twigs, filigreed with snow, to a shining radiance. Snow coated the ground and the shadows cast along it by the sun glowed burning blue. Francie and Miss Theresa talked, but Mrs Falconer walked on through the sharp vivid morning, and the thoughts she was thinking were pungent like the morning air. 'All is not lost,' cried a voice within her heart. 'If I have been a fool in my imaginings, why, to be a fool may be the highest wisdom. If I have been a fool it was because I loved. To love is to pass out beyond yourself. If I pass beyond myself into the service of a cause, surely I can bear the stigma of fool.' And she was elated, walking rapidly over the melting snow. 'The thing,' she thought, 'is to find how I can help him to prove that Louie affair.'

At Knapperley there was shouting and confusion: but, thanks to the fall of snow, the flames had been mastered. A part of the roof had fallen in. Miss Barbara stood with her legs planted apart, hands in her jacket pockets, contemplating the destruction with an infinite calm. Garry emerged from the building, half-clad, pale and weary, the gauntness of his face emphasised by the black streaks and grime that smoke and charred wood had left on it. He came out brushing ash from his clothing with his hands and spoke in an anxious tone to Miss Barbara.

'Can't find a sign of him. Looks as though it began in that room, too. The bed's destroyed. But not a sign of the man.'

'Ach,' said Miss Barbara, unperturbed. 'He's been smoking in his bed again. He'll be far enough by now, once he saw what he had done. Many's the time I've said to Johnnie, "Smoke you in my beds again and we'll see."'

Garry gave vent to a whistling laugh. 'Well, we've seen.' He returned to his labour among the debris. The little crowd that had collected ran hither and thither, talking and making suggestions. Miss Barbara stalked upstairs. Garry thrust his head from the gap where an upper window had been. From beneath, with his blackened face and protuberant ears, he had the appearance of a gargoyle.

'Friends,' he shouted, 'my aunt is obliged to you all. There's not much harm done, but without your help it would have been much more.'

'You'll need to hap up that holie in the roof, lad,' interrupted one of the men.

'I'll do more than hap it up—I'll mend it. I've been talking to Morrison here, the joiner. He can't take on the job, he's short of men and too much in hand as it is. But he says I'll get the wood.'

'Ay, ay, Mr Forbes, fairly that,' said Morrison. 'But for working, na man, I'm promised this gey while ahead.'

'Well,' said Garry, 'my leave will soon be up. I mean to start myself this very day.'

At these words, 'My leave will soon be up,' Mrs Falconer felt a queer constriction of the heart. The folk began to move away, but Miss Barbara, thrusting her head in its turn from the blackened hole, cried, 'Step in-by, the lot o' you there, and get a nip afore you go.' Miss Craigmyle and Mrs Falconer, looking round a moment later for their escort Francie, and failing to find him, it was clear that he had been enticed by Miss Barbara's offer. Had he not drunk the golden fire the previous night? 'A cappie o' auld man's milk,' Miss Barbara said, pouring the whisky. The two ladies made their way indoors.

'I'll just be bidin', then,' Francie was saying.

Garry talked to him with earnest and eager gestures.

Francie had offered himself as a labourer in the rebuilding of the fallen portion of roof.

'You'll never take him on,' cried Miss Theresa. 'The body has no hands. His fingers are all thumbs.'

'His father, he tells me, helped to build your own house. And his brother was a noted craftsman.'

'You've a bit to go to fetch his brother and his father to your house. The fellow's never been a mile from a cow's tail, he'll never do your work. He's a timmer knife. I don't like to hear of you taking him.'

'You can like it or loup it. I've engaged him.'

'You're a dour billie to deal wi',' said Miss Theresa. 'There's no convincing you. But you'll be cheated. Wait till you see if I'm not right. Your fine fat cash will be gey lean work. But I see you don't care a craw's caw for anything I may say.'

Francie's foolish, happy face remained unmoved throughout her diatribe; but when she added, 'We'll go in-by and tell your wife where you are,' he bounded to his feet, thumping the table till the dishes rang.

'Na!' he roared. 'That's what you wunna do. She can just sit and cogitate. She can milk the kye there and try how that suits her and muck the byre out an' a'. Such a behaviour as she's behaved to me! Past redemption and ower the leaf. Dinna you go near, Miss Craigmyle. She'll maybe sing sma' and look peetifu' yet.'

Mrs Falconer said in a low, hurrying voice to Garry, 'If there is anything that we could do—'

'Nonsense, Nell,' came brusquely from her sister. 'Keep your senses right side up. What could you do?'

The sisters went away.

At the Weatherhouse Lindsay came disconsolate to breakfast. She hardly heeded the excited talk about the fire. 'It's no affair of mine,' she thought impatiently, and going to the window she gazed into the chilly garden.

'It's like winter come back. At this time of year, to have snow.'

'Hoots, bairn, it's only April. Did you never hear of the lassie that was smored in June, up by the Cabrach way?'

The sun had not reached the garden. The grass was covered with a carpeting of snow, except for dark circular patches underneath the trees; but the carpet was too meagre to have the intensely bright and vivid look that snow in quantity assumes. Birds had hopped over its surface, which was marked by their claws. The delicate crocus petals were bruised and broken, and early daffodils had been flattened, their blooms discoloured by contact with the claggy earth. Only the scilla and grape hyacinths, blue, cold and virginal, stood up unmoved amid the snow.

And how cold it was! Although the sun shone beyond the garden, melting the foam of snow that edged the waves of spruce, yet the air was bitter, searching its way within doors, turning lips and fingers blue.

'The milk's not come,' said Kate. 'Oh, that's the way of it. I always said Francie did the milking. Well, we've enough to last us breakfast.'

When breakfast was over, Miss Theresa put on her outdoor things.

'Now really, Tris, where are you off to? Haven't you had enough of gallivanting for one morning?'

'To see about the milk,' said Theresa, who was agog to discover how Bell was taking her husband's mild desertion.

'Well—I'll come too.'

Mrs Falconer hardly knew why she wished to go any more than she had known why she rose from her bed to see the fire. She seemed to be driven by a force outside herself.

'These things are real life,' she thought. 'That must be it. I ought to pay more heed to what other people are doing, not wrap myself up in my wicked fancies.'

The sisters made their way along the soft, wet cart-road. The first member of the family they came upon was the young boy Sid, who hodged along the road, hands in his pockets, spitting wide, in perfect imitation of Francie's gait and manner.

'Poor brutes, I don't believe they're ever milked,' Theresa said.

Bell greeted them with fine disdain. When Francie had first courted her, twenty years before, she must have had a bold and dashing beauty. Even yet she was handsome, in a generous style, and her black eyes had lost nothing of their boldness. Until Francie had wedded her, after the death of his brother Weelum, she had had a rude appetite for life but no technique in living. The spectacle, however, of her faithful and humble lover, claiming her in steadfast kindness after his long frustration, gave Bell a rich amusement. For the first time she ceased to follow her momentary appetites, and studied in a pretty insolence how best to take her entertainment from her marriage. She was therefore furious at Francie's disappearance.

'You can whistle for your milk,' she said. 'I wasna brought up to touch your kye, dirty greasy swine. Guttin' fish is a treat till't. The greasy feel o' a coo's skin fair scunners me.'

'Stellicky's milkin' the kye,' interrupted the little boy, who was keeking at the visitors round the edge of the door.

'Haud yer wisht, ye randy. Wait you or your da comes back.'

'But where is he?' gravely inquired Theresa.

'Whaur would he be? On the face o' the earth, whaur the wifie sowed her corn. Up and awa and left me and his innocent weans in the deid o' night, that's whaur he is. America, he's been sayin' gey often, I'll awa to America. I'll let him see America whan he wins back. I'll gar him stand yont. If he's to America, I'll to America an' a'.'

It was evident that she had received no hint of Francie's whereabouts, and the absence of the devoted drudge had wrought upon her finely. She was purple with wrath. The sisters went to the byre, where the small Stella, clad in an enormous apron, with a brilliant red kerchief knotted over her black hair, was milking the two cows. Stella saw the ladies, but paid not the slightest attention to their advent, and continued to milk with an important air, manoeuvring her little body, slapping the cows and addressing them in a loud and authoritative voice. Stella was in her glory.

'When you're done, we'll take our pailful,' said Miss Theresa sharply.

The girl looked round in an overdone amazement, kicked her stool from under her, swayed her little hips beneath the trailing apron and shoved the nearest cow aside. 'Haud back, ye—' she commanded, using a word that made the Weatherhouse ladies draw in their breath.

'You can bring that milk as fleet's you like,' said Miss Theresa. 'I'll give you your so-much if I hear you speak like that again.'

Stella tilted her chin and jigged her foot. In the darkness of the byre, clad in the old apron and the turkey-red kerchief, she glowed with an insolent beauty. Miss Theresa returned to the house, but Mrs Falconer remained at the byre door, watching the girl. Stella finished her milking, but instead of carrying the pails to the milk-house and giving the waiting customers their milk, she thrust the cows about, flung her stool at the head of one that refused to budge, and began with frantic haste to clean the byre. Mrs Falconer made no remonstrance. There was something in the impudent assurance of this nine year old child that frightened her and saddened her. When she heard the same wicked word tossed boldly from the childish lips, she thought, 'Well, this is reality, indeed. Why did I never think before of all that this implies?' and she began to talk to the child.

Stella was ready for an audience.

'And do you often milk?' Mrs Falconer had inquired.

'Oh, he learned me, but he never lets me. I did it all myself,' she added, with a gleaming toss of the head. 'She said'—she jerked her elbow towards the house—'she said, "Let the lousy brutes be." And she padlocked the door and wouldna let me in. But I waited till she went out to the yard, and I after her and up with a fine big thumper of a stick. "Give's that key," says I. But losh ye, I had a bonny chase or I got it out of her. Round and round, it was better'n tackie any day. "Deil tak ye, bairn," she said, "you fleggit me out o' a year o' my growth." "If it comes off you broadways," I says, "you needna worry." '

Mrs Falconer did not ask for the milk. She continued to watch the bouncing child.

Stella made the most of her audience. She talked large.

'Ken whaur I got my head-dress?' she asked, flaunting the Turkey cotton. 'I got it frae my Sunday School teacher. I'm in a play. I've got to speak five times. Ay, gospel truth, I hae! Molly Mackie has only four times. Gospel.'

She struck attitudes, strutting about the byre and mouthing her words.

'Ken this, I have that handky on my head in the play. Ay have I. Teacher she says, "Now, girls, fold them all up and we'll put them in this box." ' (Whose voice was she mimicking, thought Mrs Falconer. The little brat had put an intonation into it that was curiously familiar.)

'But Stella, how have you the handkerchief here?'

The girl burst into noisy laughter and went through a rapid but effective dumb show. Mrs Falconer gathered that she had brought the handkerchief away thrust into the neck of her frock.

'But Stella, that was naughty. Your teacher will be disappointed.'

'She hides things herself,' said Stella carelessly. 'Ay does she. Gospel.' When she said *Gospel* Stella breathed noisily and crossed her breath with her forefinger. 'I'll tell you,' she rattled on eagerly. 'Teacher has a ring she keeps hine awa' down her neck. She's another ring that she keeps on her finger, just its marra. Twins!' The girl giggled with delight at recounting her story. 'Ken how I found that out? She aye bides ahin whan we're learnin' the play, a' by hersel. So one night I thought I'd see why, and I leaves my paperie with the words in ahin a desk and then goes marchin' back to look for it. So I sees her standin' there and one ring danglin' on a ribbon kind of thing, and the t'other ring aye on her finger. And she stuffs the ring intil her bosom, and my, but she got red. She's right bonny whan she blushes.'

The girl grasped her little nose with her fist and squinted, laughing, over the top of it to Mrs Falconer, who said severely, 'You are a naughty girl, Stella. You should never spy on people.'

'Tra la la, la la la la,' sang Stella hopping about the byre. 'I wunna tell you any more.' But she could not keep it in. Immediately she began again.

'Ken what it is she does whan she stays ahin? My! She's play-actin'. Just like us in the play. I think she'll be to say her piece at the concert an' a'. It's awful nice. It's just rare. I've found the way to climb up and see in at the window, and I've seen her ilka night, and naebody else has had a keek. They'll get a rare astonisher at the concert the morn, ay will they. Well, she pu's off the ring that's aye on her finger and dirds it down on the floor. "You hateful thing," she cries. Syne she jerks the other one up out of her bosom, louses the string, and puts the ring on her finger. This way.' The child was an astonishing little mimic. Her pantomime was lifelike. She began now to kiss the imaginary ring, holding her head to the side and rubbing the third finger of her left hand to and fro against her lips.

'Syne,' continued Stella, 'she turns the ring round, so that the stone's inside. And then she makes on to shake hands with somebody, and she says, "Do you take this woman to be your wedded wife?" "I do." Whiles after that she starts to greet and whiles to sing. I dinna ken which it really is, but we'll see the morn. I hope she'll be dressed up. She kens it rare. It's auld John Grey's ring,' she added carelessly.

'Whose?'

'Auld John Grey's, him that's head o' the Sunday School.'

'Surely, Stella, you call him Mr Grey.'

'What for? He's just auld John Grey. He's a rare mannie. You can scran anything off him. If you go in about whan he's delvin' he gives you sweeties and newses awa' to you. Ae day I was newsing awa' and the rain cam on. Loshty goshty guide's, it wasna rain, it was hale water. The rain didna take time to come down. So he took me in to his hoosie and the body that makes his drop tea spread a piece to me. And syne he gied me a pencil that goes roun' an' roun' in a cappie kind o' thing. It was in a drawer with preens and pencils and orra bits o' things—some pictur's that he let me see and bits o' stone wi' sheepy silver. And away at the back o' the drawer there was a boxie wi' a window for a lid, and yon ring was in there. I kent it fine whan I saw it again. She had scranned it off him, same's I did a preen wi' a pink top.'

'But when was that, Stella?'

'Oh, a while sin'. I dinna ken. Afore the New Year.'

'Was it before his son died, do you think?'

'The chiel that made the guns? Na, na. A long while after that.'

'And who is your Sunday School teacher?' asked Mrs Falconer.

'Miss Morgan, of course,' Stella answered, with a contemptuous stare for her visitor's ignorance.

The long lean woman positively shook where she stood.

'Stella, my dear,' she said, swallowing hard, 'you know you shouldn't take away Miss Morgan's handkerchief. What will she say when she doesn't find it in the box?'

Stella gave a loud and scornful laugh.

'Bless your bonnet, she'll find it there all right. I'll have it back afore she sees. Though, of course, after the play's done—' She broke off laughing, and leaping about in fantastic figures through the byre, she sang, 'It's half-past hangin'-time, steal whan you like.'

'So young, so shameless and so smart,' thought Mrs Falconer sadly. The warm byre oppressed her and she stepped to the door, opening her collar to the chilly air; but seeing Theresa at the same time step from the door of the house, she went back to the byre and lifted the two pails of milk.

'Is that milk not ready yet?' cried Theresa, appearing in front of the byre.

'Just ready,' Mrs Falconer answered, and balancing her body between the pails she carried the milk to the milk-house.

Miss Theresa had had a good fat gossip.

'It seems Francie's hinting at leaving them,' she told her sister. 'All talk, I fancy. If he goes to America, the wife says, I go too.' Miss Theresa laughed. 'They'll need a good strong boat and a steady sea before they take that carcase across the ocean. She had made the ground dirl, chasing round like that and the lassie after her. I'm glad to hear somebody can keep her in her neuk.'

Mrs Falconer walked home in troubled soliloquy. Reality had pressed too close. Her thoughts swirled and sounded in the narrow channel of her life, crashing in from distant ocean. Lindsay's betrothal, the fire, the young man's imminent return to the war, Francie's revolt, the pitiful spectacle of the child Stella in her vigorous vulgar assault upon life, the mystery of Louie Morgan's play-acting with the rings, her own shame, her mother's cruelty—smote her like thunder. From the hurly-burly of her mind one thought in time detached itself, insisted on attention. What had Louie done? What did the strange story of the rings imply? If the ring that had been David's mother's was indeed lying in the box in John Grey's drawer some time later than David's death, how came Louie to possess it? She turned the theme about in her head, puzzled and afraid. If it was true, as Garry maintained, that Louie had never been betrothed to David Grey, could she have given colour to her story by clandestine appropriation of the ring—in short, by stealing it? Mrs Falconer felt like a country child alone for the first time in the traffic of a city. What am I to do? she thought, what am I to do?

In the afternoon Mrs Falconer went to call on John Grey's housekeeper. This elderly woman, deaf and cankered, had few intimates and knew little of what went on beyond her doors. Gossip passed her by. 'And as for the master himself,' she would say to Mrs Hunter, 'he says neither echie nor ochie. I've seen me sit a whole long winter night and him never open his mouth.' She had therefore heard nothing of the interrupted Session meeting, nor of the speculation that Mr Garry Forbes had set going with regard to Miss Morgan.

Mrs Falconer bundled some wool beneath her arm. 'I can give her a supply for socks,' she thought. It made an excuse for her call. But the mere need to summon excuse put Mrs Falconer to the blush. How mean a thing it was to lurk and spy, in hope of proving ill against one's neighbour! Truth must be served, but if this were her service, surely it was ignoble. She sighed and rang the door bell; rang again; then knocked loudly on the panels. At last a step shuffled to the door.

'I'm that dull,' the old woman said. 'Folk could walk in-by and help themselves or ever I knew they were about.'

'I don't suppose many people would want to do that.' Strange point of departure for the interview!

'You never know, Mrs Falconer. Folk's queer. And Mr Grey, good soul, thinks ill of nobody. There's nothing in this house under lock and key. Forbye the meat-safe, Mrs Falconer, and for that I wouldna take denial. Since ever my dozen eggs went a-missing, that I found a hennie sitting on in the corner of the wood, and them dead rotten—I put them into the bottom of the safe, till Mr Grey would dig a hole and bury them. And in-by there comes a tinkey. "No," I says, "my man, I've nothing." But when I went outside, lo and behold, my eggs were gone. He had had a bonny omelette that night. Unless, as I said often to Mr Grey, he sold them for solid siller to some poor woman in the town. Poor soul, she had had a gey begeck. So after that I says, I'll have a key to my safe. If it's rotten eggs the day, it may be firm flesh the morn.'

She had led her visitor in, and rambled on, paying little heed to interpolations, which had, in any case, to be shouted at her ear. Mrs Falconer therefore gave up the attempt to talk, and sat listening.

'And you think nobody would want to help themselves? I'm not so sure, I'm not so sure. I'll tell you what I found here one day. My fine miss, the old minister's daughter, Miss Louie Morgan, right inside the parlour, if you please, with the master's drawer beneath his bookcase standing open and her having a good ransack. A good ransack, Mrs Falconer, minister's daughter though she be. "The master gave me leave," she says, "and you didn't hear me ring, so I just came in." He gave her leave right enough, I asked him. For the Jumble Sale, she says. "The things are no use to me," he said, "she is very welcome." He would give away his head, would the master, you could lift his very siller in front of him and he would be fine pleased, but don't you touch a flower. Pick a rose or a chrysanthemum and you needna look him in the face again.'

Mrs Falconer's mouth was parched, her lips were shaking. She had asked nothing, but the answer she desired had fallen directly in her ears. She was sure now that Louie had taken the ring. The Jumble Sale took place three months after the death of David Grey. But perhaps Mr Grey himself had given her the ring, to seal a betrothal left incomplete at the young man's death? Mrs Falconer put the thought away. No, no. The concealment of the ring, her stealing to the drawer unseen, Garry's certainty, all convinced her; and she was overwhelmed besides by the thought that she had been led straight that day to the discovery. The sense of urgency that had driven her to Knapperley in the night, and to Francie's croft in the morning, so that Stella's remarkable story came to her knowledge, and now the immediate relation by the housekeeper of Louie's conduct, amazed her like a revelation of supernatural design. 'I have been led to this,' she thought.

She rose to go, shouting at the old housekeeper an excuse for her unusual visit.

'There would be no mistake though you came again, Mrs Falconer.'

'But what must I do next?' she pondered as she went away.

Kate, bringing home the messages that same afternoon, overtook Louie Morgan on the road.

'I'm thinking of applying for a Lonely Soldier,' said Louie. 'To write to, you know. Wouldn't it be splendid?' And without giving Kate time to reply she hurried on, 'We must all do something to help the poor men. Or a war-time orphan to bring up. I've been thinking of that. Two of them, perhaps. Uplands is so much too large for mother and me—we'd easily have room for two. Isn't it a splendid idea for people to take these poor orphans and bring them up?'

'Excellent,' said capable Kate; but privately she thought, 'Heaven pity any child that is brought up by you.'

Louie blurted, 'I suppose you think I am making a fool of myself.'

'No. Why should I think so?'

Without answering, Louie burst suddenly into a side road and walked away.

She had just come from Knapperley.

Garry had laboured hard all day. Knowing that unless he saw the repairs completed before he left, the house would remain as it was and rot, he set to work at once to clear away the damaged material. Miss Barbara, keen for a space, volunteered her aid. She was strong as a man. Francie too, worked manfully. As the morning wore on people came in twos and threes to look at the scene of the fire. Miss Barbara's eccentric ways, above all her curious taste for lighted windows, gave rise to many explanations of the outbreak. Nor did the sight that met the eyes of the inquisitive lull the tales; for through the gap in the roof, moving about among the beams and on what was left of the flooring of a low attic, could be seen three figures, the tall lean soldier, the clumsy crofter and the brawny woman, sawing, scraping and hammering to the rhythm of an uproarious song:

I saw an eel chase the Deil
Roun' about the spinnin' wheel.
And we're a blin' drunk, boozin' jolly fou, ma jo!

Garry, swinging through the work in his enthusiasm, shouted as lustily as the other two:

> I saw a pyet haud the pleuch,
> Wha's fou, wha's fou?
> An' he whussled weel eneugh,
> Wha's fou noo, ma jo?

He broke off, however, at the sight of Miss Theresa Craigmyle among the spectators below. Theresa had hastened
back, to lose nothing of the excitement, and found herself
well rewarded.

'They had had a dram,' she declared later at the Weatherhouse. 'Bawling out of them like that.'

'And what more fitting?' inquired Lang Leeb from her
corner. 'My tuneless daughters don't understand that work
goes sweetest to a song. Did you never know that they built
a pier in the harbour of Aberdeen three hundred years ago
to the sound of drum and bagpipes? They don't work so
wisely now. Knapperley roof will be a wonder.'

A wonder it bade fair to be. Miss Barbara tired soon
and went to the stable. Francie fetched and carried, but
the young gaffer having left him alone for a spell, he began to follow his own devices—which were various. Garry
returned from attending to some matter on the ground and
saw Francie, without plan or instruction, cut gaily into the
new wood that he had brought from the carpenter's shop.
He had hacked and hewed recklessly, but, like his father
in the Weatherhouse parlour, though without his father's
justification, was so highly pleased with himself that Garry
stood abashed, unwilling to remonstrate. It was part of his
creed that a man should take pleasure in the work of his
hands, and to quench Francie's pleasure gave him the same
sense of constricting life that he had felt in quenching Miss
Barbara's candles. He set Francie's haggard boards aside.

He was called to the ground again, and before his return the post came in and he found Lindsay's letter. The
note was curt: 'Garry, I can't marry you. I'm sure I'm
not the right kind of wife for you. I'm sure I'm not.'
Garry pocketed his scrap of paper and climbed to the attic.
Francie had mismanaged his tools again. Garry cursed and
set to work himself, hoping to prevent further mischief by
adroit advice and order. As he worked, however, his heart
grew cold. Lindsay's note settled hard upon it like a frost.

He worked dourly on; but nothing prospered. In his first enthusiasm to restore, he had been sure of what he had to do. Now he found checks and miscalculations. He had to stop and realise that he was uncertain how to proceed.

Just then he saw, foreshortened on the ground below him, the figure of Miss Morgan. She beckoned. He turned his back. But she called, 'May I not speak to you? Indeed it is urgent.' He went down.

Miss Theresa Craigmyle came near at the same moment. 'Can't you keep away?' he thought angrily. He knew that her visit was an idle curiosity, and had enough regard for the reputation he wished Miss Morgan to retain to ask Louie to enter the house.

'I want you to understand,' Louie began, 'I'm sure I didn't make it clear: in allowing my possession of the ring to become a symbol, a kind of rite, you realise that I had passed beyond the material vehicle to the spirit. Can I make you see? The material symbol was of no moment. I mean, it's some justification for my keeping the ring. I simply didn't see it as a piece of someone else's property. It was just an agglomeration of matter that symbolised what was unseen. I wonder if you understand?'

'I understand,' he said slowly, 'that you want to talk about yourself. But I am busy.'

'Yes, I want to talk about myself. I know, I know I do. To you. Not to anyone else. I can have no peace until you understand that I am not a common thief. You are doing yourself an injustice if you think that. You degrade yourself by your misjudgment. I have to make you see. I feel that I am needful to you, to open your eyes to new ways of judgment—'

He turned away. 'Excuse me, I am very busy.'

'We are all needful to one another. Even I to you. But you don't think so.'

'Excuse me.' He went away.

Louie went home, and meeting Kate Falconer on the road, proposed to adopt an orphan.

Garry returned grimly to his task. He was inexpressibly weary. The muddled disorder of the garret oppressed him.

Mrs Hunter came in her comfortable way and tried to make him eat.

'You never lippened to yon craitur,' she said, spying out the disorder of the land. 'Pay the body and send him hame.'

Later she recounted the affair to her neighbour John Grey.

'That Francie Ferguson—he wouldna cut butter on a hot stane. What a haggar' he's made. You would be doing a good deed, Mr Grey, to give the laddie a hand. He's dirt dane. I took him a bowlie of broth, but he's never even lippit it.'

John Grey went round to Knapperley and said to Garry in his quiet, unassertive way, 'You'd better let me give you a hand there.' He craned over among the rafters to look at Francie's mismanagement. 'Tchu, tchu, tchu,' he said, and began to work rapidly and surely.

Behind his back Garry paid Francie twice the sum he should have had for the completed work, and dismissed him.

'Your wood's unseasoned,' said Mr Grey. 'It's too dark to work tonight. Tomorrow's Saturday. I'll give you a hand in the afternoon.' He showed the younger man with a quiet tact where he had gone wrong in his work and how to remedy the faults. 'You haven't handled wood very much.' It was impossible to feel resentment. Garry swallowed his pride and set himself to learn.

But when at length he went to bed he was overwhelmed in a sense of failure. He could not mend a roof, nor chose a workman, nor love a woman. He could not now even vindicate his friend. He relit his candle, to read once again Lindsay's letter, which he knew by heart. All the self-distrust of his nature, inherited from a timid father and the grandmother whose utmost remonstrance was a sigh, had risen in him at the reading of her note. In vain, from boyhood up, he had sheltered under a bravado, a noisy clowning or proud assumption of ability where indeed he felt none; nevertheless at moments, suddenly, this ogre of self-distrust rushed out and bludgeoned him. He had never discovered how much he was indebted to the ogre. His later reputation as a man with surprising stores of curious knowledge had its foundations there. The shame he felt at being found at fault or ignorant sent him furiously to learn, and he never forgot what was bludgeoned in; but his sensitive heart, wroth to show a wound, suffered in the process. So now tonight, when Lindsay had found him at fault, he was overcome with shame.

'She thinks I'm all wrong about Louie, and I can't tell her. What a confounded mess everything is in!' He wished he was back at war. This land he had thought so empty was proving unpleasantly full. Wisely he slept on it and woke refreshed in a windy sunrise to think, 'I'm blest if I let Lindsay go like that.' Less than ever in the sanity of morning did he wish to see the mob gaping over Louie's theft; for all the subtlety of her excuses, theft it was. But Lindsay had to know, and should know, well and soon.

In the same wind of sunrise Mrs Falconer lay, very still beside her sleeping sister, and prayed, as she had prayed at intervals throughout the night:

'Help me, O God, in all that I may have to do.'

She was sure that she had been divinely led to her strange discovery, and in spite of her shrinking from the public stare, had made the dedication of herself to Garry's service. Her knowledge must be used to help his cause. She had prayed till she was worn out.

TWELVE

Concert Pitch

Breakfast was just ending when Miss Theresa remarked, 'And a pretty picture they made, the three of them, bawling out of them on the head of the house. He's as daft as Bawbie herself. He had a real raised look, they said, at that session meeting. Oh, I forgot, Lindsay, he's your young man. I haven't got accustomed to that yet.'

'Then you may spare yourself the trouble.' Lindsay's voice was curt.

'Eh? Now, Lindsay, you needn't be so short. You know I always say just what I think. There's no manner of doubt that the young man is strange. They are all saying it. So it's just as well to know what you are taking in hand if you're taking him.'

'Which I don't happen to be doing.'

Kate gave the girl a curious look. Lindsay continued, 'Oh, go ahead, Cousin Tris, tell us all you saw and did. He's not my young man. Say just what you think.'

'What I think,' said Miss Theresa, 'is that he's a young man you'd be better without. That Louie Morgan's setting her cap at him and like to get him, I should say. Not a soul did he pay heed to, and him up there on the roof, but as soon as she came in about, down he comes and goes straight to her. Never even saw that any other body was there. O ay, Louie knows what she's about, gazing at him with all her eyes. He had her into the house right away, and him so busy with his roof. No saying how long they stayed there.'

'Brute!' Lindsay pushed back her chair and walked out.

'What would you make of that?' asked Theresa. 'Is she marrying him, or is she not?'

Kate knit her brows and said nothing.

'Of course she's marrying him,' said Miss Annie. 'You've such an ill will at the boy you can't see the good in him. You scare the bonny birdie with your clapper of a tongue.'

The bonny birdie could be heard upstairs, banging a drawer shut. Kate followed her.

'You mustn't take Aunt Theresa too hard, Linny. It's just her way. She's got into a habit of speaking like that.'

'Damned impudence. And I was a damned ass to tell her what I did.'

'What language, Lindsay!'

'I know it's what language. I've been brought up to use tidy language, haven't I? My mother would be finely shocked if she heard me. But life isn't tidy, you see, Kate, and that's what I'm discovering. Louie making up to him indeed.' She jammed her hat on her head. 'I'm going to Knapperley.'

'But Linny, that was only Aunt Theresa's idea—'

'Idea or not, it's abominable. Making eyes at Garry? Someone will pay for this. I could face the devil naked.'

'My dear, don't be so upset—'

'Do you never feel about anything, Kate? You should fall in love. Then you would understand.'

She banged the door, crashed like a cataract down the stair, collided with Paradise, shouted, 'Sorry, sorry,' as she ran. The house door slammed.

Kate, left alone in the bedroom, pressed her hands upon her breast. Her lips drew together in a line of pain. But in a moment she relaxed and began carefully to make the beds.

Halfway to Knapperley Lindsay met Garry seeking her with the same fury of decision with which she was seeking him.

Later, as they walked towards Knapperley, a mournful Lindsay said, 'I can't believe it yet. She talked so beautifully. Made life seem so strange and big. I can't explain. It wasn't like anyone else's world. But Garry—I like the ordinary world best. Only—listen, that hateful Cousin Tris. Oh, I know I shouldn't hate her, but she's always right, always right. And since that grocer let out about the way she sneaks things, she's been on her high horse—you can't imagine! She's just aching for a chance to be splendidly right in front

of everyone. And I was ass enough to say I'd given you up.
Idiot! And now she'll crow and say she always knew it
wouldn't last. Listen, you must take me to that concert
tonight, claim me in front of everyone, let her see if all her
havering about you is right or wrong. You will come, now,
won't you?'

The afternoon sped by. In aiding John Grey, Garry
worked happily and well. At fall of dark, Mr Grey said,
'That will have to do tonight. I've promised to look in at
the concert. It's not much in my line, but the children will
be acting. They are expecting me to come.'

Garry called in the approved fashion at the Weatherhouse
door to convoy Lindsay to the school.

'Going off with him, Lindsay,' said Miss Theresa. 'I
thought you said you had given him up.'

'Given him up? Who? Garry? But what an idea,
Cousin Tris.'

'What were you saying this morning, then?'

'Oh, that—really, if you can't understand a little quiet
irony!' Miss Annie listening remembered the slamming of
the doors. 'I don't think much of your sense of humour,'
concluded Lindsay gravely, and walked away.

'People should say what they mean,' rapped Miss Theresa. 'I always say what I mean myself.'

She set out for the concert with Mrs Falconer and Kate.
Ahead of them on the road skipped Stella Dagmar, accompanied by her mother.

'She's fatter than ever,' commented Theresa.

'It's here's-an-end-and-I'll-be-round-in-five-minutes if
you wanted to measure yon. As I live, she's wearing
a new scarf.' She whipped round on the road, and saw
Francie following with the *loonie*.

'So there's you, Francie. You've been giving your wife
a present, my man.'

Francie rubbed the side of his nose and sniffed.

'What other would I do with the siller he gied me?'
he asked apologetically; and added, with a happy sheepish
grin, 'It sets her grand.'

The play went well. Stella flaunted her scarlet kerchief,
Miss Morgan 'managed' both visibly and audibly, there

was ample applause. The children scattered to their parents among the audience, and Louie took a curtain to herself, bowing and posturing. She had a charming mien, and her dress of filmy green set off the soft gold of her hair. As she stood in the packed, hot classroom savouring the clapping and the cheers ('Oh, we'll give her a clap, just for fashion's sake,' said Miss Theresa), Louie's spirit floated out into its own paradise. To be admired—she craved it as one of her profoundest needs. She threw back her head and smiled at the noisy crowd. The moment seemed eternal, it was so sweet. Slowly and dreamily she turned away and sat to the piano, striking a chord. Now she would play.

But between the striking of the chord and the first note of her music (which was never sounded), Mrs Falconer stood up in her place. She had not known herself what she was to do. White, erect, stern, she had sat through the entertainment like a woman hewn from stone; but suddenly, at sight of Louie posturing and smiling, her teeth began to chatter. 'False, false, false,' she thought. She was not conscious of getting upon her feet, nor did the voice that cried aloud above the chattering and the laughter seem to come from her throat; but the astonished assemblage saw the rising of the white stern figure, saw the thin lips move, and listened as she cried, 'Friends, there has been a wrong done here amongst you. That woman yonder is a thief. Round her neck you will find a ribbon, and on it she carries a ring. Will you ask her where she got that ring?' Louie's face was ashen. She was conscious of the glare of eyes, but all she could do was to shake her head and smile. 'The ring is Mr Grey's,' cried Mrs Falconer, and sat abruptly down. Her knees had given way.

Into the moment of astonished silence Stella's voice broke shrill. Stella had clambered up and was dancing on the seat in her excitement.

'It's a blue ribbon,' she shrieked. 'Oh, Miss Morgan, say your piece. "Do you take this woman to be your–" '

Her voice was drowned in the hubbub that arose. Someone pulled her off the seat and put a hand across her mouth. Stella battered herself free with two strong and skinny hands.

And then John Grey stood up. He had been seated with both hands laid on the head of his staff, a stout cherrywood staff, short, tough and seasoned like himself. He rose in his place and stretched a hand over the turbulent assembly.

'Now, now. Now, now.' His gentle voice would not carry. He stood with a hand stretched out and made a half-articulate sound of grieved annoyance, then rapped on the ground with his staff. In a moment the noise fell.

'There was no need for this bustle. I knew where the ring had gone to.'

Louie gave a gasping cry and made blindly for the door. A hulking overgrown farm lad, a *halflin* not yet old enough for war, thrust his clumsy boot across the passage to trip her. She stumbled and recovered; but John Grey, leaning from his place, hooked the handle of his staff into her filmy clothing and detained her. He detained her long enough to work his way out from among the people, then took her arm in his and led her from the room in courteous silence.

The hubbub recommenced; but Garry leaped to a form and shouted above the din.

'Friends, I'm sorry this has happened, but Mr Grey is sure to have some explanation. Don't let's spoil the concert, since we're all together. Let's sing something.'

He began to sing a rattling song, then another. The chorus was taken up with a will. That concert was remembered for years in Fetter-Rothnie—Garry Forbes's concert, they called it. They sing his songs and repeat his yarns today.

'I did myself ill with laughin',' declared Mrs Hunter.

As Miss Morgan herself had requested, Garry said a few words about the Front. But such words!—droll, gargantuan, unforeseen. Each tale was greeted with a hurricane of laughter, each chorus shouted in a lusty heat. The folk trooped out at last into the night, laughing and warm.

Garry wiped the pouring sweat from his face.

'That *was* fun,' Lindsay said, linking her arm in his. 'Garry, how can you keep so solemn when you tell those ridiculous stories? You didn't laugh once.'

'Never felt less like laughing in my life.'

She looked at him, and grew suddenly grave.

'You mean—you were doing it to keep them from—'

'From talking about her. Yes, of course. Fill up their heads with something else. It's an off-chance that they won't say quite so much about it as they'd have been sure to say if the concert had gone to bits. Good God, the thing was indecent! Do you realise what I feel like? I began it, of course. But to throw the common theft to the mob was mean. What on earth induced her?'

'She's a horrid old woman, thrusting herself into the limelight, that's what she is,' cried Lindsay, in her hard, clear, indignant voice.

Mrs Falconer, walking behind them, heard.

She had not yet ceased to tremble. From the moment when her knees had given way beneath her and she had sat down, her body had shaken without remission. She was deadly cold. Garry's quips, the laughter and the choruses, had passed over her like winds. They sounded in her ears, but brought no meaning. She was wholly given over to one idea, that at last she had achieved something in the world of real endeavour. Its results, its value, she was incapable of considering. All she could feel was that she had made the thrust, though the mere bodily effect upon herself was beyond belief. Yet, though her flesh was shaken, her mind was not. She felt as an arch-angel might who, returning from an errand on the earth, reports to God that his mission is fulfilled: no angel could be surer of the divine compulsion.

When therefore Lindsay's clear indignant cry, 'She's a horrid old woman, that's what she is,' came upon her ear, she did not at once understand its significance. She was, indeed, still wandering in her own pleasaunce. But instantly Theresa began to talk. Theresa had only a moment before made up on her sister on the road, having had words to exchange with sundry other curious persons. Now she demanded news. Ellen had to speak; and Theresa's impatience would not let her wait until the Weatherhouse was reached: she must needs call the lovers back to hear and to discuss.

So it was that Ellen was forced at last out of her dream, and learned that she had done the very thing that Garry was working to prevent. Standing there on the road, in the chill spring night, she heard him say, 'I'd give a good deal for this not to have happened.' The spring sky was hard and clear as Lindsay's voice.

'I meant to help you,' stammered the old woman. Old was what she felt, she who had been so young, feeling the spring in her coursing blood upon the moor. They talked interminably. Even in bed, Theresa's tongue ran on. But Ellen lay impassive. She had not even prayed that night. She was dumb.

THIRTEEN

Proverbial

The throng that passed out from the schoolroom singing
Garry's songs and repeating his stories took away also a
lively curiosity over the incident he had striven to make
them forget, and inevitably it was linked with the earlier
incident of Garry's outbreak before the Session. Matters so
strange were worth the breath it cost to thresh them out.
The wars had little chance of a hearing in Fetter-Rothnie
for the next forty eight hours, by which time, thanks to
Jonathan Bannochie, Garry's reputation was established in
a phrase.

Out of the cold, clear night a wind came blowing. It
gathered strength all day, till in the late afternoon nothing
was at peace upon the earth. Trees and bushes swirled.
Boughs were wrenched away and tender leaves, half opened,
sailed aloft or drifted in huddled bands about the corners.
Twigs and sand battered against the windows and struck
the faces and necks of those who went outside. One had no
sense of light in the world. The smooth, suave things from
which light habitually glisters were wrinkled or soiled in the
universal restlessness. Blossom was shrivelled. 'I can't hear
a single bird,' Lindsay complained. 'Only the crows.'

Lindsay stood by the window, where she had stood the
other morning to watch the snow upon the garden. Now the
garden was changed anew. But while it had lain sealed and
mute beneath the snow it was less hard to believe in the life
within it than now, when this frenzy of motion tormented it
from end to end. This was not the motion of life. How just,
that Dante in his vision of love that has strayed from its own
nature should see it punished by the blare and buffeting of
such a wind as this. No silence, to hear the myriad voices,
no quietude, to contemplate and recollect. No fineness of

perception. A wind of death.

But Lindsay felt only that the garden was ugly, and the howl and clatter set her teeth on edge. She could stay no longer in the warm room. She could not stay even in the garden. The fury of the wind within its enclosure, where the daffodil trumpets were flattened like paper bags and the air was full of strippings from the branches, seemed more withering and ruthless than on the open moor. On the moor the blast swept on without obstruction. The whole grey sky tore forwards to the sea. Even from the hill-top one saw the huge white bursts of foam that grew fiercer and more numerous from moment to moment. Lindsay ran all the way to Knapperley. She could not keep herself from running. When she turned aside her head she could hardly breathe, the wind drove her nostril in with such violence. But she wanted to run. She wanted to dance and to shout above the clamour of the hurricane. Nothing could have pleased her better than to fly thus upon the wings of the wind towards her lover—faster and faster, riding the gale like a leaf. She was glad to merge her will in the larger will of the tempest, for she knew now that she had merged it in her lover's will. Since the morning when he had told her of Louie's perfidy and she had recognised that her own judgment had gone astray, she had had no more desire to trust herself. She had wept, indeed, for the revelation she had had of the evil that is in life; but now, how free and glad she felt! Running thus before the wind, she had entered into the peace that is beyond understanding: she was at one with the motion of her universe.

At Knapperley she pushed open the door and ran up-stairs. She felt free of the house now. She had accepted Miss Barbara. What a child she had been to fear her! As she had been a child to fear Garry's love. The sea was, after all, not so very wide; and earth, primitive, shapeless, intractable (as exemplified in Miss Barbara), was everywhere about one, and could be ignored. Roots, if one thought of it, must grow somewhere—in the customary earth.

She ran singing up the narrow stairway, and found Miss Barbara shaking with a jolly mirth beside the ruins of the tinker's bed.

'There's wounds,' she said, 'and growths and mutilations, bits rugged off and bits clapped on to the body
of man that is made in the image of his Maker.. Them
and their war up there'—she nodded upwards to where
her nephew was at work—'they mutilate their thousands,
they chop off heads and hands and fingers, they could take
Johnny's cranny from him, but could they make another
Johnny? What's the use of your war, tell me that. You're
making tinklers right enough, I'll grant you. They'll be all
upon the roads, them that wants their legs and them that
wants their wits and them that wants a finger and a toe, like
Johnny. But ach! For all your shooting and your hacking,
Johnny's beyond you. Your war won't make him.'

'But you know,' said Lindsay, who had listened in amazement to this novel point of view upon the war, 'wounding
people isn't all that the war does.' She would have proceeded
to expound as best she could Garry's gospel of a rejuvenated
world, had Miss Barbara not cut her short with a decisive:
'Fient a thing does the war do that I can see but provide you
tramps to tramp the roads. Wounds and mutilations—that's
what a war's for and that's what it fabricates.'

'O Garry, may I come up?' Lindsay cried, turning
her back upon the crass earth without perceptions that she
divined Miss Barbara to be. 'May I come up the ladder?'
she cried, singing, and climbing, she thrust her head above
the attic floor and sang, 'Mayn't I hold something for you?
Or hand you up something? O Garry, mayn't I help?'

Already the gap in the roof was covered. Garry had
stripped a tumbled shed of its corrugated-iron roofing and
fixed the sheet upon the boards he had already nailed in
place. In the wild fury of the gale the iron sheeting had
worked loose, and kept an intermittent clatter above their
heads. The wind too, entering by nooks and holes, shrieked
desperately round the empty room. The old house groaned
and trembled.

'Garry, have you been at work all day? Garry, won't
you stop, one little minute—and kiss me? Now go on. I
love to watch you work. And I do love to be here. We're
so respectable. I went to church this morning, Garry—just
myself and Cousin Tris. Kate's back on duty, you know.

And—Garry, it was so strange. Cousin Ellen—'

She stopped, leaning from the top step of the ladder upon the garret planks, and was silent so long that Garry, dragging boards across the floor, stopped too and looked at her.

'Well, what of Cousin Ellen?'

She raised her eyes to his. Unshed tears were gleaming on her lashes. The tin patch rattled on the roof. The wind roared round the garret, raising the sawdust in whirlpools, and out of grimy corners the cobwebs streamed upon its current. And Lindsay said, 'I'm all afraid of life. I thought I wasn't, but I am. We're so cruel to one another, aren't we?' she continued. 'At least over at the Weatherhouse we are. I don't suppose we mean it, but we are. Cousin Ellen came down all ready dressed for church and Cousin Theresa said, "What! Nell you fool, you can't mean to go to church today. Show yourself off in public, after what you did last night." And Cousin Ellen said, "You would take my very God away from me." And she marched out on to the moor. "But what's worse in me than in your pails?" she turned back to ask. "If I'm not ashamed, why need you be?" They won't leave each other alone. Pails, pails, pails, and, Making yourself a public show, I never saw! It went on all dinner-time. I couldn't stand it any more, I ran away. And old Aunt Leeb sits there and chuckles. Oh, she's cruel! She's worse than they are. She's happy when she can say a thing that hurts. She's like the Snow Queen—she looks at you with those sharp eyes, and it's like splinters of ice that pierce you through. There's only Paradise that you can feel comfortable with.'

'Perhaps that's why you called her Paradise.'

'Oh yes, no one will be uncomfortable in Paradise, do you think? But I used to think no one could be uncomfortable in the Weatherhouse, and now it's all so changed. Garry, won't you marry me soon and let me be always with you? I feel so safe with you.'

But not, thought Garry, when later in the day, having taken her home, he was striding back across the moor: not because he was safe with himself. Her perfect trust was, of course, delightful: but oddly, in just those matters where she had yielded most generously to his opinion, he had himself become unsure. Even with regard to his aunt— 'But I'm not afraid of her any more,' Lindsay had said, 'I think she's splendid'—something of the girl's terror had gripped his own soul. While she, safe in his arms, had recounted her moment of panic, he too, had become afraid of his aunt: as of something monstrous, primitive and untameable, not by any ardours to be wrought into place in the universe of which he dreamed, a living mock to his aspirations. Yet how triumphantly herself! The corrugated iron clattering at that very moment on the roof of Knapperley was witness to that.

And over Louie Morgan also he was unsure. Lindsay was no longer her champion; but, strangely, she had championed herself. There was a queer twisted truth in what she had said. David too, had felt it. More bitterly than ever he regretted having thrown her to the mob.

Reaching Craggie on his homeward journey, spent with labour and thought, he suddenly turned aside and, bursting into Mrs Hunter's kitchen, cried, 'Feed me, for God's sake.'

'Weel-a-wat, laddie, come in-by.' Mrs Hunter thrust him in a chair and spread the cloth.

Food was never out of view in Mrs Hunter's kitchen. Enter when you would, plates were there, heaped high with girdle scones, oat-cake, soft biscuits. Jam was in perpetual relief. Syrup and sugar kept open state.

'A puckle sugar's that handy,' Mrs Hunter would say, throwing a handful on a dowie fire.

'I canna bide a room with nae meat about it,' she added. 'If Dave now came in at the door and him hadna had a bite a' the road frae the trenches, a bonny mother he would think he had gotten. And him sending hame his pay to keep the laddies at the school.'

Seizing the loaf, at Garry's request, and throwing to her youngest boy, seated at the fireside, the hearty hint: 'Will that kettle be boiling the night, Bill, or the morn's morning for breakfast?', she began to cut slice after slice of bread, until the whole loaf lay in pieces on the table. Jake, her husband, shook his head.

'There's nae need for sae mony a' at aince,' he said,

in a low voice. 'You can aye be cuttin' as it's called for.'

'I canna dae wi' a paltry table. If it were Dave now, in another body's house, you wouldna like it yoursel.' And she seized a brown loaf, slicing until it, too, was piled high upon a plate.

'I grudge nae man his meat, but there's nae call for sae mony a' at aince.'

Jake remained with his worried eyes fixed on the table. A lifetime of laborious need was in the look he bent upon the piles of bread.

'Never heed him, Mr Garry. I've a gingerbread here.' She cut that too. 'Are you feelin' like an egg, Mr Garry? There'll be a hotterel o' folks in here afore the night's out, see if there's nae. There's aye a collieshangie here on a Sabbath night. And I'll lay my lugs in pawn but it's you they'll have through hand, my lad. A bonny owerga'un they're givin' the twa o' you, you and Miss Morgan.—What kind's your tea, Mr Garry?—Ay, ay, there's been mair mention of you this day in Fetter-Rothnie than of God Almighty.'

Indeed, before Garry had well eaten Jonathan Bannochie came in, and with him others.

'Here's a young man has a crow to pick with you,' said Jonathan, pushing forward a half-witted lad in the later teens. 'You're terrible smart, a bittie ower smart whiles for us country chaps. What way now did you nae wait last night for the lads and the lasses that were ready with their sangs and suchlike? Here's Willie here had his sang all ready and him just waiting a chance to get it sung. But na, nae chance.'

'Indeed I am sorry,' said Garry, rising in confusion. 'I didn't suppose—I supposed Miss Morgan—well, that she had charge of all the programme, and when she was gone that it would fall to pieces.' He stammered an apology to the half-wit, who stared grinning.

'O ay,' said Jonathan. 'Anything to shield the lady. Ay, ay, the first thing that came handiest.'

Again, as when he stood before the Session, the young man felt a fury of rage against this mocker who could penetrate among his secret thoughts. Stammering a further apology, he went out.

'Try her in the tower, Captain Forbes,' quoth Jonathan, with a stolid face. A mutter of laughter ran about: the old story was remembered, had very lately been revived. Well out into the hurricane of wind, Garry could distinguish a louder laughter and Jonathan's voice clear in the general guffaw.

He walked into the anger of wind with his head down. Jonathan's parting barb was in, and rankled. At the moment he wanted to have Louie in the tower, wanted to have her alone, wanted simply to have her. And apology was not the need. She was in his blood like a disturbing drug. He knew that she had already turned to his pursuit, and his soul had sickened at the knowledge; but suddenly he realised that he wanted to seize her, to give her what she hankered after, make her taste to the dregs the cup she wantoned with. He went straight to the house of Mrs Morgan, and was shown in.

Louie sprang from a stool by the fireside and faced him screaming. Her lips were livid, her eyes blazed.

'How dare you come here?' she screamed. 'How dare you? How dare you? Haven't you done me enough harm already, exposing me like that? They all know now. You've ruined my name. And you promised not to tell, you promised.'

Her voice ran on, high-pitched, terrific in its morbid energy. Scarlet blotches showed upon the greyness of her face. Bags of skin hung under her eyes. The possession went from him. His fury of lust for strange knowledge was dead. He began to explain that his promise had not been broken.

She did not listen. The high-pitched voice screamed on. And now she was beating her hands against a chair and laughing because she had drawn blood.

'Oh, this is terrible! Oh, this is terrible!' moaned Mrs Morgan. The elder lady rocked her body back and fore, staring uneasily from her daughter to her guest. 'I shall never be able to give a hand with the tea again,' she moaned.

Garry shook the house from him and its dark sultry atmosphere, but in the howl of the wind he continued to hear Louie's hysterical screaming. He hated both himself and her. Sounds were swallowed in the gale. Nothing lived in the steady pouring noise but its own insistence. Even thought went numb. He let himself be driven before the blast as Lindsay earlier had done, but for him there was no joy of surrender. All that tormented—the whining shell, the destructive sea, lust, folly and derision, brute and insensate nature's roar—was in the cataract that crashed about his ears. To run before this enormous wind put him to shame, as though he had let himself be routed by unholy forces. Of purpose he overreached Knapperley and battled back, and in the tussle felt some control upon himself return. When therefore in the shelter of the house he distinguished voices, he was able to give them a wary attention.

The April night had almost come, but a drab gleam showed the figures of three or four men, curious like so many others, who were retreating from a survey of the burnt house. Unperceived, Garry heard the story of the fire recounted by a man who had indeed been present, but had rendered hardly the effective aid his boast suggested. The unseen listener smiled; but heard on the instant the voice of Jonathan Bannochie, who said, 'You would need Garry Forbes to you, my lad.'

Laughter greeted the sally. The braggart was known.

Garry remained hidden. The bandying of his name moved him to wrath.

'Well, well,' said another voice, 'he made's sit up over Miss Morgan, anyway.'

'Mrs Falconer did, you mean.'

'Ay, where got she her information, would you say?'

'Where she always bides,' said Jonathan. 'Hine up on the head o' the house, like Garry Forbes and his twa fools.'

Garry strode into the open.

'Good evening, gentlemen, you are having a look around. Rather dark, isn't it? Perhaps you'd like to see inside? Hine up on the head of the house, if you want to.'

And he suddenly began to laugh.

'Do come in,' he said. 'The night's young, and my aunt has a blazer of a fire. You're not so often round by Knapperley that you need to go so soon. Come away in.'

He ushered them suavely to the kitchen, lit a lamp and shepherded the party to the damaged room. A boisterous mirth took hold of him.

'Up you go,' he cried, pointing to the ladder by which Lindsay had climbed. It stretched into shadows, through the gaping hole above them that showed like a blotch of darkness upon the plaster. The wind still shrieked through the broken window and the sheet of iron clattered overhead.

Garry acted with a reckless gaiety. A fortunate mockery came to his aid, to assuage his own pain and bewilderment. He mocked at his aunt and Johnnie, Francie, himself, with a tongue so blithe and impudent that his guests felt its invitation to laughter and joined in his mirth. His laughter was quite unforced. The interlude had been high comedy; even his own part in it he could recount with appreciation of its comic values. He swaggered, sang again the drinking song. 'Garry Forbes and his twa fools,' he cried, laughing, and catching the noise of the sheet of iron that clattered on the slates, 'Hark to yon fellow—hine up on the head of the house, like Garry Forbes and his twa fools. The old house has got a dunt on the rigging, like the folk that bide in it. But you can't deny,' he added, with a persuasive gleam, 'that Francie showed spirit. I loved it in the man. A fine large folly we both showed, he to attack the thing he couldn't do, and I to let him. Ha, ha, we want more of that spirit in the world!'

They returned to the kitchen. Garry heaped wood upon the fire and fetched Miss Barbara's whisky. Only Jonathan refused to drink.

'Drink, man,' said Garry roughly, but turned away from him at once and talked to the other men. The talk flowed rich and warm as the whisky. Garry began to speak of the war, not in the sardonic humour of his overnight stories, but with the natural sincerity he used in speaking to John Grey. His guests gave him back of their best. They told him, in shrewd and racy idiom, how a countryside took war: food, stock, labour, transport.

'There's mair goes on here than the King kens o',' said one.

A very old man sat next the fire. His face was crunkled

and dry; he rarely spoke; but tonight, holding the glass
of whisky in a trembling hand, as the liquor slowly warmed
his old blood, he too began to talk.

'Your war—your war—surely it's gey near lousin' time.
What's come to a' the young men that they must up and to
the wars? In my young time we kent the way to bide whaur
our business was. I was fee'd for ane-an'-twenty year to sup
brose ane-an'-twenty times a week—nae gallivantin' frae
toun to toun whan I was a sharger. But there's nae haudin'
the young men in 'aboot the day. My lassie's loon, he's but
a bairn, he must be aff an' a'. "Come rattle in his queets wi'
the poker," I says to her. "That'll learn him to keep to his
work." War—it wunna let a body be. It's lousin' time, I
tell you.'

'It won't be lousin' time till we've won the field,' said
Garry. And he looked strangely at the very old man. How
easy, if one could regulate all life by a single duty: a ploughman his field to plough, a cobbler his boot to patch; a life
without glory and without failure, without responsibility
for oneself.

'Won!' mocked Jonathan across his thoughts. 'This
war will not be won. What's your belligerents? Twa fools,
playing Double Dummy and grand pleased with themselves.
Both'll think they've won, but there's neither won nor lost.
A farce all the ways of it.' He added, in a voice hardly
audible, his face to the fire and a smile playing about his
mouth, 'Twa fools, hine up on the head o' the house—'

Garry argued hotly. 'I don't know, I can't explain it,
but I believe we are in some way fighting the devil. Have
you no belief in the sanctity of a cause?'

'None.'

'And the rights of the small nations? National honour?'
Jonathan chanted:

> Peter my neebor,
> Had a wife an' couldna keep her,
> He stappit her in a hole in the dyke an' the mice
> eat her.

And at Garry's impatient movement, 'You needna get hot,
Captain. You think much the same yourself at bottom. All
the mercy a war shows to any is to them that gets their

pooches filled. I'm told there's some that way,' he added, 'not that I know of it.'

Garry cried on a reckless inspiration, 'You would need Garry Forbes to *you*.'

The roar of laughter that went up from the others told him that the shaft went home. He watched Jonathan, throwing back his head and laughing too.

'Him!' said Mrs Hunter, when later he questioned her. 'He would skin a louse to get tallow. O ay, I'm told he's made a tidy bit out o' the war. A country cobbler—you would wonder, wouldna ye? But he must have a smart bit o' siller laid by and there's folks in debt to him round and round. There's places up and down that's changed hands since the war, folks bought out and businesses shut down, and some grand anes wi' new-got siller set up in their braw establishments, and Jonathan's got his nieve packed tight, ay has he that. He kens mair than he'll let on, but folk has an inkling. He kens the ins an' the oots o' maist o' the places that's come to the hammer hereaboots.'

Garry sat in Knapperley kitchen and watched the man. He changed countenance not at all, but laughed the matter by, saying idly, 'Garry Forbes would have his own ado.'

The phrase was established.

The following evening Jonathan said, in his own shop before a half dozen witnesses, to Mally Sandison who swore that she had paid the boots when she brought them to have the 'tackets ca'ed in,' 'What's that, mistress?' Jonathan said. 'Paid, said ye? You would need Garry Forbes to you, I'm thinking.'

The joke went round. It penetrated the more surely for being more than joke, or joke not fully understood. It puzzled the consciousness of Fetter-Rothnie, but remained on its tongue. The phrase became the accepted reproof of falsehood.

For the other phrase of Jonathan's coinage, 'Hine up on the head o' the house, like Garry Forbes and his twa fools,' that also passed into current speech, but baldly, a jesting reproach to those who attempted what they could not overtake. Like other phrases debased by popular usage, it lost the first subtle mockery it took from the brain of its originator. The intelligence of its victim alone apprehended it; he knew (as Jonathan did likewise, else he would not have mocked) that his folly on the housetop was a generosity, a gesture of faith in mankind.

Returning by the dark avenue when he had seen his guests to the gate of Knapperley on the Sunday after the concert, Garry heard a noise among the bushes that was not caused by the wind, and immediately a stone hit him on the shin-bone. He thrust his way among the bushes and dragged a captive to the open. His match flared in the wind and went out, but gave him time to see the half-wit whose song had not been sung. He spoke kindly to the lad, who wrenched himself free with evil words and made off.

The wind poured on—a south-wester like an elemental energy. Garry stood awhile in the fury. The shriek of wind brought to his mind the flying shells, and he thought of troop ships and minesweepers riding the storm. Only those without imagination, he felt, could love the wind. A tree crashed. He shuddered, and a longing seized him to have done with sick-leave and be again in battle. The danger that was abroad in the tortured night of wind cooled and braced him. 'I'm fit now,' he thought, 'I must get back. Damn that man and his talk of futility. It's a battle about something and I must get back.'

Jonathan's cynical smile recurred to his mind, and the roar of wind changed in his ear to the roaring of their ridicule as they made phrases of his name. That also seemed an elemental energy, and the screaming of a woman sounded through it, elemental too, destructive as the hurricane.

He slept at last, and the wind fell.

FOURTEEN

April Sunrise

He awoke before the dawn. There was no sound at all, no motion in the house or wood. The silence was unearthly, as though the wind had blown itself out and with it all the accustomed sounds of earth.

Birds brought back the normal world. Sounds began anew. Garry threw himself from bed and went outside.

The morning was like a flute note, single, high and pure, that for the moment of its domination satisfies the ear as though all music were in itself; but hardly has it sounded when the other instruments break in.

Life recommenced. Dogs barked, cocks crew, smoke rose, men shouted, women clattered their milk pails. Soon figures moved upon the empty fields. Somewhere a plough was creaking. Garry turned his head towards the noise and searched the brown earth until he saw the team. Seagulls were crying after it, settling in the black furrow, rising again to wheel around the horses. As he watched, the sun reached the field. The wet new-turned furrow was touched to light as though a line of fire had run along it. The flanks of the horses gleamed. They tossed their manes, lifting their arched necks and bowing again to the pull: brown farm horses, white-nosed, white-footed, stalwart and unhurrying as the earth they trampled or the man who held the share.

From where he watched Garry could see a long stretch of country. Jake Hunter's croft was visible. Jake was bowed above a heap of turnips, slicing in his slow, laborious fashion. Mrs Hunter sailed across the stackyard in a stream of hens. And on his steep, thin field Francie Ferguson walked, casting the seed. It was his moment of dignity. Clumsy, ridiculous, sport of a woman's caprice and a byword in men's jesting, as he cast the seed with the free ample movement of

the sower Francie had a grandeur more than natural. The
dead reached through him to the future. Continuity was in
his gait. His thin upland soil, ending in stony crests of whin
and heather, was transfigured by the faith that used it, he
himself by the sower's poise that symbolised his faith.

That gesture, of throwing the seed, seemed to the man
who watched the most generous of movements; and he was
glad to associate it with Francie, whose native generosity he
had seen and loved. His blind anger of the previous night
flared suddenly anew. 'Garry Forbes and his twa fools,' he
muttered. 'I had rather be Francie and capable of a generous folly than these others with all their common sense.' His
own wild mockery of both Francie and himself had had last
night a harsh wholesome savour; this morning it felt like a
disloyalty.

At that moment Mrs Falconer appeared among the trees.

The strong family resemblance among the Craigmyle
sisters had never seemed to him so marked as when he saw
Mrs Falconer walking towards him from the wood. She had
an almost truculent air. Theresa herself could not have put
him right with more assurance.

'So you like a sunrise, too,' she said in an abrupt, hard
way. 'Well, I wanted to say, I believe I crossed your
wishes the other night, letting them know about that Louie.
I thought you wanted them to know. But it seems you
changed your mind.'

'Oh well, you see—' The accusation in her tone annoyed
him. 'A matter of common theft—pretty low down to expose
that, don't you think?'

'Well, I'm sorry. But it was for—' She was about to
add '—your truth that I did it,' but something in his
face made her pause. He was grey and haggard. She left
her sentence incomplete. 'I'm sorry,' she repeated humbly.

'Her neck's thrawn now. Much good may it do us all.'

Mrs Falconer found nothing to answer.

'Don't you worry,' he continued. 'It amuses people.
One should be glad to add to the gaiety of mankind.
They've made a joke of it already. They seem to find me a
pretty good joke hereabouts.' With his arms folded on the
top of a gate he was leaning forward to watch Francie. 'See

that seed-casting machine over yonder?'

'What? Where? Machine—I only see Francie Ferguson.'

'What's he?'

'Mrs Falconer stared.

'Why, he's the crofter at the place by us, just over the field. But you know Francie. It was him you—'

Again she left her sentence incomplete.

'Jerked up like a marionette on the roof at Knapperley, for folk to laugh at. So it was.'

'You spoke of a machine—'

'Men like machines walking. Somewhere in the Bible, I believe. I thought myself he was a man. I'm glad that you agree.'

'Captain Forbes, I'm afraid I don't quite understand you.'

He straightened himself from the gate, stretched his arms, and laughed.

'No, I suppose not. It's quite simple, though. I chose to employ Francie because I liked the spirit of the man. He's ignorant, he's clumsy, but—well, I love him. The men of sense—oh, very decent fellows, I had a drink with some of them last night—have made a laughing-stock of both of us. I could forgive it for myself. I can't forgive it for Francie. And I can't forgive them because I joined the laugh myself. Logical, isn't it? If you're laughed at, always join the laugh. It takes the sting out. But then you see—I laughed at Francie too. They made it seem, if I could put it so, a necessary condition for my entering *their* kingdom.' He ended with passion, 'They conspire together to prevent my loving men.'

Mrs Falconer turned away her eyes. His passionate face, dark, unshaven, haggard, moved her with an emotion that she dared not countenance. Gazing intently at the clear blue hills she let fall the words, 'They too are men.'

And suddenly the man at her side, at whom she could not look, burst out laughing. His laughter resounded through the quiet morning. Jake Hunter, several fields away, lifted himself from the turnips and shaded his brows with his hand to search in the direction of the noise.

'It's Mr Garry up there,' said his quicker-eyed wife. 'He has ways real like his aunt. I've seen her rumble out the

laughin' an naebody by. Well, a laugh's a thing for twa or
for twenty, says I, nae for a man an' him himsel'.' Even her
sharp eyes had not made out Mrs Falconer's sombre figure
against the trees.

Garry stopped laughing and said to Mrs Falconer, 'It's
such an obvious thing to say, isn't it? That's why it is so
confoundedly clever of you to say it. Inspired, I ought to
say. Clever is a stupid word. Yes, that is the brutal fact:
they too are men. As much a part of things as I am. One
knows it at the Front, but here—I'm angriest of all, you
know, because I mocked at Francie. And yet I suppose I
couldn't have mocked at myself without mocking at him
too; and it was only when I had laughed at myself, last
night, with these men, that I began to feel I was a part
of things here.' He interrupted himself to say, 'But all
this is boring you. And listen—this Louie business: of
course I wanted David cleared. But when I found about
the ring—well, any man would have shut up. I felt pretty
beastly, I can tell you, when I saw them all agape. Anyhow,
it was John Grey's business after that, not mine. I had told
her, you see, that I would take no action. But you—I don't
want you to—'

'I acted on an impulse,' she said, smiling bravely. 'It
was cruel of me. I had just come to know. If I had thought
about it longer, I'd have seen it was no business of mine.'

'Please don't blame yourself. Perhaps it's best—'

'Well, I'm glad I met you to apologise,' said Mrs Falconer
calmly. 'I'll say goodbye just now.'

Garry went homeward thinking still of her reply: 'They
too are men.' It seemed to him the wisest saying he had
heard. He looked again at the wide leagues of land. And
a curious thing happened. He saw everything he looked at
not as substance, but as energy. All was life. Life pulsed in
the clods of earth that the ploughshares were breaking, in
the shares, the men. Substance, no matter what its form,
was rare and fine.

The moment of perception passed. He had learned all that
in college. But only now it had become real. Every substance
had its own secret nature, exquisite, mysterious. Twice already this country sweeping out before him had ceased to be

the agglomeration of woods, fields, roads, farms; mysterious as a star at dusk, with the same ease and thoroughness, had become visible as an entity: once when he had seen it taking form from the dark, solid, crass, mere bulk; once irradiated by the light until its substance all but vanished. Now, in the cold April dawn, he saw it neither crass nor rare, but both in one.

He looked again at this astonishing earth. And suddenly for the second time he laughed aloud. Mrs Falconer, gone not so far but that she heard him, stopped upon the road. She could not understand why he laughed, and she felt chill and sad.

'Both crass and fine,' he was thinking; but he was thinking no longer of the land, but of the men. Not irradiated by an alien light, but in themselves, through all the roughness of their make what strange and lovely glimpses one could have of their secret nature! 'Each obeying his law,' he thought.

Around him he noted that the woods were flaming. A fine flame was playing over the leafless branches, not gaudy like the fires of autumn, but strong and pure. The trees, not now by accident of light but in themselves, were again etherealised. For a brief space, in spring, before the leaf comes, the life in trees is like a pure and subtle fire in buds and boughs. Willows are like yellow rods of fire, blood-red burns in the sycamore and scales off in floating flakes as the bud unfolds and the sheath is loosened. Beeches and elms, all dull beneath, have webs of golden and purple brown upon their spreading tops. Purple blazes in the birch twigs and smoulders darkly in the blossom of the ash. At no other season are the trees so little earthly. Mere vegetable matter they are not. One understands the dryad myth, both the emergence of the vivid delicate creature and her melting again in her tree; for in a week, a day, the foliage thickens, she is a tree again.

For the first time Garry was in the country at the moment when this very principle of life declared itself in the boughs. 'As fine as that,' he thought, 'from coarse plain earth.' But if one surprised them at their moment, men had the same bright fire.

Mrs Falconer walked home.

Theresa asked, 'Where have you been stravaigin' to at this time of the morning? To get the air! Well, the work stands first, I always say. There's all the windows to clean after that gale. We can't see a thing for dirt.'

Lindsay was coming in from the garden. The grass was quite covered with twigs and torn leaves, with cypress berries, with pine needles and cones. And under one tree, an arm of which had been riven from the trunk, Lindsay had found a nest with an egg and three naked mangled nestlings tumbled on the ground. But saddest of all was the death of the bird she was holding against her body.

'Look, quite dead. I found it lying there. Oh, Paradise, could it be the mother of those gorbals? How pitiful—'

'No, no.' Paradise was touching the soft cold form with her misshapen fingers. 'This one was flying. See, his neck is broken. He had been driven by the wind against a bough. They're frail things, birdies. Many a one the gales bring down.'

'Oh! But can't they fly clear? Can't they see where they are going?'

Paradise shook her head. 'What's a fluff of air and feather against a hurricane? I've seen them rattle down in dozens.'

Lindsay held the dead bird against her breast, smoothing the silken wings and bosom. 'See, see.' She lifted a wing with gentle fingers and displayed a patch of warm bright russet in the hidden hollow.

'Such small, small feathers. Oh, its loveliest part is hid away.'

Mrs Falconer stood apart and watched. She had not offered to show the bird to Cousin Ellen.

'She loves the bird more than me,' thought the woman sadly. And she winced again at the remembrance of Lindsay's scornful words after the exposure of the theft. But as though she had divined a secret chagrin, the girl came softly to her side, holding the bird.

'See, Cousin Ellen.' She displayed the russet pool beneath the wing; and thinking that Ellen was sad because of Theresa's reprimand, she whispered, 'I'm cleaning windows, too—oh yes, I want to help.'

It was afternoon before she went to Knapperley. Garry was on the roof.

'Come down, come down. Have you been there all day?'

He nodded, nails in his mouth, and continued to hammer. Shortly he came down.

'Well, I've discovered a thing I never knew—how slates are put on.'

'Oh, you've slated it. Where's your iron sheet today?'

'Dangling by one tooth this morning. So I gathered what was left of the slates. No, I haven't slated it. Or only a bit. I'll have to get more slates. But I've fixed all that were usable. Come up the ladder and I'll show you. They go on like this—each one overlapping other two.'

'Yes. But stop for a little now, Garry.'

He came down, but almost at once began to clear away the drifts of rubbish that the wind had left.

'Will you be always like this when we are married, Garry? Always at work?'

'Expect so. There's so much to do. I'll tell you what, Linny, the war seems a colossal bit of work to get finished, but ordinary life's going to be a bigger. Coming back here, and finding all the queer individual things people do and think—it's frightened me. To get them all fitted in—I don't see how it can be done.'

The faces came on him in a mob–Francie, Jonathan, Jake, the tramp and the half-wit, Louie, Miss Theresa Craigmyle, Miss Barbara: the substance from which all his fine new kingdoms must be built. He would have liked to repudiate the knowledge he had just gained of human nature: how could one proclaim an ideal future when men and women persisted in being so stubbornly themselves?—And at that moment Miss Barbara rumbled round the corner of the house with a wheelbarrow.

'Build a house,' she said with scorn, as she set down the barrow, which was piled with earthy boulders. 'Build a house, mend a house, that's what your common bodies do. O ay, you're Donnie Forbes's grandson right enough. A Paterson of Knapperley never turned their hand to building houses.'

'And what are the stones for, aunt?'

'I'm putting up a cairn.' She stooped to the barrow handles and continued on her way.

'To commemorate the war?' shouted Garry.

'Deil a war. The fire, my lad, the fire.'

FIFTEEN

Whom the Gods Destroy

For Mrs Falconer, she watched Lindsay, all quick excitement, gather her possessions from the windowed bedroom and drive away, rosy and laughing, by her father's side. Then she climbed the stair and sat down in her empty room. She had never felt so desolate. The past came freely to her memory, and she recalled her dismal marriage, its ending, her humiliation at Theresa's hands on her return. But none of these things had troubled her as she was troubled now. For many weeks she battled against a sense of guilt. But what had she done wrong? Even if she had erred in her public denunciation of the sinner, she had acted in good faith, had meant well. The shame that overwhelmed her was too deep and terrible to have sprung from that. The weeks passed, Lindsay was married, and very slowly Mrs Falconer began to understand. Lindsay's words rang often in her ears—'a horrid old woman, thrusting herself into the limelight'—and at first they made her indignant ('to think that of me, to think that of me'), but after a time she saw that they were true. She had accused Louie so that Garry might be pleased with her.

During these months Mrs Falconer had grown pinched and wan. She sat much alone, with hands interlocked, eyes staring. When spoken to she started and spoke at random. Lang Leeb's appreciation of these phenomena was delicate. Fine barbs went quivering into Ellen's mind. A woman of sixty, pining for a man not half her age, was a spectacle to earn the gratitude of gods and men: so seldom do we let ourselves be frankly ludicrous.

In August Ellen acknowledged to herself that her love for Garry was an egotism. Her sense of shame and guilt grew heavier, not because she had discovered its cause,

but because of the revelation she had had of the human
heart, its waywardness and its duplicity. She had known
quite well what her mother and sister had thought of her
infatuation, and had despised them for the vileness of their
thoughts. Now for the first time she herself felt evil. 'It was
only myself I thought of all the time.' Her sense of escape,
of flight into a larger world, was illusion.

She ceased to pray. Prayer, too, was an illusion. 'Your
God of Comforts'—she understood it now. Her God had
always been a God of Comforts from whose bounty, as
she fashioned her petitions, she had taken precisely what
she wanted. One could go through a long life like that,
thrilled and glowing as one rose from prayer, and all the
while be bounded horribly within oneself. The God who had
constrained her in her flaming ecstasy of devotion, whose
direct commands she had obeyed in denouncing Louie, was
created from her imagination: a figment of her own desire.

She continued throughout that winter to go to church,
because it did not occur to her to cease the practice; but
the services were torture. She looked in horror at the people
as they prayed. 'How do they know that there is anything
there? Any God at all? I can never trust again what I feel
within myself.'

One day in April as she walked alone, a bird flew low,
alighted near her, pecked and tugged among the withered
grasses, flew up in swift alarm, lit again. She watched,
then sharply as though the words were spoken, she heard
Lindsay's eager question, 'What is his name? But don't
you love birds, Cousin Ellen?'

Yes, yes, I have always loved them, she thought—their
grace, their far swift flight, the cadence of their song—as
I have loved all beauty, that is a part of my undying self,
possessed eternally, the kingdom within my soul. Yet because she could not name the bird that flew up and hopped
in front of her, a miserable sense of failure came across her
spirit. She went home and found her sister Annie.

'I saw a bird just now,' she began, then choked. She
had not spoken all that year to anyone about the things
that filled her heart.

'There's lots of them about,' said Miss Annie.

'Yes. It flew away and came back again. I wonder what it would have been.'

'What kind of bird?'

But Ellen could not answer. She knew neither its colour, nor shape, nor the length of wing or beak. She rose abruptly and went upstairs. The sense of shame and failure came over her with renewed intensity. It was absurd—because she did not know a bird's name; but as she sat miserably by her window she saw all at once that it was not only the bird's name of which she was ignorant: it was the whole world outside herself.

She had never felt so much abased, so lonely in the multitude of living things. It was spring, they were around her in myriads; but she did not know them. They had their own nature. Even the number of spots upon an egg, the sheen on wing or tail, was part of their identity. And that, she saw, was holy. They were themselves. She could not enter into their life save by respecting their real nature. Not to know was to despise them.

And so with men. One could not be taken into other lives except by learning what they were in themselves. Ellen had never cared to know. In her imaginings other people had been what she decreed, their real selves she ignored. 'I have despised them all.' She felt miserably small, imprisoned wholly in herself.

From that day her new life began; slowly, for she had consumed herself in shame, and at first had neither strength nor faith enough to live on new terms. Moreover, she was sixty one, and, from the monotony with which life in the Weatherhouse had passed, set in her habits. For a time she entertained wild projects: she would go away, work in a slum, learn life. But she had no money. The war was over, Kate was again in a paid situation. One day she drew Kate aside, mumbling.

'I can't make out what you're saying, mother.'

'If you could let me have some pocket money, dear. You know I've none at all.'

'But you never want for anything, mother, I hope?'

'No, no. It was only—just to have it, dear. But it doesn't matter.'

'Of course you shall have money, mother. I should have thought of it before.'

Kate gave her a few shillings.

One day she went to town. Excited, but calm through the magnitude of her purpose, she made her way to the Labour Exchange, and stood, fumbling among words, at the advisory bureau.

'No, that is not what I wanted. No, no.'

The woman who watched her with shrewd and kindly eyes guessed at a tragedy: a gentlewoman fallen on evil days. But when she understood what the worn, haggard old woman wanted, she was silent through astonishment.

'I thought there were so many openings for welfare workers,' stammered Mrs Falconer.

'But you have no training—and your age—but perhaps you must, you have nothing to live on.'

'No, it's not that—I just wanted to get away from home.'

'Oh! Then if you don't need the money, there is voluntary work that you could do.'

Mrs Falconer went bitterly home. Another fine fancy was smoke. She had pictured herself a successful social worker. 'And I wanted to get away from home because I couldn't bear to hear their remarks—to see me humiliated, that's what it is. Confessing that my life's been all amiss till now.'

These essays in sincerity hurt her. 'But it's only through sincerity that I can reach anywhere beyond myself.' She must be sincere even with the birds and the wild flowers she had begun to study, to know their real selves that she might enter their life. Kate's shillings had bought her certain textbooks, but her study halted. Birds moved so swiftly, she forgot so soon, her manuals were poor, and by her untaught efforts it was hard to identify these moving flakes of life and the bright, multitudinous flowers. Identify—discover their identity. She had never valued accurate information, holding that only the spirit signified, externals were an accident; yet when she found that by noting external details she could identify a passing bird or a growing plant, a thrill of joy passed through her heart. She was no longer captive within her single self.

These moments of bliss came rarely in a long, slow time. That summer she ceased to go to church. God—was there a God? And where could one discover His identity? She had believed all her life in this comfortable God who revealed Himself to her spirit in ecstasy and beauty; but her ecstasies had been a blind self-indulgence. No sincerity in that. 'I can't find God in the forms of a religion that has let me go so terribly astray, that has shut me away from everything but myself.' *

Her sisters were aghast when she would not return to church. Annie's was a genuine distress. 'Ah, but you should go to church, you should go. We should all go to church as long's we're able.' Miss Annie herself, crippled and serene, set out each Sunday morning alone, an hour before the time of service, to make her slow, laborious journey.

'You might at least keep it up for appearance sake,' Theresa hectored. 'We've been a kirk-going family all our days. There's no need to be kirk-greedy to do the respectable thing. A pretty story they'll make of it, a Craigmyle and left the kirk.'

Some time after her rupture with the church, Mrs Falconer met the young Stella walking in dignified aloofness on the moor. Stella was in disgrace. Convicted of petty thieving, she had received a reprimand in face of the assembled Sunday School.

'Oh, Stella,' began Mrs Falconer, shocked at the bravado with which the girl flung out her story.

'Oh, yes,' interrupted Stella coolly. 'Tell me, like all the rest of them, that God is watching all I do. I don't believe it. There's not a God, He's just a make-up. So there!'

Mrs Falconer was silent. Stella, who had anticipated good game in the way of shocked remonstrance, inquired impatiently, 'Well, aren't you going to preach a bit to me about it?'

Mrs Falconer answered humbly, with her grieved eyes on the girl's face, 'I can't do that, Stella. I don't know if there is a God.'

Stella stared and cried, 'Well, you're a straight one. I like you for that.'

Perhaps I have done wrong, she thought, saying that

to the child. But no, nothing could be wrong that strove to establish truth. But I was striving to establish truth by exposing Louie. Life was past belief, complicated, huge. The God she had served judged all men by their motives. She had a glimpse now of a darker, more terrible God who judged results. How could it be enough to mean well? One came afterwards to repudiate one's own motives, to see that one was responsible in spite of them. One's true self, which one had not known, had worked. Surely if there was a God, it was one's real self that He judged.

Her mind turned to Louie. They had shut Uplands and gone away for a time. 'She'll get a man and not come back at all—see if she doesn't,' Theresa said. That was the kind of cruel thing that was said of her on all hands now. 'And I delivered her up to it,' thought Ellen. For years to come she was to see Louie degenerate because people knew her for what she was. But did they? She came to her deepest understanding of Louie when she saw that she was like herself, and built rashly on a foundation of her own imaginings. How could people understand that? 'But I understand. I know how it had all seemed to her.' She dwelt on the resemblance till she could hardly distinguish between herself and Louie. 'And people needn't have known her false pretences if it hadn't been for my false pretences.' She remembered Garry's tale of his delirium in the shell-hole. 'I thrust her in, I am rescuing myself.'

'Ah,' she thought, 'here is one person outside myself whom I really know.' And she went to seek Louie.

But some years had passed by then, and Mrs Falconer had made other attempts at knowing people.

It took her many months after the failure of her first grandiose designs to face again her need for entering other lives, and many months more to find a way.

One day she came home from town and said abruptly, 'Well, I'm going to help at the Working Girls' Guild. Tuesday evenings.'

'I'm sure it's a good thing, poor lassies!' said Paradise, who saw nothing incongruous in Ellen, with her old-fashioned dress and ideas, moving in the generation of post-war factory girls.

Nor did Ellen see her incongruity. Tuesday evenings were her excitement. The rude, boisterous life she met provided an experience. She came home too excited to sleep. 'Now, soon, I shall win the confidence of these girls. They will tell me all their lives, their secret thoughts.'

She did not guess that she was herself a problem to the leaders of the Guild. The girls made merciless fun of the hat that perched high above greying coils of hair, of the old-fashioned full skirt and the leather belt drawn tight to a meagre waist; still more of the smile with which she followed them about and the queer questions she put. And she could not do things. Each worker was armed with knowledge: one could guide the dancing, one tell stories, one teach gymnastics or dressmaking. Mrs Falconer had no asset.

'She's such a good soul,' the workers said, 'you don't want to hurt her, but really—she's in the way.'

'Oh, let her keep coming. She enjoys it. There's always something she can do.'

'The girls like her, though they laugh.'

'But she shouldn't be so tall. Old women oughtn't to be tall. They're not so lovable.'

They began to give her hints. She listened humbly, while students and youthful graduates told her how modern psychology decreed that working-girls should be treated. She took her lessons home and brooded over them.

For two years the centre of her life lay here. One evening she found Stella Ferguson in the Guild room, all staring eyes and open ears.

'I'm in a shop,' said Stella contemptuously. 'I'm fourteen. Ay, in the town: *I* wasn't going to your country shoppies, do you suppose.'

Some weeks later a bold girl burst indignantly up to the leader. 'Look here, I'm not going to have that old-clothes wife prying into my affairs. Cheek, I call it.' She let fly a stream of ugly oaths.

The leader was compelled to tell Mrs Falconer that she had been unwise.

'That girl, poor soul—her home and people don't stand

inquiring into. She's ashamed. One has to go very warily.'

Mrs Falconer understood after the conversation she had that evening with the leader that she had been of no great use at the Guild.

'You have been of great use to me,' she said humbly. 'I have been happy—but I won't come again.'

'Oh, please do! Come back sometimes and see us.'

Ruthless to herself, Mrs Falconer saw that her eagerness to know the intimacies of the girls' lives had been for her own sake, to quicken her life.

The following Tuesday she answered Theresa's, 'Isn't it time you were away?' with a proud plain 'I'm not going back. They think I'm too old for that work.'

The shy, baffled soul, entering upon her quest too late, with no key to open other lives, would take no consolation from deceit. It was about this period that she began to brood on Louie Morgan; and one day, though the two women had not spoken since the night of the concert, she set out to visit her.

The door was opened by the Morgans' servant, a middle-aged woman with sleeves pushed up to reveal enormous red elbows.

'It's Miss Louie you're seekin', nae the mistress?'

She led Mrs Falconer to the door of a room, within which someone was speaking.

'There's company—I won't go in.'

'Ach, she's just play-actin', ben you go.' The red-armed woman pushed Mrs Falconer in, but without announcing her, and shut the door.

Mrs Falconer stood amazed.

Louie held a teapot in her hand and was pouring tea. She moved with an elegant air around the table, filling cup after cup, and spoke to each guest in turn: but the guests were not there.

On the empty chairs Mrs Falconer seemed to see dark, menacing figures, guests with suave manners that covered a deadly leer.

A hot fervour took possession of her.

She cried aloud, 'Mr Facing-Both-Ways, Mr Two-

Tongues, My Lady Feigning.'

Louie set the teapot askew upon a chair in her astonishment.

'Oh, go away—my mother is out—what are you wanting?' Her eyes glared, but in a moment she recovered
herself and began to posture.

'I'm sorry. I didn't hear you announced, Mrs Falconer.
Do sit down.' She waved her hand at the cups of tea. 'I was
expecting guests. When I heard the bell ring I thought they
had arrived, and I was pouring the tea to be ready. Do have
some.' She thrust a cup into Mrs Falconer's hand. The tea
was already cold.

She was extravagantly dressed, but the lace at her throat
was torn and her fingernails were dirty. Her face, oppressed
by powder, and her hair, which had straggled beyond its
cut, gave her an air of sloven tawdriness; and she continued
to posture and trill.

Mrs Falconer put the cup down and said, in a harsh,
loud voice, 'I don't like the guests at your party. Don't
pretend not to understand me,' she continued. 'I don't
like your party, and I don't like the guests you entertain.
You are entertaining ghosts, demons, delusions, snares,
principalities and powers. You are entertaining your own
destruction.'

The voice hardly seemed her own, but she could not
check it. It poured on without intermission, crying a thousand things that she had brooded over, but to which she had
given no language.

'Truth, truth—it must be truth. You mustn't compromise. If you would save yourself alive there must be no
dallying with the false deities of the imagination. Things
as they are. People as they are.'

Scarlet spots burned on Louie's face and throat. She
began to retaliate, a fierce and insolent screaming.

'You—you—don't you know that you are to blame?
You gave me away. *He* never meant them to know. It was
you. And then you come and talk!'

'Yes, yes, I am to blame. We are both to blame. We must
help each other to find the truth. No more compromise. But
perhaps it's easier for the old not to compromise with life:

the young have so much longer to live. But you mustn't let yourself give in. Let me help you—'

'You fool!' burst from Louie's lips. 'I never want to see your face again.'

Mrs Falconer drew back in paralysed affright.

At that moment the big-boned servant came in to the room carrying a tray.

'Take your tea, the pair of you,' she said, and thrust the tray carelessly among the cups of cold tea upon the table. But Louie, ignoring the interruption, screamed miserably on.

Mrs Morgan's step and voice were heard.

'Not a word,' cried Louie. 'Not a word before my mother. Have you no sense of decency?'

Her whole demeanour altered. She laughed and chattered, a wild roguery possessed her. Gleams of graciousness returned.

Mrs Morgan accompanied Mrs Falconer to the door.

'Dear Louie! You must excuse her. She's so excitable. So natural in the circumstances. He may be arriving any day. Such a delightful man! We met him when we were staying in the south. Of course, we are not saying much, but you may be sure that I shall give my consent.'

The one elderly lady smiled benignly up into the face of the other; and Mrs Falconer, almost without her will, said softly, 'Yes, yes,' and patted the hand her hostess gave her in farewell. The round, pleased little lady smiled up again at her gaunt, tall guest.

'We mothers,' she murmured.

But Mrs Falconer went out on to the road shaking her head and muttering hard. All that evening she could not hold her peace. Words and broken sentences spurted from her lips, until at last Theresa said, 'What ails you, Nell, at all? If you want to say something, speak it out'; and Ellen, as though she had waited for the bidding, rose and spoke.

'I've been frightened of you all my life, Tris—I'm not frightened any longer. But I've seen a thing this afternoon that's frightened me. There's nothing to fear in all the world but deceit. Nothing at all. And I've seen it, I've seen it. I've seen a deluded woman—and he wakened her up from her

idle dreams as he wakened me—despising truth, feeding
herself on error, pouring her cups of devil's tea—'

'Where were you at all this afternoon?'

'At the Morgans'.'

'Oh, it's Louie you're meaning. Deluded, you may say.
Their woman Eppie'll tell you the things she does.' Theresa
prepared to expatiate, but Ellen cried, 'It's myself I mean.
It was myself I saw. That's what I saw—myself. I'm inside
Louie, and I'm a part of her deceit. God's in her, the God
I can't get at—'

'You're raving, lass,' said Paradise. 'Feel her hands,
Tris, she's in a fever.'

'—and for all my life to come I must proclaim it, that
God's shut up inside us all and can't get out. I pushed her
in, you see—'

Mrs Craigmyle, half rising in her corner, looked with
sudden apprehension at her daughter. Ellen's face was
chiselled now, its untouched innocence was gone; and as,
for a moment, her mask of careless mockery let fall, Mrs
Craigmyle bent forward to look at the raving woman, the
old resemblance between the faces became strangely clear,
both thin, both shapely and intent, and each significant.

Mrs Falconer's illness, which was tedious and severe,
gave rise among the neighbours to such comments as:
'She's breaking up.' 'The poor old soul; they say she's
terrible mixed.' 'Auld age doesna come its lane, but better
the body to go than the mind, say I.'

Ellen's body in time recovered; but a change had come
upon her. Nothing was in her head but the horror and sharpness of truth. She talked of it fiercely and incessantly to any
who would listen. Her humble demeanour altered to one of
angry pride. She could go to school to life no longer, since
what she had learned was already more than her wits could
rightly stand.

When her strength had returned she would slip away
on Tuesday evenings and visit the Guild.

'Truth, my dear—no, no, I don't mean not telling lies.
It's big, it's all one's life, all everyone's life, and no one
finds it.'

They saw very quickly that all she wanted was to talk,

and let her be. One evening when she seemed more unsure of herself than usual they hesitated to let her go out upon the street alone; but one girl cried, 'I'll take her home, the craitur. She's real like my old granny. Many's the time I've taken her along. Come on, granny.'

They went off arm in arm.

The next time Mrs Falconer appeared in the Guild room Miss Theresa arrived on her heels, breathless, and apologised with many words; but paused, going, at the door, to indulge her natural inquisitiveness; and Mrs Falconer, stumbling back across the room, her head thrust forward, as she had run across the garden to intercept Garry Forbes, caught hand after hand that was held eagerly towards her, and patting them softly between her own, said, 'A little dottled, my dears, a little dottled. You must just forgive me.'

'Kate,' said Miss Theresa, 'you mustn't give your mother money. She wanders away.'

Kate gave her aunt a shrewd, considering look.

'I suppose she would wander away whether or not, Aunt Tris, and if she does, surely it's better she should have money to fetch her back. In any case, she's not so dottled as you would make out. A fixed idea, if you like, that's all.'

And when Mrs Falconer pulled her daughter aside, Kate gave her, smiling, what she wished.

At times a great bodily weakness came on her. She lay wasted and shrunken, very still, her face no bigger than an ailing child's, but the eyes shone out from it with full intelligence. She spoke seldom, unless her mother were in the room, when beckoning the old lady near, she would speak in a strong, firm voice.

On one such occasion she said, 'There is a God, but I have seen not even the shadow of His passing by. When one has found the secret being of all that lives, that is God. I have hardly begun, I have hardly begun. My life is ending and I have not seen Him.'

Another day she pondered, 'Am I old? I felt so young. I thought I had endless life ahead, and I have not. They say that I am old. I didn't believe that I could die, but I suppose I shall.'

Mrs Craigmyle answered, 'There's no need to get old, my lass. A body can be just the age he wants. For shame on you, get up, get up.'

Later, her strength come again, she would rise and stalk, erect and gaunt, upon the moor; or, gathering flowers, bring them to Paradise to name. 'That's tormentil,' said Paradise; or milkwort it might be, or eyebright; and Paradise would name them to her day after day. Or drawing her chair close in beside her mother's, she would talk with a strange wild clatter, by the hour.

In the last years of her life Mrs Craigmyle ceased to torment her second daughter, and when she died the old lady would not be consoled.

The Epilogue

Lindsay came by chance to the Weatherhouse on the day that Mrs Falconer died.

'Well!'' thought Theresa. 'Nine years married and three bairns. Could one believe it?' She looked again at Lindsay's girlish figure and the happy candour of her eyes, veiled for the moment under a profound pity.

'Cousin Ellen,' Lindsay was thinking. 'Dying.' Death was remote and terrible. She had seen no one die; but there flashed back into her mind the recollection of a dead bird she had held against her bosom in this very room. 'I showed it to Cousin Ellen,' she remembered. 'That russet patch beneath its wing.' It comforted her vaguely that she had shown the beauty of the bird she mourned to the woman who was dying now. 'I didn't love her very much,' she thought. 'She interfered.' The gaunt, grey face upon the pillow horrified the watcher. 'I showed her my bird,' she thought, 'I showed her my bird.'

Mrs Falconer lay dazed and blank. 'Jumps out of bed!' thought Lindsay. 'She looks as if she could not move a foot.' But Theresa had explained that they had brought her down from her own high room. She couldn't be left alone a minute—would be up and running on her naked feet to the window. 'We couldn't be trotting up and down that stairs all day.'

'No, indeed,' said Lindsay, in her soft, commiserating voice. 'With Cousin Annie so lame, too—you must have so much to do.'

'Oh, not so much more,' answered Theresa tartly. 'If it's in the house you're meaning, all that Nell did in the house was neither here nor there. She's been about as much use this long while back as her mother, and less. Stravaigin' about on that moor at all hours. "You would need a season ticket, that's what you would need," I said to her. And muttering away to herself, you never heard! As wild as Bawbie Paterson herself, and she's a byword, though she be your husband's aunt, my dear.'

'Oh, you needn't tell me,' said Lindsay, with a glimmer. 'We can't stay in the house now. It's unspeakable. She's beyond everything.'

'It's a marvel to me that you ever stayed.'

'Indeed, yes,' said Miss Annie. ' "You must have taken her up wrong," I said to Tris, that first time after the war, when she came in and told us that Francie's wife had seen you arrive. And never to send us a line.'

'But that was Garry all over,' said Lindsay, laughing again. 'Up and away when he took it into his head. I couldn't have sent you a line.'

'Well,' thought Miss Theresa comfortably, 'I wouldn't be married to a man that's the byword and laughing stock of the place.' And she looked again at Lindsay with amazement. Happy—there was no doubt of it. Now who could have foretold that such a marriage would turn out well? 'It's these modern styles that does it,' she said aloud, with a nip to her tone, surveying the girl's lissome grace.

'I'm glad to see you don't show off your knees, Lindsay,' said Miss Annie.

Miss Annie had said, when the preparations for Lindsay's wedding were toward, 'I would like to hear that she was getting a good white wincey gown, but I don't suppose she will.'

'A byword and a laughing stock,' repeated Miss Theresa to herself. His name in everyone's mouth. *You would need Garry Forbes to you; Hine up on the head o' the house like Garry Forbes and his two fools*; and though *like seeking needles among preens* was an old phrase, *or sane folk among fools* had been added to it locally because of Garry. Mrs Craigmyle herself had made the addition, with a meaning eye upon her daughter Ellen. Theresa remembered the occasion well: an occasion when Ellen had said, unexpectedly, that Garry Forbes was liker a Christ than any other man she knew. A Christ—now what did she mean by *a* Christ? It gave them all a queer

shock, coming like that from Ellen's gaunt, pale lips. Annie
had said, 'Well, Bawbie now—she's never in the kirk from
one year's end to another, and I doubt the young man's much
the same.' Theresa remembered that she herself had cried,
'Well, there's no need for blasphemy about it,' and it was
later the same evening that Mrs Craigmyle, using the phrase
like seeking needles among preens, added *or sane folk among fools*.

'And indeed it's real hard whiles to tell the one from
the other,' thought Miss Theresa complacently.

But there was no doubt of it, Lindsay was happy. Miss
Theresa regarded her again. 'But when you've got your
poke', she thought, 'you just have to be doing with the pig
that's in it.' Even when the pig was one whose grumphs and
squeaks made something of a family scandal. 'Old Garry's
just hanging on for the next Coal Strike,' Frank Lorimer
had said. 'Wait till you see—he'll come out strong, stronger
than this time.' Some of his utterances had even been in the
papers. A horrid disgrace. A mere asking for ridicule. Miss
Theresa wondered that Lindsay would put up with it, but
she didn't seem to care—just laughed and said, 'But that's
the kind of thing that Garry does.' Well, she might repent it
yet. Nine years was not so very long a time, and the wedding
had been hasty enough, in all conscience. Theresa remembered how Mrs Robert Lorimer had come out to give them
the news.

There they were, preparing for a marriage in the grand
style a fortnight ahead; and that very morning, in the
drawing-room at home, Lindsay had become Mrs Dalgarno
Forbes; and the bridegroom was returning to the trenches
the following day.

'Oh,' Theresa had said. 'Active service again. I thought
he wasn't fit.'

Mrs Robert explained that it was his own desire. 'Would
get himself sent. And it appears he was able enough all the
time. It was just his nerves.'

So it had been a gey hasty affair, Annie supposed. And
Mrs Robert told them that even the minister was not to
be had in time, and so that old done man, the Reverend
Mr Watson, tied the knot. 'And if he didn't forget the
ring!—pronounced a benediction on them, and the ring

still in the best man's fingers, and him fidgeting about and not knowing what to do. Such an unfortunate affair.'

'Well, well,' Theresa had said. 'Who will to Cupar maun to Cupar. That's her getting married in May. And the service all in a snorl. And no wedding frock and no party.'

'And her father,' continued Mrs Robert, 'he would blurt out anything, would Andrew. He said right out, "You're in a terrible hurry," he said, "come back and pay your loaf." And then they got the ring put on.'

'Sic mannie sic horsie,' old Mrs Craigmyle had said with a chuckle. 'Andrew's his father's son. You'll never see a Lorimer trauchled with overmuch respect for the kirk. And us all to come out of a manse, too.'

'And then,' Mrs Robert had proceeded, 'when he turned to kiss his wife, she actually skipped into his arms. Kicked her heels up—a regular dancing step. The trickiest you ever saw.'

'Oh, well,' Theresa had said, 'she grat sore enough about that wedding not so long ago, and she'll maybe greet again for all her dancing.'

'Yes, that was what I said,' she thought. 'And then mother began with her ballads.' She remembered perfectly what her mother had sung. She had sat aloof, as usual, just listening. One might be sure that in time she would put in her word. A song, most likely. She diddled away at old tunes most of the time. Hitherto, since Mrs Robert had arrived, she had spoken nothing but that chuckling proclamation of Lorimer disrespect. A gey life she and her brother must have led the old Reverend! But with her mind on the walled manse garden she reflected, 'He was real fond of a funnie himself.' Theresa was half a Craigmyle, a dourer folk than the Lorimers—dour, hard of grain, acquisitive; but even Theresa had spent hilarious days in her grandfather's patch of wood. And as she sat watching her sister die, Theresa's mind was a pleasant jumble of apple trees and the ploys of a pack of bairns, through which Lindsay's eager dance step and her mother's nine year old singing recurred like a refrain. The very tune came back and the mocking words:

He bocht an aul horse an' he hired an aul man

An' he sent her safe back to Northumberland.

It was then that Ellen had interfered. Opening her mouth
for the first time, 'That's a cruel inference, mother,' she had
cried sharply. Neither Theresa nor Annie paid much heed
to what their mother sang. She was always singing, though
there had been little singing since Ellen took ill. Dowie, the
old lady was, peering anxiously. She wasn't in the habit of
caring. Theresa thought it strange. 'It's the callow that worry,' she said to herself. A very old woman like her mother
was past feeling strongly.

'What did the old ballads signify?' she thought, reverting
to the wedding; but Ellen was always finding that her mother meant something—meant more than she should, Ellen
intended to say. Well, and if she had meant to hint that
the marriage might turn out ill, it was no more than they
all thought at the time. 'But we were wrong, and it's a mercy,' she thought, daft Bawbie Paterson's nephew though he
was. Would Bawbie have gone to the wedding now, she pondered; and with the black trallop hanging down her back?
'There was nothing amiss with the song, I'm sure,' Theresa
said to herself. 'Mother had a rhyme about the ring too, if I
could remember it:

a guid gowd ring
Made oot o' the auld brass pan, ay, ay.

But they had all cried out against that one—a sluttish
thing, not to be associated with Lindsay. Mrs Craigmyle
had let them cry, humming away at her tune, pleasuring
herself with the unsavoury words.

The dying woman began to mutter restlessly. Miss
Theresa put aside these ancient thoughts and went to
the bedroom.

'How she speaks!' Miss Annie said to Lindsay. 'Such
conversations as she holds, you never would believe. She's
been taking a lot to your husband, my dear.'

'To my—to Garry? But how strange! Why, she hardly
knows Garry. Talking to Garry?'

'Talking, my dear, and answering too.' Miss Annie broke
off. 'But you never know what a body will say when they're
dottled.' She sighed a little, looked towards her mother, and
shook her head. The thought had come to her that to speak

to Lindsay of Ellen's infatuation was less than kind. 'I remember,' she began again, 'when I was but a little thing,
an old, old man—'

Her pleasant voice ran on; but while she told her story
she looked again, anxiously and in a puzzled way, at her
mother. Lindsay, too, looked at her aged grand-aunt who at
ninety four, straight as a pine-bole and with all her faculties
unimpaired, was seated on the high-backed sofa, knitting
at her shank; but her eyes, Lindsay noticed, never left her
daughter's face—Ellen, her second daughter, dottled and
dying at sixty nine.

The muttering continued.

'Poor old craitur!' said grand-aunt Craigmyle.

And her voice had still tune to it.

'Yes,' said Miss Annie, reading Lindsay's thought, 'it's
the old generation that has the last in it, I say to mother.
There's Mrs Morgan now, as blithe and active at her tea-
makings as ever you saw, and Louie a poor wasted thing.'

Louie Morgan! thought Lindsay. Strange that she should
be mentioned then. Lindsay's thoughts, like Miss Theresa's,
had been travelling in the past. And Louie Morgan, as well
as Cousin Ellen, had had her part in the singular drama that
preceded that hasty marriage service.

She said aloud, 'I haven't seen Louie for—oh, such
a long time.'

'And needn't seek to,' said Theresa, returning from the
bedroom. 'She's not a sight for self-respecting eyes. The
drink. She's drinking hard. Bleared. And her stockings
cobbled with a yellow thread. That's you and your religion
and no meal in the house.'

'Religion—is she so pious, then? She used to pray—'

'Oh, pray tonight and pray tomorrow. She would pray
your head into train oil. But no one minds her—her big
words and her grand speeches. They know what to make
of *her* declarations.'

Lindsay had a movement of compassion for poor simple
Louie, outcast from the love and reverence of the earth.

'But she wasn't saying them that time,' she thought
and remembered how she and Garry, when she had stayed
at the Weatherhouse before her marriage, had come on

Louie kneeling in the wood as though in audible prayer; but when they came behind her, what she was saying was ludicrous. 'I'm on the Fetter-Rothnie committee—may I introduce myself?' she was saying. And she smirked to an imaginary audience. They had laughed about it often afterwards, though Garry didn't like her to tell the story in public. 'Oh, leave her alone,' he always said. But what harm did it do, Lindsay would ask, with people who didn't know her? Aloud she said, 'Fancy Louie coming to that! Poor soul! I liked Louie,' she added in a moment. 'She used to take me for walks— long ago, when I was a little thing. And tell me stories. She had a dog—Demon, wasn't it? Oh, I remember how he could run. Through the wood. I can see him still.'

'Nonsense!' rapped Miss Theresa. 'Louie had never a dog.'

'But I remember. I can see him. A whippet hound he was.'

'Nonsense! She hadn't a dog. She wanted one—one of the Knapperley whippets, Miss Barbara's dogs. But old Mrs Morgan wouldn't have an animal about the place. Louie kicked up a waup over not getting it, I can tell you. And after a while she used to pretend she had it—made on to be stroking it, spoke to it and all. A palavering craitur.'

Lindsay looked doubtfully.

'Did she? I know she pretended about a lot of things. But Demon—? He seems so real when I look back. Did she only make me think I saw him? He used to go our walks with us. We called to him—*Demon, Demon*—loud out, I know that.'

She pondered. The dog, bounding among the pines, had in her memory the compelling insistence of imaginative art. He was a symbol of swiftness, the divine joy of motion. But Lindsay preferred reality to symbol.

'Queer, isn't it?' she said, coming out of her reverie. 'I remembered Demon was a real dog.'

She was unreasonably angry with Louie, as though by her own discovery of Demon's non-existence Louie had defrauded her of a recollected joy. And Garry had proved her a cheat. Lindsay's mind reverted to all that had followed that odd encounter in the wood, and so came back to Cousin Ellen. She shifted a little on her chair, bringing her eye into line with the open door and the muttering old woman who lay on the bed; and suddenly Mrs Falconer began to shout, 'They have despised him and rejected him. Cry aloud, spare not. A stubborn people who will pay no heed.'

Theresa stood over her, saying, 'Now, now. There, lie down again. Weesht ye, weesht. It's all right.' But Annie, who had caught the Biblical cadence of the words, folded her knotted and swollen hands together in her lap; and Ellen continued to shout, harshly and without intermission, tossing her long, fleshless arm above her head.

That evening Lindsay, who was on holiday at her old home, said to her father, 'Daddy, you must go out and see her. No, I don't mean Cousin Ellen. She wouldn't know you, of course. I mean old Aunt Craigmyle. She was always so fond of you. Perhaps you could comfort her a little.'

'Comfort!' grumbled Andrew Lorimer. 'The old lady never needed much comforting that I could see. You don't take things hard at ninety four, bairn.'

'Oh, I know, daddy. I know she never seemed to care about anything. She looked at us all as though she were reading about us in a book. But she is distressed—really she is.'

'Oh, well, we'll see.'

Andrew Lorimer took his car and ran out the nine odd miles that separated the Weatherhouse from the city, and by that time Mrs Falconer was dead.

'Oh, Andrew, I'm right glad to see you,' said Annie, who opened the door to him. 'Come away in. Mother's so dowie. I never saw her so come-at.'

'Eh?' said Andrew.

He remained standing on the doorstep.

'What a brae that is!' he grumbled. 'It's not fit for any car. I've a rheumatic here,' he added, feeling his shoulder. And because he wished to protract the moment before he must go in and talk to his aunt, he asked, 'How's your own rheumatism, Ann?'

Miss Annie looked down at her shapeless lumps of hands. 'It's as much as I could do to open the door for you,' she said. A gleam flickered on her pleasant face. 'I've aye been handless, Andrew, but I'm getting terrible handless among the feet forbye.'

Andrew allowed himself to laugh. He felt less constrained. He disliked heartily the job on which he was engaged; but he had always enjoyed Miss Annie.

'What'll I say to her?' he queried, following her across the threshold. 'You'd better tell me what to say.'

He sat down beside his aged aunt and began to tell her about his rheumatism, wresting his shoulder round to show her where the pain lay; but all the while he spoke his thoughts were on the woman who had just died. He realised that he was thinking of her as an old woman. 'But she can't be old,' he thought. She wasn't so much older than himself when they were all bairns together, the three Lorimer boys and the three Craigmyle lassies, and played in the Manse garden at Inverdrunie, and grandfather Lorimer gave them prizes for climbing the elm trees. 'To keep them out of the apple trees,' he explained to his wife. What a climber Paradise had been, with her long foalie's legs! Tris and he were of an age, and Ellen some three years older. Not yet seventy, then. Pretty near it, though. And he thought, seventy years without event. Oh, to be sure, there had been the episode with that Falconer chap who let her down so badly; but that must have meant four years at the most—long ago. Kate—why, Kate must be going on for forty. And at that moment Kate Falconer entered the room.

An able-looking girl—he had forgotten that she looked so well. Matron in some sort of Children's Home, and exceptionally capable, they said. Looked as though her wits were at her service. She could do well for herself, if she liked—marry well. There couldn't be much money in that Charity Home business, anyway, though he supposed Kate would take what she was offered and make no bones. She wouldn't push for her own advantage. Took that from her father. Couldn't hold off himself. Let any shaver cheat him. And then slipped out of it all and left his wife and child without a copper. Kate wouldn't have a penny but what she earned. Yes, she would marry.

'That's Stella Ferguson gone up the road,' said Miss Theresa, who was adjusting a blind.

A moment later came a sharp ring at the bell. Kate went to the door.

They heard the stranger ask in a loud, challenging voice, 'What are the blinds down for?'

Kate's soft answer was inaudible.

'She's not dead? Her? Lord alive!' The girl broke into noisy blubbering.

'Stella Ferguson?' said Andrew Lorimer. 'Oh, yes, old Jeames's grand-child. No? I remember, I remember.' With a movement of the head towards the noise of her sobbing, he added, 'I suppose that's the etiquette of mourning with that stamp.'

'No,' said Paradise, 'that's not a pose. Stella has a warm heart. A bold bessy but a warm heart. She's done well for herself, Stella has, she's a smartie. She's typist at Duncan Runciman's and making good money, though she's but eighteen. Quite my lady now, and keeps her mother in her place. But she has a warm heart. When Mr John Grey died—they found him dead in bed one May morning, a year past, and all the days he lay, you would have said a lying-in-state—not a cloud, not a breath of wind. Summer in its glory. Halcyon days they were—you would have thought his very garden knew. Well, Stella came and brought her flower. Gean blossom it was—black the next day. And so his cousin, that had come because he had none of his own, she threw away the shrivelled thing. Stella was like a play-actress—ramped and raged. Picked the very branch out of the rubbish heap and put it in his hand again. "I'll not take another," she declared. "I said a prayer over that, I did. I don't say a prayer so often that I want one wasted." So her bit of blossom went to the grave with him,' concluded Paradise. 'Quite right to leave it too, I think.'

Andrew Lorimer had gone only a little way down the hill on his journey home when the girl Stella, leaping from the dyke on which she had been seated, intercepted him.

'Look here,' she said. 'They don't like me much in there. My mother was a bad woman, and they think I'm a bad girl, but I'm not. Gospel.' As she said *Gospel* the girl breathed noisily and crossed her breath with a forefinger. 'But if I'm not a bad girl,' resumed Stella, 'it's to that precious saint lying dead in there that it's due. My eye! They don't none of them know the kind she was. Never goes to church, doesn't she? She was a stunner, I can tell you. Look here, she's got to get my roses in her hand.'

She displayed a cluster of hardy yellow scotch roses.

'Stella,' said Mr Lorimer, stepping from his car, 'if you were the worst sinner that ever was, you'd have the right to pay your tribute to the dead. But you're a good honest girl. Come with me.'

And, quite unconscious of the high scorn in the look that Stella cast on him, he led the way back to the Weatherhouse.

'You can come and put it in her hand yourself, Stella,' Miss Theresa said.

So Mrs Falconer lay that night, white and still, her face, beset so long with pain and darkened by failure, serene at last, and the rose of the girl Stella in her hand.

A Pass in the Grampians

INTRODUCED BY
RODERICK WATSON

Contents

Introduction

'Sail not beyond the Pillars of Hercules' is the phrase that ends the tale of Martha Ironside's growing-up at the conclusion of Nan Shepherd's first novel, *The Quarry Wood*. Martha decided to stay at home, to find fulfilment in rearing her adopted child and by working as a schoolteacher for the local community. 'Life was stranger than they had supposed', and Martha has 'acquiesced in her destiny and so delivered herself from the insecurity of the adventurer.' It is a tribute to *The Quarry Wood*, with its unfailing eye for character, local detail, and the transformation of the ordinary, that Martha's decision does not seem to be a cowardly or a narrow one. Nevertheless, those pillars haunt Nan Shepherd's work, and they are symbolised again in the title of her last novel, *A Pass in the Grampians*, which closes with Jenny Kilgour, at the age of sixteen, deciding to cross that pass by leaving her beloved grandfather's remote hill farm to seek the bright lights of London and an entirely different society.

The pass in the Grampians (like the Pillars of Hercules at the straits of Gibraltar), is the symbolic gateway to a world beyond the Mediterranean, which is to say beyond the golden 'middle world' of our childhood and adolescence, and Shepherd's last novel returns to the questions of her first, which are questions about what you take and what you leave on such a journey. Nor were these questions irrelevant to her own circumstances, as someone who chose to live and work her whole life as a teacher of teachers in the town of her birth.

No one could be surer of the value of place than Nan Shepherd was about her beloved North East, and Andrew Kilgour and his three younger brothers (who are professors of Divinity, Classics and Medicine) are almost ironically complete emblems of traditional Scottish Presbyterian probity. Yet her account of Kilgour himself is entirely serious and in keeping with her own passionate feelings for the metaphysics of landscape and the possibility of existential values greater than any individual creed:

> For the sheep farmer, seventy years of intercourse had made the moor sit to him more closely than the most supple of garments. . . . He had made his covenant with the moor: it had bogged him and drenched him, deceived, scorched, numbed him with cold, tested his endurance, memory and skill; until a large part of his nature was so interpenetrated with its nature that apart from it he would have lost reality. His love for it indeed was beyond all covenant. Like his love for Jenny, it had the quality of life itself, absolute and uncovenanted.

The old testament authority of this passage is unmistakable, nor is it being mocked.

Andrew has acted as a father to Jenny ever since his son Bill was killed in the Great War and Jenny has become the lively spirit of the place—a sunny child loved by all, and especially, perhaps by Kilgour's spinster daughter Mary, who works in London but returns to Boggiewalls every summer, hoping to find—needing to find—everything unchanged. But things cannot remain for ever the same, nor is this idyllic scene all that it seems at first.

Here, as in all her novels, Nan Shepherd has an acute sense of the life of women in her time. Andrew Kilgour's daughter, Mary has escaped to a more glamorous life in London, but the price of her escape was that Jenny's mother should stay behind to manage the farm—Kilgour being a widower long since. As a reminder of what is at stake in the question of who you are, and what you choose or allow to happen, there is always Jenny's mother in her 'eternal grey jersey—this year's, last year's, sometime's'. Jenny's mother has faded to not much more than a cipher in the little family, almost a servant in the background, dispossessed of status by her husband's death and taken for granted in the kitchen or the farmyard, with her hands 'ingrained with black and rough as graters'. In one of the novel's most moving scenes Jenny explains (in all the sweet blindness of her own youth) why she must have compassion for old Durno, without realising that her mother, too, needs her care, as she lies in bed with a headache, quietly mourning her own 'lost life'.

Yet even Aunt Mary's escape was not so very vital after all, for she comes to recognise that her career has been no more than a matter of 'methodical and tireless industry', lacking the spirit she sees and loves and wants to nurture in Jenny, and lacking, too, the vulgar energy that she hates in Bella Cassie, the orphan girl who was brought up with her as a sister. The same Bella couldn't stand the rural life and when she was sixteen she left the farm to seek her fortune. Now, eighteen years later she has come back as 'Dorabel Cassidy' a noted singer, determined to build a bright new bungalow among the old hills, and to liven up the neighbourhood with her bohemian friends and her love of music and parties and motorcars and her own glorious and shamelessly egocentric appetite for life.

The scene is set for a subtle contest for Jenny's future, between Bella and Mary and old Andrew—each of them with their own claim to Jenny's allegiance, each of them with their own truths and their own stories to tell. Once again, it is Nan Shepherd's Chekhovian compassion which marks her as a remarkable stylist, for every character in the novel is allowed their own dignity and his or her own space to breathe. Mary's unrequitable love for Jenny is as touching as the elderly Ellen Falconer's longing for recognition in the eyes of Garry Forbes from *The Weatherhouse*. And even old James Durno, faithful shepherd to the farm whom we come to see as a satyr-like and secretly spiteful old man with dirty habits and a violent past, even he is given his own paradoxical peace in the end as 'a wreck' that 'two violent women'—his wife and his daughter—have made of him.

As always with Shepherd's work, beyond the romance of Jenny's dawning sexuality and the melodrama of local scandals and Bella Cassie's hidden origins, it is finally the mystery of human identity, and even of sheer Being itself, that is at issue. Shepherd uses her characteristic imagery of landscape and light to catch the inner sense of our condition, playing symbols of solidity and fluidity against each other throughout the novel.

Thus the dilemma of Jenny's adult identity is represented as a choice between mountain and ocean: between the 'mountain grandeur' of her grandfather's love and Bella Cassie's 'encroaching, tumultuous, cruel, endlessly altering ocean-love. . . . If she is frail, she will be crushed between them, deformed for life through this her first battering of the elements.' The same question was posed earlier in the book, as a choice between 'I AM', representing the egocentric fluidity and flair of Bella and her talent as a singer, and 'I LABOUR' which is the way of Jehovah and the grandfather, and all the patriarchal weight—and the fineness, too—of the Scottish Presbyterian work ethic.

Which one will Jenny keep? And what will she leave behind? This is the very question which lies at the heart of so many books in the modern Scottish literary canon—not least in *A Scots Quair*, in the last scene from *Grey Granite* between Ewan Tavendale and his mother, in which the young man reminds Chris that '*there will always be you and I, I think, Mother. It's the old fight that maybe will never have a finish, whatever the names we give to it—the fight in the end between* FREEDOM *and* GOD.' Lewis Grassic Gibbon's formulation leaves it up to us to decide which is which in this case, and indeed his masterpiece ends in an impasse between the two, with Ewan leaving on a hunger march to London, and Chris in effect returning home (or perhaps retreating) to her rural origins at the back o Bennachie. Nan Shepherd's heroine also loves her home:

> She loves it as her very life, she will praise it for ever as the only life worth having, but she must know the other. She must find a thousand answers to a thousand questions. She must get beyond the Pass.

Shepherd has Jenny recognise that when she returns in future she will have to seem 'the same being as she went, with the same standards, the same pieties and disdains' or else her grandfather will break his heart. But she also knows that change is possible and that change is upon her as she commits herself to 'places unauthorised by the tradition of her people' and 'with the perennial expectancy of youth, she foresees her own difference, her unique and eternally intangible self.'

Nan Shepherd does not disguise the greenness of Jenny's hopes, but she values them too, as a necessary step towards life, love, energy, self, 'strangeness' and most of all, change. Without these qualities there is nothing but the darker side of the kailyard, a world of repression and shame in which 'time was accomplished; it had no further progression but turned back eternally upon itself.'—A kind of 'madness', in other words, as Andrew Kilgour himself recognises, as he takes leave of old Alison Durno, a dedicated churchgoer and one of a long line of religiose monsters in Scottish life and letters—a woman whose 'stillness appalled, like the terrific immobility of a whirlpool.' Shepherd can recognise the strength of such characters—'Her body, hard and dry like brown sticks, held somewhere a reserve of prodigious power'—but this is a power which must be overcome, and which Jenny must leave behind.

And she starts her journey under the vulgar tuition of no less than Bella Cassie, the fat orphan girl who came home to swank. A spiritual descendant of Emmeline in *The Quarry Wood*, or Bawbie Paterson and young Stella in *The Weatherhouse*, Bella is one of Nan Shepherd's most memorable creations—greedy for chocolate cake, greedy for life, greedy for recognition, incapable of shame and still possessed by the fury of being at thirty-four years of age. She casts off the 'disgrace' of her past and wears her chosen stagename with pride, and stands as a glorious refutation of genetic inheritance, or predestination, or *The House with the Green Shutters* and all its gloomy kin:

I'm Dorabel Cassidy, amn't I? Durno! What does being a Durno matter? I'm what I've made myself, amn't I? I'm Dorabel Cassidy. I'll finish the house—oh yes, I'll finish it. I'll get the pink tiles. And turrets. And all the things

you hate. And I'll let it to someone who isn't afraid of
having a good time. Someone that won't put on their
spectacles whenever a cow moos and look to see what's
making all the din. And I'll come back myself—oh yes,
I will. I'll come back. . . . You're all tied to your daddy's
coat-tails up here right enough. Who was her father? Who
was her mother? What was her great grandma's table-linen
like? I'm Dorabel Cassidy, I tell you.

High time, Dorabel. It's been a long wait. There are more
of you now in Scottish literature. Welcome back.

Roderick Watson

ONE

Durno

In a two-roomed cottage on the edge of a moorland, an old man was relating to his sister an event of the day just ended. He was a snivelling old fellow, dun-skinned, and wearing, even in the house and though the time was April and the door stood open to a blue vista of hills and an evening of peculiar splendour, a heavy cloth cap with lappets that came down close over the ears. He sniftered as he spoke and now and then raised an elbow and rubbed his sleeve roughly across his nose.

'That'll salt the Lairdie's brose to him,' he chuckled.

He slouched into his seat by the table, drew the platter of oatcakes towards him and, crumbling off a corner, began to eat.

'Ay, that'll salt his brose,' he repeated, the words coming thick through his mouthful of oatcake.

The sister to whom he recounted the affair paused in her task of dishing the savoury mess of stoved potatoes for the meal. She set the pot back upon the hob, laid her spoon on a plate, and, standing erect by the table, said grace in a firm and even voice. The old fellow continued to chew, audibly, and hardly was the grace over when he plunged again into his tale. His sister took her spoon and scraped the remainder of the potatoes on to the plate. She listened, but did not speak. There was no reproach in her saying of the grace, nor defiance in his continuing to munch. It was his custom to fall to upon the food as soon as he saw it, and hers to ask the blessing in a plain, reverent, unemphatic way, as soon as she saw him ready to eat. Each was perfectly aware of the other but paid no overt attention.

These two, James and Alison Durno, brother and sister and both close upon seventy years of age, were amazingly

alike in cast of feature and in build. They were insignificant
in person and both crooked, from a lifetime of labour and
exposure; but while he slouched, she held herself rigidly
erect. Both had high cheek-bones, big noses and determined
chins, but his eye roved, with a glitter now sensuous, now
ironical; hers was steady and austere. The faces of both
were seamed, their lean fingers hard and brown like heather
roots; but while her face also suggested the tough hardness
of heather wood, his was like a dirty fungus.

'Well, there's me,' he said, dunting with the handle of
his knife upon the table. 'There's me, half-ways up yon
steep bit of the brae. Yon steepest bit of all, t'other side
of the Pass. And here's my lady, with her bit car. "You
brute," she says. O ay, nothing mim-mou'ed yonder. "You
brute," she says, "clear off them sheep. You've made me
stop on this blamed hill," she says, "and I don't believe
the car'll start again now." "There's been sheep on this
blamed hill," I says to her, "since long afore you or your
bit cars were heard o'. It's an auld drove road, and sheep
have the first pick." "Pick your eyes," she says. "Clear this
road for me." "O ay, ma'am, O ay," I says. You should
aye be polite, Alison, you should aye be polite. It's cheap
saying Ay. But a sair chase I had with that bla'guards o'
sheep—a sair weary trauchle. And aye I took the other keek
at my lady—a scarlet bonnet on her head and the two bold
eyes of her making a great conversation. "O ay, my wife,"
says I to myself, "I know you." And, "Ay, ay, my mannie,
I know you," says the eyes. She got some tired waiting
or the sheep would move, though. Ay, some tired. She
maybe minded on a bit pilgate her and me had the last
time we met, forbye'—he put up his hands and smoothed
the ear-flaps of his dingy cap, pressing them thoughtfully
against his ears—'and her birse was up if her car wasna,
and she cairded me in some style, I'm tellin' you. O ay,
the wordies sounded grand.'

He chuckled, rolling the words again on his tongue,
where they tasted good; and he watched his sister with
malicious relish. But if the words had sting, she gave
no sign.

Chuckling still, he rose and shut the door. There was a

cosiness about the shut room that seemed to improve the flavour of the words, kept their juices in.

'O ay, a lady and no mistake,' he said, sitting down again. 'She had gotten education, yon one. She fair made the adjectives fly.'

He looked again at Alison, narrowly. Her face did not flicker. She sat and ate with a stern impassive calm.

'Ay, she had gotten education. Not like you and me, Alison wumman. Plain horse sense has served us all our days. Now where, think you, would she have gotten that? Education—that's a commodity you pay for, Alison my lass.—You're not asking me what like she was, eh? A fine tall woman, she was that, well set up, none of the likes of you and me, Alison, nippit little bodies that we are. A handsome dame, broad in the shoulder. Ay, for a woman, uncommon broad in the shoulder, byordinar broad. I've seen her like afore, but it was thirty years ago, I'm thinkin', and maybe a bittie on to that.'

Alison said then, 'If it's Bella you're telling me you've seen, say it out and be done.'

'Bella.'

The name seemed to last for ever as he turned it on his tongue. The old woman gave no sign of impatience, but her very eyes listened. The old fellow took his time. He had his joke, and it pleased him mightily. He was a happy man, seated there by the hot smoking fire, shovelling food into his mouth and blinking with his watery eye.

'Bella was not her name,' he announced at last. 'Oh, she's a proud one, yon! "Bella," says she, "that old runt of a name," she says. "Like a wart sticking on your nose. You call me Bella again, Durnie my lad—" "I beg your pardon, ma'am," says I, "you're Mistress Gib Munro." "O, am I?" says she. And she laughs gey lang. "I'm Dorabel Cassidy the singer, and don't you forget it." Dorabel Cassidy.'

Old Alison lifted her eyes and looked searchingly in her brother's face. Her lined old countenance, brown and life-bitten as it was, had a singular purity in its look. It was a shapely old face, controlled and sweet. Not an easy face. A face as of one who had watched too long and too earnestly the wide emptiness of moor and the terrible mountains, expecting an event that did not come. In that desolate country, where time goes by seasons and not by the packed minutes of cities, Alison Durno seemed to be saying, *Ye know not the hour.* But if it was a Day of Judgment that she looked for, there was nothing craven in her attitude. Now, listening to her brother, though she knew that he tormented her with deliberation, she had no resentment in her heart, but waited quietly for what would come.

'Ay, a singer. She had a grand voice. I learned her a power o' sangs masel, and right bonny they sounded in her bairn's voicie. She would come to Durno all right when he had a sang or a sweetie, ay would she. Ay would she. Maybe the auld man can sing a sang yet, maybe he'll sing wi' her yet for all her grandeur. She's a somebody, I tell you. Dorabel Cassidy—who'd a' thought of making that out of plain Bella Cassie? She's had her picture in the papers too, a lot o' times, and bitties printed about her. Ay, and she sings on the wireless.'

Alison said, 'Did she tell you all this?'

'She did that, and something besides that'll make you cock your lugs. She's like her mother afore her—needs an audience. All her fancy secrets, look her road and out they pop at the first glint o' your e'e. Ay, even to auld Durnie, the lousy tyke. But he had aye a way wi' him where the weemen were concerned.'

Alison scraped up the last ridge of her potatoes, with the extreme care of the poor. Her brother had not been at home for the mid-day meal, having crossed the Pass the day before, to bring back a flock of sheep from the south for Andrew Kilgour, the farmer whom men called the Laird. So Alison had contented herself with oatcakes and milk in the middle of the day, and this meal was their dinner. She rose now, tumbled an end of mutton bone from her plate into the fire and set the dirty plate on the dresser. Then she walked to the door which her brother had shut, set it open and stood in silence by it, as though she needed air.

'If her mother was once like that,' she said at last, 'she learned to heed her tongue, poor lass, long ere she was the age of this one.'

She heard his chuckling laugh behind her, but did not

turn. Before her the evening stretched, blue and transparent; behind was the murky room; and she stood listening to the old man's laughter with a desperate pity in her soul. Like a recording angel, she knew, she alone among men, why he laughed and why he needed pity; but her face remained impassive and controlled. So may the recording angel look, who, doomed to listen with unalterable mien to the long tale of human frailty, is yet permitted to pass no judgment upon what he hears.

He continued to chuckle, choking over his food, grunting half-intelligible words.

'She's coming back in style. There'll be a four-five with their eyes agape or Bella's done. It's her that's putting up this new house next door to the Laird's bit moor, no less. Bella Cassie doing the like o' that. Bella Cassie!'

The gratification in his voice thickened the air in the dark room. 'Ay, ay, Laird Kilgour, little as he likes the notion of a house stuck down by the cheek of his estate'—he gave the word an inflection of mockery that was not lost on Alison—'he'll like it less, I'm thinking, when he hears who'll be bidin' in the house. But shut you the door, wumman.'

Alison shut it.

'Alison, lass'—he gleamed at his aged sister round the flap of his bonnet—'you'll make a grand wife to some man yet. A woman that does as she's bid is worth a man's findin'.'

'You'd be some ill off wanting me yourself, I'm thinking.'

'I could surely make my sup brose to myself.'

Alison came behind him and stood, erect and grave, looking at the fire.

'There's maybe more than brose that you need from me,' she said.

He began to grumble a reply, but the words broke. Purple blotches showed upon his face. He grew cold. But they understood each other very well, these two old creatures. Alison said no more. She resumed her habitual silence, he continued a muttering in which the name of Bella Cassie could be heard.

Then a bicycle bell began to ring, sharp and exuberant, coming nearer and nearer.

Alison turned her sweet old face to the door.

'That'll be the bairn,' she said.

A voice sang out, 'Anybody in?' and in a moment Jenny Kilgour was in the room.

Jenny at sixteen, all legs and arms and quick eager grace, golden-skinned, innocent as the sun—grand-daughter of that Andrew Kilgour, nicknamed the Laird, who was like to be so ill at ease over the building of Bella Cassie's house—perched herself on the shabby rest of Durno's chair and put an arm about his neck.

His face, like an old toad's back, wrinkled with pleasure.

TWO

Peggy

When Jenny reached home, night was already falling. She heard the edgy rasping of a file and made straight for her grandfather's workshop. He filled the doorway, bending to catch the last light on the broken hammer shaft he was strengthening with an inset of iron. Jenny watched, loving as she always did the deft movements of his hands.

'Stand out of my light, you limmer. Your father wasn't a glazier.'

She laughed, and moved away, and asked after the sick calf, and said, 'The kitties will see to-morrow,' and was back again as close to him as before. But now he had driven the iron bar down the middle of his hammer shaft, and knocked the shaft home in the hammer head, and tested his work, and tidied away his tools, and locked the workshop door. Jenny thrust her arm through his. Tall though she was, he towered far above her. She liked to glance upwards at his face and see the vast bushy eyebrows against the sky.

They looked at the calf. 'See, Jenny, that pail. Fetch some logs in with you, Jenny.' Her grandfather's commands were terse. She obeyed them blithely. Speech with him was for need, not pleasure. He met her chatter with a grunt.

But when she said, 'Durnie's got a horrid boil on his neck. I put my hand on it by mistake,' he answered, 'You leave Durno's boils to Alison. Didn't your mother tell you you weren't to put your arms about him, eh?'

'But I've always put my arms round Durnie.'

'Huh. You do what your mother says. Don't you let Durno be familiar with you.'

'As though I should!' said Jenny scornfully. But then she had been familiar with Durnie from her babyhood. She had sat on his knee while he told her the most astonishing queer

7

stories about fire-flaughts, and judgments of God out of
the heavens, and thunder-stones, and men who sank to
their noses in the snow, 'and not a dratted thing could
they remember after for a week.' And he sang astonishing
queer ballads about sailors and admirals, that seemed to
Jenny the very ecstasy of romance. But best of all were his
hands. Durnie's hard brown hands could do astounding
things. He had been shepherd at Boggiewalls for over
thirty years and Mr Kilgour valued him for his skill with
the lambs. All young things were safe with Durno—calves
and foals, puppies and kittens and ducklings, and little birds
out of nests, long-necked naked gorbals that he lifted out
for Jenny to see and replaced so tenderly that even the
mother birds did not seem to be alarmed. Grown-ups
exclaimed in wonder over Durno's way with young things,
but Jenny knew it was all his hands. Of course Grand-dad
and Maggie and her mother couldn't know. They hadn't
been carried, and lifted on to palings, and steadied along
the top of dykes, and caught as they swung themselves out
of trees, and made to skim over long heather and boulders
as though they were doing it themselves. So they couldn't
understand why young things trusted him. As for his face,
'He isn't dirty,' Jenny insisted to her mother. 'He's quite,
quite clean. It's just the colour that makes it look like that.
He's as clean, really, as Neil's pads when he hasn't been
out in the wet.'

Jenny in fact was so familiar with Durnie that what her
grandfather meant was quite lost on her; but the part of
her that was almost growing up said, 'As though I should!'
because that was how girls who were growing up felt. Really,
however, Durnie lived in her consciousness much as Neil
did, a part of the physical world, with whom she held a
happy animal communion. He did not enter the moral
order, and her mother's attempt to place him there ran
over Jenny as a burn runs over boulders, leaving them
untouched. Even the drop at Durno's nose gave her no
disgust. She used to play secret games with it, counting
under her breath to see how many she could count up to
before it fell, just as she did with the raindrops outside the
window when she wakened early on rainy mornings.

But though her grandfather's warning against familiarity made no real impression on her, she judged it wise, having a young animal's objection to discomfort, to change the theme; and she said, 'O, Grand-dad, that reminds me, who was Bella Cassie?'

'Bella Cassie? She was an orphan lass that was brought up with your father and your Aunt Mary. What d'you want to know that for?'

'Oh, *that* Bella. I forgot that was her name. *Her!* I know about her—Maggie says she was a gutsy lump.'

Kilgour gave his queer short grunt. 'Maggie had an ill-will at her, right enough. But give the lass her due—there was a lot of good in Bella—it wasn't greed but need that made her eat the way she did. She was an enormous lass—neither your father nor your Aunt Mary was small, but she, for all she was the youngest, was bigger than either. She would stuff anything down her throat—grain and bran and sharps—I've seen her stuff her mouth with chaff, and many's the sore stomach she had eating green berries. Nobody grudged the bairn her meat, but it was a strange sight whiles to see her hammering the food in at her mouth as though she were feeding a steam mill.'

'And what came of her, Grand-dad?'

'She went away. She was a shop-girl for a bit—a tobacconist's shop. Then she got married, away about England. What's put you on to Bella?'

'Durnie said—he gave me a message to you about her. Imagine it being that Bella! I didn't remember—he said when I asked that you would tell me all about her.'

'He said that, did he?'

They were crossing the stack-yard, and in the waning light the old farmer stopped, looking about him uncertainly. Then he moved a few steps and stood between two of the stone foundations on which later in the year the ricks would be built. A little plant of groundsel grew between them. Stooping he picked a head of it and stood for a moment crumbling it in his fingers. Then he threw the fragments down and said to Jenny:

'Bella Cassie's mother met her death just there.'

Jenny stared in the dim light at the crumbled weed.

'There? In our stack-yard? But how?—Do tell me, Grand-dad. How horrible!'

Kilgour was silent. At last he said:

'She was thatching a rick. She could thatch with any man I met, could Peggy. A great broad-shouldered woman she was, she could do a man's work, indoors or out, all came alike to Peggy. She was kitchen woman here before Maggie's day, but in the harvest she'd be out labouring with the best.'

'Yes, and the rick?'

'Well, she tumbled off—that's all. Landed on her head and broke her neck.'

'How horrible!' repeated Jenny. Her eyes went back in spite of her to those broken crumbles of groundsel; as though she were seeing a woman's broken body.

'Don't you hate thatching ricks here now?'

'It happened more than thirty years ago. The thack's been put on a sight of ricks in here since then.'

He stood musing all the same, though seventy years' familiarity with a savage and inimical nature left him unmoved by accidental death, on the life if not the death of the silent broad-shouldered woman who had fee'd herself to him thirty-three years before. She had made her condition, and he had kept it far beyond the bargain. Not only had her child come with her, but after the woman's untimely death he had given the child a home; till at the age of sixteen she had chosen her own fate. She had not come back, and now Kilgour thought of his deed in taking the orphan girl in as a matter ended and done with long ago. He had no idea that his act was about to return upon him, searching powerfully into the lives of himself and his children. So incomplete is every action at the time of its performance.

'Yes,' he said reflectively, 'a bairn that lived her own life in spite of you. Like a puckle tansies in a park.'

'Oh,' said Jenny, who had forgotten Bella, 'Durnie said to tell you—it's her, Grand-dad, it's this Bella'—she caught her arm through his again and came close against him— 'who's building—*that*.' She jerked her elbow backwards. It was too dark now to see, but Kilgour did not need to see. And Jenny knew. The miserable bungalow that they all hated was never completely from his mind. Not that it was a bungalow yet. A month ago the foresters had finished clearing the wood. Then the corner, that abutted on their piece of moor, had been fenced off, and amid the untidy litter of bark and jags of fir branches, of trampled grasses and ruts where the trunks had been dragged bumping on their chains behind the straining horses, the foundations for the house had been cut. And they knew that a lady from England was building a bungalow there.

'Eh?' said Kilgour.

'Imphm,' Jenny answered.

Shortly she continued, 'But it won't be so bad now, will it, Grand-dad?'

'How that?'

'Well, someone you know, besides a quite unknown person. Somebody you know wouldn't make it a freak.'

'Oh, you think that, do you?—You go in to your lessons, Jenny.'

'Well, anyhow, Grand-dad, you can jolly well tell her, can't you, when it's her, not to make a freak of it.'

'Can I?'

'You brought her up, didn't you?'

She said it with such solemnity that, not knowing Jenny, one would have thought her as ingenuous as she seemed. But a moment later her merry laugh rang out on the quiet night.

'You go in to your lessons,' repeated her grandfather.

'Aren't you coming? What is there still to do?'

'Nothing, nothing. In you go.'

She paused in the open doorway, looking back at his great form against the night.

'All right, and you go and have a good think about the house.'

Her soft teasing tones stole round him like small April rain. In the light from the opened door their eyes met. And both were flooded with a deep and sure content.

THREE

A Kincardineshire Family

He stood with his back against the grey stone house in which he, and his father before him, had been born—Andrew Kilgour, seventy years of age, six foot two in height, strong and shaggy as a carthorse.

The house was plain and solid, built to resist the blasts off the mountains and the battering of sleet. For months in the winter, snow lay piled about its doors, or its yard was filled with slush and mud. Bitter frosts came in April to blacken the buds and cold rains to delay the sowing. In the high fields the corn might lie unripened into November and then rot where it lay. The arable land was thin and scanty; but Boggiewalls grew only for its own needs; the black-faced sheep were more important than the crops; and wherever one went, on its sloping and uneven fields, one was conscious of the moor and of the hills. The heather was like a dark tide licking round the edges of the fields. At ploughing time it seemed to lick a little further in, so like was the new-turned earth to the brown hill. Between the fields were dry-stone dykes, tumbled in places, grey and lichened, and in one field a great rocky boss rose up, covered with whin and clumps of heather. They called it the hillock, and violets grew there in spring.

In spring too there were days as sudden and unexpected as those violets, incredibly blue, and sweet to the senses. In June the light was clear as crystal and the air like life; and on a hot day in August the blaze of colour from miles of heather, its heady fragrance, the hum of the bees that frequented it, swung together in sweet confusion to the brain.

Far below splashed the tumbling burn. The water sparkled like light and tasted cold and pure. The Kilgours drank their water neat and pitied those who required to contaminate theirs. Folk in towns didn't know the taste of water. Nor did they know the tang of air, nor the mountain clarity of skies at night. The Kilgours believed to a man that the clean sound natural things—pure air and water, the sound of burns and the smell of earth, and plain country food—were the finest things in the world. Not that they were bigoted in their belief. They were a laughing family, and a highly successful one; and perfectly able to appreciate the fleshpots. But, they said, the other is better, and made witty jests at their own expense for neglecting what they profoundly loved. Alexander, the second brother, who was a Professor of Divinity, was something of a connoisseur in whiskies. But then whisky was pure and sound, almost as natural a food as water itself; at any rate until the war. John, the third of the Professors, whose subject was Materia Medica, swore that the worst effect of war to Sandy was the defilement of whisky, and spiced his jest with a Rabelaisian list of ingredients to be found in the post-war stuff. David, the third brother and second of the Professors, was a connoisseur in printing and a collector of rare editions.

For out of this bare house between the hills and the tumbling burn had come a succession of scholars such as arises now and then in a humble Scottish home—sound men, country bred, strong in the pursuit of knowledge, upholding tradition and handing it on deeper and stronger than they found it, their lives rooted in the soil and in the past. Such men go out from their simple homes to the company of the wise and the great, enter a society to which they were not born, and adapt themselves to it by the sheer soundness of their nature and a courtesy that comes of right thinking and respect for themselves and others; and go back to their homes, completely unashamed of their origin and their people, without a trace of condescension, and take part in the old pursuits, discuss the old interests, as naturally as they eat the plain country fare in the stone-flagged kitchens.

The Kilgours were such a family. The father of these four men, of whom Andrew, now seventy years of age, was the first, had been a sheep farmer in a small way. The mother came of merchant stock, a woman of tempered steel, who ruled her sons and edged their ambition. Both died early; but not before they had shaped their sons' lives, taught them to live hard, to laugh at deprivation, and to leave unfinished no task to which they set their hand. They were powerful men, no bookish cast about them. When they returned to Boggiewalls they were still of a piece with its rough and noble strength. David, who taught classics at the Antipodes, came seldom; but when he did, the other brothers saw to it that they came north at the same time. The Gathering of the Pro-fessors, the people said; and on Sunday it was a sight to remember, the four tall men walking together to the Kirk, and filing slowly into the pew. Folk nudged one another, and whispered, 'Here's the Laird and the Pro-fessors.' They were proud of the Kilgours, who were, of course, proud of themselves, in a genial open fashion, knowing their achievement good and quite beyond the need of boasting: like a good harvest.

Alexander, in true Scottish style, was educated for the Church. At thirty-five he filled a Chair of Divinity. Two members of his Presbytery, before the appointment, were overheard to say, 'We don't want Kilgour of Inverald—he has far too acute a mind for a Professor.' And indeed Alexander, in a short while, had a wasps' bike about his ears. 'As bad as Smith o' Aiberdeen,' cried the critics. Alexander Kilgour, however, had not only the advantage of teaching ten years later than Robertson Smith, he had also the Kilgour habit of success in all he put his hand to. He retained his chair, silenced the mutterers by tact and suavity, and gave width of outlook to a succession of young Scottish divines. His urbane persuasiveness of manner, however, covered a true prophetic zeal. He was passionate for enlightenment, drunk on the word: though in this matter too the pre-war whiskies were the best. The ageing man would sit with brooding brows over the later distillations.

David, the third boy, was a serious youngster. Professors' wives invited him to tea and he went under protest, grudging the time. But they could not make him talk. 'Do you care about *anything*, Mr Kilgour?' said an exasperated lady.

'I have a passion for the Classics,' he replied. Later he taught in a Colonial University, and it was rumoured that to learn Latin in the Antipodes one must first learn Scots: which rumour did David an injustice; for though, like his brothers, he retained the broad vowels of his country speech, his English was singularly pure and correct—nearly as pure as his Greek. He showed a pretty wit in his reception of the rumour, maintaining stoutly that he upheld the good sound Scots pronunciation of Latin against the clipped English fashion. He fell readily into the Doric, however, when he heard the shibboleth, using it pithily and with humour; and he loved to recount a good Scots story, saying that for salt and subtlety these were unmatched, and, at their best, great art, in which, as in a perfect lyric, not a word could be altered. An admirable companion to the few, he hated social functions and had a countryman's carelessness over dress, attending his lectures in shabby old clothes and relishing his students' affectionate derision. Once he chanced upon a sheep farmer by the roadside and fell into talk. 'You're frae the Nor-East,' he said. And they talked of sheep and the ways of farmers. After a while the man eyed the Professor's clothes and said, 'Was ye wantin' a job?' 'I've got a job.' 'Ye're lucky.'

John, the youngest, was the most brilliant of all. Strong on logic, as became a Scot, he read for honours in Mental Philosophy, and carried off every prize and scholarship available in his subject. 'Ay, and he's gone to show them how to do things at Oxford,' said the glen; after which he served his term as an assistant Professor. But coming home for the Long Vacation, he said to Andrew, as he helped him to subdue a rearing colt that refused to be shod:

'I'm thinking of taking Medicine.'

Andrew, as head of the house, drew a long face. Sandy and David were called to council. But the mother said tranquilly:

'Your father doctored horses. A sick beast would have him out on a night not fit for a dog to be out in. To the furthest end of the parish if need be. Ay, and a sick bairn didn't often see me in my satin gown at the cheek o' the fire. It's an inherited attribute and we are bid not to quench the spirit.'

Doctor John remained an ill lad to argue with. He could hold his tongue too well. He would let his opponent talk the heart of his matter out, then demolish him with one well-aimed blow. Argument was dearer to his soul than doctoring, and his *Philosophy of a Physician* was regarded with profound admiration in the glen, though no one bought a copy.

Standing on this spring night beside the wing he himself had added to the old house, Andrew Kilgour did not review his brothers' achievements, but all they had done and become was present in his consciousness as part of the bedrock of being, the established and accepted order of things: just as the hills, though now barely visible as dark shapes against the sky, were so present, an eternal and accepted reality. On every side of him lay hills, the many-snouted Grampian range. To the south they formed a rampart up which the Pass road climbed. North was the wide Dee valley, into which their burn, by way of a larger tributary stream, found its course, and beyond that were hills again. Hills reared their angry crests to the westward, nosed along the east to find the sea.

Present also in his mind, though not deliberately reviewed, was the thought of his own son, Bill, who was killed in the war. The young Professor, the people had called him, saying that he would beat his uncles yet. And so he would, the old man thought. And Mary, his daughter, taken from school at sixteen, when her mother died, to keep his house, to milk and cook, feed beasts, rear poultry—how well he remembered Mary, already a woman grown as she seemed to him, purposeful, efficient, stable as a sheep-dog, neglecting nothing, scamping nothing, yet finding time, at any lull in the work, for the studies she had been compelled to drop. And never grumbling. In all the eight years she had kept his house, he had never heard Mary utter a word of regret for the life she had hoped to follow. But when her chance came, she was ready. Like a shot that goes clean to its objective, Mary had marked down her widowed sister-in-law. Milly and the child will come here, she had said at once. Well, he need never regret that—he had got Jenny. Nor had he demurred at the time. He had let Mary go her own way and she had been justified. Give Milly time, Mary had said, she'll fall to it yet. Mary had an amazing way of making people do what she believed they could do. So Bill's young wife and the baby girl had come to the farm; and Milly had made her mistakes, but he had suffered them quietly, believing human kindliness to be better than efficiency. And behind Milly was always Mary—Mary dashing home for week-ends from the University, putting things right, helping Milly to find her feet, never, he knew, letting Milly down before her father-in-law or the serving people. Never claiming her old place as mistress of the house. She had been completely fair to Milly. Now, completely fair, just, efficient, tireless, she ran her little typing house in London.

And Jenny—Bill's child, true to breed, making for knowledge like a cockerel for his dish. Another long-legged cockerel spanging across the corn-yard.

But with the thought of Jenny the bewildered pain that had kept the old man out of doors suddenly sharpened. He remembered the day when he had most fully realised how much he loved her, and how powerless he was to ensure her happiness.

FOUR

The Laird

On a day in March, a year before, Jenny and her grandfather were burning heather on the moor.

Spring, Jenny thought, was come indeed. She sniffed the pungent odour of the burning, and was glad at heart as she always was when fire was lighted out of doors—fire, not the kitchen wench they usually made of her, but a free spirit, running under the sky. Suddenly she started back, as the smoke came acrid in her eyes and nostrils.

'Grand-dad,' she cried, 'it's blowing the wrong way.'

Kilgour had already seen. He was gazing into the sky. Jenny followed his gaze. There, against the infinite unclouded blue, she saw two plumes of smoke, that from their own fire and another, drift together and mingle in one. Fires were burning high up on the watershed, where the Pass road gleamed, the smoke of which blew steadily upon a south-east wind straight for the spot where they had lit their fire: but the smoke of this second fire streamed up, strong and hasty, before a wind from the north-west. North-west lay the snow-clad wilds of the Cairngorms, and so swiftly had the wind whirled out of the spaces of the sky around their awful corries, that the lashings of its tail still eddied in the contrary direction.

Instantly both man and girl saw what the change of wind would do. Their fire, that had at last taken a sure hold upon the heather, was running steadily upon a young larch plantation.

Now were Jenny and the old man caught in a timeless absorption of spirit. Each forgot that the other was there. Fire, earth, space, the wind—in labour with these elemental things they became as it were dissolved into their own elements. Memory was gone, and consciousness of

selfhood, and all the intricate coils of living. They drew
back at last, by common consent, for the fire was mastered.
With blackened hands and faces, smoke in their clothes and
hair, they stood and watched the hot smoking earth, where
fluffs of flame still burst and twigs glowed unexpectedly.
They became again aware of themselves. Their eyes met,
and they smiled.

'Ay, Jenny,' the old man said, 'that gave you a fright?'

'Fright!' said scornful Jenny.

'Well, it frightened me. I'd have been wae to see the
plantin' go.'

'Oh, yes!' Jenny said quickly; and she looked at the
small trees.

The words conveyed little of what passed between the
two as they spoke. As their eyes met, and turned to range the
brown tumble of hills and the width of sky, and met again,
with the look in them that only love can bring, both were
filled with a content too deep for words, or even thought.
To be at one was natural to them as breathing. The man
was seventy and the girl fifteen, and from the time she could
walk she had shared her grandfather's pursuits, at first in
small ways suited to her small endurances, but increasing
in range and magnitude as she grew, until now the look
that they exchanged, on this clear spring day beside the
charring heather, carried in it the consciousness of all that
they had seen, smelt, heard, known and undergone upon
the moor.

For the sheep farmer, seventy years of intercourse had
made the moor sit to him more closely than the most supple
of garments. He knew every sheep path, each spring, bog,
peat hag, each gash torn out by cloudburst and the deep
riven tracks of burns in spate. He knew the mires left by
the snows, and the treacherous footing when snow covered
the myriad inequalities of the ground. He could find his way
when clouds blotted out the landmarks, and on clear days
could tell each blue peak and gully in the distance; and knew
how far each was away, although sometimes they seemed no
farther than a sheep would stray on a winter afternoon, and
sometimes more distant and evanescent than a cloud. He
knew the foxes' holes and the lithe motion of the adders,

the swoop of the kestrel, the white hares that vanished up the hillside like a streak of smoke. He had made his covenant with the moor: it had bogged him and drenched him, deceived, scorched, numbed him with cold, tested his endurance, memory and skill; until a large part of his nature was so interpenetrated with its nature that apart from it he would have lost reality. His love for it indeed was beyond all covenant. Like his love for Jenny, it had the quality of life itself, absolute and uncovenanted.

The shift of wind sent the workers now to the further side of the burn, where they lighted another fire. In a while Kilgour said:

'Jenny, you must guard this yourself, lassie. There's naught to fear. The flame won't leap the burn. And yonder's old Durno on the Grassdams roadie—you can call him to your aid if so be you think fit. I'm for up the hill a bit, to ca' that two-three sheep down to shelter. There's a storm clapped in atween yon pair of winds.'

The air was still clear, and a pure and radiant sun, now near its setting, touched the easterly hummocks and hill-tops to a benign beauty. But Jenny did not think of disputing her grandfather's prophecy of storm. She watched him climb the stony path and heard his words of command to the dog Neil, then turned and shouted to old Durno, waving her arms and running to meet him. Eyes less accustomed than Jenny's and her grandfather's would hardly have made out the old man's figure on the moor.

Durno sniftered, though the sun was pleasant, and the one eye that was always red and watery seemed to leer as he said, 'Ay, so your grandpa was wrong for once about his wind.'

'Well,' Jenny said, 'Grand-dad couldn't know there would be two opposite winds at the same time, could he?'

'What way couldn't he? He knows a mortal lot, your grandpa.'

'I know he does. Everybody knows he does,' cried Jenny, laughing and battering off Durno's advances with a quick little movement of the hands that she had. She didn't care any longer to be *kittled*, though she knew quite well that Durnie was never so happy as when he had something soft and warm under his hands. She had cuddled up to him like a lamb herself when she was small. He said things to grown-up people that were as gritty as gravel in your shoes, but to the child he was always as patient as an old dog; so now she felt no more resentment when he tried to tickle her under the arms than she would have felt had the dog put his paws on her shoulders and licked her face; and she beat off Durno, laughing and saying, instead of 'Down, boy, down,' 'What a tease you are, Durnie!'

'Ay,' said Durno, 'I'm a grand hand at it. And so the bit plantin' near came by a mishanter. Imphm.'

He shuffled with his clumsy feet among the blackened heather stumps. Feathery white charrings eddied about his legs and the pungent smell grew stronger.

'Ay, that's what comes of owning a bit of grun', you see,' he said suddenly. 'Cark and care, fire and destruction. The Laird would lay his head easier on the bolster were he a landless lad the like o' me. The muck that sticks upon the soles of my boots, that's a' the grun' I own, or am like to own till the grun' owns me.'

'You seem quite merry about it, anyhow, Durnie,' said Jenny, still laughing as she jumped up and down on the smoking ground beside her friend.

'O ay, ay am I that,' Durno answered, leering with his watery eye. 'I thank them that's above, I've nae been ill to serve wi' the good things of this world. I'm like to die contented in the same station of life whereunto I was born.'

'Well, I suppose we all do that,' said Jenny. 'Except the people you read about in the newspapers.'

'I'm nae that sure,' said Durno. He lifted his head, which had been bent towards the heather he was stamping, and took a long stare hillwards to where the farmer could be seen driving on his sheep; then he caught the edge of his sleeve between his fingers, drew the sleeve slowly from elbow to wrist across his nose, and dashed the drop that had been hanging there to the ground with a contemptuous shake of the arm.

Jenny was so much accustomed to Durnie's snifter and the drop at his nose that she gave no thought at all to the movement.

'Grand-dad's coming down again,' she said happily, with the little smile playing at her mouth.

His stately figure was between her and the sun. He was all dark, with a bright glow of light at the edges. The half-dozen sheep ran in front of him, Neil trotted soberly at heel; and behind them was the moor, seen, like the man, dark against the light of heaven, yet it radiated, like him, by the very light that showed its darkness.

Durno scratched and said, 'Ay, Laird, you're plantin' the trees and other folks are ruggin' them down.'

Kilgour said, 'Ay, Durno, that's a bonny evening. Taking the trees down, are they?'

'They're to be cutting on Monday—the Ardie wood, I'm told.'

Kilgour made a little movement of tongue against teeth.

'So! Never the spruces? Well, well, they say he needs the cash.'

'Ay, and the Hairyhillock's to go.'

'What's he cutting that for? He'll get little enough for that. Poor stuff. Spunks and kindling. Boxes for kippered fish.'

'Ay, but he needs the cash.'

'He'll plant again, one hopes.'

'There's talk o' building.'

'Building?'

'Ay, that'll sort ye, Laird. A curran pink shanties on the Hairyhillock head.'

Kilgour mused, looking in front of him, and said nothing. Durno asked at last:

'You're saying nothing to that, are ye?'

The other returned to himself and said, 'I'm sorry to hear it, as well you know.'

'Oh, I know fine,' answered Durno, 'but what you've such an ill-will at I fail to see. Folk needing a bit roof to cover their heads—it's but natural.'

Kilgour, musing still, scarcely looked down from his great height upon the snivelling fellow yapping at his feet. He knew Durno's humour, and rarely bent himself to take note of it. He said, however, 'If they knew how to build, they might build and welcome. But these fancy houses—'

Jenny interposed to say, 'But you know, Grand-dad, you always talk as though any new house were a crime. And people must have houses, as Durnie says. I suppose it's really people, and not houses at all, that you don't want to come.'

'Well,' he answered, smiling down on her, 'perhaps that's it. We couldn't do with many more folk hereabouts, could we?'

'Oh, lots. The place is big enough.'

'Ay, but, Jenny, put your lots of people in, and the place 'll shrink. The place 'll shrink. It'll be another place. And they'd be other people. 'Twould be the end of us, my lass.'

'Graves and things,' Jenny said. She tilted up her small golden-brown face, with the look on it that wiled the heart from him, so sedate it was and yet so full of mischief, as though she were a mountain burn in which one found a pool as still as crystal, but live with the sparkle that told of energy suppressed and soon to be again released.

'There's more ends than the grave,' he answered, smiling. But to-day not even Jenny's piquant face, so lovely, so arrogant for all its prim withholding of laughter, could lift the heaviness that had settled on his heart. The full content of early afternoon had gone. As Durno spoke, fear had silently invaded his citadel; and now he walked on, disturbed and reluctant, paying no heed to Jenny's chatter with the old henchman. As he walked he cast his mind over all the years of life he had spent in that moorland place—glad, grateful memories arose on every hand. His own boyhood came before him—a sense of space, of freedom, of days without beginning or end and hills remote as Paradise. Everywhere that he turned his eyes he had ranged with his brothers. Each hill had become earth. Long days of herding came to mind; weathers too, for they were of the very stuff of experience. When he looked this way and that, a blizzard, a cloudburst, a hot sweet still day of summer, glanced from among the shifting clouds of memory; or clear starlight in the lambing season, or darkness howling in their teeth as they fought their way across the yard.

He saw again his father, patient and grave; and old Bess,

the earliest collie of his recollection. He had thought once that Bess was as much part of the established order of life as the great crag on Clochnaben, and as indestructible. He could not picture Bess without seeing his father: except in the most vivid of the pictures, when she would trot, one day, intent and solemn, down from the drove road that crossed the watershed; and give one short bark at the shed corner, and walk with Olympian assurance to the kitchen door. The boys would be at the door before her, shouting, 'Mother, here's Bess!' and their mother would come eagerly out.

'Ay, Bess, lass,' she would say; and to the boys, 'Your father'll be home within the six hours, laddies. See that all's straight for his coming.'

Their mother was always right. No matter how many days their father had been absent, crossing the mountains with his sheep, when Bess trotted home he was never more than six hours later.

Farmers had motor-cars nowadays, Kilgour reflected. He had seen a man sit in his car and herd home the cattle he had bought at the Mart. His heart warmed to the thought of Bess, bounding ahead of her master over the mountain paths, and changing her pace for the last quarter-mile to the gravity that befitted her tidings; and calling Neil, he spoke to him, putting in his voice all that old gladness of boyhood.

Then he himself had learned the drove roads. He remembered the first time he had gone with his father, climbing up and still up to the Pass, while the great crag changed shape behind them and new peaks came into view; and then the summit and the leagues of undiscovered country that were lying there below him, blue and incredible as talk of death. He was an eager lad, doing a grown man's work long before he had attained a grown man's strength and stature. At sixteen he was his father's shepherd, trudging two miles an hour with the flocks to the southern markets. He knew all the hill roads, each pass that crossed the mountains. By the time he was nineteen he had absorbed his father's stock of wisdom; and at twenty he was master of the farm and the herds. At the first meal after his father's funeral, the mother had stood, erect and stern in her black clothes, behind the dead man's place.

'Andrew,' she said, 'you will sit here.'

It was the first time in his life that he had resisted his mother's authority. Something fierce and unprecedented surged within him. All his life he had sat in the same place at table, looking straight to the hill and the sky beyond; and at every meal he ate he raised his eyes and scanned the weather. He could not change his seat. Lifting his father's great chair, he carried it to his own place.

'I'll take his seat, mother,' he said, 'but I'll keep to my old place.'

At every meal since he had raised his eyes in the old way to scan the sky.

In later years his brothers had come to him, one by one, and thanked him for the sacrifices he had made to enable them to reach success; for his quiet faithful life at the old farm. He had grasped each friendly hand in his own dark, knotted and hairy fist, and had felt grateful for their understanding and appreciation. But deep within himself he knew that he did not merit their praise. His had been a chosen way of life no less than theirs. He could never have gone out as they had gone, leaving the tumble of brown hills and the sheep paths and drove roads of his youth. To these his fate was thirled. Soon there was no man in all the valley who knew more than he did of the country; and because his knowledge was always accurate and willingly shared he became an authority among his neighbours. He had skill too with animals and acted—like his father before him—as vet for many miles around; and when he came to wed, his wife was the one for a merry crowd about her and great tables spread with plenty. There was no woman in all the land her equal for setting a company at ease or making a platter of oatcakes seem to each man the meat and drink he liked best in this world. So the pair throve, loved and honoured by all who knew them. At times Kilgour's temper was masterful. 'He's a dour billie to deal wi', yon loon o' yours,' a purchaser had said to his father when the young man first negotiated a sale alone. 'Ay,' answered the dying father, 'he's a formidable lad.' But the chances of life, combining with the integrity of his nature, had kept this temper noble by giving it room. When he laid down the law, it was a law so wise, beneficent and just that to question it would have been idleness. His reputation and his honour were equal; and the dominion that he held over his neighbours was expressed in their familiar name for him, the Laird. Even *Lairdie* had no rancour, but a shrewd affection. Behind the name lay the people's realization that this man had identified himself with the land, he and it so interpenetrated that neither was wholly to be understood without the other.

After a time, when the estate on which his farm lay was broken up, he bought his own land, and the bond between him and it grew even closer.

So as he glanced around him on this spring evening he was reminded on every hand of a life filled with honour, in which he had done the thing he delighted to do. Like other men he had had sorrows: his wife had died twenty years before and his only son was killed in war. But here he was, at the age of seventy, possessing abundantly the things that most men strive for in life—honour, love, health, material goods, power over others. Yet he sighed and felt heavy at heart as he walked, for what Durno had told him grieved him immoderately. He looked at the woods that were to be cut—already he could see buildings there, and the thought that created them made them appear vile and slim, the jerry-built fancy houses that he hated; and it seemed to him that he was looking at the end of an order that he loved. In this valley, beset with moor and hill, had been fought one of those centuries-long battles between man and elemental forces that go to make an age. As man's knowledge of the elemental forces grows, he alters the weapons and mode of attack by which he compels the universe to yield him what he wants; and a new age begins. Kilgour was dimly aware that such a period of growth was in being around him; that men were advancing from knowledge to knowledge at an incalculable pace, and that the relation between man and the great elemental background of his existence was changed. *His* life had been lived on the assumption of an immediate personal experience, through a finely tempered body, of elemental nature. Winds, waters, signs of the sky, shapes, colours, smells, sounds, the feel of things—these were to him, and the men like him, no pattern on the edge of life but the instruments of living. Their own senses, their trained observation, their memory, were the weapons they opposed to the old antagonist Nature; and through countless generations they had fought such a battle as had brought them not only the means of livelihood, but a respect and love for the antagonist they had come to know so well. On these conditions there had grown up a life that had its own dignity, and power, and joy.

As the old man brooded, looking up and down the valley, his eye resting now on the homesteads, now on the brown ploughed fields and the bare hills, now on the surrounding sky, he might have been the encompassing mind that gave the country and its people significance. In him at that moment the life of generations of men like himself was focused, at a focus point of pain. One mode of life had proved itself, achieving worth and beauty; and he saw that it was like to perish.

'It's a fine site for a house,' Durno's voice said at his side.

Kilgour's dreaming mind came back to itself and he looked critically at the wood that was to fall, judging. Yes, a good site. The houses would stand high to the sun, with the burn dashing over rocks below, and a long view to the hills. But who would wish to build in that remote spot?

'We had much to thank the railway for,' he said.

'The railway?' said Jenny. 'But it's miles from here.'

'Ay, and so we were suffered to remain ourselves. When they built the railway, these passes over the hills fell out of use. But it seems they are to be the busy roads again. Yonder'—he turned his head towards the Pass—'that was the high-road once from south to north.'

'Yes,' cried Jenny eagerly; 'Macbeth came that way, didn't he?'

'They killed him at Lumphanan,' said the old man. 'He must have crossed the river at Potarch. So your uncles told me once. But which of the pass roads he took to reach the river they did not know. Ours perhaps.'

'Oh, I wish it could be ours,' cried the girl.

'And they said the great Montrose came over the passes there like a sheep dog. Like my father's old Bess.'

'Who knew the way home herself,' Jenny said, smiling her happy smile. 'And came quicker than any man could walk.'

'They used to say Montrose did that.'

'Well, who do you think will come by it next?' said Jenny, turning to the Pass with eyes that shone.

The focus in Kilgour's consciousness narrowed suddenly to a point intolerably sharp: Jenny, welcoming life with that look in her eyes. And here was a life whose validity he had proved, but which he could not ensure to her.

'You'd better come in, Durno, since you're here,' he said abruptly, 'and have a bite with us.'

Already Jenny had bounded ahead, racing the sheep dogs.

That was the day whose memory came so savagely upon Kilgour's consciousness as he stood, more than a year later, knowing now that a house would be built and who was to build it. And again there came upon him the sense of an order ending. Who will come next? Jenny had asked. Here was her answer. He remembered Bella's ungoverned and blatant nature, her terrible vitality, how she had snatched at life, careless what she destroyed so long as she could grab what she had coveted. The demons of speed and din would come with Bella, the dreadful tides of a new and incomprehensible life, that had already, he knew, submerged the cities, would rise pounding against the hills.

FIVE

Bella Horrida Bella

In July Bella came to Balbriggie Inn to watch the progress of her house. In the same month Mary Kilgour came home on holiday.

At the farm, little buzzings of talk had risen many times over the house. They described it to one another at supper-time, they ran across to look in the evenings and on Sunday afternoons examined it carefully and in detail. Then the work claimed them again till someone said, Saw you ever the like—the walls up already! Or, Well, really, these blocks of cement—just the rubbish of stones, who would put that in a house? And the excitement began again.

Mary pursed her lips when she saw it, and said, 'Is it as bad as that?'

Mary was a strongly-built, straight-backed woman of thirty-six, with a pleasant open face and eyes that missed nothing. Her hill country breeding showed still in her straight carriage and elastic tread. She walked heel to the ground, calmly, without flurry in her movements; and her senses were keen and unspoilt by the confusion of sounds, smells and movements she had constantly to be sorting out in London. Jenny and she walked across the fields arm-in-arm, talking eagerly. They were always together when Mary came home. Mary had to be shown where the nests were this year, and where they shot the fox; and Jenny had to hear about the manuscript on lilac paper, tied up with lilac ribbons, that Mary's staff had had to type, and about the funny Frenchman who came to the office.

'There's a funny shy boy painting up above Balbriggie,' said Jenny. 'You know, the kind of picture that you don't know what it is. It's all right in Paris and places like that, but rather odd when you know it's the Grassie Burn and Craig Clach, don't you think?'

'Like a manuscript that came in last month,' Mary said. 'I couldn't make head nor tail of what it meant. The words were all in the wrong places. But the author thanked me for the beautiful typing, so I suppose he meant them like that.'

'And I found a dead fawn under that cliffy bit of rock, Aunt Mary. The loveliest black feet it had—oh, and its eyes were pecked out.' Mary could see the fawn too, she had found one lying just like that when she was a girl. They looked at each other, and both felt the same sweet pity for the spoilt life.

Then they had to visit the farms and the cottages. Mary sat in the ingles and drank black tea that had stewed for half-an-hour on the hobs; or went formally to high tea in the front parlours, with crochet eight inches deep on the tea-cloth, the best china, butter in silver dishes with glass insides, girdle scones and oven scones, crumpets, shortbread, three kinds of cake and three of jam, all home-made, besides the meat roll, eggs, and chutney in glass bottles, that began the repast. Mary didn't mind which she had, she was the same to everyone, and the people said, 'A fine lass, Mary Kilgour, no London airs yonder.'

The farmers said, 'Ay, Mary, you havena found a man yet, away about England?'

Mary laughed light-heartedly, and answered, 'I'm much too busy to think about that, I assure you.'

So dismissing one conversational stand-by, they turned to another and said, 'Your old chum Bella Cassie's setting up house beside you.'

'So I see,' Mary answered, speaking lightly. She tried to change the subject, for she couldn't bear to talk in public about things that mattered so much; but it was of no use. They all described the house to her, and she took it with a good grace and told them honestly what she thought about such houses.

'Your father's not as you would say pleased about it,' they commented, and she said, 'No, he's not.'

Bella hadn't been two days at Balbriggie before she came

to the farm. She floated into the Kilgour waters, magnificently large, flying the scarlet scarf, a small gentleman in
tow on either side.

The time was evening, and hay harvest. Jenny and
Maggie, the squat square-faced kitchen woman who swung
along at an incredible speed on her diseased hips, had been
working in the field all day. Even Mary, though London
had softened her muscles and taken the endurance from
her skin, had donned a cotton overall and worked for
awhile with the rest. Now they sat at supper, jesting
among themselves, filled with the delicious lassitude that
comes of long hours in the open and physical weariness
that has been just not too much for the strength. Kilgour
sat in his accustomed place and lifted his eyes to watch
the weather. Old Durno, bidden to stay, since his services
were wanted later, bantered with Maggie and had boiling
water tipped over his ankles for his pains; but he paid no
attention—he was too old a hand to be disconcerted by
that. Mary showed her scratches and laughed at the blisters
on her hand. Jenny's mother, Mrs William Kilgour, in her
eternal grey jersey—this year's, last year's, sometime's, the
jersey never changed—thrust back the wisp of hair that
straggled on her shoulder. She had given up caring for
her appearance, her hands were ingrained with black, and
rough as graters. Mary still held out her blistered hands;
Jenny's mother looked at them and for a moment almost
hated Mary, because she had used her for her own escape.
Yet she had been so fair, so just, deferring to her always as
mistress, but without a hint of patronage. 'I couldn't have
done it,' thought Mrs Kilgour. And who could hate Mary,
with her open happy face?

Mrs Kilgour smiled, a small hidden smile. Jenny would
escape too. 'You'll need some cold cream to that,' she told
her sister-in-law; and her momentary annoyance died away
in the sense of happy contentment pervading the room.
The clean scent of clover was still in their nostrils, the sense
of strenuous work accomplished, of hunger satisfied with
food, relaxed their bodies. It was a moment untouched
by anything but its own fullness. No one thought. Their
minds were drugged and easy. Mary forgot London, Jenny

forgot the untasted world, the old farmer himself forgot the passing of his kind. Only Durno remembered, not released from consciousness of himself, like the others, by the effort they had shared. He still sat grinning in his little self, and thought of the bungalow that was now growing fast, and of how it irked the Laird, and nursed gleefully his own deep sense of satisfaction over its progress.

It was just then that with a snort from the horn a car ran into the yard. Jenny jumped and cried, 'Oh, a car the colour of mustard. With scarlet spokes. Do come!' They crowded to look. It was like an advertisement hoarding in the dim summery pleasantness of the yard.

'Well, I declare,' said Maggie, 'it's yon Bella Cassie.'

A little hum filled the room. Its tranquil air went quite away. Maggie swung across to open the door. Jenny gave Mary's hand a squeeze and whispered, 'Oh, what will she be like?' Mr Kilgour held out his hand to Bella.

'Ay, Bella, so you've gotten your way back again.'

Bella cried gaily, 'Hullo, Lairdie! You weren't looking to see me, now were you? And here I am.'

The kitchen was full of happy sounds. Chairs were placed. Bella wouldn't go to the parlour. Maggie cleared away the dishes. There was a cheerful bustle of welcome. The wood fire crackled. Everyone was a little excited. The bungalow came silently in and sat among them.

Though it was eighteen years since they had seen her, there was no mistaking Bella now. She might have walked out of the back door last week, with her cheap cardboard case finished to look like leather, and her impudent copper hair puffed out in front. There was less hair now, and a good deal more flesh, but it was the same ruddy face and the same style in the walk. Bella carried her curves like a queen.

'Mercy!' she exclaimed, gazing round the room, 'there's the same old mutton.' She pointed to the china effigy of a sheep that had stood time out of mind above the plate-rack. 'Some mutton by this time, eh? And you, Mary, quite the lady now, aren't you?'

'Quite,' Mary said.

'Oh, well,' Bella commented, sweeping her glance over

Mrs Kilgour's humble jersey, 'it's much better, a married woman for mistress in a place like this.'

'Oh, much,' Mary replied. Her chuckle was discreet. She kept her smiling eyes on Bella, and in them was the sublime Kilgour appreciation, so sure of its own worth that it could relish the crudest joke against itself.

Bella was still looking hard at the drab dragged greyness of Mrs Kilgour's jersey. She herself was smart as paint in her scarlet cap and scarf, and she carried a scarlet bag that would have held her head had the idea ever occurred to her of hiding it. As it was her head stayed very high and splendid on her shoulders and she looked round at the room in a sort of wonderment that it was still the same. She remembered exactly how the polished pot lids hung, reflecting the panes of the window, so that a dozen dwarf windows, complete with screens and tiny geranium plants, seemed to live suspended in a remote high world along the wall; and how the stone flags under the linoleum bulged in places, making smooth, worn bits in the pattern; but for all its familiarity the room was quite unlike her memory of it, fading away indeed out of all recognition into a shadowy nonentity. Nothing seemed real until she let her eyes rest again on the magnificent old man who sat opposite, his white hair still abundant, his bushy brows accentuating the light that dwelt steadfast in the eyes, the dark hairy knuckles laid on the rests of his chair and the feet set apart, solid upon the floor.

Solid—that was the word; but in the queer nonentity of all her other impressions of the room, Bella had the sense of his solidity as not a physical attribute: as though all that he stood for—his rock-like stability, industry and honour—had solidified into a symbol in the likeness of Andrew Kilgour, farmer at Boggiewalls, among the Grampian mountains, but so much more real than the actual man who bore that name that Bella shuddered. The body in front of her was a solid body by virtue of existing not only on the plane of the actual present but also on that of Bella's recollection and of a timeless and impersonal idea, and it presented itself to Bella's consciousness with an impact of such force and hardness that she recoiled, and the harpies that had darkened her journey from the Inn to Boggiewalls flocked impudently back around her head.

She withdrew her eyes from Kilgour, almost with an effort, and cast them round on the two men who had come in her train. One of them, little old Dr Parks, who came every summer to the Inn, sat with mouth drooping open and inane eyes fastened in adoration upon Dorabel.

Instantly the squareness, the sharp solidity of Mr Kilgour began to melt. He was a man like other men again. Dorabel smiled.

She flaunted her two male champions as she flaunted the pink tiles of her bungalow, a slap in the face to the man who had ruled her childhood.

For it was Andrew Kilgour as much as anything that had brought Bella Cassie back to Balbriggie. He had no sort of comprehension of the depth of Bella's revolt against the plain wholesome life that satisfied his instincts so entirely. He had given her, as he gave his own children, sound training, the means of clean living and healthy knowledge; and he had been profoundly sorry for her when she wanted a different kind of life. Bella at sixteen, snatching angrily at the vulgar excitements and ostentations for which Boggiewalls had no place, moved him to a grave pity. He had no idea that her nature demanded a kind of life quite alien from his; that art, of which he knew nothing, and the sparkle of busy intercourse, the headlong rapture of creation, though higher in degree, were yet the same in kind as the things that Bella craved. 'Poor silly lass,' he said of her, when he heard how she hung from the door of the tobacconist's shop, catching at every straw of approbation, trolling out songs in the public street, getting herself talked about . . . Her pink-tiled bungalow, slapped down at his very doors, was a defiant self-justification.

But as she sat reviewing her company at Boggiewalls, no one could have guessed how excited she was.

Maggie rocked on to the other hip and nudged Durno with her elbow, whispering, 'Hold on your hair, here's a jollification'—a truer word than she knew where the old reprobate was concerned: but *his* satisfaction was as little to be divined by the company as was Dorabel's excitement.

Or less. For he sat sardonic in his corner, munched oatcakes and drank burbling from his saucer; and wiped the drop from his nose with his elbow as he always did; but the eyes glittered in his old toad's face. ·

Dorabel's excitement was profound. She had no more respect at thirty-four for Andrew Kilgour's notion of life than she had at sixteen; nor had she any intellectual grasp of the validity of her own. But she knew that it was good, and she meant to show it him. Yet deep and recalcitrant lay a respect for the man of which she herself had hardly gauged the strength. In a smothered corner of her nature it had all the tenacity and strangeness of love. She explained that to herself, not as the effect of his nature on hers, but by reason of a secret belief that had come to her by rumour and been accepted and enlarged by pride. She believed, on the strength of a rumour that had been current for a short while, that she was the child of the man who had kept her and brought her up out of pity. That her mother was his servant woman she was well aware, and he himself, when he heard of her own marriage, had sent her a wedding ring, saying that it was her mother's and that her mother had run away from a husband she had grown to hate and taken refuge in service. But with the arrogance of youth that thinks it knows so much, and the blindness of a preconceived idea, Bella had decided that the story was a lie; and she longed, far more deeply than she understood, now that a section of the world had approved her, to win his approbation also and in time his acknowledgment.

So she descended on Boggiewalls fearful, and elated, and obstreperous, with a male in either hand and a pink bungalow at her heels; and already little Dr Parks was serving her well. His gaping adoration had acted as a solvent for that terrific solidity that had alarmed her. She laughed, an easy triumphant laugh, and cried:

'Mercy, and Maggie! You and me were always at loggerheads, eh, Maggie? The same smart tongue, I bet you have.'

'Oh, I have aye my answer,' said Maggie dryly.

'And some answers there were no questions to, I'll be bound. Well, you didn't none of you expect to see me coming back a swell, I'll take my oath for that. A swell in my own right, too. Perhaps you think because I married Gib Munro—'

Mary knew that Gib's name would come up sooner or later. Already at the tea-parties they had said their say. 'What way did he take yon woman for a wife?' they asked her. 'Did ever you hear the rights of that, Mary?' 'I suppose he wanted her,' Mary said, with her pleasant quiet smile. 'A queer match for the minister's son, anyway,' they answered. Mary had the same unperturbed look on her face now as she said to Bella:

'And so Gib's made his fortune, I hear.'

Gib can make his fortune, she was thinking. Gib married Bella—that finished him as far as Mary was concerned. He could build all the shoddy toy houses he liked—made a good thing of it too, they said. He could afford to put one up for his wife. Gib, exploiting the gulls. Vulgar shanties for the jerry-built mob. Funny to think that Gib had been her play-fellow—but then he married Bella. A barbarian, then.

Mary, being a Kilgour, despised the barbarian; but having also the natural goodness of the Kilgours, as of apples, or well water, had no sourness in her mind. Her feeling was merely part of the apple flavour, the perfect Kilgour assurance that their values were right.

'Oh, Gib's made his pile,' Bella said. 'But I'm better known than Gib, I can tell you that. I'm Dorabel Cassidy. But perhaps you have heard me sing?'

'No,' Mary answered, 'I haven't.'

'What a pity,' Bella said.

Mary caught the eye of the young boy who was Dorabel's second swain, and surprised in it such a black fury that she looked at him a second time. Nice boy, she thought. Good hands. And ashamed of his company. But why is he here then?

'Barney,' said Dorabel, laughing as though it were a splendid joke, 'is just mad with me for dragging him in here. He lives in a tent and cooks a sausage by the light of Nature.'

Jenny smothered a gurgle against her grandfather's shoulder.

Jenny had all this while been watching the incursion with a frank curiosity. When Bella clamoured, Jenny drew her brows together in a way she had. When Bella praised herself, in a loud and cheerful voice, Jenny threw back her head and laughed; but catching the eye of the young man who cooked a sausage by the light of Nature, checked in her laughter and turned her cool and appraising eyes on him. He was the funny shy boy whom she had seen painting pictures on the hill. Confused, he flushed and looked away. Solemn and unwinking, Jenny continued to stare at the lady.

'And what about the strawberries?' Dorabel was asking. 'Great feeds we used to have.' She made succulent noises with her lips.

'And cream, of course!' Her face was all creased with enjoyment. 'I just adore eating. Don't you?' And she flashed round on Jenny.

Jenny was still regarding her intently with a grave and unmoved countenance; but at the question she broke into a radiant smile that transfigured her small clear face. 'Of course,' she said. And she wrinkled up her nose and squeezed her eyes shut as though she were savouring the delicious fruit upon her palate.

In a few minutes she bore in a bowl of the fruit and a jug of cream, and served the guests. Her bare brown legs thrust into canvas shoes, one bare brown arm half raised as she poured the cream, and her cool head inclined over Dorabel's hot splendour, she had a sheathed and virginal grace that enchained her Aunt Mary's eyes. In the year since she had seen the child, how lovely she had grown. 'She'll soon grow up,' Mary thought; and the thought gave her a pang. How unspoiled she was, and how she made Dorabel's peony bloom seem vulgar. There was no kinship at all, Mary felt, between the girl's enchanting grace and the woman's loudness. The afternoon would pass, taking away for ever its accident of meeting, and no meeting was possible between two such natures but the accidental. Mary did not think these things, but felt them, deeply, below consciousness, where the dark tides run that have danger and glory in their running.

Other eyes than hers were on the group formed by the woman and the girl.

'Beautiful, beautiful,' fell from the enamoured doctor's lips.

Mr Kilgour heard, and thought the praise was for Jenny. His eye lit and he grew warm with pleasure as he always did when she was praised. 'Sir,' he said in his deep resonant bass, 'she had a grandmother who presided over a heel of cheese as though it were a whole kebbuck.'

'Sir,' answered the doctor in his senile pipe, 'she needs no ancestry.'

'I should think I didn't,' Bella said, catching the words but unaware of what had gone before. 'But who said grandpapas? I'm Dorabel Cassidy, that's who I am. You can chuck all this stuff about the family tree. When you can sing like me nobody cares a hoot where you come from, I can tell you that. Up here of course you like to know all about a person, who he is and all that, but in the world, I assure you, nobody cares. When you can sing like me that's enough.'

The old farmer saw the mistake into which he had fallen but was not disconcerted. He answered, 'You had a grand voice, Bella, we'll need to hear it again.' And turning to the boy in the corner, said, 'Sup up your berries, lad. You look as if a sup more cream would do you good. Come in about as often as you like while you're camping. There'll aye be a bottle of milk for you, or maybe some cream. Won't there, Milly?'

'Barney,' Dorabel cried, turning also to the boy, 'you should do a portrait of Jenny. Do her and me together.'

'I don't do portraits,' said the boy, frowning.

'I declare!' said Dorabel. She caught up her bag and ran her fingers through the papers. 'See here, isn't that a portrait? And jolly good too, I say.'

They looked.

The paper showed Dorabel. Her mouth was wide open, a sheet of music was in her hand, her bosom swelled visibly as one watched. One looked in alarm to see if she was actually as ample as that.

'No, I don't like it,' said Jenny's mother, who was excited by the thought of a portrait of Jenny.

Jenny said gravely, 'One of my great friends is an artist too—Sammy Low.'

'Jenny!' breathed her mother.

'Well,' said Jenny calmly, 'he is a great friend of mine. He drives the Balbriggie bus,' she explained, turning to Bella, 'and he has painted two panels in his bus with views of Balbriggie House. Jolly good views they are. Quite recognizable.'

The boy gave her a stare of savage scorn. She returned his stare, coolly insolent. But a moment later she flung back her head and laughed. It was a hearty resounding laugh, not in the least a laugh of mockery or irony. She was not laughing at him, nor at Bella, nor yet at Sammy who painted panels of his bus, but simply at life, that contained them all and was so absurd and so delightful.

'Well,' said Bella, laughing with her, 'I'll tell you what, you'll come to dinner with me at the Inn some day. Barney, you shall come too. Get a decent meal once in a way. You, too, Mary,' she added.

Mary had a dry little smile at her lips. Not superior. Just amused. As she watched Bella gobble her strawberries, while Jenny poured more cream in her plate, and Dr Parks said benignantly, 'Sweets for the sweet, Dorabel,' Mary was thinking, 'Just the Philistine one expected her to be.'

'How good of you,' Jenny's mother was saying.

Good! Mary thought. To invite us to dinner! And she felt a sharpness on her palate. The barbarian in his own place, yes; one could shrug and be amused. But in the place of the Kilgours, never!

Jenny crossed the room and gave Bella back the sheet of paper; and Bella held it at arm's length and smiled joyously at herself.

'See,' she said to Jenny. 'That's me too. And that. That one was in the *Sunday Gavotte*.'

The two heads were bent together quite a long time over the pictures. 'What appalling egotism,' Mary thought.

'Ay, Bella,' boomed Mr Kilgour's great voice, 'you're not telling us about this spunk boxie you're setting up on the Hairyhillock head. They tell me your husband's the contractor. I thought better things of Gib Munro. Has he forgot his good Scots birth that he thinks yon knap-at-the-wind'll stand the kind of winter we get up here? Yon walls'll rumble down like a heap o' screes.'

'Oh, Gib knows what he's about,' said Bella. 'Gib's houses are all over the place.'

'Imphm.'

'Grand-dad means,' laughed Jenny, 'that that's what yours will be. All over the place.'

'It's going to be a great wee house,' said Bella.

They all talked. They all had something wise to say about a house.

Except old Durno. While the others talked he leaned cautiously forward, a furtive smile upon his loose-lipped mouth, and grabbed Dorabel's bag, which had fallen unobserved to the floor. Maggie after a time saw him gloating over the bundle of papers he took from it. He stuffed them in his pocket when he caught her look.

'Hey, there,' said Maggie, giving him her accustomed nudge in the side with her elbow, 'that's the lady's. You canna take her orrels. She's nae like us ordinary bodies. She's a singer.'

'The law of property's the same, for singers and a' other body. Findin's keepin'.'

'Findin' your granny! Hey, Jenny, Durnie's poochin' the lady's proclamations.'

Bella swirled round and dived in the old fellow's direction. She wrenched her bag from his hand and the bundle of papers from his pocket. Durno gave a sort of chuckling acquiescence to her actions. He resisted just enough to be able to relish her determination and strength. He sat smiling under the boiling crest of her indignation, as she fluttered the papers and arranged them.

'Where's Barney's sketch?' she demanded.

Durno's smile died out and he insisted stolidly that all the papers were returned.

'There was a two-three tumbled out on the floor,' he said. 'You might thank me for picking them up to you instead o' swearin' at me like a carter at his jaud. It'll be on the floor still if it's nae among the rest.'

'Oh, Durnie,' cried Jenny, jumping suddenly on his knee and battering him with her hands, 'you put one in another pocket. I saw you.' She began to wrestle with him. But for all her quickness she could not reach the pocket.

'Jenny,' said her mother, 'must I tell you again that you are not to touch Durno?' Mrs Kilgour looked sidelong at the artist, biting her lip because he was witness to Jenny's familiarity with the old serving-man.

Jenny paid no attention. She was still struggling with Durno, panting in her excitement. 'You hold this arm,' she cried to Bella.

'Me?' Bella answered in a loud passionate tone. 'Angels in white clothing wouldn't make me touch him.'

Her loud voice made a sort of explosion in the room. They were all silent and looked at her.

Still warding Jenny off, Durno put a hand to his ear and began with a slow caressing movement to pull its long lobe. His ears, uncovered now from their overlapping bonnet, were seen to be large, and across one of the lobes there ran a whitish scar. Jenny remembered how she had sat on his knee, long ago, and stroked the scar as he was doing now. 'How did it come, Durnie?' she had asked, and he answered that his sweetheart bit him. A funny kind of sweetheart, Jenny said. Sweethearts *are* funny, he replied. Who was your sweetheart, Durnie? A lady the height of your grandpa, he had answered. Jenny laughed till she thought she would never stop, to think how funny Durnie must have looked beside a lady the size of that. Is your sweetheart dead now, Durnie? Ay, she's dead now . . . But it wasn't the dead one that bit me, Durnie had said afterwards. Oh, can you have two sweethearts? Jenny asked. It's whiles been heard of, Durnie answered. Jenny had said that night, 'Oh, do you know, Durnie's had two sweethearts!' And her grandfather just gave a short funny little laugh. But that was long ago, when Jenny was a silly little girl.

To-day she sat on his knee and watched him pull the ear-lobe with the scar; but she watched too for a chance to reach his pocket, and did not observe the steady way he looked at Bella. Bella glared back.

But only for a moment. Suddenly she broke into resounding laughter.

'Let the deuced thing go,' she cried. 'Barney'll make me another. He'll do you after, Jenny.'

She turned her back on Durno, gathered up her gloves and prepared to go.

'Durnie, you have it in your pocket,' said Jenny in a low tense voice.

'Not me.'

'Will you cross your breath?'

Durno crossed his breath.

'Well, let me see that paper. There, that one I can just see.'

He pulled a paper from his pocket and spread it out for her.

'You haven't any other?'

'Not me.'

Jenny slipped from his knee and accompanied the visitors to the car. Singing as she returned, she cried, 'Isn't she fun?' Mary raised her eyebrows, then stretched her arms with a lazy grace. 'It's good to have your body tired and not the rest of you,' she said, as though annulling the whole encounter with Bella. Nevertheless she looked after Jenny with a keen, considering look.

Jenny went to the scullery and helped Maggie with the dishes.

'Maggie,' she said after a while, 'Durnie wouldn't tell a lie, would he?'

'Auld Durnie? He's coorse, auld Durnie. Coorse as a rotten neip.'

'But he wouldn't tell a lie? Not after crossing his breath.'

'Jenny,' said Maggie earnestly, 'do you see me?' She raised her back from the washing basin, that Jenny might see her squat ill-favoured face. 'You wouldna call me bonny, would you now?'

'Really, Maggie—you know I have never thought about it.'

'Well, I'm *nae*. And hark you here, Jenny, the man that would make up to the likes o' me is nae to be lippened to. Put not your trust in princes nor in them that says fair words to a foul face. Durnie—trust him wi' your tattie skins but nae your tatties. He's a coorse auld brute.'

'I don't believe he took it at all,' Jenny said, with an obstinate lift of her chin. 'What would he want it for, anyway?'

He wanted it for this. In his own home, late that evening, he sat talking with his sister Alison.

'Ay, Alison, you havena seen that same lady from London you were sae sair mad about. O ay, you saw the scarlet cap of her whizzin' by. It's a wonder she wouldna stop and speak and you that keen to get a word with her. Here, just you have a keek. That's the lass.'

Alison looked soberly at the stolen picture, which he guarded jealously in both his hands.

'Ay,' she said, 'so that's the lass.'

'A fine rantin' woman, Alison. Worth a' that Kilgours thegether, Professors and the lot. You'll nae cow yon one in a hurry, the Laird'll nae get her over his knee to whack her hurdies. A grand stummack to her and teeth with the strength of a bull.'

He put up a hand and fondled his ear.

Alison stood erect before him. Her lined old face had its habitual sweet reserve. She spoke without fear and without emphasis.

'You leave her alone, Jamie. Let the lassie be. You've wrought her enough evil, surely. Let her be now.'

'Heh? Me wrought her evil? What evil have I ever wrought the lass? Eh?—But you've a puckle queer notions in your head, Alison. It's maybe evil, by your way o't, to be alive at all.'

'Life is the Lord's,' Alison answered.

'Then what ails you at me for having given the lass her life, eh? Ay,' he said, his face darkening, 'life and an honest name. Nae corner work yonder. Cassie? She's a Durno, as clear born as yoursel, Alison. Nae Cassie about her but her hurdies and her bold red lips. Yah'—he made an inarticulate sound of hatred between his mumbling jaws—'take my bairn from me, would she?' And he mouthed curses as ugly as his working face.

'Jamie, Jamie,' said Alison, laying her hand gently on his shoulder, 'you loved her well but you loved her to both your perditions. Let her lassie be. She hated you too sore for any patching up to come to good. You'll have to meet her at the Judgment Seat and see what peace 'll come of that afore you dare to claim the Durno in the girl. Peggy—may God in His mercy deal with her—Peggy cast off your name and your remembrance and your part in her bairn; and when you came on her again—'

'Ay, ay,' he interrupted, snarling out of a black mouth, 'are you setting up for God Almighty Himself?'

'May He pardon my presumption,' Alison said. 'Whiles I think I am all the God Almighty you will give heed to. But face you Peggy first at the Seat of Judgment, ere you think to break her stern decree and win the child.'

Silence fell between them. The old man smoothed his paper and gloated over Bella's face.

'I know you hanker after the lass, Jamie,' said Alison after a time, 'as I do myself. We're auld bodies and we've none belonging us—we'd like right well to see one of our own come in-by and sit down by the fireside.'

'Speak for yourself,' he snarled.

'Jamie,' said the old woman after another pause, 'you were a right merry young chap once, the best of company, never a cross word for anybody.'

'Ay, till you weemen began your nyatterin',' he said.

SIX

Dinner-Party

Evening was still as the page in a book. The small burn made five separate sounds.

Bella's voice rose into the silence, singing. She sang because she was happy, and was happy because she sang. Her splendid body made her feel happy, so did her powerful lungs and her throat; but best of all was the thought that at Boggiewalls she had been a success. They had been struck by her, she could see that. Wouldn't she show them, these Kilgours! Her big jolly face was creased with enjoyment. This was what she loved—people, plenty of people, and still more people, and all made happy by the exuberant life in Dorabel. But those Kilgours, what a breed! Jehovah by their way of it said I LABOUR, not I AM. Horrible deity, making the earth in his own image. If you're not industrious, you don't exist for them. And mind you, they like it.

Vividly the days came back on her now. She remembered the early morning tasks—carrying milk-pails, carrying water, feeding hens. Then the long trudge to school, in every sort of weather. Often there were eggs to carry to the shop, and bags of groceries that the children brought home upon their backs. Then an endless succession of jobs—washing dishes, making up the hen's meat, dragging branches from the wood, chopping sticks. The very smell of the stick-shed came back. She saw it, a dim low place with an uneven floor of beaten earth. The cheese-press was at one side, giving out a sourish odour of drying cheese; and over the saw-stalk, to and fro, to and fro, Bill and Maggie drove the two-handled saw. Bill whistled as he worked, or jested with Maggie in clear boyish tones; and always he stopped the movement of the saw just before they had sawn their log through, and with a little uncertain rasp the

saw worried out a new notch and the steady rhythm began
again. Sometimes Andrew himself looked in and said, 'Is't
piece-work you're on, or by the hour?' and the rhythm of
the saw would quicken. Then Bill took the long trunk, held
together now by little more than the underside of the bark,
and raising it in his strong hands rapped it sharply on the
end of the saw-stalk—knock, knock, knock. At each knock,
with a sharp crackle of sound, a log broke off and bumped
to the floor; and Mary from her corner caught them and
chopped them for kindling; or with a dull thud they fell
where Bill flung them on the big pile that was waiting for
winter. Bella could hear the thud, and the sharp insistent
crack of the kindling wood under Mary's axe. Mary wielded
the axe with a quick sure movement of the wrist, on and
on, silent for the most part, completely satisfied. But in the
other corner of the shed, silent too, but silent from a sense
of powerlessness and despair, another child was crouched.
Her sullen hands took the potatoes—an insane multitude
of potatoes—one by one from the pail of water, and cut
away the earthy skin, and gouged out the eyes, and one
by one dropped them in the iron pot. On and on, on and
on. She knew she was the one spot of discontent within the
shed. In a short while Bill and Mary would go in and bend
absorbed above their lesson books. Or Bill would be away
over the moor, peering and seeking, finding out all he could
of the ways of birds and insects. Finding out—that was his
passion. Mary's passion was arranging—organizing things,
getting them in their places. But Bella wanted colour and
lights and music and dancing. And cities. Cities crammed
with people. Noise and movement, not the eerie desolation
of the moor. Well, she had had them, and in rich measure.
She could smile at a stick-shed.

   She smiled, humming against her full red lips; and meanwhile her restless fingers were roving amongst Barney's
possessions. Brushes, pencils, saucepans, underwear—she
teased her way through them all, tossing them out of place
with a jest. The tent was pitched on the brae above the Inn.
Dorabel had not been there a day before she scooped up boy
and tent together into her greedy palm. She squeezed paint
out of tubes as though it were an essence of life that she must

not miss. In much the same spirit she had crammed oilcake down her throat in childhood. Her inordinate appetite for food had been indeed an inordinate appetite for experience, that she, and those around her, were equally too ignorant to direct into its proper channels. Even now, though she had discovered many new modes of experience, life ran most readily for her in the worn channels. She grabbed, and gulped, and stuffed, because in her youth, life was not to be trusted, but coerced. Its surest rewards for her were still the physical and the immediate.

So, full of cream and a jolly, good-natured contempt, she watched the boy's quick pencil.

'Me again?'

The sketch showed her licking cream from a spoon.

'Christopher, what a fattie!'

It was a merciless caricature. Into it the boy swept his disgust with himself for biting her apple. But she took it with such unfeigned delight that he liked her more than ever.

'Mercy,' she cried. 'Do you suppose I don't know I'm greedy? If I don't look out I'll have a figure like the gasworks. But what's the good of cream unless you eat it?'

He replied (and the thought his own words called up was like a bar in the symphony of silence and enchantment that filled the evening): '*Therefore are feasts so solemn and so rare.*'

'What's that mean?' Dorabel questioned, playing from the wrong score. Then she laughed. 'That's the way I was brought up, I tell you, all right. You too, I suppose. Here's a plum. Wash your hands now. Say thank you. And be good for a week. Lord, what a way to live! And a week after: Mind, you had a plum last week—be good.'

'It is one way of life, of course,' Barney said, still drawing busily. He had had his plum, his family had let him have this sketching holiday, then he must be good for a week that was to last, he felt, all his life: he must let himself be trained to teach drawing, be 'art master' to a pack of boys. He had to earn a living, hadn't he, and repay his people for sending him to Art School? They took it for granted he would teach, and had no idea at all of his revolt against their gentle tyranny. He would have died sooner than confess to anyone that this was the first time he had gone on holiday apart from his family. Yet the next moment he found himself telling Dorabel.

'Good lad,' said Dorabel. 'I bet you're fond of your family, all the same? I knew you were! So'm I, you know. Of these Kilgours, I mean. But then they want you all to be one sort. Now you and me, we're different.'

'Some devil made me, I think.' The symphony of solemn feasts, of thin green skies and the falling notes of water, was rent now, the wrong score was predominant. In it were angry bars of contempt against Dorabel who thought that he and she were of one spirit, and a fiercer anger against himself for despising her. He crumpled his sketch and tossed it away. She picked it up.

'Well, don't cast it at that old fellow's feet,' he said.

'Me cast? There's a difference between theft and a free gift, my lad. I'll make a free gift of my belongings to James Durno when he grows a second pair of ears, not before. Did you see it, Barney? Did you see that mark across his ear? I never dreamed it would show like that. After eighteen years.' She bared her sharp strong teeth. 'I did that, Barney. I bit him. I got my teeth clean in.'

The boy's face expressed his deep disgust. He said nothing, brooding with his chin between his hands.

'Well, he kissed me, filthy beast. I'd as soon meet that man as I would a corpse rotten from the ground. I loathe him.'

'I suppose it was your first kiss,' the boy said, looking up. A dull flush spread on his brow.

Dorabel's laugh pealed through the quiet evening. 'Go on, I was sixteen. What's the old fellow to me, anyway?' she added, smiling on the boy; and she stretched her arms with a movement lazy and ample as the sea. It surrounded and engulfed all the Durnos and Kilgours of the world, leaving only Dorabel riding its crest in careless supremacy.

Already he was drawing her again. To catch that movement, its fullness, its complete *Dorabelity*—that was it. Here was a woman wholly herself. In catching her identity he would catch his own. He worked with an intent absorption.

'Me again?' cried Dorabel. 'Well, you are a lad.'

From that day on he had only one subject: Dorabel, and still Dorabel; as though in reading her riddle he would read the riddle of himself and of the universe. He drew her all day long. He followed her about, watching her, seeking the passionate core of life in her that blazed with such abandon. But his pencil could not swagger, its line could not dart to heaven, nor base itself broadly enough on earth, to capture Bella. He drew her with feet planted apart, with leg crossed over the knee and thighs like pillars, with bellowing mouth; he drew her shoving food down her gullet, and spitting raisin seeds from her lips.

She laughed at each, and appropriated them all. He made a movement to retrieve them, but gnawed a lip and turned away.

'Let them go,' he said to himself, 'they're only trials. But I'll do one yet that you won't get a hold of, by Jove.'

Aloud he said, as Dorabel sat arranging her spoils, 'Portraits of Celebrities at Different Ages.'

'Can't have that,' Dorabel said. 'There's not a single picture of me sooner than seventeen. Not even a measly snap. That's what comes of growing up poor. A cast-off. There were pictures taken of Mary and Bill all right. Dear lambies. Sailor collar and velvet bonnet. As good as gold. Oh, I'm not caring. Only these "Different Ages" stunts are rather jolly, don't you think? If they were ever to ask me, I'd have to say—Oh, I'd say, Childhood unmentionable. All records suppressed.'

Barney took his pencil and began to draw. In a while he handed her the paper.

'Beginning to your collection,' he said.

'Me?'

'Imphm. Age four or thereby.'

The child sat square and solid, legs thrust apart, she possessed the ground by the very way she sat on it. The shoulders were set, mouth gripped upon cheeks that bulged with food, the fists were crammed. Truculent eyes looked straight into the years ahead.

'Mercy,' cried Dorabel, 'did I look like that? What a joke!' She gloated over the picture, and showed it off at

Boggiewalls. They all crowded round to see. Maggie shoved an impatient head under her master's arm.

'Tut, Maggie,' said he, but held the picture down so that the squat serving-woman could look.

'My certes,' Maggie exclaimed, 'what way did he manage yon? Had he a photo?'

Old Kilgour handed back the picture to the artist. 'Well, well!' he said. But he said it with an amused and open smile. Bella laughed too.

'They think that's art,' said Barney with a bitter thrust. But his face too wore a smile—a suppressed smile of triumph.

'You've taught me to draw,' he told Dorabel later on.

'Me! I don't know a thing about it.'

'I know. But by just being yourself. Don't you see what it's meant to me? You've never "sat" to me, you've never posed. Do you think I care though you're greedy, and drink too much, and swagger about like a high wind? Or laugh'—he added, as her laugh broke loud across his words—'without intelligence or choice. Do you suppose I care? You're the first person I've met who has the courage to be absolutely sincere. You don't give a fig for rules of conduct, or whether it's done or not done. You can't think what it means to me that you were brought up under the same code as I've been. And there you are—the code just doesn't exist for you. No principles. No prearranged scale of values. No manners. The egoist simple and supreme. Oh, I know it's nothing new. But you see, I never met it before; I didn't believe it was real. You've given me just what I needed for my art. See—I couldn't draw like that before. Lifeless conventional stuff. Like—you've to get hold of that before you can create.'

'Well I never,' said Dorabel. 'How you do talk.'

One day Dorabel's husband, Gib Munro, arrived. He too came over the Pass in his car; and stopped to pick up Maggie, who was trudging home to her mother's house. He recognized Maggie, though he had not been in the place since his father's death, fifteen years before, and even called her by her name. Maggie came limping home at night in high feather.

Mr Gilbert Munro was affable and workmanlike. He rated the workmen soundly because the house was not further on, and said, 'Bless me, Mary, you're not a day older.' The tone paid the compliment, but his appraising eye suggested, 'You're never out of the bit.'

'Well,' Mary said, 'you've changed, anyway.'

'I should hope so,' said Mr Munro, rubbing his hands.

Mary's face remained smiling and her voice light; but something darkened far within, like the darkening on the face of a deep pool in the forest. No one knows that it is there, nor why its face has darkened.

Mr Munro also continued to smile.

'A good while since we used to squat in the barn and philosophize,' he continued, without a trace of embarrassment. 'We had some high-falutin notions in those days, hadn't we? Dorabel cured me of that. What realists you women are, to be sure. Here was I, creating a fine fancy kingdom—young man's paradise and all the rest of it. She brought me to earth with a bump, all right. She's a great girl, Dorabel. No nonsense about her. Take things as they are and get the most out of them. Don't waste your life crying for what you'll never be. Be what you are and use what's there. That's Dorabel's creed, and, I tell you, it gets you there all right. We've had a merry spin along the road.'

Bella appeared, Jenny laughing at one shoulder, the stark-faced boy at the other.

'Another poor young devil she's putting guts into,' said Mr Munro, glancing aside at Barney. Then he winked to Mary. 'She'll teach him all right. In her position there are always lots of fellows after her. Hear her sing, you know. She's fine on a platform—looks well, pity you couldn't see her. Paints, does he, this youngster? She'll knock some sense into him. These painting lads have a heap of nonsense in their heads. Can't see life as it is. All distorted, upside down. Coated with inhibitions, as I was. She'll send them flying. Like sunshine making the Johnny cast his greatcoat, don't you know. We had a pretty cold upbringing in these parts, hadn't we, Mary? Needed an inhibition or two to keep us warm.'

The shapes that swum in the black pool moved again.

Vanished into a darkness too profound to fathom. As though
one might drop through and go on falling without end.

Mary asked—with her head up—'I hope you don't regret
your upbringing?'

'Well!' he laughed. 'Not since I had Dorabel to help
me out.'

'I wouldn't alter an inch of it,' said Mary with a sudden
passion. 'I had the happiest childhood in the world.'

'And an equally happy adjustment to the world afterwards, I suppose?'

'Equally happy.'

'Come on, Mary, be honest. Confess you had a lot to learn
and a damn lot more to unlearn when you left this place.'

'To learn, yes. Of course. To unlearn, nothing. Nothing
whatever. Why should you expect me to deny my place and
my people? My tradition? I think it's the loveliest tradition
on earth. I'm proud of it. I wouldn't belong to anything
else for worlds. I hope it may go on unchanged for ever.'

'And very nice,' said Mr Gilbert Munro, applauding.

Mary rarely lost her temper. She merely said, 'You're
the perfect modern barbarian, Gib.'

The modern barbarian. No sense of the past nor regard
for the future. No responsibility towards either. Slaps the
shoddy house down, destroying the continuity of a tradition,
spoiling the heritage for those that come after. And Mary let
her eyes rest on the house—inimical eyes, that harboured
the enormous and implacable resentment of those who
have grown into possession of what they value and cannot
understand why anyone should take it from them.

He wasn't like this once, she thought. He had ideals.
Bella's made him into this. A smoulder of shame ran
through her—the old feeling of dull unreasoning shame
that rose in her body every time she thought about Gib.
Sometimes at night she used to awake shivering and think:
How could he have married her? How could he? Bella
Cassie, that lump. But next day she worked harder than
ever. Gib had no more place in her life. He wasn't her kind
after all. Now, as she met him again after fourteen years, she
realized how right she was. Gib was, most perfectly, all the
things she despised. Realist? she thought contemptuously.

Opportunist, rather. And smiling there in such complete assurance. Amused by Mary, as Mary ought to be amused by him. Would have been amused elsewhere. But not here. Not in the place of the Kilgours.

At breakfast the following morning Andrew Kilgour said, 'Tell that young man Munro to come along some time. I've a lot to say to him about his house. I'll tell him what it'll be like, come the New Year.'

Jenny looked up from her porridge with a gay derision. 'You're *much* too late, Grand-dad. He's away. He left last night. A house a day, you know—that's his allowance.'

Kilgour grunted.

'You don't think them worth more than that, do you?' mocked Jenny from a solemn mouth.

The next day Dr John Kilgour, the professor of medicine, with his daughter and her children, came over the Pass, on their way to the mountains. What fun there was! What darling children! What a jolly bustle! How they ran, and shouted, and carried trays of food! Jenny chased the children round the yard. The dogs barked. Everyone was delighted.

Dr John was as tall as his brother, but slighter, and stooped. His brows were shaggy, his eyes looked out from under them keen and unsparing. He saw Bella and turned his head, following her. 'Who's the Jezebel?' he demanded in his deep strong voice.

They took him round the end of the steading and showed him the house. He looked, and said nothing, while they described to him what he was looking at.

'Have it out,' he growled.

'Like an appendix, Uncle John?' Jenny said, putting up her laughing mouth.

'Huh. Malignant tumour. There's roots to that,' he added, turning to his brother. 'Once in, in for good.'

That evening Kilgour, coming in from the field, found his daughter Mary, in a plain black evening gown, laying the table for supper. Mary had revelled all day in the smell of clover, of bog myrtle, of pines hot in the sun, of bracken and moss, of the heady honey scent of bell heather, of peat smoke and new-sawn wood. She had gone sniffing in the stick-shed for the sheer delight of smelling. The stick-shed had a pleasant instancy in her memory, suggesting long untroubled busy days, filled with activity and endless content. She liked to be busy, to do things with her hands as well as with her head, to touch earth and grass and have a hill under her again; and it did not disconcert her in the least to eat in the kitchen, nor to lay the supper, now, though she was already dressed for Dorabel's dinner-party. She would have been just as happy in gingham as in georgette, but liked the georgette very well. Laughing, she showed her father her scratched and sunburnt forearms, that contrasted vividly with the white shoulders that her evening dress revealed; but she made no effort to cover the traces of her outdoor work.

'So you're gallivanting to-night, you and Jenny,' said the old man.

'If you like to call it that. I'd rather stay at home. But since Jenny's going—'

Her father gave his deep short grunt. 'Huh. What were you thinking might come over Jenny?' He added, and Mary knew quite well it was not of Jenny he was speaking, 'Poor silly lass, she's had her way. Still, for old times' sake we must show her friendliness.' He moved to the window and stood looking across the moor to Bella's house.

Mary stood beside him.

'Couldn't you have done anything, father?' she said. 'It's wicked, a thing like that pushing its nose in here. It'll never settle into this landscape. Never. I thought there was one place left where I could escape from the cheap vulgarity of the times.'

'So you don't want to change the old place, Mary?'

Mary said 'No,' and meeting her father's eyes conveyed in the single word all the affection that bound her, as it bound the whole Kilgour breed, to its home.

'I'm not sentimental over it,' she added lightly. 'I'm not saying I'd want to stay here always. I'm very happy in London, but I don't want to find this place different.' And looking once more across the moor, she said, 'Couldn't you have bought the land, father? It marches with yours.'

'In these times?' said Kilgour, shaking his head, with a

movement that made her feel a very little girl talking of what she did not know. But she was not a very little girl, and she knew very well. She knew just how hard it was to farm, and how little profit the possession of land brought to anyone; and how bad the season was, so that the turnip seed rotted in the wet ground and even the second sowing came up only in scattered patches. Mary had a vision of her father going slowly from drill to drill, dropping seed in the gaps from an old tin in which he had bored a little hole.

'And anyway,' said Kilgour, 'she'd just have got another bit.' He looked kindly at Mary. 'People like us would need to be buying the whole earth, by what I hear of it.'

'And that could not stop our tears,' quoted Mary, with a smile. She felt better and lingered on beside her father. There he stood, vast and stable as a hill. Where he was, the bases of life seemed sure. Then she ran upstairs to look for Jenny.

Jenny was standing in the middle of her room, clad in a soft green dress that her mother had made for her; and she looked so lovely that Mary stood by the door and gazed, feeling a fierce joy because the child was so gracious. Jenny gave her one of her sudden incandescent glances.

'Isn't it the loveliest frock?' she asked.

'Yes,' answered Mary; but she had no eyes for the frock. At that moment she felt a glad protective love for Jenny. She would have liked to keep her always as pure and virginal as she looked just then; and because she knew Jenny was too fiercely alive for that to be possible, she was shaken by a sudden storm of fear.

Jenny's mother came into the room and looked her daughter over.

'Mummy would like me dressed up every night,' said Jenny, laughing, to her aunt. 'Think of it, she would like me to go to town to school.'

'She's so wild,' said Mrs Kilgour. 'She rides the horses bare-backed in from the field.'

'Well, why not?' said Mary. 'I did that myself.'

'But not only here. On the Home Farm horses. And in the bothies with the men. And just look at her hands,' continued Mrs Kilgour, catching her daughter's hand and displaying its discoloration. 'Dipping sheep, hoeing turnips—anything you like out of doors. But will she undertake any regular task in the house!'

Jenny made a face. The pure virginal quality of her features vanished rudely. She looked lovelier than ever.

'But think, Aunt Mary, to town to school! And miss—oh, everything. All the lovely cold nights out at the sheep, and everything. When I can bike to Balbriggie and get down in Sammy Low's bus to Carnbannie.'

She went off singing at the pitch of her voice, but turned back to say to her mother, 'It's the loveliest frock, mumsie. Thank you so much for making it.'

'A sop to me,' thought her mother bitterly.

Jenny continued to sing and skip along the road.

'How excited you are,' said Mary.

'Excited!' scoffed Jenny. She asked presently, however, 'Will there be waiters and people like that? You know, I've never had a meal in a hotel. I've never had late dinner.'

Mary smiled indulgently. The child was ingenuous! But in a moment she hardened. Bella Cassie to be providing Jenny with her first taste of sophistication! And she said with a kind of scorn, 'Well, you won't meet much to trouble you in a country inn.'

Jenny said no more, and Mary failed to see that she was troubled. But in Bella's bedroom, where they took their coats off, Jenny blurted out, 'Really though, Dorabel, are there any waiters? I don't know what to do, you know.'

'You perfect dear,' Bella cried, catching her hands. 'Of course you don't. But there's nothing on earth to worry over. It's just the maids. Oh, don't I remember,' she cried, still holding Jenny's hands, 'the first time Gib took me out to dinner. "What're you dressed up in those togs for?" I said, as soon as he came to the door. "Taking me to dinner! Hors d'œuvres and things like that! I simply couldn't. You come in here, we'll dine here," I said. "There'll be no grandees to wait on us and see the wrong things that I do." And so we did. I raced out and bought all sorts of stuff. Out of tins, you know. Salmon and sardines, and a bottle of mayonnaise. And Gibbie made me sit swanking like a lady, while he did the waiter stunt. Oh, we went on laughing till midnight over it! But next night we went to the Palace—he wouldn't let me off. Lord,' cried Dorabel, throwing back her head and laughing in her clear extravagant voice, 'what a stew I was in! But there's no grandees here,' she added, looking down at Jenny again. 'See, that's how I looked then. And that's me in the dress I wore at my first concert.'

She began to show off a collection of photographs. It was for that that she had taken her guests to her own bedroom.

Jenny loved the photographs. She felt delightfully secure in Dorabel's presence: things were sure to be right. And downstairs they found Barney, in his baggy tweeds, silent as he always was in company. Jenny was completely happy now. She began to tease Barney, with whom she was already on good terms. She had poked through his tent furnishings as brazenly as Dorabel had done, and, unknown to her family, had learned to drive the rattling old two-seater in which he carried his stuff from place to place. She had even unearthed the landscapes he had been doing before settling in upon Dorabel, and had sat a long time with puzzled brows over their unlikeness to the familiar world. He allowed her to poke and question to her heart's content, and answered neither her comments nor her questions.

Dinner was an exuberant meal. Everyone in the room became perforce of Dorabel's party. Dr Parks was there, and there were also a couple of anglers, and the wife of one of them, a fat jolly woman; and endless laughter, and a succession of stories. Later, Dorabel turned on her portable wireless set, but cried impatiently, 'This old fogey's no good!' and next she set her gramophone spinning and a woman's voice rose splendidly above the voice that was still talking from the radio. Dorabel listened enraptured, watching Jenny and Mary. Jenny jumped up, clapped her hands and cried, 'It's you!'

'Yes,' Dorabel said. She stood over the gramophone with her right hand raised ('like an auctioneer,' Mary thought). 'A voice of purest melody,' continued Dorabel. 'Like syrup, isn't it? You know'—she tilted her hand—'pours from the soul.'

Jenny's face was quite grave, but behind Dorabel's back

she too tilted her hand with the motion of one who holds a spoon. Her eyes met Barney's, he scowled.

When the song was ended, Dorabel wound up the gramophone and began it again. This time she sang as well. One shut one's eyes and there were two Dorabels, diverging just enough to assure one there were two. One opened them again, hastily, in panic lest the two were really there. It was a drunkard's reduplication.

Still later they all went out, wandering across fields to visit Dorabel's house. The evening light had an astounding clarity. One saw every detail of the earth for miles around. Even the figure of the old shepherd crossing the moor was picked out clearly, as though heaven set its seal on what was habitually indistinguishable from the earth. Mary wished she were not in that noisy company, and wished the noisy company were not in that radiant land, and wished she did not feel so superior. But there it was, she did! And not erroneously, of course. These people didn't belong to the clean honest clarity of her mountains. She did. A mile away, in the golden transparency of the light, she saw quite clearly the grey house of Boggiewalls; and she knew that the racket of Dorabel and company would be distinctly heard through the still evening. She wasn't pretending that life here was perfect, of course. She knew well enough how mean and poor it could be, empty, and even vitiated when spirit did not inform its labours. But at its best—as in her father, for example, her whole family—how rich and satisfying, honest and sure a life it was, with its own fineness and dignity. And how she loved it and hated to think it might have to pass. Her father lived still in the old self-contained way of the days before transport. He mended his own cart-wheels and laid his own pipes for a water supply off the hill, and thought shame to be dependent on any man. And of course Mary realized that that mode of life was done for.

But though she had just disclaimed it in front of her father, she was indeed sentimental over her place and her people, and could not trust humanity sufficiently to believe that a new mode of life could at some future period develop character as strong and finely-grained as that of her own race. So in her soul she despised all who were not, like herself, resolute and reliant, with simple tastes and unspoiled appetites. Her years in London notwithstanding, she was a country woman still.

Suddenly a diversion occurred. Shambling through one of the half-built rooms they found the old shepherd fellow Durno. Dorabel screamed. Indeed he had startled her, coming on them unexpectedly like that. She grew quite passionate over it, drove him out with harsh threats, forbade him her doors. Durno wiped the drop at his nose with the back of a dirty hand and rubbed the hand on the seat of his trousers; and grinned as he went.

'Well, that's the old fellow gone. Now let's have some fun!' In an instant Dorabel had invented a game, they were all hopping across the rubble blocks that were lying untidily behind the house. Miss a block, you were in the water. Now you're off! Now you! You're drowned, you're out!

Mary felt superior about that too. She didn't mean to, with anyone else she would have played the silly game and been happy; but here she couldn't play. They were such shoddy things, these rubble blocks, not the good stone out of the land. And when the game was over, Mary wouldn't go back to the Inn. Why, they were half-way home, it would be nonsense to go back, and it was growing late. And—she thought but did not say—the walk home through the night, cool, clear, silent, disturbed by nothing but the floating fragrances of earth!

'But Jenny wants to come,' said Bella. Well, I'm not going to be a fool over this, thought Mary angrily. She laughed and said, 'Well, of course Jenny can go if she wants to.'

Jenny went.

SEVEN

Night Out

'Sing it, Jenny,' Dorabel commanded.

It was past midnight now. Jenny was drunk; a very little from the wine (which she had never tasted before) and a great deal from the excitement.

She sang as Dorabel told her to.

Dorabel had them all singing, as she had had them all playing her silly game. Nothing seemed silly while she did it. All was natural, as though life flowered so and in no other way; and fleeting and unregretted as a flower, the moment passed.

It seemed even quite natural to Jenny that Dorabel was planning what they were to do in London. Barney of course was going to paint. Jenny couldn't quite remember what she would do, but she knew she was to be there, and it all seemed perfectly right and delightful.

'But I must go now, really I must,' she said after a long time more. She couldn't exactly recollect what they had done in the interval. Only the room was full, quite full, of Dorabel. Going away was like pulling yourself out of the sea on a hot day, and you drenched through and through with the water. But Jenny knew she must go away.

'My dear!' Dorabel said. She came in front of the girl and caught her hands, pulling her to her feet; and stood so, swaying their linked hands in and out with a rhythmic motion. 'Of course you shall go. We'll have the car round, just in a moment.'

Jenny laughed at the thought of the car. For her, who walked, or cycled, the roads, at any hour and in any weather! As well send an aeroplane for the wild geese as a car for Jenny.

'But let's all go,' said Dorabel. 'It's such a night. Come out, all of you, and see the night.'

The night was like a thin mellifluous cascade of water. Jenny did not know the meaning of its magic potency. She did not know why she felt bewitched, and she did not understand the dark urgent horror on Barney's face. His car was there already by the door. Jenny's senses were like the wind in far, very far away forests and glades. Nothing was quite clear, but everything was being said, an eternal re-pursuit of meaning. She remembered having said she would go in Barney's car, if Dorabel would come too; and Dorabel had promised; but now she cried, 'We'll all go—we'll go up the Pass and see the sunrise.'

And everybody talked and laughed, and looked up at the vast naked sky.

'Jump in, Jenny,' Barney said, suddenly at her side. Without thinking, Jenny jumped. He pulled the door sharply shut and in an instant they were off, racing unsteadily among shadows.

'But Dorabel?' Jenny said.

The car continued to rock along the road.

'She said she would come if I went in your car,' persisted Jenny.

Barney laughed.

Jenny knew laughter only as delight. This laughter was different. The car swayed and rocked in it as though it were rocking through a sea; and Barney, sitting at the wheel, seemed to be driving it on not by its engines but by the compressed energy in his own body.

Jenny didn't understand. She thought the evening must have been as good to everyone as it had been to her. But to Barney it had not been good. He had realized quite clearly that he was in love with Dorabel, and his breeding revolted. In the raw life she offered he saw his own salvation from gentility; yet a sense of evil pursued him, he felt himself unclean.

'That was a hedgehog we passed just now,' said Jenny.

Barney could have killed the hedgehog. But Jenny didn't understand. Hedgehogs, galloping clumsily out of the glare of the headlights, were part of the infinite magic of the night.

Only she wanted Dorabel to share and enhance the magic. She looked back, leaning to the wind. But neither throb of engine nor the movement of a light indicated that the other car had started. And still Barney impelled his vehicle on with his whole body's passion. They were already far past the farm. Now, Jenny thought, the bridge. The narrow hump-backed Bridge of Dye. She heard the roar of the water far below. Her breath choked her as the car rocked between the parapets. Now switchback over the hump and away, up the long slope like a bird. Her excitement grew and grew as they raced. She forgot Dorabel and the other car. Utterly she had forgotten the farm. Their movement was the one reality. The black shapes of hills, the rutted road, changing subtly under their lights, the unfathomable sky, were no more than the framework that held this exhilaration, gave it position in time and space.

Now the wind freshened in their nostrils. They were up. Barney drew the car in close to the heather. There was an apple sharpness in the air, a sense of billows in the dark distances. The sky was like a wave that creamed above them and rolled them under. Their summit was far under seas and they walked heavily, as though their drowned bodies clung on them.

Jenny couldn't understand it, couldn't understand it at all. She had never felt like this before.

But far away, clear through the silence, came the throb of a car, thin and small.

'She's coming, you see,' Barney said.

Jenny breathed, 'That's good.'

'Blast her!' said Barney.

Jenny felt as though the world had been knocked out from under her. Her lips said, inadequately, 'Whatever for?'

'So you're in love with her,' said Barney.

'In love? How silly.'

'For God's sake, Jenny, get out again. Before she has you, hand and eye and mind, as she's got me. My God, you don't know what she is.'

'Well, if you don't want to be in love with her,' said Jenny calmly, 'why do you stay? And waste your time doing all these silly drawings.'

'Did you say waste?'

'Well, Grand-dad says so.'

'Oh, so you discuss me, do you?'

'Of course,' said Jenny, in genuine surprise that he should ask such a thing.

'Waste! But I forgot, your notion of art is panels painted in a bus with pictures of Balbriggie House. Quite recognizable.'

'Well, I'd rather have them than some of your horrid pictures of Dorabel,' retorted Jenny; and then paused in sheer astonishment. Whatever were Barney and she at each other's throats like this for?

'So you think they're horrid? Well, you'd better have a look at this one.'

He struck a match. 'Recognize it?' The match went out.

'It's a picture of Venus,' Barney's voice said through the darkness.

Jenny said, 'Oh.'

'Want to look again?' He struck a second match. His eyes glared out of dark holes in his head; and for the second time Jenny saw the likeness of a naked woman, superb, enormous, an incarnation of brute force. One foot was set forward as though her stride encompassed the earth.

'Recognize it?' asked Barney again.

'You said it was Venus.'

'It's a portrait of Dorabel.'

Dorabel like a sun-ripe fruit—and this Colossus, fat-bellied, with knees like clubs.

'Well, is it like her?'

'But I never saw Dorabel without her clothes.'

'I suppose you think that's clever.'

'No, I don't. Whatever are we quarrelling like this for, Barney?'

'I'm not aware that we are quarrelling. But if you can't see that that's a great picture—' He broke off and said indignantly, 'Wasting my time! Wasting! These sketches are the only things I've done that are any good. You might say all I did before was wasted, if you like. This one, for instance—it's immense. It's the best I've done. It's her soul. The principle of her life. The lust of the flesh, the lust of the eyes, the pride of life. She's like that—that's *her*. Cruel, utterly remorseless. She'll take you, and use you, and crush the life out of you, and never know she's done it. She eats you up—wolf, wolf! And when you hear her, Wolf! you rush to be eaten.'

Jenny listened. Life flooded in and swamped her landmarks.

'My God,' Barney went on, 'and you can't see the genius in that. When you're old, Jenny, that'll be one of the famous pictures of the world. I'll paint it yet—I'll turn that sketch into a picture that will make men shudder. The *Venus* of Archibald Barnet. Tremendous conception, they'll say.'

Again Jenny had the sense of life at flood. Universes not yet realized disturbed her brain. She had no words at all for what she felt, but she leaned her chin upon a lump of rock and cast down her eyes as though in an exquisite and troubling meditation. Barney remembered Rodin's girl with the chin on rock—as soft, as immobile as the stone Jenny stood. Then suddenly a convulsion shook him.

'The fool I am! The damned fifth-rate imitative double-blind fool. Thought I was original, did I? What a conception. What force. What genius. What a jest. Jupiter, what a jest! Barnet's *Venus*! Rodin's *Balzac*, to the life. Its very attitude. Oh, ye gods, what a jest.'

He snatched the paper from his pocket and tore it into shreds. The fragments floated into the night, that gave no sign of having received a scattered godhead.

Barney sat down on the heather and bowed his head on his knees. It was indeed a godhead that he had scattered on the night. In the sketch he had just destroyed he had tasted for the first time a clear Paradisal joy. He had escaped from his blundering art-school efforts into upper air. He felt free, and light, as though mortality had ceased to weigh on his creations. Now the ecstasy was gone. He was no god; and unless Dorabel made him a god, he was cheated. His young fastidious integrity insisted that for his art alone he had allowed himself to be bewitched. For his art he would allow all things. Yet he was in horror now lest this experience should turn out to be merely sordid, should befoul him and destroy his integrity. Jenny, standing there so still, so virginal, seemed to his tortured brain the pattern of his unravished self, and he wanted to smite, and break her too.

But now through the quiet night came the racket of the approaching car.

'Don't let's go,' said Barney, lifting his head. They could hear Dorabel's voice, the shouting of their own names.

'Don't let's go. We'll make a noise, and laugh, and shout, and Dorabel will produce an enormous amount to eat. Stay here, Jenny.'

An insane desire seized him to put off on Jenny the responsibility for his own decision. If Jenny would stay now, a spiritual emanation from the vast clear night, he would take it for a sign. He would go away. He would do landscape again. But Jenny, quite unconscious of herself as an instrument of destiny, and less spiritual than she looked, wanted noise and food. She wanted the full-blooded life that Dorabel held out, and she had none of the boy's fear at taking it. Only, her excitement was too strong and new for her to know yet what to do with it, and she spoke scornfully to keep herself in hand.

'If you think your silly picture of Dorabel is better than Dorabel herself, I'll leave you to it.' And she ran quickly across the heather, feeling that in another minute she might disgrace herself, and cry.

Dorabel had all the food that one could wish, and bottles of things, and coffee in Thermos flasks. The jolly angler was there ('though what's to come of my fishing to-morrow I don't know') and his fat wife, and Dr Parks praising Dorabel's idea in his thin reiterative tones. They filled the heaven with noise and the earth with the litter of their feast. But Jenny was suddenly too tired to live. She tried to eat, but the food was like timber in her mouth; and she tried to tell Dorabel that she must go home, but Dorabel was not listening. So she lay down with her head on a clump of heather and in a moment was sound asleep.

She awoke in a soft confusion. Sleepy eyes and sleepy ears, noises she could not quite distinguish, the sense of clear light. Suddenly she remembered, and realized that dawn had come. She pulled herself up on an elbow, and stared. An austere light, without splendour, revealed the wreckage of their night. Bottles and papers were tossed about, and ends of unwanted food. The fire they had danced round looked tawdry now, like a shrivelled flower. The angler was asleep, flushed, and snoring open-mouthed. His wife shivered and grumbled. Her face was a ghastly grey. Dr Parks sat like an image, with vapid eyes adoring Dorabel. Barney talked terribly, on and on. He was very drunk, and his secret discontent seethed from his lips. He would never paint, Dorabel had ruined him, she had eaten his soul. Create? How could one create who had squandered his integrity? A lot she knew or cared—glutted her lust for power, that was all she did.

'Get on,' Dorabel said. She was as pleased as a peacock.

Just then the sun came up. Serene and still, light flooded the earth. Dorabel handed drinks about.

'Drink to the sun,' she cried.

They raised their glasses, toasting the sun. Only Barney tossed the spirit wrathfully upon the fire, that flared in blue bodiless flames. The reek tainted the air for a minute like an emanation from his own tormented soul.

Jenny drew smiling up and poured hers also on the fire, with a secret movement as though she performed a rite, yet jesting frankly when they saw her action. But how could they know what dreams she had—how the dawn wind, high on that mountain pass, blew the white flame of living to a fury in her soul. Like every Kilgour in youth, Jenny now, at sixteen, was all alight with the fury of being. They had all had it, that passion to lick up the world in their progress, though the other passion in their blood, for sheer success, had taught them all to master and direct the blaze. But Jenny had no thought of mastery. Not yet. So far it was enough for her to be. In the future, she supposed, she would do as the rest of the family had done—go to college, work, succeed. They all succeeded. But the future was nebulous, a shimmering and unconsidered certainty, like dawn next year. Till now she had been utterly satisfied with what was—with driving the cart through bare brown November fields to carry home the filled potato sacks—climbing the hills by her grandfather's side, while Neil and Brand drove down the sheep—learning the whistle and the intonation that the dogs obeyed—never labouring beyond her strength nor continuing at any task that turned irksome, spoiled favourite as she was, yet loving so well all the out-of-doors activity of the farm that she worked eagerly on at tasks that most girls of her age would have found irksome long before.

But now, suddenly, this solid, sweet, rich content was invaded. She had looked on Dorabel, and all her nature quivered and sang. She was in love, oh, terribly in love, and the summer dawn, flooding the earth, flowed over her like an ocean, washed her under to such immensity as she had never yet conceived.

'Come in my car, Jenny,' smiled Dorabel. 'You're too precious to trust to Barney when he's drunk.'

Jenny was glad. But even so, Barney frightened her, speeding his car up behind them on the narrow uneven road, so that twice his bonnet almost touched them, and swerving to pass them where the slope was steepest and the road curved most abruptly.

'The bridge,' Jenny thought, delirious with apprehension and delight. Dorabel shot the long car up between the parapets. She too was driving at a reckless pace. Barney roared after them. The lovely ancient bridge dreamed on, unscathed above its burn.

And now Jenny was at home. She had come home late before from dances and winter parties, and knew where the key was hidden in the ivy by the window. But before she found it, her mother opened the door.

'Of course not,' Jenny had said scornfully when Dorabel asked if they'd be angry; but when she saw her mother's face she felt as though she had fallen through leagues and leagues of space on to a different planet.

Not anger was on her mother's face, but fear.

'But, mother,' Jenny said, 'why should Grand-dad mind? I've been late at a party before.'

'But this is different,' said her mother, devouring the girl with sombre eyes. 'You did enjoy yourself, darling?'

'Oh, rather! We saw the sun come up. It was glorious.'

Her mother sighed and kissed her. Jenny submitted to the kiss; and leaving her stained and crumpled frock in a bunch on the floor, was asleep, if that were possible, before she was in bed.

She reached the breakfast table, however, only a little late.

Her grandfather said, 'Fine junketings for a hay harvester.'

Jenny hung her head and looked abashed.

He said no more, but Maggie took up the theme and would not let it drop.

'Mercy, Jenny, yon was a rabble. You had us all out of our sleep, roarin' by like a farmyard. Yon Bella's like a steam mill—clatters the louder the aulder she grows.'

Mary and Mrs Kilgour were annoyed with Maggie. They were both aware that for almost the first time in her life Jenny had displeased her grandfather; but Maggie clumped on with bucolic insensitiveness.

'It wasn't Dorabel really that made the noise,' said Jenny, flushing. 'It was Barney.'

'Barney!' said Mary. 'He doesn't look the sort to make a noise.'

Mary's feeling of disgust against Bella grew deeper. This nice boy—was she to make a Philistine of him as well?

Jenny felt sore. Last night's throbbing sense of glory was not gone. All this talk of *should* and *should not*—what had it to do with the sense of glory? It *was*, and there was an end of it.

After a wicked time of wet and cold, the weather had turned to honey. The hay was already dry. Jenny and Mary went again to the field; and the work went on, steadily but without the former merry friendliness. The constraint annoyed Mary, who said frankly (as they gathered by the dyke for the tea that Jenny went to fetch at ten o'clock), 'At least, father, you should blame me and not Jenny, if you must blame someone. Though I can't see any sin about it.'

'I can fight my battles for myself, thank you, Aunt Mary,' said Jenny's clear voice. She set down the jug of tea and the basket of cups. 'Grand-dad is quite right. It's horrible to

twist night into day and yell and scream as we were doing.
I was drunk too, if you want to know.'

'Were you, though!' said Mary, smiling.

But Jenny paid no attention to her aunt. For all the pride
in her lifted chin, as she poured out tea and handed it about,
her eyes turned always to her grandfather, like a chidden
dog that waits for the first gleam of returning favour on his
master's face.

Her grandfather gave merely a half-contemptuous grunt
and swallowed his tea at a single gulp.

But after the mid-day meal he said, looking keenly at
Jenny, 'You're some tired, my lass. You're needing a rest.
Go you and lie down awhile.'

Jenny lay on her bed and slept so soundly that her mother
had to waken her at supper-time. And supper was late. For
they had worked on into the clear golden evening. The hay
was in.

'Maggie's wrocht like two this day,' said the old man,
pleased with his work.

'Ach!' said Maggie, trundling her squat body from hip
to hip. 'I'm as broad's I am lang, it maks nae odds on my
shoulders.'

The tears came in Jenny's eyes.

Supper over, she followed the old man to the door, saying
humbly:

'Grand-dad. I'm sorry I stayed out all night. But there
was nothing—really and truly we did nothing—nothing
wrong.'

The old man stopped short, with a look of extreme
displeasure on his face. Then he took his pipe from his
pocket and walked on; but halted in a moment and lit it
carefully, while Jenny remained silent and perturbed. At last
he said, using the name that had been her grandmother's,
'Janet, that was a word that should never have passed your
lips, nay, nor come to your thought, as it came not to mine.
But there's an end of it, lass. Go you now to the milking, for
Maggie has wrocht famously and must be clean forfochten.
And see you get soon to your bed to-night. You're a growing
lass, Jenny, and need your rightful sleep.'

But when he came in towards ten o'clock and found her

flying across the stack-yard and Maggie lurching after at an incredible speed, and both pursued by Charley the hired loon, he gave her no rebuke but put out his great sinewy arms and caught her as she ran, crying, 'Here she is, Charley, man. I can beat you young lads yet.' And then ran dodging from her to the door. Jenny stopped the uproarious caper of her own accord: which was out of the common, for she was always the last to weary of a game or prank.

She leaned a moment against the house wall, recovering her breath, ready to go in and sleep again; and Durno came by with a sheep dog at heel.

'Ay, Jenny,' he chuckled, 'I'm hearing you were all blin' drunk last night.'

'Dorabel wasn't drunk,' said Jenny sharply.

'Eh? But I bet you she had as good a jorum as the rest. It would tak a gey bucketful to blin' yon lady. Ay would it though.' And calling his dog, 'Hey, lass, here!' he went off muttering, 'Ay, Liz, ye auld hussy, ay, my girl, they'd blin' you sooner than they'd blin' yon same fine deemie. She'll beat you, Liz. She'll beat you, my lass.' And so muttered and chuckled himself out of sight.

'Durnie's terrible fine set up wi' himsel,' said Maggie. 'Coorse auld deevil.' And she jerked a hip derisively in his direction.

Her derision, had he seen it, would only have edged old Durno's pride and joy.

EIGHT

Dance of the Deadly Sins

On the same day Dorabel was engaged in combating the young painter's reaction to the night.

'Oho,' she mocked, 'he's ashamed this morning, is he? What about? Not of being drunk, Barney? What's the good of being ashamed? Shame's a frost, all right. Shame shuts you up. Send shame to the devil, where he belongs, and get on with the job.'

The boy was ashamed that he felt himself ashamed; and ashamed to remember that he had told Jenny the truth about Dorabel; and furious with Dorabel because he had traduced her.

'Oh, cheer up,' said Dorabel.

Cheer up! he thought. That was all she could say. Cheer up. She hasn't the ghost of a notion that I shall be a great painter. She thinks of nothing but her fun. I have to find my soul—this symbolic stuff's no good. Draw her arm like a ham and her fists like potato chappers—she always escapes. Cheer up! You were at grips with the profoundest problems of all time and she told you to cheer up.

Dorabel of course meant it. She couldn't bear people not to be jolly.

'You're so deadly serious about yourself, you know, Barney. You're as solemn's a spurtle. Look at me!' She seated herself on a low stone dyke and clasped a hand on each shoulder, hugging herself and rocking to and fro. 'I mayn't know much, not your planes and cubes and all that rot you talk about, but I know how to laugh at myself. I know I'm fat, and greedy—you could as soon slim an egg as slim me—and I never know where my things are, I mislay everything but my tongue. But lord, I can laugh at it all. I'm like pigs and giraffes and all those creatures,

71

dromedaries and things—people have to laugh at me. Gib
says they'll let me off a few centuries down below for just
making people happy. But heavens, if the punishment down
there is not being let to laugh, that'll be a catastrophe for me
right enough.' She pronounced it cat-a-strofe, not because
she didn't know better, but because she thought it amusing.
'A rare sight I'd look then—like a bun with the currants
picked out.'

Having thus given herself the benefit of confessional,
Bella marched away.

Barney sat at his easel and tried the landscape; but Bella's
march, the way she flung her splendid leg, got between him
and the trees. Her leg wasn't a branch, it was a leg. It moved.
Moved of its own volition, as branches didn't unless you
got right inside their identity and surprised them. Bella
wasn't esoteric, she was common life, yet her secret had
to be surprised before you captured it. He began drawing
Bella's leg on the edge of his canvas.

Next day he went to her picnic.

Dorabel was now as pleased as half-a-crown. Everyone
knew her. With her scarlet cap and a bright yellow dress
she had, and her great height, she walked about like a
petrol pump in a land where houses and garments alike
seemed to grow out of the colouring of the place; and she
had notions about that house of hers that made a filling
station seem demure. She thought the other houses about
as elegant as turnip-tops, and was proud of the stir she
made with hers.

The sun shone every day, and every day the red-and-
yellow car took the picnickers to a new spot.

Mary would not picnic. That was not a matter for
astonishment. Mary peels her apple with delicate precision
and removes the core; nothing is wasted. Bella bites, and
at the third luscious mouthful, tosses what is left of hers
away. Orchards must be plundered for Bella's need.

Jenny had no scruples over the apples. She fixed her
strong white teeth in everything that Dorabel held out.

'That kid can enjoy herself, can't she just!' Dorabel
said.

They ate meals in wild corners, that were strewn at their

departure with caramel papers, cigarette ends, fruit skins and Kodak film cartons, sometimes a sardine tin and some smashed bottles as well. They carried a gramophone and drowned in jazz the seven singing voices of the mountain burns. Jenny didn't mind—there were always burns, but Dorabel was a new universe. Dorabel would set the gramophone in the middle of a village, outside the Inn where they had lunched, or on an open space beside the war memorial, grab Barney or little Dr Parks, and begin to dance. People stared. Children cried derisive words. No one saluted the glad spontaneous gaiety of the action. Only now and then trippers in passing charabancs leaned out to laugh and wave.

One night Dorabel and Barney danced for seven hours at the end of the Boggiewalls farm road.

Dorabel's frolic expressed no more than a thoughtless delight in being. She couldn't stop dancing.

'Let's see how long we can keep it up,' she said.

'Oh, do,' cried Jenny. She climbed on a paling, curled her toes in round one of the wires and leaned forward, chin in her hands, to watch.

Maggie lurched down.

'My certies, they're fond of a job,' said she.

'That's forty-five minutes,' Jenny cried.

Charley the hired loon cried 'Hooch!' and snapped his fingers. His mother sauntered across the field from her cottage, knitting, and chatted to Maggie.

'They're fond of a job, I'm sayin',' Maggie repeated.

The music jigged on, everlastingly.

'That's an hour,' Jenny cried. She bounced up and down on the paling, making the strained wire creak.

Dorabel waved her hand and laughed. Sometimes she sang a few notes. Barney went round with his mouth shut, a little grim.

The music stopped. The little doctor threw himself upon the portable wireless box. Dorabel chanted, flicking the notes off her lips with a careless grace.

At that moment, as she turned, she saw Andrew Kilgour. He stood very still on the road, and watched.

The sweat was pouring off Dorabel now, her face was like

boiled beetroot. When she saw Mr Kilgour she sawed with her partner's arm and tossed her body impudently from side to side. As she passed she grabbed the little doctor's handkerchief and wiped her streaming face. 'Delighted, my dear,' murmured he. And in some queer land that none of them knew, foreign voices broke in gusty laughter.

On and on.

Dorabel couldn't have stopped now.

'Give's something to eat, Jenny,' she cried.

Jenny jumped from the paling and ran to the car. She thrust chocolate in their hands. The dust rose from under their shuffling feet. At one corner the grass was trodden bare. Far away, the long blue slope of the hills melted against a golden afterglow, and took form again in pure cool shapes that seemed hardly of this world; and the waves of sound, washing around the globe, frothed for a moment among the silent hills.

Froth indeed it seemed to Andrew Kilgour. Old Durno was beside him now. With his arms crossed on top of a grey stone dyke Durno leaned forward, his face dingy and runkled like an old boot, and with little more expression. These two old men watching the frenzy were like the darkness of older time. They were ribs of the earth. The land made men like these because she needed them; and made them in her own image because she knew no other way. Well, man was outwitting her at last, stealing her secret resources, creating himself. But in what image? The earth, become conscious as it were in Andrew Kilgour, so fully were her qualities embodied in him—her strength, patience, faithfulness, her wholesome vigour and enchanting peace, her heavy reiterations and profound satisfaction in herself, knowing that she was good—the earth, embodied in Andrew Kilgour, stood watching, pondering what image man the creator could use for himself once he had discarded her.

Not that Andrew supposed these two shuffling mari-onettes were the image. To him they seemed like spoilt attempts tossed to perdition. But why try new patterns when the old was so good? Men should be satisfied with what they were. For to Andrew there was but one pattern of humanity. His brothers, though pursuing different ends, still conformed to the pattern. There was recognition between him and them. But here there was no recognition. These human beings convulsed him with wrath; and turning away, he said to Jenny:

'Come you to your bed, Jenny.'

Jenny cried, laughing, that she must see the end.

'To see how long they'll keep it up, you know.'

'Eh? What for?'

'Well, just to keep it up.'

The old man looked round and saw the mountains where he pastured his sheep, the fields disciplined from moor, saw at a glance the heavens and earth and man and the beasts that fed thereon, and saw, as it seemed to him, a kingdom where no energy was expended without purpose. This dance was waste, to delight in it a degradation.

'You're some easy served, my lass,' he said to his grand-daughter, and went off towards the house; but turned back to say:

'Is the chickens' meat made up for the morning?'

'Maggie's been doing that,' faltered Jenny.

'Ay? I thought it was your job.'

'Ach,' said Maggie, who was listening with her big ears a-shake. 'The bairn has her holidays. I can do the chickens fine mysel. There's nae muckle comes amiss on my shoulders.'

Kilgour did not even look at her, but went, finally.

Jenny stood poised, one half of her nature flying out to follow the old man who till now had been as her very self. She had loved and approved his precepts. The secret principle of her life was at one with his; and so profound was their community of loves and interests that it had not yet occurred to Jenny that she could stand at the centre of her universe and not find him there too. But then she turned, and there was Dorabel; and the very skies streamed away, dark and urgent, tumbling her world into space. Oh, she must see the end, must see the end! In endurance how like a god! The tense excitement of counting the minutes—it was a new mode of being, a revelation.

Bounding she overtook the old man and flung her arm round his shoulder.

'Grand-dad, I must see it out—it's too exciting. I shan't be late. They can't keep it up much longer now.'

The words said only half. She was laughing up into his face. Eyes, mouth, the live and eager countenance, said more than Jenny knew. He too felt disruption in that secret heart of life where they had been one.

Jenny flew away again, kissing her hand to him as she ran. Her disobedience in itself gave her a thrill. She had disobeyed her mother a thousand times. That was an essential part of getting the most out of life. But this disobedience involved herself. She was doing violence to her own soul. No question about it, however, the violence must be done. All eager laughter, dimpling, incoherent, she came running back to Dorabel.

To whom however she was of small importance now.

A diabolic energy was loosed in Dorabel. She too had affair with her own soul. She was dancing for her soul. She danced with the same vehemence of will with which she had lain screaming on the floor when thwarted in her childhood. No one could move her then but Andrew, and even he sweated again ere he lifted the bulging mass of muscle; her whole will turned to flesh. Now her whole will was flesh again, was muscle stuck limpet-like, not to a kitchen floor, but to the mechanical movement of a dance.

Sometimes she screeched, sometimes sang a note or two. Barney's face was blank. And Bella's flouted self-hood drove them on.

Each movement, each gesture of Mr Kilgour was generating power within her. She was hardly aware of Durno, who still leaned on the dyke, nor of Maggie, rubbing her eyes with coarse knuckles. They were so much landscape.

The landscape shifted. Maggie nudged Durno and said, 'Ay, ay, you and me's the common dab—we're nae so ill-off for a job as some folks seem to be. We need our legs to win our meat.'

'Ay?' said Durno, turning his dark face slowly towards her. 'Ay? You'll be a bit hampered, lass, when you get down below. They're grand dancers there. They spin round in the flames like tee-totems.'

'Ach,' said Maggie, 'the Deevil wunna set the likes o' me to the dancin'. I'll get to empty the aace doon the midden.'

'There's nae aace to yon fires, Maggie. Ye spin roon' and roon' in them till ye're brunt clean awa'. And still ye maun spin on, a mere appearance of yersel.'

'Mercy on us!' cried Maggie. 'Ye're gey well acquaint wi' hell-fire, it seems.'

'Ay, I whiles give it a thocht. I've an auld runt o' a sister yonder that kens it gey well, forbye.'

'Lord have mercy,' Maggie said, 'ye auld sinner that ye are, you may go to the Deil and I wish him a good bargain, but ye'll nae meet Alison doon-by, my lad.'

Durno slowly straightened himself from the dyke and walked out into the road.

'Alison has gey mis-shapen thoombs,' he said. 'She'd be some handless kind wi' the harp.'

He turned his back on Maggie. It was now almost dark. Durno walked straight towards the dancers, but in the dingy light his figure was unperceived. And in addition to the coming of night, in Bella's soul something dark and terrible was beginning to happen. A part of her secret self was being drawn out from her after the retreating form of old Kilgour. Her superb self-hood was invaded; and the invader was love. For the first time in her life Bella found herself loving against her inclinations and desires. Something within her nature was rending; the living substance of her self, in its most secret and infinitesimal subdivisions, was pulling slowly asunder. All other loves she had known had augmented her possession of herself. Now she was pierced. And his contempt was a fire in her feet.

To see the Laird so ill-suited was honey in the mouth to Durno. He could have hugged Bella for it. He stepped on sturdily towards her—she was a blaze of white light on his vision and he had to go.

That was the very moment that little Dr Parks chose to switch on the lights of the car.

And there was Bella, spurned by the one man, whom she loved, and spurning the other, that loved her, like dirt from under her feet. She had not a notion of her own strength, and rage and humiliation so had her that she didn't rightly know what she did. Her arm swung out and the old man tumbled sprawling on his face like the toad that he was.

'Steady on!' Barney said, checking in his step.

But Bella latched her fingers in his again and drove on.

Durno picked himself out of the dust and let loose a torrent of words that hadn't the commonest decency to wrap them up. Bad words they were and bad they sounded. His worst enemy wouldn't have wished to hear him speak them out before the Lord. Jenny slipped from the paling in her consternation, and stared. And suddenly there was Mary, grave-eyed, staring too. She had come down to bring Jenny home.

Mary didn't stare for long. She turned on Jenny with a quick protective gesture.

'Hadn't you better come in, Jenny?' she said.

Jenny nodded, slid her hand into her aunt's and went away.

But for a long time she knelt on a chair at her high bedroom window, unassuaged by the tenderness of Mary's kiss. Her body was taut and vibrant. The lights of the car, the crying music, seemed to scarify her very flesh; and there swept over her the tumultuous pain of loving someone too unlike herself. She was racked, but the rack was heavenly. With every wave of pain that swept her she mounted higher and higher to an intolerable crest that would not break. Clenching her hands, she beat them on the ledge of the window, mechanically keeping time to the jig of the tune.

Her mother in the next room heard, and suffered horribly.

Mary heard, and was angry. The child shouldn't get excited like that. And over this cheap-jack vulgarity!

Andrew Kilgour was already asleep. He slept sound till the grey of morning, rose in his accustomed fashion, and went out. Bella and her partner were still turning like mommets on the road. He gave them one glance and went to his work.

As soon as Bella saw him, and saw that he had seen,

she heaved a great sigh, detached herself from Barney, and crossed to the car.

Barney's head jerked, his limbs doubled up. He sat down on the road.

NINE

The Unsheathed Claw

'Your grand-dad says,' began Mrs Kilgour.

Jenny was eating her breakfast alone. Her eyes were heavy still with sleep.

'Your grand-dad says you're not to go about with them any more. I'm sure I don't know why he should. And her asking you to London and all.'

Jenny said nothing. But when she had finished breakfast she took her bicycle out to ride to Balbriggie.

'I promised,' she said. 'I promised to go across this morning. I don't break my promises.'

She marched out of the house and found her grandfather.

'Ay, Jenny,' he said, 'are you helping your mother this morning? She's to be boiling berries, I understand.'

'Jam!' thought Jenny. 'He would die if he didn't get his jam.'

And it did not seem strange to her to be thinking such a thought, although it was she who defended the old man's love of sweet things against her mother, who knew they were bad for his rheumatism; even raiding the jam cupboard gleefully on his behalf.

'I *have* to go to Balbriggie, Grand-dad,' she said. 'It's a promise.'

He said, 'You can go this once then, and tell her it's the last time.'

She went away with her head held high.

At the mid-day meal she was in her seat to time, but she panted, and her fair skin was flushed. She did not tell them that she had sat on the stair at the Inn, waiting for Dorabel to awake; and at last in desperation had stolen to her bedroom door, and opened it by soundless inches, and stared burning-eyed at the tousled heap of Dorabel in the bed.

After the meal Mary said, 'I haven't been up Clochnaben since I came home. Come up this afternoon, Jenny?'

The girl turned smouldering eyes upon her aunt; and turned away again, in a disdainful silence.

Mary went hot. She remembered the great crag on Clochnaben, that looked so friendly and familiar from the farms, like the hunched back of an old labourer; but from one angle on the moor grew sinister, like a hooked claw. That unsheathed claw was in Jenny's eyes.

Jenny herself was quite unaware of it. She had no feeling of disdain towards Mary. Only she was hardly conscious that she was there.

Mary went out alone and her eyes fell on Bella's house. She thought, 'What a nuisance she is, coming here to upset us all. I wanted this holiday to be so free—nothing to spoil it. And now everything's spoilt.'

But deeper than any conscious thought was a raging horror against life because it was unfair. An integrity was menaced. It wasn't right. The Chosen People should possess the land.

And such a land to be possessed! And such a day for the possessing! A day of lazy clouds that turned and floated. In the hollows of the tumbled land, blue shadows hung like portions of the heaven. To come from the city here and lose one's tranquillity—Mary resented it as an affront.

But, she thought, her sense of humour coming back, my remoter ancestors were not exactly tranquil. If they had hated anyone's person and presence as I do Bella's, they'd have made short work of his house. Burned it out, himself out or in as his luck happened. His wife fled or dying in her agony, his daughter falling on the spears. But to-day we are civilized, she thought, and I can't purge my beloved land of Bella's house by means of fire. How much wiser and better if I could.

Seeing her father, she told him, with a dry smile, what had just passed through her mind.

'Ay,' he said, 'but Boggiewalls would burn as well as her bit boxie.'

'Yes,' said Mary with a sigh. We destroy ourselves, she reflected, when we destroy the things we hate.

They both looked across at the house.

'If you hadn't brought Bella up,' said Mary slowly, 'that house wouldn't be there.'

Kilgour did not reply at once. Then he said, 'Were you grudging her her upbringing, then?'

Mary answered, still very slowly, as though she were drawing into the light of her own mind for the first time what she was about to say, and was not perfectly sure what would come forth: 'You could hardly expect me to have liked her much, could you?'

'You seemed to get on well enough when you were bairns.'

Mary was silent.

'And in any case,' pursued her father, with his eyes still on the house, 'if it hadn't been her, it would be some other body. Times are changing, we can't stop that. I'm too old to understand the new ways, I'll go on as I've gone, but the new have to come, here as elsewhere, I'se warren.'

'But,' said Mary with a passionate scorn, 'they needn't have come like this. Vulgar and nasty. Nor so soon. If it hadn't been for her, this place needn't have been touched, not for a long time yet. If Bella hadn't grown up in this house, that lovely hill would be unspoilt.'

'Tut, Mary,' said the old man, 'you mustn't miscall the past because of what comes out of it. It was all done for the best. It learned you forbearance, too, my lass, and how to keep the peace with a nature different from your own.'

'Did I *need* it?' asked Mary, smiling.

'It did you no harm, and you've profited by it, I've small doubt, in dealing with all sorts as you do to-day. But even if your mother hadn't kept the bairn—your mother was right fond of her, mind you, she was a merry affectionate bairn when she wasn't in her tantrums. I can hear her voicie singing *The Lord's my Shepherd* and *Now Israel may say*—neither you nor Bill was much good at the singing; it gave your mother a lot of pleasure to teach her—'

He paused, revolving in his mind the Sunday morning readings, when his wife's clear sweet tones mingled with

Bella's lusty charge. Bella was the best singer in the room; she knew it, she felt important and sang with all her might, waiting with an expectant thrill for the deep boom of Kilgour's own voice, that came in, true and strong, on the last note of every verse. The old man remembered how she used to turn and watch him, how their lips moved together and the last note swelled and echoed in triumphant unison.

'Even if what?' asked Mary, who was waiting for the end of his sentence.

'Eh? What was I saying? Even if we hadn't kept the bairn—you couldn't remember, Mary, you were too young, but you should have seen her facie when she spied her mother in a heap at the bottom of the rick she fell from; your mother couldn't comfort her for days—ay, even if we had let her own folk have her then, your house there would be here all the same, she'd have grown up here in any case.'

'Her own folk?' Mary repeated. 'What folk had she? I know her mother was your servant, who broke her neck falling off the rick. I thought she had no one else.'

'Ay, so you thought. So you were meant to think. So she thinks herself to this day. But I don't know—I see small good myself in such concealments.'

'But who—' Mary began. She could go no further. She had a sensation of choking.

'Durno was her father. He and Peggy, poor lass, were man and wife. But what are you gaping for, Mary, what ails you?'

'Go on,' Mary said, 'tell me more. She hated him and ran away.'

'And he found her out and pestered her. The Lord alone knows what he did to make her hate him like that. But she was a strange wild woman, Peggy, not of our folk at all; you wouldn't know what she was thinking or wanting under that still black look she had. And every woman canna be like your mother, Mary my lass. Anyway, a sad mess the pair of them seem to have made of their matrimonial charter. Well, and when she fell off the rick and broke her neck he wanted the bairn—lambies and bairns, he can handle them both fine.

He was some sore at not getting his own lass, small blame to him.'

'You wouldn't let him have her?'

''Twas Alison, not me. Alison had the promise out of me, and out of him as well, though how she managed that the Lord and her own conscience know the best—she had the promise, that the girl was never to know who her father was. Peggy willed it, and Peggy's will it was to be, though it's my belief the woman nearly broke her heart, and his as well, in carrying out the promise. What sense was there in that?'

'Father,' said Mary in a low tense voice, 'did you never hear what people said, that she—that you—'

She choked. It was too painful to put into words even now what she had heard with horrified recoil in her childhood, and forgotten for so long that she stood amazed at remembering it now.

But her father gave his deep grunt and answered, 'They soon took their tongues off that. Much good it did them and no ill to me. Stories like that couldn't live where your mother was, Mary. Ill-will was some like rotten seed where she was about—it made no show.'

Mary's breath came fast. Things that had had no meaning fell into place. Durno, always hanging around Bella. Nosing about her house. Unable to keep away. And Bella hating him—Mary could see that; though she did not know how even in her girlhood he had hung about his daughter, following her at nights, snatching an embrace that roused the passionate girl to fury. Mary did not know that he bore the mark of Bella's teeth in the lobe of his ear, but she remembered how Bella had struck him down the night before. If ever naked hate looked from a woman's eyes, it looked then from Bella's.

With the terrible candour of hatred, Mary knew clearly that Bella still believed the old idle rumour of her birth ('You think I'm a nobody, I'm as good as you,' she had said once with a furtive triumph), and if she discovered that Durno was her father she would flee in abject humiliation.

For a moment Mary was overwhelmed by a storm of exultant passion. Her mouth was dry. The way was found to drive Bella out. In less than a minute it had passed: one did not stoop to measures such as that. But the passion left her trembling, her knees gave way, she gripped the stone dyke behind her for support. She had looked in that moment into the pit of hell, and the words were wrenched from her almost without her own volition, as though she had discovered there knowledge she was without before: 'She could murder him, I think.'

'Huh,' said Kilgour, giving his curt deep grunt, 'murder's not so easy done.' But thoughtfully he added, 'I might be taking a turn up-by to Alison.'

Mary was still shaking from the glimpse she had cast into the hell of which her own nature was capable. She stood against the dyke, her hands behind her pressed hard upon the coldness of the stones, and watched her father's slow deliberate bulk pass out of sight. How she loved him, his sufficiency, his rectitude. That Bella should—but at the thought of Bella the black storm swept up and enveloped her again. Bella, the grabber. Grabbing everything. Gib—but that didn't matter, Mary was just and acknowledged that. She had never loved Gib, he was only her playfellow. But Bella had grabbed—just slid her hand out, and there he was, fast inside. The very way she had slid her hand out and pinched the plums—you saw the fist at her mouth afterwards and the greedy tearing teeth. Faugh! and the juice running on her chin. Gib in her fist, just like that, and she tearing into him. She had stolen something from Mary then, though Mary herself had never understood it—she had stolen Mary's desire and capacity for love.

And that impudent assumption—that she was a Kilgour. One of themselves. Couldn't Alison have kept the girl? A Kilgour—grabbing that too.

Mary hadn't known before that hatred could exist so intense as she was feeling now. Simply hadn't known it. Her face worked, mouth twisted. She, Mary Kilgour, the serene, adequate Mary, who held her world in a bright mastery, to be shaken so! Her feet raced of themselves. Faster now, and faster, and keep thinking about Gib, about the plums, and Bella's finger in the milk-pans, with the thick cream dropping on her pinafore, keep thinking about

Alison, and one's indignation because she had not kept the child—anything, rather than allow the worst thought of all to reach the surface.

But it bored through in the end. She couldn't walk fast enough to keep it under. Suddenly she saw, quite clear, against the wood, Jenny's piquant face, grave, just crumpled at the eyes and mouth with mischief. Jenny. Bella, grabbing everything. Even Jenny.

When Bella grabbed Gib, Mary felt only disgust and contempt. But this was pain such as she had never before endured. She stood still under its impact—quite motionless. Her whole vital energy was absorbed by the pain, and her body might have been a stone.

TEN

Alison

Meanwhile Kilgour was stooping his shaggy head under Alison's doorway.

He sat knees apart, his big hairy hands hanging down between them, and looked at the small erect figure of Alison, where she stood with one hand poised on the dresser. Her sober gaze came straight to his.

'So, Alison,' he said. 'Have you seen this niece of yours?'

'Nay, Mr Kilgour, what would a fine lady the like of her do visiting me?' asked Alison. 'Even if she knew that she had any cause. She's far above us now, and it's not that I'm not proud and thankful, but we hanker for a sight of our own and a word with our kin. James there, he's that proud at seeing her and meeting in with her whiles, I can't tell you.'

'And why should not you have the same pleasure, Alison?' said Kilgour, looking at her keenly.

'Fine you know why that can never be.'

'Alison,' he answered kindly, 'is't not time to bring this concealment to an end? What purpose does it serve?—O ay, I know what you would say, but Peggy's been in her grave these thirty years and more, and why should the dead lay their hand so heavy upon the living? You both want the lass, and here she is like to settle among us—I say nothing of my own regret at the manner of her coming—I'm an old-fashioned man and I like the old-fashioned ways. But that's no reason why you and your brother should stand back any longer. I've thought so for some time, and what they tell me she did last night ca's in the nail.'

Alison's countenance grew sterner while he spoke.

'He cried out all night,' she said, 'against her. A black

thankless breed. Like her mother—the Cassie pride. He was sore hit, Mr Kilgour. Not the tumble—that was neither here nor there. But he loves her and it was a sore affront.'

'Then, Alison, it's time you had her told the truth. She's without rein upon herself—she might do him a hurt.'

'That would be a small matter, Mr Kilgour, beside the loss of his immortal soul. Peggy must give him back his word before the Seat of Judgment ere he is clear to joy in the flesh or the issue of the flesh.'

'You carry this too far, Alison,' said the old man, raising his head and looking her full in the eyes.

'Is any length too far, Mr Kilgour, where a soul is to be saved? There's neither near nor far there, but life or the pit of everlasting destruction. And do you think a cowp in the dust, or the like, or even to have the lass know we were her folk, would turn me aside from what I've set my life to the doing of? We come of decent folk, Mr Kilgour. Our mother was a woman upright in all her ways. I mind well, when I went to my first place—I was twelve years old and I had never had a penny-piece to spend before. So when a packman came in about to the door, with ribbons and pirns and the like, I bought myself a lace collar and off I set to the Kirk with it. You know a bairn's pride, Mr Kilgour. I had never had lace upon my neck before. But some speirin' body told it to my mother—not in any ill spirit, but turning the matter over as they will do where there's little to think about. So my mother hid herself by a broom bush, as I came paidlin' on through the dust of the road to Kirk, and out she flies and grabs the collar off my neck, and says, "For shame to you. I'll have no daughter of mine stravaigin' the roads like a Jezebel. The Kingdom of God is not to be won by scarlet and fine linen but by the subjugation of the flesh." I never forgot my lesson, sir, bairn though I was.'

Kilgour grunted, 'A lace tippet surely could never stand between you and your salvation.'

'In the hands of the Author of all Evil, sir, Mr Kilgour, a less matter than a tippet will serve. Ay, the lesson sank in. And well it was for me that I learned it when I did. For what with Jamie's wild ways, and the weary years my mother lay like a log of stone, Mr Kilgour, I had need of it. "Alison," my mother would say to me, "you maun cling to Jamie. Save him as a brand from the burning." And she would sigh and say, "O Lord, wherefore hast Thou afflicted me with a son like unto a stinging nettle? He that was fed upon the sincere milk of the Word—"'

'Ay,' said Kilgour, 'cheese can be gey strong whiles.'

The old woman shook her head with a slow, humble movement.

'I know he has offended,' she said. 'And may I be forgiven, but the one thing I live for now is his salvation. I had a lad once, like the rest, but I sent him away. I wept a whole night for that. "Alison," my mother demanded, "what are you bubblin' and greetin' about?" "Mother, I've a festered stob." "Deil dry your tears with a heather besom." Fine she knew it was no festered stob that made Alison Durno greet.'

'Well, well, Alison,' said Mr Kilgour, 'you have done your duty by your brother. But what hinder would it be to his salvation, or your own, to save this lass of his from losing hers? As she's like to do if she goes walloping about in this way. Bid him tell the lass that she's his own.'

Alison repeated the slow movement of her head.

'Then I shall speak to him myself,' said Kilgour. 'Last night's pliskey must not be played again.'

'Before the living God,' cried the woman, 'do not. As you respect yourself, sir, Mr Kilgour, make no mention to him of his humiliation. He hates you that bad that to meddle in this matter would hardly be safe.'

'Hut, Alison! You're raving, woman. You keep yourself to yourself more than needs, and brood on this old past affair till you canna see the cow for its own tail. What way would it not be safe for me to give him, and her too, a line of my mind?'

Alison answered, unmoved:

'For the hate he bears to you.'

Kilgour, watching her, pondered. She stood there like an image, unbending, her whole will concentrated on a purpose. Her stillness appalled, like the terrific immobility of a whirlpool. Her body, hard and dry like brown sticks, held somewhere a reserve of prodigious power.

'H'm,' said Kilgour, 'I have never flattered myself that he liked me, though his hate should be no such great matter, surely. I gave him a rough handling once, when I caught him slinking in my cornyard at dead of night. I had no knowledge then that the woman was his wife, though I could have done no other if I had known. It was after that night that poor Peggy told me the truth of things, poor lass, thinking for her own self-respect that I should know.'

'He bore you no grudge for that, Mr Kilgour. Maybe 'twould have been better for all had you done the same the other time.'

'What other time?' asked Kilgour.

'Bad he may be and bad enough, but James has never had an ill-will at them that licked him fair and true. It was your forbearance he could not abide. I've heard him girn and gnash his teeth at you, and the foul words spitting from the mouth of him like hailstones dirling from a roof, and all because you had done him a kindness. There was no forgetting for James of what he owed you, and each new benefit but cankered with a deeper hive.'

'Surely,' said Kilgour, 'I have never showed him such by-ordinar kindness that he need take it so much to heart.'

'You sheltered his wife and reared his bairn—'

'The one worked for her wage and the other you maintained.'

'You knew the wretched woman's story, Mr Kilgour, and held your tongue.'

'As any would have done, surely.'

'And kept your counsel on the shame of that accursed night.'

'What night?' asked Kilgour.

'The night before Peggy came by her end, poor hapless bairn.'

'Ay, and what like a night was that, that you remember it so well? You talk in riddles, Alison.'

Alison lifted her head and looked straight and solemn into Kilgour's eyes.

'So you indeed know not,' she said, 'how Peggy came by her death?'

'By her death? Ay, very well. She broke her neck in my own stack-yard falling from a rick that she was thatching.'

'A willing fall, Mr Kilgour.'

Kilgour slowly brought his hands to rest upon his knees. He watched Alison's eyes, not taking his own from them, as though following the weight of a stone falling in their depths.

'So that was it,' he said at last.

The stone had fallen, he fathomed the infamy that weighted the old woman's silence.

'She vowed,' Alison pursued, 'to take her life if he should touch her again. And that night—he was an agile chap then—he climbed in through her window in your own house. He swore you saw him at it, for you crossed the yard as he dropped to the ground—'

'No, not I.'

'You were seeing to a sick beast, he says. And all these years he swears you've spared him, and you're roddens in his mouth.'

'So help me Almighty God,' said Kilgour heavily, 'I never knew a word of this, no, nor suspected it.'

'I have carried that guilty secret in my heart these two-and-thirty years,' pursued the old woman, not altering mien or attitude, 'and had thought to carry it to my Maker as Peggy carried it before me, though whiles the burden has been a weight upon my soul like the last shovelful of earth that will soon lie upon my grave. And other whiles I've thought, maybe 'twere better it should come out and he take his punishment in front of all the world. When I saw him so careless, ay, and going with other women, he that had sent one woman to her account in loathing and despair, I thought, better let him be punished now, if that perchance might save him from the wrath to come. Not that he hasn't suffered for it, Mr Kilgour,' she continued earnestly. 'I've been a faithful remembrancer, since that black day when I came in and found him warming his hands before the fire. I came in and said, "There's been an accident at Boggiewalls. Peggy's been killed," I said, for no suspicion of the thing was in my mind. He went the colour of yon old pot, and I never saw a man so cold. It was a chill autumn night and a storm rising—you could hear it beating up around the bens. And aye as the wind soughed the sairer, he huddled in the closer to the fire; and it came on me then all at once, that lassie had been done to death as surely as though he smote her down. He had a dram, and better than a dram, inside him ere I got him to his bed that night, but that didna warm him, nor all my hot blankets and pigs. By the morning his teeth stopped chattering, but his feet were like a corp to the feel, and whiles on a winter day I've thought, he's never been right warm since that hour. He loved Peggy, Mr Kilgour—ay, and loves her daughter, though she flouts him like a lousy dog.'

Kilgour sat for awhile in silence ere he said:

'And Peggy made you promise the girl was not to know her father?'

Alison shook her head. 'Why should she that? She never thought to leave her life so soon, poor lass. There was no promising. I but knew it was her will.'

'Well, Alison, the girl's a woman grown long since. Headstrong and unbridled—you can see the sort of thing she does. He's ripe for mischief, and so is she. He can't keep off her, any more than he could off Peggy. Give her the clue, woman. She's good at heart, she'll come to. For this tale you've told me—it's past and gone. Leave it there.'

'I never thought to tell it—'

'Well, you've told it to me. Let that be an end of it, save as between him and his God. Bella need never know. Nor ought to know. No, nor no other body.'

Alison walked slowly away from the dresser. She moved a hand across her brow and stirred the fire as though unconscious of what she did.

'Huts, woman,' said Kilgour a trifle impatiently, 'your fire's fine. It'll last you till bed-time if you let it be.'

'It's queer to me to have it all said out,' Alison answered, continuing to poke aimlessly in the fire. 'What will you do, sir? Perhaps you will think we ought to leave this cottage. We're old to begin anew, but it was a new start when we shifted here when Peggy ran from us, and we can start anew again, the Lord willing.'

'Bide where you are. What would you want to leave for?'

'Mr Kilgour, sir, would you shelter such wickedness as ours?'

Kilgour grunted. 'We'll save some more wickedness, if you please.'

'The folk will scorn us, biding on with such a story at our heels. Many's the time I've scorned myself, thinking that if you knew you'd put us to the door. And rightly too.'

'Alison, you're havering. Clap shut your mouth, with your Peggy inside it for good and all. It's nobody's business and nobody is to know. Least of all must Bella herself be told. Tell her who she is—that she's got to know, or he'll hang around till one day, and then it'll be too late.'

'If he does her a mischief,' began Alison.

Kilgour laughed shortly. 'Fient a mischief will he ever do. He'll girn and grumble, but he's a poor hand when it comes to the deed. It's her I'm feared at. She's strong—stronger than her own knowledge, and as ill to thwart as a cloud-burst rummlin' from the hill. She'd have as much compunction on him as the hoodie craw that pecks out the eyes of a poor ewe fallen helpless on her back.' He gazed a minute into the fire, then said, 'And now tell me, Alison, is't you or is't me that's to do the telling?'

Alison sat down then, the tears standing in her old eyes.

'Indeed, Laird,' she said, wiping her face in her apron, 'I'm some upset. Here's me greetin' like a bairn that hasna grat since I gave my lad his leave. But you canna mean, Laird, that the story's to be latten be? Many's the time in the watches of the night—'

'See you here, Alison,' said Kilgour again. 'The past is past. We've no say there and the best we can do is to say nought. But we have a say in what's to be, and we'll e'en take it. Will you or will I do the saying?'

Alison mastered her tears. 'You would tell the lass she is his daughter?'

'Ay.'

As the old woman wiped her face, she stood erect once more, controlled and resolute as Kilgour had always known her.

'No, Mr Kilgour,' she said, 'that must not be.'

'Tut—' he began.

'Would God, think you, pardon such a weakness now? After all these years, to fail in my word and go before Peggy with a broken faith?'

'I am not God,' said Kilgour shortly, 'nor in His counsels.'

He was angry with her obstinacy. 'Thrawn as a buckie,' he muttered. 'She keeps by herself till she can't see any way but her own.' But as he looked at her he saw clearly that for her the present had little significance: Bella might smite her father down and Alison would care for nothing but how it might affect old Durno's soul. It crossed Kilgour's mind that if by some dire accident the thrust were mortal, Alison would see in it the hand of God, divine retribution for Peggy's fate. In her brother was all life's meaning; for in that grim hour when she saw him huddle to the fire, time was accomplished; it had no further progression, but turned back eternally upon itself.

Unsatisfied, he was compelled at last to leave her.

'This is madness,' he muttered, and went back ill-pleased to Boggiewalls.

ELEVEN

Fatherhood

Bella bounced out of slumber, stuffed herself with food and crowed, with her mouth full, over her achievement. Seven hours, they get into the papers for the like of that—well, for not much more. Well-known singer and partner. Already she had forgotten—having hardly heeded at the time—old Durno's intrusion into the game. And the Laird must have been impressed. 'I've made him wipe his glasses this time,' she gloated. Obtusely smiling, she made for Boggiewalls.

Mary was returning from her solitary walk with a steady hand upon herself. She might sin in despising the barbarian, but barbarian she would not be. Coming again in sight of Bella's house, she started, remembering that earlier in the afternoon she had thought of Bella's coming as a nuisance. Nuisance! the word was silly; and something went deadly cold within her heart. She felt as though she had completed a long and perilous journey through desolate snows, but when she tried to think of the journey's beginning she could remember nothing except that a very long time had gone by. And she realized with astonishment that the daily worries of her typing-house, which she had come here to forget, and of which she talked as though they were of tremendous import, were really of no moment at all compared with what was happening to her now. She had been forced in to the quick of her life.

Jenny, seeing her aunt approach, seized Maggie's pail and began to feed the chicks. Mary did not speak to her. 'I can't force her love,' she thought; and then she thought how horrible it was to be thinking thus of Jenny, whose love she had taken for granted as one takes for granted that water is wet. Jenny was like someone moving very rapidly past her, whose eye she failed to catch.

Maggie lurched across the yard and said to Jenny, 'D'you mind Muckle Sandy, him that drives the baker's van?' Her face was all creased with laughing. 'Yon's him that's just awa'. He's grand suited the day, is Sandy. There now, listen to yon.' They heard him hoot a fanfarade on the van's horn. 'A noisy skellochin' brute as ever you came across,' said Maggie, still laughing; 'but mind you, Jenny,' and she nudged Jenny in the ribs with her elbow, 'a man that's to be trusted to the bittermost farthing.'

'I'm sure he is,' Jenny said.

'Ay, but, Jenny, it's nae just that. D'you mind yon night, Jenny, yon time you speired about auld Durnie, and I said, Put not your trust in princes nor in them that says fair words to a foul face? Makin' up to me, the coorse auld deevil. Weel, but, Jenny, it's nae a'thegether true, for there's Muckle Sandy—he's askit me, Jenny. He's in a marryin' mood, it would seem.'

'Oh, Maggie, you mean that you're engaged. How heavenly!' Jenny caught Maggie's squat red hands and jigged her round the yard.

'Ay, but I've nae said the word yet, Jenny,' panted Maggie, who was forty-six years old and had spent half of them at Boggiewalls. 'Keep a man aye waitin' a wee, Jenny, it sooples them for marriage, or so they say.'

The horn went trumpeting and tootling again.

'Mercy on us,' cried Maggie, 'he's backin' the van. Can he nae keep awa', the great gomeril?'

She ran with incredible speed, toppling from leg to leg, trundling her hips.

But Muckle Sandy had backed the van to give passage to Dorabel.

Maggie stopped. She made a sour lip.

'She needna think she's the only one that can get a house to dwall in,' Maggie said.

Jenny stood as still as Maggie. She too had begun to race towards Muckle Sandy's van; but she did not race to Dorabel. Her face had gone white. She had left no message at the Inn in the morning and Dorabel did not yet know that Jenny mustn't come with her.

'Joy is my name,' chanted Dorabel. 'Jo-oy-oy.'

She stood there, laughing in the terrible security of herself.

Mr Kilgour walked round the corner of the steading on the way back from his talk with Alison. Bella saw him. She was instantly more conscious of him than of anyone else who was present, even herself; and she cried, loudly so that he could not fail to hear, 'Hop in, Jenny, hop in. What do you think—should I be stiff to-day or not?' She threw out her long splendid leg. 'Come on, in with you to the car.'

Her grandfather's deep grunt sounded behind Jenny's ear.

Mary stood tense and silent. Again the thought came to her of driving Bella out through her own humiliated pride, and this time the idea did not seem so revolting. Her mind persuaded itself that Jenny must be protected against Bella's vulgarity. Her father had been shocked by Bella's treatment of old Durno; Mary hoped he was to tell her, now, who she was. She wanted her pride to be repelled and herself to go away. She wanted her to behave badly, so that Jenny would see how selfish, vulgar and nasty she really was. And this seemed to her a righteous anger and a good desire. Yet a feeling of unease pursued her, as though the pit into which she had looked might open again before her feet.

Jenny heard her grandfather's grunt with a queer lifting of the heart. She had not told him that she hadn't told Dorabel. She must say it now, or he would blame Dorabel, think she had come to defy him. She said it. The clear tones sang upon her lips.

'Come on, Jenny,' Dorabel cried again. 'Barney's too stiff to turn.' She flung the other leg forward, thrilled by her own good beef and blood.

Mr Kilgour walked up with his even tread. His hand on Jenny's arm, he said quietly to Dorabel, 'Jenny'll need to be staying at home some more than she's been doing. She's been some frivolous of late. It can't be all holiday with us working folks, you know, Bella.'

That bounder, Bella's leg, stopped its advances, and executed an impatient schottische movement against the ground.

'Jenny has holidays a long time yet,' she suggested. 'You surely don't mean to make her work all the time.'

'It's a ploy she likes, the farm work,' said the old man, pressing Jenny on the arm.

There was no answering flash.

Bella burst into derisive laughter.

'We're not having her careering round the countryside like this,' resumed the farmer. 'You'll get a name to yourself, Bella, with these goings-on.'

Dorabel's leg, still impatient, responded: What better could I wish?

'So Jenny will stay at home in the meantime. You'll need to make up your outings wanting her in the future.'

Dorabel brought the leg to rest. 'But I need Jenny,' she said. 'I must have Jenny.'

Jenny lifted her head and gave her a glance disturbing as the honk of wild geese in autumn, unbearable with intimation of departure.

'But I want Jenny,' reiterated Dorabel. 'I *need* her. I *want* Jenny.' She repeated the phrase like an incantation. Some god to help her now, now that she is about to perceive what she has known all along!

'You'll be talked about, Jenny,' she cried. 'Think of it!' The idea was too funny. It clumped about in Dorabel's mind like a clumsy elephant, making crashes in the undergrowth. 'Some of us would give a neat little pile for that end, you know,' she said. 'But anyway, isn't Jenny old enough to choose? Jenny, will you be talked about? Will you come with me to London, as you said you would?'

Pain contracted Mary's heart. Wasn't she going to take Jenny to London herself when she was old enough? And Jenny felt as though icy water had struck her flesh. She had not mentioned London (except to gratify her mother, wily little mouse that she was), and now her grandfather would think she had deceived him.

She stood there, lids drooping. By flashes she eyed Dorabel. The glance was lit by supplication and a lovely far inwardness, as of a dream that was its own pure light. She trembled there between two loves—the mountain grandeur of her grandfather's, and Dorabel's encroaching, tumultuous, cruel, endlessly altering ocean-love, musical till now as summer seas. If she is frail, she will be crushed between them, deformed for life through this her first battering by the elements. She is sweet, she is ardent, is she also strong? Darkly she understands that if she yields her will to either of them now, even to her grandfather to whom she owes obedience, she is lost. Her own nature teases her, unreal and tantalizing as a gossamer, more fateful than the stars. Issue it must have towards what it loves, or return upon itself in confusion. So she stands there. Like a flame, like a jet of water, she is blown by contrary winds from her true shape, yet momently resumes it and is herself.

The mountain holds her by its vast serenity. Had her grandfather stormed, or played the tyrant over her, she might have defied him now. But when he laid his prohibition on her, in the morning, he had been so quiet and considerate that she could not revolt. She could not answer Dorabel. She heard the old man thank her for the invitation and decline it.

'I'll pay her expenses, you know.' Dorabel's voice grated, the sea lost its music.

Mary struck in: 'Jenny will come with me to London when she's old enough.'

'To a Summer School, I suppose!' yelled Dorabel. 'A Holiday Course for the Improvement of her Mind. My God! You're going to ruin that lovely child. Spoil her life as you tried to spoil mine. I only want to give her a rattling good time, and buzz, buzz, like frightened flies, round you all come. Jupiter, she'll go to some man's head yet! *You*'ll shove her in a university, take all her sparkle out, make her as flat as the water you get in railway trains. As dull as your dirty hills.'

'Hut, Bella,' said the old man, 'you're havering, lass.'

His tone, the gesture with which he pushed the flat of a hand over his eyebrow, dismissed the whole stupid accusation. Conviction pelted on Bella like a hailstorm.

'Oh, I see what it is—you don't want me here. You don't want my house. I know you don't like it—I knew that. It's not your style, it's not plain, and useful, and solid, it's not a potato. You don't want it here, you want to shove me out.'

'Nay, nay, Bella—'

'Neigh, neigh, neigh, neigh!' she mocked, desperate. Jenny had not said a word. 'It's queer that people like me everywhere else. A favourite, I am. That's a queer thing, isn't it? What do you make of that? But here—you don't like me, can't do with me.' The incredible red-hot truth shrieked out of her. 'I'm not human. Some sort of species, that's what I am. Nobody wants me here.'

Jenny threw her head back. She couldn't believe it was Dorabel shrieking in that animal abandon. She couldn't quite understand why. And she was too late by a second. Her 'O Dorabel, I do,' was shattered by a hoarse chuckling throatiness. Durno had clutched his daughter from behind.

'Hold you your head up,' he chuckled. 'What ails you at yersel that you need heed a puckle Kilgours? Whan the flood comes lippin' up there'll be nae word o' boot-laces. Kilgour'll run as fleet as them that's nae Kilgour.'

Bella heard the malicious mouthing with a spasm of panic. She was afraid of this insistence on what she wasn't. She dragged Durno's rough cold purple hand off her arm and gripped it in merciless iron fingers that delighted the old fellow's heart.

'And who—' she began. She was going to say, 'And who gave you the right to speak to me?' But he burst out, unable to contain himself: 'Your father, my dawtie.'

Bella asked no questions. Illumination shot backward over a lifetime. Glaring at the scar her teeth had left in his offending ear lobe, she stuttered: 'So that was it. Pawing at me.' Then clear and loud: 'Dirty little ferret.'

She relaxed her grip. As though her fingers alone had supported him, he sank upon a stone. No vituperation this time, only dumb defeated suffering. The bloodshot eye glared. His substance shrank, the elephant hide sagged and wrinkled. His eyes were fixed with an unseeing stare, as though in the mere looking they had seen all they would ever see again, on the rickyard where Bella's mother had slipped his grasp for ever.

Jenny glided up to him. Without a look at either her grandfather or at Dorabel, she put her young arm round his shoulders.

And at that moment Mrs Kilgour wandered out of the kitchen door, dragging the grey jersey about her throat.

'Jenny,' she said, 'haven't I told you you're not to—'

Jenny neither stirred nor spoke, only moved her head with a slow negative movement. Andrew Kilgour looked at his daughter-in-law and repeated Jenny's movement of the head.

'But I needn't speak,' said Mrs Kilgour. 'You pay no attention to me.' She dragged the grey jersey close up to her throat and disappeared again within the house.

All the while Bella had been shouting: 'You think you've got me hipped. You think I'll stick my tail between my legs and slink away with my house in my teeth and save you any more trouble. I tell you I'll be damned if I do. I'm Dorabel Cassidy, amn't I? Durno! What does being a Durno matter? I'm what I've made myself, amn't I? I'm Dorabel Cassidy. I'll finish the house—oh yes, I'll finish it. I'll get the pink tiles. And turrets. And all the things you hate. And I'll let it to someone who isn't afraid of having a good time. Someone that won't put on their spectacles whenever a cow moos and look to see what's making all the din. And I'll come back myself—oh yes, I will. I'll come back. He'll die some day. He'll have to die. I wouldn't set foot in the place as long's he's here. I loathe him. But if you think you're done with me you're much mistaken. I'm going to stay away, am I, because your name happens to be Kilgour and his happens to be Durno and my mother was called Cassie and mucked out your byre? Jerusalem! You're all tied to your daddy's coat-tails up here right enough. Who was her father? Who was her mother? What was her great grandma's table linen like? I'm Dorabel Cassidy, I tell you. I'll live in that house though you Durn my door to atoms.'

Her florid face was like a ripe black plum; but her singer's chest, full and easy, swept her on without distress.

Durno began to cackle, a gasping toothless laughter through which the words spat. 'She'll be upsides wi' you yet, Laird. She'll last you out. She'll be cocked up on the hill head when you and me's baith aneath the grun'.'

Jenny did not withdraw her arm, but she stood very still and straight, looking away.

But Mary knew that Bella was defeated. Though she had had to die for it she could not keep the smile of triumph from her lips.

She would have recalled it if she could. Bella's face changed horribly. A look of diabolic madness came on it. She scrambled in and sent her car reeling along the road.

Twenty minutes later Mr Kilgour said to Maggie, 'What are you gaping there for, Maggie, with a face like a nor-wast moon?'

Maggie pointed.

Smoke was pouring out of Bella's house.

They found her seated on a barrow, watching it burn through blubbered eyes from which the tears still streamed.

'Don't put it out,' she shrieked. 'Don't put it out. D'you think I'd live here now? D'you think I'll ever want to see this place again?' And to Andrew Kilgour she said, 'I hope you're happy now,' with an intonation of despair that marked her wounded love. But the tang of love in the brew that Bella was drinking no one detected. If her act was a burnt-offering, it was a perverted, sadistic and troublesome burnt-offering, which to a Kilgour reeked of insanity, or, more simply, sin.

'I'll get my head in my hands from Gib for this all right,' Bella cried.

She had drenched the flimsy structure with petrol before she fired it, and they saved nothing.

Jenny's mother had gone to her room.

'Oh, mumsie,' Jenny cried, 'you do look bad. Have you one of your headaches? Wait, I'll get the eau-de-cologne.'

Mrs Kilgour shuddered, pulling the grey jersey closer.

'You have always been kind to your mother, haven't you, Jenny?'

Jenny paused, one hand on the knob of the drawer, and stared.

'I have always tried to be,' she faltered.

'Oh yes, kind!' Mrs Kilgour burst out. 'Do you suppose kindness is what—' She bit her lip. When Jenny brought the eau-de-cologne she said, 'Thank you, my darling.'

Jenny brought a cushion and said, 'You know, mumsie, I had to stick by Durnie to-night. She was his daughter, you know, and treated him like that. You do understand, don't you?'

She looked down on her mother, love and compassion for the old man radiant in her eyes, smiting like the young sun-god on a mortal anguish beneath his comprehension. Her mother, smitten, answered, 'Yes, darling, I do understand.'

When Jenny had gone, she lay with closed lids, between which there slowly trickled a tear, then another, for her own lost life.

Jenny was in her own room. A thousand years had passed since she was there. Dorabel had repulsed her, blindly pushed her away and fled.

'Leave her for to-night,' counselled Mr Kilgour. 'You can try again to-morrow.' But the repulse burned in Jenny's heart like guilt. She wanted to fall on her knees and beg Dorabel's forgiveness, prostrate herself for being a Kilgour, for being Jenny, for not being Dorabel.

Crouched on the pillow, she fell asleep; awoke and moved her aching neck; and, far away on a pale sky, saw with astonishment the faint uninterested stars of summer. She had to recall her mind a long distance to understand what they were doing there; and slipping out of bed she looked at them, turning them over and over in her head and finding no explanation. She leaned out, feeling the ivy beneath her hand. Each leaf had a queer immediacy. The stem was thicker than her arm. Suddenly her mind cleared. The stars were only stars, their faint remoteness had no meaning. The ivy was a path to Dorabel. She dressed, caught the stem, and swung.

TWELVE

Mary

So in the morning Jenny wasn't there. Her bed had been slept in, but the sheets were cold.

'Mercy,' said Maggie, 'she's awa. The car went buzzin' by at the back o' five o'clock. Bag and baggage. Boxes tied on ahin, and yon Bella sitting up as large as life at the lug. There was another body aside her, small-like. Yon was Jenny, as sure's I'm born to die.'

Mr Kilgour stood scanning the broken ivy beneath Jenny's window. Drawing his bushy brows together he looked downward and aside at Mrs Kilgour and Mary.

'Hut!' he said. 'Even if she's off with her, what harm would you expect her to come by? Bella won't capsize her car upon the Mounth.'

'She hasn't any clothes,' muttered Jenny's mother. 'I could send them on.'

Mary did not speak. Her face was drawn. The sockets had eaten inwards, destroying her semblance.

'She'll come by no harm,' repeated her father. 'Jenny can stand off herself. And Bella's good at heart.'

Mary's reason acquiesced; but reason had little to do with Mary's sufferings. Asleep or waking she had felt all night the searing of her lips by her own smile of triumph, and the withdrawal of Jenny's hand. Going home, after Bella had thrust Jenny off and rushed away with streaming tears, Mary had taken Jenny's arm in hers, not speaking at all, and gently clasped her hand. Jenny quietly withdrew the hand.

'She will never know what Bella made me suffer,' Mary thought, passionately seeking her own justification.

Turning her back on her father with a muttered, 'I know, I know,' she strode off with long steps into the wood.

The branches parted and her virgin mind looked out, watched her with a grave, still regard. A disconcerting glimpse of her ancient self, unexpected, a vision that had travelled the round of space and returned to be caught by the apparatus that sent it out: herself as she was a million million years ago. That was the girl who grew up accepting Bella as one accepts all the persons of one's childhood, with no more responsibility for them than for people in a tale. There she is now, earnest and innocent, sixteen years old, Jenny's age, taking on her own young shoulders her dead mother's labours. How was she to know how much of her mother's wisdom was lacking in her own methodical and tireless industry? That is the girl, looking at Mary now. Pardon her! She is shouldering her heavy burden, she has given up what she wanted most, her university career, she neither grumbles nor repines, her father gives thanks for her in his stricken heart; but the fourteen-year-old Bella can't abide her rule. Bella rushes off and leaves her bed unmade, holes are in her stockings, she gossips with a lewd and easy tongue, in the evenings she is always out with boys. Mary kneels by her bed at night and prays for help in her exacting task.—Pardon the girl now. But Mary cannot pardon her. She is appalled by her discovery of herself. All these years, through her happy and successful life, she has kept this core of live and burning hatred in her heart. Her smile—she is sure of it—gave Bella's house to the flames. Her condemnation is in the withdrawal of Jenny's hand. But how make expiation to a Bella who does not know that she too owes an expiation? What expiation can she make save to learn to love her? And Mary is not yet ready for that.

But Jenny loves her—Jenny, whom she has carried on her back, teased and told stories to, who was always there when she came home, part of life, a portion of its necessary grace and goodliness.

Mary cannot understand that love. She could learn to tolerate Bella, she could treat her with irony or the attribute called Christian charity; but that in Bella's presence the sources of her nature should flow from their deepest springs, her spirit feel the quickening that is love, this is beyond her credence.

Mary stretched her hands out blindly. They groped and found nothing. Her lips worked. She knew that she was praying, but the words that formed upon her lips had no significance; only in a deep black solitude of soul her whole being was in supplication. She was beseeching the God of her fathers to keep Jenny. No other God must claim that delectable possession. If Jenny had gone with Bella, she was alien. A paroxysm of pure irrational terror seized Mary, atavistic, the countryman's ancient fear of what is unlike himself. Keep Jenny—O God, keep Jenny a Kilgour!

When she came to the edge of the wood, there was Jenny, running from the hill. She shouted, waved her arm, ran eagerly to Mary.

Jenny hadn't gone. Jenny was sound. The horrible sense of an alien and incomprehensible future was lifted, and Mary felt the sweat pouring on her face.

'It wasn't you,' Mary said; 'in the car?'

Jenny wore a cold puzzled frown.

'Gone away—with Bella?'

'What on earth would I do that for?'

Mary's panic was over. She understood that Jenny's cold hostile tone covered her own suffering. But before she could speak again Jenny said rapidly:

'Durnie, Aunt Mary—he's had a stroke, I think. I found him on the hill, nearly up at the crag. He's unconscious. I brought him down on my back. Grand-dad—I put him down by the mossy pool—where's Grand-dad, do you know?'

'You carried him? On your back?'

'Oh, I forgot,' Jenny said with a deadly clarity, 'I'm not allowed to touch Durnie, am I?'

Mary controlled herself and said, 'Grand-dad's in the barn. Now, what can I do? Alison—shall I go there? Or for the doctor?'

'Oh, Aunt Mary,' said Jenny in a quick rush, 'would you? Not Alison, I'll go to her myself. But the doctor—you could take my bike.'

As they went home Mary was silent, thinking what she could do to salve Jenny's hurt. But she did not know just what the hurt was, and Jenny was no longer a child, she must find her own salvation. 'If only she doesn't shut me out,' Mary prayed.

Mr Kilgour said only, 'Ay, Janet, lass.'

She looked up and saw his eyes; and said, as simply and confidently as she had brought him her broken toys in childhood, sure that there was nothing he could not mend: 'Durnie, Grand-dad—he's had a stroke, I think.'

Maggie came toppling from the door. 'Hi, Jenny, here's a piece, you must be as empty's a bagpipe.' She added, with the indecent haste of a bearer of considerable news, 'The foreman's been at the Inn. Yon was the car right enough. And who, think you, is off with her? Yon painter laddie, nae less. And handed his ain auld hurdy-gurdy o' a car to Willie Baxter—a tip, nae less, to put in his pooch, what think ye!'

'Well,' said Jenny fiercely as she trundled out her bicycle, 'he wouldn't get two pounds for it, selling it—he told me so.'

She looked at none of them, but in a cold violent way took off her bicycle pump and blew up a tyre. In spite of the noise she made, however, she heard her grandfather say, 'The boy was a good boy—what's he done that for?'

Mary went chill. To her it was a dreadful thing that this young man had done. She remembered his good hands. A nice boy. Grabbed. Ruined. So this was your Bella. Shame overwhelmed her, she could not breathe.

'Aunt Mary,' came Jenny's clear tones, 'the bike's ready. Will you go?'

Mary put her hands on the handlebars, just touching Jenny's as they relinquished hold.

'If you go to the Post Office at Balbriggie and get them to put through a message, that would be quickest,' Jenny said, issuing her orders with a cold authoritative air.

'Yes, I'll do that,' Mary said, taking the order.

She jumped on the cycle, her heart was racing, the pedals turned with a frantic instancy that had no connection with her body; and as she raced on she did not think of Bella, nor the young painter, who had finished themselves now; nor yet of Durno, who was done for too; but only of Jenny. The surface of her mind repeated, The old man is ill, I must hasten; but she knew quite well that ten minutes more or less would make little difference to Durno. She couldn't go slower, it was beyond her own volition, the things in her that were deeper than will or knowledge drove her on. Her whole body was exultant, she felt power in her limbs and skin and the very way her nostrils filled themselves with air; but she did not understand that this was because Bella had gone away disgraced and Jenny had stayed behind. When Jenny withdrew her hand, she was not accusing Mary; only the child's hurt spirit could not brook interference. In a little while Mary would find and salve her hurt. And as a mountain tarn is fed, secretly, by springs that rise beneath its own waters, so into Mary's consciousness, yet beneath its surface and hardly to be apprehended, rose visions of the wise and good ways in which she would make Jenny happy, feeding her own vast need to keep the girl at the centre of her life.

THIRTEEN

Jenny

The hard core of herself in Jenny's being remained inaccessible. She was as secretive as frost, stealing on the familiar landscape of herself with a movement no one could detect or influence. Nothing seemed to have changed. The incessant activity of the farm went on and Jenny took her daily part. Her animal spirits beguiled her into sallies of gaiety, the cold hostility was gone from her manner and she was everyone's friend as she had always been. Yet the girl could no more be reached than the north wind.

Mary tried, and was completely foiled. One black night she recognized that it was for her own need as much as Jenny's that she wanted to help her. She faced the knowledge squarely, as she had never faced the issue between herself and Bella over Gib; but Bella's violent contact had ruptured the protective casing in which Mary lived. She was no longer sure. She even saw that she might not be able to give Jenny what she needed. She felt humbled and small, and the feeling was pure pain.

The day came for Mary to go. There was a bustle of departure. 'Next year,' they all shouted. The dogs jumped and barked. Jenny ran to the end of the departure platform and waved and waved as the train drew out. 'Next year,' she cried. Then life went on. The dark came sooner. The first elm leaf grew yellow. The barley was brown.

In August the lambs are taken from their mothers. Jenny is there, intent and eager. She is in dungarees. Her arms are spread to catch a lamb that rushes to the wrong enclosure. One by one she holds the plunging, frightened creatures till they are marked. She would like to act the drover. Now that Durno is on his back, she wants to set out with the dogs and take the flock to its new master. Her grandfather grunts. He has sold the lambs to a man whose own shepherd is come to fetch them.

'You!' he booms. 'You would have my flock at the scamper the whole road, you nickum.'

Jenny's brows go up. She hunches her shoulders and mimics Durno's trudge, then throws a swift glance backward and springs to her height, laughing.

August ends, she is in school again. She is working hard this winter. Next year she will go to college. *Shove her in a university*—she ponders Bella's phrase, marvelling; but she is quite determined to be shoved. Every morning she cycles to Balbriggie and travels in Sammy's bus. Sometimes she sits by Sammy, chattering, leaning across to take the wheel; but there are days when she sits alone and gazes, but sees nothing; or stares, with the upright line between her brows, at Sammy's paintings, which are recognizable. She always knew they were absurd; now she torments herself to know why; and to know why she likes them, for all their absurdity.

Gib Munro comes, with a face like a muddy day, 'to see the remains', says Jenny, and wind up the contracts. At supper-time they tell each other that he has come, and agree that he has been hardly used. 'The mourning coach went back at a quarter to five,' Jenny says, but glances round quickly and turns red. The very air of the room rebukes her flippancy. She wants to cry, but must not let them guess her bewildered pain.

Jenny's childhood is over. A million years remove her from the Jenny who stole out of sunshine into the dim wood, stepping softly, because it was a place enchanted. The natural magic in the bright air will never be wholly hers again. She is as old now as Adam discovering evil, and the knowledge of the moral law. She has come to judgment and herself must be the judge.

So she ponders the things she has seen and heard. They leave their images in the pool of her mind; and her thoughts have the terrible importance of all first ponderings on good and evil. Vain and foolish thoughts, perhaps, but reflections have their own reality apart from the reality of what is reflected.

One morning in September the ground is white. How cold it is! The hills have come nearer through the night, and stand there, white and silent. The sun gleams on their pure, still peaks. That afternoon wild geese fly overhead, making for the south. The sheep huddle together, dingy yellow against the purity of the snow.

Next day the snow has melted. The burns clamour. The hills are brilliant now, scarlet and gold and blood-red, as mosses and blaeberry leaves, birches and bracken and *rowans*, are touched by frost. The air is pure and strong; the nostrils dilate, the blood flows fast and fierce as the lungs breathe it in. Jenny races on. Her young blood is bounding, filled with the cold intoxicating brilliance of a mountain October; and as she races on, and rings her bicycle bell from sheer exuberance of spirit, she knows it is the last year she will go carolling thus, with cold fingers and stinging cheeks, to meet the morning. This free clear life will end. She wants it to end—oh, God, she wants it to end. She loves it as her very life, she will praise it for ever as the only life worth having, but she must know the other. She must find a thousand answers to a thousand questions. She must get beyond the Pass.

And her blood sings, Dorabel, Dorabel, Dorabel. Jenny can bide her time. She is not nearly done yet with Dorabel, and she knows it. Even if she never sees the woman again in the flesh (and oh, please Hercules and Bacchus and all such forceful deities, she may!) she is not done with Dorabel. For Dorabel has been Jenny's initiation into herself. She has told no one of the July night when she swarmed up Bella's balcony, intent on comforting, and found herself forestalled; nor of her flight, dry-mouthed and shaking, to the hills. Loyalty would keep her lips shut, in any case; but there is more than loyalty at work, there is a profound dark insatiable need, a thrawn refusal of her whole being to accept what she is told and does not apprehend. Dorabel and Barney are persons, she likes them, they are not codes, the life that tumbles so fiercely through her limbs has felt its kinship with their life and must find its own terms of acceptance or repudiation.

'I can't help it,' she thinks. 'I *like* Durnie, and Barney,

and Dorabel. Grand-dad's good to them because he's good
to everyone, but he doesn't really like them and I do. And
I'm not going to stop even though they're not our kind.
Aunt Mary can think me vulgar and stupid if she likes.'

These thoughts, simple and innocent as they are, thrill
her like the closing on her flesh of a mountain pool, make
her gasp with the elation of far and dangerous adventure.
She sees the Pass, that is the symbol of her going. Beyond
it her grand-uncles, her father and her aunt, went each in
turn. She will go too, her grandfather will not grudge her;
yet by some strange prescience whose springs are dark even
from herself, she knows that she must return over the Pass
the same being as she went, with the same standards, the
same pieties and disdains, else he will break his heart. It
excites her profoundly to feel that she may be different, that
beyond the Pass she may find a new self seeking its nurture
in places unauthorized by the tradition of her people. With
the perennial expectancy of youth, she foresees her own
difference, her unique and eternally intangible self.

In November she says to her grandfather: 'Grand-dad,
Durnie would like you to come and see him, to-morrow, at
ten minutes past four. Ten past four; you won't forget?'

He goes. Jenny is already there. There is a heavy
stumbling in the next room. Supported by Alison, Durno
is trailed through. His eyes are set and glassy, one of them
protrudes and his lip sags. It is the first time Kilgour has
seen him out of bed since his seizure. A kirkyard deserter,
Maggie calls him. There he is, a dingy rotting carcase, that
a girl of sixteen could carry on her back, the wreck that these
two violent women, Peggy and her daughter Bella, have
made of him. A squandering destructive pair, destroying
his temples, the one her body, the other the house that
was the symbol of his gratification and revenge. Kilgour
thrusts his hand through his abundant white hair, dumb
in his pity.

But a chuckle comes from the grey lips. 'That gars ye
claw whaur it's nae yokie.'

Kilgour takes his hand from his head and sits where Jenny
puts him. 'Hush!' Jenny says.

Suddenly a voice rises, singing. Instantly Kilgour guesses,

he looks behind him and sees the wireless box, and Jenny's happy face, lighted like a child's with her secret.

'She sent it, Grand-dad,' she says. 'She sent it herself.'

Bella's voice fills the room, Durno rocks himself in his glee. His whole being expands with joy, the vacant eyes glitter.

'And the *Radio Times* too, Grand-dad,' says Jenny, nodding with a sidelong gleam, 'all nicely marked in red.'

As they go home, Kilgour says, in his customary phrase, 'Bella has a good heart.' It is the first time he has spoken to Jenny of Bella.

Jenny's arm is in his, she presses close against him in the darkness.

'How can she have a good heart and yet be bad, Grand-dad?' she asks softly.

'Ay, Jenny, that's a poser.'

Jenny feels her heart beat in her neck. She presses still closer, and says:

'She has a good heart, and she's generous, and greedy, and noisy, and vulgar, and I like her, and I'm going to see her again some day.'

She waits in an agony of impatience for his answer.

'Well, well, Janet,' he says, giving her her grandmother's name that he uses only in moments of tenderness.

He thinks, but does not say, 'Ay, if she wants you then,' and ponders, half aloud, 'We were maybe some to blame ourselves, it's hard to tell.' In a little he adds, 'If you could wile her back here, even for an hour, before that poor old pair are gone, you would do a good deed.'

Jenny shudders, but conquers the impulse. Pity and horror are in the eyes with which she looks on Durno now. Because she has altered, so has he. She hardly likes her hand upon him now, but she has never allowed herself to flinch from his touch. For Alison she has a new depth of reverence.

By spring the old fellow can walk without assistance. In the sweet March days, before the last of the spring storms blunders off the hills, painfully and with many halts, he makes his way to the hillock above the farmhouse. On one such day he sets out early, carrying a box. Inch by inch he wins his painful way to the hillock and sits there in the sun, exhausted. His eyes glare and are vacant. He gasps for breath. But he tugs his old watch from a pocket and waits, counting with the terrible impatience of the paralytic. The moment comes. Bella's voice soars across the yard and enters the farmhouse window. Her father gloats over every sound and rejoices because he thinks that he is annoying Kilgour.

Kilgour sends Charley to carry back the box.

Alison is watching, she comes to meet him. In one arm she takes the box, with the other she supports his body and guides his steps. She is hard, she is tough, there is infinite endurance yet in her brown wrists and tranquil face. If a heavenly visitant came to Alison to-morrow and said, There is no Judgment, you have lost your life for a delusion, her sweet eyes would not change.

'Another *Radio Times*,' Jenny says, when she comes home from school and is told the episode of the song. 'Isn't she great?' She throws her head back and laughs heartily.

'I wonder she wouldn't be black affronted to lift her voice up here,' says Maggie. 'A bad lot.'

'But she's so funny.'

'I wonder to hear you, Jenny Kilgour,' retorts Maggie sternly.

Maggie has a ring, the vanman brought it on Bannock Day. Mrs Kilgour had baked pancakes, a button, a brass ring and a thrupenny were inside. The vanman got his pick with the rest; Maggie came running out with the plate and he said, 'Well, here's a bannock for yourself,' and gave her a rolled-up pancake with the ring inside. What fun there was, what congratulations, how they laughed in the early February dusk with the headlights of the van throwing long shafts of light across the yard! When Dr Alexander Kilgour, the reverend Professor, visited his brother, Maggie came, blushing, and hiding the ring under her apron, to show him it and receive his blessing. At the May term she is leaving to be married.

So, 'I wonder to hear you, Jenny Kilgour,' says Maggie, with a look like Judgment, and Jenny is abashed. Maggie has always been there and Jenny has deferred to her as an elder. But she says sturdily:

'Well, if she's bad, I must be bad too, because I like her,' and is comforted, remembering her grandfather's words.

Jenny stays very near her grandfather all that winter. In the house her mother despairs of her. Her shoes are tossed down where she takes them off, her clothes are never mended, her room is not tidied. But she will trudge miles through wind and rain after a strayed sheep, where the fence is broken she holds the posts while her grandfather drives them in, helps him to strain the wire, hands him the staples. When the spring evenings come she sits beside him on the bench by the door, not speaking at all, her body just touching his: as though in touching him she touched an elemental virtue.

Jenny has no such thought. He is merely her grandfather, whom she loves more than anyone else in the world; yet, with the same profundity and directness as she knows that she is knit with Dorabel, she knows that if she loses touch with him she loses a portion of her identity; and she knows this by virtue of the dark unconscious forces that are perceived in reverie and apprehended through the breathing and the blood. Of these it is not well to speak. For the only words that can express them are dark words, without profit to the reason.

So she sits there, dreaming. What Dorabel has meant to her, what her grandfather has meant to her, both are involved in her unknown future, that her unknown self must discover. Her life is rooted deep in earth, its ample rhythms are in the movement of her thought. But Dorabel has crossed her path. Fear, fascination, torment and limitless desire are in her blood. She loves the slow deep satisfactions of the earth, but she has glimpsed now the wild lovely stormy things that stir and pass, once it may be in a life-time, not subject to the march of the seasons nor the regular recurrences of earth. How shall she gather these, how recognize them when they come, how learn to live not for the anticipated certainty—ploughing, seed-time, harrowing and harvest—but for the incredible fugitive approaches of an order whose laws she may not fathom?

So she pauses, like a bather at the cold pool. She will slip under, but not just yet; and meanwhile familiar things have a new instancy. Rime stands up like fur on the bramble leaves, a blackbird flutes before dawn, Jenny lifts a sleepy head and knows its meaning and is asleep again before she can fix it in her memory. A star burns at morning, and the air is full of voices. One afternoon a doe is standing by the kitchen door, she bounds away in terror when the dogs start up, barking. The milk freezes in the basins on the milk-house shelves, the burns run out from caves of snow. Next winter, Jenny thinks, I shall be in a street.

Excitement chokes her. The world is too big. Her own small part has been so full and good. How can she hold all that is to come? She is like a child crying that its egg is too full because it runs over. She touches her grandfather for reassurance.

He knows more than she dreams of what is passing in that bright head, but he does not speak. He will not disturb the sacred earth in which the miracle of growth goes on. He has given her the nurture of sun and wind and rain, now he lets her be. But she never turns to him without the welcome of his whole nature meeting her, she can never ask his help but it is hers, nor offer him her own but he makes use of it.

Yet both are aware that it is the end. Their perfect unity is over. For him it is an end inevitable and foreseen, that has come, as such ends always must, too soon. But for her it is a beginning, and not an end, to anticipation. She thinks she knows the old farmer through and through. She is the surprise. She waits, still as a puss but ready for the pounce, and dreams of her own strangeness with the invincible expectancy of youth.

The Living Mountain

A celebration of
the Cairngorm Mountains
of Scotland

INTRODUCED BY
RODERICK WATSON

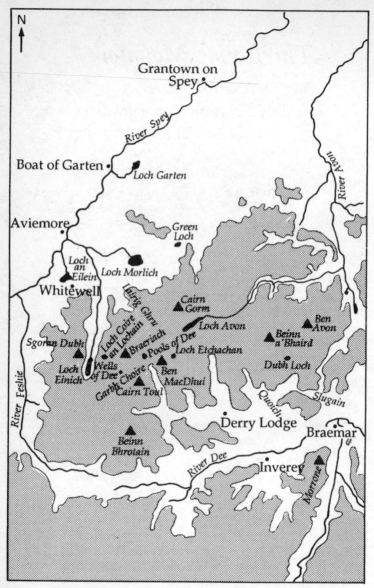

The plateau and a few place names.

Author's foreword

Thirty years in the life of a mountain is nothing—the flicker of an eyelid. Yet in the thirty years since this book was written many things have happened to the Cairngorms, some of them spectacular things, things that have won them a place in the Press and on the television screens:

Aviemore erupts and goes on erupting.

Bulldozers *birze* their way into the hill.

Roads are made, and re-made, where there were never roads before.

Skiers, swift, elate, controlled, miracles of grace and precision, swoop and soar—or flounder—but all with exhilaration.

Chair-lifts swing up and swing down (and a small boy falls from one and is killed).

A restaurant hums on the heights and between it and the summit Cairn Gorm grows scruffy, the very heather tatty from the scrape of boots (too many boots, too much commotion, but then how much uplift for how many hearts).

New shelters are sited for climbers. A cottage at Muir of Inverey is enlarged and fitted up as a place of resort for Cairngorm Club members, the members themselves laying the flooring and erecting the bunks.

Glenmore houses and trains those ready to learn. Skills are taught and tested. Young soldiers learn the techniques of Adventure. Orienteers spread over the land (but the Lairig Ghru, so far, is not to be tamed as part of a national 'way').

Reindeer are no longer experimental but settlers.

The Nature Conservancy provides safe covert for bird and beast and plant (but discourages vagabonds, of whom I have been shamelessly one—a peerer into corners). Ecologists investigate growth patterns and problems of erosion, and re-seed denuded slopes.

The Mountain Rescue service does its magnificent work, injured are plucked from ledges by helicopter, the located, the exhausted carried to safety.

And some are not rescued. A man and a girl are found, months too late, far out of their path, the girl on abraded hands and knees as she clawed her way through drift. I see her living face still (she was one of my students), a sane, eager, happy face. She should have lived to be old. Seventy men, with dogs and a helicopter, go out after a lone skier who has failed to return, and who is found dead. And a group of schoolchildren, belated, fail to find the hut where they should have spent the night. They shelter against a wall of snow, but in the morning, in spite of the heroic efforts of their instructress, only she and one boy are alive.

All these are matters that involve man. But behind them is the mountain itself, its substance, its strength, its structure, its weathers. It is fundamental to all that man does to it or on it. If it were not there he would not have done these things. So thirty years may alter the things he does but to know it in itself is still basic to his craft. And that is what, thirty years ago, I was striving to do in this manuscript. It was written during the latter years of the Second War and those just after. In that disturbed and uncertain world it was my secret place of ease. The only person who read the manuscript then was Neil Gunn, and that he should like it was not strange, because our minds met in just such experiences as I was striving to describe. He made a couple of suggestions as to publication, but added that in the circumstances of the time a publisher would be hard to find. I wrote one letter at his instigation and received a courteous and negative reply and the manuscript went into a drawer and has lain there ever since. Now, an old woman, I begin tidying out my possessions and reading it again I realise that the tale of my traffic with a mountain is as valid today as it was then. That it was a traffic of love is sufficiently clear; but love pursued with fervour is one of the roads to knowledge.

August 1977

Contents

Introduction

Nan Shepherd loved the Cairngorms and her prose meditation on that love, *The Living Mountain*, takes us to the wellsprings of her imagination and her sense of what it is to be a living being at large in the world, precariously balanced between the mysterious realms of organic and inorganic matter.

Written during the end and the aftermath of the Second World War, the manuscript of *The Living Mountain* was kept for nearly thirty years before it was finally published by Aberdeen University Press in 1977. Shepherd called it 'a traffic of love', adding cannily, 'but love pursued with fervour is one of the roads to knowledge'. That passion for knowledge, and the passion *of* knowledge and *in* knowledge, is entirely characteristic of her nature. It was an insight which led her to produce one of the most astute essays on Hugh MacDiarmid's later poetry at a time (1938) when few other critics understood or valued his quest for 'The Impossible Song'. And the same mixture of spirituality and scientific precision can be found in her correspondence with Neil Gunn when she was receiving treatment for a glandular imbalance which led her to suspect that her former poise, and her sense of self, might be no more than 'the result of a generous supply of thyroid—an accident of matter.' (Letter to Neil Gunn, 24 February, 1948.)

Nan Shepherd's sense of the precariousness of whatever it is that 'separates us from non-being' can be felt in all her novels, especially when she considers the further reaches of our inner lives, and those remote and intuitive insights that come like a flash in the dark.—One thinks of Bawbie Paterson in *The Weatherhouse*, suddenly perceived as a 'dancing star'; or young Martha's shiver—'until she felt as enormous as the sky'—at her first sight of the Auroral northern lights in *The Quarry Wood*. Shepherd's fiction is particularly rich in such descriptions, and they are almost always linked to effects of landscape or weather. And this is appropriate enough, one might say, for the changeable North East climate. But these descriptions point beyond the merely material, to a haunting sense of immanence and unity which Nan Shepherd sought and found in the hills all her life.

Writing to Neil Gunn about his books *Wild Geese Overhead* (1939) and *Second Sight* (1940), she explained what it is she feels at such moments, and how much she admires Gunn's own translation of them into the written word:

> To apprehend things—walking on a hill, seeing the light change, the mist, the dark, being aware, using the whole of one's body to instruct the spirit—yes that is the secret life one has and knows that others have. But to be able to share it, in and through words—that is what frightens me. . . . It dissolves one's being. I am no longer myself but a part of a life beyond myself when I read pages that are so much an expression of myself. You can take processes of being—no, that's too formal a word—*states* is too static, this is something that moves—*movements* I suppose is best—you can take movements of being and translate them out of themselves into words; that seems to me a gift of a very high and rare order.
>
> (Letter to Neil Gunn, May 1940)

This passage shows Shepherd's clear affinity with the more Zen-like moments of Neil Gunn's muse, a connection which can be seen even more clearly in the opening page of her meditation on 'Water' in *The Living Mountain*: 'Like all profound mysteries, it is so simple that it frightens me. It wells from the rock, and flows away. For unnumbered years it has welled from the rock, and flowed away. It does nothing, absolutely nothing, but be itself.'

Among the Shepherd manuscripts in the National Library of Scotland is the following poem, called 'Achiltibuie', drafted and dated 4 October, 1950. Here again we sense her characteristic experience of how the organic and the inorganic can meet and mingle at moments of heightened mental and physical exertion:

> Here on the edge of Europe I stand on the edge of being.
> Floating on light, isle after isle takes wing.
> Burning blue are the peaks, rock that is older than
>   thought,
> And the sea burns blue—or is it the air between?—
> They merge, they take one another upon them,
> I have fallen through time and found the enchanted
>   world,
> Where all is beginning. The obstinate rocks
> Are a fire of blue, a pulse of power, a beat
> In energy, the sea dissolves,
> And I too melt, am timeless, a pulse of light.

Shepherd's published poetry (*In the Cairngorms*, 1934) is equally striking in its imagery of air, light, water and stone; and when she writes again about the Cairngorms in *The Living Mountain*, she asks herself where this sense of dissolving comes from. Is it part of the landscape, or part of herself?

> . . . this nonsense of physiology does not really explain it at all. What! am I such a slave that unless my flesh feels buoyant I cannot be free? No, there is more in the lust for a mountain top than a perfect physiological adjustment. What more there is lies within the mountain. Something moves between me and it. Place and a mind may interpenetrate till the nature of both is altered. I cannot tell what this movement is except by recounting it.
>
> 'The Plateau')

And recount it she did, in her poetry and at key points in each of her novels. But the fullest expression, and the most complete exploration and indeed *analysis* of what it was she felt, was reserved for *The Living Mountain*.

The prose style of this little book is at once austerely intellectual and passionately felt—'love pursued with fervour' is indeed 'one of the roads to knowledge', and it is 'knowledge', rather than 'feeling' that seems to be Nan Shepherd's route to the sublime. In this respect her writing can be traced back to the Wordsworth of *The Prelude*; and here she shares another link with Neil Gunn, whose autobiography *The Atom of Delight* is equally deeply suffused with the Wordsworthian spirit. And there's a connection, too, with the later MacDiarmid and the Carlylean austerity of *his* pursuit of stones and spirit on the high places and the raised beaches of the world.

In the penultimate passage of her book—called 'The Senses'—Shepherd comes to the conclusion that the living mountain *lives* because of our own conscious engagement with it. Without that outgoing address, the world, and ourselves in it, would be truly dead:

> It is, as with all creation, matter impregnated with mind
> . . . It is something snatched from non-being, that shadow
> which creeps in on us continuously and can be held off by
> continuous creative act. So, simply to look on anything,
> such as a mountain, with the love that penetrates to its
> essence, is to widen the domain of being in the vastness
> of non-being. Man has no other reason for his existence.

'Man has no other reason for his existence'—there speaks the true spirit of MacDiarmid and Carlyle! But 'to look on anything . . . with the love that penetrates to its essence'—this is what lies at the heart of Nan Shepherd's humane vision as a novelist. Indeed, the austerity of her final position should not blind us to the wealth of everyday detail and delight to be found in *The Living Mountain*, as a record of the birds, the plants, the stories and the people of the hills, and also as a personal diary of the many years she tramped the great rolling mountain tops of Scotland's central massif.

Nan Shepherd was no sentimentalist, and as a dedicated member of the Deeside Field Club, her love of the country was entirely practical. Former students and colleagues fondly remember being lectured on the 'sinfulness of dropping sweetie papers about the countryside' and how, even in the remotest mountain bothies, Nan instructed them on how best to air the sleeping bags and pack the bedding. Yet, these acts too, as the Zen pupil will tell you, are holy; and the closing words of *The Living Mountain* are entirely in keeping with this sense of discipline and humble privilege—qualities which marked Nan Shepherd's whole life, in her dealings with her family, in her relationship with her students, and in her insight into the blighted and also the freely flowering lives of so many women in her novels.

I believe that I now understand in some small measure why the Buddhist goes on pilgrimage to a mountain. The journey is itself part of the technique by which the god is sought. It is a journey into Being; for as I penetrate more deeply into the mountain's life, I penetrate also into my own. For an hour I am beyond desire. It is not ecstasy, that leap out of the self that makes man like a god. I am not out of myself, but in myself. I am. To know Being, this is the final grace accorded from the mountain.

Roderick Watson

ONE

The Plateau

Summer on the high plateau can be delectable as honey; it can also be a roaring scourge. To those who love the place, both are good, since both are part of its essential nature. And it is to know its essential nature that I am seeking here. To know, that is, with the knowledge that is a process of living. This is not done easily nor in an hour. It is a tale too slow for the impatience of our age, not of immediate enough import for its desperate problems. Yet it has its own rare value. It is, for one thing, a corrective of glib assessment: one never quite knows the mountain, nor oneself in relation to it. However often I walk on them, these hills hold astonishment for me. There is no getting accustomed to them.

The Cairngorm Mountains are a mass of granite thrust up through the schists and gneiss that form the lower surrounding hills, planed down by the ice cap, and split, shattered and scooped by frost, glaciers and the strength of running water. Their physiognomy is in the geography books—so many square miles of area, so many lochs, so many summits of over 4000 feet—but this is a pallid simulacrum of their reality, which, like every reality that matters ultimately to human beings, is a reality of the mind.

The plateau is the true summit of these mountains; they must be seen as a single mountain, and the individual tops, Ben MacDhui, Braeriach and the rest, though sundered from one another by fissures and deep descents, are no more than eddies on the plateau surface. One does not look upward to spectacular peaks but downward from the peaks to spectacular chasms. The plateau itself is not spectacular. It is bare and very stony, and since there is nothing higher than itself (except for the tip of Ben Nevis) nearer than

Norway, it is savaged by the wind. Snow covers it for half the year and sometimes, for as long as a month at a time, it is in cloud. Its growth is moss and lichen and sedge, and in June the clumps of Silene—moss campion—flower in brilliant pink. Dotterel and ptarmigan nest upon it, and springs ooze from its rock. By continental measurement its height is nothing much—around 4000 feet—but for an island it is well enough, and if the winds have unhindered range, so has the eye. It is island weather too, with no continent to steady it, and the place has as many aspects as there are gradations in the light.

Light in Scotland has a quality I have not met elsewhere. It is luminous without being fierce, penetrating to immense distances with an effortless intensity. So on a clear day one looks without any sense of strain from Morven in Caithness to the Lammermuirs, and out past Ben Nevis to Morar. At midsummer, I have had to be persuaded I was not seeing further even than that. I could have sworn I saw a shape, distinct and blue, very clear and small, further off than any hill the chart recorded. The chart was against me, my companions were against me, I never saw it again. On a day like that, height goes to one's head. Perhaps it was the lost Atlantis focused for a moment out of time.

The streams that fall over the edges of the plateau are clear—Avon indeed has become a by-word for clarity: gazing into its depths, one loses all sense of time, like the monk in the old story who listened to the blackbird.

> Water of A'n, ye rin sae clear,
> 'Twad beguile a man of a hundred year.

Its waters are white, of a clearness so absolute that there is no image for them. Naked birches in April, lighted after heavy rain by the sun, might suggest their brilliance. Yet this is too sensational. The whiteness of these waters is simple. They are elemental transparency. Like roundness, or silence, their quality is natural, but is found so seldom in its absolute state that when we do so find it we are astonished.

The young Dee, as it flows out of the Garbh Choire

and joins the water from the Lairig Pools, has the same astounding transparency. Water so clear cannot be imagined, but must be seen. One must go back, and back again, to look at it, for in the interval memory refuses to recreate its brightness. This is one of the reasons why the high plateau where these streams begin, the streams themselves, their cataracts and rocky beds, the corries, the whole wild enchantment, like a work of art is perpetually new when one returns to it. The mind cannot carry away all that it has to give, nor does it always believe possible what it has carried away.

So back one climbs, to the sources. Here the life of the rivers begins—Dee and Avon, the Derry, the Beinnie and the Allt Druie. In these pure and terrible streams the rain, cloud and snow of the high Cairngorms are drained away. They rise from the granite, sun themselves a little on the unsheltered plateau and drop through air to their valleys. Or they cut their way out under wreaths of snow, escaping in a tumult. Or hang in tangles of ice on the rock faces. One cannot know the rivers till one has seen them at their sources; but this journey to the sources is not to be undertaken lightly. One walks among elementals, and elementals are not governable. There are awakened also in oneself by the contact elementals that are as unpredictable as wind or snow.

This may suggest that to reach the high plateau of the Cairngorms is difficult. But no, no such thing. Given clear air, and the unending daylight of a Northern summer, there is not one of the summits but can be reached by a moderately strong walker without distress. A strong walker will take a couple of summits. Circus walkers will plant flags on all six summits in a matter of fourteen hours. This may be fun, but is sterile. To pit oneself against the mountain is necessary for every climber: to pit oneself merely against other players, and make a race of it, is to reduce to the level of a game what is essentially an experience. Yet what a race-course for these boys to choose! To know the hills, and their own bodies, well enough to dare the exploit is their real achievement.

Mastering new routes up the rock itself is another matter.

Granite, of which the Cairngorms are built, weathers too smoothly and squarely to make the best conditions for rock-climbing. Yet there is such challenge in the grandeur of the corries that those who climb cannot leave them untasted. The Guide Book and the *Cairngorm Club Journal* give the attested climbs, with their dates, from the end of last century onwards. Yet I wonder if young blood didn't attempt it sooner. There is a record of a shepherd, a century and a half ago, found frozen along with his sheep dog, on a ledge of one of the Braeriach cliffs. He, to be sure, wandered there, in a blizzard, but the men who brought down the body must have done a pretty job of work; and I can believe there were young hot-heads among that hardy breed to whom the scaling of a precipice was nothing new. Dr George Skene Keith, in his *General View of Aberdeenshire*, records having scrambled up the bed of the Dee cataract in 1810, and Professor McGillivray, in his *Natural History of Braemar*, tells how as a student, in 1819, he walked from Aberdeen University to his western home, straight through the Cairngorm group; and lying down to sleep, just as he was, at the foot of the Braeriach precipices, continued next morning on his way straight up out of the corrie in which he had slept. On a later visit, searching out the flora of these mountains, he seems to have run up and down the crags with something of the deer's lightness. There are, however, ways up and down some of these corries that may be scrambled by any fleet-footed and level-headed climber, and it is doubtless these that the earlier adventurers had used. The fascination of the later work lies in finding ways impossible without the rope; and there are still many faces among these precipices that have not been attempted. One of my young friends lately pioneered a route out of the Garbh Choire of Braeriach, over rock not hitherto climbed. To him, one of the keenest young hillmen I know (he has been described, and recognised at a railway terminus, as 'a little black fellow, load the size of himself, with a far-away look in his eyes'), the mere setting up of a record is of very minor importance. What he values is a task that, demanding of him all he has and is, absorbs and so releases him entirely.

It is, of course, merely stupid to suppose that the

record-breakers do not love the hills. Those who do not love them don't go up, and those who do can never have enough of it. It is an appetite that grows in feeding. Like drink and passion, it intensifies life to the point of glory. In the Scots term, used for the man who is *abune himsel'* with drink, one is *raised*; *fey*; a little mad, in the eyes of the folk who do not climb.

Fey may be too strong a term for that joyous release of body that is engendered by climbing; yet to the sober looker-on a man may seem to walk securely over dangerous places with the gay abandon that is said to be the mark of those who are doomed to death. How much of this gay security is the result of perfectly trained and co-ordinated body and mind, only climbers themselves realise; nor is there any need to ascribe to the agency of a god either the gay security, or the death which may occasionally, but rarely, follow. The latter, if it does occur, is likely to be the result of carelessness—of failing in one's exaltation to observe a coating of ice on the stone, of trusting to one's amazing luck rather than to one's compass, perhaps merely, in the glow of complete bodily well-being, of over-estimating one's powers of endurance.

But there is a phenomenon associated with this *feyness* of which I must confess a knowledge. Often, in my bed at home, I have remembered the places I have run lightly over with no sense of fear, and have gone cold to think of them. It seems to me then that I could never go back; my fear unmans me, horror is in my mouth. Yet when I go back, the same leap of the spirit carries me up. God or no god, I am *fey* again.

The *feyness* itself seems to me to have a physiological origin. Those who undergo it have the particular bodily make-up that functions at its most free and most live upon heights (although this, it is obvious, refers only to heights manageable to man and not at all to those for which a slow and painful acclimitisation is needful). As they ascend, the air grows rarer and more stimulating, the body feels lighter and they climb with less effort, till Dante's law of ascent on the Mount of Purgation seems to become a physical truth: 'This mountain is such, that ever at the beginning below 'tis toilsome, and the more a man ascends the less it wearies.'

At first I had thought that this lightness of body was a universal reaction to rarer air. It surprised me to discover that some people suffered malaise at altitudes that released me, but were happy in low valleys where I felt extinguished. Then I began to see that our devotions have more to do with our physiological peculiarities than we admit. I am a mountain lover because my body is at its best in the rarer air of the heights and communicates its elation to the mind. The obverse of this would seem to be exemplified in the extreme of fatigue I suffered while walking some two miles underground in the Ardennes caverns. This was plainly no case of a weary mind communicating its fatigue to the body, since I was enthralled by the strangeness and beauty of these underground cavities. Add to this eyes, the normal focus of which is for distance, and my delight in the expanse of space opened up from the mountain tops becomes also a perfect physiological adjustment. The short-sighted cannot love mountains as the long-sighted do. The sustained rhythm of movement in a long climb has also its part in inducing the sense of physical well-being, and this cannot be captured by any mechanical mode of ascent.

This bodily lightness, then, in the rarefied air, combines with the liberation of space to give mountain *feyness* to those who are susceptible to such a malady. For it is a malady, subverting the will and superseding the judgment: but a malady of which the afflicted will never ask to be cured. For this nonsense of physiology does not really explain it at all. What! am I such a slave that unless my flesh feels buoyant I cannot be free? No, there is more in the lust for a mountain top than a perfect physiological adjustment. What more there is lies within the mountain. Something moves between me and it. Place and a mind may interpenetrate till the nature of both is altered. I cannot tell what this movement is except by recounting it.

TWO

The Recesses

At first, mad to recover the tang of height, I made always for the summits, and would not take time to explore the recesses. But late one September I went on Braeriach with a man who knew the hill better than I did then, and he took me aside into Coire an Lochain. One could not have asked a fitter day for the first vision of this rare loch. The equinoctial storms had been severe; snow, that hardly ever fails to powder the plateau about the third week of September, had fallen close and thick, but now the storms had passed, the air was keen and buoyant, with a brilliancy as of ice, the waters of the loch were frost-cold to the fingers. And how still, how incredibly withdrawn and tranquil. Climb as often as you will, Loch Coire an Lochain remains incredible. It cannot be seen until one stands almost on its lip, but only height hides it. Unlike Avon and Etchachan, it is not shut into the mountain but lies on an outer flank, its hollow ranged daily by all the eyes that look at the Cairngorms from the Spey. Yet, without knowing, one would not guess its presence and certainly not its size. Two cataracts, the one that feeds it, falling from the brim of the plateau over rock, and the one that drains it, show as white threads on the mountain. Having scrambled up the bed of the latter (not, as I knew later, the simple way, but my companion was a rabid naturalist who had business with every leaf, stalk and root in the rocky bed), one expects to be near the corrie, but no, it is still a long way off. And on one toils, into the hill. Black scatter of rock, pieces large as a house, pieces edged like a grater. A tough bit of going. And there at last is the loch, held tight back against the precipice. Yet as I turned, that September day, and looked back through the clear air, I could see straight out to ranges of distant

7

hills. And that astonished me. To be so open and yet so secret! Its anonymity—Loch of the Corrie of the Loch, that is all—seems to guard this surprising secrecy. Other lochs, Avon, Morlich and the rest, have their distinctive names. One expects of them an idiosyncrasy. But Loch of the Corrie of the Loch, what could there be there? A tarn like any other. And then to find this distillation of loveliness!

I put my fingers in the water and found it cold. I listened to the waterfall until I no longer heard it. I let my eyes travel from shore to shore very slowly and was amazed at the width of the water. How could I have foreseen so large a loch, 3000-odd feet up, slipped away into this corrie which was only one of three upon one face of a mountain that was itself only a broken bit of the plateau? And a second time I let my eyes travel over the surface, slowly, from shore to shore, beginning at my feet and ending against the precipice. There is no way like that for savouring the extent of a water surface.

This changing of focus in the eye, moving the eye itself when looking at things that do not move, deepens one's sense of outer reality. Then static things may be caught in the very act of becoming. By so simple a matter, too, as altering the position of one's head, a different kind of world may be made to appear. Lay the head down, or better still, face away from what you look at, and bend with straddled legs till you see your world upside down. How new it has become! From the close-by sprigs of heather to the most distant fold of the land, each detail stands erect in its own validity. In no other way have I seen of my own unaided sight that the earth is round. As I watch, it arches its back, and each layer of landscape bristles—though *bristles* is a word of too much commotion for it. Details are no longer part of a grouping in a picture of which I am the focal point, the focal point is everywhere. Nothing has reference to me, the looker. This is how the earth must see itself.

So I looked slowly across the Coire Loch, and began to understand that haste can do nothing with these hills. I knew when I had looked for a long time that I had hardly begun to see. So with Loch Avon. My first encounter was sharp and astringent, and has crystallised for ever for me some innermost inaccessibility. I had climbed all six of the major summits, some of them twice over, before clambering down into the mountain trough that holds Loch Avon. This loch lies at an altitude of some 2300 feet, but its banks soar up for another fifteen hundred. Indeed farther, for Cairn Gorm and Ben MacDhui may be said to be its banks. From the lower end of this mile and a half gash in the rock, exit is easy but very long. One may go down by the Avon itself, through ten miles as lonely and unvisited as anything in the Cairngorms, to Inchrory; or by easy enough watersheds pass into Strathnethy or Glen Derry, or under the Barns of Bynack to the Caiplich Water. But higher up the loch there is no way out, save by scrambling up one or other of the burns that tumble from the heights: except that, above the Shelter Stone, a gap opens between the hills to Loch Etchachan, and here the scramble up is shorter.

The inner end of this gash has been howked straight from the granite. As one looks up from below, the agents would appear mere splashes of water, whose force might be turned aside by a pair of hands. Yet above the precipices we have found in one of these burns pools deep enough to bathe in. The water that pours over these grim bastions carries no sediment of any kind in its precipitate fall, which seems indeed to distil and aerate the water so that the loch far below is sparkling clear. This narrow loch has never, I believe, been sounded. I know its depth, though not in feet.

I first saw it on a cloudless day of early July. We had started at dawn, crossed Cairn Gorm about nine o'clock, and made our way by the Saddle to the lower end of the loch. Then we idled up the side, facing the gaunt corrie, and at last, when the noonday sun penetrated directly into the water, we stripped and bathed. The clear water was at our knees, then at our thighs. How clear it was only this walking into it could reveal. To look through it was to discover its own properties. What we saw under water had a sharper clarity than what we saw through air. We waded on into the brightness, and the width of the water increased, as it always does when one is on or in it, so that the loch no longer seemed narrow, but the far side was a long way off.

Then I looked down; and at my feet there opened a gulf
of brightness so profound that the mind stopped. We were
standing on the edge of a shelf that ran some yards into the
loch before plunging down to the pit that is the true bottom.
And through that inordinate clearness we saw to the depth
of the pit. So limpid was it that every stone was clear.

I motioned to my companion, who was a step behind,
and she came, and glanced as I had down the submerged
precipice. Then we looked into each other's eyes, and again
into the pit. I waded slowly back into shallower water. There
was nothing that seemed worth saying. My spirit was as
naked as my body. It was one of the most defenceless
moments of my life.

I do not think it was the imminence of personal bodily
danger that shook me. I had not then, and have not in
retrospect, any sense of having just escaped a deadly peril.
I might of course have overbalanced and been drowned;
but I do not think I would have stepped down unawares.
Eye and foot acquire in rough walking a co-ordination that
makes one distinctly aware of where the next step is to fall,
even while watching sky and land. This watching, it is true,
is of a general nature only; for attentive observation the
body must be still. But in a general way, in country that is
rough, but not difficult, one sees where one is and where
one is going at the same time. I proved this sharply to
myself one hot June day in Glen Quoich, when bounding
down a slope of long heather towards the stream. With
hardly a slackening of pace, eye detected and foot avoided
a coiled adder on which the next spring would have landed
me; detected and avoided also his mate, at full length in the
line of my side spring; and I pulled up a short way past,
to consider with amused surprise the speed and sureness
of my own feet. Conscious thought had had small part in
directing them.

So, although they say of the River Avon that men have
walked into it and been drowned, supposing it shallow
because they could see its depth, I do not think I was
in much danger just then of drowning, nor was fear the
emotion with which I stared into the pool. That first glance
down had shocked me to a heightened power of myself,

in which even fear became a rare exhilaration: not that it ceased to be fear, but fear itself, so impersonal, so keenly apprehended, enlarged rather than constricted the spirit.

The inaccessibility of this loch is part of its power. Silence belongs to it. If jeeps find it out, or a funicular railway disfigures it, part of its meaning will be gone. The good of the greatest number is not here relevant. It is necessary to be sometimes exclusive, not on behalf of rank or wealth, but of those human qualities that can apprehend loneliness.

The presence of another person does not detract from, but enhances, the silence, if the other is the right sort of hill companion. The perfect hill companion is the one whose identity is for the time being merged in that of the mountains, as you feel your own to be. Then such speech as arises is part of a common life and cannot be alien. To 'make conversation', however, is ruinous, to speak may be superfluous. I have it from a gaunt elderly man, a 'lang tangle o' a chiel', with high cheek bones and hollow cheeks, product of a hill farm though himself a civil servant, that when he goes on the hill with chatterers, he 'could see them to an ill place'. I have walked myself with brilliant young people whose talk, entertaining, witty and incessant, yet left me weary and dispirited, because the hill did not speak. This does not imply that the only good talk on a hill is about the hill. All sorts of themes may be lit up from within by contact with it, as they are by contact with another mind, and so discussion may be salted. Yet to listen is better than to speak.

The talking tribe, I find, want sensation from the mountain—not in Keats's sense. Beginners, not unnaturally, do the same—I did myself. They want the startling view, the horrid pinnacle—sips of beer and tea instead of milk. Yet often the mountain gives itself most completely when I have no destination, when I reach nowhere in particular, but have gone out merely to be with the mountain as one visits a friend with no intention but to be with him.

THREE

The Group

My first climb was Ben MacDhui—rightly, since he is the highest—and by the classic route of Coire Etchachan; and from that first day two ideas persist. The first is that a mountain has an inside. I was well accustomed to hills, having run from childhood on the Deeside hills and the Monadhliaths, those flowing heights that flank the Spey on the other side from the Cairngorms, an ideal playground for a child; and the end of a climb meant for me always the opening of a spacious view over the world: that was the moment of glory. But to toil upward, feel the gradient slacken and the top approach, as one does at the end of the Etchachan ascent, and then find no spaciousness for reward, but an interior—that astounded me. And what an interior! the boulder-strewn plain, the silent shining loch, the black overhang of its precipice, the drop to Loch Avon and the soaring barricade of Cairn Gorm beyond, and on every side, except where we had entered, towering mountain walls.

Years later, I had something of the same sensation inside the Barns of Bynack, that enormous black cube of rock that lies like a Queen Anne mansion on the side of Ben Bynack. One can walk up a sort of staircase within and look out by a cleft as though from a window.

The second knowledge I have retained from my first ascent is of the inside of a cloud. For, from a few yards above Loch Etchachan to the summit, we walked in a cloud so thick that when the man who was leading went ahead by so much as an arm's length, he vanished, except for his whistle. His wife and I followed the whistle, and now and then when we were too slow (for he was an impatient lad), he materialised again out of the cloud and spoke to us. And alone in that whiteness, while our *revenant* came

and went, we climbed an endless way. Nothing altered.
Once, our ghostly mentor held us each firmly by an arm
and said, 'That's Loch Etchachan down there.' Nothing.
The whiteness was perhaps thicker. It was horrible to stand
and stare into that pot of whiteness. The path went on.
And now to the side of us there was a ghastlier white,
spreading and swallowing even the grey-brown earth our
minds had stood on. We had come to the snow. A white
as of non-life.

That cloud, like others inside which I have walked, was
wet but not wetting. It did not wet us till, almost at the
summit, it broke in hard rain, and we could at last see the
corries, scarfed in mist. Some clouds savage the wayfarer
on the heights—clouds from below, up here they are rain,
or sleet—some nuzzle him gently but with such persistence
that he might as well walk through a loch. Or the wet may be
more delicate, condensing in droplets on eyebrows and hair
and woollen clothing, as has happened by morning with the
dew after a night outside. Or the cloud may be hardly more
than a sensation on the skin, clammy, or merely chill. Once
I was inside a cloud that gave no sensation whatever. From
within it, it was neither tangible nor visible, though as it
approached it had looked thick and threatening. We were
on the flank between Sgoran Dubh and Sgor Gaoith, on
a cloudless day of sun; and suddenly there was the cloud,
making steadily toward us, with a straight under-edge about
the 3000 feet level. We thought: we're in for it! But nothing
more happened than that the sunshine went out, as though
a switch had clicked; and in some twenty minutes the sun
clicked on again, and we saw the level under-edge of cloud
pass away across the Einich valley. Inside the cloud had
been just dry-dull.

To walk out through the top of a cloud is good. Once
or twice I have had the luck to stand on a tip of ground
and see a pearled and lustrous plain stretch out to the
horizons. Far off, another peak lifts like a small island
from the smother. It is like the morning of creation. Once,
on Lochnagar, we had watched the dawn light strike the
Cairngorms, like the blue bloom on plums. Each scarp
and gully was translucent, no smallest detail blurred. A

pure clear sun poured into each recess. But looking south, we caught our breath. For the world had vanished. There was nothing there but an immense stretch of hummocked snow. Or was it sea? It gleamed, and washed the high hills as the sea washes rock. And came to an end, as most seas do somewhere, with the Glen Lyon Mountains, Ben Lawers and Schiehallion, standing up out of it like one of the long twin-peaked islands of the west. A sea of mist invading the heart of the land, but sucked up by the sun as the hot day went on.

Seeing the Cairngorms from other mountains, Lochnagar or the Glen Lyon heights, emphasises them as a group. From the latter their great lift can be clearly seen, their mass and squareness. They tower up in a blunt pyramid. The height of high hills can, of course, be appreciated only from others of equal or at least approximate height, but this is not merely a matter of relative stature. There is something in their lift, their proportions and bearing, that can only be seen when one is somewhere near their own size. From below, oddly enough, they are not so majestic. This can be best seen with the Cairngorm group from Geal Charn in the Monadhliaths, which, though not even a three-thousander, stands erectly over against them across the Spey valley. Coming steeply down its front, one watches the high panorama opposite settle into itself as one descends. It enchants me like a juggler's trick. Every time I come down I want promptly to go back and see it all over again. A simple diagram explains the 'trick', but no diagram can explain the serene sublimity these high panoramas convey to the human mind. It is worth ascending unexciting heights if for nothing else than to see the big ones from nearer their own level.

From the hills of lower Deeside, the plateau nature of the group is most clearly seen, for only the long table of Ben Avon and Ben a' Bhuird is in view. As one follows up the Dee valley, Cairntoul appears, dominant. By Lochnagar, the whole façade is clear, sculptured in block and cleft and cornice, with which the light makes play. It is best at morning, when the cliffs are rose-red. The phenomenon lasts about an hour, precipice after precipice glowing to rose and fading again, though in some conditions of the air the glow lasts longer, and I have seen, in intense still summer heat, not only the corries but the whole plateau burning with a hot violet incandescence until noon. Sunset also lights the corries, but this must be seen on the other side of the group. From the Lochnagar side summer sunsets are behind the Cairngorms, but winter sunsets touch them obliquely. From Lochnagar, too, can be seen what is not often seen except by going to it or to those parts of the plateau just above it, one of the most secret places of the range, the inner recess of the great Garbh Choire of Braeriach.

On the hills still further west, from Glas Maol on the borders of Angus, the Cairngorm group seems to grow gently out of the surrounding hills, its outlines melting into harmony with theirs. Its origins may be different, but like them it has been subdued by the grinding of the ice-age, and here more than anywhere else the common experience shows. From Ben Ouran at the head of Glen Ey, one looks straight into the Lairig Pass, and sees the plateau split in two by the cleft that runs right through it. But from the mouth of the Ey valley, on the hillside a mile or so from where this stream joins the Dee, one is surprised by a new vision of the familiar range. Here one realises: these are mountains, not a shattered plateau; for they are seen as peaks piled on peaks, a majestic culmination. This effect is most marked when the long flat top of Braeriach is veiled, as it is so often, in mist, while Ben MacDhui towers up like the giant he is, flanked by the peaked cone of Cairntoul and reinforced by the lesser and nearer peaks of the Devil's Point and Cairngorm of Derry. These peaks seem to hang splendidly aloft above the eye, giving a new sense of the grandeur of these mountains. But moving further round, south-west and west, one finds only a lump-mass, rounded and unshapely, with no dignity except bulk. This is the back of the mountain, like the back of a monster's head: at the other side are the open jaws, the teeth, the terrible fangs.

The north-east view, from the Braes of Abernethy, directly opposite to this lumpish back, has the gaping jaw and the fangs. It is a place of swift and soaring lines. This is Cairn Gorm, from which, though it is only the fourth summit in height, the whole group takes its name. These plunging precipices frame Loch Avon. Here is Stac Iolaire, the Eagle's Crag. Cairn Gorm has the finest complement of lochs—Loch Avon, the small and lovely Loch an Uaine, whose waters have the green gleam of old copper roofs, and Loch Morlich, the perfect mirror of the three great corries on the Speyside face. The edge of cliffs hangs 3000 feet above the smooth water, which is broad and long enough to hold the whole majestic front, corries, ridges and foothills, that jut like a high relief from the block of the plateau. On a still day it has a dream-like loveliness.

This whole north-west face, the three Cairn Gorm corries and the three on Braeriach, rises steeply from moor, so that walking along the plateau lip, one has the sense of being lifted, as on a mighty shelf, above the world.

FOUR

Water

So I am on the plateau again, having gone round it like a dog in circles to see if it is a good place. I think it is, and I am to stay up here for a while. I have left at dawn, and up here it is still morning. The midsummer sun has drawn up the moisture from the earth, so that for part of the way I walked in cloud, but now the last tendril has dissolved into the air and there is nothing in all the sky but light. I can see to the ends of the earth and far up into the sky.

As I stand there in the silence, I become aware that the silence is not complete. Water is speaking. I go towards it, and almost at once the view is lost: for the plateau has its own hollows, and this one slopes widely down to one of the great inward fissures, the Garbh Coire. It lies like a broad leaf veined with watercourses, that converge on the lip of the precipice to drop down in a cataract for 500 feet. This is the River Dee. Astonishingly, up here at 4000 feet, it is already a considerable stream. The immense leaf that it drains is bare, surfaced with stones, gravel, sometimes sand, and in places moss and grass grow on it. Here and there in the moss a few white stones have been piled together. I go to them, and water is welling up, strong and copious, pure cold water that flows away in rivulets and drops over the rock. These are the Wells of Dee. This is the river. Water, that strong white stuff, one of the four elemental mysteries, can here be seen at its origins. Like all profound mysteries, it is so simple that it frightens me. It wells from the rock, and flows away. For unnumbered years it has welled from the rock, and flowed away. It does nothing, absolutely nothing, but be itself.

The Dee, however, into which through its tributary streams all this south-eastern side of the Cairngorms is to drain, takes its headwaters not from one only but from both halves of the central plateau. The gash that divides the two halves (the Cairntoul and Braeriach from the Cairn Gorm-Ben MacDhui side), the Lairig Ghru, is so sheer and narrow that when mists roll among the precipices, lifting and settling again, it is sometimes hard to tell whether a glimpse of rock wall belongs to the mountain on which one is standing or to another across the cleft. High on the Ben MacDhui side, though 300 feet lower than the wells on Braeriach, two waters begin a mere step from one another. One runs east, falls over the precipice into Loch Avon and turns north to the Spey; the other, starting westwards, slips over the edge as the March Burn and falls into the Lairig Ghru. Eventually, turning south and east, and having joined the water that flows out of the Garbh Choire, it becomes the Dee. But where it falls into the narrow defile of the Lairig, its life seems already over. It disappears. A little further down a tiny pool is seen, and still further down two others, sizable pools, crystal clear and deep. They have no visible means of support, no stream is seen to enter them, none to leave; but their suppressed sparkle tells that they are living water. These are the Pools of Dee. The March Burn feeds them, the young Dee, a short way beyond the lowest of the pools, is plainly their exit. I can conceive of no good reason for trudging through the oppressive Lairig Ghru, except to see them.

Through most of its length the Lairig Ghru hides its watercourses. On the other side of the watershed, towards the Spey, this havoc of boulders seems quite dry. One is surprised when suddenly a piece of running stream appears in the bottom, but it is soon swallowed again. Finally, where the precipitous sides of the gash widen out, and the storms of centuries no longer have rained successions of broken boulders on to the stream beds, the burn at last gushes into the open, a full strong stream of crystal water.

It is not only in this narrow defile that the fallen and scattered boulders cover the watercourses. I have sat among boulders on an outer face of the hill, with two low sounds in my ears, and failed to locate either. One was the churr of ptarmigan, the other the running of water. After a long time,

I saw the ptarmigan when he rose with a movement of white wings from among the grey stones he so closely resembles, but the water I never saw. In other places a bottle-neck gurgle catches my ear and where I thought there were only stones, I can see below them the glint of water.

The Cairngorm water is all clear. Flowing from granite, with no peat to darken it, it has never the golden amber, the 'horse-back brown' so often praised in Highland burns. When it has any colour at all, it is green, as in the Quoich near its linn. It is a green like the green of winter skies, but lucent, clear like aquamarines, without the vivid brilliance of glacier water. Sometimes the Quoich waterfalls have violet playing through the green, and the pouring water spouts and bubbles in a violet froth. The pools beneath these waterfalls are clear and deep. I have played myself often by pitching into them the tiniest white stones I can find, and watching through the appreciable time they take to sway downwards to the bottom.

Some of the lochs also are green. Four of them bear this quality in their names—Loch an Uaine. They are all small lochs, set high in corries, except for the Ryvoan Loch, the lowest and most decorative. Perhaps I should say, decorated. It lies within the tree level, which none of the others do, and has a lovely frieze of pine trees, an eagle's eyrie in one of them, and ancient fallen trunks visible at its bottom through the clear water. The greenness of the water varies according to the light, now aquamarine, now verdigris, but it is always pure green, metallic rather than vegetable. That one which hangs between a precipice and sloping slabs of naked rock on the face of the great curve of cliffs between Braeriach and Cairntoul, has the sharpest beauty of the four—a stark splendour of line etched and impeccable. Ben MacDhui and Cairngorm of Derry have the other two, less picturesque than the first, less exquisite than the other. The Spey slope of these mountains has the best of it with lochs, but the Dee slope has the lovelier burns—they fall more steeply, with deep still pools below the falls.

Two of the lochs are black by name—the Dubh Loch of Ben a' Bhuird, and the Dubh Loch that lies in the second cleft that cuts the plateau, the Little Lairig; but they are black by place and not by nature, shadowed heavily by rock. That the water has no darkness in it is plain when one remembers that the clear green Quoich runs out of the one loch and the Avon is fed by the other. In winter the ice that covers them has green glints in it, and in April dark streaks run through the glinting ice, showing where the springs are already running strong beneath. In summer I have stood on the high buttress of Ben a' Bhuird above the Dubh Loch, with the sun striking straight downward into its water, and seen from that height through the water the stones upon its floor.

This water from the granite is cold. To drink it at the source makes the throat tingle. A sting of life is in its touch. Yet there are midsummer days when even on the plateau the streams are warm enough to bathe in. In other years on the same date the same streams surge out from caves of snow, and snow bridges span not only the Dee on its high plateau but the Etchachan in its low hung corrie; and fording the Allt Druie, which is too swollen to cross dryshod, I have been aware of no sensation at all, not even of the pressure of the current against my legs, but cold.

The sound of all this moving water is as integral to the mountain as pollen to the flower. One hears it without listening as one breathes without thinking. But to a listening ear the sound disintegrates into many different notes—the slow slap of a loch, the high clear trill of a rivulet, the roar of spate. On one short stretch of burn the ear may distinguish a dozen different notes at once.

When the snows melt, when a cloud bursts, or rain teems out of the sky for days on end without intermission, then the burns come down in spate. The narrow channels cannot contain the water, which streams down the hillsides, tears deep grooves in the soil, rolls the boulders about, brawls, obliterates paths, floods burrows, swamps nests, uproots trees, and finally reaching the more level ground, becomes a moving sea. Roads that were mended after the last spate are stripped to their bones, bridges are washed away. My path comes to a place where I had forgotten there was a bridge—it is a mere plank over a ditch. The plank hasn't been moved, but now it lies deep under a roaring race of water twenty feet wide. I try to ford it, and almost at once the water is mid-way between knee and thigh, and my body is tensed with the effort to stand erect against its sweep. I step cautiously forward not lifting my feet, sliding them along the bottom as an old gamekeeper has taught me, but before I reach the middle I am afraid. I retreat. There is another way round.

But sometimes there may not be another way round. Standing there with the racing water against my thigh, I understand why, in days when there were few bridges and the ill-made (or un-made) roads went by the fordable places, so many Scottish streams had a sinister reputation. Avon had an ill name for drownings, like Till of the old rhyme. Even within my lifetime, both Spey and Dee have had many victims.

For the most appalling quality of water is its strength. I love its flash and gleam, its music, its pliancy and grace, its slap against my body; but I fear its strength. I fear it as my ancestors must have feared the natural forces that they worshipped. All the mysteries are in its movement. It slips out of holes in the earth like the ancient snake. I have seen its birth; and the more I gaze at that sure and unremitting surge of water at the very top of the mountain, the more I am baffled. We make it all so easy, any child in school can understand it—water rises in the hills, it flows and finds its own level, and man can't live without it. But I don't understand it. I cannot fathom its power. When I was a child, I loved to hold my fingers over the tap at full cock and press with all my puny strength until the water defeated me and spurted over my newly-laundered frock. Sometimes I have had an insane impulse to hold back with my fingers a mountain spring. Absurd and futile gesture! The water is too much for me. I only know that man can't live without it. He must see it and hear it, touch and taste it, and, no, not smell it, if he is to be in health.

FIVE

Frost and Snow

The freezing of running water is another mystery. The strong white stuff, whose power I have felt in swollen streams, which I have watched pour over ledges in endless ease, is itself held and punished. But the struggle between frost and the force in running water is not quickly over. The battle fluctuates, and at the point of fluctuation between the motion in water and the immobility of frost, strange and beautiful forms are evolved. Until I spent a whole midwinter day wandering from one burn to another watching them, I had no idea how many fantastic shapes the freezing of running water took. In each whorl and spike one catches the moment of equilibrium between two elemental forces.

The first time I really looked at this shaping process was in the Slugain valley on a January day. The temperature in Braemar village had fallen the previous night to −2°F. We had climbed Morrone in the afternoon, and seen sunset and the rise of a full moon together over a world that was completely white except for some clumps of firwood that looked completely black. (In Glen Quoich next day the ancient fir trees far up the valley had the same dead black look—no green in them at all.) The intense frost, the cloudless sky, the white world, the setting sun and the rising moon, as we gazed on them from the slope of Morrone, melted into a prismatic radiation of blue, helio, mauve, and rose. The full moon floated up into green light; and as the rose and violet hues spread over snow and sky, the colour seemed to live its own life, to have body and resilience, as though we were not looking at it, but were inside its substance.

Next day a brilliant sun spangled the snow and the

precipices of Ben a' Bhuird hung bright rose-red above us. How crisp, how bright a world! but, except for the crunch of our own boots on the snow, how silent. Once some grouse fled noiselessly away and we lifted our heads quickly to look for a hunting eagle. And down valley he came, sailing so low above our heads that we could see the separate feathers of the pinions against the sky, and the lovely lift of the wings when he steadied them to soar. Near the top of the glen there were coal-tits in a tree, and once a dipper plunged outright into the icy stream. But it was not an empty world. For everywhere in the snow were the tracks of birds and animals.

The animals had fared as we did: sometimes we stepped buoyantly over the surface of drifts, sometimes sank in well above the knees. Sometimes the tracks were deep holes in the snow, impossible to read except by the pattern in which they were placed; sometimes the mark of the pad was clear, just sunk into the snow surface, and at other times only four, or five, spaced pricks showed where the claws had pierced.

These tracks give to winter hill walking a distinctive pleasure. One is companioned, though not in time. A hare bounding, a hare trotting, a fox dragging his brush, grouse thick-footed, plover thin, red deer and roes have passed this way. In paw depressions may be a delicate tracery of frost. Or a hare's tracks may stand up in ice-relief above the softer snow that has been blown from around them. In soft dry snow the pad of a hare makes a leaflike pattern. A tiny track, like twin beads on a slender thread, appears suddenly in the middle of virgin snow. An exploring finger finds a tunnel in the snow, from which the small mouse must have emerged.

But while birds and tracks (we saw nothing four-footed that morning) amused us as we went up the Slugain, our most exquisite entertainment came from the water. Since then I have watched many burns in the process of freezing, but I do not know if description can describe these delicate manifestations. Each is an interplay between two movements in simultaneous action, the freezing of frost and the running of water. Sometimes a third force, the blowing of wind, complicates the forms still further. The ice may be crystal clear, but more probably is translucent; crimpled, crackled or bubbled; green throughout or at the edges. Where the water comes wreathing over stones the ice is opaque, in broken circular structure. Where the water runs thinly over a line of stones right across the bed and freezes in crinkled green cascades of ice, then a dam forms further up of half frozen slush, green, though colourless if lifted out, solid at its margins, foliated, with the edges all separate, like untrimmed hand-made paper, and each edge a vivid green. Where water drips steadily from an overhang, undeflected by wind, almost perfect spheres of clear transparent ice result. They look unreal, in this world of wayward undulations, too regular, as though man had made them. Spray splashing off a stone cuts into the slowly freezing snow on the bank and flutes it with crystal, or drenches a sprig of heather that hardens to a tree of purest glass, like an ingenious toy. Water running over a rock face freezes in ropes, with the ply visible. Where the water fell clear of the rock icicles hang, thick as a thigh, many feet in length, and sometimes when the wind blows the falling water askew as it freezes, the icicles are squint. I have seen icicles like a scimitar blade in shape, firm and solid in their place. For once, even the wind has been fixed. Sometimes a smooth portion of stream is covered with a thin coat of ice that, not quite meeting in the middle, shows the level of the water several inches below; since the freezing began, the water upstream has frozen and less water is flowing. When a level surface has frozen hard from bank to bank, one may hear at times a loud knocking, as the stream, rushing below the ice, flings a stone up against its roof. In boggy parts by the burnside one treads on what seems solid frozen snow, to find only a thin crisp crust that gives way to reveal massed thousands of needle crystals of ice, fluted columns four or five inches deep. And if one can look below the covering ice on a frozen burn, a lovely pattern of fluted indentations is found, arched and chiselled, the obverse of the water's surface, with the subtle shift of emphasis and superimposed design that occurs between a painting and the landscape it represents. In short, there is no end to the lovely things that frost and the running of water can create between them.

When the ice-paws crisped round the stones in the burns, and the ice-carrots that hang from the ledges, are loosened, and the freed ice floats down the river, it looks like masses of floating water lilies, or bunching cauliflower heads. Sunset plays through this greenish-white mass in iridescent gleams. At one point (I have heard of it nowhere else) near the exit of a loch, the peculiar motion of the current among ice-floes has woven the thousands of floating pine-needles into compacted balls, so intricately intertwined that their symmetrical shape is permanently retained. They can be lifted out of the water and kept for years, a botanical puzzle to those who have not been told the secret of their formation.

Snow too can be played with by frost and wind. Loose snow blown in the sun looks like the ripples running through corn. Small snow on a furious gale freezes on the sheltered side of stones on a hilltop in long crystals; I have seen these converge slightly as the wind blows round both sides of the stones. Another fixation of the wind. Or the wind lifts the surface of loose snow but before it has detached it from the rest of the snow, frost has petrified the delicate shavings in flounces of transparent muslin. 'Prince of Wales Feathers', one of my friends has called a similar materialisation of wind and frost. Snow can blow past in a cloud, visible as it approaches, but formed of minute ice particles, so fine that the eye cannot distinguish them individually as they pass. Set the hand against them and it is covered by infinitesimal droplets of water whose impact has hardly been felt, though if the face is turned towards them, the spicules sting the eyeball. Such snow lies in a ghostly thin powdering on the hillside, like the 'glaister o' sifted snaw' that fell on the head of the old Scots minister in his ill-roofed kirk.

The coming of snow is often from a sky of glittering blue, with serried battalions of solid white cumuli low on the horizon. One of them bellies out from the ranks, and from its edge thin shreds of snow, so fine one is hardly aware of their presence, eddy lightly in the blue sky. And in a few minutes the air is thick with flakes. Once the snow has fallen, and the gullies are choked and ice is in the burns, green is the most characteristic colour in sky and water. Burns and river alike have a green glint when seen between snowy banks, and the smoke from a woodman's fire looks greenish against the snow. The shadows on snow are of course blue, but where snow is blown into ripples, the shadowed undercut portion can look quite green. A snowy sky is often pure green, not only at sunrise or sunset, but all day; and a snow-green sky looks greener in reflection, either in water or from windows, than it seems in reality. Against such a sky, a snow-covered hill may look purplish, as though washed in blaeberry. On the other hand, before a fresh snowfall, whole lengths of snowy hill may appear a golden green. One small hill stands out from this greenness: it is veiled by a wide-spaced fringe of fir trees, and behind them the whole snowy surface of the hill is burning with a vivid electric blue.

The appearance of the whole group, seen from without, while snow is taking possession, changes with every air. A thin covering of snow, through which the rock structure breaks, can look more insubstantial than the most diaphanous blue—a phantom created from reality. When the snow is melting, and the plateau is still white but the lower slopes are streaked and patched, against a grey-white sky only the dark portions show; the plateau isn't there, the ridges that run up to the corries stand out like pinnacles and aiguilles. Later, at evening, the sky has turned a deep slate blue, identical with the blue that now washes the bare lower stretches of the mountains, and the long high level summit of snow, with its downward-reaching tentacles, hangs unsupported.

When the mountains are at last completely covered in with snow (and it doesn't happen every winter, so unpredictable is this Cairngorm weather—the skiers may wait far into the spring in vain for the right depth and surface of snow), then on a sunny day the scintillation is bright but does not wound. The winter light has not the strength to harm. I have never myself found it distressing to the eyes, though sometimes I have walked all day through millions of sparkling sun spangles on the frosty snow. The only time

I have suffered from snow-blindness was at the very end of April, by which time, five or six weeks after the equinox, this northern light has become strong. I have heard of a strange delusion that the sun does not shine up here. It does; and because of the clarity of the air its light has power: it has more power, I suppose, in light than in heat. On that late April day, after some halcyon weather, a sudden snow storm blew up. It snowed all night—thick heavy snow that lay even under the next day's sunshine. We were going to the Dubh Loch of Ben a' Bhuird, with no intention of a summit, and I had taken no precautions against exposure; I had expected neither frosty wind nor hot sun to play havoc with my skin, nor had I had till then any experience of strong light upon snow. After a while I found the glare intolerable; I saw scarlet patches on the snow; I felt sick and weak. My companion refused to leave me sitting in the snow and I refused to defeat the object of his walk, which was to photograph the loch in its still wintry condition; so I struggled on, with his dark handkerchief veiling my eyes—a miserable blinkered imprisonment—and in time we were shadowed by the dark sides of the corrie. I was badly burned that day too; for some days my face was as purple as a boozer's; all of which discomfort I might have avoided had I remembered that snow can blow out of a warm sky.

It is not, however, such freak storms that are of moment, but the January blizzards, thick, close and wild—the *blin' drift* that shuts a man into deadly isolation. To go into such conditions on the mountain is folly; the gamekeeper's dictum is: if you can't see your own footsteps behind you in the snow, don't go on. But a blizzard may blow up so rapidly that one is caught. The great storms, when the snow beats down thick and solid for days on end, piling into the bowls of the corries, pressing itself down by its own weight, may be seen gathering over the mountains before they spread and cover the rest of the earth. I watched the preparation of the storm that was called, when it broke upon the country, the worst for over fifty years. I watched, from the shoulder of Morrone, the Cairngorm mass eddy and sink and rise (as it seemed) like a tossed wreck on a yellow sea. Sky and the wrack of precipice and overhang were confounded together. Now a spar, now a mast, just recognisable as buttress or cornice, tossed for a moment in the boiling sea of cloud. Then the sea closed on it, to open again with another glimpse of mounting spars—a shape drove its way for a moment through the smother, and was drawn under by the vicious swirl. Ashen and yellow, the sky kicked convulsively.

All this while the earth around me was bare. Throughout December the ground had been continuously white, but in the first week of the year there came a day like April, the snow sunned itself away and the land basked mildly in the soft airs. But now the commotion among the mountains lashed out in whips of wind that reached me where I stood watching. Soon I could hardly stand erect against their force. And on the wind sailed minute thistledowns of snow, mere gossamers. Their fragility, insubstantial almost as air, presaged a weight and solidity of snow that was to lie on the land for many weeks.

In the corries the tight-packed snow stands for many months. Indeed, until a succession of unusually hot summers from 1932 to 1934, even in July there were solid walls of snow, many feet thick and as high as the corrie precipices, leaning outwards from the rock and following its contours. There was snow worth seeing in those old summers. I used to believe it was eternal snow, and touched it with a feeling of awe. But by August 1934, there was no snow left at all in the Cairngorms except a small patch in the innermost recess of the Garbh Choire of Braeriach. Antiquity has gone from our snow.

It was in the storm whose beginnings I have described, during a blizzard, that a plane containing five Czech airmen crashed into Ben a' Bhuird. That its impact was made in deep snow was clear from the condition of the engines, which were only a little damaged.

Blizzard is the most deadly condition of these hills. It is wind that is to be feared, even more than snow itself. Of the lives that have been lost in the Cairngorms while I have been frequenting them (there have been about a dozen, excepting those who have perished in plane crashes) four were lost in blizzard. Three fell from the rock—one of these a girl. One was betrayed by the ice-hard condition of a patch of snow in May, and slipped. All these were young. Two older men have gone out, and disappeared. The body of one of these was discovered two years later.

Of the four who were caught in blizzard, two died on 2 January 1928, and two on the same date in 1933. The former two spent their last night in the then disused cottage where I have since passed some of the happiest times of my life. Old Sandy Mackenzie the stalker, still alive then, in the other small house on the croft, warned the boys against the blizzard. As I sit with Mrs Mackenzie, now, by the open fireplace, with a gale howling in the chimney and rattling the iron roof ('this tin-can of a place', she calls it), and watch her wrinkled hands build the fir-roots for a blaze, she tells me of the wind that was in it. I listen to the smashing of this later gale, which has blown all night. 'If you had been getting up and going away the house would have been following you,' she says, knowing my habit of sleeping by the door and prowling at all sorts of hours. And remembering how I crept down into my bag last night, I picture those two boys lying on the floor in the empty house, with the roof rattling and the icy wind finding every chink. Not that they had cared. They asked for nothing but a roof. 'And salt—they asked for salt.' Strange symbolic need of a couple of boys who were to find no hospitality again on earth. Her old bleared eyes look into the distance. She says, 'the snow would be freezing before it would be on your cheek.' John, the son, found the second body in March, in a snow drift that he and his West Highland terrier had passed many times. 'But that morning,' he told me, 'she was scraping.' 'You will not be finding a thing but in the place where it will be', says the old woman. She had fetched the bellows and blown the logs into a flame. 'Sandy used to say, *The fire is the finest flower of them all*, when he would be coming in from the hill.' She makes the tea. But she has brought the storm in to our fireside, and it stays there through the night.

The other two boys went over Cairn Gorm in the kind of miraculous midwinter weather that sometimes occurs, and slept the night at the Shelter Stone beside Loch Avon. They were local boys. In the July of that year, on a very fine Sunday when we had gone out at dawn and had an empty hill all morning to ourselves, we saw with amazement a stream of people come up the hill the easy way from Glenmore and pass over and down to the Shelter Stone. We counted a hundred persons on the hill. They had come to see the place where the two boys slept and to read their high-spirited and happy report in the book that lies in its waterproof cover beneath the huge balanced boulder that has sheltered so many sleepers. That they would not reach home when they set out that morning after writing it, they could not dream. One of them was an experienced hill walker. But they reckoned without the wind. The schoolmistress of the tiny school at Dorback, which lies under Cairn Gorm on the Abernethy side, told me, of that wind, that her crippled sister, crossing the open space of the playground, was blown from her feet. And five miles from Glenmore and safety, crawling down Coire Cas on hands and knees, the boys could fight the wind no further. It was days later till they found them; and one of the men who was at the finding described to me their abraded knees and knuckles. The elder of the two was still crawling, on hands and knees, when they found him fast in the drift. *So quick bright things come to confusion.* They committed, I suppose, an error of judgment, but I cannot judge them. For it is the risk we must all take when we accept individual responsibility for ourselves on the mountain, and until we have done that, we do not begin to know it.

SIX

Air and Light

In the rarefied air of the plateau, and indeed anywhere in the mountain, for the air is clear everywhere, shadows are sharp and intense. Watch the shadow of a plane glide along the plateau like a solid thing, and then slither deformed over the edge. Or pluck a feathery grass, brownish-pink and inconspicuous; hold a sheet of white paper behind it and see how the shadow stands out like an etching, distinct and black, a miracle of exact detail. Even the delicate fringe inside the small cup of the field gentian throws its shadow on the petals and enhances their beauty.

The air is part of the mountain, which does not come to an end with its rock and its soil. It has its own air; and it is to the quality of its air that is due the endless diversity of its colourings. Brown for the most part in themselves, as soon as we see them clothed in air the hills become blue. Every shade of blue, from opalescent milky-white to indigo, is there. They are most opulently blue when rain is in the air. Then the gullies are violet. Gentian and delphinium hues, with fire in them, lurk in the folds.

These sultry blues have more emotional effect than a dry air can produce. One is not moved by china blue. But the violet range of colours can trouble the mind like music. Moisture in the air is also the cause of those shifts in the apparent size, remoteness, and height in the sky of familiar hills. This is part of the horror of walking in mist on the plateau, for suddenly through a gap one sees solid ground that seems three steps away, but lies in sober fact beyond a 2000 foot chasm. I stood once on a hill staring at an opposite hill that had thrust its face into mine. I stared until, dropping my eyes, I saw with astonishment between me and it a loch that I knew perfectly well was there. But it couldn't be. There wasn't room. I looked up again at that out-thrust brow—it was so near I could have touched it. And when I looked down, the loch was still there. And once in the Monadhliaths, on a soft spring day when the distances were hazed, valley, hills and sky all being a faintly luminous grey-blue, with no detail, I was suddenly aware of a pattern of definite white lines high above me in the sky. The pattern defined itself more clearly; it was familiar; I realised it was the pattern of the plateau edge and corries of the Cairngorms, where the unmelted snow still lay. There it hung, a snow skeleton, attached to nothing, much higher than I should have expected it to be. Perhaps the lack of detail in the intervening valley had something to do with this effect.

Rain in the air has also the odd power of letting one see things in the round, as though stereoscopically. The rays of light, refracted through the moisture in the air, bend round the back of what I am seeing. I have looked at a croft half a mile away lying into the hill, with a steading and a cow, and felt as though I were walking round the stacks and slapping the cow's hind quarters.

Haze, which hides, can also reveal. Dips and ravines are discerned in what had appeared a single hill: new depth is given to the vista. And in a long line of crags, such as the great southern rampart of Loch Einich, each buttress is picked out like Vandyke lace. Veils of thin mist drifting along the same great loch-face look iridescent as they float between the sun and the red rock.

For the rock of this granite boss is red, its felspar is the pink variety. Crags, boulders and scree alike are weathered to a cold grey, but find the rock where it is newly slashed, or under water, and there is the glow of the red. After a winter of very severe frost, the river sides of the Lairig have a fresh redness. Here and there one can see a bright gash where a lump of rock the size of a house has fallen; and a very little searching beneath reveals the fallen mass, with one side fresh, or broken into bright red fragments; while nearby is a dark boulder that has lain there for long enough, but from which a red chip has now been struck by the impact of the falling rock.

Or under water: the Beinnie Coire of Braeriach is the least imposing of all the corries—a mere huddle of grey scree. But through it runs a burn that has the effect of sunshine, so red are the stones it hurries over. Farther along the same mountain face, through the deep clear water of Loch Coire an Lochain, even when a thin mist quite covers it, the stones at the bottom are still intense and bright, as though the water itself held radiance. All round the margin of this exquisite loch is a rim of red stones, where the lapping of the water has prevented the growth of lichen.

Thin mist, through which the sun is suffused, gives the mountain a tenuous and ghost-like beauty; but when the mist thickens, one walks in a blind world. And that is bad: though there is a thrill in its eeriness, and a sound satisfaction in not getting lost. For not getting lost is a matter of the mind—of keeping one's head, of having map and compass to hand and knowing how to use them, of staying steady, even when one of the party panics and wants to go in the wrong direction. Walking in mist tests not only individual self-discipline, but the best sort of interplay between persons.

When the mist turns to rain, there may be beauty there too. Like shifting mists, driving rain has a beauty of shape and movement. But there is a kind of rain without beauty, when air and ground are sodden, sullen black rain that invades body and soul alike. It gets down the neck and up the arms and into the boots. One is wet to the skin, and everything one carries has twice its weight. Then the desolation of these empty stretches of land strikes at one's heart. The mountain becomes a monstrous place.

I think the plateau is never quite so desolate as in some days of early spring, when the snow is rather dirty, perished in places like a worn dress; and where it has disappeared, bleached grass, bleached and rotted berries and grey fringe-moss and lichen appear, the moss lifeless, as though its elasticity had gone. The foot sinks in and the impression remains. One can see in it the slot of deer that have passed earlier. This seems to me chiller than unbroken snow.

But even in this scene of grey desolation, if the sun comes

out and the wind rises, the eye may suddenly perceive a miracle of beauty. For on the ground the down of a ptarmigan's breast feather has caught the sun. Light blows through it, so transparent the fugitive spindrift feather has become. It blows away and vanishes.

Or in a drab season, and feeling as drab as the weather, I stand on a bridge above a swollen stream. And suddenly the world is made new. Submerged but erect in the margin of the stream I see a tree hung with light—a minimal tree, but exquisite, its branches delicate with globes of light that sparkle under the water. I clamber down and thrust a sacrilegious hand into the stream: I am holding a sodden and shapeless thing. I slip it again under the water and instantly again it is a tree of light. I take it out and examine it: it is a sprig of square-stalked St John's Wort, a plant whose leaves are covered with minute pores that can exude a film of oil, protecting it against the water that has engulfed it, in like manner as the dipper, plunging into the stream has a film of light between him and the water. I think of the Silver Bough of Celtic mythology and marvel that an enchantment can be made from so small a matter.

Storm in the air wakes the hidden fires—lightning, the electric flickers we call *fire flauchts*, and the Aurora Borealis. Under these alien lights the mountains are remote. They withdraw in the darkness. For even in a night that has neither moon nor stars the mountains can still be seen. The sky cannot be wholly dark. In the most overcast night it is much lighter than the earth; and even the highest hills seem low against the immense night sky. A flash of lightning will draw them close for a brief moment out of this remoteness.

In the darkness one may touch fires from the earth itself. Sparks fly round one's feet as the nails strike rock, and sometimes, if one disturbs black ooze in passing, there leap in it minute pricks of phosphorescent light.

Walking in the dark, oddly enough, can reveal new knowledge about a familiar place. In a moonless week, with overcast skies and wartime blackout, I walked night after night over the moory path from Whitewell to Upper Tullochgrue to hear the news broadcast. I carried a torch but used it only once, when I completely failed to find the gate to the Tullochgrue field. Two pine trees that stood out against the sky were my signposts, and no matter how dark the night the sky was always appreciably lighter than the trees. The heather through which the path runs was very black, the path perceptibly paler, clumps and ridges of heather between the ruts showing dark against the stone and beaten earth. But it amazed me to find how unfamiliar I was with that path. I had followed it times without number, yet now, when my eyes were in my feet, I did not know its bumps and holes, nor where the trickles of water crossed it, nor where it rose and fell. It astonished me that my memory was so much in the eye and so little in the feet, for I am not awkward in the dark and walk easily and happily in it. Yet here I am stumbling because the rock has made a hump in the ground. To be a blind man, I see, needs application.

As I reach the highest part of my dark moor, the world seems to fall away all round, as though I have come to its edge, and were about to walk over. And far off, on a low horizon, the high mountains, the great Cairngorm group, look small as a drystone dyke between two fields.

Apparent size is not only a matter of humidity. It may be relative to something else in the field of vision. Thus I have seen a newly-risen moon (a harvest moon and still horned), low in the sky, upright, enormous, dwarfing the hills.

SEVEN

Life: The Plants

I have written of inanimate things, rock and water, frost and sun; and it might seem as though this were not a living world. But I have wanted to come to the living things through the forces that create them, for the mountain is one and indivisible, and rock, soil, water and air are no more integral to it than what grows from the soil and breathes the air. All are aspects of one entity, the living mountain. The disintegrating rock, the nurturing rain, the quickening sun, the seed, the root, the bird—all are one. Eagle and alpine veronica are part of the mountain's wholeness. Saxifrage—the 'rock-breaker'—in some of its loveliest forms, *Stellaris*, that stars with its single blossoms the high rocky corrie burns, and *Azoides*, that clusters like soft sunshine in their lower reaches, cannot live apart from the mountain. As well expect the eyelid to function if cut from the eye.

Yet in the terrible blasting winds on the plateau one marvels that life can exist at all. It is not high, as height goes. Plants live far above 4000 feet. But here there is no shelter—or only such shelter as is afforded where the threads of water run in their wide sloping channels towards the edge of the cliffs. Whatever grows, grows in exposure to the whole vast reach of the air. From Iceland, from Norway, from America, from the Pyrenees, the winds tear over it. And on its own undulating surface no rocks, or deep ravines, provide a quiet place for growth. Yet the botanist with whom I sometimes walk tells me that well over twenty species of plant grow there—many more, if each variety of moss, lichen and algae is counted. He has made me a list of them, and I can count them. Life, it seems, won't be warned off.

36

The tenacity of life can be seen not only on the tops but on lower shoulders where the heather has been burnt. Long before the heather itself (whose power to survive fire as well as frost, wind, and all natural inclemencies is well known) shows the least sign of life from the roots beneath its charred sticks, or has sprouted anew from seed hidden in the ground, birdsfoot trefoil, tormentil, blaeberry, the tiny genista, alpine lady's mantle, are thrusting up vigorous shoots. These mountain flowers look inexpressibly delicate; their stems are slender, their blossoms fragile; but burrow a little in the soil, and roots of a timeless endurance are found. Squat or stringy, like lumps of dead wood or bits of sinew, they conserve beneath the soil the vital energy of the plant. Even when all the upper growth is stripped—burned or frosted or withered away—these knots of life are everywhere. There is no time nor season when the mountain is not alive with them. Or if the root has perished, living seeds are in the soil, ready to begin the cycle of life afresh. Nowhere more than here is life proved invincible. Everything is against it, but it pays no heed.

The plants of the plateau are low in stature, sitting tight to the ground with no loose ends for the wind to catch. They creep, either along the surface, or under it; or they anchor themselves by a heavy root massive out of all proportion to their external growth. I have said that they have no shelter, but for the individual flower there is the shelter of its group. Thus the moss campion, *Silene*, the most startling of all the plateau flowers, that in June and early July amazes the eye by its cushions of brilliant pink scattered in the barest and most stony places, has a habit of growth as close-set as a Victorian posy. Its root too is strong and deep, anchoring it against the hurricane, and keeping its vital essence safe against frost and fiery drought, the extremes and unpredictable shifts of weather on the exposed plateau. In these ways this most characteristic of the plateau flowers is seen to be quite simply a part of the mountain. Its way of life lies in the mountain's way of life as water lies in a channel.

Even its flamboyant flowers are integral to the mountain's way of life. I do not know how old the individual clumps may be, but judging from the size to which these close-knit cushions grow, some must have endured the commotion of many winters. Most of the mountain flowers are long livers. The plant that races through its cycle in a single season could never be sure, up here, of fruition—there might be no successors. Death would dog, not only the individual, but the species. Yet even the long livers must renew themselves at times, and it is on only some of the summer days that insects can fly to the mountain top. So the *Silene* throws this ardent colour into its petals to entice the flies.

Lower on the mountain, on all the slopes and shoulders and ridges and on the moors below, the characteristic growth is heather. And this too is integral to the mountain. For heather grows in its most profuse luxuriance on granite, so that the very substance of the mountain is in its life. Of the three varieties that grow on these hills—two Ericas and the ling—the July-blooming bell heather is the least beautiful, though its clumps of hot red are like sun-bursts when the rest of the hills are still brown. The pale cross-leaved heath, that grows in small patches, often only single heads, in moist places, is an exquisite, almost waxen-still, with a honey perfume. But it is the August-blooming ling that covers the hills with amethyst. Now they look gracious and benign. For many many miles there is nothing but this soft radiance. Walk over it in a hot sun, preferably not on a path ('I like the unpath best,' one of my small friends said when her father had called her to heel), and the scent rises in a heady cloud. Just as one walks on a hot day surrounded by one's own aura of flies, so one walks surrounded by one's own aura of heather scent. For as the feet brush the bloom, the pollen rises in a perfumed cloud. It settles on one's boots, or if one is walking barefoot, on feet and legs, yellowy-fawn in colour, silky to the touch, yet leaving a perceptible grit between the fingers. Miles of this, however, stupefies the body. Like too much incense in church, it blunts the sharp edge of adoration, which, at its finest, demands clarity of the intellect as well as the surge of emotion.

To one who loves the hills at every season, the blossoming is not the best of the heather. The best of it is simply its being there—is the feel of it under the feet. To feel heather under the feet after long abstinence is one of the dearest joys I know.

Scent—fragrance, perfume—is very much pertinent to the theme of life, for it is largely a by-product of the process of living. It may also be a by-product of fire, but then fire feeds on what lives or what has lived. Or of chemical action, but if there are obscure chemical processes at work in the dead stuff of the mountain, they give little indication to my nose. The smells I smell are of life, plant and animal. Even the good smell of earth, one of the best smells in the world, is a smell of life, because it is the activity of bacteria in it that sets up this smell.

Plants then, as they go through the business of living, emit odours. Some, like the honey scents of flowers, are an added allurement to the insects; and if, as with heather, the scent is poured out most recklessly in the heat of the sun, that is because it is then that the insects are out in strength. But in other cases—as the fir trees—the fragrance is the sap, is the very life itself. When the aromatic savour of the pine goes searching into the deepest recesses of my lungs, I know it is life that is entering. I draw life in through the delicate hairs of my nostrils. Pines, like heather, yield their fragrance to the sun's heat. Or when the foresters come, and they are cut, then their scent is strong. Of all the kinds that grow on the low reaches of these mountains, spruce throws the strongest perfume on the air when the saw goes through it. In hot sun it is almost like a ferment—like strawberry jam on the boil, but with a tang that tautens the membranes of nose and throat.

Of plants that carry their fragrance in their leaves, bog myrtle is the mountain exampler. This grey-green shrub fills the boggy hollows, neighboured by cotton-grass and sundew, bog asphodel and the spotted orchis, and the minute scarlet cups of the lichens. Its fragrance is cool and clean, and like the wild thyme it gives it most strongly when crushed.

The other shrub, juniper, is secretive with its scent. It has an odd habit of dying in patches, and when a dead branch is snapped, a spicy odour comes from it. I have carried a

piece of juniper wood for months, breaking it afresh now
and then to renew the spice. This dead wood has a grey silk
skin, impervious to rain. In the wettest season, when every
fir branch in the woods is sodden, the juniper is crackling dry
and burns with a clear heat. There's nothing better under
the girdle when scones are baking—unless perhaps small
larch twigs, fed into a fire already banked. Once, striking
thick loose snow from low juniper bushes before walking
through them, I surprised myself by striking from them
also a delectable fragrance, that floated on the wintry air.

Birch, the other tree that grows on the lower mountain
slopes, needs rain to release its odour. It is a scent with body
to it, fruity like old brandy, and on a wet warm day, one can
be as good as drunk with it. Acting through the sensory
nerves, it confuses the higher centres; one is excited, with
no cause that the wit can define.

Birch trees are least beautiful when fully clothed. Exquisite when the opening leaves just fleck them with points of
green flame, or the thinning leaves turn them to a golden
lace, they are loveliest of all when naked. In a low sun, the
spun silk floss of their twigs seems to be created out of light.
Without transfiguration, they are seen to be purple—when
the sap is rising, a purple so glowing that I have caught
sight of a birchwood on a hillside and for one incredulous
moment thought the heather was in bloom.

Among drifts of these purple glowing birches, an occasional rowan looks dead; its naked boughs are a smooth
white-grey, almost ghastly as the winter light runs over
them. The rowan's moment is in October, when even the
warmth of its clustering berries is surpassed by the blood-red
brilliance of its leaves. This is the 'blessed quicken wood',
that has power against the spirits of evil. It grows here
and there among birches and firs, as a rule singly, and
sometimes higher than either, a solitary bush by the rivulet
in a ravine.

October is the coloured month here, far more brilliant
than June, blazing more sharply than August. From the gold
of the birches and bracken on the low slopes, the colour
spurts upwards through all the creeping and inconspicuous
growths that live among the heather roots—mosses that are

lush green, or oak-brown, or scarlet, and the berried plants, blaeberry, cranberry, crowberry and the rest. Blaeberry leaves are a flaming crimson, and they are loveliest of all in the Rothiemurchus Forest, where the fir trees were felled in the 1914 War, and round and out of each stump blaeberry grows in upright sprigs: so that in October a multitude of pointed flames seem to burn upwards all over the moor.

This forest blazed with real fire in the early summer of 1920. One of the gamekeepers told me that forty of them were on the watch for ten days and nights, to keep the fire from spreading. And by night, he said, the tree trunks glowed like pillars of fire.

Not much is left now of this great pine forest. Yet in the glens that run up into the mountain, there are still a few of the very old firs that may have been the original Caledonian forest. Old trees still stand in Glen Einich, as they do at Ballochbuie on the other side of the mountain; and by the shores of Loch an Eilein are a scatter of enormous venerable Scots firs, their girth two and a half times the span of my (quite long) arms, the flakes of their bark a foot and a half in length and thick as books, their roots, exposed where the soil has been washed away above the path, twisted and intertwined like a cage of snakes. Here and there also, notably by the sluice gates at the exit of Loch Einich, can be seen, half-sunk in the bog, numbers of the roots of trees long perished.

This sluice dates, like those on other of the lochs, to the late eighteenth century, when the ancient wood rang with the activity of the fellers. The trunks ready, the sluices were opened, and the trees guided down on the rush of water to the Spey. There is a vivid description of it, as a child remembered it, in Elizabeth Grant of Rothiemurchus's *Memoirs of a Highland Lady*. When the timber was first realised to be a source of wealth, and felled, small sawmills were erected on the various burns—tiny clearings, with the saw, a but and a ben and a patch of corn; but soon it was found more profitable to float all the timber downstream to the Spey, where it was made into rough rafts and so carried to Fochabers and Garmouth. The very sites of these ancient sawmills are forgotten. Today come the motor lorries, the sawmill and all its machinery making a compact township for the time that it is required; and outsiders, not the men of the place, fell and lop and cut. Only the old ways still linger here and there as where a native horse, tended by a man deep-rooted in the place, drags the chained trunks down from inaccessible corners, and is led back for the night to one of the ancient farms on the edge of the moor.

The first great cutting of the forest took place during the Napoleonic wars, when home-grown timber was urgently required. A century later we have seen the same thing happen. In 1914 and again, and more drastically, in 1940, the later wood has gone the way of the former. It will grow again, but for a while the land will be scarred and the living things—the crested tits, the shy roe deer—will flee. I tremble especially for the crested tit, whose rarity is a proud distinction of these woods.

I have heard people say that they have watched in vain for these exquisite tits, but, if you know their haunts (I shall not give them away), they can be conjured easily from a tree by simply standing still against its trunk. You have heard the stir and small sound of tits, but at your approach they are gone, there is not a bird to see. But stand quite still, and in a minute or two they forget you, and flit from branch to branch close to your head. I have seen a crested tit turn itself around not a foot from my eye. In the nesting season, however, they will scold like fishwives. I have been scolded at by a pair of them with such vehemence that in pure shame for them I have left their tree.

How fierce was the rush of water when the ancient sluices on the lochs were opened, an eighty-year-old woman made plain to me when she told me how it was once used to outwit the gauger. For a drop of the mountain dew was made on the far side of the Beinnie, in a thick place beneath Carn Elrig where I once lost my path; and when the man who made it had the word passed to him that the gauger was on the way, he had no time to hide the stuff. Indeed, then, when the word came to him, he was nearer the sluice than the still, and to the sluice he went—I can see him *spangin'* on, heel to the ground, with the loping stride of the Highlander bent on business. So when the exciseman came, turbulent water raced between him and the drop whisky. And no crossing it that day at the least. Nor perhaps the next.

Gaunt remnants of pine trees high on the mountain sides show that the earlier forest went further up than the present forest does. Yet here and there a single seed, wind borne or dropped by a bird, has grown far above the main body of the trees. Some of these out-liers show the amazing adaptability of this tree. They can change their form at need, like any wizard. I know one, rooted a few paces from a 2900 feet summit, a sturdy plant but splayed to the mountains and almost roseate in structure, three feet across and not more than five inches in height. There it clings, plastered against the arid ground. I shall watch with much interest to see how much larger it will grow, and in what direction.

Dead fir roots, left in the soil long after the tree is gone, make the best kindling in the world. I know old women who look with the utmost contempt on paper as a fire-lighter and scorn to use more than one match to set a fire going. I know two such old women, both well over eighty, both living alone, one on the Spey side of the mountains and one on the Dee, who howk their fir roots from the moor, drag them home and splinter them. Then you may watch them, if you visit their frugal homes when the fire is out, build the *rossity reets* (we call them that on the Aberdeenshire side) into a pyramid with their brown hard wrinkled fingers, fill the kettle with a cup from the pail of well water, hang it on the *swye* and swing it over the blazing sticks. And before you have well settled to your *newse* the tea is made, and if the brown earthenware teapot has a broken spout ('my teapot has lost a tooth'), and tea splutters from it on to the open hearth and raises spurts of ash and steam, you can call it a *soss* or a libation to the gods as you feel inclined, but it will not make the tea less good nor the talk less racy.

Of the inconspicuous things that creep in heather, I have a special affection for stagmoss—not the hard braided kind but the fuzzy kind we called 'toadstails'. I was taught the art of picking these by my father when I was a small child. We lay on the heather and my fingers learned to feel their way along each separate trail and side branch, carefully detaching each tiny root, until we had thick bunchy pieces many yards long. It was a good art to teach a child. Though I did not know it then, I was learning my way in, through my own fingers, to the secret of growth.

That secret the mountain never quite gives away. Man is slowly learning to read it. He watches, he ponders, patiently he adds fact to fact. He finds a hint of it in the 'formidable' roots of the moss campion and in the fine roots that the tiny eyebright sends into the substance of the grass to ease its own search for food. It is in the glaucous and fleshy leaves of the sedums and the saxifrages, through which they store the bounty of the earth against the times when the earth is not bountiful. It is in the miniature size of the smallest willow, whose woolly fluff blows about the plateau as the silky hairs of the cotton grass blow about the bogs. And in the miniature azalea that grows splayed against the mountain for protection, and lures the rare insects by its rosy hue, and flourishes, like the heather, on granite; whereas granite cannot meet the needs of many of the rare mountain flowers, that crave the streaks of limestone, or the rich humus of the micaschist—like that rarest of all, found in only one spot in the Cairngorms, the alpine milk-vetch, its delicate pale bloom edged with lavender, haunted by its red-and-black familiar the Burnet moth: why so haunted no one knows, but no milk-vetch, no Burnet moth. On a wet windy sunless day, when moths would hardly be expected to be visible at all, we have found numbers of these tart little creatures on the milk-vetch clumps.

The more one learns of this intricate interplay of soil, altitude, weather, and the living tissues of plant and insect (an intricacy that has its astonishing moments, as when sundew and butterwort eat the insects), the more the mystery deepens. Knowledge does not dispel mystery. Scientists tell me that the alpine flora of the Scottish mountains is Arctic in origin—that these small scattered plants have outlived the Glacial period and are the only vegetable life in our country that is older than the Ice Age. But that doesn't explain them. It only adds time to the equation and gives it a new dimension. I find I have a naive faith in my scientist friends—they are such jolly people, they wouldn't fib to me unnecessarily, and their stories make the world so interesting. But my imagination boggles at this. I can imagine the antiquity of rock, but the antiquity of a living flower—that is harder. It means that these toughs of the mountain top, with their angelic inflorescence and the devil in their roots, have had the cunning and the effrontery to cheat, not only a winter, but an Ice Age. The scientists have the humility to acknowledge that they don't know how it has been done.

EIGHT

Life: Birds, Animals, Insects

The first time I found summer on the plateau—for although my earliest expeditions were all made in June or July, I experienced cloud, mist, howling wind, hailstones, rain and even a blizzard—the first time the sun blazed and the air was balmy, we were standing on the edge of an outward facing precipice, when I was startled by a whizzing sound behind me. Something dark swished past the side of my head at a speed that made me giddy. Hardly had I got back my balance when it came again, whistling through the windless air, which eddied round me with the motion. This time my eyes were ready, and I realised that a swift was sweeping in mighty curves over the edge of the plateau, plunging down the face of the rock and rising again like a jet of water. No one had told me I should find swifts on the mountain. Eagles and ptarmigan, yes: but that first sight of the mad, joyous abandon of the swift over and over the very edge of the precipice shocked me with a thrill of elation. All that volley of speed, those convolutions of delight, to catch a few flies! The discrepancy between purpose and performance made me laugh aloud—a laugh that gave the same feeling of release as though I had been dancing for a long time.

It seems odd that merely to watch the motion of flight should give the body not only vicarious exhilaration but release. So urgent is the rhythm that it invades the blood. This power of flight to take us in to itself through the eyes as though we had actually shared in the motion, I have never felt so strongly as when watching swifts on the mountain top. Their headlong rush, each curve of which is at the same time a miracle of grace, the swishing sound of their cleavage of the air and the occasional high pitched cry that is hardly like the note of an earthly bird, seem to make visible and audible some essence of the free, wild spirit of the mountain.

The flight of the eagle, if less immediately exciting than that of the swifts, is more profoundly satisfying. The great spiral of his ascent, rising coil over coil in slow symmetry, has in its movement all the amplitude of space. And when he has soared to the top of his bent, there comes the level flight as far as the eye can follow, straight, clean and effortless as breathing. The wings hardly move, now and then perhaps a lazy flap as though a cyclist, free-wheeling on a gentle slope, turned the crank a time or two. The bird seems to float, but to float with a direct and undeviating force. It is only when one remarks that he is floating up-wind that the magnitude of that force becomes apparent. I stood once about the 2500 feet level, in January when the world was quite white, and watched an eagle well below me following up the river valley in search of food. He flew right into the wind. The wings were slightly tilted, but so far as I could judge from above he held them steady. And he came on with a purposeful urgency behind which must have been the very terror of strength.

It was this strong undeviating flight on steady wings that made a member of the Observer Corps (my friend James McGregor reports—the Observation Post was in his highest field and his croft, I believe, is the highest in Scotland) cry out in excitement, 'Here's a plane I can't identify! What's this one, do you think?' McGregor looked and said, without a glimmer, 'That's the one they call the Golden Eagle.' 'Didn't know there was such a one,' said the other; and he could hardly be convinced that he was looking at a bird and not a plane. And just this morning, in my own garden on Lower Deeside, fifty miles from the eagle country, I caught sight of three planes very high against white clouds, wheeling in circles round one another, and my first amazed reaction was 'Eagles!'

Mr Seton Gordon claims that the Golden Eagle rises from her eyrie clumsily, especially when the air is calm. I have never had, I was going to say the luck, but I should say rather the assiduity and patience to see an eagle rising from the eyrie, but I have watched one fly out from the vicinity of an eyrie, alight in heather some distance away, rise again and again alight, and there was nothing noteworthy in its movement. It is the power in the flight that enthrals the eye. And when one has realised, as probably one does not do at first, that it is a power which binds the strength of the wind to its own purpose, so that the more powerful the wind the more powerful is the flight of the bird, then one sees how intimately the eagle, like the moss campion, is integral to the mountain. Only here, where the wind tears across these desolate marches, can it prove the utmost of its own strength.

To see the Golden Eagle at close quarters requires knowledge and patience—though sometimes it may be a gift, as when once, just as I reached a summit cairn, an eagle rose from the far side of it and swept up in majestic circles above my head: I have never been nearer to the king of birds. And once, on the edge of the Braeriach side of the Lairig crags, I saw an eagle soar out below me, glinting golden in the sun. And I have seen one near on a hillside, intent on something at his feet. But getting close to him is a slow art. One spring afternoon, while I was idling among the last trees on the Speyside end of the Lairig path, watching the movement of tits, a voice by my side asked: 'Is this the way to Ben MacDhui?' and looking down I saw what at first glance I took to be a street gamin of eleven. I said, 'Are you going up alone?' and he said, 'I'm with him.' So turning I saw behind me a second youth, lanky, pasty and pimply, hung round with gadgets. They were both, perhaps, even the undergrown one, nineteen years of age, and they were railway workers who had come all the way from Manchester to spend their one week's leave in photographing the Golden Eagle. And please, where would they find one? I told them of some of my encounters. 'And could you have photographed that one?' they asked. They knew, I found, the books. Those two weedy boys had read everything they could find on their subject, and though they had never been in Scotland before, they had walked in the Lakes. 'The distances,' I said, 'are different. Don't try Ben MacDhui till tomorrow, and take the whole day to it.' And I remembered an old shepherd in Galloway, whom I had asked which spur of the hill I should take to go up Merrick. When he had told me, he looked at me, and said, 'You've not been up before? Do you know what you're undertaking?' 'I've not been up before, but I've been all over the Cairngorms.' 'The Cairngorms, have you?' His gesture dismissed me—it was like a drawbridge thrown forward. So I said to the boys, 'Don't go up Ben MacDhui today—it'll be dark in another four or five hours. Go on by the path you're on and see the Pools of Dee and perhaps look around the corner into the great Garbh Coire.' 'Will there be ledges there?' they asked; and repeated that what they had come for was to photograph the Golden Eagle. I never saw them again—I hope I dissuaded them from going up Ben MacDhui that day—I didn't even attempt to dissuade them from photographing the Golden Eagle. The eagle itself probably did that quite effectively. But I liked those boys. I hope they saw an eagle. Their informed enthusiasm—even if only half informed—was the right way in.

Imagination is haunted by the swiftness of the creatures that live on the mountain—eagle and peregrine falcon, red deer and mountain hare. The reason for their swiftness is severely practical: food is so scarce up there that only those who can move swiftly over vast stretches of ground may hope to survive. The speed, the whorls and torrents of movement, are in plain fact the mountain's own necessity. But their grace is not necessity. Or if it is—if the swoop, the parabola, the arrow-flight of hooves and wings achieve their beauty by strict adherence to the needs of function—so much the more is the mountain's integrity vindicated. Beauty is not adventitious but essential.

Strong flight is a characteristic also of another bird that haunts not the precipice but the plateau itself—the small unassuming dotterel. You are wandering one summer day on a plateau slope when your ear catches its plover-like cry. You pause and watch—no bird is there. Then you move softly towards the sound, and in a moment one bird, then another, rises in short low flight, comes to earth again and runs, crouched to the ground like a small grey mouse.

Shape, movement, colour, are all so mouse-like that the illusion almost might deceive you, were it not for the vivid black and white of the head, the glowing breast, and the white tail feathers. You wait, and soon the birds forget you. On one slope, off the recognised route to any particular destination, a nesting place or perhaps a gathering place for flight, of these small birds, I have seen them by the score, running a little way, and pausing, and running on again, almost domestic in their simple movements. Yet in autumn this humble bird flies straight to Africa.

The other bird that nests on the high plateau, the ptarmigan, is a home-keeper. No flights to Africa for him. Through the most ferocious winter, he stays where he was born, perhaps a little lower on the slopes, and dressed for winter by changing to the colour of the snow.

The creatures that dress like the snow to be inconspicuous against it—the ptarmigan, the snow bunting, the mountain hare—are sometimes cheated. They are white before the mountain is. When blue milkwort is still in blossom on the last day of the year, it is not surprising to see a white stoat blaze against a dull grey dyke. Few things are more ludicrous in Nature than a white hare 'concealing' itself, erect and patient beside a boulder, while all round it stretches a grey-brown world against which it stands vividly out. A white hare running over snow can be comical too, if it is running between you and the sun—a shadowed shape, with an odd ludicrous leggy shadow-skeleton, comical because the shadows alter the creature's shape. But if the sun is behind you and strikes full on the running hare, only the ears show, and a dark thin outline to the back. If the snow lies in fields, the running hare may not be noticed at all, till it flakes off at the edge of the snow patch, gleaming white. Breaking suddenly into a hollow, I have counted twenty white hares at a time streaking up a brown hillside like rising smoke.

Deer on the other hand are conspicuous in snow. In a completely white world, one can see from a high shoulder a herd feeding a thousand feet beneath, vivid black specks on the whiteness. But then they do not need to hide themselves from peregrine and eagle. Actually in winter and early spring, their coats are greyish, the colour of dead snow, bleached heather and juniper and rocks.

Stay-at-home though he be, the ptarmigan has power in his wings. In startled flight, his wing-beats are so rapid that the white wings lose all appearance of solidity, they are like an aura of light around the body.

Like all the game birds, ptarmigan play the broken wing trick when an intruder approaches their young family, to lure the enemy away. I have had the trick played on me so many times that now I hardly notice the parent birds, but always and eagerly I watch the behaviour of the young. Once near the summit of Braeriach, I halted dead at the rise of one, then the other parent, seeking with my eyes for the youngsters. There was one, three feet away, another nearer, and another. My eyes came closer and closer to myself—one ptarmigan chick was not two inches from my boot. Seven of them crouched within a radius of a foot or two, and they might have been birds carved from wood for all the life they showed. I stood for a long time and as long as I remained motionless, so did they. But at last I yielded to the mounting temptation (which I try always to resist) to touch and fondle one of these morsels. So I stooped to the one nearest my boot. And instantly the whole seven, cackling, were off. A noisy undignified scramble, contrasting strangely with their carved immobility.

Very near the summits, on the most stony braes nest the snow buntings. Both in song and in person these small creatures have a delicate perfection that is enhanced by the savagery of their home. Sit quietly for a while in some of the loneliest and most desolate crannies of the mountain, where the imagination is overpowered by grim bastions of the rock, and a single snow bunting will sing with incredible sweetness beside you. To have sat on one of the high stony fields around seven of a clear summer morning, when the sun has just drawn up the morning mists from the corries, and seen the stones come alive with small forms like flakes of the stone blown eddying upon the air, is to have tasted a pleasure of the epicure. Watching carefully, one sees that two of the dozen or so birds are males, the rest are the members of their two young families. The females are already about the business of bringing out a second brood.

Ranging the whole mountain mass are the hoodies, black and grey, the mountain scavengers. Wheatears bob and chuckle on the boulders, or flash their cheeky rumps as they fly to another stone. And in the burns of the highest corries the white-dickied dipper plunges beneath the water. A lonely song by a solitary burn reveals the golden plover. But why should I make a list? It serves no purpose, and they are all in the books. But they are not in the books for me—they are in living encounters, moments of their life that have crossed moments of mine. They are in the cry of the curlew sounding over the distances, and in the thin silver singing among the last trees that tell me the tits are there. They are in an April morning when I follow a burn to its sources, further and further into a fold of the hills, and a pair of long-tailed tits flash and are gone and come again. Or in a December afternoon of bitter frost when a dozen of these tiny tufts, disproportionate and exquisite, tumble from a tree beside a frozen stream. Or a July day when one small tree holds thirteen crested tits. Or in a March day (the only time I have found anything attractive in the grouse) when against the snowy hillside a pair of these birds pursued each other in lovely patterns of flight. Or in the mating ecstasy of the kestrel, or the fighting blackcock suddenly discovered one morning in a clear place among juniper. Or in the two woodcock that follow each other night after night low over the trees just beyond where I lie still awake outside the tent.

And so many that I have omitted. Just as I have omitted so many exquisite flowers—dryas, timeless as white jade, bog asphodel like candle flame, the purple-black hearts of cornel. I have missed the wagtails, yellow and pied, and the reed bunting precise as a dignitary in his bands, the seagulls and oyster catchers come up from the sea, the crossbills and the finches, and the wrens. But I cannot miss the wrens. So tiny, so vital, with such volume of voice. It may not be fact, but in my experience the wrens are more numerous on the Dee side of the range than on the Spey side. In the high tributary valleys, Glen Quoich, Glen Slugain, among the last of the trees, they are common as eyebright. There's a skeleton of a fallen tree in Glen Quoich, a vast leggy thing, all the legs to the ground and the trunk a ridge of spine above them, a magnificent example of prevailing wind—twinkling through its bony ribs I have watched a family of nine young wrens. And once in Glen Slugain a pair of golden bumble bees (as it seemed) sped past me in a whorl of joyful speed. But it couldn't be—they were too large. I stalked them. They were young wrens.

It was near the leggy tree that I saw rise some way off down the stream, a bird so huge that I could only stare. It wheeled and vanished. Two enormous wings, with a span that I couldn't believe. Yet I had seen it. And there it was coming back, upstream now, the same vast span of wing: no body that I could see; two great wings joined by nothing, as though some bird had at last discovered how to be all flight and no body. And then I saw. The two great wings were a duck and a drake, following one another in perfect formation, wheeling and dipping and rising again with an unchanging interval of space between them, each following every modulation of the other; two halves of one organism.

Wild geese are only passers here. One blustering October day I watched an arrow-head of them, twenty-seven birds in perfect symmetry, flying south down the valley in which I stood. I was near the head of a deep glen, the watershed rose steep above me. Up there the wind must be ferocious. The geese were there now. They broke formation. Birds flew from one arm of the wedge to the other, the leader hesitated, another bird attempted to lead, their lovely symmetry became confused. It seemed as though the wind were beating them back, for the whole line, blunt-headed now, edged round, one bird leading and then another, till they gradually rounded the top of the glen and were flying back the way they came. As I watched, they flew into a cinder-grey cloud, in an undulating line like the movement of a fish under water. The dark line melted into the darkness of the cloud, and I could not tell where or when they resumed formation and direction.

It is tantalising to see something unusual, but not its ending. One January afternoon, in a frozen silent world, I saw two stags with antlers interlaced dragging each other backwards and forwards across the ringing frozen floor of a hollow. Their dark forms stood out against the snow. I watched till dusk came on and I could barely see but could still hear the noise of the scuffle. It is the only time I have seen this phenomenon of interlocked antlers, and as I have always been told that stags so caught cannot extricate themselves and fight on till one or both die, I wanted badly to see what happened. I went back next day but found no stags, dead or alive. The crofter-ghillie in whose house I was staying said that they probably saved themselves by the breaking of an antler.

The roaring of the stags set me another problem to which I have not found a definitive answer. On one of those potent days of mid-October, golden as whisky, I was wandering on the slopes of Ben Avon above Loch Builg. Suddenly I was startled by a musical call that resounded across the hill, and was answered by a like call from another direction. Yodelling, I thought. There was such gaiety in the sound that I looked eagerly about, thinking: these are students, they are hailing one another from sheer exuberance of spirit. But I saw no one. The yodelling went on. The yodelling went on all day, clear, bell-like and musical; and it was not long till I realised that there was no other human being on the mountain and that the stags were the yodellers. The clear bell notes were new to me. I had heard stags roar often enough, in deep raucous tones. Bellowing. The dictionary would have me believe that belling is merely a variant of bellowing. For me belling will always mean the music of that golden day. All the time I listened, there was not a single harsh note.

But why? That is what I don't understand. Why sometimes raucous and sometimes like a bell? Hillmen whom I have asked give different suggestions. That the bell notes are from young stags and the raucous from old. But against that, one gamekeeper sets the tale of a gruff-voiced bellower that the shooting-party to a man declared would be an old beast and that turned out when they got him to be comparatively young. That the note changes to express different needs. But that theory does not seem to be borne out by the way in which two stags kept up an antiphon one day in my hearing, the raucous answering the bell across a ravine with absolute consistency. That stags are like human beings and some have tenor voices, some bass. Then were they all tenor stags on that morning when the hill broke into a cantata? All young? or all tenor? or all in love with the morning?

Normally deer are silent creatures, but when alarmed they bark like an angry dog. I have heard the warning bark far off on a distant slope and only then been aware of the presence of a herd. Then they are off, flowing up the hill and over the horizon. Their patterns against the sky are endless—a quiet frieze of doe and fawn and doe and fawn. Or a tossing forest of massed antlers. Or with long necks to the ground, feeding, like hens pecking. Those mobile necks are a thought uncanny at times. I have seen five necks rise like swaying snakes, a small snake-like head on each, the bodies hidden. Five hinds. And I have seen a hind turn her head to look at me, twisting her neck around until the face seemed to hang suspended in air alongside the rump and some atavistic fear awoke in me. Bird, animal and reptile—there is something of them all in the deer. Its flight is fluid as a bird's. Especially the roes, the very young ones, dappled, with limbs like the stalks of flowers, move over the heather with an incredible lightness. They seem to float; yet their motion is in a way more wonderful even than flight, for each of these gleaming hooves does touch the ground. The lovely pattern of the limbs is fixed to the earth and cannot be detached from it.

Indeed there are times when the earth seems to re-absorb this creature of air and light. Roes melt into the wood—I have stared a long time into birches where I knew a doe was standing and saw her only when at last she flicked an ear. In December an open heather I have found myself close upon a feeding red doe so like her background that I had thought the white scut another patch of snow. She becomes aware of me, her ears lift, her head goes sharply up, the neck elongated. I stand very still, the head drops, she becomes again part of the earth. Further up on the slopes one can watch a fawn learning his hillcraft from his mother, pausing in exactly her attitude, turning a wary head as she turns hers.

But find a fawn alone in a hidden hollow, he will not endure with his mother's patience. It is not easy to make a doe move before you do, but when the fawn, after his first startled jump to the far side of the hollow, stands to gaze at you on the other side, if you keep perfectly still he grows restive, moves his head now side on to you, now front, an ear twitches, a nostril, finally he turns and walks away, like a reluctant but inquisitive child, pausing at every third step to look back.

I have never had the incredible fortune, as a young doctor I know once had, of seeing a hind give birth; but I have found very young fawns, left by their mothers beside a stone on heather. Once I had gone off the track to visit a small tarn. Something impelled me to walk round the back of the tarn, scrambling between the rock and the water, and then to continue downwards over a heathery slope that is not very often crossed. From the corner of my eye I noticed two or three hinds making off; and a moment later I came on a tiny fawn lying crouched into the heather near a stone. It lay in an oddly rigid way, the limbs contorted in unnatural positions. Could it be dead? I bent over it—very gently touched it. It was warm. The contorted limbs were fluid as water in my hands. The little creature gave no sign of life. The neck was stretched, stiff and ungainly, the head almost hidden; the eyes stared, undeviating. Only the flanks pulsated. Nothing moved but the pulsing flanks. There was no voluntary movement whatsoever, no smallest twitch or flicker. I had never before seen a fawn shamming dead, as young birds do.

A young squirrel, caught upon his own occasions, will behave like the young fawn you have surprised walking out alone: both are a little reckless about humanity. I have come upon a small squirrel the size of a well-grown mouse, on the ground under fir trees, scampering from cone to cone, picking up each in turn, scrutinising, sampling, tossing it away, with a sort of wilful petulance in his movements such

as I have seen in small children who have too many toys.
He becomes aware of me, pauses, eyes me, eyes his cone.
Cupidity and caution struggle within him, I am quite
still, caution loses, he goes on with his game among
the goodies. When he stops to crunch, I move forward.
At last I move so near that he is suddenly alarmed.
He makes for a huge old pine tree whose bark hangs
in scales so thick and solid that his small limbs can
hardly compass them. He can't get up; and now, like his
red-gold parents, he wallops his thin long ribbon-like tail,
not yet grown bushy, in a small futile way, and scrabbles
against the mountainous humps of bark. At last he is up,
he runs out on a side branch and jeers down at me in
triumph.

Other young things—leverets in the form wrapped in
silky hair—fox cubs playing in the sun in a distant fold
of the hill—the fox himself with his fat red brush—the
red-brown squirrel in the woods below, whacking his tail
against the tree-trunk and chattering through closed lips
(I think) against the intruder—gold-brown lizards and
the gold-brown floss of cocoons in the heather—small
golden bees and small blue butterflies—green dragon
flies and emerald beetles—moths like oiled paper and
moths like burnt paper – water-beetles skimming the
highest tarns—small mice so rarely seen but leaving a
thousand tracks upon the snow—ant-heaps of birch-twigs
or pine-needles (*preens*, in the northern word) flickering
with activity when the sun shines—midges, mosquitoes,
flies by the hundred thousand, adders and a rare strange
slowworm—small frogs jumping like tiddly-winks—rich
brown hairy caterpillars by the handful and fat green
ones with blobs of amethyst, a perfect camouflage on
heather—life in so many guises.

It is not just now sheep country. The sheep were cleared
to make room for deer; today in one district the deer
are giving place to Highland cattle, those placid and
abstemious beasts to whom thin fare is a necessity and
whose shaggy winter mats protect them from the bitter
winds. They look ferocious and are very gentle—in this
resembling some of the blackface ewes, hags as ugly as sin

that are found in every mountain flock, grim old malignants whose cankered horns above a black physiognomy must, I feel sure, be the origin of the Scots conception of the Devil.

NINE

Life: Man

Up on the plateau nothing has moved for a long time. I have walked all day, and seen no one. I have heard no living sound. Once, in a solitary corrie, the rattle of a falling stone betrayed the passage of a line of stags. But up here, no movement, no voice. Man might be a thousand years away.

Yet, as I look round me, I am touched at many points by his presence. His presence is in the cairns, marking the summits, marking the paths, marking the spot where a man has died, or where a river is born. It is in the paths themselves; even over boulder and rock man's persistent passage can be seen, as at the head of the Lairig Ghru, where the path, over brown-grey weathered and lichened stones, shines as red as new-made rock. It is in the stepping-stones over the burns, and lower in the glens, the bridges. It is in the indicator on Ben MacDhui, planned with patient skill, that gathers the congregation of the hills into the hollow of one's hand; and some few feet below, in the remains of the hut where the men who made the Ordnance Survey of the eighteen-sixties lived for the whole of a season—an old man has told me how down in the valley they used to watch a light glow now from one summit, now another, as measurements were made and checked. Man's presence too is in the map and the compass that I carry, and in the names recorded in the map, ancient Gaelic names that show how old is man's association with scaur and corrie: the Loch of the Thin Man's Son, the Coire of the Cobbler, the Dairymaid's Meadow, the Lurcher's Crag. It is in the hiding-holes of hunted men, Argyll's Stone on Creag Dhubh above Glen Einich, and the Cat's Den, deep narrow chasm among the Kennapol rocks; and in the Thieves' Road that runs south from Nethy through prehistoric glacial overflow gaps—and somewhere on its way the kent tree (felled now) to which the prudent landlord tied a couple of his beasts as clearance money. It is in the sluices at the outflow of the lochs, the remnants of lime kilns by the burns, and the shepherds' huts, roofless now, and the bothies of which nothing remains but a chimney-gable; and in the Shelter Stone above Loch Avon, reputed once to have been the den of a gang some thirty strong, before the foundation stones that hold the immense perched rock shifted and the space beneath was narrowed to its present dimensions: wide enough still to hold a half-dozen sleepers, whose names, like the names of hundreds of others, are recorded in a book wrapped in waterproof and left within the shelter of the cave.

Man's presence too is disturbingly evident, in these latter days, in the wrecked aeroplanes that lie scattered over the mountains. During the Second World War more planes (mostly training planes) crashed here than one cares to remember. Like the unwary of older days who were drowned while fording swollen streams, or dashed from the precipices they attempted to climb, these new travellers underestimated the mountain's power. Its long flat plateau top has a deceptive air of lowness; and its mists shut down too swiftly, its tops are too often swathed in cloud, pelting rain or driving snow, while beneath the world is in clear sunlight, for liberties to be taken with its cruel rock. I stood one day on the Lurcher's Crag and heard the engine of a plane, and looked naturally upwards; but in a moment I realised that the sound was below me. A plane was edging its way steadily through the great gash that separates the two halves of the plateau, the Lairig Ghru. From where I stood, high above it, its wing-tips seemed to reach from rock to rock. I knew that this was an illusion and that the wings had ample room; that the boys who shoot their planes under the arch of a bridge, or through the Yangtze gorges, had the same exuberant glee as the boys below me were doubtless experiencing; yet if mist had suddenly swept down, that passage between the crags would have been most perilous. And even in the brief time needed to negotiate a plane through the Lairig, mist might well descend in this region of swift and unpredictable change. I have experienced this. Out of a blue sky cloud has rushed on the mountain, obliterating the world. The second time I climbed Ben MacDhui I saw this happen.

I had driven to Derry Lodge one perfect morning in June with two gentlemen who, having arrived there, were bent on returning at once to Braemar, when a car came up with four others, obviously setting out for Ben MacDhui. In a flash I had accosted them to ask if I might share their car back to Braemar in the evening: my intention was to go up, the rag-tag and bob-tail of their company, keeping them in sight but not joining myself on to them. The request was granted and I turned back to say farewell to my former companions. When I turned again, the climbers had disappeared. I hastened after them, threading my way through the scattered pines that lie along the stream, but failing to overtake them and hurrying a little more. At last I got beyond the trees, and in all the bare glen ahead, I could see no human being. I could not believe that four people could have walked so fast as to be completely out of sight, for my own pace had been very fair. Prudence—I had only once before been on a Cairngorm—told me to wait; I had begun to suspect I had out-distanced my company. But I couldn't wait. The morning was cloudless and blue, it was June, I was young. Nothing could have held me back. Like a spurt of fire licking the hill, up I ran. The Etchachan tumbled out from under snow, the summit was like wine. I saw a thousand summits at once, clear and sparkling. Then far off to the south I saw a wall of cloud like a foaming breaker. It rolled on swiftly, blotting out a hundred summits a minute—very soon it would blot out mine. I threw a hasty glance around, to fix my bearings, and pelted down towards the ruined surveyors' hut, from which the path downwards by Coire Etchachan is clearly marked by cairns; but before I reached it I was swallowed up. The whole business, from my first glimpse of the cloud to the moment it washed over me, occupied less than four minutes. Half a mile down, drinking tea in the driving mist by the side of the path, I found my lost company still ascending. On another occasion, seated by a summit cairn, gazing through a cloudless sky at peaks and lochs, I found myself unable to name some of the features I was looking at, and bent close over the map to find them out. When I raised my head, I was alone in the universe with a few blocks of red granite. This swiftness of the mist is one of its deadliest features, and the wreckage of aeroplanes, left to rust in lonely corners of the mountains, bears witness to its dreadful power.

Man's touch is on the beast creation too. He has driven the snow bunting from its nesting-sites, banished the capercailzie and reintroduced it from abroad. He has protected the grouse and all but destroyed the peregrine. He tends the red deer and exterminates the wild cat. He maintains, in fact, the economy of the red deer's life, and the red deer is at the heart of a human economy that covers this mountain mass and its surrounding glens. There are signs that this economy is cracking, and though the economy of the shooting estate is one for which I have little sympathy, I am aware that a turn of the wrist does not end it. The deer himself might perish from our mountains if man ceased to kill him; or degenerate if left to his wild; and on the crofts and small hill-farms wrested from the heather and kept productive by unremitting labour, the margin between a living and a sub-living may be decided by the extra wage of ghillie or under-keeper. Without that wage, or its equivalent in some other guise, the hill croft might well revert to heather.

These crofts and farms and gamekeepers' cottages breed men of character. They are individualists, gritty, tough, thrawn, intelligent, full of prejudice, with strange kinks and a salted sense of humour. Life here is hard and astringent, but is seldom kills grace in the soul. The best of them are people of many skills, inventive at supplying their needs, knowledgeable on their own ground and interested in a number of things outside it. They are not servile but avoid angering the laird; upright, though 'the Birkie up yonder' comes near enough to the thought most of them hold of God; hospitable, but never 'senseless ceevil', keeping a cool sense of proportion over what matters: though there are exceptions, to be sure, as where wouldn't there be?—a

man who 'wouldna part wi' a yowie (fir cone) off his
grun'', or a woman who has 'put her eyes on my lustre
jug', or again a generosity that will have sugar in your
cup whether you want it or not, 'to take the wildness off
the tea'.

Life has not much margin here. Work goes on from dark
to dark. The hay is brought in in August, the oats (with
luck) in October: but at Christmas they may still stand,
sodden and black in the tilted fields. And one night, before
you know it, stags may have broken in and ravaged the
growing crops. The crofter's wife can't go to her brother's
funeral in January, because the cows are beginning to go
dry and if a stranger milks them they may cease to yield
altogether, and there's the income gone and milk to be
bought *for-by*. The water must be carried from the well,
through drifted snow or slush, unless the crofter himself
has ingenuity and useful hands, and has brought his own
water supply from the hill to the house; and even then
it must be watched and tended through the rigours of a
mountain winter.

Sometimes there is no well—no spring rises within reach
of the house, but all the water to be used must be carried
from the burn, up steep and toilsome banks. Then the
washing is done in the centuries-old fashion, down at
the foot of the banks in the burn itself—sometimes on
a windy day I have seen smoke rising, and caught the
wink of fire, and coming near seen a great cauldron in
a sheltered nook beside the burn and figures of women
moving around it.

In these crannies of the mountains, the mode of supplying
elemental needs is still slow, laborious and personal. To
draw your water from the well, not even a pump between
you and its sparkling transparency, to break the sticks you
have gathered from the wood and build your fire and set
your pot upon it—there is a deep pervasive satisfaction in
these simple acts. Whether you give it conscious thought
or not, you are touching life, and something within you
knows it. A sense of profound contentment floods me as
I stoop to dip the pail. But I am aware all the same that
by so living I am slowing down the tempo of life; if I had

to do these things every day and all the time I should be shutting the door on other activities and interests; and I can understand why the young people resent it.

Not all the young want to run away. Far from it. Some of them love these wild places with devotion and ask nothing better than to spend their lives in them. These inherit their fathers' skills and sometimes enlarge them. Others are restive, they resent the primitive conditions of living, despise the slow ancient ways, and think that praising them is sentimentalism. These clear out. They take, however, the skills with them (or some of them do), and discover in the world outside how to graft new skills of many kinds on to their own good brier roots. An unfortunate proportion want white-collar occupations, and lose their parents' many-sidedness. For the young are like the old, various as human nature has always been, and will go on being, and life up here is full of loves, hates, jealousies, tendernesses, loyalties and betrayals, like anywhere else, and a great deal of plain humdrum happiness.

To the lovers of the hills whom they allow to share their houses these people extend the courtesy that accepts you on equal terms without ceremonial. You may come and go at your own times. You may sit by the kitchen fire through the howling winter dark, while they stamp in from the byre in *luggit* bonnets battered with snow. They respect, whether they share it or not, your passion for the hill. But I have not found it true, as many people maintain, that those who live beside the mountains do not love them. I shall never forget the light in a boy's face, new back from the wars and toiling by his father's side on one of these high bare mountain farms, when I asked: well, and is Italy or Scotland the better? He didn't even answer the question, not in words, but looked aside at me, hardly pausing in his work, and his face glimmered. The women do not gad. The day's work keeps them busy, in and out and about, but though they do not climb the mountains (indeed how could they have time or energy?) they do look at them. It is not in this part of the Highlands that 'views is carnal'. 'It's a funeral or a phenomenon if I'm out,' says one gamekeeper's wife, but in her youth she ran on the mountains and something of

their wildness is still in her speech. But even within families
there are differences. Of two sisters, brought up on the very
precinct of the mountain, one says 'None of your hills for
me, I have seen too much of them all my days,' while the
other had spent weeks on end in a small tent on the very
plateau. One of the truest hill-lovers I have known was
old James Downie of Braemar, whose hand-shake (given
with a ceremonial solemnity) sealed my first day on Ben
MacDhui. Downie had once the task of guiding Gladstone
to the Pools of Dee, which the statesman decided must be
visited. Now the path to the Pools, from the Braemar end,
is long though not rough, shut in except for the mountain
sides of the Lairig Ghru itself; and the Pools lie beneath the
summit of the Pass, so that to see the wide view open on
to Speyside and the hills beyond, one must climb another
half mile among boulders. Gladstone refused absolutely to
stir a step beyond the Pools. And Downie, the paid guide,
must stop there too; an injury which Downie, the hillman,
never forgave. Resentment was still raw in his voice as he
told me about it, forty years later.

But while they accept mountain climbing, and are
tolerant to oddities like night prowling and sleeping in
the open ('You would think you were born in a cart-shed,
where there wasna a door'—and when one rainy summer
night we did actually set our camp beds in the cart-shed,
what fun they had at us, what undisguised and hearty
laughter), yet for irresponsibility they have no tolerance
at all. They have only condemnation for winter climbing.
They know only too well how swiftly a storm can blow up
out of a clear sky, how soon the dark comes down, and how
terrific the force of a hurricane can be upon the plateau; and
they speak with a bitter realism of the young fools who trifle
with human life by disregarding the warnings they are given.
Yet if a man does not come back, they go out to search for
him with patience, doggedness and skill, often in appalling
weather conditions; and when there is no more hope of his
being alive, seek persistently for the body. It is then that one
discovers that shopmen and railway clerks and guards and
sawmillers may be experienced hillmen. Indeed, talking to
all sorts of people met by chance upon the hill, I realise how

indiscriminately the bug of mountain feyness attacks. There are addicts in all classes of this strange pleasure. I have talked on these chance encounters with many kinds, from a gaunt scion of ancient Kings (or so he looked), with eagle beak and bony knees, descending on us out of a cloud on Ben MacDhui, kilt and Highland cloak flapping in the rain, to a red-headed greaser, an old mole-catcher, and an errand boy from Glasgow.

Many forceful and gnarled personalities, bred of the bone of the mountain, from families who have lived nowhere else, have vanished since I first began climbing here—Maggie Gruer, that granite boss, shapely in feature as a precipice, witty, acrid when it was needed, hospitable, ready for any emergency, living with a glow and a gusto that made porridge at Maggie's more than merely food. Day or night, it was all one to Maggie—no climber was turned away who would sleep on a landing, in a shed, anywhere where a human body could be laid. Nor did she scruple to turn a man out of that first deep slumber of the night, the joyous release of an exhausted body, to give his bed to a lady benighted and trudging in at one in the morning. James Downie—short, sturdy figure, erect to the last, with a hillman's dignity in his carriage; teller of stout tales—of a prince, a statesman, a professor, measuring themselves against his hill-craft; the first women to climb under his guidance, in trailing skirts and many petticoats; the hill ponies he hired for them from a taciturn shepherd who hid in his shanty and gave no help in seating 'the ladies'—'I likit fine to see you settin' them on the shalts'—the stern discipline he exacted from his lady climbers. Indeed there was a stern and intractable root in this old man. Some of his stories were very funny, but he did not laugh much. The stern grandeur of the corries had invaded his soul. There was nothing tender or domestic about him; unmarried, he *bothied* by choice in the bothy of his own croft, leaving the house to his sisters. 'He's nae couthy wi' the beasts,' his nephew's wife confided to me once. ''Deed, he's real cruel to them whiles.' The last time I stayed on the croft, during his lifetime, he insisted on carrying my bag all the way to the bus. I remonstrated, but was treated as I suppose he treated his lady climbers long before. 'I shall not do it again,' he said. 'I shall not see you again.' He was dead a few months later.

Then Sandy Mackenzie, the mighty gamekeeper on the Rothiemurchus side, already a done old man when I knew him, warming his body in the sun; and his second wife, Big Mary, surviving him for many years, dying at ninety, half-blind but indomitable. Tall, gaunt and stooped, her skin runkled and blackened from the *brook* of her open fire, her grey hair tousled in the blowing wind, she had a sybilline, an *eldritch* look on her. When I saw her last, a step-daughter had taken her from the lonely cottage, that I had shared so often—had tended her, washed her grey hair to a pure fleece of white, scrubbed her nails and her hands that were soft now because she could no longer heave her great axe or *rug* fir-roots from the ground, and dressed her in orderly black, with a lacy white shawl on her shoulders. It took my breath away; she was too exquisite—a spectacle; but the earthy and tempestuous was her truer element. She belonged there, and knew it. 'I was never one for the housecraft,' she told me once. 'I liked the outdoor work best, and the beasts.' Alone there with her ageing husband, she talked to the hens, to the old horse and to the cow, in the Gaelic that was her mother tongue. When the old man died, the cow was taken to the farm across the moor. 'May there be no more Whitewell cows here,' said the woman who milked her. 'We have not the time to be speaking to them, and will she let down the milk without you speak?'

Sometimes, as her sight failed on her, the loneliness oppressed her, for she had an avid interest in other people's lives, and books could no longer fill her need. 'The news will be sour on me before I will be hearing it,' she would complain. And she turned the news about upon her tongue—of one, 'she's a bad brat'; of an infatuated man, 'he doesna see daylight but through her'; of a widower, 'it put the quietness on him, losing Mary.' For the few weeks of the year that we over-ran her cottage, she was as full of glee as we were ourselves—teased us and joked with us, though her passionate interest in every detail of our lives was never ill-mannered: she understood reticence. And the morning we left, while we collected 'meth' stove and frying-pan, and stuffed the sleeping bags and folded the camp-beds, she would send the flames crackling up the great open chimney to boil the kettle for our last ritual cup of tea; and the tears were standing in her eyes. Her hunger for folk, all the waywardness and oddity of their lives, was unappeasable. Yet, when the laird offered her a couple of rooms in another cottage, shut in and low-lying, but among people, she would have none of it. The long swoop of moor and the glittering precipices, the sweep of air around her dwelling, held her in spite of herself. I am glad that she died in her own house, between a winter with one friend and a winter with another. One blustering late September day I stepped off the train at Aviemore, to be met at once by my friend Adam Sutherland the guard. 'Do you know what has happened now? They are burying Big Mary at one o'clock.' I was in time to walk the two or three miles to the ancient kirkyard, dank among trees by the river, and to follow the men who carried the coffin down the long wet path from the road. Someone (whom I bless) had made a wreath for her, from heather and rowan berries, oats and barley and juniper, the things she saw and handled day by day. Close by lies Farquhar Shaw, survivor of the famous fight on the Inches of Perth, who troubled the neighbourhood so that when he was dead they set five heavy stone *kebbucks* upon his flat tombstone, to keep him under. I like to think that she lies near him, who was of as strong and stubborn an earth as he.

For, yes, she troubled her neighbourhood, as he did his, if on a smaller scale. Not in an evil way: there was no malice in her. But she was salt and salt can be harsh. She was thrawn as Auld Nick, and only God (so they tell me) can turn him aside from what he wants to do. That she set problems for those with whose lives hers was interlaced, I can well believe. But she had her own integrity, rich and bountiful. I feel that I want to say of her, as Sancho Panza, challenged to find reasons for continuing to follow his master, of Don Quixote: 'I can do no otherwise . . . I have eaten his bread; I love him.'

For the living—those who have instructed me, and harboured me, and been my friends in my journey into the mountain—there are some among the many[1] whom I must name: the other Mackenzies of Whitewell, old Sandy's family, and the Mackenzies of Tullochgrue; and most especially Mrs Sutherland, Adam's wife, herself a Macdonald rooted in the place, a woman generous as the sun, who has cherished my goings and my comings for quarter of a century; and James Downie's nephew Jim McGregor, and his wife, friends to thank heaven for, who on the Dee side of the mountain, as the Sutherlands on the Spey, have given me the franchise of their home.

These people are bone of the mountain. As the way of life changes, and a new economy moulds their life, perhaps they too will change. Yet so long as they live a life close to their wild land, subject to its weathers, something of its own nature will permeate theirs. They will be marked men.

1. Those named are now, with the exception of Carrie, daughter of Sandy Mackenzie, all dead, but their descendants live on.

TEN

Sleep

Well, I have discovered my mountain—its weathers, its airs and lights, its singing burns, its haunted dells, its pinnacles and tarns, its birds and flowers, its snows, its long blue distances. Year by year, I have grown in familiarity with them all. But if the whole truth of them is to be told as I have found it, I too am involved. I have been the instrument of my own discovering; and to govern the stops of the instrument needs learning too. Thus the senses must be trained and disciplined, the eye to look, the ear to listen, the body must be trained to move with the right harmonies. I can teach my body many skills by which to learn the nature of the mountain. One of the most compelling is quiescence.

No one knows the mountain completely who has not slept on it. As one slips over into sleep, the mind grows limpid; the body melts; perception alone remains. One neither thinks, nor desires, nor remembers, but dwells in pure intimacy with the tangible world.

These moments of quiescent perceptiveness before sleep are among the most rewarding of the day. I am emptied of preoccupation, there is nothing between me and the earth and sky. In midsummer the north glows with light long after midnight is past. As I watch, the light comes pouring round the edges of the shapes that stand against the sky, sharpening them till the more slender have a sort of glowing insubstantiality, as though they were themselves nothing but light. Up on the plateau, light lingers incredibly far into the night, long after it has left the rest of the earth. Watching it, the mind grows incandescent and its glow burns down into deep and tranquil sleep.

Daytime sleep, too, is good. In the heat of the day, after an early start, to lie in full daylight on the summits and slip in and out of sleep is one of the sweetest luxuries in life. For falling asleep on the mountain has the delicious corollary of awaking. To come up out of the blank of sleep and open one's eyes on scaur and gully, wondering, because one had forgotten where one was, is to recapture some pristine amazement not often savoured. I do not know if it is a common experience (certainly it is unusual in my normal sleep), but when I fall asleep out of doors, perhaps because outdoor sleep is deeper than normal, I awake with an empty mind. Consciousness of where I am comes back quite soon, but for one startled moment I have looked at a familiar place as though I had never seen it before.

Such sleep may last for only a few minutes, yet even a single minute serves this end of uncoupling the mind. It would be merely fanciful to suppose that some spirit or emanation of the mountain had intention in thus absorbing my consciousness, so as to reveal itself to a naked apprehension difficult otherwise to obtain. I do not ascribe sentience to the mountain; yet at no other moment am I sunk quite so deep into its life. I have let go my self. The experience is peculiarly precious because it is impossible to coerce.

A 4 am start leaves plenty of time for these hours of quiescence, and perhaps of sleep, on the summits. One's body is limber with the sustained rhythm of mounting, and relaxed in the ease that follows the eating of food. One is as tranquil as the stones, rooted far down in their immobility. The soil is no more a part of the earth. If sleep comes at such a moment, its coming is a movement as natural as day. And after—ceasing to be a stone, to be the soil of the earth, opening eyes that have human cognisance behind them upon what one has been so profoundly a part of. That is all. One has been in.

Once, however, I fell asleep where I would not have chosen to do so. We were on Braeriach. It was a day with hazed horizons and a flat view that had little life or interest; so we lay on our faces just beyond the summit, as near to the edge as we dared, our bodies safe to the earth, and looked down into Coire Brochain. The burns were full and everywhere there was the noise of waterfalls.

We watched them drop, pouring on and on over the rock faces. Far below us on the floor of the hollow, deer were feeding, small moving specks. We watched them move. Then the sun came out and warmed us, and the pattern of movement and sound made us drowsy. Then abruptly I awoke and found myself staring down black walls of rock to a bottom incredibly remote. It is actually, I believe, some 2000 feet from the summit to the bed of the burn below; to the bottom of the inner corrie, where the deer were still feeding, is not much over a thousand; but to that first horrified stare, dissociated from all thought and all memory, sensation purely, the drop seemed inordinate. With a gasp of relief I said 'Coire Brochain,' turned round on my back, eased myself from the edge, and sat up. I had looked into the abyss.

If the depth of its insensibility is the boon of daytime sleep on the mountain, nights under the sky are most delectable when the sleep is light. I like it to be so light that I am continually coming to the surface of awareness and sinking back again, just seeing, not bedevilled with thought, but living in the clear simplicity of the senses. I have slept in the open as early as May and as late as the first week in October, a time when, in our odd and unbalanced climate, there is usually a splash of radiant weather.

My one October night without a roof was bland as silk, with a late moon rising in the small hours and the mountains fluid as loch water under a silken dawn: a night of the purest witchery, to make one credit all the tales of *glamourie* that Scotland tries so hard to refute and cannot. I don't wonder. Anyone caught out of doors at four or five on such a morning would start spelling wrong. *Faerie* and *glamourie* and *witcherie* are not for men who lie in bed till eight. Find an October night warm enough to sleep out, and a dawn all mixed up with moonshine, and you will see that I am right. You too will be mis-spelled.

I do not like *glamourie*. It interposes something artificial between the world, which is one reality, and the self, which is another reality, though overlaid with a good many crusts of falseness and convention. And it is the fusion of these two realities that keeps life from corruption. So let us have done with spells.

Most of my nights out of doors have been simple summer nights, and I like waking often in them because the world is so beautiful then, and also because wild creatures, and birds, come close to a sleeper without suspicion. But there is an art in waking. I must come fully awake, and open my eyes without having moved. Once, sleeping in the daytime, I jerked awake, to find that a young blackbird, accustomed to feed from the hand, had been walking along my leg. He had asked for his alms in the odd throaty chuckle he affected, too deep in pitch to penetrate my sleep. And once a chaffinch touched my breast. In both these cases I was so lightly asleep that I felt the contact and was awake in time to catch the startled flight of my visitor. If only I had not been such a fool as to jump! But then my sleep had been broken. No, it must be a natural awakening: my eyes were closed, and now they are open, nothing more than that; and ten yards away from me a red deer is feeding in the dawn light. He moves without a sound. The world is entirely still. I too am still. Or am I? Did I move? He lifts his head, his nostrils twitch, we look at each other. Why did I let him meet my eyes? He is off. But not for far. He checks in his flight and eyes me again. This time I do not look at him. After a while he drops his head, reassured, and goes on feeding.

Sometimes I have floated up from sleep at dawn, and seen a roe, and sunk back into sleep again before my conscious mind had registered the thing. The glimpse remains a vision, wholly true, although I could not swear to it in court. When I wake for good that morning I have forgotten it. Later in the day the thought teases at the edges of my brain—*But did I dream that roe?*—and because I can't be sure it haunts me for a long time.

Or the paling below my sleeping place may be alive with finches. I have counted twenty of them when I opened my eyes. Or tits, turning themselves about in the engaging way these morsels have. Of all the tit family the one who does this to perfection is the rarest of them, the tiny crested tit, whom I have seen more than once showing himself about, now back, now front, now side, keeping each pose for a moment before flirting to a new one on a higher or a lower twig. A finished mannequin.

At other times the ear awakens first. Snipe are drumming. Then I sit up in the bag and search the sky to see the lovely downward swoop. Sometimes it is still too dark (even in a Scots midsummer) to see the pattern of movement, only the zooming fall hangs on the ear.

Out of sleep too I have heard the roaring of stags; but these are no longer outdoor nights. The nights then are cold and dark, and the roaring is fearsome as it comes from the hills that are usually so silent. The silence may be broken by another roaring. When the snows melt, cataracts sound in my ears all night, pouring through my sleep; and after many days of rain I have waked to hear the burns come down in spate, with a duller and more persistent roar than that of the stags, but in its own way as fearsome.

ELEVEN

The Senses

Having disciplined mind and body to quiescence, I must discipline them also to activity. The senses must be used. For the ear, the most vital thing that can be listened to here is silence. To bend the ear to silence is to discover how seldom it is there. Always something moves. When the air is quite still, there is always running water; and up here that is a sound one can hardly lose, though on many stony parts of the plateau one is above the watercourses. But now and then comes an hour when the silence is all but absolute, and listening to it one slips out of time. Such a silence is not a mere negation of sound. It is like a new element, and if water is still sounding with a low far-off murmur, it is no more than the last edge of an element we are leaving, as the last edge of land hangs on the mariner's horizon. Such moments come in mist, or snow, or a summer night (when it is too cool for the clouds of insects to be abroad), or a September dawn. In September dawns I hardly breathe—I am an image in a ball of glass. The world is suspended there, and I in it.

Once, on a night of such clear silence, long past midnight, lying awake outside the tent, my eyes on the plateau where an afterwash of light was lingering, I heard in the stillness a soft, an almost imperceptible thud. It was enough to make me turn my head. There on the tent pole a tawny owl stared down at me. I could just discern his shape against the sky. I stared back. He turned his head about, now one eye upon me, now the other, then melted down into the air so silently that had I not been watching him I could not have known he was gone. To have heard the movement of the midnight owl—that was rare, it was a minor triumph.

Bird song, and the noises birds make that are not singing, and the small sounds of their movements, are for the ear to catch. If there is one bird-call more than another that for me embodies the spirit of the mountain, it is the cry of the golden plover running in the bare and lonely places.

But the ear can listen also to turmoil. Gales crash into the Garbh Choire with the boom of angry seas: one can hear the air shattering itself upon rock. Cloud-bursts batter the earth and roar down the ravines, and thunder reverberates with a prolonged and menacing roll in the narrow trough of Loch Avon. Mankind is sated with noise; but up here, this naked, this elemental savagery, this infinitesimal cross-section of sound from the energies that have been at work for aeons in the universe, exhilarates rather than destroys.

Each of the senses is a way in to what the mountain has to give. The palate can taste the wild berries, blaeberry, 'wild free-born cranberry' and, most subtle and sweet of all, the avern or cloudberry, a name like a dream. The juicy gold globe melts against the tongue, but who can describe a flavour? The tongue cannot give it back. One must find the berries, golden-ripe, to know their taste.

So with the scents. All the aromatic and heady fragrances—pine and birch, bog myrtle, the spicy juniper, heather and the honey-sweet orchis, and the clean smell of wild thyme—mean nothing at all in words. They are there, to be smelled. I am like a dog—smells excite me. On a hot moist midsummer day, I have caught a rich fruity perfume rising from the mat of grass, moss and wild berry bushes that covers so much of the plateau. The earthy smell of moss, and the soil itself, is best savoured by grubbing. Sometimes the rank smell of deer assails one's nostril, and in the spring the sharp scent of fire.

But eye and touch have the greatest potency for me. The eye brings infinity into my vision. I am lying on my back, while over me huge cumuli tear past upon a furious gale. But beyond them, very far away, in a remote pure sky, there float pale exquisite striations of cloud that can hardly be detected. I close one eye and they recede, only with both eyes open do they come into sharp enough focus for me to be sure that they are there. So now I know that the mountain makes its own wind, for these pale striae float almost motionless, while still the gale above my head drives the monstrous cumuli on. It is the eye that discovers the mystery of light, not only the moon and the stars and the vast splendours of the Aurora, but the endless changes the earth itself undergoes under changing lights. And that again, I perceive, is the mountain's own doing, for its own atmosphere alters the light. Now scaur and gully take on a gloss, now they shimmer, now they are stark—like a painting without perspective, in which objects are depicted all on one plane and of the same size, they fill the canvas and there is neither foreground nor background. Now there are sky-blue curves on the water as it slides over stones, now an impenetrable tarry blackness, slightly silvered like tar. The naked birches, if I face the sun, look black, a shining black, fine carved ebony. But if the sun is behind me it penetrates a red cloud of twigs and picks out vividly the white trunks, as though the cloud of red were behind the trunks. In a dry air, the hills shrink, they look far off and innocent; but in a moisture-laden air they charge forward, insistent and enormous, and in mist they have a nightmare quality. This is not only because I cannot see where I am going, but because the small portion of earth that I do see is isolated from its familiar surroundings, and I do not recognise it. Nothing is so ghostly as mist over snow. On a March day, I am climbing into the corrie that holds Loch Dubh; the snows have melted from the lower slopes and the burns are turbulent. They can be crossed only on snow bridges, levels of snow down which runs a sagging uneven line that shows where the water is pouring underneath. Further up, it is all snow. And now the cloud sinks down on me, a pale mist that washes out all the landmarks the snow had not already obliterated. Rocks loom out of it, gigantic, monstrous. The lochan below Loch Dubh seems enormous; the steep climb beyond it towers upward so giddily into nothingness that I am assailed by fear: this must be the precipice itself that I am climbing—the lochan was the loch. I have passed it and am clambering towards the cliff. I know it can't be true, but the dim white ghostliness out of which stark shapes batter at my brain has overpowered my reason. I can't go further. I scramble downwards, and the grey, rather dismal, normality below the mist has a glow of comfort.

On another misty day—a transparent mist—I saw a peregrine falcon fly out from a precipice. There were the curved and pointed wings, the rapid down-beat of the pinions. Yet I stared incredulous. I was gazing upwards at a fabulous bird. No peregrine could be of such a size. It was only when he stood still on the air, before sailing back to the crag, that I believed my own eyesight; and it was only then that I understood what Hopkins meant when he wrote:

> To see the eagle's bulk, render'd in mists
> Hang of a treble size.

Mist, oddly, can also correct the illusions of the eye. A faint mist floating in a line of hills brings out the gradations of height and of distance in what had seemed one hill: there is seen to be a near and a far. In something the same way, the reflection of land in glassy water defines and clarifies its points, so that relative distance and height in a tumble of hills, so deceptive to the eye, are made clear in the loch reflection.

The eye has other illusions, that depend on one's own position. Lying on my back, and looking across the Garbh Choire to the scree slopes above Loch an Uaine, I see them as horizontal; just as from immediately below it, the Lurcher seems a horizontal plain with erect rock masses rising from it. One year we pitched our tent below the curve of the hill above Tullochgrue, on the far side from the Cairngorms. We looked out on a field that ran upwards, and above it the whole line of mountains, cut off about the 2500 feet level: the intervening moor and forest had vanished. As I lay night after night outside the door of the tent, watching the last light glow upon the plateau, I had an odd sensation of being actually myself up there. My field felt the same height, I also lay bathed in the afterglow that had gone from all but the summits. Half-closing the eyes can also change the values of what I look upon. A scatter of white flowers in grass, looked at through half-closed eyes, blaze out with a sharp clarity as though they had actually risen up out of their background. Such illusions, depending on how the eye is placed and used, drive home the truth that our habitual vision of things is not necessarily right: it is only one of an infinite number, and to glimpse an unfamiliar one, even for a moment, unmakes us, but steadies us again. It's queer but invigorating. It will take a long time to get to the end of a world that behaves like this if I do no more than turn round on my side or my back.

Other delights the eye can catch—quick moments that pass and are gone for ever: spray blown like smoke from a mountain loch in a gale; a green gleam on the snow where I know a loch lies, caught before I can see the water itself; Loch Avon, glimpsed on a rainy day from the side of the rocky burn above it, as deep a green as Loch an Uaine itself; a rainbow wavering and flickering, formed on a small shower blown by a furious wind; the air quivering above sun-filled hollows on drowsy summer afternoons; a double rainbow, dark sky in between, arched over the river, its reflection stretching from bank to bank.

How can I number the worlds to which the eye gives me entry?—the world of light, of colour, of shape, of shadow: of mathematical precision in the snowflake, the ice formation, the quartz crystal, the patterns of stamen and petal: of rhythm in the fluid curve and plunging line of the mountain faces. Why some blocks of stone, hacked into violent and tortured shapes, should so profoundly tranquillise the mind I do not know. Perhaps the eye imposes its own rhythm on what is only a confusion: one has to look creatively to see this mass of rock as more than jag and pinnacle—as beauty. Else why did men for so many centuries think mountains repulsive? A certain kind of consciousness interacts with the mountain-forms to create this sense of beauty. Yet the forms must be there for the eye to see. And forms of a certain distinction: mere dollops won't do it. It is, as with all creation, matter impregnated with mind: but the resultant issue is a living spirit, a glow in the consciousness, that perishes when the glow is dead. It is something snatched from non-being, that shadow which creeps in on us continuously and can be held off by continuous creative act. So, simply to look on anything, such as a mountain, with the love that penetrates to its essence, is to widen the domain of being in the vastness of non-being. Man has no other reason for his existence.

Touch is the most intimate sense of all. The whole sensitive skin is played upon, the whole body, braced, resistant, poised, relaxed, answers to the thrust of forces incomparably stronger than itself. Cold spring water stings the palate, the throat tingles unbearably; cold air smacks the back of the mouth, the lungs crackle. Wind blows a nostril in, one breathes on one side only, the cheek is flattened against the gum, the breath comes gaspingly, as in a fish taken from water—man is not in his element in air that moves at this velocity. Frost stiffens the muscles of the chin, mist is clammy on the cheek, after rain I run my hand through juniper or birches for the joy of the wet drops trickling over the palm, or walk through long heather to feel its wetness on my naked legs.

The hands have an infinity of pleasure in them. When I was a girl, a charming old gentlewoman said something to me that I have never forgotten. I was visiting her country home, and after lunch, going for a walk with her niece, I picked up my gloves from the hall table where I had laid them down. She took them from me and laid them back on the table. 'You don't need these. A lot of strength comes to us through the hands.' Sensation also. The feel of things, textures, surfaces, rough things like cones and bark, smooth things like stalks and feathers and pebbles rounded by water, the teasing of gossamers, the delicate tickle of a crawling caterpillar, the scratchiness of lichen, the warmth of the sun, the sting of hail, the blunt blow of tumbling water, the flow of wind—nothing that I can touch or that touches me but has its own identity for the hand as much as for the eye.

And for the foot as well. Walking barefoot has gone out of fashion since Jeanie Deans trudged to London, but no country child grows up without its benediction. Sensible people are reviving the habit. They tell me a tale up here of a gentleman in one of the shooting lodges who went to the hill barefoot: when he sat down for lunch the beaters crowded as near as they dared to see what manner of soles such a prodigy could have. But actually walking barefoot upon heather is not so grim as it sounds. I have covered odd miles myself here and there in this fashion. It begins with a burn that must be forded: once my shoes are off, I am loth to put them on again. If there are grassy flats beside my burn, I walk on over them, rejoicing in the feel of the grass to my feet; and when the grass gives place to heather, I walk on still. By setting the foot sideways to the growth of the heather, and pressing the sprays down, one can walk easily enough. Dried mud flats, sun-warmed, have a delicious touch, cushioned and smooth; so has long grass at morning, hot in the sun, but still cool and wet when the foot sinks into it, like food melting to a new flavour in the mouth. And a flower caught by the stalk between the toes is a small enchantment.

In fording a swollen stream, one's strongest sensation is of the pouring strength of the water against one's limbs; the effort to poise the body against it gives significance to this simple act of walking through running water. Early in the season the water may be so cold that one has no sensation except of cold; the whole being retracts itself, uses all its resources to endure this icy delight. But in heat the freshness of the water slides over the skin like shadow. The whole skin has this delightful sensitivity; it feels the sun, it feels the wind running inside one's garment, it feels water closing on it as one slips under—the catch in the breath, like a wave held back, the glow that releases one's entire cosmos, running to the ends of the body as the spent wave runs out upon the sand. This plunge into the cold water of a mountain pool seems for a brief moment to disintegrate the very self; it is not to be borne: one is lost: stricken: annihilated. Then life pours back.

TWELVE

Being

Here then may be lived a life of the senses so pure, so untouched by any mode of apprehension but their own, that the body may be said to think. Each sense heightened to its most exquisite awareness, is in itself total experience. This is the innocence we have lost, living in one sense at a time to live all the way through.

So there I lie on the plateau, under me the central core of fire from which was thrust this grumbling grinding mass of plutonic rock, over me blue air, and between the fire of the rock and the fire of the sun, scree, soil and water, moss, grass, flower and tree, insect, bird and beast, wind, rain and snow—the total mountain. Slowly I have found my way in. If I had other senses, there are other things I should know. It is nonsense to suppose, when I have perceived the exquisite division of running water, or a flower, that my separate senses can make, that there would be nothing more to perceive were we but endowed with other modes of perception. How could we imagine flavour, or perfume, without the senses of taste and smell? They are completely unimaginable. There must be many exciting properties of matter that we cannot know because we have no way to know them. Yet, with what we have, what wealth! I add to it each time I go to the mountain—the eye sees what it didn't see before, or sees in a new way what it had already seen. So the ear, the other senses. It is an experience that grows; undistinguished days add their part, and now and then, unpredictable and unforgettable, come the hours when heaven and earth fall away and one sees a new creation. The many details—a stroke here, a stroke there—come for a moment into perfect focus, and one can read at last the word that has been from the beginning.

These moments come unpredictably, yet governed, it would seem, by a law whose working is dimly understood. They come to me most often, as I have indicated, waking out of outdoor sleep, gazing tranced at the running of water and listening to its song, and most of all after hours of steady walking, with the long rhythm of motion sustained until motion is felt, not merely known by the brain, as the 'still centre' of being. In some such way I suppose the controlled breathing of the Yogi must operate. Walking thus, hour after hour, the senses keyed, one walks the flesh transparent. But no metaphor, *transparent*, or *light as air*, is adequate. The body is not made negligible, but paramount. Flesh is not annihilated but fulfilled. One is not bodiless, but essential body.

It is therefore when the body is keyed to its highest potential and controlled to a profound harmony deepening into something that resembles trance, that I discover most nearly what it is *to be*. I have walked out of the body and into the mountain. I am a manifestation of its total life, as is the starry saxifrage or the white-winged ptarmigan.

So I have found what I set out to find. I set out on my journey in pure love. It began in childhood, when the stormy violet of a gully on the back of Sgoran Dubh, at which I used to gaze from a shoulder of the Monadhliaths, haunted my dreams. That gully, with its floating, its almost tangible ultramarine, *thirled* me for life to the mountain. Climbing Cairngorms was then for me a legendary task, which heroes, not men, accomplished. Certainly not children. It was still legendary on the October day, blue, cold and brilliant after heavy snow, when I climbed Creag Dhubh above Loch an Eilein, alone and expectant. I climbed like a child stealing apples, with a fearful look behind. The Cairngorms were forbidden country—this was the nearest I had come to them; I was delectably excited. But how near to them I was coming I could not guess, as I toiled up the last slope and came out above Glen Einich. Then I gulped the frosty air—I could not contain myself, I jumped up and down, I laughed and shouted. There was the whole plateau, glittering white, within reach of my fingers, an immaculate vision, sun-struck, lifting against a sky of dazzling blue. I drank and drank. I have not yet done drinking that draught. From that hour I belonged to the Cairngorms, though—for several reasons—it was a number of years until I climbed them.

So my journey into an experience began. It was a journey always for fun, with no motive beyond that I wanted it. But at first I was seeking only sensuous gratification—the sensation of height, the sensation of movement, the sensation of speed, the sensation of distance, the sensation of effort, the sensation of ease: the lust of the flesh, the lust of the eyes, the pride of life. I was not interested in the mountain for itself, but for its effect upon me, as puss caresses not the man but herself against the man's trouser leg. But as I grew older, and less self-sufficient, I began to discover the mountain in itself. Everything became good to me, its contours, its colours, its waters and rock, flowers and birds. This process has taken many years, and is not yet complete. Knowing another is endless. And I have discovered that man's experience of them enlarges rock, flower and bird. The thing to be known grows with the knowing.

I believe that I now understand in some small measure why the Buddhist goes on pilgrimage to a mountain. The journey is itself part of the technique by which the god is sought. It is a journey into Being; for as I penetrate more deeply into the mountain's life, I penetrate also into my own. For an hour I am beyond desire. It is not ecstasy, that leap out of the self that makes man like a god. I am not out of myself, but in myself. I am. To know Being, this is the final grace accorded from the mountain.

Glossary

aace ashes
Ablach, tiny undersized creature
anent, over against, concerning
antrin, one here and there
a'thing, everything
aweirs o', inclined to
barkit, covered as with bark, peeled
begeck, disappointment
begrutten, tear-stained
ben the hoose, inside, further into the house or next room
besom, hussy
bide bydin, stay, remain; staying
bike, wasps' nest
birse, vb., to force, press upwards; *n., to have one's birse up,* one's temper roused
birstled, cooked till hard and crisp
bit, little, scrap of
blake, cockroach, beetle
blate, shy, diffident
blaud, dirty, soil
blin' drift, drifting snow
blithe, happy
bog-jaaveled, completely at a loss
bourrach, small group, swarm

bow-hoched, bow-legged
brear, first small blade appearing above the ground; *brears o' the e'e,* eyelashes
broch, halo
brook, soot
brose, oatmeal and milk or hot water
buckie, limpet
bung; ta'en the bung, taken offence
byordinar, unusually
byous, beyond the ordinary
caddis, dust, fluff
ca'ed, driven
cairded, scolded
canalye, Fr. *canaille*
cantle up, brighten up
cantrip, piece of mischief
canty, lively, cheerful
cark, care
chappit, (thumb), hacked
chau'mer, chamber, bothy
chiel, lad
cloor, dent, blow
clorted, covered with mud
clout, rag
clyte, fall
collieshangie, animated talk
coorse, bad
connach, devour, spoil
contermashious, contradictory, obstinate

85

crack, gossip

craiturie, little creature

a crap for a' corn and a baggie for orrels, an appetite for absolutely anything and then some (literally: a bag for leftovers)

creish, fat

crined, shrunk, shrivelled

curran, a number

dambrod, chess-board

dander, to have one's dander up, temper roused

dawtie, pet, darling

deave, deafen, torment with insistence

deemie, farm, kitchenmaid

deil, devil

delvin, digging

dicht, wipe

dingin' on, raining or snowing hard

dirds, bangs (vb)

dirdums, daein' dirdums, doing great things

dirl, ring, vibrate

doit, small copper coin

dour, stubborn

dowie, spiritless

drookit, soaked, drowned

drummlie, physically upset

dubbit, covered with mud

dubs, mud

dunt, a blow

a dunt on the riggin, not all there (dent in the roof)

dwam, faint, swoon

(neither) echie nor ochie, not the smallest sound

e'en, eyes

eident, diligent

ettlin', desirous after

f=wh

fa, who

fan, when

fat, what

faur, where

fairin', present from the fair

fash yersel, put yourself to trouble

fee'd, hired

ferlies, wonders

fey, peculiar, other-worldly

ficher, fiddle, fidget

fient, never! not a! (lit: devil!)

flan, gust

fleggit, startled

flinchin, deceitful promise of better weather

foo, how

forbye, besides

forty-fitted Janet, centipede

forfoch'en, exhausted, fought done

fleg, fright, frighten

flist, storm of temper

fou', drunk

ful, proud

fyle, soil, make dirty

gait, way

gar, cause to

geal-cauld, ice-cold

geet, child

gey, rather

a gey snod bit deemie, a rather neat little maid

geylies, considerable

gin, if

girn, fret

girse, grass

glower, scowl

gomeril, fool

gorbals, nestlings

graip, fork (for land work)

grat, cried

greetin, crying

guff, smell

gumption, sense, vigour,
  initiative
gype, stupid person
gyte, ga'en gyte, gone out of
  one's mind
haggar, clumsy hacking
halarackit, high-spirited,
  rowdy without
  offensiveness
halfin, teenager
hantle, a good deal
hain, save, spare
hairst, harvest
hap, cover up
havering, talking nonsense
heelster-gowdie, upside down
hine awa'/up, far away/up
hippit, stiff in the hips
hirple, limp
hive, a skin sore
hotter, boil vigorously
hotterel, a swarm
howff, draught
howk, dig
hurdies, hips
ilka, each, every
ill-fashioned, inquisitive
inen, in among
ingan, onion
jaloose, guess, suspect
jaud, (common) woman
kebbuck, cheese
keek, keeking, peek, peeking
kink-hoast, whooping-cough
kowk, retch
kitties, calves (a pet name for)
kittled, tickled
kye, cattle
lave, rest
legammachy, long story
  without much in it
leuch, laughed
lift, sky
limmer, hussy

lippen, trust
to lippen to, to trust
loon, boy, lad
louse, loosen, unharness
lousin' time, end of the
  working day
lowe, blaze
lugs, ears
mavis, song thrush
mim-mou'ed, primly spoken or
  behaved
mishanter, mishap, disaster
mommets, dolls, puppets
mowse, right (with sense
  of Latin *fas*), *nae mowse*,
  nefas, uncanny
my certies, indeed (emphasis)
neips, turnips
neuk, corner
newse, chat
nieve, fist
nimsch, fragment
nippit, pinched, narrow
  in outlook
nowt, cattle
nyatter, nag
nyod (an exclamation,
  lit: God!)
ootlin, outsider, outcast
or, before
orra, odd, miscellaneous
orrels, bits and pieces
oxter, arm-pit, *vb.*, to put the
  arm round
pech, sigh
penurious, particular, ill
  to please
pi, pious, sanctimonious
pilgate, quarrel
pleuch, plough
pliskey, trick, escapade
pooches, pockets
preens, pins
puckle, a few

puddock, frog
pyet, magpie
pyockie, poke, bag
queets, ankles
raivelled, confused
rary, go about noisily, clamour
rax, stretch
reeshle, rustle
rickle, a structure put loosely together, loose heap
rive, tear asunder
roarie-bummlers, (noisy blunderers) storm clouds
roup, a sale or public auction
rug, pull
sair, sore
sair weary, very tired
sark, shirt
scalin', dispersing
scran, scrounge
scunnered, disgusted
scutter awa', do things slowly and not very thoroughly
scuttered, fiddled about
shaltie, pony
shank, stocking being knitted
sharger, half grown creature
sharn, dung
sheen, shoes
sheepy silver, flakes of mica (in a stone)
shog, push
sic mannie sic horsie, like master, like man
skellochin', shrieking
skirp, splatter
sklype, clumsy worthless person
smeddum, vigour of intellect
smored, smothered (in snow)
snod, neat
sonsy, of generous proportions
sooples, supples, softens

soo's snoot, pig's nose
sotter, untidy dress
sowens, a kind of fine-meal porridge
spangin', walking vigorously
speir, ask
spoot-ma-gruel, any unappetising food
spunk, match
spurtle, a round stick for stirring porridge
stap, stuff
steekit, shut
stew, dust
stob, splinter under the skin
stite, nonsense
sumph, heavy lout
swacker, more supple
swage, loosen, make easy
sweir, lazy
tackie, tig (child's game)
tangle, icicle, seaweed
tansies, ragworts (plants)
teem, empty
teen, temper, mood
thole, endure
thraw, to wring
thrawn, obstinate
thrums, scraps of thread
thirled, bound, tied
timmer knife, wooden knife (useless)
tine, loose
tinkey, tinker
trauchle, n., trouble, heavy toil
trig, neat
tyauve, struggle
wae, woeful
wantin, lacking
waur; name the waur, worse; none the worse
warstle, wrestle
waucht, draught

wersch, without savour, insipid
whammlin', jogging
whiles, at the same time
whin, gorse, furze bush

wrocht, worked, laboured
yird, vb., to give a blow
yon, that
yowies, pine cones

CANONGATE CLASSICS

Books listed in alphabetical order by author.

The Land of the Leal James Barke
ISBN 0 86241 142 4 £4.95
The House with the Green Shutters
George Douglas Brown
ISBN 0 86241 549 7 £4.99
Witchwood John Buchan
ISBN 0 86241 202 1 £4.99
The Life of Robert Burns Catherine Carswell
ISBN 0 86241 292 7 £5.99
The Complete Brigadier Gerard Arthur Conan Doyle
ISBN 0 86241 534 9 £4.99
Dance of the Apprentices Edward Gaitens
ISBN 0 86241 297 8
Ringan Gilhaize John Galt
ISBN 0 86241 552 7 £6.99
A Scots Quair: (Sunset Song, Cloud Howe, Grey
Granite) Lewis Grassic Gibbon
ISBN 0 86241 532 2 £5.99
Sunset Song Lewis Grassic Gibbon
ISBN 0 86241 179 3 £3.99
Memoirs of a Highland Lady vols. I&II
Elizabeth Grant of Rothiemurchus
ISBN 0 86241 396 6 £7.99
The Highland Lady in Ireland
Elizabeth Grant of Rothiemurchus
ISBN 0 86241 361 3 £7.95
Highland River Neil M. Gunn
ISBN 0 86241 358 3 £5.99
Sun Circle Neil M. Gunn
ISBN 0 86241 587 X £5.99
Gillespie J. MacDougall Hay
ISBN 0 86241 427 X £6.99
The Private Memoirs and Confessions of a Justified Sinner
James Hogg
ISBN 0 86241 340 0 £3.99
Fergus Lamont Robin Jenkins
ISBN 0 86241 310 9 £4.95
Just Duffy Robin Jenkins
ISBN 0 86241 551 9 £4.99
The Changeling Robin Jenkins
ISBN 0 86241 228 5 £4.99

Most Canongate Classics are available at good bookshops. If you experience difficulty in obtaining the title you want, please contact us at 14 High Street, Edinburgh EH1 1TE.